THE BOOK OF
HUMAN SKIN

MICHELLE LOVRIC is the author of three novels – *Carnevale*, *The Floating Book* (winner of a London Arts Award and chosen as a WH Smith Read of the Week) and *The Remedy* (longlisted for the 2005 Orange Prize for Fiction) – as well as two children's novels, *The Undrowned Child* and *The Mourning Emporium*. She combines her fiction work with editing, designing and producing literary anthologies including her own translations of Latin and Italian poetry. Her book *Love Letters* was a *New York Times* bestseller.

Lovric divides her time between London and Venice, and holds workshops in both places with published writers of poetry and prose, fiction and memoir.

BY THE SAME AUTHOR

NOVELS
Carnevale
The Floating Book
The Remedy

NOVELS FOR CHILDREN
The Undrowned Child
The Mourning Emporium

THE BOOK OF
HUMAN SKIN

MICHELLE LOVRIC

BLOOMSBURY

LONDON · BERLIN · NEW YORK · SYDNEY

First published in Great Britain 2010
This paperback edition published 2011

Copyright © 2010 by Michelle Lovric

The extract from *Holy Feast and Holy Fast: The Religious Significance of Food
to Medieval Women* by Caroline Walker Bynum, published by University
of California Press, copyright © 1987 by the Regents of the University
of California, is reprinted by permission of the publishers.

The moral right of the author has been asserted

Bloomsbury Publishing, London, Berlin, New York and Sydney

36 Soho Square, London W1D 3QY

A CIP catalogue record for this book is available from the British Library

ISBN 978 1 4088 0964 8
10 9 8 7 6 5 4 3 2

Typeset by Hewer Text UK Ltd, Edinburgh

Printed in Great Britain by Clays Ltd, St Ives plc

www.bloomsbury.com/michellelovric

ARTS COUNCIL
ENGLAND
LOTTERY FUNDED

Vile and contemptible is the book which every body likes.

Thomas Spooner of Lemon Street,
*A Compendious Treatise of the Diseases of the Skin,
from the Slightest Itching Humour in Particular Parts
only, to the most Inveterate Itch*, 1724

Part One

Gianni delle Boccole

I want to tell ye the story of Marcella Fasan, someone have got to do it.

Ye wunt believe it.

Ye'll say, 'No girl were ever so sinned agin, tis like Job in a dress. Tis a dirty lie, Gianni. Ye have took me for a fool.'

And I would say, Listen.

This is going to be a little uncomfortable.

Minguillo Fasan

If you ever see a portrait of a nun, you should know she was a dead woman when it was painted. Nuns may not have their portraits painted while they are alive, a nun's face being nobody's business, not even her own, not even her brother's.

If I had known that fact when I set out to discover what had happened to my sister, I would have saved myself a voyage and a disease, and I might never have laid a hand upon a fatal book of human skin, making cannibals of my nine remaining fingers.

Now it takes very little to disgust the Adorable Reader, so I'll not stay dwelling on all the unpleasantness of things for a small while yet, or after the very first chapter I'll risk having to open letters adrip with indignation along the lines of 'What a thing to say and me with a mouthful of hot wine and the wall just recently distempered white!'

And of course the first thing that the Dearly Beloved Reader asks Himself when He opens a book, and lets a voice have at Him, is – 'Do I wish to go on a long walk in the dark with *this* person?' He has a choice. So I (Minguillo Fasan, enchanted etcetera) shall be making every effort not to irk but to beguile. And to be mindful of my duty to give pleasure even in the recounting of disgustful memories. To smuggle in the sinewy meat, as it were, under the light, sweet pastry.

In this spirit, let us go back to the wishbone, to the clean fork of the beginning of things, when there are certain items that the Enquiring Reader really needs to know in order to dine well on the said meat of this story. The Dull Reader may at this point betake His stupid rectum to His preferred armchair in the Coffee House, and pick up His penny journal, satisfied in knowing that there is nothing between *these* covers for Him. So.

To begin with the fascinations.

The portrait of my sister Marcella arrived unexpectedly in Venice, having travelled by donkey down the scarcely credible slopes of El Misti in Peru, whence it was taken by boat to Valparaiso (of incomparably lush memory), where it was impounded for three days in a damp customs house. By the time her face was released from imprisonment, my sister's skin had pocked. Flakes had fallen even from the pupils of her eyes, leaving numerous tiny white highlights that gave the erroneous impression that she was not only living, but lively in the flesh.

My sister was never a lively girl. I saw to that. Marcella always looked like tuppence worth of dead, even when she was alive. Not at all the kind of thing I went for, myself.

What is that?

What?

The Reader has a wonderful story that the whole world would love to hear?

La-di-da, etcetera and so forth. I know what. The Reader should scratch His scribbling itch and tell *His* tale by all means. And I'll just have a little nap.

A wonderful story? The whole world?

Mine is much better.

And I am not even born yet.

The two wretches who shall beget me are fumbling towards my conception, none too fast. They've already made a mistake: a girl called Riva.

And as for Marcella, the object and heroine of this entire tale? Well, for *her* the Eager Reader must wait even longer, but we'll find ways to fill up the time, eh?

Gianni delle Boccole

Ile regret it till my dying day if I live that long that I niver knowed to write a direy when I were young. Now I must remember myself of evry thing peace by peace, God-on-a-stick!

I were nothin more than a kitchen lad, borned under the kitchen table as it appened, for my Ma were a cook at the Palazzo Espagnol. My father were a itinnyant pedlar who wernt seen agin in these parts after he shone my Ma his wares, as ye mite say. Our kind Master Fernando Fasan hallowed her to keep me, e'en tho twere her second offents for I alredy had a half-sister Cristina by a passin coalman.

My crib were set below that kitchen table, so in my first years I saw mostly the broad bords of its underside insted o the sky. I have two memmaries, the one o my Ma's lovin face peepin under the cloth to kiss me reglar. And t'other of her *tortellini in brodo* that were a wonder prazed upndown the Grand Canal.

Our Ma were carrid oft by the Small-Pox when I had jist six years. That could of been very poor for me n my sister. Yet by the kindness of my Master Fernando Fasan, Cristina n I was not turned out nor yet sent to the nuns.

'But you are one of us, young chap!' that's what my Master sayed seriusly oer his spectickles to sixyearold me. 'How could we do without you, Gianni?'

We was set to makin ourselfs youthful by turning the spit on the fire and runnin for kindling.

Cristina doated on me, and all t'other laydies o the house were that kind too, especially the maid called Anna what were jist three years older n myself and were little, pretty, proper n fine.

By that time my Master Fernando Fasan ud took himself a andsome fat wife with a towering hairdo. My Master hisself were freakwently way in Peru, where he done his busyness. But all were did proper in his absents. There was the grate bankwets for t'other nobbles, balls in season, card tornyments and so on.

Like all laydies of her stashon, my Mistress Donata tookt an assistant husband what kindly presided when my Master were way, and een sumtimes when he come back, seein as how the assistant husband Piero Zen and the marrid husband Fernando Fasan was like the lovingest pare of brothers ye ever seen. The very walls thesselves was warm in them days with their feckshonit laffs n shouts, Sweet Little God!

A little daughter, Riva, were borned to my Master and Mistress. There was more bankwets, and grate snootfuls of wine for the servants too. My sister Cristina were straitway pointed number four nussmaid and twere a pleasure for her, for ye could hear the little one chucklin in her crib all hours o the day. In onour of the new babe, my Master Fernando had a garden o roses n lilacks planted in our courtyard. He leaved a space, sayin summing Ile not soon forgit, 'There will be more children, and more flowers for us.'

Swear I got more sweet memmaries from those times than ye got hairs. In retrospecked, twere as if we was makin o the Palazzo Espagnol a perfeck bower, a vegetable paradise on earth, for Marcella Fasan to be borned into.

We was more than sorry each time my Master Fernando had to sail agin for Peru. Twas vilent times in that far place. There was stories comin out o there to make yer hairs turn white n curl up yer toes.

Sor Loreta

I was warned against writing this.

I ask all you who read it not to think badly of me because I had the bold presumption to set down this text, given that I am utterly ignorant and without graces.

Should any Christian cast his eyes on this work, he must understand that it is not my own arrogance but the will of the Lord God that flows down upon the page through these worthless fingers. He should take sustenance from my words as he might swallow the Blessed Eucharist.

That same good Christian should naturally look on the testimony of the Venetian Cripple and her friends as the saliva of the Devil turned to ink and spat upon paper.

I shall start with the first of my significant memories. That was the long death of Tupac Amaru II. It lasted from ten in the morning till five in the

10

afternoon, which thoroughly pleased all devout persons. It happened in Cuzco, Peru, where I was born. It was 1781, and I had twelve years.

Tupac Amaru had revolted against the Spanish rulers and the Holy Mother Church of Peru. This peasant defied even the Inca nobility, who denounced him for an upstart. With his murderous campaigns Tupac Amaru had denuded whole Spanish towns of the servants of God. So now they made a holy example of him.

He was made to watch his wife, his eldest son, his uncle and his brother-in-law all tortured to death in the Plaza de Armas, a worse insult on account of that it was once the sacred square of the Incas themselves. Then the soldiers brought Tupac Amaru himself to the front of the wooden platform. The crowd roared, and me with them. A little Indian boy in front of us muttered, '*Chapetones pezuñentos!*'

Stink-hoofed Spaniards, is what the brat said. For those who are in league with the Devil often use his filthy epithets upon the Holy Innocent.

First they cut out Tupac Amaru's tongue.

I clapped my hands when I saw that. I had so many feelings crowding my breast that I cannot write them all down. For even then I knew that whoever suffers the greatest pain feels God's sweetness the most. *Deo gratias*.

Then they harnessed four horses, one to each of Tupac Amaru's limbs. The horses failed to pull him apart, so the soldiers hanged, drew and quartered him instead. Afterwards they cut off his head. This inspired intense prayers and much shouting. I myself did both things, kneeling upon the ground and crossing myself. My father looked away. My mother covered her eyes, and in that moment I suspected a horrid thing: that there might be a trickle of Indian blood in her veins. Her dark beauty was so different from my own sore thing of a face.

From that time, I had no mother. Once I began to doubt her *limpieza de sangre* I could no longer look into her eyes or accept her caresses.

Parts of Tupac Amaru were strung up as a warning to anyone else who might have thought of freeing the *sambos* and rousing up the Indians. His head was sent to Tinta, where he was born, and given its own private hanging. Then it was impaled upon a stake. His traitor arms and legs were sent to four different towns for the same treatment. *Deo gratias*.

Gianni delle Boccole

Scuse me but I am slightly on one this evenin, Chicken-shitting God!

Ask pardon, ask pardon, sirs, madams. I am playing the thing dredful fine. I know ye'll think me wanting in the head.

Ye see. Twere one on them skinny slivers o Tupac Amaru as reached Venice all them years later wernt it? But by that time it had got isself bound round a book. Twere nowise one as would of been much injoyed by the original owner o the binding, savin his grease.

A filthy thing. That book were all kinds o evil. Ye wunt want it in the ouse. But my young Master Minguillo Fasan, with his bad blood and his desiccrating heart, he would jist love that book, wunt he? And he would get a feroshus plan for it and lead us all to Hell.

Yet back then in 1781 we still had a few good times left. Venice haint niver heared o Napoleon Bonypart, and Napoleon Bonypart haint yet dreamt o crushing ancient empires under his little foot. Kings' and Doges' heads was still resting stoutly on there shoulders without the least thought o falling blades.

The reverlushon in Peru were at last bloodily finishing and the Fasan silver mines was safe again, and the Fasan warehouse in Arequipa too. Here in Venice, the Palazzo Espagnol were tethert to the water like twernt going anywheres, but the sad truth were that a bad sea were arising.

From the inside.

Some few men like my old Master Fernando Fasan was still big on trade. But *they* had to float all the branchlets o there famlies with small doles n grate big partments. Whole hants-huncles-cuzzins-nevvies was borned, growed up n died, doing nought but stork the unearned ducat. Them parasites niver bethought thereselves on taking care o the partments what they had acquired without a drop o swet on there own part. No more than a tapeworm thinks o sprucing up its humane host. I had nightshirts with more backbone n sents of duty than them relatives o my Master Fernando Fasan.

So een at our Palazzo Espagnol, specious rooms that was onct proud n painted slowly by slowly slid into dismal grottoes. When a room finely died in blaze o mould, them nobble bedbugs jist shutted the door on it. More doors shut, intire floors was handed oer to the umidity. And so our whole city lay a-rutting, cankered with meanness and indolents.

We dint know it, only because we choosed not to know it.

There were no star to warn us; no signs nor wonders in the air to say: 'Watch out, things is going to the bad on a buggy.'

To say, 'Nothin, not happyness nor Venice, is for ever.'

The only thing we knowed were that my Mistress Donata Fasan were onct more with child and that her skin were irrupted with weals n wens like ye wunt believe. Swear it were the miserablest pregnancy. And Anna told us the strangest thing: the babe inside my Mistress were kickin that hard n cruel that her belly were black with bruises.

Doctor Santo Aldobrandini

The book of human skin is a large volume with many pages of villainy writ upon it.

There are people who are a disease, you know.

As I go my rounds, I still hear it said – even by their victims – that there are no truly evil persons born in the world: just misunderstood unfortunates. Some wrong done in early life has monstered such creatures quite against their will.

While I dress stab-wounds or roll poultices on beaten wives, I often wonder – *why* are we so lenient towards abominable human beings, yet we declare unequivocally against Cancer, for example, or the Small-Pox?

If we put out an illness, we rejoice. There is no lyric moment of regret for its passing.

Now your human villain stalks the world much the way the Small-Pox roams the blood and wrecks the body's integument. He hurts. He disfigures. He kills. He'll do it again, if not stopped. So why do we hesitate to 'cure' his evil? Do we try to understand the feelings of the Small-Pox scab? Do we perfume the stink of the Small-Pox pustule with excuses?

There are people who are a disease, and it is purely our indulgence that makes a plague out of them.

No one talks of things like this. But I have always liked to write them down and have them keep company with other musings of mine.

In Peru there are nuns who keep fleas in bottles for the companionship of something lively in their quiet cells. So did these written thoughts of mine serve me for many years. In the absence of mother, father, sister or brother, I was always grateful for the quill and the flutters of paper seeming alive under my fingers, especially in the lonely hours when there were no more patients to tend, and in the aching years when I was denied the company of she whose thoughts are my book and whose heart is my Host.

Sor Loreta

Our town of Cuzco was stacked high with the craggy follies of the Incas – forts and palaces dedicated to their barbarous gods. How those graceless offerings must have disgusted our true Creator!

With the death of Tupac Amaru II, a quietness began to fall in Peru. At first, little spasms of revolt still shuddered through the ignorant valleys, rather as a dead snake still moves, not understanding that God has wished it dead. But gradually everyone grew quiet, from the Indians, the mixed-blood *mestizos*, the African *sambos* to the real white Spanish like myself. Inca portraits, names, dances, clothes and their pagan funeral rites were outlawed, so that they might cease to be sorry for being conquered and instead grow to love the gentle dominion of the Spanish and the Mother Church. But the Indians were too ill-bred to understand that it was all over with their gods. Secretly, some still clung to the old infidel ways.

It was not long after they cut up Tupac Amaru that I was taken by a little Indian servant girl to see her family hovel. No doubt she hoped to excite some charity by her poverty. However, she claimed she wanted to show me something particular. She was filled to the brim with excitement. Inside the house, she opened a cupboard under the stairs and my eyes fell upon a mummy with the skin still on and the teeth grinning through leather lips. He was sitting up on his haunches and dressed in splendid rags.

'Is my great-grandpa,' she declared, thumping his shoulder affectionately. A little lump of dried gristle fell off in a puff of sour air.

'Why does your great-grandfather sit up like that when he is dead?' I enquired innocently. 'Should he not lie down in his grave like a Christian?'

The servant told me, 'Because he comes to dinner by us when the dinner is good. All us grandpas do so.'

Then she picked up a seashell and blew a soft sad note through it. I shook my head because it was one of the forbidden *pututo* trumpets that the Indians used in their heathen mourning.

Mistaking my expression for awe, the servant girl next gave me a gruesome tale of the peasant daughters chosen for the honour of sacrifice. 'Them girls was called *capacocha*,' she breathed reverently through her gapped teeth. These *capacochas* were taken from their families at the age of four and sent to the priestesses to be raised.

She told me a scandalous thing then: the Inca house of the priestesses, who were called Virgins of the Sun, once stood in exactly the same place occupied by our own Christian convent of Santa Catalina! The two buildings, one heathen, one holy, shared the same foundations. Where pure young novices now fasted and scourged themselves for the glory of God, the pagan girls used to be fattened up for sacrifice with llama stew and maize.

My servant licked her lips, 'They aten meat most every day!'

After that they cut their hair off, apparently, and took them on a long journey up a mountain to a shrine.

'Then did they murder the little girls?' I whispered.

'Oh no, they girls did it of theyselves. They was give maize beer and coca leaves to make em feel sleep-sleep and byenbye they was left lone.'

'So they starved to death?'

'Some of em got sick before they died. So high up there, the *puna*, you know. Make everyone sick sometime. Like the old uns. They must clean big vomits off my great-grandpa when he did die,' she observed, pointing to a dried green mess like lichen on the mummy's sleeve.

I left that house with a horrible vision of the great-grandfather's corpse at table with a napkin wrapped under his ragged chin while they poured soup through him on to the floor. But then I remembered that those people were too poor and vulgar to use a napkin.

Naturally the Holy Mother Church frowned on the Indians' keeping and worshipping their ancestors in the house. The Christian *conquistadores* had hunted down nearly all those mummies hundreds of years ago, so it was exceedingly rare to find one now. I was happy in more ways than I can write down because I knew God had chosen me to specially extirpate this idolatry. Indeed, in my twelve-year-old eyes, my servant's deceased great-grandfather personified to a nicety a Graven Image. I hastened to my Confessor and told him what I had seen.

The officers of God had a special way to treat those infidel mummies. They broke them. They bent them out of shape, they wrenched out the teeth, they made them look pitiable and defeated, so the Indians could not think highly enough of them to worship them any more. In the same way, when the Spanish took all the gold from the Inca temples, it was not at all motivated by a lust for treasure, but because our Holy Fathers wished to show the Andeans that those heathen deities were worthless.

The servant girl did not return to our house for one week. When she did, she showed a beaten face. She dared not look at me, but she sat outside my door and wept her story through the keyhole. Her father had raised his hand against her. This was because my Confessor and his officers had told him how they came by their information, before they thrashed the great-grandfather to clumps of bone and hair and dropped him into a chamber pot with the shards of the *pututo* shell that would never more utter its pagan moans.

'I thought you was my friend,' the servant girl moaned. 'I took you to mine.'

So Satan tempts the righteous to pity the wrong. I knelt on my side of the door and poked my little finger through the keyhole right into her eye. She fell backwards and crawled away, sobbing humbly. I was pleased to see she had learned a little of the ways of Our Lord.

It was in those days that I began to read the life of Santa Rosa of Lima with more than simple fervour in my heart. Santa Rosa was the very first saint of the New World. Unlike myself, she was cursed with physical beauty. They called her Rosa because her complexion was as petals, and her cheeks bloomed an adorable pink. Her lovely face carried the weight of her family's earthly ambitions: she was supposed to marry a fortune.

Everyone loved her looks but Rosa despised them, for she did not wish to marry anyone except God.

She barely slept, constantly fasted, abjured all flesh. She mortified her delicate skin with continual floggings and a hair shirt. Her family chastised her and even tried to stop her with stern edicts. This only inspired Rosa to more ardent acts of worship.

One of her innovations was to rub lye into her hands, and pepper into her face. She cut off her flowing hair, thrusting a wreath of roses over her shorn head. Inside the flowers Rosa concealed a brace of iron spikes. Later, she dared to skewer her head with a long pin.

Finally, when she was twenty and her beauty was ruined, her family submitted to her will. She became a Dominican tertiary. Taking a vow of poverty, she left her comfortable bedchamber to live in a small grotto in the garden. There she undertook good deeds for the Christian poor and tended to the deserving sick with her own hands.

She rarely ate or drank, except for a draught of gall infused with bitter herbs that deadened every sensation in her mouth. Even as she raked her flowers, or made lace to sell for the destitute, she dragged around a heavy wooden cross fastened to her back. Soon she began to tell of visions, divine visitations and voices in her head. Once, when she gazed for hours in rapture at a painting of Christ, she caused His face to grow wet with perspiration.

People laughed at her. Her own family denounced her behaviour as a form of madness. Even this she endured with fortitude, gladly taking on the ridicule of the world as another penance to bring her closer to her Holy Bridegroom.

Eventually Rosa could no longer walk or even stand upright. In her last weeks she took to a marriage bed she had designed herself, consisting of stones, sharp shards of broken pottery, jagged pieces of glass and thorns.

God permitted her to use herself like this until she was thirty-one, when He finally rendered His most devout Virgin unto Himself. The people of Lima immediately regretted their nasty hilarity about Rosa and rushed to behold her pure, shattered body. So many people crowded the Cathedral that it took days to get her corpse to burial. Before long, those same people who had mocked her began to comprehend the miracle of Rosa's life. She was canonized the patron saint of Lima, of Peru, of gardeners and florists, and all people who are derided for their religious fervour. She became famous all over the world, and her painted image was hung in great churches everywhere, even as far away as that wickedest of cities, Venice.

For so the immoral always lust after the beauty of true goodness, even in the midst of their most flagrant iniquity.

In the top drawer of my bureau I assembled lye, pepper and a long pin for my thin hair.

The death of Tupac Amaru continued to live in my heart. I rehearsed the scene again and again in my mind: the knife dropping through his tongue, the messengers carrying ragged pieces of him in five directions. I got a little length of chain from the blacksmith and I hit myself with it when I thought about Tupac Amaru, but only in the secret places of my body. For I did not yet want anyone to know that I would be a nun and scourge myself for the rest of my life.

When I was nearly thirteen years old, and my mother presented my trousseau chest, I judged it timely to announce my decision.

My mother and father were surprised. My father's textile mill flourished. My fine dowry was often spoken of. My mother exclaimed, 'Isabel Rosa!' – for that was my name in those days – 'You will hate to be sealed up in a cloister.'

And I declared loudly, 'I would like it above all things, to be enclosed in the love of the Lord Jesus Christ.'

I changed my tone to a persuasive one: 'I shall pray all day and into the night to lessen *your* time in Purgatory.'

They exchanged glances muddied with guilt. My parents were imperfect in their pious observances. I had more than once confessed on their behalf.

My mother, to whom fashion was religion, protested, 'You will own nothing. Everything will be the property of the convent. Even your clothing will come from the common wardrobe.'

'I shall not notice what I wear. I shall be like a child at its mother's breast without the slightest care or thought for mundane things. All shall be provided.'

'You may one day have . . . longings that would be fatally repressed in such an atmosphere,' my mother coughed delicately, tinkling her bracelets.

I answered, 'The sweet Lord loves me so much that He will never allow me to serve and be subject to men, concerning myself with base matters like housekeeping and cooking. He does not wish my body riven by childbirth. He wants me joined to no one but Himself.'

'Come child, you are not so ugly that you shall not find a husband in Cuzco eventually,' my father told me. 'We shall see to it, somehow.'

'You profane the pure spirit of the Lord,' I admonished them. 'Our most Holy Father adores all His creatures, even the plainest in His sight.'

'The nuns may be unkind to you,' my father stated baldly. 'Yours is not an easy face to love, Isabel.'

I said, 'It is most likely that they will envy me for God's mark on my face. The Scriptures have shown that the holiest souls have always been assailed by the Devil's wickedness in the form of envy. Yet those who are persecuted are ever gloriously sustained by our Beloved Father, and indeed chosen for His Favourites.'

My parents remained in terrible anguish for they did not want to lose a child. They had no other. My own feelings suffered vexing pricks for I wished all the pain to be on my part only.

My mother came to me cajolingly, and asked once more, 'Would you not like to be married, Isabel? And have children to love you?'

And I replied, 'To me marriage would be like the martyrdom that the ancient tyrants inflicted upon the Holy Ones – by tying them to putrid corpses until the horror, melting corruption and frightful stink brought about a slow, dreadful death.'

I refused to study such sinful subjects as French and arithmetic, and read only my Bible and my Life of Santa Rosa. I demanded to confess every day and announced all my defects scrupulously. I rejoiced in the penance for my every lapse. I was so steeped in obedience to our most Holy God that if my Confessor had commanded 'Put your hand in the fire!', I would have rushed to do so and left it there until the last cinder dropped off the stub of my wrist. Indeed, I regretted that my Confessor put me to such pallid penances as he did.

I dragged my mattress away and slept on a bare plank. I ate little more than the communion wafer. I found it disgusting to abandon prayer in order to take bodily food. I would eat only at the direct order of my Confessor, and even then reluctantly. People in the street stared at the jutting bones of my face, perhaps already aware that they were beholding the most spiritual virgin in Cuzco, if not all Peru. My pangs of hunger were like church bells tolling in my stomach: I exulted in them and my mastery over them.

I felt distant from other human beings, as if I already occupied a higher region. When other people spoke to me I saw white puffs of air come out of their mouths, like cotton. I could not hear them properly unless they spoke to me of God. I continued to scourge myself, and spent many hours in a state of oblivious ecstasy.

Then my bloodied linen was discovered by the servant girl, who took it to my parents.

The next day my Confessor told me, 'You must go easy and temper your great fervour.'

He asked me to bring him my whips and chains. When I did so he was dumbfounded at how many they were, and how cruel was their construction. He ordered that I might not scourge myself without permission from him. I stated God's truth: 'There is prejudice in the minds of ignorant people against these devout practices, but I had not expected to find it in a priest.'

He locked my whips and chains in his cupboard and sent me home. My parents spoke to me then in grave, reproving tones, and I saw that my Confessor had acted in collusion with them.

I grew sad and vague for some time after that betrayal. I had so many miseries that I could not write them all down. I was shocked to realize that all these people less devout than myself were in fact *envious* of my special gifts.

I woke in the night and twisted and kneaded my skin as hard as I could without making myself gasp – for the little Indian servant had been put to sleep in my room with instructions to raise an alarm if I began to scourge myself. That girl told my parents that she had seen me touching myself under my blankets. They gave orders that at night I was to be trussed up like a roasting bird, with my four limbs tied to the bedheads just as if I was Tupac Amaru with the horses. My Life of Santa Rosa was taken away from me.

I contented myself with Santa Catalina. She knew she was married to Christ, for she received a vision in which she wore as a wedding ring the Holy Prepuce that was circumcised from His body. When she was just a child she threw herself into the boiling waters of a spring near her house in order to burn the skin of her face and body and so discourage human suitors. She ate almost nothing and barely slept. So respected was this virgin, unlike myself, that she ended up telling Popes what to do.

When they took my Santa Catalina away too, my soul rebelled inside my body. I scrubbed my face with the pepper and lye that I had hidden in my bureau drawer. With my head on fire, I ran into the kitchen and plunged my face in a *caldera* of boiling water, at the same time sticking the long pin into my right ear. I fainted before I could see what I had done.

20

The first thing I remember after that is a little hand reaching under the covers of my bed. It belonged to the Indian servant girl.

'Lemme look at you,' she said, lifting the sheet to see my face.

'Dunt see nuffink different,' she observed. 'You was always ugly right through like a hole in the ground.'

But the damage must have been considerable, for even my mother could not bear to look at me any more. God had marked me out, and my mother's soul was too weak to behold the miracle. My parents now acceded to my wishes. I was taken away from Cuzco and sent, under the protection of a reliable *arriero*, to the convent of Santa Catalina in the fabled white city of Arequipa.

Doctor Santo Aldobrandini

Perhaps this is why I have always loved the skin: because it is both the story and the storyteller. My own book shall be prefaced with a touching paradigm.

Most days I deal with the living, but once, in Peru, I was brought the body of a little girl found up on the higher reaches of El Misti mountain. The magistrates wished me to pronounce on the manner of her death before they buried her. An apprentice surgeon panted to anatomize her, for there was no medical school in Arequipa at that time and the doctors had to learn their trades in wet ways.

I laid the little girl out on my bench. I had read of such cases, yet it still shocked me to see a child so mistreated.

A death from starvation manifests as follows: a shrivelled integument coated with a brown, bad-smelling excretion. Beneath the paper-like epidermis, surgeon's fingers will locate muscles in a state of atrophy. Without even cutting, the surgeon knows that he shall find the gall-bladder bloated with bile but the liver under-sized. The heart and lungs will be bloodless, sunken; the empty stomach collapsed and ulcerated. The bowel, if extracted, shall show itself void, shrivelled and translucent.

I could not bear to think of the girl's body being ransacked now.

21

'The child was sacrificed to a local god,' I told the apprentice surgeon. 'Pray do not cut her. You shall gain nothing by anatomizing her, for the death took place at least three centuries past.'

I called in the next, yet-living patient, but my mind dwelled sadly on the horror of the little victim's lingering death.

Some people see skin simply as a texture, that holds in place all the important organs, as a sack holds a squirming haul of fish. Few know what a strong lens reveals of that sack: a tendinous, membranous, vascular and nervous intermixture of fibres. The colour of skin, like a biographer, betrays the secrets of the inner constitution. The Sanguine of character show themselves in a vermilion epidermis. Those of a Bilious personality will be dry-skinned with a yellow cast to their complexion. The Melancholicks are leaden of hue. The Phlegmaticks are soft and white. In sickness, the skin peacocks its colours: livid, fiery, bluish, pale, purpureous.

Then there's what happens to us: also tattooed upon our faces. The skin's an anxious entity, even in the nicer touches of pleasure. Its eruptions are our souls' troubles and delights made visible to all in blushes, blanchings and gooseflesh. I suppose this is why fanatics mutilate their own flesh. I am reminded of one such I personally encountered but a short time ago. Her scourged and mutilated skin was her signpost. The striated lettering advertised: 'God loves me. I am specially marked out for His favour.'

But was it God's *favour* that my little mummified girl wore on her tortured body? I attended her burial, alone with the priest and the grave-digger in the windswept Chavela cemetery. Her final grave is marked only in my memory. I threw a winter rose and a sugared cake into the pit that swallowed her. For a moment I imagined those skeletal fingers clamouring around the sweetmeat, and my own skin hunched away from my bones, feeling terror and dreadfulness, and worst of all, an emptiness in the heart of the world.

Yet I also knew even then that there is a God, and that He is good.

Because of Marcella Fasan's laughter, and her skin.

Minguillo Fasan

I trust the page-turning finger of My Reader stays in supple condition? And that His Mercenary Soul remains requited by the sheer worth of paper between the skins of this book? Excellent. Every good dog deserves a bone.

Now the vulgar generality of Readers, I find, craves particulars of parentage, provisioning, points-in-time, et dreary cetera and prosaically so forth. For that vulgar generality, I furnish the following, quite unwilling.

I was born in a *palazzo* on the Grand Canal. That is, our *palazzo* in our city of Venice, some years before that latter lady's death. Her executioner: Napoleon; his minions: the Venetians themselves; her judges: my own Kind Reader (many warm hellos to Him again!) and all posterity.

People called it the Palazzo Espagnol, the Spanish Palace. Golden-Book Venetians, we had married into Spanish silver back when the Spaniards were first richly picking the New World. Fat on silver, my ancestors had commissioned a Tiepolo to paint the New World's oldest and most futile saint, Rosa of Lima, for the Gesuati church on the Zattere. Our family dealt in silver, we had silver in our veins and we spoke Spanish as easily as Venetian inside our home. Until Boney came upon us – patience, I pray you! – Spanish-ness gave our family pleasure and distinction, if you can call it that. The Cultivated Reader shall of course know this, that to straddle two languages, to have a tongue in the ear of two tongues, what a very good and superior feeling that imparts.

In those days the treasure-house of Spanish silver was in the pitted belly of Peru. The Spaniards kept a greedy grip on their colonies, but my father, with his Spanish blood, found ways of dealing there, especially since he began to trade also in the red bark of the fever tree, that was indispensable to the Venetian quacks for their electuaries, balsams and expectorants. Also in The Milk of the Candelabra Cactus, efficacious against no disease but, in the utterance, so delightful on the anxious ear. My father's customers were the finest apothecaries in Venice, for those New World drugs had a specially profitable ring to them, as in 'new', meaning not yet proven to be from-top-to-bottom useless.

But look, the midwife and the surgeon are hastening to my birth-chamber!

My mother Donata Fasan shuddered me out on the thirteenth of May 1784. She nearly died of it, I am told. The clock had not long struck midday when my little face first appeared, the wrong way round and awkward with it. My mother screamed and fainted away with the pain. The Reader should take note: even at this evanescent glimmering of our tale, my mother's weakness was such that it might have withered me and this story inside her. However, the attendant physician dragged me out of that red womb into this drab-coloured world. And there you have it, our adventure begun.

If the Reader hungers for pathetical fallacies in the natural world to conflate His literary pleasure, let Him look no further. There are times when literary devices truly seem superfluous! For the unvarnished fact is that the world verily shook in the minute I was born: far away across the ocean, at noon on that same thirteenth of May, an earthquake tumbled down ten cities in Peru. Imagine: mountains decrusting themselves, the earth grinning open in chasms to swallow little black apostrophes of people! Yes, Dear Reader, let us mark it one more time for general satisfaction, the earth's skin as well as my mother's was fissured the day I was born, and both would bear the scars of it for ever.

The news from Peru was not all bad. Indeed, what some might call a disaster was soon proving profitable for me and my fortunes. The earthquake, you see, opened up free, *gratis*, three deep, new veins of silver in my father's mines in the South Americas.

Already, all around my cradle were silver rattles, silver cups and silver reflections from the Grand Canal. My sister Riva shook silver earrings above my head to make me cry.

She would be sorry later.

Gianni delle Boccole

Weasly little mincer he were from the start. The son o the house were borned and yet there were very little rejoysing, on account of how he had near split my Mistress in half, Brute God! At first there was poorish few hopes o Donata Fasan's life. Then she rallyed a little and we should of felt reliefed. Yet we did not. We dint know nothin of all them lives lossed in Peru, but we still felt desprit sad at the Palazzo Espagnol them days, for reasons we couldn't fathom of ourselves.

The babe hisself ailed and puled. However, he were quite clearly set on livin, whether his Mamma perisht or no.

Now his sister Riva were a notable pretty infant. But he weren't nothin nice to look on, this first son o my Master Fernando Fasan. There were not a devil's mark on him, nothin ye could point a finger at an remark 'orrible!' Not yet. Yet

Nose, eyes, privities all in the right places as ye mite say. Maybe the eyes a little close together. He had that kind o weak repungent face that people fall into staring at, can't help thereselves, drawn down like into a deep drownin well. There was things about that babe what made evryone stand on there nerves. People would approach the cradle smiling, and draw back, confust n unhappy. Swear that butterflies dropt dead if they flewed oer him.

That little Minguillo give oft summing dark into the air. It seems ridikilus to say it, when we talk ovva little infant here. Yet the facts is, no matter how Anna scrubbed him, he let loose a kind o fog what smelt like a blacksmiths. They put popery in evry corner of the bedchamber but that smell niver went way. It felt on yer skin zackly like a hot grinding kind o hate.

My Master and my Mistress was that upset by it. They lookt crossways at each other, sif to ask, 'What did we make?'

Now I wernt sittin on the bedpost, but I believe that was the end of all doings atwixt em, sept perhap the onct, by which Marcella were made.

Only little Riva dint seem to feel nor smell the black fog of her baby brother. She jist laffed and shook her silver earrings at him.

Poor sweet darlin little fool. Pig ovva God!

Sor Loreta

Throughout the ten-day journey from Cuzco to Arequipa I looked with a reproving eye upon the world from which I would shortly be removed. I saw not one thing that I regretted to leave, not the mountains, nor the lambs, nor the fields of vulgar asparagus. And certainly not the ignorant curiosity of strangers' faces turned towards the raw shipwreck of mine.

I had eschewed mirrors as the Devil's trinkets since well before I plunged my face into the boiling water. Now my fingers told me that the cooked skin had settled into meaty furrows and that a nostril had fused in melting to the left cheek. One eye would not open evermore. Even from my blind side, however, I could feel them staring at me, those shallow people who had never heard of God's Grace, who would spend a leisurely time in Purgatory. Fortunately I could not hear half their taunts as the long pin had left me profoundly deaf in my right ear.

We were two days from Arequipa when three peaks rose insolently against the azure sky.

'El Misti,' the *arriero* told me, 'Chachani. And that is Pichupichu.'

Below them the countryside was starkly divided into grey slabs of desert butting up to the snaking terraces favoured by the Indians, who had diverted God's natural streams to colour these steppes a vicious, unnatural green.

'Like the hanging gardens of Babylon,' I observed under my breath. 'This does not feel like a Godly place.'

As always, my instincts were to prove correct.

It was on May 13th 1784 that I first heard the bells of Arequipa striking midday in the distance.

We were approaching the outskirts shortly after, when the bells began to

26

ring again, but crazily, as if beaten with sticks by children. Even as the air shook, the earth began to shudder, throwing the men off their horses. My buggy tipped me on to the grass. I fell straight to my knees and commenced to pray with my one eye wide open so I could see God's great work in progress. A rumbling convulsion threw a whole mountain down, ingulfing flocks in the field.

I knew that God had chosen me to witness his Uncreation for a reason.

The spectacle lasted as long as a psalm. Then silence fell. The outlines of the town were blurred with dust.

A few hours later, our party was edging through streets rent by great chasms. The sun shone down on the dismemberment of indigo-blue, red and ochre-painted stones. Arequipa had collapsed as a flower dies, with its dropped petals spread out in a bright nimbus of colour.

'Even in His destructions, God makes beauty for the sinless to enjoy,' I marvelled.

The men who accompanied me were silent, disbelieving. Occasionally they roused themselves to tell me the names of the areas we passed through, 'San Lázaro' – steep labyrinths populated by Indians, 'Santa Marta' – where they showed me the episcopal palace and two convents, Santa Teresa and Santa Rosa, hooded under vast walls. All were branded with God's displeasure in the form of gaping holes and collapsed walls. A grand warehouse stood unroofed and windowless. The *arriero* told me, 'Belongs to Fernando Fasan, Venetian merchant.'

Venetians in Arequipa! Ambassadors from Sodom and Gomorrah!

Worse and worse, I thought. I felt a shudder running through me like a premonition, for even then I was prescient and alert to evil where duller souls saw only facts.

'Why?' the townspeople moaned everywhere, pulling limp and bloody bundles out of the rubble. The women were clad in the ruins of frivolous dresses. Under their flowery skirts I saw torn red stockings running into buckled black slippers. There were vents in their fitted jackets from which the lace spilled out. And yet these women, got up as harlots, sported crucifixes at their breasts! I was surprised at the paleness of their skins. The thicker taint of Indian blood made the citizens of my old home Cuzco much darker.

But there must be blackness in the Arequipan soul.

'Why?' indeed! It seemed that I alone understood that when the Almighty wishes to punish the wickedness of mankind, He sends forth messages in earthly manifestations. They must be crude, as humanity's understanding is just so.

I myself understood this earthquake of May 13th 1784 as a sign to show that my new mission was to strenuously break the rocks of ignorance that had confounded Arequipa for too long. I, frail creature that I was, would be the Minister of His wrath. From my virgin breasts would flow the milk of His righteousness.

For the purest and simplest creatures are ever made the instruments of His will. Even flies and lice have been harnessed as messengers of Divine Justice, and have taught wicked people many a stern lesson.

Doctor Santo Aldobrandini

As the self-appointed scribe of that great storyteller, skin, I work nightly on my manuscript. There is a certain joyful urgency for its delivery.

I naturally begin the tale with the earliest afflictions. The physician can identify neglected babies by their rashes. Folds of their own skin rub together; the friction chafes. Sometimes a fluid is exuded, acrid enough to inflame the local mischief. Presently a raw, hurting surface is produced.

Babies afflicted in this way are prone to fits of angry crying, which can make them unpopular, and leads to further neglect, and worse rashes. A little washing in tepid water, and the application of a calendula lotion will soothe. Yet more than anything it is the loving touch of a feminine hand that cures Intertrigo. In some cultures the mother's adoring gaze is believed to physic and fatten a baby more than her milk. Not having known such a thing myself, and being persistently lean, I've always suspected some truth in this folk-wisdom. And I have sworn that the first baby of mine shall be gazed and smiled at until his whole skin lights up like a candle; or hers. No child shall ever be fed such ocular love!

But, to return to purely medical matters: infants must be allowed a regular access of fresh air to the integument. Confined babies are also prone to Red-gum, or Tooth-rash, pearly white pimples that appear over the face, neck and arms.

Uncared-for babies suffer more often than loved ones from Branny Tetter, in which the skin falls off in pale cereal-like scales. Neglected, the condition advances to small nutty lumps and weeping fissures under the hair. It's simply cured by a little glycerine-of-borax.

Yet someone must notice it and care about the shedding skin enough to apply the medicine, and to cradle the child in their arms while it cries as the cold salve is smeared on the little hurting head.

Minguillo Fasan

My commiserations to the Erudite Reader: this part of the story's prattled out by a little baby in a crib, so what can He expect by way of pleasantly sophisticated atrocity? Feeble infant concerns shall be the Reader's concerns for a little while yet.

Milk, for example, features much at this point.

No wet-nurse would take me, so I clamped my jaws on the maternal breast and sucked.

The first of my mother's crimes, for which she would in time be punished, was this: she tried not to look at me, even when I bit. As for the milk, I swear it tasted *unwilling*. She let her eyes rest lovingly upon my sister Riva, dancing her dolly in a corner of the room. I had to feed on second-hand sweetness, intercepting my mean portion of mother-love by stealth.

The Compassionate Reader cries out in pity for the poor Venetian *bambino*, whose mamma begrudged him even the tender liquid of life. Whose mamma never once dropped a kiss on his face, never diddled a little finger of his between her own.

'How did that feel?' the Reader asks tenderly.

It felt stinking.

It felt shameful, and it tasted of iron, for my toothless gums champed so hard on my mother's flinching teats that I drew blood.

And still she looked away, handing me to a nursemaid with a bottle and never once asking for me back. My father, call him forty years old then, did not ask it of her. How could he? – he did not come into the nursery, even.

Look at my parents, turning their backs on me. It was not good, and soon it would not be safe. The Old-fashioned Reader will smell the milk curdling; see a new slant to the story starting here, a story with a bad end. I am sure I hope so myself.

I glanced around my cot, which fewer and fewer people visited. And my eye settled in that corner, on my sister Riva, she whom my mother preferred to me.

Sor Loreta

It took us the best part of a day to pick our way through the broken town to the convent of Santa Catalina.

At the heart of the city, we discovered that God had of course spared His cathedral all but the most minor marks of His displeasure. Yet rumours were relayed to us that Santa Catalina had lost many cells, and that a part of the novices' quarters had collapsed. I was not slow to draw my conclusions from that.

Indeed. From the first, my reception at the convent was lacking in respect. The whole place was in undignified disarray, with the earthquake cited universally as the excuse. But the *earthquake* had not painted the cloisters those lurid blues and fleshly terracottas! The *earthquake* had not grown those heathen flowers and fruits in the courtyard where a bare crucifix would have sufficed! Not was it an excuse for the smells of sumptuous and fatty foods floating out of every cell.

The *priora* did not take the trouble to greet me personally, on the pretext of tending to the injured. Men with wheelbarrows walked among the fallen stones, and brazenly eyed the chattering nuns. I sensed a deeper disorder in the undisciplined staring and giggling that met my own appearance at the convent gate and ushered me all the way to a cell where the air was still rich with falling dust.

The earthquake soon settled into memory. Its scars were sewn up with ribbons of new-laid stone. Months passed, yet I myself could not settle into my new life.

For in the very cloisters of Santa Catalina, I found myself exposed to a place more godless than the streets of Cuzco. Imagine my disappointment to discover that the souls of the sisters of Santa Catalina were light as feathers and that those nuns shirked all spiritual duties in their pursuit of the sensual pleasures of the table and the music-room.

Loneliness is the curse of the righteous. I had fondly imagined that to enter a convent would bring my soul every consolation it had so long sought. But my life at Santa Catalina was from the first burdened down with heartache and insult, for there was no sister in that whole convent who recognized a special creature when she saw one in me, nor greeted her with joy. In fact, the feathery nuns did not fail to goad me in a thousand vexatiously pricking ways. And when they were not tormenting me, my company was shunned by everyone, as always happens to those whom God has chosen, for the Ignorant are legion, and this shall continue until the very Last Day.

One morning, alone in the church, a vision of Christ came to me: He took the form of a lovely little child hovering just above the communion chalice. I cried out so loudly that everyone in the convent heard me and came running to behold the sight of my most extraordinary piety. After that my lips grew dry with longing every time I contemplated the Host and I licked them repeatedly so as to be able to continue with my prayers. Rather than falling to their knees, those light sisters merely snorted with laughter every time they saw my blessed gesture. And instead of being honoured, I was jeered at when I appeared with the blood-drops of my scourging trailing behind my habit.

My faith could not be weakened by their ignorance. I busied myself with good works. With just one good eye, I could still see the smallest piece of dirt or corruption. Even though I barely ate or slept, the strength of my soul was marvellous. So I would get up and sweep the byways of the entire convent while everyone else lay asleep. And the amazing thing was that it never rained when I was about my work – that happened only in the few hours when I rested or read my *Lives* of the saints. With such small miracles, the Creator marks out those who are to live in His inner chamber of love.

31

I allowed my face to be filled with the pure illumination of rapture when emptying the heavy slop buckets and scrubbing the stoop in front of the confessionals. At table, I refused all the nicest food and took the tiniest portions only of what was completely burned or bad to show that I was unworthy of any good thing. And I would offer half of my meagre rations to other nuns, who, bloated with delicacies, rejected it mockingly. Without finishing my food, I would rise and fetch a basin to wash the feet of other nuns in the refectory, just as Columba of Rieti had done before me. But my light sisters kicked me away, or giggled, 'It tickles!' and I was forced to desist.

Any good Christian reading this will naturally be amazed to learn that soon after my arrival the *priora* herself spoke to me disrespectfully at the Chapter of Offences, the weekly meeting to discipline poor behaviour among the nuns. I was stupefied to hear the *priora* say to me, 'Beware of pride, Sor Loreta,' – for this was to be my new name – 'that you take too much pleasure in humbling yourself.'

'I am worthless in God's eyes,' I murmured. Someone stifled a laugh.

'Your manner,' the *priora* continued sternly, 'shows you think yourself far from worthless, Sor Loreta. The sisters complain that you are arrogant and that you look down on them. You cannot be surprised that they find ways to make themselves feel better. You must have seen them imitating the way you keep licking your lips when you see the Host. That is an affectation I order you to leave off from.'

I turned my deaf right ear towards her, and let her speak the nonsense that was in her heart harmlessly, thus avoiding two sins – hers in uttering it, and mine in hearing it.

Gianni delle Boccole

Swear my old Master Fernando give the boy babe one long look and betook imself to the furthest corner o the world. He were that shamed to be the author o sich an abdomenashun as Minguillo Fasan, Great Canary ovva God!

A brace o weeks after the boy were borned come the news o the devasterating of Arequipa. My Master Fernando claimed that he must see to his warehouse n mines all ripped by the earthquake. And scarce were he back but he were oft agin, under the horsepiss of 'busyness', braving all the quarantys agin the Small-Pox n the Yellow Fever. And so twent on.

We dint know scut bout it at the time, but much later twould come out that he had another reason to keep hurryin to Arequipa dint he.

Minguillo Fasan

Soon the sight of my father's face was to my infant eyes more a memory than a habit.

See how gravely he humiliated my mother by his repeated absences. Her female friends tittered, 'And is Fernando returning soon?'

'The damage . . .' my mother mouthed vaguely.

Yes, the damage. The earthquake in Arequipa might easily shoulder the blame for a number of sad deaths that the Methodical Reader shall shortly be recording in His daybook.

The Suspicious Reader cocks an interrogative eyebrow. If my father had abridged his times abroad, for example, would Riva have lived to kindle the corridors and congeries of our home with giggles and *pas-de-deux*?

In fact, I suppose not.

The truth is that even if he had stayed in Venice, my father would have done little to regulate my behaviour. In those rare times when he was among us, he could barely bring himself to speak to me. He issued no instructions for my handling. My mother showed even less interest. I was left to crawl around the *palazzo*, to eat whatever I snatched up from tray or table, and learn my manners from our guard-dogs, my scruples from our mosquitoes, and to infect the whole place with my curiosity.

The servants followed the lead of my parents. Nobody in that whole place nourished a drop of respectful liking for me. They looked the other way if they saw me. Or they did what was needful and rushed off, not liking to be alone in my company.

The Reader asks: did I care?

I did not, and nor did I fail to thrive.

Though my own mother had pushed me out of her belly and out of her heart, I still lived inside the grandest mamma a boy could ask: the Palazzo Espagnol. And was it any wonder that from my infancy I adored my home? That I loved that great Gothic pile like I loved nightfall and meat? The Palazzo Espagnol had become dam and sire to me, and I grew like the place: tall, narrow, impenetrable, with a constitution of stone. I took my first steps, unapplauded, across its courtyard. I spoke my first words, unheard, in its *limonaia*. There was not an inch of it I did not know.

To the rest of our household the Palazzo Espagnol was a leaky battleship in which they served, sweltered and shivered as it trickled to pieces around them, for there is no cure for water and Venetians do not seek one. My family and servants did not know the joy of the tiny locked chamber by the water-gate or the cobwebbed window in our private tower from which, if you climbed one hundred and seventy-five vertiginous steps, you could see planets, and own all Venice with your eyes.

They did not guess what secret tribute lay at the bottom of the well or buried under the rosebushes. They did not understand how the stairs smelled in the morning, or what feathery scabs you might find tucked into the toes of hundred-year-old slippers in travel trunks in the remotest *ripostiglio*. No, nobody loved the Palazzo Espagnol as I did.

Most of all I loved to know that one day it would be mine.

Even my seven-year-old sister Riva did not know the hidden place in the wine-store where black bottles perched on shelves like vultures, and what the drink inside those bottles could do to your insides, when mixed with sugar and ground-up glass.

I was only four years old when I taught her what she did not know how.

Gianni delle Boccole

Twere as if my brain was ate by bears. How could I of knowed to save her?

I am wiser now, but then, who would of bethought it?

I only got but a little money to put into the hero busyness, n as for

I git on a bad bust from

I know as much as a tin box bout what appened to our little angel Riva. Damn it all to Hell, it will nowise come out. Them sparkling black eyes, them sturdy little legs. She were alredy a darling ovva dancer. The coffin no bigger than a hatbox on four men's shoulders

in the funeral gondola

I wunt

Buggering God

Sor Loreta

Then I had to contend with one Sor Andreola, who had set herself up as the most devout nun in the convent, without even mortifying her flesh so that you would notice it. She merely did smallish good works in a mightily showy way. She was clever with a needle and produced a cloak for a statue of the Virgin that the *priora* decreed worth six hundred *Ave Marias*, four hundred *Salves* and fifteen days of fasting. I nearly forgot to mention the fact that Sor Andreola's skin was supposed to shine with some kind of clear light – like pearls, they claimed – though I could never see it myself. Sor Andreola was only half a year my senior, and already a professed nun.

The other sisters spoke of her with awe. When Sor Andreola fell into one of her famous raptures the novices clustered around and imitated her. That was how much they loved Sor Andreola, who sought the admiration of foolish nuns the way the Devil seeks disciples. And this burned worse than any lye or pepper on my skin. Why was Sor Andreola an object of admiration, and I, far thinner and more devout, a vehicle for sniggering ridicule?

I reminded myself that the Apostle Peter prophesied that in the weeks before the Last Day there would appear on earth many naysayers and mockers. They shall be the first to be struck down. And I comforted myself that Jesus, by subjecting me to the martyrdom of scorn, had called me to be more intimately united with Him than any other sister at Santa Catalina, and particularly more than Sor Andreola.

Renewed in my resolve, I went to the infirmary. But I was not allowed to tend to the sick women as they said that the sight of my ruined face troubled them and gave them bad dreams, and that the smell of my breath made them retch.

Sor Andreola never went to the infirmary except to hold the hands of the sick or sit by them while she embroidered her interminable chasubles and stolas, spinning silks in her fingers like a white spider. Yet for those visits she was praised and almost worshipped by the other nuns, and her presence was constantly requested.

The infirmary sisters were blind to God's design, ignorant of the fact that to look on my face was to be blessed. Not wishing them to persist in their delusions, I pressed my request upon them with strong words. I was refused with hysterical curses. So instead I washed all the infirmary filth, even the bandages and garments of two sisters who were sick with enormous stinking sores.

Secretly in the night I went to those sick sisters and kissed them on the mouth and kissed each of their sores even though they tried to kick me away with their feeble limbs. I told them that I loved their souls so much that nothing would stop me from saving them. They wept. I informed them that, like Colette of Corbie, I could effect cures by putting food I had chewed between their lips, and by spitting over their faces some water I had held in my mouth. Yet they moaned when I did this. Then, like Santa Catalina herself, I drank the very water with which I had washed away their pus, which also tasted sweeter on my tongue than communion wine. The result was that I contracted their fever and was laid out for many days.

In my rapt state I saw many visions and foretold many great events. In my visions there appeared a beautiful woman of my stature dressed in gold with many jewelled shawls up to her cheeks. If all my visions had been recorded by the other sisters, then they would have made a large book. Yet my sisters neglected to do so.

As for the aforementioned infirmary nuns who had refused me access to the sick, not much time passed before one of them came down with a tumour in her breast, another fell ill to the dropsy, the third was apparently killed by a tile falling from a roof damaged by the earthquake and the fourth and most discourteous of them succumbed to a swift pneumonia after a solitary cold bath: so it was that the four of them soon expired in the most pitiful circumstances.

No one can resist the wisdom and will of our great God.

Gianni delle Boccole

No one could pin nothin on the young Master. Nothin. Not the doctors. And not the officers of the law, what was summoned because Riva's passing were so vilent n all-of-a-sudden. The Palazzo Espagnol drained there eyes. Them yahooties took in the tapestries n marbles, and fell to bows n scrapes, dropping there brains out o there breeches. They forgot to ask yer most alimentary question. What zackly were Minguillo doin with young Riva when she died?

'Don't pertain to me,' the boy deklared, if anyone dared ask, playin with his lower lip.

Banditing God!

It broked my Master Fernando Fasan's heart, it broked all our hearts. The maid Anna and my sister Cristina was inconsolibble. I held them two in my arms and let em each cry a canal on my shoulder, poor ones.

Without een pretending not to sob, my Master Fernando Fasan askt Cristina to fold way all Riva's little dresses in a coffer, and straitway offert my sister a new post as chambermaid.

'I don't want to stay here no more,' wept Cristina, but not so's my Master could hear, of course.

It felt as if all our blood ud flowed out o the cracks in the walls of the Palazzo Espagnol, for we was left weak and wondering, like the babiest kittens isn't it.

Minguillo Fasan

As I remarked latterly, the Reader has now embarked upon a long walk in the dark with this voice of mine. Given that He'll not be hearing from the other, oblivious protagonists of this tale, I must do the necessary to keep Him by my side.

Yet not as some voices do, laying a little white hand on the Reader's heart and trembling its wet eyelashes: the Chivalrous Reader must read on, just as a Knight must save his Lady! There's no pleasing everyone. One Reader loves the confidential whisper; it makes Him feel magnificent as a confessor in his black booth. Another fixes His lectatory mandibles upon some voyeur's observations of the more interesting lives of others. Then there's the bird's-eye view, the writer serving as invisible air beneath the Reader's soaring wings. Wheedling and flattery are popular. So is a comical, ranting tone.

What? What's that? The Reader requests that I cease holding up long-winded and unflattering mirrors? Insists I provide instead a sensible account of my maturing childhood, with explanations tending to subsequent events etcetera and so forth?

Pazienza. I would not willingly infuriate, but there's little of note to tell. My sister Riva's death made everyone long-nosed as parsnips for a while. That was tedious, as treats and outings were thin upon the ground. The Venetian Republic played out its last days of gold-leafed and spun-sugar magnificence. The oil portraits of a girl artist called Cecilia Cornaro became our city's sole object of trading value. Speaking of faces, my own countenance began to take on the features that would carry it through to the end of this story, if you can call it that.

The stairs of the Palazzo Espagnol grew smaller; I became familiar with the servants' knees, thighs, bellies and eventually their faces, not that anyone turned theirs my way voluntarily. I attended briefly at an academy for young noblemen. I was sent back. Call that another story. I submitted to a priest's tutoring at home. The Reader will be gratified to know that my expensive education was not wasted on me. I had a gift for languages, as He knows already. I also grew into a great lover of books, though my tastes were most particular and possibly a little strong for the stomach of the Fastidious Reader.

When I say that I loved books, I mean that I loved not just the souls of my books but their bodies. Even before I could read, I was a fanatic for bindings, affectioned to the intimate protection and adornment jointly embodied in their snug fittings. I adored the shapeliness and firmness of books. I enjoyed their intransigent corners, their rich smells and the way they opened and lay down flat in front of me on the merest suggestion of my fingers. Then, when I learned to read, I was happy in a whole new way: in a house where everyone avoided me, the books in our library exposed their tender insides and submitted to my attentions whenever and however I wanted.

Call it a liking that I also nourished for Cristina, the plump little daughter of our former loose-legged cook. (Does the Reader not think it shows a nice side of my nature, to be attached to a human skin that was not attached to my own body? I am sure I hope so myself.)

I took my first kiss from the said Cristina, as a prelude to easing the virginity off the two of us. She spat and shook me off, 'You are not nice, Minguillo.'

'What am I then?' I enquired, my hand warm and busy down her bodice.

'You are . . . the other thing,' she stammered.

Her little brother's employment, I mentioned, hung in the balance. They were bastard orphans, the pair of them, and she grasped the thing directly. But she screamed when I twisted a little bud of a nipple to see if it would come off. I had always wondered. My researches were interrupted by the arrival of the nightsoilman. After that I did not find the cook's daughter alone again until – another episode of this account, some months later.

What? It is provoking to hint in this way? Really, I despair of the Reader who still insists on a story delivered in neat pellets like a rosary. He must learn to bear with the vagaries of a tale told the way a cat coughs, unexpectedly, and learn to like it.

My childhood withered. I suppose I was in my way content. Even though my mother avoided me and my father regarded me as he would the scab of a Small-Pox sore – with fear and distaste – I was the only son of that great house so I strode about it masterfully, slamming doors with my head held high. I celebrated my twelfth birthday (for no one else did) with a solitary re-enactment of recent events in France, deploying some chickens to interpret the roles of the French King and Queen, and a hatchet on a string to simulate *la belle dame* Madame Guillotine.

Then occurred a thing I had not seen coming. After all those years my mother was suddenly fat with child, begotten, the Reader may suppose, during one of my father's increasingly rare appearances. I watched her breasts grow lumpen with the milk. Rankling memories arose, of how she had decided to withhold those breasts from my own teeth. For six months I observed them fill and droop inside her clothes.

Another child in the house? I did not think so, I really did not.

Sor Loreta

There was a tradition at Santa Catalina that on Good Friday three nuns would be fastened to the crosses in *el santuario* as a tribute to what Our Lord suffered on our behalf. It was a great honour to be chosen for this duty, and I was diligent in my efforts to make sure that I would be among the three for my first Holy Week at the convent.

I tried so hard to be worthy of this honour that I involuntarily caused a miracle. Just like Santa Rosa, I gazed for hours with love on a painting of Christ's Passion in the church. Eventually the face of Our Lord began to look misty, and then damp, so that perspiration appeared on His brow and cheeks. I called loudly for witnesses and the *priora* came running. However, the woman was unable to see the miracle I had wrought.

'Sor Loreta,' she sighed, 'the painting is perfectly dry.'

She added, 'But I'll not deny you've the power to make a body's flesh creep. I declare I feel quite clammy and uncomfortable myself when I look at you.'

I was highly gratified, for exactly in this way had the naysayers mocked the very same miracle when it was performed by Santa Rosa herself.

But after the incident with the painting, I was denied the privilege of standing on the cross for Our Lord that Easter. Naturally Sor Andreola was chosen, and she selected her two most slavish followers to join her.

Meanwhile, it pleased God to test me and to send upon me mischievous jokes and insults, like a living worm in my bread and a black cat left locked up in my cell.

Four years went by in this way. I was never chosen for the Good Friday cross. My sufferings were always made more painful by the sight of nuns offering acts of veneration to Sor Andreola wherever she walked. Some even profanely fell to their knees, kissing the ground where she had passed.

But at that time, it being 1788, God sent a pious man at last to Arequipa, and I was convinced that he would prove my salvation, by which I mean the salvation of the sinful convent of Santa Catalina. Bishop Pedro José Chávez de la Rosa had come all the way from Spain to lay waste to the lax morals of Arequipa. He started immediately at our convent.

Like any good Christian, he was shocked at the luxurious cells of the rich nuns, who used their *peculios*, their private allowances, to surround themselves with comforts, including slaves and servants. My *peculios*, of course, I put into the missionary-box: I refused to buy myself treats while there were heathens in the world without Bibles of their own. I preferred to use the serving nuns for my menial work rather than to own a slave. The only ornaments in *my* cell were a small human skull and a Baby Jesus rendered in pure plaster.

The Bishop saw that the nuns' slaves and servants were a vice, being the eyes and ears and purses of the nuns, going forth on to the streets at will, and bringing back the taint of the outside world on their tongues and in their shopping baskets. It was as if the convent walls did not exist for those girls. Bishop Chávez de la Rosa was also dismayed to see the private kitchens of the rich nuns and the costly delicacies that were served to them on damask cloths set with silver plates while they lolled on their cut-velvet cushions like courtesans in a seraglio. He ordered all the nuns to return to the godly

41

simplicity of communal dining. He closed the bakery that produced the opulent bread and *polvorón* cakes for which the convent was famous.

Now I of course valued the world as something merely worthless and I had never been one tiny part jealous to see the sisters flaunting their jewelled silver crosses and Sèvres teacups. Nor had I envied them their slaves, or their pernicious affection for each other, shown in wanton kisses and hugs. But I agreed wholeheartedly with Bishop Chávez de la Rosa that their wicked ways must be put to an end. Therefore I wanted to make sure that he was fully informed of the many additional sins that the nuns were trying to conceal from him.

Those days that the Bishop made his investigations among us, I spent prostrate in prayer upon the icy stone floor of the church. He was obliged to step over my suffering form several times on his way to the altar. And so my own piety, the only true faith in the whole convent of Santa Catalina, was finally noticed by Bishop Chávez de la Rosa.

'What is your name, child?' he asked me.

I kept my face down on the floor. I did not wish him to be distracted by it. 'I am no one, *Ilustrísimo*,' I declared. 'I am a humble messenger.'

With my head muffled by stone, I recounted all the secret wrongdoings of the light nuns and the *priora*. I told him of my deeds of penance, my fasting, and what I had suffered in the way of scorn. I left out no detail.

He knelt down beside me and listened in silence. Then he picked up one of my wrists and turned it over in his hand.

'Poor child,' he pronounced finally, rising to his feet. 'We must see what can be done for you.'

By this, I naturally understood that I would shortly rise to a position of great authority, and preside over all those sinful ones who had sought to bring me down.

Gianni delle Boccole

Until he had eleven year, if ye dint know him intimid, twere jist possible, with yer head on one side n yer fingers crosst, to think

42

on Minguillo as a tearing-way kind ovva lad, with a morbid maginashon n a bad temper.

He dint grow any prettier. Swear that the eyes lookt closer to by the year and the mouth on im were like summing pulled in on a hook with mackerel guts. The skin stretcht oer his face so ye could see the scull underneath, trying to affright ye, ugly as a gargle, Great Toad ovva God!

At eleven he grewed the worst crop o pimples as ever bedivilled a humane skin. The repungent kind what waxes yellow, then black, what run around in colonies, settling n spreding there seed, finely digging pits in the face. Twere as if his wickedness got up evry night while he lay sleeping and writed more of his gilt on that face o his.

And that were the year that he were found tyin up my poor sister Cristina in the *limonaia*. He ud made a little wooden cross for her, and she were bound hand n foot like Jesus pon it. There were an apple in her mouth. He, in cool blood, were sharpening the knife on a grindstone. Thank the Lord. On account of as it were the shrieks n sparks o the knife what caused a passin footman to investigerate.

The Papà Fernando Fasan were of natural course way in Arequipa agin. I rusht down to the *limonaia* to see my Cristina trusst up and the fish-gutting knife a-glinting in Minguillo's hand. Twere me that restled the thing out o his fist. He dint nowise wunt to give it up, and the look he give me burnt into the back of my brain. At the last minute he twisted the blade so it went deep into my hand. None o t'other servants dared to help me. The knife stood there in the fat o my palm, uprite like a soldier.

Dint I ache to nuck im one up the bracket jist then? But Minguillo were the young Master, he were intitled. He dint bash an eyelid. I caught his eye and quickly turned back into my idiot-drooling self, the abstruse one that twere safest to be round him.

'Don't pertain to me,' he dekklared, swaggering oft. All the servants, there blood up, sayed slurs at him like they would niver ornery dare, tho naturally they waited till he were almost out o hearing.

Cristina finely spat the apple out o her mouth and begun to wail at the blood squirting out o my wound.

Anna stitched n dressed my hand, using a burned needle n a clean cloth, so there were no longlastin damidge. Except that wheniver after I saw the young Master, a stab o pain went through my palm. Sumtimes it doed that too, when he wernt there, but were up to evil elsewheres. And Cristina were taken away by kind Piero Zen, my Mistress Donata Fasan's assistant husband, to live n work in his homonymouse *palazzo*. He knew twere not safe for her no more at the Palazzo Espagnol. Anna n I messed her sorely. That were one more peace of good gone out of all our lives on count of Minguillo Fasan.

My Mistress were in her fifth month so she were spared the story o the croosyfied Cristina. For Conte Piero were worrit it mite bring on the birthing pains too early isn't it.

Doctor Santo Aldobrandini

Skin's drama will usually make its first eruption in early adolescence.

I feel a special compassion for my pimpled patients, who often come to me at that tender age when appearance is all, and all is blighted. They feel they are dying, not of disease, but shame. For the person whose face is marked in ignominy must always be conscious of the disgust of those with whom he stands at close quarters. At best, his companions pity the distempered blood they read on the raddled skin; at worst, they wonder what moral corruption is embossed in the cutaneous putrescence.

The poor sufferer runs to the apothecary, oftentimes at his – or, more likely, her – peril. In my time in Venice there were many skin preparations on the market. All promised to alchemize an ugly outbreak into silken skin with the lustre of pearls. Most were harmless waters drugged with alcohol and sugar. A picturesque name usually conjured some exotic provenance: the Grand Sultan's Elixir, The Maiden's Dew, The Milk of the Candelabra Cactus, and so on. Venetians love entertainment: such names alone charmed the gold out of the pockets of the rich. That these hypocritical juices were bought by the poor instead of solid food was the quacks' true crime.

I do not rant or preach. I would judge most of the cheaper preparations worth the few *soldi* they cost for a sense of feeling better and a mood actually lightened by the wine. Some, like Bezoar Stone (manufactured in the belly of the Peruvian llama), might in fact speed an infertile woman towards conception. And the Bark of Peru, from the chinchona tree, is known to treat the symptoms of the Sweating Sickness most effectively, though none of the above have the least effect upon the skin.

Yet for every quack that peddles pretty water, there is one who murders drop by drop. A few of these Venetian skin preparations were actually dangerous, containing poisons and corrosives that might weaken a victim for ever, or even kill at high dosage. The worst I would ever come across was also the costliest. It went by the name of 'The Tears of Santa Rosa', and was all the rage in Venice when I was a young man just setting out on my career in skin.

Whichever pharmaceutical criminal had conjured it, he aimed his sights on the rich. The nastier the taste or smell and the higher the price, the more effective such people believed a medicine must be. They adored the double sacrifice of hurting their purse and disgusting their mouth or nose: the cure would be more exquisitely imagined in this way.

Despite its rankly oversweet odour, the affluent Venetians would be constitutionally unable to resist 'The Tears of Santa Rosa'. For the hairdressers who disseminated it gave out such a picturesque tale of its provenance. They claimed that it was composed of the tears of Peruvian nuns wept into lachrymatory bottles in the snowcapped peaks of the Andes, and that a kind and infallible physician had brought it all the way across the ocean for the beautifying of Venice.

Sor Loreta

I waited for my rightful elevation in vain.

Instead, a few hours after my interview with the Bishop, I was taken to the infirmary and force-fed a meal of fatty soup, thick porridge and pieces of oil-soaked bread. My head was bound in rags soaked in herbs and I was tied to the bed.

'Bishop Chávez de la Rosa will punish you when he hears what you have done to me!' I warned through a gap in the bandages.

'Who do you think suggested this treatment for you?' The pharmacy nun Margarita, a Bolivian, grinned at me in a vulgar fashion. 'Open your mouth, there's cake for you.'

Suddenly I understood that of course the Bishop had wanted to keep me safe while he went about his work. In the busy infirmary, moreover, I was in the society of other nuns and overheard more of what was going on than I would have done in my habitual isolation. And it was God's design that I should know the daily happenings at Santa Catalina and beyond, because one day I would need to right all the wrongs that were about to take place.

For it went badly for poor Bishop Chávez de la Rosa. His righteous remonstrances to the nuns of Santa Catalina were treated with disrespect. The high-born nuns acted as if they were superior to the Bishop and frustrated his holy plans in more ways than I can write down. This must have included his plans for me, for they came to nothing.

The Bishop never came to see me in the infirmary, so he could not have known about the cruel ways in which they forced me to eat. Of course, I quickly realized why he did not visit me: if the other nuns had seen how he favoured me, they would have found even more ways to torture me. Instead, Sor Andreola came floating in, and sat beside me, sewing and whispering to me in a voice of pretended kindness. I let her stay, because I wanted to examine her at close quarters. I found nothing spiritual in her. She was definitely plumper than me. She had an insipid kind of prettiness and a bleached-looking complexion. I did not see anything that resembled the lustre of pearls on her skin.

I told her: 'I pity you from the depths of my heart, Sor Andreola.'

While I lay in the infirmary, Bishop Chávez de la Rosa fought and lost a war against the high-born nuns. When he saw how proud and disobedient they were, the Bishop suspended elections for the next *priora* and installed one of his own choice (I myself being still in the infirmary at that time). But the luxury-loving nuns rebelled and sent secret letters to powerful figures in the Church, many of whom were their uncles.

Discovering their subterfuge, the Bishop imposed harsh penances on the leaders and even denied the five most sinning sisters the Eucharist. They responded by asking their uncles to take their case all the way to the *audiencia* in Lima. The uncles obliged and the High Court and even the King humiliated the Bishop. The nuns of Santa Catalina won the right to govern themselves free of his influence.

After that, Bishop Chávez de la Rosa, abashed and sorrowing, gave up on Santa Catalina. He lifted his eyes over the convent wall and found many things to reform in the town of Arequipa. As I had done on the day of my arrival, he saw ladies clothed like harlots, and harlots done up like ladies. Bishop Chávez de la Rosa tried to make the females of Arequipa dress decently for their worship in our churches. But the women would not give up their high-hooped skirts and lewd necklines.

His attempts to rid Arequipa of its vicious *fiestas* fell on stony ground, just like the heads of the poor French King and Queen rolling on the sawdust in Paris. How could the people of Arequipa not see the parallels? Yet it seemed that the Most High chose to illuminate only the soul of His most humble daughter with this insight.

The Bishop found men and women openly cohabiting without the blessing of God, claiming that weddings were priced too high by the clerics of Arequipa. As if *this* were the reason that all the richest citizens of the town, including a Venetian nobleman named Fernando Fasan – he whose warehouse had been righteously destroyed by the earthquake of 1784 – lived in open concubinage with their mistresses.

Next Bishop Chávez de la Rosa campaigned against the number of children born out of holy wedlock in Arequipa. He soon had a thousand children, the spawn of immoral unions, safely sequestered from decent society in his new Foundling Home. The high mortality rate among the bastard offspring reflected the wicked nature of their begetting.

Little babies were buried every day, and the light nuns at Santa Catalina loved to say sentimental prayers for their souls. 'A baby mass!' was the constant cry among them, and of course Sor Andreola of the white skin must sit in the middle of everyone holding a baby doll, and soaking up their adoration as if she were the Virgin herself.

I had been allowed out of the infirmary by then. But I refused to attend the crowded baby masses. I preferred to worship my own plaster image of the Baby Jesus in the strictest seclusion. I was not sure in my heart if those flesh-and-blood foundling babies could be sinless, as everyone said they were. It was my suspicion that their feckless parents had transmitted something bad in the blood.

47

Doctor Santo Aldobrandini

I never knew my parents. The nuns told me that I was the child of fornication and dishonour. For some time I thought that Fornication was my mother's name and Dishonour was my father's. Then that foolish idea was beaten out of me too.

I was often told that I was fortunate to be an orphan in a Foundling Home in Venice, and not some infidel child left exposed on a mountain in a pagan wilderness. There were many ugly moments when I disagreed.

By the time I was eight the skin on my back was pleated with the trails of old whippings. The other side of me was concave – I had never known a full belly. But I had clear eyes and a brain that refused to be incurious about the workings of the human body, and had only the mildest interest in what the nuns called my soul. For, as far as I could see, my lively soul was the thing they were trying to whip unconscious.

The human body, though! Now there was a thing. I lay in bed at night listening to the blood ticking through my veins, working out its ways. I performed a dismal analysis upon the orchestra of coughs emitted by the other children in my dormitory. I soon came to know which coughs would fade away, and which would end with a blanket over the poor child's head and a curt prayer for his passage to the afterlife.

What I liked best was skin. Any sign of sores or rash and you would find me by the side of the suffering child. You might call it pity – but who was I to pity anyone? For me, it felt more like fondness. The nuns had done everything possible to harden my heart, yet it still opened up at the sight of a poor creature afflicted in the skin. To this day, it does that. I am still known to follow a stranger in the street, and press an ointment or a balm into his or her surprised hand: whatever is needed to cure his rash or Impetigo.

Even as a little boy, I had a way with cutaneous maladies. I could pound a poultice from the poorest ingredients scraped up from the corners of the convent, and apply it secretly under a bandage torn from my own shirt. I was beaten for ruining my clothes, but my little patients prospered; they brought me more patients with newer conditions. I did not know what these illnesses were called, yet I knew how to palliate them, it seemed by instinct, unless it was the Small-Pox that took hold. When Tommaso from my dormitory succumbed, I could do nothing more than hold his hand until he died. I held that hand so fiercely that it was white when they forced me to let go.

Furtive and roundabout ways worked best in the convent: to state my desire to be a doctor would have brought down punishments on my head for arrogance. There would be sarcastic questions as to who would pay for the training of a worthless orphan like myself. So I kept my eyes down in the classroom, never visibly distinguishing myself, never writing all I learned on my little slate.

As soon as I had mastered my letters, I began to haunt the infirmary. I befriended the old nun who worked there. Her eyes were failing: she let me read out the pharmacy receipts for her. Each one I read, I memorized. And every day I stole a little sugar or a little salt. In this way I kept alive when many of my companions did not. Sometimes I emptied some herbs into my pocket as I ground up a prescription for a sick child. Eventually I ignored the pharmacy nun's instructions, for I knew better than she what saved and what exterminated the convent's inmates, who comprised both children and fallen, destitute women.

The medical records of the foundlings and their mothers were kept in the infirmary. The lock was not too stubborn for a scalpel. I learned that my own unwed mother had died of puerperal sepsis in that very room, due to 'miasma' in the air. I sniffed the air of the infirmary archives. The dust of ages and the effluent of the drains filled up my nostrils.

The old nun was persuaded to reminisce about my birth. A medical student had delivered me, arriving hotfoot from assisting at an autopsy, his hands still wet with necrotic gore. One soul, mine, had come into the world by that red hand; another, my mother's, had left it.

My father was unknown and would stay that way.

Sor Loreta

There came to us more news from Europe of the dreadful doings of the revolutionists who hated the Holy Mother Church, her priests, and even her nuns, and persecuted them like the Christian martyrs of old.

Merchants delivered foreign newspapers to the Tristáns: this rich Arequipan family had connections in Paris. One of the Tristán *sambas* brought in a well-thumbed page to Santa Catalina and the nuns crowded round while one of my sisters who was sinfully fluent in French translated for us. Some evil-doer had drawn a cartoon of nuns being driven out of their convent.

The Godless revolutionists used laughter just as the Devil plies his pitchfork. They sneered that the convents were like bastilles. They drew the Church as a lamprey, sucking good out of the world without giving anything back. The heathens declared that *praying* for the wretched was lazy and worthless. They insisted that the nuns were not too good for housework and cooking: they should *work* for the poor and sick. Nor should nuns think themselves too fine for human husbands. They should go out and marry and procreate for the state.

'God does not make anything celibate,' one blasphemer urged.

As if those poor nuns were not already married to God! What kind of state was this, that proposed bigamy for the pure brides of Christ? Some noble nuns were even accused of subverting the revolution, because they refused to cuckold God and lived on in their communities in a blameless manner. It was not until All Saints that news of the notorious event arrived in Arequipa, an event that made all good Christians gasp: on July 17th 1794, sixteen Carmelite sisters from Compiègne had been led to the guillotine and their heads had been cut off.

In Santa Catalina our nuns were swooning with gratitude that such things could never happen here. Yet my heart was torn in my breast, for those nuns from Compiègne had been allowed God's greatest honour of martyrdom. *Deo gratias*. I wondered if there was a way to obtain some of the dirt from beneath the guillotine. The earth that had drunk the blood of the martyrs must be a most precious relic, I thought, and I wished with all my heart to have some.

And now there was talk of a long-haired Corsican. With every passing month the merchants brought more tales of his depredations. An ocean did not seem vast enough to keep that dangerous madman Napoleon Bonaparte away from us.

Minguillo Fasan

Marcella, more lately Sister Constanza, was born twelve years after myself.

The Reader sighs, 'At last!' – was this event not promised in the very first pages of my tale? And yet so much verbiage has intervened. Can all of it be relevant? No. But if the Tetchy Reader desires an argument, I defy Him to deny that He's been royally entertained along the way.

What? What's that? The birth of my sister Marcella? Why not immediately resume that interesting subject? Ah, let us not rush at it. We shall arrive there roundaboutly with more pleasure. I am sure I hope so myself.

There's a proverb quoted at the parturition of every Venetian woman, 'A lord is born in the world', which rang very hollowly that fearful year of 1796, with the French and Austrians kicking up tufts of the Veneto and Napoleon swearing quotably as ever '*I shall be an Attila to the state of Venice*'. Bitter Venetians were saying even at noble births, or perhaps especially at those, 'Ah, a *slave* is born to the world. There will be no more Venetian lords now.' All the gladness slunk out of our city, and into its place crept shame.

Marcella was born under an azure sky unmolested by the pesk of a cloud. I lingered in the courtyard, savouring my mother's birth cries, so much lustier than those of the kitten I had that morning dispatched with a rusty nail. I had left it impaled on our street door. I thought it a suitable emblem to inform passers-by that ours was that day a house of suffering, not to mention our city dying on her legs at the same time as my mother retched and ripped on her bed.

My mother's screams echoed through the corridors of the Palazzo Espagnol and flowed out of the windows down the Grand Canal. My father was of course away in Arequipa. While everyone else fussed around my mother that day, I, as the owner-in-waiting, had felt entitled to sit at my father's desk, dip his pen in his inkwell, and open all his drawers with the key he kept hidden in a notch up the chimney. I had passed the sweet hours of the afternoon picking at the yellow meat of the pimples on my chin while looking at his private documents.

Nothing detained my interest for long – until I found a document signed just before his latest voyage to the Spanish colonies.

It began, '*I, Conte Fernando Fasan, of the Palazzo Espagnol, residing in this city of Venice, being unaffected in my intellect, but knowing death a certainty yet its hour unknown, do hereby order and execute this my last will and testament in the following manner . . .*'

I looked for the words 'bequeathe my entire estate' shortly followed by 'my son Minguillo Fasan'. Then I sat up and spat. It seemed that my papà had been thrown into a flummox by my experiment on the chickens in our courtyard garden. I had explained it to them all quite patiently. The French Revolution had lately separated a number of beings from their heads in a novel way, including nuns and priests. It gave a boy ideas, made him curious. And why should skill not be involved?

My foot started drumming on the floor when I read the following statement in his will: '*My son, Minguillo, being incapacitated with a mental disorder, is not fit to inherit. Therefore I leave my possessions to my next-born child upon that child reaching its majority.*'

That next-born child was just that minute making its way into my world. My father was a bestial idiot! This will was an impossible deed! What if it was a daughter, the thing dividing my mother's bowels as I read? In our world, daughters did not inherit except where there were no viable sons. Yet I was feeling very fine and healthy indeed, what's more well engorged with living anger.

So, even before she was halfway into this world, I began to hate the thing that would be Marcella.

Footsteps and shouts echoed in the corridor. I divined that my mother was nearing her time. Perhaps the infant was suffocating in the womb? Then it occurred to me that, in the event of the demise of this being-born child, before achieving a majority, there would be no one to take the Palazzo Espagnol away from me.

I had just finished locking the ludicrous will away when I heard my mother's final piteous cry, and a faint, lamb-like bleat. I strode into the bedchamber without knocking. It smelled sweet, of blood and tears. A sheet was offering up scarlet spirals in a basin of milk. The servants scurried about, patting down clean linen, dabbing my mother's forehead. They knew better than to meet my eyes.

My mother looked up from the bed, with that expression of fret and uncertainty that she always wore when she had dealings with me. She was whiter than her pillow, and shuddered from time to time, as if her body still rehearsed the birth. The nurse held a cup of water to her lips. Some trickled down her chin into her breasts, which must ache in the stretching now, I thought. Like the below. Which must excruciate.

'Did it hurt tremendously, Mamma?'

She nodded, warily.

'Was it like a red-hot iron rod being poked up into you? Was it like when you hit something's eye with a splintery stick?'

The maids hissed quietly to each other. I heard the words 'kitten', '*misera bestia*' and '*diavolo incarnato*'. My mother blurred a feeble *stop* with her white hand.

'What have we got?' I enquired, glancing at the whimpering scrag they were swabbing down. It was bald and pink. A pink sea-creature, shelled. There was an absence between the legs.

'Is that all?' I asked. 'Will it live?'

'*Perfettina*,' the young maid called Anna murmured tenderly, discreetly throwing me the worst look she dared.

'A perfect little girl,' my mother whispered, 'a sister. You will be kind to her, won't you, Minguillo?'

I passed the hairdresser Signor Fauno on the way out. My mother's birth-turbulent coiffure was to be rebuilt on the instant. Beneath her hair, worries swam in aimless panic, like fish in a barrel. (Did the Jovial Reader ever shoot fish in a barrel? I recommend it as a most amusing pastime.) My mother's fish blew bubbles inside her tired head. Her husband was absent

53

and Napoleon was at the gates, with his long lank locks bedraggling down his excavated cheekbones. The crows of war were cruaaacing and cruaccing above us. Send for the hairdresser!

Gianni delle Boccole

There was more hairdressers than boat-builders n soldiers in Venice at that moment, jist when boat-builders n soldiers mite o been the salivation of us. The nobbles ud stopped bothering with the Grate Council. The cares o public office was way too onerous for them. When our last Doge, Manin, were told of his elekshon, he had to be helped, weeping, to his bed, God-on-a-stick! Napoleon Bonypart were on his way, and that's what we had to fight him with.

Venice believt she were a beautiful courtesan to be bargaint with for her favours. Bony saw her as a wasted old hag greased n painted up, and he valued her at half-a-sequin. He dint even pity her, that's how little he bethought of her.

It give me the Viles to remember it.

Send for the hairdressers! That's what the nobbles allus cryed when there were trouble afoot. The hairdressers ud come busslin in with there lotions n potions for the face, hair n hands. They would curl yer wig, do a *parrucca alla delfina*, dolphin style with a bag for the hair at the nape, or a *groppi*, with yer real curls cluttert all oer like honeycome.

That's what her ancestors left for our darling little Marcella, who were borned like a holy insent into her city's dying days. A plague o hairdressers, Napoleon Bonypart, and a brother ye would want to watch oer yer shoulder. Desprit.

The funning thing were, Marcella herself would of probly found summing bout it all to make her laff, spite of evrything, and a way to make ye feel better as well.

Doctor Santo Aldobrandini

My saddened city of Venice was in those days caught between Napoleon's haemorrhoids and his bladder.

Both were in an irritable state.

We Venetians should have seen what was coming to us when Napoleon took up the *terraferma* cities of the Veneto. Just at the moment those cities began to foment a little rebellion, Bonaparte's usual complaints were exacerbated by a searing itch all over his body. He scratched until he drew blood, opening a vent for his peccant humours.

In other words, he declared war on the former owner of those cities: my own Venice.

Irritation with the Venetians must have caused Napoleon to clench on his sensitive rectal tissue. Riding horseback with Venetian-induced piles could not have endeared Venice to Napoleon Bonaparte. His bladder and his anus were on fire, and the Veneto was burning as a result.

Doctors more eminent than myself would one day ruminate upon the strong streak of automania in the Frenchman. But even then, well before I grew to the Corsican's own small height, I knew a symptom when I heard of it.

There were sniggers and whispers in the dormitory that the general's genitals were notoriously infantile in form. Such a deficiency might easily breed in his glands a desire for conquests. In my secret little empire of cures at the convent, I began to suspect that Napoleon's cutaneous issues were related to his restless desire for dominance. Perhaps it was the raw pain between his legs, or perhaps it was the very passivity of Venice that aroused Napoleon to take her.

When Napoleon threatened my city, he also forced himself upon me. He made himself my muse: the discomforts of his skin would become the opening pages of my medical textbook, while throughout my youth the Corsican's integumental disorders would scar the very epidermis of my world. Napoleon was my patient, I suppose, in that my life was thenceforward in forced fealty to his, just as if I had sworn an oath to attend personally to his ills.

Minguillo Fasan

'We are not safe in our own beds,' whimpered my second cousin, our last Doge Ludovico Manin. And your man laid down the ducal *berretto* without a fight. Faced with Boney's cool ultimatum, the Great Council voted itself into extinction and scuttled out of the Doges' Palace. A few days later, three thousand Frenchmen marched through the city. Venice was no more a glorious Republic but a shabby little 'Democratic Municipality'.

It was a bungled suicide, not an honourable death. Venice was dying like a fool. Boney nailed a French cockade to her stupid, dead forehead.

The only people who fussed at all were the poor, who were losing precisely nothing. Brooding at the window of the Palazzo Espagnol, I drank up their shouts of pain. In their *palazzi*, it was rumoured, my brother aristocrats were busy turning out their treasures to sell or hide. And writing their wills, as if that would do any good when Napoleon, the biggest fortune-hunter in the world, was standing on the doorstep, with extremely itchy palms.

As soon as she was his, Napoleon took to pimping our trinket city. He sold Venice to his enemies the Austrians in exchange for something he *really* wanted, the little grey bandbox of Belgium. On his way out, he helped himself to our Bellinis, our Tizianos, our Veroneses. He kidnapped them not because he loved the art, but because he did not want the Habsburgs to have them.

Dark days they were for me, after the little pink creature Marcella was born and began immediately to become a person loved at no one's expense but my own. That baby had more followers than the infant Jesus; they were always cluttering up the nursery and gazing on her with adoration. I had to look over the tops of their heads and could no way get near her. Servants attending her simply did not hear my voice commanding them to step aside.

And the Palazzo Espagnol, my beloved, unwavering parent: even that seemed under siege now. There were stories that our new masters would billet their sordid soldiers in the best of accommodations, throwing noble families on the street with special pleasure. Then there were rumours that the Austrians planned to raze our rambling palaces and build right-angled boxes of barracks. Then the French would . . .

As the Reader observes, I passed from child to man, as Venice passed from hand to hand. If Venice was my sister, I would have considered her rifled and dishonoured. I would have been disgusted by her. And I would have wanted to punish her, hard, for what she had taken from me.

Doctor Santo Aldobrandini

A boy of nine thin years, I joined the crowds rustling like a plague of moths through the dim corridors of the newly occupied city, which to me, even then, resembled the fascinations of a many-chambered hospital. The poor were visibly pellagrous, those of citizen class were often poxed, and the nobles bore their special, inherited or expensively acquired ills.

The day the French arrived, I followed a black-robed senator, whose neck-goitre interested me. How gauche I was! The nuns had taught me nothing of how to parley with my superiors. As the nobleman paused to read a new edict nailed to a wall, I knew no better than to put my hand on his arm and ask if I might examine the swelling at his throat. I hoped to be able to suggest a cure: I had confected a poultice that had worked well on a similar condition in a fallen woman at the convent. Naturally, however, the senator shook me off and hastened away, muttering.

Staring after him, a thought struck me. A nobody from Corsica now owned the fate of my city. So a nobody fathered by Dishonour on Fornication could also choose his own destiny, might he not?

I ran away from the orphanage. I lived on the streets. I crept into hospitals, only to help. I scoured noisome pharmacy vessels in exchange for lessons. I weeded herb gardens. I ran errands for sellers of medical tracts.

And, like my muse Napoleon, I stole.

The only things I stole were books about the human body and its ills. If I could steal something that dealt with conditions of the skin I was happiest of all, for that was where my thirst for knowledge was now tipping into an outright passion.

After two years on the streets, I made the rounds of all the surgeons in Venice, offering my services as an apprentice. No one wanted me, and few would even listen to me.

I could not understand it. By then I had spent time helping the *Fatebenefratelli* at the hospital, I had read my Galen, my Avicenna, my tracts on all the diseases of dampness that commonly afflicted Venetians and soldiers. My pockets were full of useful herbs; my head was bursting with useful detail. Yet even on the rare occasions when someone allowed me to spout my knowledge, they just sighed regretfully. One surgeon went so far as to say, 'If only . . .' before he dismissed me.

'If only what?' I begged.

He shook his head. It was his servant, a youth of my own age, who kindly explained the truth to me as he showed me out the door.

'Youse too thin and poor-looking. The poor Venetians caint afford themselves a doctor. Or they go to the Jews. The rich Venetians wants somethin plump and pretty to look at when they're ailing or pretending to. A young surgeon's a sweet entertainment to them. A little flirtation makes 'em feel more better than physic. Youse too poor-mouth, and too serious, boy! It will not do. You need to find a country surgeon to apprentice on, and put yourself around some decent food while youse about it.'

'May I look in the hall mirror?' I asked the boy. I had none at my disposal in the doorways, boats and outhouses where I slept.

He patted my shoulder sympathetically as I learned the truth of his diagnosis. I looked uncared-for, which I was, and starved, equally true. Worse, I looked tragic, as if I were somehow bleeding invisibly from the heart. Given my own dilapidation, how could others believe that I might be capable of curing them?

I took the boy's advice. I made my way out of Venice, by fishing-boat, foot and cart. I felt deep dry earth crunching beneath my feet for the first time. I followed the rumours of vacant posts until I found myself a Master, Doctor Ruggiero, an irascible general surgeon in rural circumstances near Stra. There I would drink my fill of cow-warm milk and eat my height in mounds of cheap polenta. And there I would learn the Small-Pox, the Cow-Pox, scything gashes and other country ailments. And, though I could not guess it then, a shocking gunshot wound and an attempted murder would also come my way in the gentle green hills of the Veneto.

Sor Loreta

One morning I was at my solitary devotions in my cell, when suddenly there shot out of my crucifix five blood-red rays that pierced my heart, forehead, feet and hands. The burning pain made me swoon. I had a sensation of my soul rising in flight with the speed of a bullet. Exactly so had Teresa of Avila described the sensations of her Transverberation. I felt my body floating irresistibly upwards, towards where my soul soared.

When I came to myself, I saw with joy that God had not only pierced my heart and entrails with His love, but He had also awarded me the stigmata. Now I too bore the immortally fresh marks of Jesus's crucifixion on my hands, feet and forehead. I sent a *samba* running to fetch the *priora*, so that I might begin on the path to sainthood right there and then. I hoped Bishop Chávez de la Rosa himself would be summoned to witness. The *priora* arrived, panting, in a disagreeable frame of mind.

'Behold!' I announced, pointing to the red holes in my limbs.

'Behold what?' she demanded rudely. I divined that I had interrupted her at one of her many light and pleasurable activities. Next I indicated the halo that hovered behind my head since my stigmatization.

'So you painted a yellow circle on your cell wall,' she sneered, 'to sit in front of.'

Then I realized that I had just witnessed the proof of her unenlightenment. *Naturally* she could not see my stigmata or halo. She was not a blessed person.

'I pity you that you are blind to God's miracles,' I told her calmly. She stormed off.

Nor was anyone else at Santa Catalina worthy to see the mark of the Most High upon me. They stubbornly worshipped Sor Andreola, with her showy white light, and ignored the subtler mark of the Lord's love imprinted on my skin. In fact, my invisible stigmata gave them one more reason to laugh at me.

I comforted myself that Santa Catalina herself had suffered the same oppression. Her stigmata could be seen by no one but herself during her lifetime. She was content that it should be so. The opinion of the coarse rabble was meaningless for her. Yet after her death – then everyone saw the marks, and knew that she had been right and they had been wrong, and they were sorry and ashamed in more ways than I can write down.

Minguillo Fasan

My mother had entreated, 'You will be kind to her, won't you, Minguillo?'

The trouble was every single thing about my sister queued up to make me not so.

There was the will, of course, brooding in my father's unattended desk. The Empathetical Reader shall feel as if upon His own skin the chafe of its most hurtful revelation: that Marcella would some day inherit my adored Palazzo Espagnol and I would be reduced to her lowly dependent.

The infant girl herself raised my wrath by her very bitch-sized being. The smaller and more pathetical she seemed, the greater my ire in proportion, for the grosser was the injustice in that scrap being preferred to myself.

From the beginning, as I've explained, I got no more than glimpses of Marcella, usually being snatched hastily out of my sight. My blurred image from these encounters was of a milky little thing, a skinnymalink, a shedder of silent tears, a lowerer of lashes, a wearer of the palest pink. She was a hand-clinger and a singer of breathy snatches of little songs. The servants sighed over her. She never had, in any perfection, her health.

She did not appear to trouble anyone with precocious teems of brain, yet there were times when Marcella seemed much older than her years, like a statue in miniature of a saint or one of those loathsome wax dolls with a grown-up face. Her great joy in life was drawing on scraps of paper. I'll admit she showed an early talent for a likeness, but her pictures were as wispy as herself, the pencil barely touching the page. As if she could not even do that *hard*. And when she lost the use of her leg, she was just like a damaged kitten, she did not have the least idea of protecting herself. However, let us not anticipate that interesting event.

From infancy, Marcella sought the dim humiliation of obscurity the way the rain seeks the earth. Shady corners, the underbellies of beds were the places where one would most often find her. She was the second sister in every way, a second, paler printing from the same incised plate as our older sister, Riva, deceased. Marcella's were the same lineaments indistinctly placed and nuanced where Riva had been strong and vibrant. Though not for long, of course.

That incompleteness ran right through Marcella. She seemed to me a little deaf, as if her tiny ears had not been properly formed. Look at those delicate cast-down eyelids! They lacked the slash of black lashes that had defined Riva's dark smoulderers, even on her deathbed, even when her mysterious illness had excavated her belly and

Here I desist for the sake of the Squeamish Reader, who need not bother Himself, in any case, with a character who will feature no more in this story. Forget I mentioned her. So.

Marcella weaned at a politely young age and learned the use of the chamber pot. Yet at five she started waking in wet sheets. It appeared that her internal organs were deficient in the valves that should have been of unquestionable function. The maid Anna started up with the known wisdoms, dry suppers, bathing the spine at bedtime with equal parts of ammonia and alcohol, followed by hand friction with a red cloth. Through the keyhole, I saw the skin of Marcella's back painfully exalted to the texture of veal fillet pummelled for the pan.

Then there was the daytime occasional mishap when Marcella forgot to listen to the calls of nature. Or when she was prevented from attending to them. For it was in this frailty that I found my first entertainment.

Our scene is the courtyard. Having hidden her chamber pot, and nailed down the lid of the commode in her bedchamber, I would wait down near the necessary room. When I saw her making her uncertain way towards it, I would hurry in ahead of her, and take my time, watching her from the arrow-slot in the wall, into which I had inserted a sliver of mirror. I stood by my spy-hole, drinking in every momentary spasm of discomfort that creased her face, her wretched, restless pacing, her tense sitting-down on the bench with her bony little knees pressed together inside the sheath of pink silk. Even if she grew so desperate as to presume to tap tentatively on the door, I would hold back, not acknowledging her until she was obliged to tap again and louder. I heard the catch of her breath as she shocked herself by uttering a truly audible noise. Then, from behind the door, I would reproach her for indelicacy.

Eventually I would open up. I stood in the doorway with my arms crossed and dragged a lazy glance over her while she shifted from foot to foot, not daring to meet my eyes because she knew that a long parley with me would only extend her agony. Her brain was by now riveted to the rhythmic stab of need in her lower pelvis (I had brought myself to that point more than once, so that I could really taste the ecstasy of her suffering).

'Please, Minguillo, may I enter?' She indicated the desired room behind me with a shaking, translucent finger.

'Why?'

And here she was truly trapped because she absolutely could not frame the actual words in front of a man, and because she knew that in honour her brother of all men should not ask it of her either. I allowed her to shoulder that part of the guilt, to think that she personally had inspired this behaviour in me, through a fissure in her own decency. Look at that little pink lip trembling. See the tears tadpoling on the lashes. In the lower centre of her body the prods and shrieks of need grew visibly louder and more urgent. She buckled at the knee and her eyes started to turn up in her head.

Just once, I had made her faint and had left her there to wake in streaming ignominy. And that was enough to make her understand that I could do it at any time.

62

So after another minute I would let her pass, tousling her soft head with my hand as she slipped under my arm. It was the only part of my sister that I ever touched.

The only part of her I touched with my own hands, that is.

Marcella Fasan

The first moment of my sentient life was the one when my brother wrenched my kitten from my arms and threw it into the Grand Canal. It was not the sudden violence nor the piteous mew that were the revelation: it was my parents' defenceless faces when Gianni, soaked through and clutching the kitten to his heaving chest, told them what had happened. I remember their figures in stone-still silhouette against the brilliance of the nursery window. I lay in my cot, listening.

Minguillo said, 'I wanted to see if cats float.'

The kitten sneezed mightily, climbed down Gianni's leg and returned to my cot.

Minguillo remarked, 'As you see, they do.'

My parents flinched. They would not look at my brother, or at Gianni, or at me, or at one another.

Then my beloved godfather Piero Zen strode into the room. He ignored Minguillo, reached into my cot and took both me and the kitten into his arms. My parents broke from their miserable trance and crowded around me, taking turns to hug me and kiss the kitten's little nose.

My little hands stroked the kitten's wet fur and it purred forgivingly. But when it was well and dry, I asked Anna to take it down to the kitchen and not to bring it back to me. I had just learned, and the lesson was not wasted upon me, that existence would never be secure for any vulnerable creature who visibly loved me.

Piero just knew. There are men that do.

I never told him the whole truth about Minguillo's tortures, and that

63

never seemed to matter. Piero just knew to interpose himself between me and my brother at every possible moment and in a way that made the intervention seem unconscious.

'Fancy a little turn in the courtyard?' he would ask in his pleasantly cracked voice, as if he knew that if he accompanied me down there Minguillo would not come between me and the necessary room.

Piero's was the first portrait I drew, as soon as I could hold a pencil. He claimed it was a perfect likeness, and had it set in a silver frame. But I think in truth it was a fair portrait of a tall and slender wading bird, like a heron, if one could imagine a heron with the kindest face and most delicate plumage. For Piero was tall and so very slender that you could see even his skeleton was fragile. His clothes did nothing but trap packets of air around his thinness. Despite his high birth, he seemed almost apologetic about his lack of substance, stooping somewhat, stammering a little. He sometimes walked with a hand on his narrow hip, as if to reinforce its strength. His eyes were pale green and none too large; his hair that pallid sandy red that generally displeases fashionable society. His eyelashes were too weak to make a visible appearance, and his eyebrows swooped in a light, ironic arch.

Yet give Piero someone to defend, someone weaker than himself, and he was superb.

From my observations of Piero above, it is easy to see what kind of child I would grow into. I was a very little girl when it came to me that I, who could as yet only watch, might usefully employ myself by chronicling what happened to the people around me. It seemed to me that people often let extraordinary stories pass through them quite unheeded.

There should be a book about everyone, I thought, watching and watching. And my habit of watching gave me the idea to keep a diary of my own life, so as not to lose it in all the commotion of the more interesting stories of others. I first kept my diary in laborious sketches and then, when I learned to write, in words.

My pictures I gave to those who were kind to me. I even tried to court love by making portraits of my mother, her likeness snatched in glimpses during brief visits to the nursery. I fear that I was too young to dissemble, and that my pictures of her did not please, being principally depictions of elaborate hairstyles foaming around a blank face. Still, I handed them to her, trustingly, hopefully.

But my diary – no, *that* I hid from everyone. For that diary I never used a book, which would have been conspicuous: just scraps of paper that could be hastily and easily concealed. My body soon became such a public place, visited by the hands of so many doctors: my thoughts, I felt, should have a little privacy somewhere.

There was always the idea in my mind that when Minguillo killed me, as he surely intended to, something of my little presence in the world might be left behind on those pages of mine, something less tenuous than my own flesh, which seemed more insubstantial than paper or glass, and seemed to tear and spill more easily.

From the start Minguillo had an uncanny ability to oppress the bodily fluid out of me. Just his step on the threshold and I was in danger of dampness. Tears, obviously. But also the other. If the urine was coming there was nothing I could do. If Minguillo was there around me, it was certainly coming. If it was coming, it came. And with it, the unbearable sympathy of the servants whisking the wet linen away.

By the time I was five, I was cut in half: there was the top part of me that was universally adored, the *perfettina*, and a part of me that my parents despaired of.

'The bladder is not functioning well,' my parents would say, not '*Marcella's* bladder is not functioning well'. They thus avoided a familial relationship with my bladder. And from that it was a short step to not owning Marcella herself. (You see, even I begin to talk about my defective self in the third person.)

And that distance allowed them to go to war against my bladder. Cruel treatments were decreed – not on *me*, in their minds, but on the enemy, that disobedient faction, the badly behaved bladder.

My condition exercised the poetic vocabularies of the doctors. I was too high-born to be a mere incontinent. And so I was treated with violent purges for 'spurious' and 'erratic' worms in the belly. When those failed, I was dosed with dizzying alcoholic tinctures, according to the theory that my discharges were the result of 'atrophic degeneration of the kidney due to hysteric paroxysms'.

Piero would intervene, send away the quack, empty his stinking potion out of my window into the Grand Canal. But soon another doctor would step up with his fluent promises and deep black bag.

Whatever the reigning euphemism, everything to do with the bladder became an anathema to my mother. The mention of the necessary room made her flinch. The cotton cloth used to mop up my accidents was purchased by Anna on secret excursions, and it was sent out to Cannaregio to be washed. I was suffocated by concealing perfumes at all times. Watching me drink a glass of water was my mother's least favourite occupation. (She did not see Minguillo forcing the cups to my lips in private.) The very colour yellow was not popular in our *palazzo*.

'It does not matter,' murmured Piero, whispered Anna, blurted Gianni. But it did. I did not want the people I loved to be burdened by my weakness. And I was shamed by it.

And naturally shame made it worse, brought on the dangerous searing tickle at every moment Minguillo was around me, made me desperate, made my heart beat like rain, made me lose control.

Gianni delle Boccole

Anna n me, we headed Minguillo oft, when he went to her room at night under the horsepiss of saying goodnight to her. Yes, we besot to make sure she were accompany-ed wherever she goed. And when the brother was keeped way, or when he were oft huntin ducks in the lagune, why then Marcella's little problem niver let loose, as ye mite say.

But we dint allus have the vigilince what was needed. There was bruises appeared on her arms. There were sumtimes fear in her pretty eyes.

But there were summing else too, summing brewin in Marcella's eyes. Not jist fear. Not jist tears.

It were, mazin to tell, a little fire what burned inside her. And that fire were strong nuff to keep *other* folks warm.

I stood stonished as the years went by and little Marcella growed nothin but sweeter n stronger n more comical in her spirit. Ye know the pleasure ye get from a frizzle o perfume on warm young skin nearby ye? Or from the face ovva kitten suprized in a summersalt? It's a little thing but it can make ye grin all day. That was what kind o pleasure Marcella Fasan give. Evryone loved her, wanted to talk to her, sit beside her, bring her daisies n pastries. And for there pains she would draw there faces for em, little sketches on the corner ovva letter or a page from a ledger, done in humble pencil yet with sich a loving spirit to em. She caught evryone at there best. There wernt a servant in the ouse who wunt rather look at Marcella's poortret of him than his real fizzog in the mirror.

She were clever, too. She were only four when she lernt to write quicker n lightning. And then there were no stopping her writin things down. An she were quicker n lightning too, if Anna or me was caught in her room when we had no busyness to be. She would say summing pretty in a wink, what saved our skins from a raggin oft my Mistress.

When I think on what Marcella would have to do in the end, I see the root of her strength then, in that little little girl with the brother so set on hurtin her, with a body what let her down so bad sumtimes, and she so set on assolutely not bein a Poor Thing that it felt half the time as if she were takin care of *us*.

Doctor Santo Aldobrandini

My famous patient, Napoleon, suffered his first attack of dysuria at the Battle of Marengo in 1800. I never got quite close enough myself to make a personal diagnosis, but they say his urinary pain was a terrible thing to behold. He would lean against a tree, moaning as he tried to relieve himself of a burning liquid clotted with sediments. His men rather admired his symptoms, which seemed those of an amatory complaint. Soldiers appreciate a general who makes some feminine conquests to supplement his territorial ones. Yet there was no medical evidence to support a venereal diagnosis, and plenty to make the surgeon (or young apprentice-surgeon with his nose in the textbooks) suspect bladder gravel.

Napoleon's personal pain made him reckless of others' suffering. Having so often tried to bring relief to men in agony, I knew that Napoleon's illness would eventually waylay and rob him of intelligent decisions. The pain-wracked Napoleon was more dangerous than the one who had been but mildly afflicted. So just as the dictator's itches had already set a million men a-scratching at each other, now each actual illness of Napoleon Bonaparte sent ten thousand healthy men to shallow battlefield graves.

By that time I was one of his employees, a member of that unthanked, scattered crew of doctors whose lives were also dismembered by Boney's itch. My country surgeon and I were drummed into service with the Italian contingent of his army. In Egypt, Germany and the Low Countries, we saw battles fought in four languages. Blood spurted and men screamed in one universal dialect, however, as my Master, Doctor Ruggiero, often sneered, in that manner of his that so generally failed to raise the spirits of our patients.

My fingers were grooved by waxed thread, for we were dextrous tailors of human skin. My Master and I became famous amputators, jointing a man faster than gangrene could devour him in the heat of battle and stitching together the cleaved and shattered flesh in neat, swift seams. And when, for the blessed year of 1802, Napoleon briefly stopped scratching, we attended at military hospitals, where the repaired wounded eked out their shortened lives.

Sewing up torn human hide was to my Master a matter as casual as darning a sock. I could snip, patch and mend as fast as he, but I never achieved the detachment on which he prided himself. This, like so many things, annoyed him. He constantly reproached me, 'Why waste your breath talking to them? "All shall be well",' he mimicked my voice cruelly. 'I don't think so!'

Once, when our surgical table was caught in crossfire, we took refuge underneath it, and I crawled out to drag a wounded man under its modest shelter. He would need to lose the leg, but I knew we could save his life if our own were spared. My vision suddenly collapsed to stinging red and black. I thought I had taken a bullet, but it was Ruggiero's hand.

'Never do that again,' he hissed at me. 'That's one for the corpse-waggoner. Don't take meat from the other fellow's plate,' he sniggered.

Marcella Fasan

The person I loved best to draw was Anna. She was a pretty girl, and cared a great deal about that, so I was never satirical with her likeness, not even affectionately. I saw how she coveted my portraits of her by the way she smoothed them and placed them facing inwards in the pocket of her apron, to protect them.

If only Anna had been able to protect her face from my brother!

It was not long after my fifth birthday. Piero Zen was seeing to the army's depredations at his country estate. My father was still in Arequipa. The rest of us were gathered in the *chinoiserie'*d drawing-room that night, my mother hard at gossip with her friend the Contessa Foscarini, me sketching their intent faces, and Minguillo, as was his habit, raking the embers of the fire into angry volcanoes and tamping them down with the poker. Occasionally my mother murmured mildly, 'Pray be careful, Minguillo, not to let the ashes fly.'

Anna lilted in with a tray of sweet wine and my favourite spiced cakes. She winked at me, as she always did, moving towards the low table near the fire. I was winking back when she tripped over the leg that Minguillo stuck out in front of her so that he might detain the cake plate entirely for himself. The tray flew out of Anna's hand, its contents crashing against the mantelpiece.

Minguillo's new yellow waistcoat, the one embroidered with poppies and violets, was soaked through with wine. My brother, hissing with indignation, seized the red-hot poker.

Sor Loreta

It was only when I had reached my thirty-first year that I was at last allowed to take the Holy Veil. My profession had been unfairly delayed by those who were jealous of me at Santa Catalina, who spitefully claimed that I was not in my right mind.

But for some years I had displayed only the most modest of behaviour, hiding any miracles that I performed involuntarily, and also the more obvious signs of my penances. I pretended to eat. The ruling nuns ran out of reasons to prevent my promotion.

Of course as soon as I was properly married to God, I began to look forward to when I might pass beyond this false life, to when I might render my soul up to my Celestial Spouse.

In other words, I began to look for a suitably glorious way to die.

I was impatient for my martyrdom, and I was sure that it was imminent. How could God wait to take His most loving daughter to His bosom? Each night I sprinkled my cell with Holy Water before I laid me down. I begged my Confessor to give me extreme unction each day, for I expected it to be my last. He reported this to the *priora*, who came to me with hard words.

'Sor Loreta,' she thundered, 'what will you not do to get attention? I *knew* we should not have let you profess.'

I replied, 'The Ignorant have always misunderstood and feared the Chosen. And set out to worship false idols, like Sor Andreola.'

'Chosen!' she barked. 'Your jealousy of Sor Andreola and your competitive nature are the only things that mark you out.'

It was then that a miracle occurred. I began to hear with my damaged right ear. Not the vulgar yapping of the *priora*, but the lovely mingled voices of Santa Rosa and Our Lord God, both of whom assured me that I would have great and difficult tasks to perform and that I must steel myself for them, and agree to live a little longer in this ungrateful world.

'You alone, Sor Loreta,' God whispered tenderly, 'must be My earthly voice at Santa Catalina. The others shall be cast into a Great Fire.'

'How shall I serve You, Lord?' I asked, but silently, inside my head.

Santa Rosa promised sweetly, 'I shall tell You, child. How sorry shall Your persecutors be for their crimes against You when the Fiends of Hell lift their great clawed paws to rip out their plump bellies.'

The *priora*'s voice then broke in sharply upon my left ear, 'You're not listening to me, are you, Sor Loreta? I wash my hands of you.'

Santa Rosa whispered in my right ear, 'Remember, dear Sor Loreta, that the more You mortify Your flesh, the more beautiful shall You be for Your Bridegroom.'

Back in the Old World, Napoleon had fallen on the Holy Mother Church like a wolf on the fold. A terrible story came to us, that all good Christians will read with horror, of a cathedral in Bavaria that was sold to a butcher! That night I dreamed of the knives laid out on the altar, legs of ham hung from the rafters, the drooping rabbits, heavy with shot, tied in bunches from the columns. I awoke, trembling, my nose twitching with the smell of the herbed garlic sausages I had seen smoking in the Bavarian confessionals. Of course, it was only the slaves of Santa Catalina cooking luxurious breakfasts. But for a moment it seemed to me that the stink of Napoleon's sins had floated over the oceans all the way to us.

I kissed the chains that morning before I employed them to beautify my body, and I paid particular attention to my face.

Gianni delle Boccole

Poor Anna, what had been so andsome, found it hard to bare the great red weal that runned from her forrid to her lip all long the left side. I allus told her that no one notist it, but that were a lie. It were ever after the *only* thing most folks notist bout Anna, that pink shiny ribbon down her fizzog.

Marcella's scar were tinier, jist a burn-mark on her rist from where she ud tried to pull the red-hot poker outa her brother's hand when Minguillo were already bringin it down fizzlin on Anna's face. Marcella had een took a bite out o his thumb to try on

71

make him stop. But he jist flunged his little sister cross the room and got on with his busyness. Then he stormt out, shoutin for a new wainscot to replace the loorid thing stained with the wine Anna had dropt on him.

Marcella crawled out of the corner strait to Anna and held the poor burnt head in her lap. My Mistress Donata Fasan and the Contessa Foscarini had convenient feinted way the both of em, and allus sayed afterwards that they remembert nothing of what appened. But Marcella staid with Anna, and wunt be seprated from her when the doctor come to salve n so the wound. Marcella held Anna's head the whole time and sung to her soft n low awhile he stitcht the broke skin together.

After that, Marcella keeped drawin Anna's face for her, but she done the grate sweetness of showin only the rite side that were not damidged except for the spreshun of fear that allus hornted it now. After Minguillo hit her with that poker, Anna were terrified to her core and would allus shake leaflike if she were forst to be in the same room as him.

Were Minguillo punisht for what he done to Anna? No. The insident were husht up like the grave from the outside world and put out in the household as an accident wernt it. Anna ud tripped n fell in the fire, twere said. She were thereafter keeped out o the public rooms so t'other nobbles wunt have to see her face. Insted she were set to cleaning the servants' rooms hincludin that midden that were frankly my own, and lookin after Marcella n other work that keeped her generally out o sight.

Nor were Minguillo punisht for what he keeped doin to Marcella.

'For why ye do her that way, sir?'

That were my partickeler phrase, *for why ye do her that way?* Course, since Anna's face, I dint have the nessary number o guts to say it out loud. Instead I pranced with death, daring to let my eyes say it with knitty looks. Evry time she cried isn't it.

Weren't scarcely bareable to watch, the bastert brother with the sister. Twere agin Nature, Chicken-shitting God! Ask pardon, ask pardon, sirs. Madams.

I mumbled like preying, Kill the bastert, God, for why dunt Ye strike im dead n similar. And several times, to my shame, poor little Marcella overheared me, and lookt up at me in worrid wonderment. Then she runned strait oft n made me a drawin o her brother as a stiltylegged turkycock or some other ridikilus beast, with mesself drawed as a very stern farmer with a great big sheep crook. All my hatin turned to laffing in a second.

The Mamma were condemnable too if ye askt me. There is times when a blind eye is an accessability to a crime. Blind eyes n deaf fucking ears too, when Miss Marcella wept or screamed. Ask pardon, sirs! Madams! For the dirty mouth on me. The memmary of it snagged the rein o my tong back there a moment.

Ye see, Minguillo Fasan were niver a boy, not a natural child. Swear he were one o Nature's erratas. One o God's ferrule things, allus drummin his foot agin the floor under the table. So me, I got them old bull-horrors when my Master Fernando Fasan askt me to varlet for his son. Twere a grate rise from the kitchen, yet at a high cost to me in slaps to the head n dog's abuse. In exchange for learning me my letters, I were sposed, sayed my Master, to 'keep n eye' on the Young Man. I stared at him – what were he thinking? I wernt but a few years older than Minguillo. And twould o took ten eyes to hold that one under proper surveylance, and me as ye know rather wanting in the brain.

But my Master tipped me, got in a tutor for my poor hollow head. I would compost the laundry lists, I sposed at first. Then my Master sayed: 'I must return to Peru. Write me when you can. Don't be afraid, Gianni. You feel too much, young chap. You need to grow a tougher skin. And anyway, Minguillo does not need to know you can write.'

Nor would he, not niver. That were the first thing I made sure on.

And I doed as my Master telled me. Leastwise I tried. I grewed a skin thick nuff to *hide* my feelins, but I were niver grand nor nobble nuff to stop akshally having em.

In fact, twas at that time I begun to have some feelins for women. At first I thought feelins was all you got, but I guest that there were summing o my Ma in me, because soon I got to touchings too. But I were niver a wanting like my Ma, and I dint never . . . not then leastwise . . . find a girl what could unnerstand my friendship with Anna, what was perfeck chaste, or who dint get gellous bout all my menshons of Marcella. Some girls was intimated by me been razed to varlet, and by me havin my letters. It goed on like that until . . . well, it were like that for yearonyear.

I could read soon nuff, but to *write* – that were my tortshure. I could shape the letters n words, but nowise the sentences. To this day, picking up a quill gives me them old bull-horrors. Pen in hand, brains leave head, waving byebye. That's me rule. A goat danced more greaseful than I compost a piece o writin. As ye see.

There were so much I should of writed to my old Master Fernando Fasan bout what was going on in the Palazzo Espagnol them long long days of his too-long absents. It give me the Viles that I did not. I write it now, sorry fool I am.

Marcella Fasan

Why did I not tell them about Minguillo?

The truth was this. By the time I was six, I already knew that there was only one just penalty for Minguillo's crimes: his putting-to-death.

It was simple, just as pain is simple.

Pain from a pin hidden in my bread, pain from a wrenched lock of hair, pain from the bite of a *scolopendra* let into my bed. Each of those pains was a little death to me, because pain by pain, I lost any sense of being safe in the world.

A portrait of my sister Riva hung in the *piano nobile*. In front of it, I would sometimes find a maid or a footman quietly weeping. My mother always averted her eyes as she passed the frame wreathed in black silk. In the dim pockets of my infant memory nestles a vision of my father striking his head with a despairing gesture as he gazed at Riva, and Gianni swearing audibly behind him.

I grew to understand that Riva's death was somehow to be attributed to Minguillo's wickedness, and that there was nothing to be done about either.

Gianni and Anna confirmed it, by the angry, helpless things they muttered as they tended my abrasions and bruises. I learned from listening: if Minguillo chose to kill me by degrees, then no one in our household would dare to stop him. And then there was Anna's dear, scarred face to remind me daily what might be expected by anyone who got in my brother's way.

I believe that my parents were afraid of him, and spoke of him, even in my presence, in whispers, as children speak of a monstrous creature under the bed. Did my mother and father think I was deaf because I was sometimes a little faulty in the bladder? They talked over my head about me and my brother with absolute, hurting candour. Then again, have you not noticed that deafness is often attributed to people who are physically imperfect in other ways?

Only Piero remonstrated, saying, 'The boy should be made to feel some of the pain he inflicts on others. Fernando, Donata, do you not see what you are creating by your negligence?'

My father protested, 'You know, Piero, I am making provision . . .' But he had a faraway look in his eyes.

Piero wanted Minguillo disciplined, but my own young mind, with the stark simplicity of childhood, made a harder ruling. I knew that death was what Minguillo deserved. Yet with equal simplicity I knew I faced an impasse. My parents were not about to have their only son put down like a biting dog, little as they enjoyed him.

And it turned out that punishment only provoked my brother to injure me in more angry ways. Worse, my parents' feeble reproofs seemed to sanitize his crimes, and would sometimes result in acts of violence against my dear Gianni or the other servants, or terrible humiliations for them.

So I retained my dignity, and kept my friends safe, by keeping my silence. I pretended to be deaf when Minguillo insulted or summoned me. And whatever act he committed against me – I drew and then wrote it down, buried it in my diary, and never breathed a word aloud. I sketched all the ignominious beasts of the realm, each personifying one of Minguillo's little ways to a nicety. And then I folded him up, with his image trapped on the inside.

I used the occasions of his absence to go into his room, where I hid my pages in a niche behind his great armoire, which was as large as a cottage. I had but to lie on my back between its clawed feet and reach up to the cool, dusty void behind the oak. Minguillo's own room was the one place he never thought to search.

My clamorous diaries were denied him. My apparent silence had the benefit of confusing him. It was a slight and poor hand in this dangerous game, but as yet the only one I had to play.

Gianni delle Boccole

Yellow Fever in eighteen-o-three and o-four meaned my Master Fernando Fasan could not come back from Peru without months o stricked quarany. The port o Livorno got shutted down. Venice herself were tighter than a clam. For a long time there was noways of getting news to Marcella's father, een if Ide the words to put it in.

I curst myself summing feroshus as a plate-licking cur, an anchovy and a coward. For things was gitting worse. With evry month Minguillo were more wild, less humane. One day the eyes in Riva's portreet caught me and followt me down the hall. That night, with little Riva's breath on the back o my neck, I forced the words out on paper. Like pellets, twere.

I sent the letter with a brandy-merchant that I met in an *ostaria* at Rialto. He were going to Arequipa where he had some agents, what he called *factores*, to git round the Spanish trade interdicks. The pits n pocks on his face spelled it out, 'I had evry fever alredy.' Anyway it were no problem to leave Venice – it were the coming back that were prevented.

The servants got together and give me money for the letter's passage. Twere all we had, I told Mister Pocksy Merchantman, handing him the leather purse and our faith.

I companied him to the boat and waved him and my letter godspeed to South Hamerica.

In that letter I finely hexplained all what Minguillo doed with Marcella, how the servants was too fraid to say scut, the girl herself strange silent too, and – most difficult of all – how the lady

76

o the house shone a hopeless fatality bout her son. The sworm o tapeworm-hants and huncles in there dikrepitating partments wernt een worth a menshon, of course. They would stay quieter n a mouse pissin on Peruvian cotton jist to keep in Minguillo's good books, as he were the hair parent and held the keys to all there ouses.

I got flustered in the detail, rattled on like a gibbermonkey, yet a man with half a blind brain could of read the amount o desprit I were, and unnerstood that there were serius pause for concern bout his little daughter.

After all, he had *askt* me to write.

If that letter dint bring my Master Fernando Fasan back from Arequipa, quaranty or no quaranty, then he dint nowise diserve to be the father ovva livin angel like Marcella Fasan.

Minguillo Fasan

My father's letter to my mother arrived four months after his sending it.

The delay was explained by the red seal with a head of San Marco's lion and a large 'S' for *Sanità*. The letter had been *spurgata* in quarantine, passing the last part of its journey on the island of the Lazzaretto Vecchio, where it was slit open and purified by smoke. The stamp indicated that the letter was considered by the authorities to be pure of Yellow Fever, Plague and Leprosy. Unfortunately for me, my father's handwriting was none decayed by its treatment.

More fortunately I intercepted the letter before it reached my mother's breakfast tray. On reading it, my every rib of hair stood up to attention and my foot drummed uncontrollably on the marble floor under the desk.

My father instructed his wife that their son Minguillo was to be subjected to certain medical examinations by the priest-surgeons on the lunatics' island of San Servolo.

'*Some recent events have been brought to my notice. He is clearly not sane, Donata,*' my father had written. '*This must be dealt with, for the safety of the household. His conscience has not developed in the way of a normal person's.*'

I had barely finished scanning it when a fictitious gust of wind carried it out of the window and away down the Grand Canal before any inquisitive monkey might count his toes. Oh dear, etcetera and so forth.

From the smoke-scented letter, I gathered that my father had somehow got wind of my little games with Marcella. This meant spies and betrayers in the house. And that meant – investigations.

I started with my Mamma, whom I subjected to a close scrutiny. She was not my woman. I discovered no reason to suspect trouble from our priest or Marcella's pretty and pompous doctors. The servants were illiterate. So how *could* my father have heard about my activities in far-off Peru? There had been certain details. I could not touch Piero Zen, but I suspected him.

With the Yellow Fever and its quarantines providing a fine excuse, my father continued to dally in Peru. Of course, he must have thought the letter had discharged his responsibilities towards me and my alleged madness. He did not know that his instructions were floating with the discharges of a thousand privies down the Grand Canal.

Untroubled months passed. My anxieties relaxed. Watermelon was my new project. Watermelon, that engorged my sister's bladder, that I fed her night after night, assuring her that the rude red slices were the very thing she needed to keep her continent. And in her draughty bedchamber, by my order, only the tiny *scaldino* glowed with a pitiful few coals, so she was never warm about the kidney.

''Sgood for her,' I said commandingly, and waved a handsome leather book when the servants protested. They did not know that it was the admirable *Justine, or the Misfortunes of Virtue*, by the esteemed (at least by me) Marquis de Sade.

Even if the servants hated me, books loved me and passed me on to their friends. Sade took me by the hand to Rousseau who led me to one interesting fellow, Thomas Day. This enterprising Englishman had adopted a foundling girl to bring up as a wife. His Sabrina had then been subjected to a number of imaginative disciplinary methods. For example, she was obliged to learn stoicism through having hot wax dripped on her arms. She acquired composure by allowing her tutor to shoot between her petticoats.

It was not hard for me to find a gun, but more difficult to find the privacy to practise with it. A whole summer long I thought on it, imagining the bullet passing through the linen, like a little black rabbit jumping out of a snowy burrow.

Doctor Santo Aldobrandini

After five bloodied years on battlefields and in field hospitals, my Master Doctor Ruggiero was himself gouged in the side by a stray bullet. Some said it came from one of our own soldiers whom he had affronted with his surly tongue. Ruggiero wanted attendance on his way home to the Veneto, so he brought me back with him. The war was over for me awhile, at least Napoleon's war.

I was still at war with the hurts and ills of human skin, however. Now I treated patients not in shattered platoons but in the solitude of their own suffering beds, be they in hovels or villas. I was moved by the way the poor ones constantly apologized to me for the mundanity of their illnesses, 'after all you've seen on the battlefield, Doctor'. And I was appalled by the rich, who, untouched by war, revelled in the most minor symptom and expected me to furnish a picturesque title for it, and still more picturesque remedies, as if for them illness was just another diversion. It was rarely the head of the household I attended. Such men were not often ill: they were too busy. It was their dependent children, cousins and nephews who languished under their cut-velvet coverlets. Like tapeworms, these lesser creatures hovered in the homes of their great host, ruthlessly extracting the nutrients up until the moment of his death, when they would show a rare burst of energy in locating a new, vigorous victim to fix their simpering mandibles upon. Poisoning was not beyond these sons, daughters, cousins and nephews, nor sly stranglings.

It seems likely that my famous patient, Napoleon, had also been infected by a parasite as he lay in one of his long baths back during his Egyptian campaign of 1798–9. Worn out and filthy after massacring two thousand Marmalukes at the foot of the Sphinx, the Corsican took himself to the tub.

It was my diagnosis that larvae from some microscopic creature lurking in that warm water then entered his integument and coursed into his bloodstream, by which way they congregated in his rectum and bladder. In those hospitable places they would have laid their own eggs and founded colonies of sons, daughters, cousins and nephews that would survive as many generations as their host lived human years.

Napoleon had himself crowned Emperor in 1804. He was thirty-six, the prime of life. Or he would have been so, had the parasites inside him not been industriously devouring his vitals, and, with them, his vitality. Within four years he would nurse a pallid little paunch, lose the vigorous growth of his hair and worst of all, his famed ability to do without sleep. He would grow garrulous where he had once been terrifyingly silent. His ability to make a lightning decision and follow it through – that would now evaporate, possibly sucked out of him by a hundred little mouths busy down below.

That next year, 1805, was the one I would always remember – firstly, because it was the year I was called to attend to the suppurating wounds of one Matteo Casal, a madman who had attempted to crucify himself.

And also because it was the year I first came face to face with the young Marcella Fasan.

Gianni delle Boccole

My guts shrivvelled inside me wheniver I watcht the bastert brother fondling his gun. With that gun in his hand he were a different person, purposed, but with the soul completely gone from the body. He were fixin to do summing bad, we all knowed it.

Trudgical to say, nothin had appened as a result of that letter I so struggled oer. My old Master Fernando Fasan ud eventually come back from Peru for a brief spell, but he niver menshoned it to me. Perhap my letter got lossed? Perhap my writin were ineligible? Perhap he ud not believt me and decided to hignore it? Or ud not wanted to believe me? He treated me with the same kindness as in the old days, just a bit sadder n more disdrackted than before. My old Master were depresst in his spirits. Twere clear his heart were sore, or, the servants gossiped, elsewheres.

Wherever his heart were, his eyes was sartin not on his boy. He niver tookt the necessary steps. Niver tookt his son by the scuff of his neck and shook a partickle o the Fear-o-God into him.

We tried to keep an open eye on the little girl, but we was not allus there. When the famly goed to there country villa on the Brenta, they had there country servants. They wernt none too vigilant, them bumpkins, and they dint know scut bout nothin.

Do ye know what they done for her poor little problem? I heared about it later, after . . . They give her a fox pasting, they did. Some country remedy, some old wise tale, for women's troubles in there inward places as ye mite say. And ye can be sartin that Marcella, not to offend, jist smiled thank ye when the maid worked up a salve ovva fox's limbs and his grease, with old oil n tar. Marcella would of let her apply the fox paste to her woman's parts and put up with the smell for the sake o not hurting the girl's feelins no dout. That would be Marcella. And maybe she had some hopes of it too, for in them days the girl still wanted allus to believe the best.

A fox pasting! But what they should of did, the waggots, was simply keep an eye on her at all times.

Where, for why n what the hell were they bout when he finely got her?

'Tell me,' I ordered the country footman when I got ahold of him, 'or Ile give ye a Peruvian Pander, which is kin to a Chinese Burn but with more burn to it.'

Bednaw have that appen to ye, I tell ye.

Minguillo Fasan

We Venetians left our latest rulers, the Austrians, a task they must have loved deep in their efficient souls, that of turning our magnificent Republic into a minor department.

The fiddly little matter of government was taken out of our fine white hands and placed in the ink-spotted fingers of petty officers who rejoiced in the minutiae of forms and pettifogging statutes. We shrugged and went about our business, that is, our pleasures, as before. We had got used to being ashamed of ourselves. Sitting in a warm bath of our own filth, we ceased to smell our disgrace.

The Yellow Fever abated. My father returned from Arequipa after a mild case of the Small-Pox. He had tried one of the newfangled vaccinations. But instead of passing through him with a quick salutation, the malady had briefly taken hold. He was weaker, and older in his face. By contrast, I felt vigour surge through me whenever I saw his stooped outline at the water-gate.

He never mentioned the letter that he had sent, the one asking for the surgeons to examine my brains and blood for the spores of madness. He could not have been too suspicious about what happened to it: many letters went astray or arrived so smeared with vinegar or smoke from the quarantines as to be unreadable. If he spoke of it to my mother, it was in a place where I could not eavesdrop. In any case, I knew she would set herself vehemently against such a project. My father might run off to the South Americas whenever he pleased, but she would have to stay in Venice and endure the shame of a son locked up in an attic or with the lunatics on San Servolo. Her dear friend the Contessa Foscarini would never have let her forget it.

Life took on a semblance of its old normality. In the spring and winter I was taken daily by gondola to the Collegio di San Cipriano on Murano for my lessons in reading, writing, arithmetic, French, English and Latin.

A little setback occurred when an impertinent magistrate of the *Sanità* sent a curt letter to my parents, insisting that I might no longer roam around Venice 'without a responsible escort'. I know not which of my spicy little pranks brought this on, but the Reader may be sure it was one of many.

From June to October our family still went to our villa on the mainland set in its garden planted *all'inglese* with shaped bushes and pink roses. The *villeggiatura* passed in furious employment for me, as I was permitted without reproach to trap songbirds on limed twigs and do with them what I wished, so long as Cook might have the corpses later to turn on sticks of rosemary. Marcella, as the Sentimental Reader would expect, entertained a drivelling love of all things Green. She adored to ramble about the grounds with a pencil and a piece of paper to draw trees, flowers and our very picturesque dovecote with its cooing inhabitants.

The Lascivious Reader may at this point wish to loosen His clothing.

The summer of 1805, Marcella was nine. I was twenty-one and knew the intimate company of a maid for the first time, a great fine agricultural lump of a girl, thickly furred in the thigh and arm. The Germans say 'where there is hair there is pleasure': I traced the hairs all the way to where they coarsened, and had my fill of prodding her little shame-slit and her little shame-tongue while she stared up at me, scarcely crying at all. For a few coins, all summer long I jottled in her petticoats twice in the morning and three times at night.

The Inquisitive Reader enquires: why did I wait so long to get on top of a girl? I'll disarm Him by admitting I had a little difficulty in managing the thing, the first hundred or so times I tried it. The Venetian whores had laughed at me diminishingly. The Palazzo Espagnol maids were too quick and clever to find themselves alone with me. It was only in the agricultural girl that I found the satisfactory blend of compulsion and submission that enabled me. Once launched, however, there was to be no stopping my career in venery. After that, all the rooms of my imagination were lined with soft human skin. My own may not have been pretty, but I was comfortable in it, and now even more comfortable inside someone else's.

That fine hot season flew faster than some days do. I was caught out and put out when the first *caccia* of the autumn delivered a fine bloodied stag to our door, which meant it was time to go back to Venice.

That year a little less of Marcella returned to our *palazzo* than had gone out to the villa.

Sor Loreta

I continued to be surprised that Bishop Chávez de la Rosa did not come to seek me out in the convent.

Then one morning at breakfast I saw a vision in a pale ingot of butter on the trestle. In it, a greasy yellow Bishop Chávez de la Rosa writhed in mortal combat with a bird that looked like a dove. What churning and pecking and strangling I saw taking place in that butter!

Afterwards, when I recovered my senses, I was troubled. Why should the Bishop fight with the Holy Spirit in the form of a dove? Perhaps I had been wrong to support his endeavours to reform Arequipa? Perhaps his failure to promote me was in fact a sign of some secret turpitude? Had that prevented him from carrying out his plans? Had God punished him, nipped and pecked at his ambitions?

It seemed that my vision was correct. For the talk was all of Bishop Chávez de la Rosa leaving town with none of his reforms accomplished. There was more concubinage and fornication in Arequipa than ever. Why, even the aforementioned Venetian Fernando Fasan had fathered an illegitimate child on his Arequipan mistress Beatriz Villafuerte. That woman and her growing bastard continued to live in luxury and attended mass at Santa Catalina every Sunday. Beatriz Villafuerte insisted on displaying herself in a Venetian shawl of deepest red. Bishop Chávez de la Rosa allowed her and the boy communion as if they were decent Christians.

Subtly, I ceased to mention the Bishop's name. Obsessed with their light pleasures, not one of my sisters at Santa Catalina noticed my change of heart.

Minguillo Fasan

The world knows – because I've informed it so – that I meant only to test her nerves, as Thomas Day prescribed, but she twitched and screamed, and there you are, a leg shot through the knee and ever after useless to her.

This much I'll let drop: on the day itself the process was not entirely scientific. It was true that I was up to the armpits exasperated with that tiny oh-so-demanding bladder, which forced every family excursion out of shape, and I had seized that gun in vexation rather than in the spirit of education. I was out of sorts, contemplating the prospect of our return to Venice, of leaving all those dives in the dark I had so enjoyed on the hirsute maid, of resuming grey city life with its dull restrictions and the doughy presence of the Austrians to remind us odiously of our fall.

The more I thought about it, the more I reasoned that Marcella's weakness had become my personal cross to bear. Because of her, I could not go about the town, to take even the gaudy ghosts of pleasures remaining to Venetians of our mortified age. So many times Marcella's bladder had stopped a good excursion in its tracks. If Marcella might not go somewhere, then it had become the iniquitous case that I might not go either. For, as the Reader will remember, thanks to that pedantic magistrate, I was not permitted out unsupervised in public. There was no servant who could be bribed or threatened to take me out on his own, so all excursions were to be conducted *in famiglia*. I might not even go alone to the marionette theatre in San Moise, where I so loved to watch the wooden husbands beat their cloth wives with hammers.

I wallowed morosely in the memory of the past Palm Sunday. I had been deprived of the parade by an eruption to Marcella's health. She had developed a high fever and the house was in an uproar with three different quacks attending and Piero Zen quarrelling with them all. *She* was perfectly suited, tucked up in bed with one of her drawing blocks. I was the one in pain. Palm Sunday was one of my favourites. On that day, from the Basilica – its mosaics sunlit like an illuminated manuscript – a bounty of pigeons was released. The populace might capture them and do what they liked with them if the baying seagulls did not dismember the grey birds first. In the confusion, I always contrived to lose my guards for precious minutes. No one remarked on a noble youth with two or three pigeons stuffed under his armpits on his way to somewhere undisclosed.

Yes, Marcella had picked a poor moment to cross my path, that golden autumn day on the Brenta. As she walked across the courtyard with the inevitable drawing block in her hand, said I to myself, 'She'll not get where she is going so smug so fast oh no.'

The Comprehending Reader feels this too, of course – that there are moments when a body has to send the blood back to the heart. I started wondering how I could make my mark on that little white muzzle of hers.

All summer long I had daydreamed of Thomas Day's exercise with the petticoats and the musket. As I carried my fowling-piece into the garden of our villa, I was already framing my highly credible explanation. It went along these lines: by invoking the loud noise of the gun just as she went to relieve herself, I would teach Marcella's bladder an involuntary fear of and aversion to emptying. I had already turned down the relevant page in Thomas Day's book, ready to demonstrate my unwrinkled reasoning and good intentions.

The Reader will also comprehend that my father's mistaken will was still in my mind. *He* was already back in town on business, attended by my mother and her hairdresser. If a man takes his eyes off his family, he shall pay for it somehow.

'This is going to be a little uncomfortable,' I whispered to myself.

The little black rabbit exploded with a beautiful nimbus of red out from among the snowy petticoats.

The blood was not all hers. The gun jerked in my hands and a piece of the metal casing flew off, taking with it a large piece of my index finger.

Servants came pouring out of the house like maggots out of a corpse. No one attended to my amputated fingertip. They clustered round Marcella, weeping and screaming. She lay silent, uncomplaining, and cried out only once, when they lifted her on to a pallet of wood to take her into the great hall. I trotted along behind.

The servants knew no better than to staunch the bleeding with a dirty handkerchief. I took myself to the minstrels' gallery for the best view of what would happen next.

Surgeon Ruggiero arrived promptly with a young nobody of an apprentice. The hardbitten doctor parted the ways through the weeping servants, tutting and issuing peremptory instructions for boiled water and clean rags. Your man inspected the wound, and declaimed showily on same. My shot, it turned out, had penetrated her left knee at an awkward angle. The pellet of lead had torn into the structure, lacerating and shredding the tissue of the joint itself. Proudly, he flourished a pair of unusual forceps, with a hollow roundness forward and a few hooks curled in that part.

'Can you hear me, child?' he asked Marcella, who lay silent, unless you count the faint stutter of her blood falling on the flagstones. She was the only one *not* weeping apart from me, up in the minstrels' gallery. I sucked on my finger-stub, while she lay on her back like a marble saint, her martyrdom painted red across her leg.

Her open eyes sought me out up in the gallery. She held on to me with her eyes, until I felt nausea and fear lolloping in my belly. My skin felt too tight and my foot drummed on the floor. I did not love our country house as I loved the Palazzo Espagnol. It had not sired me. I could not feel so safe here as in Venice.

But hush! The surgeon bends to whisper something to my sister.

I imagined, as shall the Empathetical Reader, that Ruggiero was saying, 'This is going to be a little uncomfortable.'

She nodded. I leaned over the rails of the minstrels' gallery to watch him arrange her body in the same position in which it had taken the bullet. Then he opened the joint and flushed out with hot salt the shot, the fragments of bone and cartilage, the blood clots and the debris of her petticoat. Finally he reached inside with the unusual forceps.

Marcella's drawing block dropped on the floor with a resounding slap. I guessed she had been clutching it against the pain.

I was amused to see that the sound caused the surgeon's young apprentice to turn to stone and make an utter *casino* of his duties. That wan stripling would never make a surgeon! Marcella's concern was all for the youth and she begged the servants to bring him water. Then a piece of bone and a lump of shot fell in the surgeon's bucket, and she too departed from consciousness.

Doctor Santo Aldobrandini

Ruggiero never lost an opportunity to use me for his foil, particularly in noble houses. He loved to pretend I was but a novice in surgery, needing to be taught everything, by which device he might, in comparison, highlight and aggrandize his own expertise. It also gave him an opening to dazzle his audience with a terrifying medical vocabulary. Where simple terms would have sufficed, and indeed served better for clarity, Surgeon Ruggiero resorted to pomposity and Latin. The frescoed hall of the Fasan villa was, of course, the theatre of his dreams.

My Master quickly decided not to amputate. He cleaned, dressed and tourniqueted, applying a calendula lotion to arrest the haemorrhage. I was kept busy mixing our faithful battlefield balsam of terebinth and Peruvian, the linen pledgets dipped in oil of turpentine and our special buttons of tow, in which was wrapped vitriol, grossly pulverized.

'See, boy,' he instructed at frequent intervals, 'like this.'

The hall was fairly illuminated by the onlookers' admiration. It was to be much regretted (by Ruggiero) that the noble parents of our patient were away in Venice. For my part, I wondered at the Conte and Contessa leaving such a little girl under the supervision of the servants. I supposed there was some great ball in town.

I had not yet seen the girl's upper body, blocked from my view by the considerable bulk of my Master. But I noticed that her delicate little shoes – spattered with blood – were smaller than my hand.

As we elevated her leg, a thick block of paper fell open on the floor. I glimpsed a pencil portrait of a male servant in livery. Skill and, it seemed, love, announced the man's good heart over his homely features. It was at this point that I first raised my eyes above the girl's knees: just as my Master buried our worn forceps in her leg.

Then I disgraced myself.

When Ruggiero barked 'ligaturing needle!' I was unable to move or speak. I stood staring dumbly at the girl's face, and I heard my Master only dimly, as if a soft helmet had been pulled over my face. Ruggiero repeated his order, and yet still I was incapable of twitching a finger. In the end Ruggiero elbowed me aside, delving into our layette of knives and needles with his own brusque hand. I stumbled, kicking over the bucket of blood and bone in a wincing clatter.

Now I had accompanied my Master to Napoleon's battlefields before my voice broke, and I had seen men split from thigh to neck, and hip to hip. I myself had burrowed for bullets in writhing flesh without flinching. So why did I now lose my grip on my profession?

It was not the mashed knee that lost me the use of my tongue and limbs. It was the face of the girl who had been mutilated. I had never seen such skin, its owner's sweet nature so clearly legible upon it. I was only sixteen and I had not treated a noble girl before; or any girl of this age. Napoleon had not sent any our way. I was surprised by a feeling of tenderness I had not experienced since I treated my little companions in the convent. Since that time, I had not rehearsed in affections of the heart, not even in friendship. Two years on the streets and Ruggiero's testy temper had seen to that.

One long look I had, while the sun fingered the villa's frescoes and the soft hair of our patient. She met my gaze, and smiled. A silent moan escaped me. It was like offering a beautiful but empty Murano goblet to someone dying of thirst. The little girl could not have been more than nine years old, and yet I felt – and this is the strangest of it – *mothered* by her. I felt as if I had known her a long time, since before I was born, and that her tenderness and humour were things I might take for granted, as I had never taken anything for granted in my life.

I did not lay eyes on the brother, not that day.

By the time I came to my senses, the girl herself had mercifully fainted away. Ruggiero employed a footman to hold the injured parts in apposition while he ligatured the arteries, and joined the parted flesh first with plaster and then with thread. Seeing that I was no use, I crept out of the great hall, back to our trap, where I hid my ignominy behind the horse.

Ruggiero beat me when we returned to his rooms. I had embarrassed him in the great house.

And that was just the beginning of what I would suffer, and gladly, for Marcella Fasan.

Minguillo Fasan

For several days they despaired of the leg altogether, and at times her life hung in the balance. I thoughtfully sent a note to the local undertaker who came and looked over my sister with a proprietorial air and a measuring eye. That must have been discouraging for her.

But for some reason Marcella warded off the gangrene.

My agricultural girl told me, 'Your sister's too pure to rot, that's what they're saying in the servant hall.'

She would not soon forget the slap she earned by that. Then I got her riding rantipole while her tears dropped on my face, which was, in fact, the way I conceived the dazzling idea for 'The Tears of Santa Rosa', about which the Patient Reader shall hear a great deal more in due course.

Unlike Marcella's, my flesh proved insultingly mortal. The damaged finger turned yellow, then red and then black. I hid it as long as I could but the putrid smell attracted unkind comment. A frill of numbness was spreading towards my hand. In the end Surgeon Ruggiero unceremoniously lopped the digit off. I had lost my index finger, my pointing finger, my stabbing-on-the-table-to-prove-a-point finger, my eye-poking, shame-slitting finger. I kept it in a leather box until the worms found it.

Meanwhile, Marcella continued to improve. The undertaker pouted and finally ceased his daily visits, unlike the servants, who never now left her alone for one minute. Now there was always someone hovering outside her door and at least one of them in with her, day and night, no matter what time I went there.

Gianni delle Boccole

Some foible bout an accident, bout Marcella being in the way of his gun when he fired it! Some cheap story bout a speriment. Scuses lame as a tree!

Minguillo come back to Venice a few days later looking disingenious like a clever ape. No dout, when he bethought on his poor sister what he had cripplet, he fetid hisself for a genius.

'Now he's for it,' I bethought. But his Papà's spirit were too broke to give the boy a proper dissiplin.

I wondered tho, *For why dint Minguillo jist kill her outright? When he could o, easy?*

Sor Loreta

Bishop Chávez de la Rosa departed, leaving Arequipa to fulfil its destiny as the Sodom and Gomorrah of the South Americas. I did not grieve at his going. He had failed to distinguish the one pure soul at Santa Catalina, which proved that he had never been a blessed person.

I alone truly understood the reasons for Bishop Chávez de la Rosa being driven out of Arequipa in disgrace. God wanted it that way. I realized now that He had brought the Bishop all the way to Arequipa only so that He might enlighten me. My Celestial Spouse had proved His special love for me once again, for He wished me to know that my visions were immaculate and that I should in future trust in them as lesser creatures did in the Holy Scriptures.

Of course none of my light sisters shared this knowledge of my uplifting: none of them except one, who had recently joined our order. It seemed to me God's design that Sor Sofia entered the convent the same day – October 21st

1805 – that the evil church-crusher Napoleon was defeated by the British at Cape Trafalgar, though of course we did not get news of that glad event at Santa Catalina until the year's end.

From the first moment I saw Sor Sofia across the refectory table, I knew that our lives would be intertwined. This was not because she was sweet and soft like a kitten but because my Celestial Spouse and Santa Rosa whispered clearly into my deaf ear that I must love this new sister with all my might for it was laid down on high that she and I should be together.

Doctor Santo Aldobrandini

The girl would live, but after my humiliating performance in the great house I was not allowed to see her.

Ruggiero set me to drying the Small-Pox scabs he collected whenever he could. He had some eccentric theories about uses for the brown crusts. I hated to handle them, but I sweetened my labours with daydreams of the noble girl's incomparable skin and uncomplaining amiability. Between blows, Ruggiero had told me that, when I had swooned, all her thoughts had been for *my* comfort!

On the first day of winter my Master stumped back into the house in a frightful mood. Our cures had worked all too well, and the girl had been taken back to Venice for the fashionable town quacks to practise on.

What would they do to her? In those days the French orthopaedists were the idols of the Venetian doctors. Discreetly I made my way to Ruggiero's bookshelf, crowded with volumes on his obsession, the Small-Pox, and took down Nicolas Andry de Bois-Regard's *Orthopaedia: or, the art of correcting and preventing deformities in children*. I groaned.

There would be hose made of dog-skin and shoes with leaden soles to force the leg out of its protective crippled clench. The thigh and calf would be washed in stinking Oil of Worms, roughly frictioned with Oil of Lilies, poulticed in the leaves and roots of marshmallows and the whole leg bathed in boiling tripe broth and then run under freezing cold water to contract the ligaments. A roasted salt herring might be placed on the abused leg then, to draw out the humours. All this prior to binding with paste-board, splints of wood and small plates of iron.

I looked in the mirror by the bookshelf – was I yet well-fleshed and handsome enough to go to Venice, and attend the daughter of one of the city's richest merchants?

The answer was an unequivocal no.

Minguillo Fasan

Back at the Palazzo Espagnol, my father called me into his study. 'You're not ever going to be up to much,' he stated matter-of-factly, with a kind of deadness in his voice. He was not angry with me. Ludicrously, he acted as if I was some kind of lunatic. He spoke slowly, as to a foreign person.

'Every family has its bad seed,' my father said flatly. I noticed then how lustreless his eyes were, and how steeply his shoulders stooped. 'Piero is right . . . it's the duty of the parents to bury that seed where it shall not grow.'

The Reader shall be marking Piero Zen's name in His daybook for future attention.

My father roused himself to announce with a faintly contemptuous finality, 'So I'll not be sending you to the university in Padua, as I had once hoped . . . You'll be a house-boy. I suppose I'll be working to keep you in idleness until the end of my days.'

I did not dignify this with an answer, but my silent thoughts were busy. *In what way can this be a surprise to you, Papà? And why should I work? You have worked: surely that is enough embarrassment in the family. And how could you think – except that you understand nothing of me – that I might ever want to live away from my darling Palazzo Espagnol?*

He sighed, 'My first son shall be like Venice, a thing kept alive for hypocritical reasons, but of no utility.'

My first son? Was he planning other sons? My eye flew to the drawer where his will was kept. I cursed my ill luck. I had reasonably expected that my sister's literally diminished being would force him to re-make the will in my favour. It seemed that part of my plan had gone severely awry.

Rather like my sister's limb. The shot leg twisted inwards, as if shy of presenting its wronged self to a curious world. Nutrition of the lower limb was compromised. It soon dwindled to a twig-like frailty. To compensate, her sound right foot turned otherwise to an unnatural angle and commenced to swell, so that Marcella had the appearance of a club foot, and a limp that she would never lose.

A newfangled French surgeon moved his traps into the nursery, which soon smelled like a fish market. Once I passed by Marcella's room to see her lying on her couch with a large roast herring sizzling on her damaged leg. I would have got closer, but the valet Gianni appeared from nowhere with some stupid questions about my evening attire.

When Marcella was allowed out of her chamber of tortures, she simply carried them with her. The French surgeon confined her leg in leather equipment heavy with buckles and straps, which surrounded the lower part of her pelvis in a brutal ligature. In order to carry all this around, she needed a crutch.

Ah well, 'twas all to my purpose. With apologies to God, of course, for rearranging his design of my sister's body. Clanking like a suit of armour, Marcella could not hurry to the necessary house to relieve her bladder. She could not hurry anywhere. The chamber pots she requested did not always arrive in time: sometimes the servants were delayed in the corridors running errands for her brother. Marcella still struggled not to embarrass herself, yet that was no longer always possible. And so she descended a rung lower in the scale of human function.

Meanwhile, I was not daunted in my pursuit of Thomas Day's theories. In fact, I conquered and surpassed them, inventing new training methods far more vigorous than his own, especially efficacious now that Marcella could not run away from me. I supplemented my readings with the work of Pinel on the treatment of French female lunatics. Interesting, very interesting. There were other days when I walked in the tracks of the medical charlatans and their gigantic promises.

After months of apparently good behaviour on my part, even the servants slackened slightly in their vigilance. They had their own pelts to take care of, after all. There were a few times of the day and night when my parents were not there to intervene in my treatments. But my greatest ally was my sister herself. Marcella, it seemed, still would not give me away. I had told her that I would shoot her properly if she did.

I taught her to fall down into a faint at the sound of my voice: 'Die, Marcella!'

And she would lie there until I gave her permission to live again.

They might hate me, but Marcella protected me with her silence. As did the death – under cloudy circumstances – of that pedantic magistrate who had once decreed that I might go forth only under supervision. As far as I was concerned his edict died with him, melting in the froth bubbling out of his blue lips. No one at the Palazzo Espagnol challenged me. It was almost as if they were happy when I left the house.

I did not care when I found offerings in my room.

Who's afraid of a pig's heart stuck with thorns and nails tied to the fireplace?

Sor Loreta

Sor Sofia never laughed at me, but instead sympathized with all my travails. She picked apple pits out of my veil and beetles out of my water when the other sisters put them there. We passed many hours of silent prayer together. Sometimes we prayed so late that I told her to stay with me in my bed, so as not to catch cold on the way back to her own cell.

Sor Sofia's was a purer beauty than that of Sor Andreola. My friend's little white face seemed to me like a flower. God made flowers for our pleasure, and so I enjoyed her. When she came into the room I always felt a constriction in my heart as when I was in the rapture of prayer.

Sor Sofia was becomingly quiet, yet her looks said much. I felt that she supported me in every thought and deed. Once she exclaimed, 'Sor Loreta, if you had been a man, how far you would have gone in the world!'

'Hush, child,' I told her. 'There are ways in which a bride of Christ may shine brighter than any man.'

I believe she replied, 'You are so brave to scourge and fast as you do. Death itself holds no sting for you! With your courage, you might have gone to war! Who could have resisted your strength? You would have swept all before you.'

'I must fight God's war here in Santa Catalina, even though the world knows nothing of my sacrifices.'

'Yet one day your sacrifices will be known – is that what you think?' she asked.

I cast my eyes down modestly then, to my volume about Santa Rosa, of which I knew every word by heart, but particularly the last pages, where, after her death, everyone in Peru was sorry for treating her badly and venerated her greatness.

'Like Santa Rosa!' breathed Sor Sofia, and without saying anything to confirm or deny her words, I embraced her.

At that moment Santa Rosa herself whispered in my ear, 'Dearest Sor Loreta, everything You feel and do, however unusual it appears in the eyes of others, You shall do for the glory of God and Me.'

Part Two

Gianni delle Boccole

They brought her back to Venice a broke thing in her body.

The day they carrid Marcella indoors I seen summing I dint like one bit in her mother's face. My Mistress Donata Fasan dint rush to her daughter's side. She sayed to Anna, 'Make her decent before I go to her.'

Decent? Then I unnerstood. In the mind o my Mistress, a cripplet daughter were a bit like our downfalled Venice, really. Marcella were layed out – still livin – in an open coffin where everyone might look at what remaned with horror while pretending pity. That were not tall the kind o daughter that ud serve a nobble lady in Venetian High Sausiety.

I myself were frit that Ide find Marcella a cringin thing, pologizin for what Minguillo done to her.

But Marcella's spirit dint lie down n die.

She outright refust to be the sad heroin o some trudgical opera.

She askt for me n Anna soon as she were fairly in the ouse. We arrived to find Piero Zen alredy at her side. There was apples n cakes n books n paper n pastels spred out all oer the bed. Conte Piero ud filled the room with flowers.

And they was, without a single word bout the shot leg, laffing at what she drawed.

Soon we was too, tho I was cryin as well.

Marcella Fasan

I drew a cartoon of it, of how I had fallen through a trapdoor into invalidhood. My whole body had fallen on bad times; it was insolvent; it was pillaged by gangs of doctors' fingers; it had no respect from anyone any more, except of course from my lovely Piero, Anna and Gianni.

My parents summoned surgeons from as far away as Paris. There was always some bearded pomposity palpating my thigh or laying something sticky in a bag on my knee or lacing me into leather girdles that put an agonizing compression on my haunches. Worst were the culinary cures, by which the doctors tried to hot-baste me to wellness. I mitigated my humiliation by making satirical sketches of those preposterous torturers. And I soothed the burning pain by drawing the smoke rising from my leg and the Palazzo Espagnol cats deserting their comfortable perches in the kitchen to see what was cooking in the sickroom.

But flamboyant physicians with bottles of crushed millipedes – and still less my secret sketches of them – were never going to restore me to my parents' *perfettina*. The twisted limb was one thing, but the consequent exacerbation of my bladder's bungling was what finally orphaned me in their hearts. It had always been nervous, but after I was crippled, my bladder became positively frantic. My previous problems seemed almost enviable now.

A cripple had got into their daughter's body. It must have seemed an insult to the memory of their *perfettina* to transfer their love to this thing that had usurped her place, who huffed around in contraptions hoisted on ugly buckles like farm machinery. In Venice – the least barnyard-like of fairy tales! I overheard the Contessa Foscarini advising my mother to send me to a country cottage, where I might harmlessly shell peas on a stoop, or to one of those ramshackle tenements on the Lido where the rich hid their imbecile children.

'Ah,' I realized then, 'deformity makes people like Chiara Foscarini think that you are stupid!' I looked down at the drawing in my lap. Indeed, my pencilled self-portrait showed my nine-year-old self crammed into a tiny baby carriage. Even when she struggled out and proceeded boldly on to the next page, it was with the cripple's buffoonish way of walking.

See, once again even I speak of Marcella the cripple in the third person, just as I drew her. For I too was at times able to distance myself from Marcella's damaged body, and to watch the *perfettina* descend into the *povera creatura*. Like any fable, it had a satisfying, plummeting feeling about it, the kind best shown with long vertical lines in the background, all going in one direction.

Cripples are the Devil's work, they say.

I, of course, was Minguillo's. Those days I usually drew him as a hairless black dog, but from behind, without showing his face.

Only Piero dwelt on the facts of the matter, urging my mother to 'put a rein on that boy' and saying darkly, 'Next time it may be worse.'

But my parents earnestly wished to forget *why* I was crippled, for what did it say of their negligent protection of me? Worse, popular wisdom decreed that no creature – not even a Minguillo – is conceived except of parents who carry all his defects in their own germ plasm. My mother and father could not confront such a gruesome thought. And so my parents gradually persuaded themselves, and never contradicted visitors who thought so, that I had been born with my deformity, and that being a cripple was an essential part of my nature.

My pencil began to reveal fear in people's eyes when they beheld me – me, the slightest, least fearsome creature imaginable. Even my hair was soft like chicken-down. The very cartilage of my nose was translucent in the sunshine. But that, I was learning, is what frightens people: creatures who are weaker and rarer than themselves. I drew caricatures of elegant baboons, their eyes and tails askew with terror – fleeing from a tiny mouse – with my features – in a wheeled chair.

Alone in my room, I drew thrilling scenes of myself running away to the circus where I became a leading Artist of Deformity. In Venice, giants, dwarves and bearded ladies were a flourishing business. For these outrages of Nature, there was always repulsed fascination – and some coins. People will pay good money for a gratifying wave of disgust.

But to be mildly deformed – no, no, that, in reality, I was discovering, brings only ignominy and obscurity. My pencil ranged over the page with increasing fearlessness, but my life shrank. I was not much produced. Excursions in my wheeled chair were confined to the remote and poor parts of the city. My parents could not afford to be embarrassed by such a daughter as I had become. Mothers of my parents' acquaintance had of course stopped grooming their sons to marry me the day the first doctor strapped me into the resplendently ugly regalia of crippledom.

Perhaps I was even then already halfway to being a nun in the eyes of other people; a sexless, shambling creature. Being deformed, I was discovering, eclipses every other difference – of gender, race or age. Deformity lives in another kingdom, dreaded and shunned as if misfortune were contagious.

Yet I did not quite become what my parents saw – a mild, accepting victim. They desired that in me, and so I gave the appearance of it to them as a gift. Mostly, I obliged by staying in my room, where I read my way through the Palazzo Espagnol library, and made copies of the portraits in the house, delivered to me one by one by kind Gianni. I wrote my diary. I drew, energetically and ambitiously, but secretly.

And in comporting myself so I completed the process my parents had started: I forked myself in two. Outwardly I was meek as a novice. Inside me, silently, grew a defiant creature who had not accommodated her reduced prospects in any way whatsoever. The more passive I seemed, the more determined I grew to re-shape not my body, for that seemed impossible, but my situation.

Minguillo watched my visible descent with lucid satisfaction.

But Minguillo had no more insight than a hairless dog drawn from behind.

Oh yes, he knew when I hurt, when I burst, and when the iron teeth of the leather harness bit into my skin. Such primitive things dogs can know about other dogs.

I, on the other hand, was doubly endowed with insight. It was meat and salt for me that I had thoughts of my own, and that Minguillo could not penetrate them.

I was not my parents' *perfettina* any more: and they were not my parents as they had once been. Instead, I had Piero. I had Anna and Gianni.

And I would have that other kind of love too. It would one day circle and land in my heart and take me away from the cruelty. I was, against all the odds, even then quite sure of it.

Minguillo Fasan

Now, if it isn't asking too much of the Kind Reader to concentrate a little . . . please. If the style and temper of my effusions have not at first seduced, pray be assured that their charms shall soon steal over you. I am sure I hope so myself.

Not long after Marcella's accident, my father set sail again for Arequipa (which means, by not unhumorous coincidence, 'Yes, stay' in the local Quechua dialect).

My mother thereafter explained that if he attempted to return, my father would be promptly clapped inside the elegant halls of the *priora*'s house on the Lazzaretto Vecchio with its wistful view of Venice, for weeks of quarantine against whatever pox was currently crusting the shores of the Mediterranean.

'And of course he's needed in Arequipa. Everyone knows the Spanish *factores* cannot be trusted,' my mother told her friends, subtly fingering a silver picture frame. Yet certain rumours were winging down the Grand Canal.

What's that? The Reader's eyebrow lifts a little? He would like to know if my mother was stupid, or absurdly innocent? Yes, both, but in this case I believe my mother simply chose not to suspect. Anyway, the woman was not deprived of husbands.

My mother's *cicisbeo* Piero Zen ate at our table each evening. His daily bouquet arrived with a sugary sonnet tucked among the petals. He excelled in his duty of holding up a mirror to my mother for others to read. That mirror declared, 'Behold my lovely mistress, the delightful object of my affections.'

The *cicisbeo*'s function was ornamental, rather like his flowers. I was head of the household in my father's absence. My duties were minimal. I did what any noble young man in Venice did. I annoyed my father's clerks on the mezzanine floor of the Palazzo Espagnol. I rifled the petty cash. No one dared force a chaperone upon me nowadays. I went where I pleased and did same. I held forth on lewd subjects at Florian, until the owner of the *caffè* requested me to take my business, if you can call it that, elsewhere. I gondola'd to a Spanish brothel in Cannaregio where the whores sold me the use of their hides. I supervised my little sister as and when I could find her.

I waited for my father to come home, in order to settle the matter of his will. There was a confrontation brewing between us. Before I found the will, I had only his distant disdain to tolerate. True, I had not loved noticing how other men treated their sons to manly embraces and lingering looks of pride when they brought them to our home. But I had entertained no particularly strong feelings against my father.

Regular inspections of the hiding place revealed the will unchanged over the years: my father was allowing a paltry matter to become a serious one. His every hour – 'Yes, stay'! – lingering in Arequipa, and even the risky nature of the journey back, imperilled my prospects. I now cultivated a poisonous asperity in my father's regard, slowly petting it into industrious hatred.

Meanwhile, I was developing a distracting interest in fashion that mirrored my mother's, though of course I went deeper and harder into the thing than she did. The Elegant Reader will have observed for Himself that not for nothing are we humans the only creatures not fully satisfied with the snug vestments we're born in. I was less satisfied than most. And soon people began to talk of my clothes in tones usually reserved for acts of God. Not everyone could bring off my cravats, frock-coats and waistcoats. Yet I captured and held the attention of people who might otherwise have treated me peremptorily or hurried away from me.

I developed other ways of increasing my stock. I made people wait for me. I took an extraordinarily long time to tie my cloak on leaving for an appointment, while all the servants stood by. I was always the last into the gondola, watching out of windows for signs of impatience and rumbles of contempt before I let myself be seen. Then I descended with majestic slowness, drinking up the hate.

Sor Loreta

Even with Sor Sofia's sweet prayers added to mine, our Heavenly Father did not fulfil my great desire for an early death. I began to believe that the priests who governed Santa Catalina were also my enemies, for each time I confessed to them some new transgression by one of the light sisters, they thanked me, and tantalised me with hints of a rise in my estate, only to cast me down when the next election brought me no closer to a position on the council of nuns.

I was called to an interview with the Chaplain, who continually wiped his forehead as he pronounced, 'Sor Loreta, you must moderate the fury of your scourges. Indeed, the Devil may enter into the scourge and cause it to perversely delight the flesh, in which case to scourge is to behave impurely. Which is not to be God's true servant, is it now?'

I turned my deaf right ear to these words. I returned to my cell, where Sor Sofia was waiting for me.

There were times when I thought I could not live without Sor Sofia by my side. I worried about her day and night for she was subject to a weak stomach and frequently confined to the infirmary. Since the incident with the sores, I was no longer permitted to enter in there. Instead, like Lidwina of Schiedam, I made a point of going to stand very close to anyone who suffered from a headache or toothache, so their suffering would become mine. I did this in church so that they could not move away from me.

At those times when Sor Sofia was forced away, I suffered a loneliness that sent me to lie on the stone floor of the church for hours on end. Only in Sor Sofia did I find that humility, love and gentleness with which I had always desired to surround myself.

Yet the vicious light nuns of Santa Catalina were not content to leave us alone in our mutual devotion. Some whistled like men in a *chichería* when they saw me walking down the Calle Sevilla with Sor Sofia. Little drawings were pushed under my door, showing myself and Sor Sofia naked and embracing in obscene positions. Others mocked my renowned physical strength, showing me lifting the delicate Sor Sofia in one hand.

So evil minds will seek to extract some kind of impurity from even a perfect love.

Gianni delle Boccole

An ouse without a proper Master soon runs downhill. At the Palazzo Espagnol, we was going that way, not slowly by slowly, but feroshus fast. Minguillo weren't truely Master of imself let lone anyone else. Least that's what I besot to tell myself in them days, that Minguillo were more wackaloon than devil-in-pantaloons as ye mite say.

Now I pause to cross myself for I am thinking on his face.

Twere at this junkshure that he started to *look* rampin mad. He gangled round loose in his joints as a hyena. The pimples, they was a-sworming. His hair were greased back like a rat what had swum up a drain, or least that's how I allus saw im after Marcella made a sketch o same, a wet rat sittin on the head ovva airless dog all shone from ahind. But twernt funning really. It rot fear in the soul. His eyes had that pinpoint stare. The colour had emptied out of em. They had no more n a shadow o blue, like turned milk. He had only to fasten his two eyes on a body, and that body would be took with the shakes, Swine ovva God!

His clothes were the talk o the taverns. He ran to prancy damask and silk frock-cotes in colours that dint nowise love one another, and he favored tock hats like crumpilt cats hangin oft one side o his spotty head.

Bein so very vizable, his reputation were well rigged bout the town. He were by now swinging round Venice's for-sale laydies limn by limn and not letting one *etto* of lust or drunkness pass him by. If there were a cockfight, or a stringing up ovva mogul dog, or a catfight mong whores, ye was dead sartin to find Minguillo Fasan there with his coin on the nastiest contestant. And if anyone got took bad as a result, he would strut off, grinning like a shot fox, sayin his usual 'It don't pertain to me'.

We was happyer when he were out on the lamb. For inside our ouse he went bout crookeding the running of things, so that evry servant had his or her life upsided down beyont any sense. The cook were made to wash the slop buckets. The gardener was got up in tight livery for digging the roses. We was subjeckted to all-of-a-sudden lining-ups in the *piano nobile*, to slaps cross the eyes n kicks in the pants, and awful, awful hurting insalts that made us small n shamed in our own n each other's eyes.

We swallowed it hole. We was thinking on our positions. We had to not direckly offend Minguillo, who had power oer us like an Eguptian Farrow! Piero Zen could not save us all, not like he ud saved the skin o my sister Cristina by takin her to his own *palazzo* for a maid back when Minguillo ud shone a parshality for her.

A servant what had got hisself dismist from one of the grate ouses would be out on his scuppers. He mite as well present hisself direckly at the almshouse: he wunt find other work. So we ate our shame and doed our work.

The only thing we should have been shamed o was not watching out sufficient for Marcella, when she most needed the shield o our eyes from her bastert brother. What mizworms we was, minding out only for ourselves, when we alredy knew zackly and full well what he was caperble of.

Sor Loreta

Then the *priora* came to tell me that I must not keep Sor Sofia in my cell through the night, and that I must moderate my expressions of love towards her.

'I shall never do that. It is God's design that I should live in love and harmony with my sister Sofia.'

'You defy me?'

'It is our duty to defy those who try to make us act against God.'

The *priora* looked smug then, as if I had just uttered the one thing that would please her the most.

'If you insist, Sor Loreta. As long as you are in this convent as God's servant it is I who decides how you must be disciplined. And I have decided,' she announced, 'you may not see Sor Sofia any more until you show that you are capable of humility and obedience. Now we shall see what kind of love you have for her.'

Minguillo Fasan

It came over me that my mother's *cicisbeo* took an excessive interest in Marcella. No choice could have been less fortunate for his sympathies. Piero Zen's proper duties were laid down: to be my *mother*'s confidant and private entertainment.

He was not supposed to dote upon her *daughter*.

Or interfere in the business of his lady's son, who had come into his majority, and who should do as he pleased in all matters.

It had been going on for far too long. I remembered him dandling the baby Marcella on his knee with a detestable naturalness before my father came back from Arequipa and claimed that privilege. Pieraccio was never discomforted when the number one Papà returned. Ludicrously, he appeared to think Marcella should have as many grown men devoted to her as possible.

Since her accident, Pieraccio would personally carry Marcella up the stairs. He was forever nuzzling her thin little neck with smile-laden secrets. He sat her by his side at dinner, discussing art and literature with her in uncondescending terms. He had her served first, when the platter should have come to me by right. For that alone, I thought, he should be hurt. When I passed her bedchamber at night, I could hear him reading Goldoni and Gozzo to her, and her tiny voice almost loud with laughter. Between Pieraccio and the servants, who clung to her like drops of sweat, it was almost impossible to find Marcella by herself.

And when I did, I discovered that Piero Zen had given her a little silver bell, which tinkled like angels percussioning in heaven if anyone lifted her bedcovers, summoning her ugly maid Anna and for some strange reason also my own valet Gianni. In seconds, he would come hurtling into her room, shouting, 'Is there anything we can do for you, sir?'

How did the oaf already know it was *me* lifting the covers?

Between the valet and Pieraccio there was some understanding that infuriated me, for Gianni was my creature and had no right to make associations of his own. I divined that Piero tipped the little jackanapes heavily – that was the only possible explanation.

It crossed my mind that Pieraccio might know, might actually know that Marcella was due to inherit the Palazzo Espagnol. He was a dear friend of my father, in the way of *cicisbei*: a comrade in the difficult war against the caprices of women. Pieraccio had of course been present at dinner the night my poultry-guillotine was discovered in the garden. Perhaps he had consoled *both* my parents. He was no great supporter of mine: I had several times overheard him urging my father 'to make a stand against the evil', meaning me.

It burned that Pieraccio might know about the perverted will, and feel smug at my expense, for of course he could not guess that I had secretly read it. His persistent, cloying interventions in my sister's life were not to be tolerated. He made personal comments about my special clothes, sly ones. Which was why in the end I found a way to bring them both down together.

If the Reader cannot divine from the foregoing what I had in mind, I would not have Him suffer a sleepless night over it. Soon enough, He shall hear it, soon enough. I am sure I hope so myself.

Marcella Fasan

My diary from those times is full of Piero.

When he leaned to pick me up, Piero made it seem as if it was a spontaneous embrace and not a service that he offered. He did not avoid the subject of my crippled state. Unlike my parents, Piero could bring himself to ask directly, 'Is your leg hurting you today with this cold wind?'

What was more, he cared about the answer. For if it was yes, the leg hurt, then he had a plan for my sedentary diversion. If the answer was no, then he had another plan, involving an excursion or a treat.

Piero looked me in the eye when he spoke to me. Most people avoided that kind of fusion since the accident. When I was alone with Piero, my answers were boldly my own, not the passive murmurs of the congenital Poor Thing that my parents had settled upon for my career.

And Piero was not content to let me merely watch. It was Piero, a noted connoisseur and collector of art, who took me to meet Cecilia Cornaro in her studio at San Vio. It was Piero who commissioned her to paint me. The portrait, he told me, was to be a surprise gift for my parents. There's lovely Piero again: wise and subtle. For we both knew that a painting of my head and shoulders, cutting off all that was unacceptable below, could not fail to please even my mother.

Of course I knew all about Cecilia Cornaro before Piero took me to her. Cecilia Cornaro was a tremendously, perilously fascinating woman. No other noblewoman in Venice had made a career of any kind, let alone in the louche field of portrait painting. She had crept out of her parents' *palazzo* by Miracoli at the age of thirteen to become the lover of Giacomo Casanova and only-rumour-knew who else. Painting, she had learned at the hand of one of our last great masters. She quickly surpassed him. She was naturally the author of that portrait of my late sister Riva that made our servants smile and weep.

Cecilia Cornaro had painted kings and princes, had even travelled to the courts of the Habsburgs. She spoke languages as she used colour – learning everything by instinct from the skin of her clients. She was most famous for skin. Her portraits had a dewy quality about them, as if her sitters had just risen from a tousled, happy bed. If you were to believe everything that was said about Cecilia Cornaro, she had quite possibly personally tousled the bed with them, if only to extract a more lovely painting. Cecilia Cornaro's fame was such that she was no longer required to be respectable.

Piero told me that it was probably better for our visit to her studio to remain a secret between us, at least initially. 'If it turns out as I hope, many things shall change,' he said thoughtfully, 'though of course, that depends entirely upon how you two ladies take to one another.'

As our gondola shot across the Grand Canal towards San Vio, it occurred to me that there was one thing that I had never heard about

Cecilia Cornaro: that she kept a female friend. Her intimates and her yet more cherished enemies were all men. The nub of it was this: Cecilia Cornaro's tongue was notoriously barbed. The salons and *conversazioni* of Venice – those few that had survived Napoleon – crackled with reports of her insolence towards those more accustomed to fawning. Senators, diplomats and foreign lords had quailed under her raillery. Women were terrified of her frank, personal observations. So what amusement would the fork-tongued Cecilia Cornaro take at the expense of a malfunctioning young girl? I felt a Poor Thing posture gripping my spine with slimy fingers.

We arrived at the Palazzo Balbi Valier, where three Istrian-stone arches framed a great courtyard inhabited by bloated white statues and a large striped cat, who looked at us with reserve. With his usual lack of fuss, Piero carried me out of the boat and up the stairs. The cat followed us, sniffing delicately at the heel of one of Piero's shoes.

Piero said kindly, 'Marcella, I'll warn you – initially, Cecilia may be a little . . . raw . . . in her manner.'

The door was open, and my first impression was of a room bursting with human life. Faces in oil and pastel lined the walls in no particular order, like people thrown together at a party that has surpassed everyone's expectations of intimacy and hilarity. Immediately I understood why people waxed lyrical about Cecilia Cornaro's painted skin. Every face was rampantly alive, each mouth seemed about to speak a tasty secret. Each pair of eyes looked at me with an expression sweetened by satisfaction.

'What vermin have you dragged in this time, cat?'

A green-eyed woman with a cloud of tumbled hair had advanced upon us while we were still trapped in the gaze of the portraits. She stood wiping her hands on a rag. A mouth-watering smell of oils and medicinal herbs charged the air. The cat ran over to her, climbed nimbly up her skirts and to her shoulder, from which vantage point he nuzzled her ear, and miaowed into it. She nodded. Her eyes travelled from Piero's face to my own, at which point the artist smiled enthusiastically, then clapped her hands as she peered closer.

It was the strangest thing – she was staring frankly at me, yet at the same time she had no recognition of me at all. This was different from the usual looks that slid quickly over me in my wheeled chair. Cecilia Cornaro was – avidly – taking in the lineaments and colouring of my face.

111

Myself as a person, my character, my likes and dislikes, my strengths and weaknesses, all those parts of me could wait, and indeed might never come into the orbit of her interest at all.

'Ah, I see what you mean, Piero. Much more interesting than the sister! Yes, this absolutely must be painted.'

'What did I tell you, Cecilia?' Piero set me down on a chair and gently turned my face towards the light. The artist paced around me, swooping in for a closer look from different angles. Cecilia Cornaro had a cat's insolence. Her clothes looked as if they might fall off with the next shrug. You would never want to stop looking at her.

Now Piero was saying something that astounded me, 'Cecilia, don't eat the girl up. And the face does not come free of charge, you know. I told you: I have come to trade it.'

'And I told *you*, I don't take pupils. And if I did,' her eyes narrowed, 'I would choose 'em myself, for their talent, if any, and not for their faces.'

My face sweltered like a hot red plum. Pupils? This was Piero's plan? To apprentice me to the greatest artist in Venice? He had always encouraged my drawing, praised my every scratch on paper. *Dear, dear Piero*, I thought, *only your fondness could make you exaggerate my skills so! I can catch a likeness, and make you laugh, but I know nothing of colour. Cecilia Cornaro is rightfully insulted that you think I might approach the hem of her dress as an artist.*

Indeed, Cecilia had turned her back on us and was rifling through the contents of a bathtub crammed with paintings and large brushes.

'Marcella, my love,' said Piero kindly, 'I am afraid that we have had a wasted visit. However, I am glad that you have met with the paintings, and their perpetrator.'

He bowed to Cecila Cornaro, who now stood fuming by her bath. He took me in his arms again and turned so that my face was in her full view, paused for a moment, then set off down the stairs.

At the bottom of the stairs he paused.

'Wait!' Cecilia Cornaro called down. Her heart-shaped face appeared over the banisters. With his back still to her, Piero winked at me.

'Piero, you old *scroccone*, you very well know I cannot bear to be constrained,' she grumbled.

'No one is constraining you,' replied Piero mildly, turning around to face her. 'This is not a forced sale. If you don't like the price, you do not have to take the face.'

'*Ghe sbòro!*' she expostulated. My skin goose-pimpled with pleasurable shock at the worst obscenity of the gondoliers.

Piero laughed. 'Your pretty ways, Cecilia!'

He took a step towards our gondola. Cecilia Cornaro uttered a frustrated little mew under her breath. Then she sighed, 'I might as well try it, though I'll not vouch for any success. The girl will not expect me to be *kind* to her just because she is a cripple, I hope.'

I spoke for the first time, and it was as myself, unmitigated: 'I should be very unhappy if you were.'

She grinned, 'That's very well, because I don't have a kind bone in my body.'

Minguillo Fasan

The Reader will understand that it is now necessary for Him to digest a little more history before He may fall with relish upon my personal tale once again.

Napoleon had changed his mind. In January 1806 he annexed Venice back into his new masterpiece *Il Regno d'Italia*.

The Austrians marched out, the French slouched back in, and Venice had a whole new paper identity. Now we Venetians were citizens, apparently, all equal in a new Italian kingdom. Equal to the peasants on the plains of the Veneto. Equal to the grape-treaders of Bassano. The whole idea stuck in our lordly craws. Yet we did not let ourselves dwell upon it. *Va bene*, shrugged the noble Venetians. Let Boney's minions print their laborious little bills and decrees. We'll still go about having our hair dressed, strutting in full fig, intermarrying with other Golden-Book families and putting our unwanted women into convents. Of which interesting subject, more anon.

I was gradually taking over the family business. My father had lost his vital spark of interest in it. I believe that his spirit finally snapped when he heard that Napoleon had returned. After Boney proclaimed *Il Regno d'Italia* my father wrote to me that I could do as I wished. He no doubt thought I would not understand his concluding sigh, '*The whole world is mad, who am I to confine the madness?*'

Now he washed his hands of Venice, which included me.

The silver that had made us rich glittered dully in my imagination. Once I dreamed of the holds of boats heavy with the gleanings of the Potosí mines, and of seeing our worked candlesticks in the salons of important *palazzi*. But since 1792 the vulgar new Americans had been minting their plebeian dollars from silver – and it had entirely lost its mystery for me. And so I set about quietly dismantling Father's network of silver agencies.

What attracted me now was less heavy and more exotic. I concentrated on our fever business, that is, brokering on the happy marriage of two inseparable but disparate items: the bitter bark of the fever tree, *Chinchona calisaya*, and the malarial miasmas of Venice. My family supplied Venice with the one, and Venice supplied us with the Sweating Sickness and therefore customers.

I set up my own quack and apothecary in an exclusive business. Inspired by my weeping agricultural girl, I had him conjure up a skin preparation – 'The Tears of Santa Rosa' – that very soon became a fashionable appendage to every noble toilette table on account of its ridiculous cost, its eye-opening perfume and its proud boast to give the user skin 'with the stainless whiteness and lustre of a pearl'. Our literature implied that the precious liquid had been wept by Peruvian nuns fed only on the fruit of the candelabra cactus in the high Andes. Sometimes we embellished the tale with assertions that these virgin brides of Christ were also blind.

Our shop was in populous San Luca. It was handsomely equipped with bottles of two-headed salamanders for those simple folk who thought they could buy good omens; we also sold spent bullets and bundles of leather flayed from black dogs for use against the evil eye, and silk ribbons for binding around warts. I called my emporium 'Novo Mondo' and my quack's name was masterpieced from old maps: 'Doctor Inca Tuparu, of Valparaiso, Chile-Peru, the noted pyretologist or fever-doctor'. Congenitally plump, he browned up nice and greasy in tinted cocoa-butter. I groomed his Spanish

114

accent myself, by the expedient of a naily collar that I tweaked whenever he failed to lisp.

Part of his exotic title had the extra joy of a little truth to it: his New World provenance. For at last, with my father too dispirited to shackle me, I had begun to travel beyond Venice. I found it much to my liking. I travelled like a king, and was treated accordingly. At the beginning I ventured only as far as Seville and then Praia in the Cape Verde Islands. But soon I was fitting myself out for my first proper journey – all the way to Valparaiso. And it was there that I had bought my quack, one red-ruptured dawn, over a table of cards.

The turkey-hipped little Roman had been washed up on the shores of Chile by a tide of debts at home. And when I encountered him in Valparaiso he was up to his dankly-feathered wrinkle in debt once more, but this time with the Chilean card sharks. He was seated around a table with five of their most scintillatingly dangerous number. That night his creditors were ready to take their money in his blood, for they had realized – with my help, for I had casually unmasked his faked title of 'Marchese' – that there was no hope of any other satisfaction. The sharks were in that final happy stage before violence breaks out, that state of extreme and jovial amity towards the victim. He was their dearest, truest friend in those luscious anticipatory moments. So do born murderers refresh their spirits. And I dipped into the joy of the occasion, exhilarated by the fumes of fear and sweat.

The Travelled Reader knows about nights like these: the air smoking over the salty port, the boats creaking on their ropes, the old women's limbs creaking behind their rancid aprons, the bedsprings creaking under the industrious whores. Candlelight and gutted glasses, and men with knives by their thighs seated round a table, drawing their business to its inevitable conclusion.

I could have simply enjoyed the show. The murderers' pleasure was contagious. Yet something made me change the condemned Roman's destiny, that is to say, give him one. When I noticed a blade ripening inside a nearby pocket, I threw a purse across the table.

'He's mine now,' I said in that free and easy way I have. 'Don't mind if I do.'

They took my cash indifferently. I had never bought a man before, and I liked it extremely. I passed the next few weeks in the agreeable pastime of training him up for his new role in Venice.

The man had marsh fever in his blood, like all Romans. Subject to the headache, the loose bowels, the vomiting, the stark fits, he was never going to win at cards or life. The disease had shrivelled him and turned his skin a New Worldish yellow that was very much to my purpose. Usefully, his fever was conjured up by the stressful nature of his educational regime, which I'll admit lacked incentives and was more built on the principle of pain. In addition, I administered certain drugs that excited watery stools and brisk, unexpected purges.

'This is going to be a little uncomfortable,' I told him, tipping another acidulous expectorant down his throat. In fever, he dreamed and raved, and told me many interesting items about his past that would serve as useful blackmailing tools later. By the end of our joint stay in Valparaiso his new-minted Spanish accent was subject to only occasional lapses that hurt him more than they hurt me.

It came into my mind that I should set him up with some kind of talismanic object, exclusive to him – all the best Venetian quacks had one. It was at this moment I first heard whispers of a book bound in human skin that had been salvaged from a shipwreck at Arica. It was said to have been made from a piece of the hide of Tupac Amaru II, the last Inca rebel, whose executed parts had been divided some twenty-five years before, and then displayed in every crevice of his country as a warning to other troublemakers.

For twenty of my finest ducats the book was mine. My *factor* in Arica brought it down to Valparaiso swaddled in linen, barely concealing his distaste. Feigning indifference, I waited till I was alone before I ran a thrilling finger over its grey-pink binding, feeling for any hidden slivers of pain. It was cool and hard, revealing nothing. Still.

As a child, I had devoured all the journal reports of Tupac Amaru's death, and the torture of his wife, and had dreamed of setting up a similar fate for a rabbit during our *villeggiatura*. They had tried to tear the rebel apart with four horses whipped in different directions – an idea that had inspired in me a very natural desire to experiment. However, I had not been allowed near the valuable horses since I had nailed one of them to the stable floor – so this plan had come to nothing.

I did not dwell on my old bitternesses. I was a happy man that day. I had in my hands that lovely thing that so well combined form and function.

Inside was sewn a cautionary tract about the sorry end of the binding's owner. I now overpasted the pages with my recipes for the drugs we would make with all the splendid poisons of Peru. On the journey home, I kept the book by me at all times, and frequently laid my hand on it while I talked to people, who surely would have hated to know that they were on parlaying terms with a man who owned a book of human skin.

I changed ships in Ancona on the way back to Venice, to avoid a tedious pause at the lazzaretto and to protect my book from the vinegar and smoky perfumes of the quarantines. I declared myself returned from 'just a short trip to Puglia'. My father had never thought to be so subtle.

The book of human skin and I were safely home. The juice and grease of my own fingers had already softened that grey-pink binding.

Sor Loreta

After the *priora* told me that I might not see Sor Sofia any more, I was not quite myself for a period. When I awoke, I was told that I had called out many unsuitable things and spoken blasphemies, as if a demon had been placed inside my body by my enemies.

For some days I floated between barest consciousness and a stupor like death. I felt that the Devil was fighting for my soul with his long green tongue in my ear and his claws touching every part of my body, but from the inside. When I was strong enough, I tried to beat him out.

I damaged my back and thighs so badly that they took away my whip and my cilice. Then, like Speranda of Cingoli, I donned the hide of a pig with the hard bristles turned in against the skin of my waist, until the *priora* had that removed from my body. So instead I wore a goatskin bound with horsehair cords like Umiliana de' Cerchi.

Though I begged to be allowed to starve quietly to death, I was ordered to attend the refectory, where I was made to eat a diet of white food that was thought good for cooling heated brains. The nuns around me glutted on bright pimentos, and colourful stews and red apples like the one Eve took from the serpent. They sniggered at my plate of white rice, white bread and a soup of strained breast of chicken. Sor Sofia had been ordered to dine alone in her cell, so as to avoid being seen by me.

I took my chipped bowl (for I still insisted on the humblest vessels) and knelt beneath the table and prayed, 'Lord, thank You for all the good things you have done for wretched me, deserving only of pity.'

'Deserving of a good kick,' laughed Rafaela, the chief of my persecutors, about whom there will be many more grievous things to tell. Rafaela then pushed her foot against my rear under the table. I fell forward into the breast-of-chicken soup with a splash.

Now before I was taken to Santa Catalina, I was entirely naïve. The world's lust for honours was entirely unknown to me, as was the duplicity of those who profess godliness in order to win themselves glory on earth. Just such evil was manifested at that moment, when Sor Andreola's voice could be heard above the table saying, 'Rafaela, pray do not show unkindness to our troubled sister.'

Without my telling them to do so, my teeth sprang into a snarl like a wild animal. For to be saved by Sor Andreola was the worst degradation except for one thing – which was that by a terrible irony the godless Rafaela was the older sister of my own beloved Sor Sofia. As a symbol of her rebellion against God's design, for Rafaela thought herself too good to be His bride, that girl had refused to take her nun's title of Sor Águeda, and was universally addressed and spoken of in her old, secular name.

To be mistreated by Sor Sofia's sister and patronized by Sor Andreola was too much for me. Suddenly the world seemed too cruel a place even for one born to suffer like myself. It was at that moment that I publicly announced a penance that would surely prove fatal. The soup in my nose made my voice sound like bees humming when I told the nuns dining above me: 'The Lord suffered on the cross without nutritious and refreshing drinks for my sake, and so I do not desire to take any either. Out of reverence for the sponge that was put to His lips, I hereby renounce all liquid except vinegar.'

'Vinegar face! Suits you!' Rafaela had no Christian virtue in her, being at all times worldly and irreverent. 'Do you ever ask yourself, Sor Loreta, what kind of God wants in his marriage bed a grown woman who's starved herself to look like a spindly child?'

And she took a great bite of alpaca stew, smacking her lips noisily. This cruel mockery was uttered while I maintained the most joyous expression on my soaked face, becoming to one who has seen her way to glory in the arms of God.

Sor Andreola lifted up the tablecloth and peered down at me with a false expression of concern painted on her face. 'Are you sure, Sor Loreta?' she asked me. 'I would be sorry to see you suffer like that. Please take a little water. It will help you think more clearly, I dare say.'

The truth was of course that *she* would never think of such a good penance. Sor Andreola had not the martyr's courageous spirit in her. Compared to my own rigour, she was merely flaccid in her faith.

After that I would take no drinks: not tea, *tisana* or chocolate or soup. I would allow enough water into my mouth to unparch my tongue for prayers and that was all. I sipped the communion wine. Otherwise I drank only vinegar.

Just such a fast had brought several saints to their marriage bed with Christ in less than thirty days.

Gianni delle Boccole

When Minguillo went way the first time, what a joy fell on the ouse, what an idol. My Mistress Donata Fasan, she begun to sing in the mornings. Piero Zen were with us the hole time it seemed, almost niver going back to his homonymouse *palazzo*. Marcella's laffter rang out all day long. Twere akshually like a famly, the three o them together round the dinner table. It doed ye a grate big good to see it.

Simple stuff. A smile here, a laff there. Famly love, cheap as dirt, good as gold. And evry day Conte Piero tookt Marcella out in the gondola for a few hours. I dint know scut bout where they went. All I cared were that Marcella returned with roses in her cheeks, with n honest appetite beside.

Marcella's little personal complaint finely faded way. With the brother gone, we took her out of the leather gear and let her midrift n her twisted leg breathe a space. She jist needed a little crutch for when she were tired. Twere a pleasure to watch her straying bout the courtyard picking flowers. She would make pretty poortrets of our favrit blooms for us servants with our own faces at the heart of each flower. We had to keep reminding her to keep wary of Minguillo's nasty little patch o poisonus monkshood n foxglove shootin up there blue heads in tericotta pots.

In them balmy days, summing motherly at last woked up inside the breast o the Mamma, what had pratically held a funeral for Marcella as the sweet little girl she formally was. With Minguillo way, with Conte Piero to courage her, I ad hopes o my Mistress Donata Fasan at last. I saw her kiss the top o Marcella's head onct, and it were like seeing a beautiful sunrise. I was undid.

'Yes,' I breathed, 'learn to love her. Do it so it stays did this time.'

They's still in a drawer at the Palazzo Espagnol, the drawings Marcella made of her mother them weeks. It were the face she drew for onct, not the more notable hair, and she got her Mamma to the very life.

Minguillo stayed n stayed way. And stayed some more. Bliss, twere. I got to wear my own face all day long, not the stupid one I keeped special for him.

Me, I preyed evry night for a shipwreck or a nice Leprosy or a nasty robber in Chile-Peru. Or a whore with a short temper and a knife under her pillow. There must be one among them, I was thinking, with a bit o gameness to her. Who jist wunt take it no more, Great Cuckold ovva God.

Val-par-eye-ee-so, that's how ye says it, Valparaiso.

Minguillo Fasan

Ah, lovely Valparaiso, where the girls were poor enough to do anything without whining. Ah, what memories of the rain beating down on tin roofs and walls while I beat down on the flesh of delicious *mesdames*! Adorable Valparaiso, that might at any moment be shook down by an earthquake, and all eighteen thousand souls living stacked up on her steep *quebradas* in danger of their lives without cease. The prospect of the deadly *temblores* put an excitement on everyone at all times. So every wretched hovel was tingling with defiant life.

I had taken up my abode at the house of a Mr French, or so he chose to style himself, where hard-worked beds with haggard curtains were offered behind a baby-pink tin facade. And it was Mr French himself who introduced me to certain Valparaisan ladies, if you can call them that, who could be induced to wear spurs and smoke cigars. Who sat *astride* on horseback and smelled like low tide after granting me the enjoyment of their persons.

I was sad to leave Valparaiso, yet with my quack trained up in the town's most famous *botica*, and the book of human skin in my pocket, my duty lay further north in Arequipa, where my father was expecting me. But my curiosity dragged me north even of that.

So instead of proceeding straight to Arequipa, I purchased a passage on the merchant brig *Orpheus*, bound for Lima. Landing at Callao, I traversed the miserable nine miles to the capital, where I was enchanted by the local fashion of the *saya*, a skirt so tight it left nothing and everything to the imagination, and even more so by the *manto*, a veil tied around the waist and then drawn over the head to expose only one roving eye. It was rampantly the most provocative thing I had ever seen. In Venice, our ladies of the 'popular' class wrapped their attractions in their *nizioletto*, which performed a similar function, but even the Venetians had never been so depraved as to show *just one eye*.

121

At first when I saw these one-eyed ladies in their regiments, for they walked about everywhere, I was unbearably excited, thinking that they had been deliberately maimed like this and that the de-eyeing of ladies was an actual profession in Lima, where poverty and humidity kept the cauldron of violence at a constant boil. I was faintly disappointed to unwrap one girl as soon as possible and find the other eye round as a pebble and bright as the sun. Savagely disappointed, so that the girl, though she knew it not, stood in danger of losing that eye on a permanent basis. But I stayed my hand, for her pimp was outside, and larger than myself.

I roamed the Calle de la Cascarilla, Bark Street, spying on the wares of the pharmacies there, taking note of the prices and the purity of the chinchona they were famous for. I negotiated a regular shipment for a sum that I would multiply thirty times when it reached the streets of Venice, though I would be losing ten per cent to the King of Spain, and one per cent to the port, and a greedy tithe to the church when each boat docked at Cadiz.

I was enjoying myself so heartily and profitably that I successfully forgot I was supposed to have stopped first at Islay, and to have made my way to Arequipa, to meet with my father. But while I tarried with my one-eyed honeys in Lima, I received a reproachful letter from the man himself. My father had finally roused himself to show a little interest in the family business, and he was not pleased to hear about my severance from silver. He wanted me to desist from all my new and imaginative apothecary activities. I was ordered straight to Arequipa to account for myself and to stop causing scandals in the ports.

'*This is not a good time for your notions, son,*' my father wrote. His handwriting wandered uncertainly over the page.

The querulous letter was enough to make me book my passage straight home to Venice from Lima, with no stopping at Islay after all. I would not be harangued and lectured like a little boy, not by a man who had secretly disinherited me, and lacked the valour to confront me with his heinousness.

I whistled on the deck as we passed Islay and its mules, waiting to take obedient sons over the mountains to their Papàs. I gave the place the shine of my teeth, and a wave of my lace-ruffled wrist. I doubted if my father would give chase. So I never got to see Arequipa that time, which was a shame in some ways: in Lima I had heard well of it and its small-footed, white-skinned ladies, who never walked anywhere for fear of growing large hoofs.

Fondling Tupac Amaru in my pocket, I thought, *What do I care for Arequipa when I have seen Valparaiso?*

I was in a hurry to get back to Venice: my 'Tears of Santa Rosa' was about to storm a market parched of beautifying novelties, all the more craved because Napoleon's insults to Venice were beginning to seem personal.

I had no idea that before too long I would be back and climbing El Misti mountain on my own account. I did not know about the Yellow Fever gnawing through Papà's parts at its leisure.

The fact was that I had narrowly missed my chance to see my father's disappointed face one last time.

Marcella Fasan

'You, you with the face on you, don't cringe in the corner. Come here in the light.'

'She is called Marcella,' Piero said patiently.

My diary records that in response Cecilia Cornaro dispatched a glance *'that would have withered a nail'*.

I limped over to her, watching the expressions fleeting across her face: irritation, pleasure, calculation. She took my chin in her hand and turned it none too gently from side to side.

'From the left, first time,' she pronounced.

No, she never was kind to me, Cecilia Cornaro. That first day in the studio she was peremptory as only she knew how. I do not believe the word 'please' was ever a part of her vocabulary. She swore like a porter. Objects flew across the room. I was grateful to see that, like Piero, she acknowledged my condition yet she treated it as she would a fly in the room; noted the annoyance of the thing and then put it in its puny place and got on with more interesting matters.

At the time I met Cecilia Cornaro I was just beginning to grow towards adulthood, and grappling with the disappointment that grew with my every inch. I mean the disappointment of others in me. It is the natural condition of a little child to be helpless, and to be loved for it. But a helpless adolescent or adult, now that is something different. No one smiles indulgently, no one ruffles hair or coddles, when a grown person limps into a room or rolls in on a wheeled chair.

Cecilia Cornaro simply did not interest herself in charity, forced or otherwise. On my arrival she pointed me towards a chair with a hole in its seat. Beneath its curtained legs was a chamber pot. I blushed to imagine the conversation that must have taken place between her and Piero in order to secure this item. Then I told myself that Piero would have handled it all with ease and delicacy, and that here, after all, was an elegant solution.

'Arrange yourself there,' she told me neutrally, the one tone that could have spared me an agony of embarrassment. The strangest thing was that, with the opportunity ever available, my bladder simply forgot its inconvenient imperative. I never once needed to make use of that chamber pot, not in all the months I spent in that studio. It was only as Piero and I swayed in the gondola towards home that I felt the soaky tickle and clenched up anxiously. Then I remembered that Minguillo was still away in South America, and I forgot every disagreeable sensation.

I kept no diary in those succeeding weeks, because I was living life instead of watching it. In the studio I was able to forget even Minguillo himself. Or, if I thought of him, it was as a thing to be valued very low. I had a new pleasure in those days. Inside my head I played out imagined encounters between Cecilia Cornaro and Minguillo, in which the artist sliced through my brother in crisp syllables.

In contrast, I felt myself honoured as the object of the artist's fierce attention. By the day of my first official visit, Cecilia Cornaro had already decided every detail of the portrait. The curtained chair was disposed in a corner by a Grand Canal window. I tried not to tremble as she advanced on me and wrapped my hair in a turban of white linen.

'The Devil in heaven, those bones!' she murmured.

'What bones?'

'*Ignorante come una talpa,*' she muttered in response. *Ignorant as a mole.*

I wanted to explain to her that I had been kept like a mole, on account of my condition, yet somehow my whole soul rebelled against acting the unfortunate in front of Cecilia Cornaro.

I had read that portrait painters liked to know the essence of their sitters. Nervously, I offered, 'Shall I tell you about myself?'

'No,' she replied without apparent malice, 'I am not interested in you because you are not yet very interesting. It will be more interesting for *you* to hear about art.'

While Cecilia sketched and then painted me, she explained how the colours were made – what insect, plant or mineral had offered up its essence to make each of those swarthy reds, browns and crystalline whites that went into mimicking my skin. I blushed when she placed a little tray of yellows in front of me – that I might see and comprehend that yellow was a rainbow in itself.

'Ictherine,' she said, 'yellow or marked with yellow. Luteous, golden yellow. Meline, canary yellow. Ochroleucous, yellowish white. Vitellary, bright yellow. Aurulent, gold-coloured. Citreous, lemon-coloured . . .'

Did Cecilia Cornaro take me for an idiot-incontinent at whose expense she might enjoy a little malicious joke about the colour of urine? No, I prefer to think she wanted, as no one had ever done, to strengthen me, to make me unflinching in the face of less subtle and more protracted unkindness. The next time, she tested me unexpectedly, wanting to know what I had retained of her lecture on the nature of colour, I surprised her by proving a most sedulous pupil. Then, and ever after, I remembered every colour and its source, and not just the yellows.

'You might as well make yourself useful,' she told me on the third visit, placing a mortar and pestle in my lap. Inside was a blue-green stone vividly grained with grey and white. 'Malachite from Peru,' she told me. 'Make me some colour for your eyes.'

Our sessions never seemed long enough, because Piero could credibly keep me away from home for only a few hours at a time. After three weeks, when I had ground all the colours in her palette, Cecilia Cornaro gave me a tray with a piece of paper and a lozenge of powdery blackness. 'Draw a circle,' she commanded.

For days on end I drew circles, until I could summon the perfect sphere without hesitation. Then it was straight lines. Then a shadow behind a circle with the light coming from different points. The charcoal wore away to nubs and still I did nothing more than nursery geometry. It was only back at the Palazzo Espagnol that I dared to make my own sketches of the great artist Cecilia Cornaro at work in the studio. I depicted her as a clever wildcat of unreliable temper, dextrously wielding a paintbrush in a blue forked tongue.

Meanwhile, the artist's portrait of me had ripened into a startling likeness, and been abandoned for a more 'theoretical' work, in which my face was part of an allegory. Then she started a third portrait. Cecilia Cornaro was not keeping to her end of the bargain or was at least stretching it beyond Piero's price.

Piero took my corner as ever. 'Enough geometry lessons, Cecilia,' he insisted. 'Let Marcella show you what she can do!'

She turned to me, 'So does poor old Piero have to fight all your battles, Miss?'

Gianni delle Boccole

Twere the happiest summer of our lives and it seemed to want to go on for ever.

Then one day the blue sky dropt into a black bucket. Grate white gashes opened up in the skin o the night. We cowered inside the Palazzo Espagnol as if there was beasts outside approaching for the kill. My poorly hand, the one Minguillo ud buried the knife in, give me pain, Sainted God! No one slept that night because we was all frit of dreaming.

We aughter been affrighted o summing else.

Marcella Fasan

Cecilia Cornaro pointed to a table on which I saw a white sheet stretched over a frame and a box of mutilated pastels, the dog-ends of her own instruments.

'I think paint is too wet for you,' she remarked cruelly and Piero stood up, ready to remonstrate.

Cecilia seemed to repent then, though she did not apologize. She at least did not re-open the wound of her joke against my now vanished incontinence. She just looked a bit rueful, as if she had eaten something that turned out to be bitter. I guessed she was quite often forced to wear that expression. Then she changed the subject. 'You may begin a portrait of your own. Your times here are so brief that it is hardly worth it to mix the oil colours that will dry up in your absence. So, pastels. Best thing for human skin and ermine, the most stupid animals in the world, about which you must draw your own conclusions, Marcella. Now, who shall you portray first?'

The medicinal smell of the pastels rose up from the box on my lap. I hesitated, feeling contempt quicken in her stare.

Piero offered, 'I'll sit for Marcella, O sweet-tempered one, if that helps.'

Cecilia Cornaro jeered, 'Piero, you weren't even worth painting when you were young. All your gifts are from your spirit. Bring some chocolate cake next time. At least it won't be a wasted visit then.'

She turned a tall mirror towards me, and I blushed to see my strained, eager face in its silvery trap.

'Paint that,' she commanded. 'There cannot but be a good result, even for a . . .'

Piero interrupted, 'I am sure the word that escapes you is "beginner", Cecilia. Though in fact Marcella has . . .'

It was as if he had not spoken. 'And depending on the result, I will find some clients for the girl.'

I bent my head lest a whinny of joy escape my mouth. That I might find my way in the world, earn a living, do something that would cause people to look at what I did, and not what I was! A prospect opened up in front of me like a door into a garden. I saw myself painting alongside Cecilia, listening to her abusing her clients; perhaps even joining in with some banter of my own.

Cripples may not be witty aloud – it comes out as bitterness. Cripples must be sweetly cheerful to protect the full-bodied who do not wish to be cast down and made miserable by our crippledom. But an artist? An artist is licensed to scintillate in wickedness, wit and wonderfulness alike!

Cecilia was perfectly aware of her generosity, and took pains to dampen the effect immediately. 'Are you prepared to actually work, for the first time in your life?'

No one speaks like that to a cripple! They speak like that to a person expected to rise to a challenge. This realization opened my own unmitigated mouth: my thoughts and words had no need to go separate ways in that studio. I observed, 'Yes, whores wanting to be painted as Allegories of Innocence, mothers wanting to be painted as Allegories of Vigilance, fathers wanting to be painted as Allegories of Eloquence . . .'

Cecilia was smirking and Piero stood up, distended to full height and almost to some width by pride. Was this why he had brought me here? I wondered – not just for the art but for the provocation?

I continued, 'And of course the armies of Venetians for sale . . . I mean the young men and women who want portraits to sell themselves as husbands and wives. It takes a sweeter nature than yours, Cecilia Cornaro, to flatter them and raise their price.'

We laughed uproariously then, the three of us, and Piero put his arm around me for a quick hug. When he let go of me, I saw he had fastened a row of pearls around my neck. Cecilia's cat rolled over to show us his spotted belly. Cecilia launched into an indiscreet tale of a noble client and we returned to work without any agreement to do so, as if her scurrilous commentary was the natural accompaniment to the thing. Piero went back to gazing at us both with adoration. My life seemed to give off that perfume that comes when you open the waxed paper inside a box of marzipan cakes.

Yet when I returned home that day, the good times were already starting to be over. Anna met me at the water-gate with the imprint of a hand red on her face. I knew that imprint. He had chosen to slap the side that was already wounded. She was holding out my leather harness in a shaking hand.

Without any warning, Minguillo was back, and slaps were being distributed like largesse among the servants.

On the same day arrived a letter from Peru which had made my mother look queasy under her tight helmet of curls.

Doctor Santo Aldobrandini

It was just as my patient Napoleon was starting to be less than he was that I had my first personal encounter with a medicine quickly grown huge in popularity.

Ruggiero sent me to examine a Venetian countess who was too ill to return to the city at the end of the summer *villeggiatura*.

I found a feeble hand, a quick pulse, a startling anaemia. The lady, who professed to thirty of her fifty years, complained of colic, cramps in the limbs, optic neuritis, a metallic taste in the mouth, constipation and scant rose-coloured urine. While she talked, I observed the blue line along her gums. That line told me, more eloquently than she could, that her health had been devastated by white lead.

'What preparations have you been using?' I asked.

She pointed to a squat purple bottle. A sniff of its violently floral contents confirmed my diagnosis. The label showed a nun weeping into a bottle of exactly the same shape, with a tall mountain behind her.

My patient clutched her belly. Pitiable creature: any prospect of a long life had been darkened by her desire to look more luminous.

Within weeks, more noble patients were presenting the same symptoms. The same bottle was to be found beside each canopied bed. I made it my business to find out more about 'The Tears of Santa Rosa'.

It was distributed by a notorious Venetian quack who styled himself 'Doctor Inca Tuparu'. He boasted of training at a famous *botica* in deepest Chile-Peru. He claimed that 'The Tears of Santa Rosa', liberally applied to outer parts, solved all noxious problems of the vitals and the glands. Yet most of all, and this was what was making the doctor's patron rich, the colourless fluid was supposed to impart the lustrous whiteness of pearls to the skin.

My Master Ruggiero preferred his Small-Pox scabs, and did not possess the necessary charm for quack doctoring. But that did not stop him being jealous of 'Doctor Inca Tuparu', or at least the quack's raging commercial success.

The surgeon showed me a florid handbill in which Doctor Inca swore the secret to his formula had been found hidden in a mysterious book bound in human leather. The proud quack also proclaimed that Napoleon himself doused his handkerchief in a bottle of Rosa's Tears every morning.

Ruggiero sniggered, 'Well, that will explain little Bonaparte's failure to thrive then!'

Sor Loreta

Then our own church of Santa Catalina was stained with a terrible deed. The Holy Fathers consented to hold a requiem mass for the Venetian merchant Fernando Fasan. His mistress paid the alms and offices from her ill-gotten gains. All the nuns except myself attended and sang hymns for that immoral man from behind the grate.

I still lay in my bed, refusing all food and all drink except vinegar.

For brevity's sake, I shall not describe my agonies of thirst. My body shrivelled to its sinews. I was stripped of nearly every sensation. When I lay in bed at night, my hip bone ground painfully into the pallet. I had grown so insubstantial that I had a sense of floating above my mattress. I lost the clarity of vision in my one good eye, and there were times when my breath came in tearing sobs.

The *priora* remonstrated, 'I must inform your parents of this course you have taken.'

I turned my head to the wall, on which I had painted many crucifixes in vinegar, though I did not remember doing that thing.

My mother wrote, '*Daughter, do not kill yourself with these absurd, exaggerated acts. You must eat and drink, or you shall die. Suicide is a sin.*'

From what seemed certain to be my deathbed, I weakly dictated a reply, happy that at last my words would be recorded for posterity: '*Mother, it grieves me that I must explain the ways of God to you, treating you as if you were my own ignorant child. But I shall do so, for the sake of your soul.*

'Mother, I must warn you against your well-known love of fine clothes and food. Sumptuous eating heats up the body, makes it sleepy and puts it in calores. Fasting clamps the spark of concupiscence and keeps the soul awake for all-night vigils. Instead of arrogantly telling me not to fast, you should take up this holy practice yourself.

'You must understand that Christ Himself is fed by my fasting. Sensuous gorging upon the forbidden apple was what caused Adam and Eve to be expelled from Paradise. Christ was forced to die on the Cross for our sins, to win our redemption and re-admission to Paradise. Now we dine on His blood and body at communion. That is all a Holy One needs to consume. Like Mechtild of Magdeburg, I desire to eat only God.

'If you should hear presently that I have died of my penances, you should be proud and feel the highest joy to be the mother of a martyr. I am going to my wedding with my beloved Bridegroom, and I rejoice to do so.'

My voice grew tired and faded away. Then I was horrified to see that the nun to whom I was dictating had stopped writing, and had let the paper drop negligently to the floor while she stared out the window with a bored expression on her face.

'Where is Sor Sofia?' I screamed. 'Why do you keep her from me?'

Then all went red in front of my eyes, and soon afterwards black.

When I woke again, the *priora* was looking down on me. She stated, 'Sister Loreta, you have suffered a crisis of the brain for several days.'

'God sends fever to those who burn hottest with piety,' I answered.

'Indeed,' she smiled, in a way that seemed to me to be satirical.

'Did my body levitate above the bed like that of Teresa of Avila as I lay unconscious?' I asked. 'Did my sisters try without success to restrain my flight?'

She laughed out loud. Of course, only the blessed can see such miracles.

'I am quite well now,' I told her. 'Please let me prove it. Give me a step to scrub or an altar to burnish or better still a chain to scourge myself with. And let me see my dear Sor Sofia, for her presence will surely soothe my fever.'

'You may not,' said the *priora* cruelly, 'see Sor Sofia unless you renounce this foolish fast and choose to exercise modest self-control like a woman of God. Think on how Sor Andreola carries herself with dignity! We have assigned Sor Sofia to her supervision.'

She opened the shutter and bright light flooded into the room. That was when I saw my first angel: a thin, filmy creature with wings iridescent like those of a fly.

Minguillo Fasan

When the news arrived that my father had died in Arequipa, I danced a little minuet around his desk and vaulted over two velvet chairs in jubilation. At last I could destroy the wrongful will. The possibility of his return had been the only thing keeping that will safe until now.

I sat in his chair, and surveyed the mahogany desk, the fireplace of tortured leonine marble, the trefoiled window that cupped our prospect of the Grand Canal. All these things were mine now, to do with as I wished. In my pocket nestled the new will I had carefully prepared for this moment. I had left it in a box with a mouse to die on it, lending it an appearance of some antiquity.

Outside rain snivelled down the guttering and coughed into the canal in yellowing gouts. My own heart's blood, meanwhile, flowed rich and treaclesome with satisfaction. I would never more suffer my father's disapproving face looking down on me, judging me, thinking me mad, making me smaller than I was. In one minute I would destroy that heinous will and all would be at rights again. My beloved Palazzo Espagnol could not be taken from me. There would be fundage for freedom, travel, fashion, pleasure and power without end.

There would be no more stint on all my pet projects! I'd be flounced, frogged and pearl-buttoned to my heart's content. I would raise my sights in terms of whores and collect all the books of human skin that had been made in the world, and I would beget new ones to commission. Tracts on childhood bound in the hides of the children of my enemies, if I liked. And I probably *would* like!

Pieraccio would be disposed of, and. And.

No respect to the Gracious Reader, but I doubt if He can imagine how perfectly, roundly, exquisitely happy I was in that moment.

Until I searched the desk that I had monitored all these years, to look for that sore document I had opened and read a hundred times, each time more bitterly.

My father's will was gone, and the thief had left in its place a fresh chicken head.

Gianni delle Boccole

My old Master's real will were a death sentence for Marcella, that much I figgered. That's for why I took it, the minit I heared o my old Master Fernando Fasan's sad passin.

Course I knowed from my secret visits to Minguillo's draws n boxes that he ud fudged hisself a new inhairitance alredy. Better he ust that lying will awhiles, that were my thinking. Least till Marcella were of age. I een hoped Minguillo would be cunning nuff for to take the fudged will to a notary what did not personly know the old Master's hand. Which he were.

I were not smart nuff to calkillate zackly persay how to make use o the bonified will, which were writed in high-falutin words that was hard to unnerstand. But I knew that the bastert brother must nowise have it in his destroyin hand.

My originl thought were to give it to Piero Zen. He would know his old friend Fernando's true hand. He would know what were needed to be did. But I esitated.

Ye see, if I shone the will to Conte Piero, Ide of shone mesself a thief n a sneakin reader o things I ud no busyness to read. So how would he trust me? He mite be abhorred at what Ide did. The Zens was the nobblest o the nobble. Them bluebloods is all of one tribe in the end. Conte Piero dint nowise look kind on Minguillo, yet he *mite* take the young Master's side agin a thieving servant. I dint think so, but I dint know so.

I havered like one on them famoused Peruvian humminbirds.

All that day long my voice serged up in my neck evry time I saw Piero Zen. Twice, I stretcht out a hand to waylay him. Yet each time my thoughts balled up in a grate tangle, like yarn that would niver know a strait line again.

That night, after twelve hours o deliberashuns, full o Dutch curry, I een rolled up to Conte Piero and begun to speak in a roundabout way, to interduce the subjeck. He ansered me kind, lookt me in the eye. And that undoed me. My tong stuckt to the roof of my mouth, so I scused myself n made myself sparse.

A few days later, we dressed in black and went to church to prey for my old Master Fernando's soul. His body ud staid in Arequipa, where his heart ud latterly lived.

After the funeral, all Venice's High Sausiety come back to the Palazzo Espagnol for a toothful o sweet wine n cake. Conte Piero n my Mistress Donata Fasan made em all sadly welcomed. The son stood lordly on the threshold twigged up in one o his most loorid fit-outs. People was conmisrating with Minguillo, callin him 'Conte' with respeck, like he were the legal hair. The tapeworm hants n huncles was brushin their long fingers all oer him feckshonitly, speshally where his pockets was.

This were the moment to open my mouth. I could of brung out the bonified will in front of evryone, esposed the truth. I could of shone evryone what a lie Minguillo were to his core. But still I sayed *gnente di gnente*, nothin of nothin, about the will. I thrastled my conshens to the ground and trampled it and give it a kick for good measure. '*Scrostati!*' I shouted at it. 'Pick yerself oft like a scab!' Yet I staid numb and past bout the room handing sweet wine to the nobbles.

I can say only this to scuse myself for letting them first preshous days pass. I started to believe we could do it, protect Marcella from Minguillo till she were of age: meself n t'other servants. Conte Piero ud help us too, without knowing nothin bout the real will.

But I dint count on Minguillo having a plan, that dirty chicken o Beelzebub, and on her falling under it, Stippled Sow ovva God!

Minguillo Fasan

Without my even noticing it, Marcella had grown to the verge of womanhood. At my father's corpseless funeral, I observed for the first time how the eyes of male visitors rested on her longer than was necessary. Even I had to admit that a disturbing prettiness had grown on those pale features of hers. It was indecent to parade such skin in public. Her face ended at her collar, and all eyes seemed to wish to burrow beneath. And why was there always a smile hovering at the corners of her mouth? What did *Marcella* have to laugh about? Even my mother had somehow softened in her regard, something I would have to deal with.

My own eyes had an involuntary addiction to the soft grey shadows between the silky droplets of Pieraccio's pearls on Marcella's little white neck. The more I looked at those pearls, the less control I felt over my fingers.

The Perceptive Reader will have guessed that this correspondent's not one to let a scruple get between him and his heart's desire. Fact is, if it was not for the gamy mystery of the missing will, I would have promised Marcella to the highest bidder then and there, and made my father's funeral a double celebration.

If it was not for the missing will, I would have had her betrothed to something noble, a lot older of course, nothing younger would take her on account of the twisted legs. There would be some raddled count who would have her. For how many times sixty goes into twelve or thirteen is always a pleasurable consideration. I imagined some hoary parsnip nudging up her cranny tentative as a winter morning. If the thing could be managed. Given the irritation of the zone, and all.

But the one thing I could not afford at this juncture was an inquisitive, acquisitive, intelligent brother-in-law; not unless I found the real will and destroyed it first. A forthcoming brother-in-law would have the right and duty to ask for certain documents in the course of the wedding transactions.

My forged will, nicely browned and spotted, would not raise an eyebrow – provided it was not closely compared to my father's real handwriting.

Yet what if the real will were to reappear at that inconvenient moment? I could see how it would work. My sister's banns would be read and the very next morning there would be your man Mister Will-Thief at the water-gate, wanting in, with a proposition.

Whoever had taken that thrice-cursed will wished me no good. And if he wished to feed on my fortune he would have no trouble in finding a dining companion in Marcella's potential husband – before or after the wedding. Then what if Marcella bred? I could not bear to imagine her in kindle with a child, another bloodsucker on my inheritance, another squalling pretender to my darling Palazzo Espagnol.

It would be the height of foolishness to allow that to happen.

There came a morning when my fingers could not keep away from those pearls of Marcella's and I found them pulling the necklace tight against her neck. That maddening smile flitted away and was replaced by a thin line of terror. Who knows what might have happened had my valet Gianni not interrupted me with some inanity about a misplaced cravat?

Gianni delle Boccole

The pearls done it. I bethought of poor little Riva n them black bottles, and I scrood my resolve together and went to get the will. I planned to innersept Conte Piero's gondola when he arrived at the Palazzo Espagnol and have a quite word with him at the water-gate.

But when I went to get it I discovert that I were not so clever as I bethought.

It were not where I left it. Where I bethought I put it. I seemed to be mistook bout where I hid it last. I must o been dranged by seein Minguillo throttlin Marcella with them pearls.

So I emptid my draws. I pulled all my pockets inside out, leavin my clothes piled up in driffs on the floor. I turned the lining of the curtins. I slit the mattress. Nothing. *Gnente di gnente.*

Marcella Fasan

'Why so quiet?' demanded Cecilia Cornaro. 'I've met noisier nuns. Not that I mind some peace after your incessant banter.'

'My brother is returned,' I murmured, fingering my pearls and the bruise on my neck that I had covered with a shawl.

'In what way does that affect this portrait of the little Contarini?'

My subject took the opportunity to stretch and yawn. Cecilia dispensed a single look and the boy resumed his pose with an expression marred by fright. I winked at him, and he began to retrieve his composure.

'Remember Marcella's poor father is recently dead,' Piero pointed out sadly.

'And this affects her *painting* how?'

A shadow fell between us and a foreign voice answered her, 'Not at all, I would say myself. That's a fine piece of work, lassie. You have the young gentleman to the life.'

Cecilia looked the intruder up and down in that way she had, as if she were running a medium-sized squirrel-fur brush over his whole body, which was large, well made and soberly clad. She stopped at his head, meeting the steady grey eyes with her own reckless green ones.

'A Scot?' she pronounced with satisfaction, as if she had deduced that fact purely from his musculature, skin and features.

'A Scot, madam. Come to see if you would do me the honour to paint my wife Sarah.' His voice softened on the name, so it came out as a two-note sigh.

'And where is the dear lady?' enquired Piero helpfully.

'Away in Edinburgh, being too delicate to travel. I would pay whatever I have, no, whatever it takes, to bring you to her.'

'Is she going to die?' asked Cecilia with characteristic subtlety.

'I fear so.' The voice did not falter, but it was even quieter now.

The Contarini boy shuddered and took his hand off the skull upon which Cecilia had insisted that he place it. In his confusion, he set it down on the dead lizard that she had splayed on the silk tablecloth in front of him to signify the supple transience of youth. He squeaked, drawing the one thing he feared above all: Cecilia Cornaro's gaze. Without a word from her, he scuttled out of the studio.

Cecilia laughed and turned a mild eye on our guest. 'Sit down, Mr Scot, and tell us about yourself.'

Hamish Gilfeather traded in miscellanies. Scottish plaid was all the fashion in Europe, and he travelled with pallets of the bright soft wool. His Italian was excellent, well flavoured with a piquant burred Scots accent. Cecilia considered him. 'Explain what makes your Sarah worth a portrait, then. A portrait by Cecilia Cornaro.'

Hamish Gilfeather smiled, 'It shall take more than one interview to tell you that.'

And Piero held out his hand, 'All the better.'

Gianni delle Boccole

I keeped lookin evrywhere for the will. I were that confust that I douted my memmary, which were niver good thanks to all them slaps to head that I got reglar from Minguillo. The more I bethought, the more confust I was, till it got that I could not een recall the zact minit of putting it down.

My next shuttering thought were that Minguillo ud been to my room and stole it back agin. But if he ud finded it, then he would of had me in for a feroshus ragging, after what I wunt of had my employment no more. Yet Minguillo treated me jist like before, perhaps with extra slaps for the worrit look on my face what he niver liked.

I askt Anna in a roundabout way, 'Did you see any bits of paper, official-lookin, bout the place? When you was tidying my room, for hexample?'

But she ritorted, 'That *casino*! Paper everywhere! And as for you . . . always showing off your reading and writing!'

Which I tookt for a 'no'. Twere a shame that my old Master Fernando Fasan, saving his grease, niver bethought to get the female servants tort their letters. Anna allus risented it, for she were clever n spoke edikated een tho she couldn't write.

I must of jist forgot the last hidin place, that were it. That's what I telled myself agin n agin.

Sor Loreta

I was surprised to find out how many days I had passed tied to my bed.

As a penance for all that time without prayer, I cleaned the dust off my crucifix with my tongue. In the dirt of my floor, I licked the shape of the cross. That dust and dirt were the only nutriments I allowed into my body for days on end, apart from the five orange seeds I sucked in memory of Christ's wounds, as Veronica Giuliani had done.

My little wispy angels continued to visit me during the hours of daylight, appearing clearly against white walls or when I looked towards the sun. I saluted them in a sweet voice, for these dear creatures were the proof that I was marked out by the Most High.

Sor Sofia was kept hidden from my sight. I was sure the sweet child would never have willingly allowed herself to be separated from me. She must have been restricted to parts of the convent where I might not go: for I was forbidden to walk near the Zocodober fountain where she lived in a large cell with her godless sister Rafaela. Then again I tortured myself with the thought that the spiteful *priora* had spoken some truth amid her lies – that Sofia had been assigned to the spiritual care of that false angel Sor Andreola, whose cell was also by the fountain.

Those wicked setters of snares, the other nuns, sought every chance to bring back my fever, leaving indecent notes inside my hymnbook, smearing my door-handle with fat, and calling Sor Sofia's name in whispers outside my window. I listed the names of those who tortured me on pieces of paper, and then I burned them. The ashes writhed like heretics and flew up in the room.

I was obliged to burn Sor Andreola's name every day. For she had contrived a new devilment in the nunnery. She had begun to pretend to have visions of the Lord, and she wrote them down. These visions were passed from hand to hand, and were universally admired. Only I remembered the words of Teresa of Avila: 'The weaker sex is ever more vulnerable to false visions sown by the Devil. The weaker sex is also more likely to pretend to possess saintly virtues, yet for selfish advancement.'

All this was perfectly and horribly personified in Sor Andreola.

Whatever Sor Andreola did became the fashion immediately. Before long, dozens of ignorant nuns were scribbling down their visions. Santa Catalina became a community of writers of fiction, each vying for the most ludicrous vision. The *priora* came to tell me that even my beloved Sor Sofia claimed a vision of her own. It was of a black bird, signifying Death, which had flown into her cell. 'He told her that she must avoid Sor Loreta, who would do her a great harm otherwise.'

I protested, 'The Devil often takes hold of an innocent pencil. This is Sor Andreola's perverted influence at work on poor Sor Sofia!'

The *priora* opened one of her slow smiles. It was then, perhaps unwisely, that I told her about the angels who came to my cell in the brightest hours and flew all around me until I grew dizzy.

'I declare this has gone beyond what anyone can bear!' cried the *priora*. She took me by the arm and marched me up to the *oficina*. Of course, with my unusual physical strength, I could have pushed her to the ground at every step. Instead I demonstrated the most abject humility.

'Wait here,' she said fiercely. 'I am sending for the doctor.'

Minguillo Fasan

I made an interesting discovery about my sister: she feared convents.

First, I noticed how Marcella averted her eyes when we passed by Corpus Domini in the gondola. And then, when walking by Sant' Alvise, I had witnessed a tug of fright wrench her limp to a bestial gallop. In church she never peered at the nuns singing behind their grates like any normal curious person. She pleaded to stay at home when my mother went to visit her confined cousins at the *parlatorio* of their convent. She would not touch the fragrant nun-baked cakes my mother brought home.

It had come to me, while I lay with one of my whores from the Spanish madam's in Cannaregio (I did some of my best thinking when I was not thinking), that the easiest way to head off a pretender to my estate was to marry Marcella immediately to God, who did not tolerate secondary husbands or property, except the little bit he demanded in exchange for His austere hospitality. The going rate that year was a thousand ducats, a fraction of a proper dowry for a noble marriage, the profit of a single smelting of 'The Tears of Santa Rosa'.

Once safely interred, the nuns' wings were clipped by poverty. They could not escape unless it was to earn their bread on their backs. Convent life prepared them for no other profession. So in the convent they stayed. Until they died.

Of course some of them had a Sapphic bent anyway, and would not have had it any other way. Otherwise, women do not run to friendship without hair-pulling or recriminations. Men together grow clannish; the ladies tend to the obnoxious.

'Why are you grinning?' asked my Spanish whore. '*¿Y qué es este libro?*'

My book of human skin had spilled out of my clothes during our preliminary skirmishes. I snatched it from under her heavy white thigh and slapped her across the face with it. No one should touch that book but me

– and occasionally my quack – she must learn that! I had to pay her twice over, for she would be out of circulation with that bruise for a few weeks. In fact, it was my last dalliance at the establishment, for the Spanish madam thereafter turned me away with a curdling kind of look, the second time with a ruffian behind her for emphasis. I put the unspent money into my drawer for 'special funds'.

For I had conceived a new vision of myself – as a collector, famed throughout the world, for my library of human leather. I had made a sparkling start with Tupac Amaru. Now that I had come into Marcella's money, I graduated to scraps of sailor hide tattooed with 'Mother' and the outlines of seagulls. I had them trimmed and bound around manuals for sea captains and instructions on how to knot ropes. But what I really craved was to enrich my collection with books already bound with historic *martyred* human leather. I dispatched letters, very specific letters, to the great booksellers of the continent.

Replies were not slow in coming, nor booksellers in dusty person, for Venice had long been a hub of their commerce. Imagine my feelings when I realized that I was not the only such collector in the world! A flat-eyed bookseller explained it to me when I tried to turn a hard bargain on something soft and musty in his back room. It turns out that anthropodermic bibliopegy has always had its secret adherents, many more than the Squeamish Reader would perhaps like to think. There were even merchants who travelled only in human books – livings and fortunes were to be made from small items of dead.

So I had to compete for my treasures? That only spiced the quest.

My rivals invented ethics for their collections. Some doctors claimed it '*congruent*' to have a book on the Small-Pox bound in pocked human flesh. There was a cardinal in Rome who preferred to portray his roseate *Dance of Death* as a sacred *memento mori*. A '*moral exhibit*' – that's what one historian called his feudal Bible bound in a village elder. '*A thought-provoking remnant of barbaric times*,' said a classicist of his *Marsyas* covered, literally, in flayed Greek.

'History', these hypocrites snivelled, had distanced these 'artefacts' from the crimes of their begetting.

I pretended no such distance. For me, it was enough that the book was inscribed 'HIC LIBER CUTE COMPACTUS EST' with someone's name in the genitive. If possible, I wanted to know the intimate details of flaying. Skin does not fall off of its own accord! The clever dealers who wanted my business provided credible biographies and especially rousing death scenes for the original wearers of my bindings.

I subjected each new acquisition to minute examinations at the privacy of my desk. I loved to speculate on which cut of flesh covered my own *Dance of Death* or my *Manual for Lawyers*. I ran a slow finger down each fold. Was that valley of shadow a turn at the groin? Or the dip of a buttock? Was that little wrinkle what was left of a nipple? And yes, I put my nose to those places too. At first, I smelled only poverty and sumac. For those who find themselves bound around stacks of printed paper are generally those too poor to complain of such treatment, who have no one to claim their remains, and who might be dyed by the – ironically, itch-inducing – juice of the sumac root to any colour that the bookbinder desires – sometimes to emphasize the pink humanity of the object and sometimes to make it disappear into the rich, lovely sheen of a riding boot.

The Reader fails to understand how a skinned skin may be beautiful? Thinks it must be wrapped around a living body or it loses its appeal? Let me educate Him in new joys, even as I educated myself!

The Sensual Reader already knows this dual joy of skin: how it feels on the inside and the outside at once. Just as one can take joy of one's own skin by touching it like a stranger's, sweetly or roughly as you please, so I gave and helped myself to those books. Under the brisk glissando of my expert fingers, the books began to give up the stories thrumming in their bindings. And my nose too grew wise to the living pain inhumed and recapitulated in those dead leathers.

My researches led me to books of human anatomy illustrated with etchings of men and women peeling off their own skins. Coyly, they lifted pendulous flaps to reveal their naked viscera. This was the pure spirit of Science: man the specimen offering his flesh willingly for the scholars' inspection. The largest organ of the body must be subject to the widest scrutiny, must it not? In his *Historia de la composición del cuerpo humano*, Juan de Valverde de

143

Hamusco's self-flayed man held up his own skin triumphantly; in his other hand was the knife with which he rendered himself *écorché*. Such books were not originally printed with human skin attached to their bindings, but in my library they soon acquired it. Thus I rewarded those books for showing me that when you flay a man there is nothing left but a wound all over.

But first, Marcella! I might not flay her and bind her round a book and stow her on a shelf, yet there were other ways to make her fit my requirements.

Once it had seeded, the convent idea took root in my head and I saw many branches growing from it, all laden with advantages for myself. To be free of that little white face! The everlasting rustle of pink silk! The always asking her to repeat herself because she spoke so low. The intolerable sight of Pieraccio indulging and petting her. The servants ignoring me and milling round her as if one of her smiles was the most craveable single thing in all Venice.

As a preliminary, I began cultivating my mother's favour. Until now it had been enough to frighten her. But I thought at this juncture she might start giving me the consideration that I had deserved all these years. Marcella was hardly a prospect for a glittering match and so could scarcely detain her interest. And my mother had been abandoned by my father just as I had. And now by Piero Zen too. Were we not natural allies?

I began to mention the convent to my mother on a regular basis. She made a point of demurring at it, but I suspected that in truth she grasped at it with a secret relish too. Delicately, I made Mamma understand that it would be quite a kindness on my part to marry Marcella off to God. Certainly, it was unusual for an only (remaining, as it were) daughter of our class to be enclosed, but my mother soon came to see that Marcella was not fashioned for the rough niceties of marital life, or strong enough for childbearing. If anyone worth having would take her, even. My mother shuddered at the thought of a making-do match with some citizen, his vanity overstimulated by Napoleon's talk of democracy. Then there was Napoleon himself: my mother had a childlike terror of the man. When I told her no unmarried girl in Venice was safe from the Corsican and his soldiers, she shrank under her curls like hot ashes in water.

Now it was just a matter of setting up a solid *illustration* of the concept, a situation which showed just how much and urgently Marcella needed to be protected from the world. Call it a question of Her Own Good. Don't mind if I do.

Pieraccio left himself open for it, always cuddling Marcella and telling her she was lovely. I did not know where he took her in the gondola, but the point was this: etiquette dictated that it should have been the mother, not the daughter, handed ceremoniously into the boat. Watching them set off one morning, Marcella chattering and smiling, Piero elegant as a lagoon heron, I comforted my fingers on the book of human skin in my pocket, and Tupac Amaru gave me an idea.

But all fully Sentient Readers will of course comprehend that Piero Zen had only himself to blame for the hasty way in which he passed from this world into the one whither he and all my dear Readers — and even little Napoleon Bonaparte — are bound.

Doctor Santo Aldobrandini

There were those doctors who insisted that Napoleon's fainting fits and nervous episodes could be attributed to epilepsy. But I could see that his fits were not exactly those of the Petit Mal or the Grand Mal, for all the reports were that he did not chew his tongue or lose consciousness entirely. Yet my eminent patient had a weakness that caused him to leave this world on a temporary basis, often at times of crisis.

I may have appointed myself his doctor at a distance, but Napoleon himself would not have welcomed my ministrations or theories.

Napoleon hated physicians and loved surgeons. He could see sense and worth in an out-of-doors man who might lop off a gangrenous leg in the heat of battle, but he had no patience with a houseboy who ground herbs with long names in a garret and used his patients as mixing bowls. He told his physician-in-chief, 'Medicine is the science of murderers.'

Napoleon's temper was inflamed, of course, by his itch. No herbs ever cured that chronic scratching of his. Quacks plastered him with foul ointments without success until the famous Corvisart prescribed a mixture of olive oil, alcohol and powdered cevadilla. A simple housewife – or a young apprentice like myself – might have cured that itch with sulphur and lard, but Napoleon by then was far beyond the ministrations of the humble and sensible.

Napoleon had left the Veneto ploughed up with furrows of uncertainty. No one knew if it was worthwhile to plant a crop that might be seized by the next passing army. The wealthy patients abandoned their villas and hid in town. Surgeon Ruggiero could no longer afford to feed an assistant. He sent me back to Venice.

He explained gruffly and without pleasure: 'You've grown some looks at last, young man. You've the appearance of something a Venetian lady would not object to see at the end of her bed.'

Gianni delle Boccole

While Minguillo were busy with his quack busyness, I set myself reglar searches of his study. I found this new thing. A little book. I dint think nothin of it at first, books nowise bein any of my favrit things in the world. But then I saw a curling-up note inside. It sayed *encuadernado con la piel de Tupac Amaru II*. And from all my years living in the Palazzo Espagnol, where Span-yard were spoke offen as Venetian, I knowed straitway what this meaned. It meaned, bound in the skin of Tupac Amaru II.

I clutched my hand way. A pucker went long my spine and my whole skin hedgehogged with horror.

In what way was I fit to touch sich a thing? In what way was I fit to touch anyone else, now that I had toucht that filthy thing? Is anyone insent what touches a book of humane leather?

Inside was the receipts and notes of the Peruvian drugs used in Minguillo's apothcry trade, hincludin how to make a skin tonic called 'The Tears of Santa Rosa'. From the look of the ingreedyents, twere the kind of thing that ud burn a hole in the side o yer belly. Save us, weeping nuns haint got nothin to do with it.

Also he ud lists o poisons long as yer arm, and underlined were the one called monkshood.

Minguillo Fasan

For ten francs the hairdresser had told my mother that Piero was taking Marcella to a discreet house to give her the kind of education not normally offered to a noble girl of tender years. I had drilled Fauno till he was fluent, so I knew just what he had said, from the first teasing 'pray, do not ask me!' to the final 'oh, do forgive me. I have said too much'.

The hairdresser had faux-confessed, 'It's the talk of the town, how your daughter comes back from her mysterious excursions – excuse my indelicacy – with a scent of strange oils about her and so exhausted that she must instantly bathe and retire, thereby avoiding the eyes of her family. And, excuse me for mentioning it, but the Conte Piero, when did he last whistle so cheerfully and look so satisfied with himself? Those . . . very lovely pearls he gave little Miss Marcella . . . ? Was that not an *unusually* generous gift for *a little girl*? My Lady, we all *so* admire your fortitude! Your dignity! No one would guess how you miss the Conte Zen's once-faithful attendance upon yourself. And of course you still look perfectly splendid, Madam, considering . . .'

Gianni delle Boccole

From the hall, I saw Anna stagger out of the Mistress's room. Her face were chalky, sept where the shiny pink scar runned down it, and her mouth open in a grimmis like a mask. Then she told me what ud been sayed.

147

Save us, but not a one of us believt it bout Conte Piero. Twere a ferocious lie.

But, coming from her hairdresser, it would of seemed like God's own truth to my Mistress Donata Fasan.

Minguillo Fasan

Our scene is the maternal bedchamber. My mamma is *déshabillée*.

Enter her faithful son, attired at the acme of fashion in rivalrous shades of violet and green. He seats himself delicately at the foot of her bed.

'Mother . . .' yours truly murmurs with tender concern. 'There is something dolorous to discuss. I know what Signor Fauno told you yesterday. And if *I* know, then . . .'

She started. Her face flushed with the wider picture: could it be that *everyone* knew that her *cicisbeo* preferred her pretty crippled daughter to his ageing mistress, she who had already been so publicly passed over for some *divertimenta* in Peru?

'What is there to do, Minguillo?' she faltered.

'Everything, Mamma,' I reassured her. 'You may count on me.'

Fauno had told me that my mother seemed not to understand. I imagined her putting on her most empty face. For her pride's sake, she would have made it seem that she could not comprehend what the hairdresser was insinuating.

Yet she had understood, and all too well. At supper, she told Pieraccio that the gondola excursions must cease, on the grounds that 'Marcella's health is too delicate for all this gadding about'.

'*Brava*, Mamma!' I thought. 'You play your part to perfection here.'

And Pieraccio too slid smoothly into my hands, burbling affably, 'Now Donata dear, have you ever seen the little sweetheart looking better? Clearly our little outings agree with her most wonderfully, and indeed we think to extend them, if anything.'

My mother dropped her eyes and snuffled like a diseased bear. I was meanwhile tapping my fingers on the table to a delightful air inside my head. Pieraccio sat still, the whole picture gradually dropping into place in his brain. He saw the trap and the trapdoor shutting on him at the same moment.

'My *dearest* Donata,' he cleared his throat, but then caught sight of her face, and stopped.

I rose and walked with magisterial slowness to Marcella's chair. For a pregnant moment I did nothing more than cast my shadow over her. Then I ripped Pieraccio's pearls from her neck, scattering the white orbs like musket fire. I snarled, 'How did you earn *these*, sister?'

Marcella opened her mouth and something tumbled out: a picturesque nonsense about painting lessons and the notorious artist Cecilia Cornaro! She told it badly. Great gaps of credibility yawned between each stammering phrase. Finally Marcella blushed into her soup, shedding sunset hues on the pale velouté of artichoke. I said coldly, 'I am ashamed for you, Marcella. You compound your sin with lies. I shall give you a hint. *This* will be your salvation.'

I made my way round the table in menacing silence. From the credenza I took Mr Diderot's fine novel *The Nun* that I had placed *en scène* earlier. Its account of the cruelties of convent life had much diverted me over the previous weeks. Now I slammed it on the table in front of Marcella. Glasses took flight and plunged, pulverizing on the marble floor. As the last tinkle subsided, I strolled over to Pieraccio, who was quite immobilized by shock. I dropped my glove on his plate.

'You have corrupted my sister and humiliated my mother,' I stated coolly. 'You shall die for it, dog. I'll see you downstairs.'

Duelling was forbidden, but within the privacy of our courtyard who was there to gainsay my orders? Piero stood up from the table. 'Minguillo, in your poor father's name . . .'

'It is in my poor father's name that I do this. Someone must defend this family's honour.' I tossed him a sword I had placed behind the door. My quack was waiting for me downstairs with my own weapon.

Pieraccio cried, 'I'll happily explain to you exactly what . . .'

'You have nothing to say that I want to hear, you old goat!'

My mother's hand flew to her hair, which she touched all over. Marcella seemed to have forgotten what her lungs were for.

'Downstairs, lecher!' I shouted. My voice was not as low or manly as I would have liked. Yet that, and the drumming of my foot under the table, were the only things that spoiled the perfection of the moment at all.

Down in the courtyard, I did not let Pieraccio raise his arm before I speared him deep in the breast and the side of the neck with the blade my quack had dipped in something that had hissed like a snake in the alembic, as well it might.

Life has silken wings, they say, but Death uses dirty iron scissors. Pieraccio retched and flailed to the ground. Doctor Inca pronounced the case imminently fatal. To show willing, I told my valet to call in another doctor.

'I believe that Conte Piero is feeling a little uncomfortable,' I smiled sympathetically, wiping my sword on the grass.

Gianni delle Boccole

Twere obvious to anyone with an eye that whatever potion killt Riva ud also tookt sweet Conte Piero way from us. When Piero Zen expired twere with Riva's zackt same symptoms: the closing o the windpipe, the blue tong, the retching up of evry last gut, the all-ovva-sudden glassy stare.

The duel were a traverty. Conte Piero believt twere a chance to defend his onour. He were going to fight the way he danced: greaseful, like a gentleman. He were still bowing when Minguillo stuck him like a pig, Brute God! Minguillo fought the way he bethought n breathed: like a murderer in an alley with a smile of forty-four teeth on his face.

Weak in the hams, I stumbled oft to get a young surgeon called Santo Aldobrandini to attend to the Conte what lay shuttering in the courtyard. I had heared good things o this youth, jist lately come to the naybourhood – that he was trained among the *Fattybenfratelli* and that he had saved a child from the Typhus when all others ud throne up there hands. He had but a short spell back set up in lodgings two courtyards from the Palazzo Espagnol. So I seen his clear eyes n kind hands for myself when one o the maids were took with the Scarlatina.

He waren't minted hisself, not by the state of his clothes, yet the boy wunt take a coin for the girl's life. Insted he askt shyly: 'If someone who can afford to fee me falls ill – call for me then.' His eyes ud twitched unhappily to the ceiling, to the floor of the nobble floor above us. Ide lookt at his jawbone stretched agin his ear as he spoke. I douted if he ud eaten that day.

Piero Zen could afford to have his skin saved, if twere a possible thing, so oft I ran to find that Doctor Santo Aldobrandini.

The young man were by good luck at his table – three olives n a peace of day-old bread in prospecked – when I arrived to fetch him. He were ready in moments, gallupped ahead of me to the Palazzo Espagnol, dropt to the ground by the Conte's fallened body. Catching up, I falled to my knees aside him with a groan. I had run my hardest yet I alredy feart it mite be too late.

The doctor rifled through the Conte's clothes, all beasty with the poor man's gore. He found what Minguillo had did, six inches of openings, alredy turnin black. He were outraged, 'There is poison in these wounds!'

'There is poison in this ouse,' I shouted back.

Then I clunkt my head down on my breastbone. Conte Piero were in peril on account of my esitation. If Ide of given him the will when I should of, then Minguillo would alredy be shutted up in prison or the madhouse, and wunt niver have put his hand on a sword or a bottle o snake again. I notist Minguillo's pet quack hovering ahind a lime-tree, what barely hid his fat belly. He could nowise make a medicine, that quack, but he could make a poison like the Devil's own apothcry.

With the Conte's head craydelled on his lap, Doctor Santo lookt up n around our courtyard, as if to unnerstand what kind o place could host sich wickedness. I saw him take it in, that there were

151

money here, and so secrets n shelter for highborned inabitants who committed bad acts jist as they pleased within them walls. His glance fell on Minguillo's little potted plantashon of monkshood and foxglove, and jolted his head.

Save us, that's when I saw it appen. I saw his gentle brown eyes flitter oer the trees n the vines and up to the window where Marcella stood, aghasted, leaking tears like milk agin the pane.

She ud witnesst the whole thing.

And I saw it, that first meeting of there gazes, that sting of knowing, jist knowing, while Conte Piero's last breaths rattled in his ribs.

Twere naught for the naked eye to see. But if a foaming challis ud been carrid in procession and delivert to the young man, it could not of been clearer to me, watching with abated breath. Piero Zen, to my mind, had jist handed oer the protecting of Marcella Fasan to this young doctor Santo Aldobrandini.

And Marcella – why she set the house on fire for him! The boy were ravaged at the sight of her. I bethought, *Please God, yer man Santo will rise from his sackcloth n ashes, and he will be the one to save her n sweep her oft her feet.*

Doctor Santo Aldobrandini

There was nothing to be done with poor Conte Zen. I gave him the tenderness of gentle hands upon him as he flailed out of this world and a kind voice uttering the sweet nursery wisdoms (or so I assumed, never having known them) such as 'there now' and 'all shall be well'.

Piero Zen struggled against his death. His was the kind of wound that makes it a cruelty to own a human skin. The poison literally ate his flesh from the inside. It would have been a mercy for the life to ebb out of him on a fast tide, yet he seemed unwilling to depart. His dimming eyes kept staring up towards the second noble floor, where the bedchambers were. There was someone in the Palazzo Espagnol he cared for too much to leave.

I did the last good service a doctor can perform for a patient. I told him that it was honourable to die now, that he had no more need to battle heroically against death. He looked into my eyes, gazed upwards one last time, and his body fell slack. As I closed his eyes, and held my hand over them for a moment, my own travelled up to the place his gaze had sought.

There, in the window, was the same girl with the skin that had made me lose all sense in the frescoed hall of the villa by the Brenta Canal. Her hair hung dishevelled around that face with the luminous sheen to it. The years had carved more beauty out of her cheekbones, lifted her eyebrows delicately, filled her lips. My tongue hung drily in my mouth with shock, for that face had never left my heart.

Marcella Fasan

There was a young doctor who came to attend to Piero. When I saw that youth, there came into my breast that same soft commotion that you feel when a bird takes flight very close to you.

Then I saw the blood darkening the flagstones under Piero's shoulders. A Dominican priest scuttled into the courtyard. I thought he had come to minister to Piero, yet he hurried past my friend's body with the merest grimace, and into the *palazzo*. I heard Minguillo shout a happy greeting.

I slumped down on the floor, where I stayed until Anna and Gianni came to find me. I was lost in bitter self-recriminations. As the last seconds of Piero's life sped away, I had gabbled ineffectually about Cecilia Cornaro. I could have opened a drawer and flourished my precocious sketches of my mother's face as tangible evidence. I could have sent Gianni running to fetch Cecilia. I could have screamed and wept, perhaps delaying Minguillo's plans long enough for Piero to be got safely out of the Palazzo Espagnol. I could have thrown my body in front of Piero's. Surely even Minguillo would not have dared to run me through in front of all the servants?

153

But I had done none of those things. And now my dearest friend was dead.

Anna put her arms around me and crushed me to her breast. Gianni mumbled comforting lies into my hair about 'dint feel a thing' and ''twas that quick'.

I gently pushed both of them away from me.

Minguillo had killed more than Piero. I had just seen what might happen to a person to whom I gave my full confidence, and who defended me: Minguillo had made it fatal. Now I would need to divide myself even in the presence of Anna and Gianni, to protect them from my brother's interested eye.

Sor Loreta

The doctor made me look towards a bright light and describe my angels.

He sighed and turned to the *priora*, as if it was not worth talking to me, 'We call them *Muscae volitantes*, sun-spots. The appearance of floating *Muscae* indicates a morbid sensibility of the retina, often caused by insufficient sleep and deranged digestion. From her wasted state, I presume the sister has been fasting? A normal person barely notices the phenomenon. However, a hypochondriacal or hysterical patient, having once detected the *Muscae*, takes such frequent notice of them that they become the subject of great anxiety.'

'But I love them! They are my angels!' I interjected.

'They are not angels, do you not understand?' hissed the *priora*.

The doctor said, 'These ocular spectres are real enough to the sister. In order to prevent further distress I shall send a pair of blue glass spectacles that she must wear during all the hours of brightness.'

The *priora* muttered, 'She'll love that, another thing to mark her out!'

In my blue spectacles, the world was suffused with the azure of God's Heaven specially for me. There were bad days, however, when it seemed to me as if God had sent a second flood to drown the worldly sins of Santa Catalina.

There were more and more bad days, for the *priora* betrayed my trust in a most outrageous manner. Even though I agreed to take food and drink, the presence of Sor Sofia continued to be denied to me. I glimpsed her only at the far end of the church or in the distance. Her eyes were always lowered. Sor Andreola fluttered around her, touching her every now and then, quite unnecessarily, with her flat white hands.

In my *hornacina* I kept a plaster statue of Our Lord as an infant in the manger. By God's design I was powerfully attracted to it, feeling great desire to hold it and kiss it, especially since I no longer had Sor Sofia to come to my cell. The Lord Himself graciously requested me to follow my desires. One night, after I had scourged myself and lay prostrate and bleeding upon the floor, I heard His words in my right ear. He spoke in a little lisping child's voice. 'My most beloved Daughter, I am but a Babe for you to tend. You must love Me and suckle Me on your love.'

Christina the Astonishing had been able to squeeze milk from her virgin breast. And when Veronica Giuliani had put an icon of the Madonna and Child to her bosom, the painted Baby Jesus had turned his mouth towards her, choosing the saint to suck upon instead of His own Mother.

So I took my little Jesus out of His crib and undid my habit and laid Him on my naked breast to drink of my love. The cool lips of the Infant had no sooner touched my skin than I began to feel a fire coursing through me. All the members of my body tingled with delight and the taste of warm honey flooded into my mouth. I was filled up with His Love for me, for He urged me to partake of His divine essence, just as He partook of mine. I knew then that I had the most potent Grace in the Lord God.

I cried out, 'Blessed are the teats that give You suck, oh Lord!'

Yet as I lay with God at my bosom, and my soul transported to another place, an impudent *criada*, without knocking, burst open the door to my cell on the pretext of delivering my clean habit for the next day. She observed Jesus at my naked breast and clapped her hands over her mouth.

Gianni delle Boccole

I found the convent contracked on his desk, sittin there out loud for anyone to read it. There were a little chit aside it what froze my heart. It sayed *'Dowry paid, date of admission to be named.'*

Minguillo ud promist Marcella to the dogfaced Dominicans, and the most remote n nastiest convent, Corpus Domini, right at the nethers o the town.

Marcella, marrid to God?

As I unnerstands it, all nuns is marrid to Jesus who is the sacrifishal Lamb. There's a little bit of Lamb in each communion waver n in evry drop of conserkrated wine. It aint in there till the priest mumbles oer the wavers n wine. Tis jist reglar provender. Then all ovva suddenly tis the bodynblood o God.

The nuns fast so that they eat there husband the Lamb n nought else. Some on them beat on thereselves with whips.

Then I dunt recall no partickeler moment in the Bible when Jesus beated on hisself. As for eating, seems to me Our Lord were allus having suppers round bout and een congering extra food out o nothing so there were plenty o good eating for all isn't it.

My poor head went a-spinnin like the empty toy tis. It allus come back to the same dredful thing. If I haint lossed the will, this would niver be appening. And now, with Piero Zen dead, and my Mistress a puppet on the son's strings, there wernt no one to tell anyways.

At leastwise, I bethought, Marcella dint know what her brother were up to with Jesus n the Lamb. There were a tiny mercy in that. She mite stay at piece a little longer.

Marcella Fasan

That night I wrote in my diary, '*There is only one reason why Piero is dead. He's been sacrificed. Minguillo means to put me in a convent. By his successful slander of myself and Piero, he has won my mother's complicity in anything he does. He has met with the priest. He will bury me alive, for I have stubbornly refused all these years to die.*'

Just weeks before, I had heard Cecilia Cornaro speak disparagingly of nuns to our Scots friend Hamish Gilfeather, who had visited us on a daily

156

basis during the several weeks he spent in Venice. He was not turned away. He was still trying to persuade Cecilia to go to Scotland and she was still enjoying that. Meanwhile, Piero and Mr Gilfeather had taken to one another in a warm instant. How the kind Scot would grieve to hear what had passed when he next returned to Venice. My mind winced away from the thought and back to that happy paint-flecked day in the studio.

'Nuns! I don't paint 'em,' Cecilia had frowned. 'You're not supposed to, not till they're dead. Yet how does anyone tell the difference? We inhabit a world of superb variety. No two flowers are identical. Nor should they be. But in the convent, all things are mashed into a forced sameness. The women are made to live together, dress the same, eat the same, crop their hair the same. It's against nature, and who can be surprised when misery and unnatural practices result?'

'Cecilia!' Piero gave a warning look in my direction.

Hamish Gilfeather had added his mellifluous growl, 'How can a wee girlie be the bride of Christ? He is her daddy too! Christ has no sex, or he is all sexes. How does that work, practically speaking? His brides are innumerable, yet I hear no one denouncing the fellow for bigamy or incest. 'Tis surely a cruel hoax to marry innocent little females off to an incestuous hermaphrodite, a perversion of everything that should be associated wi pure young lasses!'

'How we shall miss you, Hamish,' Cecilia had declared when she stopped laughing. 'Must you really leave?'

'If you continue to refuse to paint my Sarah, I must go and glut myself upon her lovely living image.'

'Godspeed,' Piero had bid him gently. 'You leave tomorrow?'

'Aye.'

I wept at my memory of the two men embracing, and Cecilia's unusually soft eye wishing Hamish well. I scribbled bitterly in my diary, *'God is surely more wicked than anything Piero was dishonestly accused of.'*

My mother would not enter my room, so I asked Anna to take a note to her.

'Please let me explain, Mamma,' I pleaded. *'It is not at all as you think.'*

That note went unanswered.

I could guess how Minguillo had worked upon my mother's credulity, scraped at her vanity and poured acidulous insinuation into cavities where it was most likely to corrode. She probably believed that Piero would have survived the duel if he had been truly innocent. And if Piero was not innocent in her eyes – then neither was I. My mother was Minguillo's creature through and through now.

I sent another note. If she could not bring herself to see me, I begged her to call on the artist herself. '*Cecilia will explain, Mamma, I promise!*'

But my mother refused to be contaminated by the world that had seemingly betrayed her. Piero had been convicted of unsuitable relations not just with me but with Cecilia Cornaro herself. I could not deny it, when my mother appeared in my doorway to ask just one barbed question in a tight voice: whether the artist and the *cicisbeo* had been 'close friends'.

My quiet 'yes' was enough for her. It was a trap. For Cecilia Cornaro's florid reputation sealed Piero's in dishonour.

'Please, Mamma,' I repeated, 'if you will not go to her, then ask Cecilia to come to the Palazzo Espagnol.'

My mother shook her head silently, and gave a warning look to Anna. 'That name shall not be uttered in this house,' she pronounced with uncharacteristic firmness. 'Your brother has decreed it.'

Minguillo appeared, grinning, at her side. I guessed he had been listening to the whole exchange.

'Dear Mamma!' he simpered, and kissed her hand. They disappeared down the corridor together.

Cecilia Cornaro, I agonized, must have heard of Piero's death, officially described as an unusual colonial malady that had overleapt the quarantines around Venice to claim a solitary victim. Anna told me that all the servants at the Palazzo Espagnol had been subjected to the most violent and true-seeming threats from Minguillo, to ensure they did not gainsay that story.

Of course I hoped that Cecilia Cornaro would miss me, make enquiries about me; that she would come in search of me, even. When she did not, I told myself that perhaps she would not wish to lay eyes on me, because I would remind her painfully of her lost friend Piero? Perhaps, I tormented myself, she believed me somehow implicated in his death? That my family had contaminated him with some disease imported from their holdings in Peru? That I might limp back into her studio with the same sickness as my returning gift?

A sad insight asserted itself. *Better she does not know the truth. If she came here to take up my part, she would get hurt. As Anna was hurt. As Piero was hurt.*

What I did not know then was that Cecilia had already left Venice on an expedition to the Low Countries. Her departure had been abrupt, within a day of Piero's murder. She had always boasted that she did not maintain ties of amity or gossip with Venice when she undertook one of her expeditions to foreign parts.

So she would hear nothing of what was to happen to me next.

Sor Loreta

The story of the Baby Jesus at my bare breast was spread around the convent by the impudent *criada*. For weeks afterwards, nuns passing outside my window made loud sucking sounds followed by snorts of vulgar laughter. They laughed uproariously when I entered the refectory. Sniggers followed me down all the little streets of the convent, and into the confessional and waited for me outside it. I knew it then: God's will would not be done until all the wickedly irreverent hilarity at Santa Catalina had been put an end to.

It soon pleased the Lord to reward my suffering. As if in answer to the disrespecting nuns, He sent a new challenge for me to contend with, to prove my purity and my perfect faith.

There was one priest who turned a lecherous eye on me, notwithstanding my damaged face, my blue spectacles and my walk made ungainly by the blisters of my penances. Indeed, perhaps it was my body so deeply marked by its devotions that inspired him to try to steal Christ's most worthy bride. This wicked priest made every effort to find me alone at my worship on the church floor, and to draw me out into unwise speech about myself, about the light nuns, about my scourging, about the death of Tupac Amaru II, but most especially about Sor Sofia.

My own pure state had given me a special gift to detect and excoriate impurity in others. As I described my pure love of Sor Sofia and the things we used to do together, the priest's breathing quickened and he began to shift

159

his position on the pew. He asked eagerly, 'So with Sor Sofia you studied and practised all the arts of how best to please your Bridegroom on your wedding night in Heaven?'

God sent a scorpion to walk across the stone flags just in front of my nose then. So I became aware of this priest's foul intentions and the lust in his heart. I feared for my virginity. And so I refused to give him obedience, ignoring the tiny penances he set for me and choosing my own superior ones.

In the rapture of communion the next Sunday, I had a vision (behind my closed eyes) of this priest holding the Host with bloodied hands and poking a black tongue out of his mouth at the effigy of the Lord. Beside him Sor Andreola, fat and naked, writhed like a *bacchante*. The chalice that held the communion wine foamed over with green liquid.

I was jubilant. My gifts had enabled me to distinguish a false Host from a real one. Just such a miracle – of detecting a false Host – had previously befallen several saints, including Lidwina of Schiedam, Margherita of Cortona and Joan the Meatless of Norwich, who had fasted for fifteen years. So I knew myself to be especially holy, to have received this vision after just fifteen days of my most recent fast!

I started to my feet in the middle of the service and cried out: 'Do not drink from the chalice! This man has contaminated the Host with his corrupt hands! Have you not seen how he gnashes his teeth at the mention of Our Saviour's name?' until I fainted away, but not before I had pointed at the priest and cried out, 'He wished to defile me!'

I nearly forgot to mention that my actual last words were, 'Sor Andreola! See how she dances lasciviously with the Devil!'

Afterwards an investigation was made and it was discovered that this priest had in fact lured many young girls of his parish into sin, and he was dismissed from the service of the Lord and excommunicated. I was called to an interview with two priests in the *priora*'s *oficina*. They told me that as a result of my holy vision (and the five young pregnant girls of Arequipa who confirmed its truth) the nuns' wishes were for once to be overruled and I was to be made not just a council member but the *vicaria*, second only in power to the *priora* herself. Behind the priests, the *priora*'s eyes flashed with ungodly hatred for me and for them. I heard her growl, 'This is madness.'

No one was laughing at me now. The faces of the other nuns were mutinous and fierce when they beheld me. For, also as a result of my vision, their favourite Sor Andreola was to be sent away to the stricter convent of Santa

Rosa, where the nuns slept in tombs to remind them of their fate. Those light nuns of Santa Catalina no longer had their silky white girl to idolatrously worship, and Sor Sofia would no longer be subject to Sor Andreola's caresses.

My little Sor Sofia, so long kept apart from me, I ordered to come into my cell now. Even if they had known, no one would have dared to oppose me. Blushing and lowering her long lashes, Sor Sofia humbly congratulated me on my rise in estate.

And now Sor Sofia admitted that by night I levitated above my bed in my sleep like Douceline of Marseilles. And Sor Sofia agreed that she too saw my stigmata burning on my skin. She was submissive to my every wish, and I caused her to make me happy in more ways than I can write down.

Doctor Santo Aldobrandini

The valet Gianni from the Palazzo Espagnol saluted me sadly in the street a few months after I tended to the dying Piero Zen.

I had been outraged but not much surprised to see that the Fasans had successfully suppressed the truth about his death. I had seen enough dynastic poisoning in the great country villas. I knew how these things worked among the noble families: Napoleon might humiliate and rob them, but he would never penetrate their secret codes and their ways of intimidating their servants.

I longed to ask Gianni what had happened to the girl with the beautiful skin. I hoped that time would erase the piteous image of her murdered friend. I wondered how the childhood injury to her leg had healed, for I had not seen below her waist when my eyes met hers at the window. I wanted to say all that.

But in what way might a youth barely off the streets ask after a young noble lady in a *palazzo*? She was no longer a child. I was afraid of impertinent enquiries tumbling incontinently out of my mouth. My face fired up red. Gianni must have thought me a foolish country ass.

Although I dared not say her name aloud to Gianni, I had been thinking of her constantly, as a naturalist thinks on a new species he has glimpsed. My mind's doting eye hovered over her, cherished and privileged, living inside that great *palazzo*.

I muttered an incoherent greeting to Gianni and rushed off, leaving him mystified in mid-sentence. Only in retrospect did I realize that he had seemed very eager to talk to me, as if there was also something on *his* mind.

Minguillo Fasan

My enemies had grown in ranks like the hairs on an old woman's wart.

Yet, like the hairs on an old woman's wart, they were nothing to keep a body awake at night. The Spanish madam in Cannaregio forbade me her fleabitten girls. So? The family of Piero Zen cut me dead in the street. That was the worst they would dare. They did not want a scandal any more than I did. The servants of the Palazzo Espagnol hated me. Bless their dull little heads. My mother was utterly compliant, depending on my every direction, her maternal love quite divorced from the daughter who had betrayed her. Only the will-thief worried me, and that far less since I had concluded negotiations with the convent of Corpus Domini.

But now I was about to take on an enemy any man would have to respect: Napoleon Bonaparte himself. A little enemy, to be sure, yet in the case of Napoleon Bonaparte, a little goes a long way.

As the Retentive Reader will remember, in January 1806, Boney had annexed Venice into his new Kingdom of Italy. It was then that he really stuck his tax tooth into us, rummaging for gold to feed his troops and men to feed the cemeteries of his battlefields in Spain and Portugal.

The Perceptive Reader will easily imagine how much askance our family's Spanish connections were regarded at that time. I was forced to come to many adroit accommodations with customers who disdained to buy our Bark of Peru, except at a 'conscientious' discount. The tide would turn one day: I noted their names in my records for future conscientious treatments of my own. My prosperity was assured, however. 'The Tears of Santa Rosa' continued to sell in vast quantities, distributed through a discreet network of hairdressers, who were, of course, much in demand, given the anxious times. Publicly, I dissociated myself from the preparation. A nobleman cannot be seen in intimate proximity with his source of pocket money.

In November 1807, Boney his great self had graced our city for a couple of weeks. We put on a tattered show for him, a *regata* or two, a stagey arch built over the Canalazzo. The little man was not much interested in the pretty stuff. Napoleon looked at Venice and saw not her caparison of romance and legend but a plate of food from which he had to flick back the frivolous garnish in order to get to the meat.

Anything that sounded like a secret was anathema to Napoleon. Small men always feel left out, I suppose, forever craning their necks to hear what the big chaps are on about. To Boney, our patrician *scuole*, which raised cash for art and charity, were a threat. Their doings smacked of clandestine meetings. The well-meaning *scuole* were dismantled, their paintings and archives carried away. Napoleon spent his time with engineers and builders. He did not soirée or fête the city's noblest sons, like myself. I supposed that he feared our breeding and elegance would highlight his own congenital inferiority.

God was another rival that Napoleon would not tolerate. Napoleon found over a hundred churches in Venice and left half as many. (The Reader's eyebrow twitches with disbelief? We are speaking here of a man who would soon arrest the Pope.) Dismantling our churches, even demolishing them, did not cause little Boney a moment's reflection. But his last act in Venice was the one that caused me personally the most crucial problem. Boney began to close down the city's convents. God knows what foments he imagined going on in *there* to his detriment. But of course, it was Napoleon's never-ending thirst for liquid assets that truly fuelled their downfall. The cloisters were slowly stripped of every portable valuable: four hundred million francs' worth, as it turned out.

When I say 'valuable', the women inside those convents were not included in the booty. They were worth nothing. Their families had paid their dowries to God, and Napoleon was now tapping on the stained-glass windows.

'Hand it over, God,' shrilled little Napoleon. And God knew what was good for him.

At Corpus Domini the priest turned deaf ears on me when I went to set the date for Marcella's admission. 'With the situation so uncertain,' he said, 'it would be for the best if you kept your sister safe at home a while longer.'

I riposted, 'Then suppose you let me have the dowry back, so that it can also stay safe at home for the interval?'

The priest peered at me, 'My son, you're not looking well. Have you tried a remedy called "The Tears of Santa Rosa"? I've heard it cures troubles like your face.'

Then he jerked a cord and a curtain fell between us. By the time I had fought my way through the waxy yellow silk, he had disappeared.

Gianni delle Boccole

As Bonypart begun to put down the convents, I got feroshus excite. Marcella mite yet be saved from the fate Minguillo were desining for her. Evry time another convent closed, I toasted Napoleon down in the kitchen and waited with abated breath for the next one.

Twere a race to the death. Marcella lookt to be fadin fast. The death of Conte Piero had curved her tiny appetite. With her appetite had gone the funning sketches. And with the funning sketches had gone the laffter. N nearly all the words.

Not that I knowed what was in her heart them sad days. Since Conte Piero died Marcella ud been shutted up inside herself. She were kind n sweet as ever, but there were summing bout her what seemed to say, 'Do ye not come too close to me.'

She dint een look pleased to see me half the time.

Marcella Fasan

The hands that had briefly tingled with pastels and oils in Cecilia Cornaro's studio – they now lay idle. In the months after Piero died, I did not have the heart to draw. I even gave up my diary. I pretended to eat, for Anna and Gianni's sake, but the skin that the artist had once rejoiced in soon stretched over my skull like an Egyptian mummy's. The wits Cecilia had teased, however, remained keen as ever, well hidden behind my downcast eyes and bent neck.

Minguillo, I had divined, was waiting for Napoleon to go away so he could put me in the convent. My freedom was now staked on Napoleon winning against my brother.

It was Napoleon's sweeping cheekbones that rescued me from my apathy: I could not keep my hands still when I thought about them. Finally I reached for my paper and pencil, and began to draw: not just Napoleon, but myself. I drew endings for my story that were different from Minguillo's plans.

I had endless privacy for my art. My mother kept sternly away. Anna and Gianni came to me whenever they could, but I gently sent them away on errands that would detain them a long time. It would not be good for them if Minguillo looked in and found them at my side. I would not even confide my fears in them: it was my gift to them to keep their peace of mind safe from such wretched speculations.

Minguillo Fasan

The Empathetical Reader can feel my frustration and disgust: how little I liked to be pinched between the ambitions of Boney and the priests, both of

165

whom wanted my money, and neither of whom wanted my sister any more than I did.

But now two consuming matters called my attention away from this ugly dilemma. One was a dose of a love-disease. The other was my impending marriage.

La vogia de cagar e de maridarse la vien tuta in t'un momento, we say in Venice: the desire to shit and to marry come upon you suddenly.

The Startled Reader asks: has yours truly fallen in love?

Love? Don't think I don't know about such things! I had podded my share of females and I was currently in full fling with three girls in Venice, separated by *sestieri*: always safer. The Indulgent Reader will excuse my mentioning it: I had taken coals in the nethers from one of them, godnobble her, and so the world of so-called love was one I held in odium at that moment.

Meanwhile, forced to endure a period of chastity until my visible infection healed over, I scratched my itches with my eyes. By which, the Reader shall understand, I set myself to look for a wife by whom I could print the family face on the next generation. If Boney was to do his worst and close Corpus Domini, there had better be a male heir of mine squalling in his cradle to defend the Palazzo Espagnol against Marcella and whomever had stolen the real will.

I wanted something fat, noble and stupid in the wife line, talented in the smallest of talk and dancing. My thrifty heart longed for a fat and stupid dowry too, to swell my charnel-house of books. And to repair my poor dry-rotting, teetering, creaking Palazzo Espagnol, lumps of which dropped off under my caressing fingers with increasing frequency. (Perhaps the Doting Reader has known this hard love, by which the more you touch, the more you lose? The afflictions of my home's skin were a torture to me.)

So. A wife.

Look at yours truly bent over the parchment! Dipping his quill in the rose-scented ink. While I waited for my scabs to drop off, I set myself up for the romance business, copying out reams of love letters from literature with a space at the top for my bride's name to be filled in. I commissioned a wooden box for love letters, its lid painted with a flaming heart. It would be my first gift to my new *fidanzata*. A heart is an overrated piece of equipment in a man, yet even I'll admit its utility when it comes to yanking a young woman in a useful direction. Not for nothing is this organ shaped like a squeezed handful of blood.

I commissioned my tailor to exceed all previous amazements. Violet taffeta is regarded with prejudice by many, perhaps because it is cheap. But when one *knows* how to wear clothes, well, even violet taffeta, eked out with scarlet ribbon, can be sculpted to a cutaway frock-coat that sets off an embroidered waistcoat like a charm. As for myself, I cultivated a great felicity of sideburns, though their reddish hue contrasted with my dark hair, among which I had Signor Fauno conjure me some of those tousled curls that were the acme of fashion at that moment.

And I consulted my book of human skin for the best potion to get a chosen bride enamoured, and a future wife docile and fertile.

I cast my eyes around the noble damsels of the city, imagining myself at itch-buttock with each candidate. As it turned out, I did not have to seek far at all for the fortunate recipient of my letters and my drugs. My perfect bride had been growing up all along in the Foscarini *palazzo*, not far from our own.

I looked forward to being a married man, I truly did. There's another amusing little Venetian proverb, perhaps the Reader knows it?

A bastonar la so dona, se delibara le anime dal purgatorio.

Beating one's own wife frees souls in purgatory.

Gianni delle Boccole

The poor girl, Amalia Foscarini, she had no idea what were comin to her. In her malignorance she tookt jist six weeks to fall under the barrage of woos what Minguillo pitcht at her. Twere as if she was drugged, she fell that quick.

Her Ma were a friend of my Mistress Donata Fasan, who neer sayed a word to warn the Contessa Foscarini that she were feedin her daughter to the wolf. But by then my Mistress were thick as sieves with Minguillo, and acted his bidding like she too were havin summing droppered in her soup.

That Amalia Foscarini, she were handsome – *bionda, bianca e grassottella* – as we like to say in Venice – blonde, fair n fat, n she were in the money. A pink heart ovva face, with the dearest little double chin, fair brows archin up and eyes almost Slav-like in blueness n upwardturningness. *Mozzafiata*, breathtaking. More to the point, her sister had jist delivert her fourth, so motherhood runned in the family as ye mite say.

And she was stoooooooooopid, Dear Good Little God! Five years at Madame Carlina's school had left her quite bare o brain. Lovely dancer, tho.

Our household loved a wedding, jist like evry *palazzo*. My Mistress tookt her chance to show how fine she mite look and Minguillo corraged her to make a show o herself in moray emrald silk that would sartinly outshine Contessa Foscarini's well-knowed pink satin.

But downstairs in the kitchen, as we turned the capons in garlic and crusted the lamb in rosemary-bredcrumb for the betrothal feast, our hearts wernt in it. Felt like twere the bride we was turning on the spit.

The wedding were a quiet one on account of as Minguillo's famly were much depleted. By him. The tapeworm hants n huncles of the Palazzo Espagnol dint make an peerance on account o not bein invited. Marcella were still disgreased in her room. She dint een come downstairs, knowin she wernt welcome and would be like the speckter at the feast.

The bride's famly was grim-faced. The contrackeds was all signed, but at the last minute some botherin stories had reacht them. We servants had made sure o that. But we ud been too sottile n too late, not darin to be otherwise.

We have a proverb in Venice:
La dona che se marida bisogna che la gh'abia do cose:
boca da porçelo e schena d'aselo.
The woman who marries needs two things:
the mouth ovva pig n the back ovva mule.

168

Dint say nothing about the skin ovvan elefant. Should of, for Amalia.

The bridle night were paneful for the bride, that much were obvious. I saw Minguillo trottin oft towards the bedchamber with that horrid book of humane skin stickin out o his pocket. I could of sworn I saw dents like its corners in the new Contessa's arm the next day.

There werent no wedding journey. Minguillo dint have no use for romantic notions like that, and anyway twere more commodius for the begetting busyness to have a wife an yer own bed vailable at all hours. The Contessa's views dint come into it tall. A week after the wedding the bride alredy had her feelins crusted with the scabs of old wounds. There was hard words atwixt her and her Mamma in the shanozzeree drawing-room, that rang through the whole house. The daughter wanted to quit the Palazzo Espagnol n her obstropilous new usband, n run home to her famly. The Mamma were having none of it.

'You belong to him now,' Contessa Foscarini screecht. 'You do what he does. You think what he does. You act as he does. What did you think marriage meant? Courtship under the same roof? Perhaps he'll go to Peru and die of fever like his father. That's the only thing to hope for . . . you'll not come trailing back home to embarrass us!'

You could see at onct why Chiara Foscarini and Donata Fasan was best friends isn't it.

Young Contessa Amalia's womb were the bit of her what reeked revenge. For she made only daughters in there, to her usband's spleenful fury. When the first one were delivert he lookt like a weasel eating briars.

He muckled her looks for that daughter. She could not go out for weeks.

After that first botched baby, Minguillo made Contessa Amalia eat a hare's belly dried, and cut into shives, the best his quack could offer for kindling a male child. She retcht on the sour meat. So he had the quack rub the hare bellies to dust for dissolving in drink. Minguillo would go evry night with this glass o dark brown juice to her bedchamber, and the whole house heared her weep each time he opent the door.

When he were out of the room, she allus reefered to her usband as 'the Churl'. It wunt oironickle at all. Contessa Amalia dint have that in her. Swear she haint a grain o humour. Twere simple deep-seeded fact, that er usband were a churl, and the girl were too dim to disguise it. If Minguillo heared it, he dint nip it in the butt, but were probly proud of it, for it shone that she were hurting.

Minguillo Fasan

If the Reader does not relish dismal accounts of Poor Things done in a pungent style, He should not read on.

My wife was instructed to treat Marcella like the eyesore she was, as the zero in the scale of inferiority in our domestic society. I did not have to say it more than once. My dove of a wife was pleasantly stupid yet not too stupid to realize her fortunes and mine lay very snugly alongside one another.

My sister had once been the prettiest thing in our house. Now my wife had taken up that role, filling it splendidly and expensively, to my enormous gratification. I did not go in for friends, but since my nuptials I had discovered the pleasures of ostentatious dinners in my home. There were plenty of noblemen on the watch for an opulent free supper in those reduced days. I was interested to see just how much rich food it took to sicken a spoilt Venetian. More than that, I loved to see the men round my table envying me the wife I had got myself, imagining me alone with her when they had all gone home to their thin spouses or to the women they had to pay for by the hour. I sat through entire dinners too smug to eat, throwing flowers to myself for my choice of a consort.

Look at Amalia's eyes drifting over men's faces like a pair of courting kingfishers! Men felt that soft blue glance feather-stroking their cheeks, even if they dared not gaze back. Look at Marcella, if she came to table at all, wasted and wordless, attracting only grimaces of pity. Like the evicted nuns, my sister these days created embarrassment in those who had to face her.

Fashions had driven waists further upwards and necklines down lately, but I did not think it necessary to refresh her wardrobe. Her outmoded gowns showed it: what did she know of the world, and of pleasing fashionable chatter? The Modish Reader takes the quip right out of my mouth: not enough to make a snake weep. So my guests averted their eyes, and made speedy and vivacious conversation with their neighbour on the other side.

Marcella sat there, watching the men watching that fine gaudy thing, my wife, and Marcella's pale face grew pointed and then pointed downwards.

I had not yet succeeded in making her a nun but she had a nun's face now. All vitality had fled from it and a dim wax had replaced the living flesh of her complexion.

Sor Loreta

At first it was good to be *vicaria*, for the *priora* had fallen ill with the dropsy and did not trouble me with any remonstrations or letters to nuns' uncles that might have me removed from my new position of authority. Instead of showing steadfastness in illness, she took to her bed, so that I became the *priora* in all but name and was able to start my great task of purification without her interference.

I made many changes to the regime of the convent to bring it back to holy ways. Laughter was no longer heard along the little streets of Santa Catalina. There was no more gossip in the courtyards. The luxurious and sensual sisters were accustomed to grow their hair long and to curl it with perfumed oils. In my first week as *vicaria*, I ordered all the nuns' hair cut short, despite their protests. I had the curls made into new wigs for all our plaster and wooden saints.

Instead of tying nuns to the cross once a year on Good Friday, I decreed that it should be done every Friday. Those who had mocked and hurt me the most were the first to feel the midday sun on their faces in the sanctuary, for in disrespecting His most loving daughter they had profaned God Himself. And my sisters afflicted with the itching scabies took their turn next. For what more

171

feeling penance could there be – as I explained to them – than to be prevented from lewd scratching by being tied at all four limbs to the Holy Cross?

And I decided that it was time to take steps against El Misti, the mountain that impudently stared down on the convent. I had read that in Europe there were those who claimed that the crude lineaments of the mountains were indecent to look upon. I agreed. Therefore I decreed that any nun seen looking up at the mountain should be punished with a long cold bath, for to stare at those untamed crags was surely to indulge in *calores*.

My head vibrated with plans, particularly for my enemies, who now cowered in their cells, awaiting my judgments. It was only because she was Sor Sofia's sister that I did not punish the wicked Rafaela hardest of all.

As *vicaria*, I still waged a ceaseless campaign to make the Holy Fathers see just how unclean was the laughing soul of this Rafaela. But it turned out that Rafaela's father had endowed the convent with rich tracts of land. The gift was attached to a contract that specified its return if Rafaela were ever to be put out of the convent. To have written such a contract, the man must have known that his wife had lain with Satan to produce this older daughter of hers.

Rafaela drew around herself a tribe of light sisters, notably Margarita, the pharmacy nun, and Rosita, who kept the gate. Wherever Rafaela was, there was laughter and irreverence, most particularly towards myself. Even the *priora* had a weakness for Rafaela, who was therefore protected from all censure.

But the godless Rafaela had one weakness of her own: the little sister whom she adored, even as I adored her: Sor Sofia, my sweet angel in earthly form.

Gianni delle Boccole

That year 1810 Napoleon Bonypart closed down the convent of Corpus Domini what Minguillo had promist Marcella to. Twere not long afterwards the building were razed to the ground.

That same day Minguillo ordered me n Anna to move Marcella out o her room, for two weeks, he sayed.

'Too long she has been closeted up in there,' he hexplained, 'I am having some men in to freshen it up.'

Then there were bangin n thumpin n the smell o dust n distemper for days on end.

I guest direckly for why Minguillo ud got them artesians in. He were searchin evry crevasse for the bonified will. I wore an oironical smile, for in the last two year Ide been oer evry inch of it alredy myself, lookin for the same thing, and I knowed all the places in the Palazzo Espagnol it twernt, hincludin that one.

Minguillo Fasan

I had no real contingency against the shipwreck of my plans. But, on the very day Napoleon finally kicked my hopes in the teeth, I conceived the seed of an idea, which I now watered with the tears of my mother.

'Mamma, I fear,' I opined experimentally one evening, 'Marcella is not sound in her mind.'

'No, Marcella has bad moments,' protested my mother. 'Sometimes I believe that she is not quite happy.'

'No, the thing does not function like that. A person is either in or out of her senses.'

Having rubbed a few more subtle reminders of Piero's alleged preferences in the salt of her wounded pride, I thrust on with, 'Anyway, Marcella is at least weak-witted. Old Piero must have guessed it, and profited from it.'

My mother swallowed hard. I continued, 'I have come to understand at last what ails her. Poor Marcella has secretly developed a religious mania. Perhaps it is in compensation for her sins with Piero? Have you observed how she lives a hermit's life in our midst, as if pretending that the Palazzo Espagnol is a convent? She keeps her eyes downcast like a nun. She never smiles. And have you seen her room lately?'

By careful design my mother had hardly laid eyes upon Marcella or her room since Piero's death.

'Come with me,' I urged.

My men had just finished their work. In Marcella's room the pretty tapestries had been wrenched off walls that were now distempered white as a convent cell. No will had revealed itself in the process, yet by stripping the room I had been investing in my inheritance in a new way. I showed my mother the prayer stool I had installed, with its little row of sharp pebbles where the knees went. I pointed to the hurtfully thin Jesus crucified above Marcella's bed. I pulled out the breviary I had placed under her pillow. And finally I leaned into the armoire and dragged out a leather whip laced with nails, which I laid in my mother's flinching hands so that she might *feel* her daughter's penchant.

'She barely eats, you know?'

'She is fasting?' whispered my mother, adding disparagingly, 'She is dreadfully thin. It really is quite deranged, to wreck what's left of her looks like this.'

'Do not worry, Mamma. I shall get Doctor Inca to her,' I reassured. 'Now that she is so reduced I suspect those harnesses need to be tightened. To do her any good, you know.'

Gianni delle Boccole

It were at that time that Minguillo's fat quack all ovva suddenly falled from grease. He were discovert at a card game where he had staked the book of his famous apothcry preperashons on a loosing streak.

Minguillo saved the book jist in time. The quack were sent way to the dredful town o Rovigo, 'for to study and improve himself', Minguillo telled us.

But Marcella's health were broke and she needed attendin to. For the first time ever luck went on our side. Minguillo sayed, 'Go get that doctor then, the cheap one who attended dear old Piero Zen.'

You could see him calkillating: Santo were poor, n so he would be tracterbull. I were oft faster than a ferrate. And Santo followt me like a bullet back to the house.

'Whatever you see up there, tell me about it first,' I warned him, pushing Doctor Santo towards the stairs. Minguillo were awaitin up there, so there weren't time to hexplain nothing more.

Doctor Santo Aldobrandini

My first sight of Minguillo Fasan should have told me everything I needed to know about him. It was not just the lurid clothes or the little panniers of fat on his hips that spoke of a chronic glandular disorder.

Faccia punctata, maggot face, and a smell of iron filings around him.

A persistent inflammation of the sebaceous glands and hair follicles had produced on his face a permanent eruption of hard, conical elevations filled with suety matter. When squeezed out of the skin such matter is emitted in a cylindrical form with the appearance of a small grub or maggot.

Maggot face is caused by enervation, intemperance, sexual abuse and a character that devours itself from the inside, and feeds on all around it.

But Minguillo Fasan was not the patient I had been summoned to attend.

Marcella Fasan

My brother's shadow fell over my bed. Then the painfully emphatic colours of his frock-coat filled my vision. Anna's cringing face hovered nearby.

'We've a new doctor for you,' Minguillo announced. Hearing the light steps on the stairs, I decided that it was best to pretend passivity and a feeble comprehension until I saw what style of a man had been washed in. I had no great hopes, given he had been supplied by Minguillo. I kept my eyes downcast when the light footsteps arrived by my bed.

'Why is she so thin?' the doctor asked immediately. His voice was low and sweet, with a slight flavour of the street to it, for all its quiet cleverness. I was certain that he assumed me a servant girl, given my ugly plain chamber and my shabby clothes.

Minguillo said blandly, 'The damage is self-administered. She is something of a religious fanatic. Young girls, you know how they can be. There's no accounting . . .'

The young man spoke out unwisely. Even more sharply than for my own pain, I flinched for him when he asked, 'How can you allow this poor girl to practise such cruelty upon herself? I cannot believe . . .'

Minguillo's lip jutted out, 'Then you cannot be in our employ here, young man.'

I glanced up and saw the boy's hunger then – his thin face, his fragile wrists, and the hair that hung in home-cut wisps around his face. And then I looked again, with a vein of fire racing from my fingertips to my head, because I *knew* this young man. This was the same kind youth who had cradled Piero's head as he lay dying in the courtyard. I had been standing upstairs in the glassed corridor; the young man was a dozen yards below me in the courtyard. He had seen me then – our eyes had locked for a moment just as poor Piero died.

But that was when I was dressed in silk, still rosy from a season of happiness with Cecilia Cornaro. From down in the courtyard he could not have seen my withered leg, my club foot. Now it gave me a strange pain in the heart, like someone clenching a fist in there, to realize that a mere eighteen months later the young man could not possibly recognize that girl at the window in the thing I was now.

All I saw in his face as he examined me was impersonal pity and a professional kindness, overlaid with shock when he discovered the latest shackles and harnesses invented by Doctor Inca for my brother's pleasure. He said evenly, 'It is my duty to attend to even self-inflicted illness, of course.'

'That's right, young man,' smiled Minguillo and he pulled a coin out of a crevice in the voluminous old-fashioned frock-coat he affected to hide the increasing oddities of his shape. It was a small coin, yet the young man took it eagerly.

'May I return tomorrow at the same hour with some poultices and a tonic for her?' the doctor asked deferentially. 'I would propose a different treatment from the preceding doctor's, which, as you can see, has hardly proved effective.'

'For the second visit we pay one half,' came the answer.

'What is she named, my patient?' the young man asked, acknowledging that the bargain was made.

'Marcella Fasan,' he was told.

At this the young man stopped short and his face grew milky-white. I watched him relive his own memory of Piero's death in our courtyard at the Palazzo Espagnol. Now he lowered his eyes to my face, and traced its ruined outlines.

'May I . . . May I speak to her mother?' he asked Minguillo.

Oh, I thought, *do not do that. Do not let him think that you care. It shall go badly for you if you do.*

Gianni delle Boccole

The poor insent lad left the nobble floor of the Palazzo Espagnol mistificated – the Mamma so passive n disintrested, as if he talkt of someone else's daughter, the brother unable to hold back a smile that struck Santo as obseen, all the while cadgin extra details of his sister's poorliness. Twere as if Santo had brought him a present, Great Robber ovva God!

Santo traled down to the courtyard with a heavy burden on his thin shoulders. I think he alredy suspected that he shunt have shone his hand to Minguillo. But he dint nowise want to believe what his insides was telling him. Who would?

I were waiting for him under the portico, where they couldn't of seed me from the nobble floor. I told him, 'Ye aint did no good by makin a scene. Minguillo Fasan abdomenates do-gooders and

177

ye've only drawn tension to yerself that could een be dangerous for ye.'

Then I finely told Santo zackly persay how Marcella had come bout her twisted leg – tho turned out o course that he knewed all bout that alredy. So I told him about the scene what had led to Piero Zen's murder, what ud appened to Marcella's poor sister Riva, and many other facts that dirted the histry o the Palazzo Espagnol.

'Why do you not go to the magistrates?' he askt, all wild bout the eyes.

'Would t'other nobbles listen to a servant runnin tales agin his Master? More likely twould be the likes of us clapt in prison or the madhouse for slander.'

'I'll not abandon her,' he swore. Then he worrit, 'She'll think I am with her brother, just another false doctor come to torture her. But there's no help for it.' He swallowed like a fish, and breathed in deeply. His poor thin neck was scarlet-red with caring.

Then a russle in the flowers made our hairs stand on there ends. Twere not safe to talk unristrained like this inside the Palazzo Espagnol where Minguillo mite come creeplin up pon us. We ranged to meet reglar at the *ostaria* in the Calle delle Boteghe, so that he could give me reports on Marcella's progress. Twere easy to draw him out. The boy ate so little that he was mock-eyed and shaggy-tonged on a glass o rough red. Poor, he was, poor as pauper soup. Out o my own stipend I stood him a plate o food when I were able.

And so I learned his story, which were the sorryest kind. He had niver sat at a table with a famly to fill it. No mother, no father, no sister nor brother. No woman neither, for the boy had not yet loved. He perhaps loved his patients, skin by skin, but no one ud ever loved him back. He dint know how it were did, that.

He talkt o the poltisses n affusions he compost for Marcella, o the healthful flush on her skin when he fed her some nowrishing broth. But course the reports that I truely gathert in the fuggy glum of that *ostaria* were about the progress of Santo's newborned love for my little Mistress, how it had bloomed from its first moment o life, when their eyes met in the courtyard as poor Conte Piero died. And how it grewed now that he saw her evry day, and had it in his hands to make her live, tho the prospecked of her death were the chapel o her brother's eye.

Marcella Fasan

My diaries recommenced. The first thing I wrote was this: '*The doctor Santo Aldobrandini now attends me. I suppose Minguillo keeps him on because he is cheap and near.*'

When Doctor Santo smiled for the first time, not just with his lips but with his brown eyes, I wrote that they were in fact '*brunneous, burnet, castaneous, castory, sepia and sorrel, with a pure white highlight like the fleeting wing of an egret glimpsed in the evening waters of the lagoon*'.

Sor Loreta

The old *priora* passed from this miserable life. Given my many good works, I expected to be promoted to her post by the Fathers. But they did not intervene in my favour this time. I supposed that some uncles had been set to persuading them. A new *priora* was voted in by the wilful council of the nuns.

This new *priora* was the worst we had yet known. My quill is not able to describe her virtues because they were so few. Also, she was already of middling years. Those who grow old sinning have more evil-doing on their conscience than those who have not been in the world long enough to ripen in their wickedness. With the election of Madre Mónica there began a period of outrageous frivolity in our convent. All this sister cared for was the music of a godless Italian named Rossini.

That woman spent four thousand francs of convent funds on a piano and printed sheet music, so that this Rossini's lewd melodies might reverberate among us and thrum on the tender strings of young girls' hearts at all hours of the day and night. The morning the piano arrived the whole of Santa Catalina was plunged into an Italian *bacchanalia*. Under the windows of certain nuns, I smelled the fumes of cigarillos. I wept that our earthly Mother should lead the daughters of God's house into luxury, vulgarity and even tobacco.

My reproaches went unheard: I was still *vicaria*, but not by the choice of the nuns, who dared to show their displeasure by acting as if I did not exist. Of course, I myself had no desire to stay alive. My life became a constant round of fasts and flagellation, such that I fell ill again, and my body no longer had the appearance of a living thing. When Sor Sofia brought delicacies to my cell, I turned my head aside and sighed. 'The sweets of this earth are not for one as me,' I told her. 'I wish to go to my reward.'

'Do not speak so,' begged Sor Sofia, but her eyes had a faraway look, as if she could see beyond my death. This cut my feelings as if with a hundred sharpened blades. I sent her away, saying, 'The next time you see me it will be in my coffin. I suppose that this will please you.'

Weeping, she departed. I forced myself to swallow the delicacies she had brought even though they tasted like ashes on my tongue.

Doctor Santo Aldobrandini

To another man, Marcella Fasan might have looked like a husked stalk. Yet nothing could destroy the beauty of her skin for me. Then there was the effect she had upon my own. When I was with her, I felt like one of the smiling *écorché* figures in the books of anatomy I had studied. I offered up my opened self willingly. Unlike the flayed Marsyas, I did not cry 'Why are you stripping me from myself?' For it was a pure and beautiful relief to shed my reserve and present my visceral being to this girl.

Despite her depleted state, I had the immediate sense that here was someone who was taking care of *me*, just as I had felt when I first saw her face at the Villa Fasan at Stra those many years past. Here was something I had never known before: the sight of me was a pleasure for her. Her smiling eye spoke it; her face flushed it whenever I entered the room.

We said nothing that a chaperoning maid might raise an objection against, yet there were transactions going on between us: glances, tones of voice subtler than a silkworm's case, that held something living inside.

The first time I saw her back down in the public rooms of the Palazzo Espagnol, her delicate shape stammered out by an ill-fitting dress, an idea blushed through me: *If she is not going to be a nun, then she could be a wife*.

I reproached myself for my vainglory. How could a noblewoman, even a crippled outcast of a noblewoman, marry a son of Dishonour and Fornication?

She soon ceased to flinch when I laid a finger upon her wrist to test her pulse. I ceased to apologize every time I did so. I began to exercise her damaged leg, removing the shameful shackles and leather stirrups that her brother had insisted on, and which his disgraced quack had apparently embraced as a useful tool of torture.

To her surprise and shy, adorable delight, she found that she could still move quite well aided only by a light crutch. I walked her around the shabby little parlour that had been assigned to her, to the walls of which were pinned her pretty sketches. They were mostly studies of flowers but one day there was a comical sketch of herself as a bony little colt, staggering on uneven legs. As I gazed at it, she handed me the crutch and walked across to the window unaided, clutching the curtains and laughing until she was out of breath. After that, she never used the crutch inside that room. She took my arm, or Anna's, if she needed it.

While she rested between bouts of exercise, she asked me to describe some of my rich and pompous patients and she sketched caricatures that turned my bitter words into hilarity.

'You need not hate them, for that hurts you too,' she explained. 'It is sufficient to laugh at them.'

She added in a quiet voice, 'In most cases.'

Then she limped over to the door and stuck her pencil in the keyhole, a little eccentricity of hers that I often observed.

I prescribed a diet that would reflesh Marcella's fragile bones, and instructed her maid Anna on aromatic herbs for her bath. Accompanied by Anna, we ventured out of doors with the wheeled chair, crutch and my arm for support. I began to love Venice more because I saw it through Marcella's delighted eyes and then reported in her sketchbook: marbled water cradled in the shadow of a bridge, a *palazzo* seeming to sway in a web of fretwork, a solitary egret question-marking the far shore in pale Gothic script.

What I longed to do was touch Marcella Fasan's downcast eyelashes.

I did not destroy myself with hopeless fantasy. I imagined not what I might do to her but what she would do to me. I imagined shreds of things, never a whole caress: three of her fingers brushing the top of my hand. Even a long look was beyond the greed of my imagination. My grandest hopes were attenuated to the fantasy that she might get something in her eye so that I could tilt her head in my hand, gently cupping the nape of her neck.

Gianni delle Boccole

Minguillo suspected naught o the sweet-hartin that were goin on under his roof. It dint enter his curst head that his sister could raise a fire o love in the soul ovva young man. He dint think it o Marcella. He dint know what a soul was anyways. And love? Swear he could nowise een spell it.

Anna done all she could to feed Marcella up on Santo's erbs. I done all I could to warm her thoughts o the little doctor of whom I had sich bold, presuming hopes. I brought up his name a dozen times a day, on any excuse, jist to see the spark in her eye.

Anna, what allus knew all the news within ten miles, told me that now the artist Cecilia Cornaro ud returned from a trip to Albania a destroyt woman, on account of some sad busyness there with a poetical English milord. There was even roomers ovva bastert baby tuckt way with the Armenian monks on an island in the lagune, what had survived Bonypart's cull o churches on account on them being skolars much as priests. Anyways, Cecilia Cornaro were no sooner back in Venice than she rusht oft to London. Now she were painting the English nobbleses' watery eyes and the tiny hairs up there pinky-grey nostrils and listening to there mutterances with that famoused sinnical look painted all oer her fizzog.

I told Marcella, 'Your friend the artist come back to Venice.'

Instead of lookin happy or eager, Marcella's face growed worrit.

I hexplained, 'Then she gone oft direckly. They's sayin Cecilia Cornaro has developed an aspersion for Venice. But look here's Doctor Santo come to tend to ye.'

Minguillo Fasan

Most wives will hate you if allowed, and my wife was no exception.

She soon learned to dread the spank of my hand on the doorknob.

I went to the papà business in earnest. I worked my wife like a peasant works the plough.

After I married I did not want any issue outside of the family. So I wore shirts-of-Venus when I saw angels in the arms of whores so ugly that they had to give change. It was a relief from my wife's soft-pastry prettiness, to lie with those vigorous dogs. Nothing amiss with an ugly woman, if she is willing. Bring them round, say I. Don't mind if I do.

Between betraying my wife I bought her gifts of jewels for I was genuinely sorry to have spent seed without utility now that I had a proper vessel for it.

My quips were sadly thrown away upon my wife. If I wanted sentient pain I had to seek out my sister and gorge upon her visible distress – for her skin faithfully supplied the most vivid chart of her suffering when I came to keep company with her.

Even though my affections inevitably soured on her, I rarely raised my hand against Amalia. My tongue sufficed in most cases for her discipline. I had an excellent knack of silencing her protests with a great economy of verbiage. But the Reader will understand that I could not restrain that hand when I saw on her dressing table a bottle of my very own 'Tears of Santa Rosa', which would kill any son of mine stone-dead inside her.

'How did you get that?' I demanded, dashing the bottle against the fireplace. Fortunately it was still sealed. I had intercepted it just in time.

'A new hairdresser came today as Signor Fauno is unwell . . .' she faltered. 'Minguillo dear, why should I not use it? Everyone talks of it. The scent is . . . but the bottle is . . . was so very pretty.'

'You would question my judgment, would you?' I advanced on her with the broken neck of the bottle still fisted.

Now the Married Reader is accustomed to such scenes of domestic bliss in His own household, so I'll not do the tedious and spell out every letter.

Gianni delle Boccole

Minguillo's wife niver came to the room, niver onct, to do the amiable or to see how Marcella doed. She ud been taught by her husband to think o Marcella as a sickly peace o vermin in the ouse. Twere as if she spoke with Marcella then some contaminating air would fly into her mouth. In fine company Contessa Amalia treated poor Marcella like a piranha.

The Contessa mite of had a drop o kind blood in her heart for all we knowed. Een if she did, she wunt dare cross her usband. So Ile nowise condem her outrite. She dint have a dog in this fight. It cost her nothin to hignore Marcella. She dint know the joy o the girl's lovely nature one bit. It would of cost her plenty to go agin Minguillo and make nice to his sister.

Yes, the wife had problems of her own.

Minguillo wunt let one small smile of Amalia's lie about loose without an owner. We was all irked to our bellies to see how Minguillo got to pimping the Contessa. He besot to make each man jealous for what he ud got. Her blonde curls, her plump hip, her blue eyes – he ud bought at the top of the market to get her, and he wanted everyone to know it.

Minguillo allus tugged her bodice down as she walked into the dining room, and slapt her cheek to make it rosyer. As if playful. Anna wispered in the kitchen that he ud ordered a brass corset for the Contessa jist a little tighter than was condoosing to yer akshual breathing.

'Look at those shoulders,' he would say, from across the table, to the men who past for friends. 'What do you think of my wife's breasts?'

The men was embarrast. But they lookt. First, on account of how very good that boosum were to look at, and second, on account of being frit of going agin anything Minguillo sayed.

At first she most obviously hated it, but after a spell the Contessa begun to drink up the men's looks like hot wine. She were proper greedy for them looks. They was her consolashun for a usband what had proved a fearful objeck.

The young doctor were sumtimes clapt in an old frock-coat of Minguillo's and drug up to supper to make up the numbers at the table. For at the last minit, guests often found they couldn't stomach Minguillo's company, much as they lusted after his dinners or his wife's boosum.

Did the young doctor look at the Contessa? Perhaps he did, but nowise with intent. A hungry person will look at a dog's food, without wishin to steal it, Sweet God! And course Santo, poor as a stone, dint dare look at Marcella, huddled in spurned one-ness at the poor end o the table, if indeed she were hallowed to be there tall.

After one on them dinners, Santo askt me, 'What is that book that Minguillo Fasan carries about in his pocket?'

I stared at him with an empty hole for a mouth. Then I told him bout the book of humane skin and the lists of poisons inside it.

'No!' cried Santo. 'Not "The Tears of Santa Rosa!"'

Then he told me that he knew of that stuff, of how it made a tempry show of white skin, yet had a slow leaden poison that burrowed its way beneath n killt.

'It is obvious why Minguillo Fasan keeps his involvement a secret,' Santo sayed slowly. 'Not only does his own pimpled face prove its inutility, but he'll know as well as I do that he's

185

sending weak vain people to a lingering death if they keep using it.'

'He knows what he's bout,' I acceded sadly.

'But Marcella . . .' he begun, and stopt with a blush.

Be careful, I bethought, *do! Dunt let Minguillo Fasan see ye looking like that.*

Minguillo Fasan

How glorious and useful a body the Reader is, allowing me a vent for every sore frustration! The Reader may take this as notice of forthcoming expostulations.

The Reader will sniff in a superior manner, and be right. *Yes*, I should have noticed the youth's fervour when he spoke of my sister. Yet I did not. However, love and coughing, as they say, always reveal themselves. The first thing that alerted me to trouble was that my sister looked better and even began to thrive. All that time I had been sadly ignorant of what kind of cure she had been getting.

The love cure.

The hands of young Doctor Santo all over her. His healing touch! Finally I saw with my own eyes what was going on between them. It was one solitary laugh I caught, like a fly in a glass jar. But it was enough.

Marcella at the window, the little doctor down in the courtyard fussing with the broken catch on his dilapidated black bag. Then he looked up, their eyes met and held. Then she actually placed her little hand flat against the window pane, and laughed. Her laughter flew through the glass and caressed his cheek. I felt it on my own and in other parts of me as well.

I had not seen Marcella laugh since before Piero Zen met his end.

'Oho,' I said to myself. It all came to me in a stripe of lightning: how little the young doctor cost me, and yet how often he came. And Marcella, she had lately seemed sealed up like a walnut – for weeks I had had no way of seeing into the red core of her pain. This was why. She had found a new Pieraccio to protect her. I had been blind. Now I was blind with fury.

A common surgeon! Who had been honoured to sit at my table! He was cheaper than the hairdresser. He lived in a dank hole. I should have divined that philanthropic gleam in his eye was lit by something else within. A memory stirred. Damn me – superfluous as that may be – if he was not also the same malnourished runt of a quacklet that my valet had summoned to officiate when Pieraccio met his putrid end!

My imagination seethed like acid eating nails inside a bottle. When and where had it started between them? Perhaps the ambitious doctor had bribed Gianni to be given the work of attending to her? Had the doting couple whispered little nothings to one another? Had they exchanged cooing *billets-doux*? Had they contrived an actual congress under my own roof? Would her little rose-coloured particular be delicate eating after all the liquid that passed almost continuously from it? No doubt she would take her turn on her back as meekly as she had taken every turn I'd done her. And let herself get tasted docile as she would take a spoonful of Balm of Gilead.

My nerves wrapped themselves in ropes around my heart.

Then I calmed myself with a certain knowledge. *Nothing could have happened.* Marcella, as I knew to my cost, was never without her maid Anna or Gianni or some other servant to coddle her. They would never have let the little pretender get to her, not in person or by letter. The little doctor had the look of poverty all over him: the pittance I paid him would not have stretched to bribing my servants the way Piero Zen must have done.

So the romance must have been all off-stage for Marcella, conducted on the invisible tight-wire between their two longing pairs of eyes. Let the Dullest Reader imagine all the worst concoctions of the most fevered blue-stockinged ladies, whose virginity is ever preserved by their homeliness, and even then He shall hardly find Himself capable of imagining the vapid fantasy that was surely my sister's affair of the heart, devoid of novelty or actual fulfilment. I resolved with difficulty not to soil my fists on the doctor's carcass. There was a cleaner way to be done with this excrescence. One that pertained to my latest, as yet evanescent deliberations on Marcella's future – *pazienza!* – nay, this plan might well beautifully expedite them!

What? What's that? No, they *could not* be together. Not under any. The Sentimental Reader should evacuate that drivelling thought from His maudlin mind on the instant. And wash His hands after.

On his next visit, I contrived to have the doctor briefly separated from his old leather bag. Intercepting him in the hall, I jovially chaffed him for its shabbiness and offered the services of my valet Gianni to polish it while he attended to my sister. He seemed nervous at my solicitude, but he dared not refuse me. I then misdirected him to a small parlour where Marcella was not waiting for him, as I had already arranged for her to be carried to the dining-room by Gianni.

Bearing the bag to my studio, I quickly penned a letter. It pretended to come from Doctor Santo Aldobrandini. It was addressed to a certain woman. I did not think it possible that Marcella knew the doctor's handwriting but, to be certain, I made a good attempt at scribal verisimilitude, using a chit for herbs I found in the bag. I gave the bag a little rub for luck and then took it to Marcella's room where I laid it on its side, the contents spilling out. I arranged the letter carefully, gaping slightly and leaning precariously against the broken latch. It very clearly invited my sister to lift it up, whereupon it would fall fully open, inviting her to make absolutely certain that it had dropped from her doctor's valise. Accidentally.

'*Impossible Object of my Fervent Desire,*' I had written, for I guessed the little doctor would go for high-flown and capitalized, '*I watch you at the table and I long for you to be mine. Yet I must revolt my hands and eyes with humbler and less delicious meat for my daily wage.*'

Only at the end of the letter did my little doctor reveal the name of the object of his desire. She was a woman whose physical perfection I had seen my sister's eyes slide all over. Marcella, ignored by everyone, also stared at she whom everyone else watched and adored.

My wife.

When I had baited the doctor's bag, I rang for Gianni. I berated him for leaving my dilapidated sister on display in the dining-room when elegant guests were due for luncheon. He knew better than to remind me I had ordered her carried there myself.

'Take her back to her room on the instant,' I thundered.

Then I had the puzzled doctor footman-ed from the empty parlour to my study, whereupon I pulled together a very choice specimen of a righteous rage.

'How dare you?' I hissed. 'A beggar at my door, practically.'

I told his confused and frightened face that I had caught him looking at my wife.

'Nobody likes a lecher, and a parasitic lecher is very upsetting for everyone. It ill behoves you to take my food and money if you're actually after something more substantial,' I told him, indicating overflowing feminine breasts and hips with economic movements of my hands. 'You shame yourself with vain delusions. You spit on my hospitality. And as a doctor, you are a complete fraud. I detect no improvement in my poor sister's condition, which is not surprising, given your attention is evidently elsewhere.'

The doctor stuttered, 'This is a fantasy, you lose the run of yourself, sir . . .'

I had a bowl of sausage stew on my desk that I had ordered up especially for this moment. I threw it over him. 'My food does not look so appetizing when you're wearing it on your shirt, does it?'

He gasped, giving me the disbelieving look of a beaten dog who had thought himself in good domestic odour.

'Begone from my household. You shall also depart from Venice altogether. I shall be having words with the *Magistrato alla Sanità*. You and your shoddy services shall not be welcome anywhere in good society now.'

He flushed to the roots of his baby-fine angel-blond hair and continued to stammer in an agitated manner. 'Your wife is nothing to me! And you must stop with the production of "The Tears of Santa Rosa". People will get sick.'

At this I admit I was taken aback. How did he know that I was the source of the Tears? And how did he know how bad it was? The safest course was to return to the high moral ground. 'You contradict me? You dare to deny what the whole world knows, having seen you devouring my wife with your eyes?'

'You are an . . . an evil person,' he whispered.

Within a day of finding the letter, Marcella had turned her head against

189

the wall and started playing dead. She stopped eating. She did not speak. Her breathing was so slight as to be undetectable.

Remarkably few die of disappointed love, however, so there was still work to be done. I marched into her room without knocking.

'This moping and starving and staring at the wall,' I remarked in that free and easy way I have, 'this is the behaviour of a madwoman.'

Marcella Fasan

I buried the hurt deep in my heart like a dagger blade. It would take years for that dagger to be pulled out, and for me to live again without a sear of grief that cut me with each breath.

I refused to drag Gianni or Anna into that abyss with me. I would not put them in danger of knowing the truth of what I had felt for Santo, and nor would I burden their loving compassion with my anguish.

Gianni delle Boccole

Santo were very shook-looking when he come out o Minguillo's study. He were still dripping with stew. At first, I bethought he had been poisont, and vomited on hisself. Then I recognized the stew, as we ud had it for luncheon downstairs. I was reliefed for it had been holesome.

I fetcht a damp rag and expunged the worst oft, tender as a nussmaid. *He* stood still, shockt like a little child betraid.

He told me, 'I've been tricked, but I don't know how.'

He could not meet my eyes. I bethought, *Also umiliated, and made to see the side of Minguillo Fasan that would chill a walrus to the bone, Great Beast ovva God!*

190

He told me his story, and I filled in the missing parts.

He moaned, 'The worst of it is . . . he's sure to have told Marcella. She will think horribly of me. She will think me a goat . . .'

I told him I would hexplain the terrible lie, I would smooth it out with Marcella.

'If she believes you. Even if she does, I cannot enter this place again. Conte Fasan has forbidden me.'

'Then we'll jist make Marcella well nuff to leave!'

Until this moment I haint niver spoke o the feelins atwixt them. Twere summing too delicate to bring to the light. Summing that nestled in the soft darkness, bit by bit growing stronger, though not yet ready to fly.

Scant years back, that Santo were o the street and that Marcella o the highest birth would of been a problem to confront. But Napoleon ud dug up the trenches atwixt the nobbles and the common people and had his eyes set on the space atwixt man n God now! – And anyway this was desprit times at the Palazzo Espagnol. So I sayed, 'I believe if ye want it, she will finely come to ye. And if she does, ye will have to look after her. Her brother will not take her back.'

Santo started like an affrighted moth. Yet I saw hope in his face. I pressed his nice-shaped hand. There wernt no more to be sayed, Dear Good Little God.

Minguillo Fasan

'You know, my sister is demented? Her religious obsession was merely a veil for her true malady – the *ninfomania*. She should not be permitted to dwell among decent, sane people.'

That very afternoon I rehearsed this opinion on my wife, who barely raised her lovely blank eyes from the card table. I saw a rare understanding there. I touched the silk of her dress, a moss green with sleeves puffed up like cats' heads. She recoiled and murmured like the dove of a wife she had better be, 'Whatever you think best, dearest.'

I thought, *There are emeralds in this for you, my dove*.

I went to my mother's room. And I proceeded to inform her about Marcella's lamentable love affair, using my imagination and my vocabulary to their fullest extents, which is to say much. I portrayed the affair as a logical continuation of the youthful depravity spawned and enjoyed by Piero. My mother quivered at my plain speech. She flinched at the commonness of the young doctor, at his presuming to lust after my own wife while goading Marcella's weakness into a new outbreak of obscenity. Then she lowered her gaze modestly, as she always did when she sacrificed Marcella, and told me that I was the head of the household now.

'*Ninfomania*,' I sighed loudly. 'The shame of it.'

All this time Signor Fauno the hairdresser had his head bent over my mother's curls, his great ear swallowing up all this information on a direct route to his great loose mouth. My sister's descent into the most sordid form of madness would be disseminated in every noble household on the Grand Canal by the next day's evening.

Gianni delle Boccole

Twere one thing to tell Santo that I knowed how things lay atwixt em. With Marcella I had to walk een more light. Since Conte Zen were took from us, I had volenteert to carry her updown the stairs wheniver twere needed. On the way down to dinner that sore day, I wispered into her neck, 'Miss Marcella, ye dunt have to stay here. If ye dunt mind not to live in splendour with grand fixins, n I think ye would not mind not to, then ye has a choice.'

She turned a confust face to me. There were summing gone from her eyes.

'Doctor Santo – I appen to know . . .' I besot.

'I cannot eat tonight.' Her two eyes froze in misery – that were her response to my menshon o Santo's name.

'Gianni, please take me back to my room,' she askt.

She sayed nothing more while I returned up the stairs. I layed her gently on the bed. She lookt at the wall with a face white as if carved out of whacks. I tried agin, 'Taint true, what you think bout Santo, ye is under a mistake. Santo would do anything for ye, Miss Marcella. Anything.'

Her voice were cold like the grey water at the bottom ovva well, 'My brother says I am to have a new kind of treatment.'

'Yer brother! Yer playing into yer brother's hands,' I told her, bold as a child, for I was affrighted at this change in her. 'How can ye think *he* is looking out for ye? Now Santo . . . he's more n willing . . .'

I could not find the words, damn my clotted tong, to do the Cupid. I bethought I would jist need to throw a little rope, and that the bridge atwixt them would be built from all them feelins nussed so strong n secret all this time. But Marcella dint hold out her hand for the rope, and I wernt ready not to be helped by her.

Marcella lookt at that wall, like it was the tablet o the Ten Commandments, and each one of em was carved in ice and sayed 'Thou Shalt Not Be Loved'.

Then Anna put her poor scarred head round the door and baconed me with her hand.

Outside she wailed, 'Minguillo has just put out such a dreadful story to the Mistress!'

Minguillo Fasan

We call it the Archipelago delle Malattie, the Archipelago of Maladies, the cluster of islands that curves around Venice like a shield. It is, in fact, a shield, which keeps the city pure of taint, bodily and spiritual. There is Santa Maria della Grazia for infectious diseases, San Lazzaro for Leprosy, the Lazzaretti, Nuovo and Vecchio, for the Plague. And finally, San Servolo, the island of the Mad.

Fortunately for me, the island of San Servolo had a faintly Iberian history that mirrored my own. Its denizens were lately *i reduci*, soldiers who were less than they were, having given a limb or two for their country. They were cared for by the *Fatebenefratelli*, the doing-good-Brothers, originally from Portugal. The Brothers were great herbalists, and respectful friends of our family. My father had cannily endowed the elegant new pharmacy on the island in 1790, so he might keep it supplied with the Bark of Peru. By then the island already had its own bloodstained operating slab, its bottled brains and marinated foetuses. San Servolo enjoyed the gruesome honour of being second only to Paris as a surgery for the amputation of limbs and the treatment of syphilis.

There were other patients. Even before Napoleon came to craze us, San Servolo had started to accept certain bad seeds from noble families, sons and daughters whose behaviour might bring down a scandal. The mists of the lagoon closed over these blue-blooded gibberers, the '*dozzinanti*', forgivingly and forgettingly.

The island was large; the accommodations generous. San Servolo flourished as a lunatickery. Soon even *pazzi* of the plebeian classes were swallowed up into its gardens and corridors. The 'furious' lunatics were confined where no one in town could hear them screaming. San Servolo came to be the home of everything that Venice did not wish to hear, smell or see – the epileptics, the congenital idiots, the raving lunatics, the deficients, the feeble-minded, the moral defectives and the women.

Of course, the Informed Reader knows that all women are potentially mad because of the rambunctious organ in their bodies most conveniently reached by the wound between their legs. For the women who defied their husbands or indulged in sexual over-enthusiasm there had bloomed a picturesque vocabulary – *ninfomania, erotomania, furore in utero, dissolutezza* et pretty cetera and so sweetly forth. Ladies of these uterine persuasions were quickly and discreetly dispatched across the water to San Servolo.

194

There was another motive to scoop the cocksmitten lady lunatics out of Venice. The great thing was to stop them copulating and breeding, and passing on their vileness. A madwoman contaminates everyone, even her own offspring, who feed on her mad blood in the womb, and who drink her mad milk from the teat.

The Reader taxes me with the sin of garrulity? Requests a change of subject more pertaining to our plot? Why so very much information on lunatics, all written so very sanely?

The Reader's opinion on the matter passes me by as does the idle wind.

For there was a good reason why I knew so much about San Servolo. The Retentive Reader will be bristling importantly now because *He*'s just recollected that moment, years ago, when I intercepted a letter from my father, proposing to send me exactly there for an examination of the brain. In later letters, I discovered he had even considered having me confined on the island, and had conducted researches into the process. But my mother, it appeared, had always dissuaded him.

Before Boney, disposal of an afflicted relative would have taken a little subtle business with my father's noble peers on the Council of Ten. But 'Il Regno' had smashed that up. Now gentlemen could no longer simply confine wives or sisters at will. Petty officers of citizen class might dip their lugubrious noses into our matters, and even prevent us. Damnably, I needed to research all the excruciating detail of all the new paperwork created by the shifting sands of state.

Gianni delle Boccole

I rusht from one t'other for some days, trying to prop the failing hopes of Santo, trying to open up the closed n bitter one-words of Marcella.

'What makes her all ovva suddenly believe the brother? What

wunt tell the truth to save his life from dying?' I lamented to Anna. 'But not the folks she has trusted her hole life?'

I wernt halfway to workin out this mistery when Minguillo acted on his threat agin Santo. The Magistrate of the Sanity, or leastwise there blue-blood patrons, had growed awares of Santo and not in a good way. One of there number come to Santo's rooms with a pair o thugs, and ordered the boy to quit Venice, 'Or it will not go well for ye.'

The thugs staid ahind to tell Santo, 'If it comes to our tension that yer spreading slanders bout a skin liquor called "The Tears of Santa Rosa", no matter where ye are, we shall find ye and put yer head in a bucket of it for a very long time.'

I found Santo staring miserably at his shabby bag like it held a bad secret. He talkt wildly o stayin and defyin Minguillo, but when he told me of his visitors and there threatenings, I sayed sternly, 'Twould be sartin death for ye to stay,' for I knowed them partikeler thugs from his describing. Santo must assolutely get out o Venice now them dogs ud got thesselves a sniff of him. Anyways the Sanity wunt let im practise his trade no more in the town.

'Where will ye go?'

'To one of the monasteries where they still practise medicine. I can learn and help with their patients. Padua, perhaps. Treviso. Somewhere beyond the influence of Conte Fasan, I hope.'

'And my young Mistress?' I pleaded.

'Does she think kindly on me again? How does she look when you mention my name?'

I had to shake my head. 'But Santo, for why let Minguillo Fasan *win* eh?'

'The brother started this devilment, but it is Marcella who now distrusts and despises me. It is Marcella who is hurt. How can I force . . . myself upon her when her confidence in me is shattered? I must find a way to prove my . . . feelings to her. And anyway, even if she could believe in me again . . . I have nothing to offer her except my devotion.'

He used that dry word 'devotion' yet what he meaned was 'adooring love'.

I longed to tell Santo about the bonified will then. But how could I? Would of lookt as if I was using Marcella's riotous fortune to tempt him to stay in Venice where he would sure as Sunday get killt. To dangle the will in front o him now, well, it would of insalted him, would of been tantymound to callin him a fortune-hunter. And then o course there were the small matter of I still dint know zackly persay where it twas.

I went to Marcella again. She were looking at the wall. Alredy she seemed thinner than a new moon agin.

'Santo swears 'tis a lie. Swears.'

She lookt at me with one small spark of hope flowring in her eyes. Then it died in front o me. There were summing fearful inprinted in her memmary that were stronger than my poor words. She hogged me close n hard for a second, and pushed me away, saying, 'Leave, Gianni, you should not be found here.'

I dint know what Ide sayed wrong, but then there were nought but silents and a heaving breast.

I warned, 'Do not do this, Miss Marcella. Dear Sweet God, it give yer brother scuses.'

Doctor Santo Aldobrandini

I had vowed I would not let Minguillo Fasan visit any more damage on the incomparable skin of his sister. But how could I treat her or look after her as long as she refused outright to see me or to hear my name?

For the second time, I had been told that I was not good enough to stay in Venice. I retraced my steps out of the city, leaving behind me everything I loved.

Minguillo Fasan

People who live in madhouses need few possessions. They need no trappings to define themselves: their empire is already prescribed. A fee to the keeper, and a few inexpensive treats sent in a basket on her saint's day, that's all a family might decently be expected to do for a mad daughter or sister.

On San Servolo Marcella would have no use for the fortune that my misguided father had planned to leave to her. Even if the real will were produced, the law stated that a madwoman was incapable of disposing her material goods in a sane fashion. In such a case, those goods would certainly revert to her entirely sane brother. This was neater than marrying her to God. Moreover, even Boney was not likely to close down our madhouses and foist our lunatics back upon their unhappy families!

Soon after the little doctor was dispatched, there appeared all the signs that Marcella's bladder had returned to its mischievous courses, as it always did when its owner was in distress. She refused to speak even to her own brother. She kept her head turned to the wall, she ate erratically and her colour drained away like melting snow from a barren quarry. These, I assured my wife and mother, were all sure signs of an advanced *furore in utero*.

My mother whimpered a bit, recanted for about half a tricksome hour, and claimed that Marcella *could* be cared for at home. I went to the nursery and plucked my daughter warm from her crib, and brought her back to my mother's parlour. I emptied the child on to her lap. The hairdresser cooed, pronouncing the baby the most perfect baby in the world. She was as yet on the bald side, but my daughter would one day be a customer.

'Is this innocence not a beautiful thing?' I demanded. 'Would you have it compromised, Mamma? Marcella has no control over her desires. Twice you've seen that already. Would she scruple at debauching a tender young niece? Can we have such a horror in our home?'

'Of course not,' whispered Mamma, holding the baby a little away from her, as if the child had already succumbed to Marcella's taint.

Outside my mother's room I palmed Signor Fauno the usual coin for his trouble. I held up my hand. 'By the way, "The Tears of Santa Rosa" – I've decided it would be advantageous to retire it for a period.'

'It is our best-selling item . . .' he protested.

'There are some rumours that need nipping in the bud. A little shortage now will be immensely stimulating for sales when we return it to the market, with a raised price on account of its scarcity. Tell all the hairdressers to cease at once. Sell off all the stock cheaply' – inspiration struck me then – 'to the Spanish madam in Cannaregio, and advise triple doses.'

Signora Sazia would be out of business in a week if she did not realize what caused all the retching in her livestock!

'But my noble customers?' the Perfumed and Curled One havered. 'They do not like to be denied. They are not used to it either.'

'We shall say that the nuns in Peru have ceased weeping in the bottles on account of some desiccating local pestilence.'

'Even better,' he gloated.

Now I had been cultivating the good Brothers of San Servolo like the tender shoots of plants, drawing them towards the light by virtue of their natural inclinations.

In my first letter to the priests, I confessed that a certain imbalance could be found in our family. I profited from my father's tentative researches into committing my own self. In that letter I told the Brothers that many, many years ago their predecessors might have received some correspondence from my dear father about a problem with a child. That child, I wrote, had now grown into a problematic young woman whose condition threatened the happiness of our whole family. Sadly, my father was no longer among us. So I wished to do as he would have done – consult our family's esteemed friends, the *Fatebenefratelli*, about the nature of my sister's illness. For if there was something to be done with the poor creature, the sainted Brothers would surely know the best course.

I caught their interest. Years had indeed passed. Any priests who could remember my father must have been retired or dead. Napoleon had pillaged all the city's and the Church's archives thoroughly. I trusted no one would look for or find the actual correspondence. Yet the Fasan name still figured largely in their account books, given our assiduous supply of chinchona and other Peruvian pharmaceutical delicacies. A certain Padre Portalupi wrote back, politely asking what he could do to help me.

I made a show of hesitation then. I thanked him effusively, but demurred '*Perhaps I have revealed too much. Some secrets are too dark to be let out. Doubtless it is better to leave things as they are.*'

'*Dear son,*' Padre Portalupi reassured me, '*we do God's work here. Your family's private sorrows are perfectly secure with us.*'

Given that assurance, I was most candid, probably more so than the doing-good Brother bargained for. I refined Marcella's condition for my purpose. I worked it this way: it is well known that cripples, like housemaids and governesses, have a tendency to madness. And like all cripples, my sister suffered from a mental distortion that reflected her physical state. I flirted coyly with Padre Portalupi's compassion, hinting that there were other matters too gross to raise before him.

And once more the priest wrote to me as I had hoped: '*Nothing disgusts us here on San Servolo. Please tell me exactly what ails your sister, no matter how terrible, and I shall tell you if we can help her.*'

Marcella, I now confided ruefully, had developed a wilful bladder malfunction, deliberately soiling herself whenever she was denied anything she wanted. Originally I had hoped that austere and calming convent life would help her. But Napoleon had dismantled the convent, leaving my sister to fester unwillingly in our home. Our affectionate mother, I scribbled, had tried to indulge her, to treat the problem with kindness, yet Marcella — and her bladder — had become every day more imperative. It had become a mania with her. My hope was that perhaps the famous water treatments at San Servolo could help.

Moreover, I told them, Marcella's animal economy was developing in worrying ways: her eyebrows were sprouting asymmetrically, and her thighs were disproportionately plump in relation to her wasted body. Her eyes were not strong. Her forehead had broadened. I did not need to translate these manifestations into symptoms. The *Fatebenefratelli* kept abreast of current medical literature: such lineaments had recently been diagnosed as commonly manifest in women with a bent for uncontrollable lewdness.

My presence was requested at the island. Our gondolier rowed me over on a sparkling day that seemed to favour all my plans, even laying emphasis on the pea-green brilliance of my slashed silk waistcoat. Not everyone could bring off that colour. The walls of the island loomed up with a fronding of trees above. A small aperture in the monolith of stone winked as our boat approached. I passed through an arched gate decorated with light-hearted ironmongery, was greeted with gratifying deference and led to a handsome parlour on the first floor. I faced a small group of men in priests' garb. One wiped his hands on an apron stained with beautifully red blood. He must have come fresh from surgery: the *medico-religioso*.

I took the lead. I spoke with expert knowledge and shining approval of the island's fashionable regime of tranquillization by twelve-hour enforced baths and stimulation by powerful jets of cold water. In hopeful tones, I suggested that Marcella's body, immune to medication, might be *educated* in that way. I concluded that I had perfect confidence in the good Brothers' ability to charm the devil out of my sister's bladder and make it a godly organ again.

The Brothers exchanged glances, though some seemed fixed on my waistcoat. I took my chance. 'There's one other matter . . . too difficult to commit to writing. Yet I owe you a fuller explanation within the privacy of these walls. It is to be feared that the constant agitation of my sister's bladder had given rise, as it were, to immoral sensations in that region,' I spoke delicately.

In the quickening crossfire of glances, I explained how Marcella was rising to the estate of woman, without being a real woman. Her body, so fragile, was suddenly wracked with the baser calls of Nature, which had drawn all her thoughts in the direction of her womb. In that super-sensitive vessel such desires had become super-dominant, and perverted her mind. It followed, as night after day, that there would be trouble – and there had been.

'She developed an obsession for a young *retainer*' – (so I styled him) – 'who attended to her. Naturally he was repulsed by her lewd advances, and his affections were certainly never engaged. But he so far neglected his honour as to encourage her, solely for fortune-hunting motives.'

Ergo, I continued, given her inability to judge between good and evil, it would be agreed by all reasonable souls, much as it would hurt me to lose her, that my sister must be confined to protect her against corruption and even a pregnancy that could be deliberately precipitated – as it were – by this unscrupulous retainer.

'I do not want to turn my house into a prison for my sister, yet I must preserve her innocence. I worry that she has become too wild to live safely in the world.'

The said villain, I concluded, would give up his pursuit of my sister's fortune only if she was removed from his reach.

'And this is not the first instance of my sister's moral incontinence,' I concluded sadly. 'Even as a child, she seduced a much older friend of my mother's.'

Padre Portalupi obliged handsomely, declaring, 'The fortune-hunter may not follow her here, and there will be nothing for him to seek. If your sister's mind is unbalanced, she may not govern property. Any inheritance is held in annulment. That is the law.'

I mimed thoughtful surprise. Then I pointed to the gardens glowing green at the end of the corridor. 'Pinel,' I suggested, naming their hero, 'advised flowery groves, yes? Even for overdeveloped voluptuous leanings?'

'You have read Pinel?'

I patted the book that bulged visibly in my pocket. 'Of course. Do you know that he trained for the Church before becoming a doctor? I read him as a concerned brother, and as a man whose mission it is to supply the apothecaries and priest-surgeons of Venice.'

They nodded serially, swallowing that whole. It was fortunate that they did not ask to see the volume in my pocket, for it was my book of human skin, which would have taken some explaining.

I touched lightly on Pinel's cures for *furore in utero*. I knew that would send the red-aproned *medico-religioso* into a ferment, for whatever they did in Paris, they soon did on San Servolo too. The Italian surgeons were in close correspondence with the French, and the rivalry ran deep.

'I understand that the womb's hysteria often manifests in an excessive flow of saliva, yet may also in exceedingly rare cases show in tears or urine, as characterizes my sister's symptoms. My humble hope is that this unusual occurrence will be of scientific interest to the scholars among you.'

The surgeon's eyes gleamed like those of a jaguar in the jungle.

'Desperate remedies, you know. I hate to think on it, but if you have to cut her, for her own good, well then, you must.'

At this morsel, the lips of the bloodstained surgeon curled into an irrepressible smile. No doubt he was aching to notch up more operations than his rivals in Paris. Padre Portalupi's face tightened with anxiety; there was clearly dissent among them.

The irony was not lost on me: the one thing that might really have helped Marcella was surgery, as there clearly existed a species of small mechanical failure in her bladder. However, if I was clever enough, they would operate upon the womb – on the principle that the hysteria, induced by the furious unemployment of that organ, was what had launched all her symptoms. And after its removal, there could never be any babies to challenge my ownership of the Palazzo Espagnol.

San Servolo was ready to receive my sister.

Finally, I re-instated my fat quack Doctor Inca, allowing him to restore himself to my good graces by several unspeakable acts of self-abasement about which the Reader need not intrigue or vex Himself. Let us just say I wanted the man back under my roof.

On a night soon approaching, his services would be indispensable.

Marcella Fasan

I looked at my wall, which Minguillo had distempered white as a novice's habit. I remembered how Santo's graceful shadow had walked upon it, growing smaller as it approached me.

Graceful as a snake, I thought now. Gianni told me Santo was forced out of Venice by Minguillo's threats.

So, I thought, *it must be true that Santo loved Amalia, for why else would Minguillo menace him and chase him off? Like a snake, Santo has shed his skin and wriggled away.*

'*I must have been mad,*' I wrote in my diary. I must have been mad to have dared to believe that Santo felt something of tenderness towards me. My eager eyes had been deceived by his sweet looks. My very first sight of his handwriting – and what could be truer than that? – had informed me in cruel detail just how mad had been my fantasies, how mad my arrogance to think I might be preferred by any man to the exquisite Amalia.

'*I must revolt my hands and eyes with humbler and less delicious meat.*' That was what he had written.

Only much later would I realize how mad I had been in those dwindling days to demonstrate my crushed hopes by my steadfast gazing at the wall, thus furnishing a perfect illustration of madness alike to all who tried to help or hurt me.

Sor Loreta

The Holy Fathers confirmed that I would continue to hold my position of *vicaria* indefinitely, even though sisters elected to office in the ordinary way must stand down after three years. My enemies, the light nuns, took their revenge in more acts of mockery and cruelty than I can write down.

Like Santa Rosa of Lima, I had always taken refuge from ridicule by throwing myself into good works, such as the growing of herbs and vegetables for the poor. My little courtyard was a paradise of cucumbers and gourds.

Santa Teresa of Avila explained that Our Heavenly Father loves the smell of flowers and refreshes His spirits upon them. So I grew flowers too.

I would have nothing but carnations, which symbolize obedience and penitence, and divine blue monkshood, whose seeds I had ordered from Cadiz, using the little part of my *peculios* that I kept for myself. No other nun could charm the roots of plants into such fecundity as mine showed. Only I – and Sor Sofia – knew that this was because I watered my little plants with drops of my own pure blood. When she saw me open my vein in the garden one evening, she took my hand and begged me not to do it. I should have taken more notice of her words in that moment. For it was the very first time that Sor Sofia revealed an unenlightened side of her character.

But I was distracted by the arrival of two new nuns from Puno on Lake Titicaca: Sor Narcisa and Sor Arabel. Both were red and raw from head to foot by their own hands. They had been sent away, I heard, because of the excesses of their penances, which had terrified the young novices of their former convent. They sought me out all hours of the day. They could not hear enough of my words and prayers. I knew that they had pledged themselves to me when I overheard the godless Rafaela refer to them as 'Sor Loreta's Jackals'.

Sor Sofia was frightened of Sor Narcisa and Sor Arabel. I saw it in her face and her little white hands that trembled whenever those two sisters were near.

Minguillo Fasan

The Sentimental Reader gives a chilly response to exits hastily stage-managed, without proper goodbyes. So let us usher Marcella off to the garden paradise of San Servolo with a touching little scene.

I went in to have one last look at my sister, who sat in her faded muslin morning dress with the everlasting white paper spread out luminous on her lap. But she had drawn nothing, and stared blankly ahead.

As usual, she started on seeing me, and lowered her eyes and then raised them to the wall. She was rising sixteen, a woman, or so the maids had told me. Certainly old enough to be declared a lunatic.

I asked her profile, 'And what shall we do with you now, Marcella?'

The wall remained the object of her fascination.

Given the support of the *Fatebenefratelli*, it had not proved difficult or overly expensive to persuade the state surgeon to write the necessary letter '*in nome della sovranità del popolo IL COMITATO DI SALUTE PUBBLICA . . .*'

To seal the bargain, I simply told him that in her state of badly saddened and frustrated *erotomania* Marcella had not only meditated upon but publicized a threat of self-destruction. That was enough. And indeed I am sure that Marcella would have wished to die, if she had known where she was going next.

I sent the hairdresser to her late at night, when the servants were abed, with specific instructions as to how to deal with her eyebrows. I admire to idolatry the Reader who has already divined what kind of a diagram I had prepared for him.

Part Three

Marcella Fasan

They came to take me in the dark hours.

Later I would learn that admissions were usually by night and most especially by full moon. The theory was that poor souls carried across the waters would be too overawed by the sight of the moon to howl at it. The moon-mesmerized patients were landed at San Servolo, wrenched from the boat and hustled through the corridors to a bed in one of the tiny rooms off the observation corridor, where they might lie alone and absorb the facts of their new lives until cock-crow.

My own journey to San Servolo was not so understated. It was necessary to uphold Minguillo's declaration that I was a '*turbolente*' and in need of stern confinement. At Minguillo's urging, the Brothers had sent my new gaolers fully equipped to show me as mad as possible: the two men had brought with them a kind of leather muff. They entered my room in the middle of the night and flipped me expertly out of bed. Without an opportunity to wash or dress, my arms were deftly strapped into the muff, with my fingers intertwined inside. The cords were then fastened around my back, so I hugged myself.

Struggling inside this equipment, I looked completely mad, of course. My sobs and screams were most convincing. Then there were my crazed eyebrows, courtesy of Minguillo's hairdresser. The young orderlies of the *Fatebenefratelli* looked on me with grim determination, and when they discovered that I was not dry, with disgust. Of course, I could not know it then, but I had just demonstrated as true everything they had been told about me.

The servants rushed down to the entrance hall in their nightshirts to protest.

'What's happened to her eyebrows?' shrieked Anna.

The San Servolites waved a white document headed with the stamp of the *Regno d'Italia* and its rampant rooster. This, I guessed, was Minguillo's work, though my brother was nowhere to be seen that night.

209

As if he could have slept through those shouted proceedings! My mother was also notable by her absence. It would be generous to suppose that Minguillo had drugged her supper.

In the midst of all the servants' wailing, Minguillo's quack waddled from his lodging on our first floor. He added his voice to those of the men, 'It is for the best. I have diagnosed her myself. The Conte Fasan has arranged it all.'

At this, the household staff dissolved into tears and farewells and exhortations of gentleness to the San Servolite men. Dear Gianni pressed a coin from his own pocket into the hand of the taller man. But I am ashamed to say I almost hated Gianni in that moment when I should have been so grateful to him. The servants were too quick, I felt, to count me as one lost.

Under the pretext of a last embrace with Anna, I whispered, 'There are a few papers in my room. Will you take them and hide them somewhere good? And tell no one?'

I wept silently all the way across the *bacino*. While we rocked and pulled through the inky water, I recalled the excited expression on Minguillo's face at my bedchamber door earlier that evening. He must have been living this scene in happy anticipation. I felt his glad eyes from behind his own room's curtains as the men carried me from our jetty to their boat.

In half an hour I was at San Servolo. By now I had realized that ardent protests would have made me seem yet more piteously demented, so I disembarked without a word or a whimper. I was escorted through a courtyard. We turned right into a stark corridor. One of many doors was nudged open by the knee of a nurse and a lamp lit inside a small, windowless cell with tall walls. I was laid into a trestle bed with a leather covering fastened all around. There was just a hole for my neck and head, which was laid gently on a pillow. That was how I passed my first few hours, blinking in the dark, my arms forcibly around myself, waiting for Minguillo's next surprise.

I was thirsty, I begged them, in the early hours. They gave me a sponge to suck. It must have been dipped in something soporific because then sleep fell like a black crow over my eyes. The next thing I knew, the sparrows were chanting outside and a priest was sitting quietly by my bed. He had a face that would have appealed to Cecilia Cornaro: so many things going on between his thoughts and his skin.

He balanced on his lap a long thin ledger, like a book of accounts. Its length was about fourteen inches and its width about eight. It was spread open, and I could see neat paragraphs underlined, six or so on each page. The priest leafed through the book till he arrived at the pages marked 'F'. There was a little space for me, bottom right, below the other madwomen of the tribes of 'F'.

'*Marcella Fasan*,' he wrote.

I stirred to show him I was awake. He hastened to remove my leather covering, so I might sit up. He showed no disgust at the dampness of my nightdress, and reached out a hand to shake mine.

'Padre Luigi Portalupi,' he smiled. 'I am pleased to meet you.'

He inscribed my notes so that I could see them, copying from the last night's document headed by the stamp of the *Regno d'Italia*.

'*Marcella Fasan, noblewoman, cripple, incontinent, conducted here by the staff of San Servolo, on May fifteenth, 1812, under the order of the police, being accused of a* Furore in utero, *with a consequent* ninfomania *that has led to a desire for immoral behaviour with a male person of citizen class.*'

He saw that I was reading what he wrote, and that it distressed me. 'I do not judge you,' and his voice was kind, 'this is a place of understanding, not punishment.'

I pardoned the Padre that he did not at first comprehend that I was the victim of a travesty. This man had only the information with which Minguillo had furnished him. And I could see, from the steady pace and quiet certainty of his writing, that he had tranquilly absorbed Minguillo's story in its entirety. Husbands he might doubt, if admitting inconvenient wives. But a brother – what reason could a brother have for wrongful committal of a sister?

Minguillo must have come over to the island well in advance to design my new fate. He would have seen to all the details. He would have acquired the crucial vocabulary. Then I remembered how I had seen Pinel's book open by my brother's bed the last time I went to his room to hide my diary.

An involuntary conspiracy had taken place. Luigi Portalupi was a good man, a decent man, who very unfortunately believed my brother, because the Padre himself had the gift of accepting unacceptable behaviour with understanding. So the priest's compassion easily extended to me, a poor *ninfomaniaca*, with an alleged *furore in utero*, and a stated history of *dissolutezza*. He would care for me even in that state. He had seen the worst human nature could conjure; he had looked after women damaged by love in every way, and now he accepted me as one of love's victims.

And indeed, perhaps I was rightfully classed as such, given Santo's love for my sister-in-law. How bitter I felt now at the charges against me – that I had lured a man into my bed! Santo had attended *my* bed solely for payment. All his desire had been for Amalia. And Minguillo had profited from it all, perhaps even setting his irresistible wife in Santo's way as a snare.

Now Minguillo would expect me to rave against my confinement. He would perhaps have our gondola row him over sometimes, just for the joy of hearing from the Brothers how desperately I pleaded my case, and how strenuously I defended my sanity.

It occurred to me that anything I said now in ignorance might be used against me. The Padre in front of me seemed kind, yet who was I to judge? My instincts had recently been proved wanting. And even if he was truly kind, was Padre Portalupi powerful? Were they all as kind as he? Unlike Minguillo, I had no idea how things operated on San Servolo, whether the inmates were treated as involuntary criminals or half-witted unfortunates by all employed there. It would be necessary to observe, to learn and to calculate how to best survive here, before I committed myself to speech.

So, from that moment on, I became a mute.

I held out my hand, indicating that I would like to see the book in which he was writing. Without hesitation, Padre Portalupi held it up to my eyes. I scanned the other entries: women admitted for *frenosi pellagrosa, melanconia con stupore, monomania impulsiva, temperamento pazzesco, melanconia semplice, frenosi alcolica.*

These were the sisters with whom I would share my life now.

Some of the entries showed a date of release – days or months after their arrival on the island. 'Returned to the family, *risanata,*' I read, 'made sane again.'

I pointed at one such entry, and smiled at Padre Portalupi. He smiled back. 'Why do you not speak, Marcella? I don't believe that you are mute.'

I shook my head, and pointed at some other entries on the page, some with crucifixes delicately drawn at the side.

'What does that mean, the little cross, is that what you wish to know?'

212

I nodded.

'That they died here.'

Gianni delle Boccole

I skulled oer secret with Anna to the island with a baskit of Marcella's little things. A priest tookt the baskit oft me and promist to give it her, kind nuff. But when we askt to see her, he sayed it were forbid, for she could not be disturbt by contact with the life what had originly damidged her mind. The priest lookt oer his spectickles at me n Anna all reproofing, as if to say, 'Do you want to make her madder with the sight of ye?'

Anna's face were orrible red n swelled up with crying, and twas true that the prospecked of her wunt cheer a body. As for me, I was so stiff with rage that I couldn't hardly sit back down in the boat, God with Horns On!

I called Minguillo a stack o swear-words out loud as we pulled way. Then some strong feelin made me look back at San Servolo. I bethought I saw a little white hand fluttering at a window. Yet then agin I wanted to see Marcella so much that I mite of made it grow in the frame o glass jist for me.

All the way back cross the lagune Anna told me dredful things what was wispered round Rialto bout San Servolo. They put women in a cold bath for one hour, six hours, twelve hours, depending on how mad they believed them women was. Under a wooden blanky that covered em to there necks so they could nowise move. Then they fizz-sicked em with bitter erbs and doused em with fifty more pail o cold water.

'That,' I sayed, feroshus grim, 'will kill Marcella faster than a gun.'

Then Anna cried so much ye would of had to put a bucket in each corner o the boat to catch all the tears.

'Couldn't Doctor Santo do something to get her out of there?' she sobbed.

'Twould be a death sentence for im to come back to Venice,' I risposted. 'I daren't een tell im where she is – he'll only come a-rushin back like lightning, which is probly jist what Minguillo wants, to loor im here for his thugs to beat on and kill to death. Santo *must not know*, ye unnerstand, Anna?'

She nodded. I swore under my breath. Minguillo ud cheated me again, he were so very smart for all-of-a-suddenness. And een if I could of found it, twere too late for me to bring out the will now that Marcella were offishal deklared a lunatick. I seen the law book pages marked with slits of paper in Minguillo's study – lunaticks can't own nothin, for they do not have the riotous possessing o there own minds.

Niver mind that the poor girl were not out of her mind no ways. Minguillo had hisself a peace o paper what sayed she was. His peace o paper were worth more than the one I ud lossed.

I had one spick of hope. The artist Cecilia Cornaro were finely back in Venice.

'Who are you?' she askt none too friendly when I walkt in the open door to her studio. Trunks n boxes n a large white bathtub was tumbled all oer the floor. She was alredy at her eezle. She saw me looking and beared her teeth. But I tested my metal and twere not found wantin. I cut to the hunt and stated my busyness. She yipped like a dog and threw a paintbrush out the window like a spear.

'The bastard!' she shouted. 'I'll see to it. San Servolo! The bastard!'

Then come a stream o words ye would not say to a gipsy with his hand in yer back pocket. Her eyes was like spirals of green when ye turn a sprig o clover in yer fingers fast as ye can. Them spiralling eyes made me too frit to otter one more word. I bethought she would go for my juggler if I did.

Summing ud appened to this Cecilia Cornaro. Some man, they sayed, had broke her heart, and now she were on the warpath agin all men who broked hearts, leastwise that is what I heared. I were sorry for her troubles, yet I were happy if her broke heart could bring any kind o vigger to the helping of Marcella.

214

Minguillo Fasan

The following may prove prejudicial to the digestion of the Squeamish Reader. For, well, well, well, it turned out to be true. Piero had indeed been taking Marcella to the artist Cecilia Cornaro for painting lessons, that is, until all such activities were brought, ahem, to a halt.

What? How did I learn this? Because the witch-haired harridan herself finally presented at the Palazzo Espagnol, demanding to be told what I had done with my sister. She still had the grime of a journey around her collar.

Our scene is my study. She clamoured her way in there, and then fell silent. She stood looking at me the way a cat scrutinizes a piece of bad meat. She examined my face as if I were not behind it. That was when it fell upon me hard, that all my noble contemporaries had got their faces painted by this woman. But my cold-hearted father had never cared enough for my face to commission Cecilia Cornaro or any other artist to immortalize it. Instead, he had got a painting done of Riva, not long before her death, as it happened. A seven-year-old daughter painted – and the son ignored!

Cecilia Cornaro seemed to be thinking the same thing. She said quietly, 'There are only two reasons why a man of quality does not have his only son painted. One is when he's been cuckolded and his wife has foisted some other man's issue upon him. The other is if that son shows himself unworthy to carry the family name to the next generation.'

She winked at me impudently, 'I would opine that I have found my man in possibility number two. The face says it all. And the clothes scream it.'

My skin tightened and my foot started drumming on the floor. No one had spoken to me like that, not since my father died. This woman had been a friend of Piero Zen. Had Pieraccio told her something to my detriment? And, if so, was this woman a model of discretion? Did she not have the ear of every vain and flighty noble, who came to her for a portrait, and required the entertainment of artistic gossip to speed the long still hours?

While I still sat with my mouth open, she bustled on to the reason for her visit: 'Now, get Marcella out of that madhouse! Why did you do a thing like that, you stupid boy? Did you really begrudge her the tiny amount she needs to exist out here in the living world?'

My mouth formed a reply but my lips opened and closed over it silently like a fish's in the water. Cecilia Cornaro took advantage. 'Go to it speedily and the San Servolites will restore your little heap of cash without too great a deduction for the inconvenience.'

Now she flashed a grin at me, as if the situation was resolved, 'In all seriousness, write your letter this minute, and I will perfect it for you – and we'll get her out before the surgeons open her up or freeze her to death in a bath. You can form your letters, can't you? One can never be sure with these bad seeds in the old families. I'll write it for you, even. Come now, set to it. You know you'll sleep easier with an upright conscience tonight.'

This rangy scrag of a woman was telling me how to live and who I was! Standing over me like an impatient governess. Who was she to speak? A person tolerated in society only because of her family and a spurious talent to flatter with a paintbrush. Her lovers notched up on her belt. Married, noble, ignoble, what did she care? Easing old worlders in her cock-loft by the half-dozen a night. And now *she* had come here to tell me my fortune and that I must fetch my sister off San Servolo?

She growled, 'If Marcella stays too long in there, she'll become one of them, at least in the eyes of everyone else.'

At which I smiled widely. 'I know,' I parried. 'It's notorious.'

For the first time Cecilia Cornaro stopped talking. Look at the colour draining out of her face! Look at the slender fingers clenching up – yes, especially look at those! She whispered, 'Marcella, why did you not tell me about your brother? Was I so . . . ?'

I had her shown out with scant ceremony. I told the servants that admittance to the Palazzo Espagnol was thereafter strictly denied to the immoral artist Cecilia Cornaro. Then I summoned certain men I knew from the Arsenale, men with bellies tautened by irregular employment. It did not cost much.

For what they did I never had any reproaches from her. She had learned something of how one deals with Minguillo Fasan.

Gianni delle Boccole

It were all oer Venice, that rotting busyness with Cecilia Cornaro's studio, n the burning of her hand. I went myself across the canal to the studio, to say sorry, for I were the one who had drawed her into this trouble.

The courtyard still had a feint smell of burning, and black ashes floated down from the beams from time to time. Peaces of faces, I guest, hornting the place. The vandals ud killed a hunnerd portraits alredy did, they sayed.

Up at her studio, there were a note stuck on the door saying, 'Gone painting in foreign parts. Cat will be hungry. Feed the brute.'

There were no need. A pile o chicken bones lay bout the floor, keeping company with fish head n fresh lamb chops, n a plate o coin left by them who haint had time to shop for the puss. So very many people ud alredy come a-seeking Cecilia Cornaro, as she would of known that they would: the cat hisself lay fat n greasy on the stoop, licking his nethers. I moved to go but the cat detained me with a paw cross my path. I dropt a coin what he batted expert into the plate, and nodded.

It were sayed about the town them days that Cecilia Cornaro ud left Venice for ever because she dint feel herself or her paintings was safe mong us. Twere a matter o shame for the city, to drive that genius woman way. So many Venetian faces lossed, because Cecilia Cornaro wunt record them now. What would appen to all them nobble famlies without faces now? How would they find rich furriners to get marrid to without there faces to send out for to advertise the bargain?

Marcella's bastert brother were heared to curse from attic to skirtin board when he could not have a Cecilia Cornaro likeness of his wife.

But I saw summing smug sneak across his face as he done so, Dog ovva God.

Minguillo Fasan

The _Fatebenefratelli_ sent me irritating little despatches about Marcella. They had misunderstood their role. The saintly doing-good Brothers wished to believe that they might cure my sister, thereby doing good by the spadeful. Padre Portalupi waxed enthusiastic about how quickly she might _come home to her family_. My crest drooped considerably when I belatedly realized that this was the desired outcome of all their treatments.

And damn her bladder too but did it not start to behave itself on the island? The especially-good Brother Portalupi boasted of the _farmacia_'s contra-diuretic potions and a diet excluding such foods as watermelon and asparagus. She was treated to warm baths instead of the twelve-hour cold ones I had so revelled in picturing.

Next Padre Portalupi wrote, under the impression that it would please me, that he had obtained excellent results in her damaged limb from the _Herbarium_ of Apuleis Platonicus. He drivelled on about wherwhet for soreness of the sinews and foot disease, hockleaf for irritation of the bladder, henbane for swelling of the privities and elder for water sickness and non-retention of the urine.

Also, the verdant peace of the island appeared to suit Marcella. I recalled now with bitterness how she had always liked gardens and greenery, until I terminated her lyrical country rambles decisively when she was nine.

At the time there were not more than fifty other lunatics domiciled at San Servolo. Marcella was kept separately from the violent ones and the poor ones. As a _dozzinante_, or paid-for lodger, she occupied a pleasant high-ceilinged room above the reception area, looking over towards the islands of La Grazia and San Clemente: a view that rivalled my own from the windows of the Palazzo Espagnol. As if that were not luxury enough, I was soon pestered by Padre Portalupi for an allowance that Marcella might purchase books to read and paper to write and draw upon.

I refused the book and paper money: '*It is my opinion, knowing her from an infant, that books would be injurious to my sister. Her brain is not to be taxed. Her animal economy will be deranged or even destroyed by too much intellectual strain. In the meanwhile, I have been reading about some very interesting new treatments of leeches applied to the pubis and thighs in cases very like my sister's . . .*'

Padre Portalupi wrote back that, while he respected my opinion, and accepted that I would not defray expenses for new books, he had decided to open the library to my sister, under supervision, that she might read history, science, languages and other improving subjects.

'*Paper,*' he declared, '*is never denied to our patients, no more than water or air.*'

His quiet defiance, and the between-the-lines implication of my meanness, filled my mouth with acid. I wanted to write and insist upon those leeches, but I dared not provoke an argument at this stage. The stamping and verifying of documents for Marcella's official committal dragged on and on, which meant that I as yet relied on informal boarding arrangements with the Brothers to keep her on San Servolo.

I received one note after another on her excellent progress.

'*Interestingly, her eyebrows have grown back to a shape of perfect symmetry.*'

'*She is no longer afraid when her door opens, but smiles tranquilly on every nurse. She has mastered some gymnastic exercises and grows stronger daily.*'

'*She follows our regime without question. Her courses are regular. She takes her medicine without protest.*'

I countered, '*But has she confessed her sins, and undergone a moral cure?*'

'*Your sister,*' Padre Portalupi replied, '*does not speak, as you know. Yet she has given us to understand by the civility and gentility of her behaviour that she is morally cured. Indeed, sometimes I worry that she grows almost too docile . . .*'

I strode up and down my study in a fury. Morally cured? Was that enough to send her home? Marcella had played her silent card well. No respect to the Gracious Reader, but can He conjure sufficient disgust for this priest's weak mind?

I supposed that I must add Padre Portalupi to my little stock of enemies, now including Doctor Santo, Cecilia Cornaro, the Spanish madam and the will-thief, all but the latter firmly and finally dealt with.

Doctor Santo Aldobrandini

I found work and a bed in a monastery near Treviso where the sick were taken in. I wrote to tell Gianni where I was, and to ask for news. For the longest time, he did not answer me. So I knew there was nothing good to tell. Marcella, I understood, still believed that I loved Minguillo's wife.

Meanwhile, after ignoring me for several years, Napoleon again took an interest in my career. If he ever needed surgeons, it would be in his new war against the Tsar of Russia.

By the spring of 1812, I was caught up in the flotsam of the thirty-two thousand Italian soldiers dragged by the currents of fate towards the Russian front with criminally few provisions to feed us. Come September, the starving Grande Armée was walking down the empty streets of Moscow, looking for bread and beds. Our resentful campfires soon burned the wooden city down. By October, we had caught sight of our true enemies: cold and the ineptitude of those who failed to keep us fed and clothed. On November 5th, the first snow fell. After that all I remember is hunger, and whiteness, and my scalpel tapping on frozen flesh.

The image of Marcella's face imprinted itself on the snow. I saw her features in the drifts, as my hands busied themselves amputating frostbitten digits. During the retreat from Moscow I learned everything I would ever need to know about the effect of cold on human skin.

It was at this time that Napoleon ceased to be my textbook. He no longer seemed indestructible. I did not see it as Napoleon losing, but as his diseases winning. My patient was failing: next it would be the turn of the priest. Only a very sick man would have spent a whole Grande Armée upon a mad delusion of snowbound empire.

I raised my head the day we limped back into Italy. For months it had slumped down with my defeats – for I counted each man I lost to the cold a grievous, wrenching failure – or hunched between my shoulders against the ice and the winds that blew from Siberia.

But that day I thought I could smell the sea, or at least a small lagoon in the crook of the Adriatic. Nothing belonged to me in that place, but I belonged there. Marcella was there. I had now seen the invincible Napoleon in mortal retreat: nothing was impossible. I no longer believed that anything could keep me from her. And I was no longer interested in reasons why I should keep away.

I returned to the monastery at Treviso and began to make plans for my return to Venice. After all those silent months, I took up my pen and wrote once more to Gianni.

Sor Loreta

There was one day when a sudden recurrence of my brain fever caused me to slap the smirking face of Rafaela, who appeared at my cell to take her sister back to her own. Perhaps I pulled her hair a little, too. They claimed I tried to gouge her eyes in my passion, yet these must be slanders for I remember nothing of it.

After that I saw Sor Sofia not at all. Madre Mónica forbade her to come to me. I was not allowed to go to her.

'You are dead to Sor Sofia,' the *priora* told me. 'I have permitted you to exploit the poor child's gentle nature for too long. This time your separation from her is final, *vicaria* or no *vicaria*.'

I had a sensation as if I was being stripped of my own skin, more painful than any scourge I had ever employed on myself. When I opened my mouth to protest, the *priora* said spitefully, 'You have your Jackals to play with now.'

It was never God's design that things should turn out this way, so I decided instead to mourn Sor Sofia as if *she* were dead.

I announced that I was fasting to save the soul of Sor Sofia from centuries in Purgatory. I used my allowance to have masses said for her. I wrote her name on the walls of my cell, picking out the letters in my own pure blood.

Sor Narcisa and Sor Arabel came to me, and offered to scourge themselves on Sor Sofia's behalf, but I sent them away with hard words. 'You never loved Sor Sofia as you should,' I told them. 'You were jealous of her.'

I lay on my bed with my body rigid in the shape of the cross. The rosary could not be pried from my hand. In that time I drank only gall mixed with bitter herbs, and, like Clare of Pisa, I allowed no solid food to pass my mouth unless it was mixed with ashes. They took away the ashes from my hearth. Then, like the Holy Virgin Mechtild of Magdeburg, I would eat only the Eucharist, and always experienced rapture and the taste of pure honey in my mouth when I did so. Back in my cell, I wept copious tears into a lachrymatory bottle, which I placed as an offering in front of my *hornacina*.

In spite of all my fasting and my flagellation, when I took my bath I could not help noticing that my body had remained as white as snow and that even though I approached my forty-third year I still seemed like a very young girl in physical appearance. I was strong as an Amazon, yet without a morsel of sinewy bulk: my strength came entirely from my soul. My breasts were almost non-existent, and my flanks were free from womanly curves. Since I began to fast, I had rarely suffered the indignity of the monthly courses that weaken ordinary women. From this I knew how much my purity had pleased my Celestial Spouse: an uncorrupted body is one of the sure signs of sanctity. This is proved in the story of Jacinta di Atondo, who had a boil removed by a sceptical surgeon, a non-believer. Instinctively feeling her holiness, he kept that boil. Twenty years later it was still as fresh and undecayed as the day he removed it. Jacinta di Atondo's boil won that surgeon over to our true God.

The *priora* came to my cell and showed her complete incomprehension of the ways of God by speaking to me severely. She tried to tell me that my feelings for Sor Sofia were unwholesome, and a symptom of my brain fever returning.

'This fever is not of earthly origin,' I told her. 'Look,' I affirmed, 'God will not allow me to eat.'

And I took up a piece of bread that lay beside my bed, and put it into my mouth. But immediately my jaws clamped on it, a great wave of nausea surged through me. The bread, against my will, was ejected from my mouth along with a jet of bile straight on to the *priora*'s habit.

I declared, 'So you must acknowledge that it is a superior force that prevents me from taking food. I can swallow only the Body and Blood of Christ. Alpaïs of Cudot lived for forty years on the Eucharist alone, and took food into her mouth only to suck the juices, spitting out the pulp. Indeed' – and I looked at the stain on her habit significantly – 'a piece of fish spat out by Alpaïs of Cudot was saved as a holy relic by one of her enlightened company.'

'True virtue is free of pride and ambition, Sister,' snarled the *priora*, wiping the bread and bile off her clothing with a disgusted look on her face. 'And why must you always talk of food? Why must I and everyone else around you always talk of what you do not eat?'

Then she spoke slowly and clearly, as if to someone deaf. 'Sor Sofia is not dead, do you hear? The other nuns – and the poor child herself – find it sinister that you carry on so. This stupid hysterical ploy will not work, Sor Loreta. Cease this ostentatious fasting and live like a humble nun. That is all you are, don't you understand? Humility of heart is what Jesus showed and asked.'

She cried out in a frustrated way, 'You have lived in God's beautiful house for three decades without absorbing any of His insight. Your soul has not developed; even your fanatical acts are tediously repetitive. Stop these exaggerated virtuosities, these pretended prodigies! If you want to attract attention with a novelty, then you should crucify your tongue instead of subjecting us all to its pompous rants!'

At this blasphemy she stopped herself short, looking ashamed. 'For that last, I apologize profoundly. You made me lose control of myself, Sor Loreta. That was my weakness. I shall go to confess directly. Nevertheless, you have been warned. One more offence and I promise you that I shall have you stripped of the title of *vicaria*. I hate to bring them into convent affairs, but even the Holy Fathers, who elevated you beyond your capacity, will see sense if I explain to them this persecution of poor Sor Sofia. So you might as well eat. Otherwise, you will die a ridiculous, and, I promise you, *obscure* death.'

It came to me then, the bitter realization, that only in the powerful position of *vicaria* could I save Sor Sofia's soul: I could not do so as a despised humble nun without worldly position. So though my heart longed to see my body dead, I forced myself to give up my vigil, keep down a little stale and mouldy bread, and return to the world.

Marcella Fasan

How many lunatics' tales does one read from their own pens? Their stories are missing, like their persons. Mad people are excluded from society. Others become the custodians of their stories. Those custodians name their conditions, as a writer names his characters.

I did not fit tidily into any of the normal categories, *frenosi pellagrosa, melanconia con stupore, monomania impulsiva, temperamento pazzesco, melanconia semplice, frenosi alcolica*. I was neither a living skeleton, nor grossly fat nor cauliflower-eared. And yet I would pass two years among other souls whose stories were in custody. I shared their table, their bread, their purges. By day I lived with the lunatics, and as one of them. Only at night did I withdraw to my privileged private room, where I resumed my habits of autobiography and sketching, having found a convenient niche behind my chimney breast in which to hide my paper.

Being a *dozzinante*, I was not required to work, but I went daily to the printing workshop and learned the science of etching. My colleagues knew nothing of my noble blood, and cared yet less. They were pleased with my nimble fingers and, when I showed that I knew colour, then they let me tint etchings for special editions by hand.

Once I was set to cutting an etching of a portrait made by Cecilia Cornaro. On that day I broke down in tears and was subjected to a rare forced bath, Padre Portalupi being away and unable to save me from his zealous colleagues.

Clearly, my brother hoped that by living with lunatics I would become one of their number. He thought that their taint would envelop me, and that I would breathe in their ravings and expel them through my own mouth eventually. And he knew, as I did, that the more time I passed at San Servolo, the more others would come to accept that I was mad.

At first I struggled to be my sane self. But it was so achingly lonely to hold myself aloof from the society in which I found myself. The priests and surgeons plainly saw me as a patient. And the patients embraced me as one of them. Those without visible deformities of their own were sorry for my mutilated leg and even bent to kiss the air near it. They threaded flowers through the wheeled chair that was sometimes used to take me round the verdant gardens. Tentative hands appeared to guide me over broken steps. The white of the bread was placed reverently on my plate.

Padre Portalupi was unfailingly kind. Only one person, apart from Piero, had ever been so gentle with me. And he – I had seen the evidence of how he had betrayed me with my sister-in-law. He had walked across my heart to get to her.

Perhaps San Servolo was the right place for me, I thought: a place for people damaged by love and life. What was I if not distorted and harmed by both?

I must revolt my hands and eyes

There was comfort to be had in acceptance, and I, increasingly, took it.

Gianni delle Boccole

Still, they wunt let us visit her. A month passed, another month. A summer. A year.

I niver stopt hoping that Marcella would show her sound brain to the doctors and that they would send her back to us at the Palazzo Espagnol. *She* were nowise the rampin mad one in the family. I bethought, *surely the doctors will see it clear*. The *Fattybenfratelli* were good men, famoused healers. They would realize they ud been sold the wrong cut o meat. Wunt they? Wunt they?

Each time I heared Minguillo tell the gondolier 'San Servolo!' I hoped, *Save us, this is the time he is not coming back. They will exchange him for his sister and keep him there.*

Each time he come back, Robber-God!

Ventually Minguillo deceased his visits. Insted Anna were hallowed to take Marcella some things ovva personal kind, and visit with her for a few short minutes.

Anna come back with her apron soakt in tears. She told me, 'Marcella is a dead woman walking. There is no light behind her eyes. She does not speak.'

'Not speak?'

'She gives out that she is mute. Why would she do that, Gianni?'

'She must fear that they wunt believe her if she speaks.'

'So she could stay there for ever, and let them think she is really mad? No! She is one of them now,' she wept. 'To see her like that!'

But Anna were wrong: I were sartin on it. Marcella had not lossed her mind. She ud put it away somewhere for safe-keeping on San Servolo. When it were safe, Marcella would be sane agin. I were sure on it, Dear Little God.

Minguillo Fasan

Finally, I received one letter that worried me more than the rest – Portalupi told me that he feared that if she stayed too long on San Servolo, my sister might become 'habituated' and incapable of leaving the island to resume normal life.

'*She must leave,*' he wrote, '*lest we do more harm than good.*'

'Habituated' had such a good ring to it. A conclusive, excluding ring, the next best thing to the tolling of a funeral bell. In fact, the word had something of the cloister about it, with the cloister's dulled finality.

But Padre Portalupi did not agree. 'Habituated' was to be avoided at all costs, he insisted, and he already saw dangerous signs of it in Marcella's behaviour.

'*It is necessary for the mother bird to push the baby out of the nest sometimes,*' he drivelled in his godly tight hand, '*for the good of the little bird.*'

I ransacked my desk for a certain piece of paper and hurried to the island, thinking of the little birds I had impaled on sticks at our country estate. I was ushered upstairs to the office of Padre Portalupi.

'Let me see her,' I insisted, without preamble. 'I would like to see what miracles you have performed on her. Because when I last saw her she was not ready to leave the nest, pushed or not.'

Padre Portalupi did not hide his surprise at my abrupt arrival. 'I could have saved you a trip, Conte Fasan. I am sorry to tell you that Marcella has specifically said that she does not wish to see you.'

'She spoke?'

'Yes, for the first time, when I told her that I considered her fit for an existence outside this place. She then said a few words, and they were all perfectly sensible.'

My little lame dog of a sister had told him something to my detriment, I supposed. She was playing with me, using this doing-good Brother as her cat's paw.

'Then how can she come home? If she won't see me?'

That silenced him.

'Given that I pay, and pay handsomely, to have her accommodated here, how is it that I have no rights to see my sister? You calmly tell me that her furious exacerbations are cured and you want to foist her back upon my household, without permitting me to see for myself if it is true! I would imagine that the officers of the *Magistrato alla Sanità* would be interested to hear of such a case.'

There dawned on Padre Portalupi's face the beginnings of an understanding that it was not convenient for him to have. Fortunately, I had come prepared with an accessory to sway his thinking in the right direction. I opened, 'Do not worry yourself unduly, Father. I could not conceive of doing anything to hurt poor Marcella. In fact, as you know, I have a strong interest in the salvation of lunatics. Researching establishments of this kind in foreign countries, I have discovered a most excellent English contraption to help Marcella when the fits of *ninfomania* come upon her, as they surely will, when she is exposed once more to the world. I have already commissioned one of *these* for her bedchamber.'

I handed Padre Portalupi a sketch. It was a crude representation of my sister with a stout iron ring riveted about her neck. A short chain passed from that to an upright iron bar bolted to the wall.

Padre Portalupi blanched. 'Th . . . *this* is how you will keep Marcella if we send her home?'

'For everyone's safety, the best course, don't you think? It can't help resting her, feeling so secure. And remember, I have male servants and women and children in the house! The fortune-hunter might be lurking! Of course, as soon as she is ready to see me, I shall take her home to the bosom of her family. It will be nothing less than a celebration for us. Why, Marcella has a baby niece she has never yet met!'

'And no nephews?'

I thought I had him cowed, but the man was cruelly apt. Again, I had a shuddering inkling that Marcella was pulling his jaw-strings from some hidden apartment. I looked around for her cornflower eye at a knot-hole in the wall. I was certain that I was being secretly watched. That sensation undermined the working of my tongue and I stammered for a full minute without coming to the end of a single word. My foot drummed on the floor. Inside my tight skin, my heart too stuttered to a standstill and I heard a sick creaking in my soul, as when a mast splinters preparatory to shipwreck.

Finally I got it out, 'A nephew is forthcoming.'

Padre Portalupi accepted my parting handshake, yet I saw doubts on his face.

The *medico-religioso* would be more tractable, I divined. I went home to write him a confidential letter. After that, there would be no more need for me to make upsetting personal visits to San Servolo.

I sealed the letter and nestled deep in my father's chair.

And so comfortable was I in that moment that I experienced a visceral, almost venereal itch to write down my triumph, an account starting with the delightful ploy of the confected letter to my wife from the little doctor Santo, who might never more return to Venice to plague us with his ineffectual seductions.

I was so absorbed in this cheerful work, dwelling on my masterful timing and subtle touches, that I did not notice my simpleton of a valet hovering close behind me with a silver tray on which reposed a midnight-blue velvet toque, the latest masterpiece by my tailor.

'*Was it not ingenious?*' I finished with a flourish, reiterating and summing up in a few simple words designed to help the Duller of my Readers comprehend such an artfully complex tale.

Then I felt Gianni's breathing on my neck.

I turned around to see him staring vaguely like a goat in a field.

Marcella Fasan

My diary from that time makes disquieting reading. I remember little of those months myself. I still worked in the print-shop but gradually the languor of the other Tranquil Lunatics invaded my own soul and I ceased to be as I was; rather I became a floating, faded self, only loosely tethered to what I used to be. Here is an extract of what I wrote, that good Padre Portalupi kept for me all these years. The words were accompanied by many a pencilled sketch of fairylike and somnolent beings in a bowery island world.

'*High windows slash light all over our faces, down to our chins, but below that we are in darkness. We bodiless phantoms steal about, lowering our heads until only our foreheads are illuminated and our brains, those diseased things, the wrongness of which had brought us here, are shown as the only living part of our bodies.*

'*Shadows of door handles frighten us.*

'*Those corridors burn up summer light like flues. And at the end of them, all who interpose themselves between us and the light turn into blurred spiders, their bulbous thoraxes and debatable quantities of limbs a terror to us. The floors are tesserated like rich honeycomb, yet broken like a derelict hive. My friends Marta and Fabrizia fear bees. This is their kingdom . . .*

'*. . . The mad are often pigeon-toed, and they hang their heads and sometimes reach into their small-clothes, looking for consolation. We will put our heads down anywhere, these heads are so heavy, against tabletops, architraves, anything to take the weight of the heads. On bad days, we slump to the floor and let our knees take the weight of these heads. Rare visitors will often see two heads* *bending together to hold up the mutual weight – what mad cyclopses we are at San Servolo, these years!*

'I speak of the Tranquil Lunatics now, like Marta and Fabrizia and Stella, who are allowed to work at their old trades and live in dormitories, which is regarded as a promotion and a sign of getting better. When they are bad, lunatics live differently.

'In their netted cages the violent lunatics roar, or poke a delicate finger out, like Hansel in the story. But we are safe from these clamorosi, inquieti, pericolosi and turbolenti. They must be isolated from us. We do not even know their names. Their enclosure allows out only their noises and one finger at a time.

'Sometimes we go to a secret place where we can watch them ripping their curtains, screaming and whistling and making themselves naked.

'They take off their clothes and they fling their private parts about for all to see, amusing those who have collected enough wits to be amused with for a temporary spell. And another one is down, on the floor, his hands up as if he is pushing a barrow . . .

'. . . This week Stella and Fabrizia are milked by the visiting French doctors of our anecdotes. How those men love to hear the Venetian lunatics raving! Stella tells me, "When we make them happy, we are given extra wine by the servants who have been bribed by the surgeons." The kind Fatebenefratelli cannot supervise every transaction on the island. Some of the most important ones are hidden from them in the workshops, in the haystacks, in the curtained part of the chapel.

'The French doctors follow us while we work. Mad people must work or our brains will devour us. Men who were farmers grow food for us. Seamstresses like Marta mend our torn costumes. Cobblers make our leather restraints. I myself colour etchings in the print-shop. When we do good work, quietly and steadily, then we are given good things from the kitchen, so we can learn the merit of giving of ourselves without fussing and displays . . .

'. . . My hands are raw with soap and water today. The mad people clean everything all of the time. We whitewash the walls, we scrub the floors, we change the straw pallets of the beds. I myself am not forced to do these things, for I am somehow different from the others, they tell me. But I do, for I know that these activities keep us clean in spirit and in flesh. All this cleanliness stops us from growing black like dirt inside and killing ourselves in dirty ways.

'I am growing flesh. They feed us at the exact same time each day, for regular habits, they say, will break our mad inner indiscipline. The refectory is under the special supervision of the priests, who are kind and always tell us to eat calmly and quietly. The clamorosi are denied the benefit of eating in company. They must eat in their cells so no one is upset when they use their bowls as chamber pots or paint the walls with porridge . . .

'. . . Fabrizia and I love to lie in the sun, when it comes, to drink the heat into our empty middles. When one of us lies in the sun, it puts it in all our minds to align ourselves to its caressing rays, and we behave madly, forming clusters of mad sunners, looking worse for our multiplicity.

'It is an airy place, San Servolo. The windiness of the island does not please everybody. When the scirocco comes, it comes hard, and the exhalations of the sea on certain days make Stella uneasy under her skin, especially at night. Marta and Fabrizia and Celia are affected by the winds known as the bora or the levante or the tramontana. On San Servolo we soon learn who howls in each wind, and who revels in it . . .

'. . . By night the dormitories are lit with oil lamps high up on the walls. Two nurses sleep in each dormitory, while four wakened ones pass the dark hours walking around and tending to every need, and exploring every little noise from the beds. The medico-religioso visits us all each night, even me, who sleeps high up in my dozzinante bedchamber. Marta says he is looking for new lunatics to chop up for his experiments. He likes to examine our skin for lesions, for we lunatics are very prone to diseases of our surfaces. By touching our spots and rashes, the hard-faced doctor with the blood on his apron reads our maladies like sheet music. All the girls put their heads under the blankets when he passes by. But we like the other priests who come, for they hold our hands and whisper gentle things in our ears that help us sleep . . .

'. . . Now it is the winter and so we are woken at six-and-a-half in the morning, and made to wash ourselves and then go out into the fresh air. We wear woollen stockings and cloth jackets, with a copetto di bambace, woolly waistcoat under our cloth coats. And berets over the tops of our poor heads. Then we are sent to do whatever work we are capable of, and the medico-religioso and his men do their rounds among us, looking for anyone who needs a special bath . . .

'. . . Now it is the spring again and they begin to rouse us at five. We wear canvas shirts, stockings, shoes and canvas jackets of mixed colours, each with a kerchief.

'There is a new girl called Lussieta who pulls her head under her clothes, leaving a wound of a neck in an empty collar and a clenched hand holding her cloth roof together with an elbow planted on a tablecloth embroidered like a field of flowers. We are all fine mathematicians at San Servolo – for lack of other employment sometimes we count those flowers on the tablecloths, the shiny tiles, the kicked and beaten skirting boards, the arched windows.

'We stare at people the way children do just before someone admonishes them severely. Marta's hair is rampant like haystacks in the wind but then we all hang our heads down, down, looking towards Hell.

'Lussieta has a dolly and she defends her with fists. If we were allowed, we would button ourselves into ten concentric shirts in case someone comes to diminish us. That way we would always have another layer of protection against what they wish to expose.

'When we eat, we put our faces too close to our bowls, for we are too anxious. If we drop our food, we will seem mad, so we eat in a mad way instead in order to assure our keepers that we are sane . . .

'. . . Cross-hatched by the shadows of bars, the man who says he knows more than me, one day leads me away with a firm hand on the upper arm. The elbow is for polite society. Fortunately a tall nurse catches us before we get to the back of the carpentry workshop. There are sharp things there, the nurse tells us kindly, and we must not be there alone . . .

'. . . We love corners and we show it by kissing them. We skim the walls like creatures at the bottom of the ocean – even we find that comical so we grin, and they say "Look, what a lunatic grin!" and it is all confirmed.

'We can furrow our brows like a field ploughed by diamond blades, and some days we like a few of our buttons undone; it means that we are only temporarily mad and could soon be buttoned up again.

'We sit low in front of our keepers, so their eyes are safely above our heads.

'We mostly sit and look at our hands, or straight ahead, or at the floor. Not at each other, because we do not trust lunatics any more than you would.

'We like to place our eyes against little slots for a long time. Keyholes. Box lids. Saucepan lids.

'You will see us crouched with our knees up around our necks more than anything else and if made to sit on a chair then we will form the perfect "S", our backs hard against the chairback, our heads bent lower than our chests, our legs splaying out and backwards.

'If there are two chairs side by side, we like to sit on the floor in the space between the two.

232

'We run to fat and thin yet we are mostly appallingly ordinary. Those who suffer with the Pellagra may be known by their smell like bread that has gone to the mould. In fact the doctors say that the insane have a particular fetor, like fermenting henbane, which can be discovered on entering their rooms first thing in the morning, when it is strongest. The French doctors declare that the breath of maniacal persons is tale-tellingly unpleasant and others compare it to stinking fish. We cannot smell ourselves, however, perhaps because we are too mad even in our noses.

'We hold our own hands nearly all the time, it is frightening to be among the smelly lunatics like this.

'We undo each other's clothing like monkeys and we cry a lot when we see the bits of the other lunatics spilling out. We are curious but not that curious.

'Marta and Fabrizia, who have the Pellagra, look up to the left and the right at the same time, as if two people are calling them at once.

'We show everyone everything that occurs to us – our toenails and a leaf on the tree are often demonstrated to visitors. We would like to retain some privacy as to our bowel movements, and even to hoard them inside us, yet our keepers are most attentive on that matter, administering purgatives at the least opportunity. And they will give us vomits too, if they can.

'On our bad days, purged and vomited, you will afterwards see us in postures as if gunpowder had blown us in the air and dropped us from a great height . . .

'. . . Sometimes we are here because we are ugly. Marta's hairline stoops, Fabrizia's ears jut, Celia's nose grows like industry, there is one girl – Marta says her mouth must have been ripped off a monkey's phizog – sometimes I feel my hands are too big for my little body. Some of us are dry where we should be moist or wet where we should be dry. We frighten people. We must be put away somewhere for our own good, so that those poor frightened people cannot hit us, which is a natural reaction, because we are so ugly or strange, and we upset them because they worry the same thing could befall them.

'They keep mirrors away from us as the sight of our mad selves will rot our brains even faster.

'Most of my friends do not talk very much. Even with Marta and Fabrizia, I do not speak. Talk has brought us all trouble. Talk will give the cutting priest an excuse to cut.

'This silence is what befalls those who are not loved, what befalls the humbler and less delicious meat, to whom others are preferred.'

233

Gianni delle Boccole

Now that I finely knowed by what dirty trick Minguillo ud divvyded them, I bethought I could put em back together.

I ud been an asp. In all that time I niver bethought of Santo bein akshual handy, insted of pining way to a flake o skin for love o her or rushin back to Venice to get himself murdered all useless. But Santo of all people would have a scuse to go to the island, with all his doctoring scills isn't it. A plan begun to unroll in my head.

I knowed where he were, at a small monastery near Treviso, working for a pittance and splintin up his own cracked heart. After he got chased out o Venice, he n me ud writed to one another, in an empty kind o way, to keep Marcella alive in our thoughts. But he had no consoling for me, and I had no good news for him, for Marcella never wanted to hear his name. So the letters ud traled way like his hopes.

By the time Marcella were took to San Servolo, the letters from Santo had deceased coming altogether. Mine to him was sumtimes returned, unopened.

But all ovva suddenly Santo ud writed to me agin. Turned out that in fact Santo had betook hisself far beyont my letters, and joined the Grond Armay in Russia. O that, he writed little.

There were a new voice in his writing. He dint just ask bout Marcella, he demanded to know bout her. He were waiting on a risposte.

I took out the dred quill and ink. I told him what had appened. About the false letter, Marcella's mad-seeming staring at the wall, the shaved eyebrows, San Servolo n all. I knowed he would come a-running. I also knowed he would be feroshus angry at me for holdin back the true story all this time.

Course twere still nowise safe for him to come home to Venice. Not as himself. Yet. But I had a plan for that continency too. Twere so bold n clever! I were sure as pigs goes into pots that twould straitway placket Santo's rage with me. And the beauty of it were – I ud seen Minguillo write in his own hand that he ud no need to visit San Servolo any more.

And yes, Santo grasped it in a minit. I dint have to put the wheedle on him, oh no. He were determined to give my plan a try and he had extra imbellishments for it too, what made it een better.

And so twere that them priests on San Servolo got thereselves a letter from a young lay-doctor by the name o Spirito, of unpeckable credenshals, who wisht to work among the Venetian lunatics and speshally to treat the flictions of there skins. He were give a most positive risposte, and in days Santo – I mean Spirito – were on his way back to Venice.

Ha! I bethought. *Minguillo will be foiled at last, this'll put some pepper in his gravy.*

And as for Santo, why, when I went for to meet him at Mestre, I found a different creecher in the altogether from the pale boy Minguillo ud sent packing. The war in Russia ud markt him. He lookt taller, more sustanshal, n een the timber o his voice had more pith to it, tho allus gentle like a dove. And there were summing more, too. He what had niver afore knowed the love ovva mother or a sister, had known at last what tis to adoor a woman, and to love her threw n threw, not jist to study her skin and cure its ills. So far Love haint did im any favours, but I bethought the new Santo had it in him to be Love's footsoldier like they say in poitry.

'I should knock you down, Gianni,' he growled at me. 'You had no right to decide what I should know about Marcella. Or not know.'

He advanced on me and I bethought I were in for a pasting. But all ovva suddenly Santo hogged me close, hard n strong. Then he laffed, a good strong laff, full of daring do.

I held my breath and hopt, Dear Good Little God.

Sor Loreta

Then a terrible thing happened. Because I had drawn attention to Sor Sofia, others began to show a special interest in her. At first this was certainly designed specially to irritate and hurt me, who was strictly forbidden intercourse with her. But quickly others began to actually see the unique beauty of Sor Sofia's soul that previously I alone had detected.

Sor Sofia was starting to attract a mob of admirers, drawn by the curve of her downturned eyelid and the pretty gestures of her tiny white hands.

It was God's design for me to keep a watch on Sor Sofia – from a distance – for I now suspected in her the stirrings of another Sor Andreola, another vain hypocrite set on her own cult. And sure enough, it was not long before others were comparing Sofia with the departed Sor Andreola, and favourably, and it got so that some of the novices knelt down as she passed, and made other blasphemous gestures of idolatry. When I myself passed by, some of the light nuns took to crossing themselves, as if Satan were among them.

Marcella Fasan

Anna came with a basket of pies and such news. I found her eyes very shiny. I tried to pull my thoughts back together. I did not start well, for it was such a long time since I had spoken aloud.

'Are you a lunatic come to join us?' is what came out of my mouth, and it was not what I meant at all. She flinched away.

'You can speak!' she cried, when she recovered herself. 'They told me you don't talk.'

'There are bad doctors here. Cutting doctors with blood on their aprons. It is not safe to show them what we think. But I talk with you, Anna. I always talked with you, did I not? With you and Gianni?'

I tried to remember how it had been between her and me, before I came here and became one of the folk of this village. This meant swimming to the surface of my mind, where the waves crashed. It was more tranquil and more slow down there below in the calm white emptiness, where I had been living with my friends for some time now.

Anna's face kept forcing me to leave the still deep, and to break the skin of my element. It hurt. It hurt. Memories surged back into my head. My heart darkened when I recalled how Santo, while all the time ministering to me in the tenderest ways, had in fact fallen in love with my beautiful sister-in-law and used his visits to me as a cover for stealing glimpses of *her*. I had seen the letter myself. I pulled my eyelids down to erase the remembered sight of it.

I did not want to think about these things any more. I wanted to be in a corner, with Fabrizia or Marta warm and quiet beside me, and to let my head slowly fill again with warm whiteness.

But Anna insisted on speaking of Santo. With that name in my ears, I could not keep my inner self white and soft and impervious to everything. It was as if someone had cast a line down into the deep where I had gone and dragged me back up, swooping and undulating, back to the cruel place where I had to remember that Santo loved my sister-in-law and desired her, and only pretended to care for me.

Yet now Anna, stumbling over delicacy, was telling me something new. She was telling me that it was not true, what I had believed for so long. She explained that Minguillo had seen how Santo looked at *me*. And how I looked at him. Then my brother had used his wife's famous fascinations as a means to his end. In short, Minguillo had written that hurting letter himself and left it for me to find.

'Gianni saw your brother writing the whole story down. He was boasting about it! That is how we found out.'

So Santo had never loved my sister-in-law? Had never written those cruel words?

I must revolt my hands and eyes

So many months of misery could not simply be wiped away by Anna's words. Perhaps this was an elaborate fiction sent to tempt me back to life on the surface? No, I could not yet think the surface a safe place.

'Stop,' I told her. 'No more.'

But she continued to speak, moving on to one more new thing, which was that Santo would soon come to the island, under a false name, to work as a doctor.

'All so he can be close to you, whom he adores!' Anna insisted, for my face was still frozen. 'You must understand, Miss Marcella. Why else would he do this, except for love of you? He is in love to his bones, that boy!'

'But my brother . . . ?'

'Minguillo wrote that he doesn't need to come to San Servolo any more. He thinks his work is done here.'

Belief stole up on me then, like a shutter opening on a sunrise. My hands prickled. Suddenly I knew it was true, everything that Anna had said. Had I ever seen Santo's handwriting before the day I found that letter? I had not. I had fallen into Minguillo's trap like a foolish mouse. Worse, I myself had rejected and hurt Santo – by Minguillo's design. My closed-tight heart burst into fragments.

One fragment was grey and sharp. Gianni and Anna, good-hearted as they were, had not seen the dangers of their beautiful plan. If the ones in authority found out that Santo was on the island for love of me, it would render apparently true everything that had got me incarcerated here. My alleged *ninfomania* would be confirmed by my seeming to lure the very man here. Then Santo, Anna and Gianni would be punished, and Padre Portalupi too, for allowing it to happen.

'Tell him not to come,' I shouted at Anna. 'It's a trap!'

I must have frightened her, using some of the ways I had learned with my fellow lunatics, rocking side to side for comfort. She backed out of the room and I heard her feet pattering fast through the corridors back to whence she had come.

Gianni delle Boccole

Anna come home lamentin n ringin her hands.

'She says "No",' Anna told me flatly.

Save us, I were that exascerbated that I screamed, 'But what of Santo? What of the plan? *For why* does she say no? Has she truely unnerstood? Did ye tell it to her right?'

'Is it a plan, Gianni? He just wants to be with her. He hasn't thought it through properly, has he? He is not her guardian. She is not of age. He cannot sign for her release and he cannot marry her. She'll get no portion of a dowry, and he has no money to keep her.'

My tong burned with the memmary o the lossed will.

I risposted, 'He can watch oer her there on the island. Where we cannot.'

'And will he keep to that simple thing? No man will watch without touching if he can touch.'

'I niver touched you, Anna. But I allus watches out for you.'

'That is nothing but pity. Who would want to touch this scar?' she pointed to her face what Minguillo ud disfiggered.

'I dunt een see that any more, Anna. I see you jist like Marcella ust to draw you.'

She snifft, and lookt halfway pleased a minute. But she were carpin on agin direckly: 'What's the good of Santo going to the madhouse?'

'Santo will see Marcella every day and he will make sure they dunt hurt her, dunt drown her in the cold bath, dunt . . . Twill set the cart among the pigeons, at the very leastwise.'

Marcella Fasan

Anna came to me once more, looking frightened. I found an old sane smile to give her. I said, 'I understand now, Anna.'

She clasped both my hands and stared into my eyes, as if looking for something inside me. She seemed to find it, for joy broke out over her face, crinkling up her scar. She hugged me and I breathed happily on her smell of ironed linen. From the depths of that embrace, I told her:

'Santo may come but he must never be alone with me. That would be too dangerous for all of us.'

After two years of calm whiteness, my life was suddenly colourful like a kaleidoscope. For Padre Portalupi informed me that Cecilia Cornaro had returned to Venice and had come straight to the island. I laughed when he said that she had spoken indelicately. The Brothers had sent her away for fear of upsetting me with her wild talk.

'I wanted her to stay,' he said, 'I could see that she loves you. And I confess that the smell of brimstone on her was strangely enthralling. I detect that it comes not from her soul, but her tongue.'

At this I smiled yet again, a smile reborn from a long time past, a smile from before the madhouse, from before even Santo: a fond, remembering smile from Piero's time with me, from those days in the studio with Cecilia, from when Anna hugged me ten times a day to her linen-scented breast. I pressed my lips to take the sane goodness of that smile on to my fingers and then I pressed my fingers to my forehead.

Padre Portalupi leaned over to me eagerly and took my fingers in his.

'Marcella,' he began. I knew he wanted me to speak to him candidly and fully. I knew he could be trusted and that he wanted to help me. I would have loved to pay him the compliment of manifest trust. But if Padre Portalupi began to defend my sanity, he would draw Minguillo's attention to himself, and how could I let him be exposed to the danger of that? Besides, Minguillo's interested eye was the very last thing I wanted on San Servolo just at that moment.

Minguillo Fasan

I received a brief note from the *medico-religioso* that the island was to receive some new lay doctors trained on the mainland in certain modern methods. 'Among them is even a doctor expert in the conditions of the skin that so often affect our lunatics,' he added proudly.

'What can it hurt?' I thought. 'Let them leech her and scrape her and marinate her to their hearts' content.'

'As some of these new methods are experimental,' the surgeon had written, 'we shall not pass on the expenses to you.'

Don't mind if I do. For, apart from my expensive obedience to the vagaries of Madame Fashion, I had an even more costly pastime to subsidize: my swelling shelves of books bound in human skin. The Acquisitive Reader will know the satisfaction of a collection that shall not see its rival in any acquaintance's salon, of an assemblage that grows slowly as a mountain on account of the rarity of the sought object.

Nor was I the passive kind of collector who sits waiting for largesse to fall into his well-padded lap. I was indefatigable in my researches. On hearing of a book of human leather upon the wrong coast of Italy, I would be in a carriage rattling towards it in less than a day.

Slowly, over the years, more and more rectangular, embossed soul-cages had come to be in my possession. Murderers' biographies rubbed shoulders with *Compleat Physicians*. I even had the German novelty, *Kinder und Hausmärchen*, a little book of fairy tales, bound in the flesh of a small girl from Kassel, where the authors, Jakob and Wilhelm Grimm, had hunted down their stories.

I was no stranger to dismembering and exalting ordinary books. Sometimes a good text and a good piece of skin just begged to be united by my wit. In pioneering spirit, I had rebound to order an English novel 'by a Lady', called *Pride and Prejudice*. A slice of thigh from the cadaver of a woman dead of puerperal fever became available to me at the same time as the novel was delivered to the Palazzo Espagnol. The original first edition of *Pride and Prejudice* was put out at a price of eighteen English shillings, but mine, rebound 'in a Lady', cost me a hundred times the price.

In general I did not read them. But I had an intimate relation with my human-skinned books. I experienced certain sensations when I touched them. I ordered and re-ordered them, sometimes according to size, sometimes according to hue or provenance: senility salaciously juxtaposed with juvenilia; philosopher elbowing priest; prim pastoral poet up against

241

thrilling highwayman. I dusted their crevices with tiny squirrel-fur brushes I had got from an artist's studio.

I ornamented some of my soul-cages with additional rivets and fearful metal clasps. In close confinement with such bad company, my human bindings suffered new lacerations, as when a shark scrapes alongside an innocent dolphin.

Pain never finishes, does it?

Marcella Fasan

A lunatic asylum is like a village. There are enemies, friends, gossip and a thread that joins all, be they nurse, warder, doctor or patient. Sane or insane, on San Servolo we were all imprisoned by the madness of some of us. For the nurses might not leave us when they wished to, but only when they were allowed to. The Brothers and the surgeon-Fathers were bound to us by taking responsibility for our care.

Isolated on San Servolo, our village was as clannish and closed as any island community in the Venetian lagoon. Indeed, some of the patients, when cured, stayed on and became warders themselves. As my drawings showed, life inside such a village is a kind of caricature of the wider life outside, with everything just a little bit distorted, as in a mirror with a fault in the glass. There are hierarchies inside a village, of both power and affection; there are winners and losers. Everything is dramatized. Everything is condensed.

Into our village came a golden-haired angel called Spirito. He had changed beyond measure in the two years that I had not seen him: more than the new substantialness of his frame, there was the deeper voice and the new quiet force in him, something stronger than muscle or bone.

Everyone loved him: the male patients, the female, the Furious and the Tranquil Lunatics, the nurses, the herb-gardeners, the bakers, the apothecaries and the cooks. The chief *medico-religioso* was the only one who failed to be captivated. Santo-Spirito was never tired; he fed everyone's need with compassionate attention. Santo-Spirito's brown eyes drew pain out of people and disposed of it kindly.

His manner was respectful, even with the self-soiled and self-tattered lunatics, the ones who needed to show him the holes in their small-clothes, the ones who craved to tell him of how they could walk on water, the ones who wanted just to hold his hand and feel his sanity and goodness through his skin. Padre Portalupi soon regarded Santo-Spirito as a son and a disciple, for they were in perfect accord on the correct and kindest methods of helping the mad. The two of them could be seen together often, walking the grounds, deep in conversation.

At first I was terrified. Yet Santo-Spirito observed to the letter my demand that he should never be alone with me. Indeed, such a thing would have been hard to contrive. My private quarters were forbidden to unaccompanied male staff, and when I was outside of them it was always in the plentiful company of other Tranquil Lunatics.

Nor did we talk together, for when I was in public I did not speak. Anna had made Santo-Spirito understand that he must allow me to stay mute, for safety's sake.

But Santo-Spirito would come to my side for lingering moments, and talk gently with the cluster of my friends, and I could almost feel the warmth of his body aligned with mine. I could hear birdsong and fountains in his voice, without listening to the words. And when his eyes fell on mine for a discreet second, I felt as if he were breathing on my eyelids softly and specifically. I had the full joy of inhaling wisps of his warm breath when my friends detained him for long minutes among us with innocent questions and lengthy replies to his own, for a well-treated lunatic is seldom anything but leisurely in the explanation of his or her condition, wrongs and tragedies.

I never knew when I might see him with his loving patients around him: in the refectory, in the garden outside the church, at the door to the operating theatre, by the pharmacy. I only knew that I would see him each day, and so it was worth awakening every morning.

Gianni delle Boccole

Satdays Santo came to the *ostaria* and give me news of Marcella.

He were learnin bout her, more evry day – the way the blue of her eyes changed colour a hunnerd times with the light, the bits o food she liked, what winds wayed on her spirit, and what ones lifted it.

'If this isn't Heaven,' he gloted, 'it is close to it.'

Yet twere a sore oirony that keeped him livin so in armony n prossimity with Marcella. He hexplained, with the smile goin a bit on the lopped side, 'We cannot marry, not while she is written up as insane. A madwoman may not sign the marriage register. Yet, as long as she stays officially mad, I can be with her every day.'

Then he went on to tell me more bout the gold of her hairs when tussled by a passin breeze, and the way she lookt in profile agin a sunset, lichening Marcella's skin to the petals o roses, and other sich gossimer stuff what is the perogertive of happy lovers.

Sor Loreta

In my vision I saw a beautiful woman very like myself in stature who watered a rose. She watered and watered that rose till it balled up and grew sickly white and clammy. Eventually the petals fell away, leaving a black bud.

Everyone in the convent came and wept with inexpressible sorrow at the passing of the lovely rose with petals as white as the skin of Sor Sofia. Only I (for it was me, in fact) remained composed, with the watering can in my hand, to show that I was the author of what had happened. With great authority, I stood over the rose till even the withered bud dropped off its stem. I told the weeping nuns, 'Understand from this parable – you must sacrifice everything you love in this transitory world, for the sake of salvation in eternity.'

But all the sensual sisters, Rafaela most of all, cast scorn on me for killing the rose. I stayed pale and silent while they abused me, soaking up their insults just as the rose had taken in the water.

Sor Sofia was nowhere to be seen in this dream. It was as if she was dead. I woke awash in more drops of sweat than I can write down.

Marcella Fasan

But then, into our village, came a bully. Later it would come out that he was a dissembling villain who had come to San Servolo with the express desire of hurting lady lunatics. Padre Portalupi was attending at another *Fatebenefratelli* hospital when this Doctor Flangini was recruited privately by the *medico-religioso*. And Santo had no chance to detect Flangini's wickedness nor to protect us from it, for it erupted before anyone had time to grow suspicious.

On his very first day among us, Doctor Flangini dismissed our nurses and lined up all the Tranquil lady patients. He walked up and down the line, striking on the arm all of us who were under thirty years of age. At the end of the line, he stood with his back to us for a moment. His shoulders were shaking. When he turned I saw the traces of laughter on his flat face.

The man is an impostor, I realized. *The Flangini are a respectable family. He is none of that. And Padre Portalupi's away. Where is Santo?*

For the first time I had an inkling of danger. I felt it in a twinge of my bladder and a prickling of pins in the backs of my hands.

'Those whom I have touched,' he bellowed suddenly, 'take one step forward.'

He ordered us to follow him to the records office. 'Line up,' he ordered peremptorily.

'One at a time,' he cautioned, disappearing inside.

Marta came out of that room shortly afterwards staring straight ahead. Fabrizia emerged blushing on fire, Lussieta in tears. We clustered around them, put our hands upon them to comfort them, yet they would tell us nothing. They were sealed up in unspeakable distress.

I started to stumble away to fetch help.

Where was Santo? I guessed that he must have been on duty far away in the operating room. Even if he were not using his surgical skills, he was often especially requested to hold the hands and soothe patients who must undergo painful cutting and bleeding.

In that moment I was prepared to confront even the *medico-religioso*, whose office was close by. But then the door of the records office squawked open and my collar was seized from behind, choking me. Doctor Flangini dragged me inside. I was discomforted to see no nurse in the room, such as normally accompanied the doctors in their private interviews with female patients.

'So Marcella Fasan, noblewoman of unblemished descent,' he remarked, looking at my *cartella clinica*. 'You have no furious symptoms. Despite your deformities, your animal economy is more than adequate for purpose. But your brother had you committed here and there's no talk of his bringing you back under his roof. So he does not love you and he does not want you back. And therefore he does not care what we do to you.'

The so-called doctor was now touching my hair with his large hand. Flangini pushed his face close to mine, perspiring visibly. He jabbed me with a finger that showed a curious bluish tint under the nail. His lips were also discoloured.

He announced, 'You shall not be able to seduce me, try as you will with those downcast eyes and that buttery fine hair of yours, and those very pretty soft breasts that make a man wish to forget the lame leg and the depraved mind.'

If Padre Portalupi had heard this, he would have sent the man away in an instant. Flangini grinned, 'Seeing as how it is the *ninfomania* that has brought you here . . .'

'It is . . . not true.' My voice, so long unused, was hoarse.

'So you talk. It says here that you do not. Why should you talk now? Are you frightened, my pretty?'

He moved closer to me; too close. I could see the hairs on his chin. His clothes did not have a good air about them.

246

'You mad little temptress!' he crooned, running a hot, rough hand over my neck.

'Please, you do not think I am insane, sir. Padre Portalupi does not think I am insane. Please.'

My pleas were savoured by him, his visible pleasure growing even as I uttered them, as if he were eating a trail of sugar up to his own intentions. He said, 'I have my own treatment for this condition, which is to tie women with their legs apart so that their thighs may not rub together to cause pleasurable sensations. For this treatment, it is better to remove any confining small-clothes.'

He flicked a knife out of his bag. It had no very medical look about it. Out of the same bag he pulled a *camiciola di forza* with eight separate ribbons for straitening the limbs.

'Please,' I entreated, 'please do not.'

He laughed.

'Do not do this. Rather nail up the door and leave me inside to die,' I whispered.

'Later,' he smiled hugely.

I must have imagined it in my terror, but I thought I heard him say then, 'This is going to be a little uncomfortable.'

Sor Loreta

Now, even if she was alone, Sor Sofia would turn away from me if she passed me in the lanes of the convent. In my nightly walks near her cell, I thought I overheard her whispering slanders about me to her sister and her new friends, the light nuns Margarita and Rosita. Sor Sofia knew private things about me, divulged in our former moments of tenderness.

Now I began to experience a burning hatred of Sor Sofia, stronger even than the love I had felt for her before. I had many visions of her in lewd postures with Sor Andreola and even with her sister Rafaela. I began to fear that Sor Sofia had gone over to the Devil. This was also proved by her treatment of me.

Marie of Oignies had fasted for forty days to drive the Devil out of a possessed nun. It seemed to me that at least fifty were required in Sor Sofia's case. I drank so little and I prayed so long that my flesh trembled and quaked, and I was forced to put my hands inside my clothes to calm myself when I was alone.

One night, standing under her window, I heard Rafaela joke, 'Oh, Sor Loreta has eaten of the Insane Root. Your woman is a complete ghoul, in love with shedding her own blood.'

I thought I heard Sor Sofia's laughter tinkle out of the window. Sor Sofia, who had once been the joy of my eyes, suddenly turned ugly in my sight. Where I had nourished perfect love for her, I now knew her to be my enemy, and therefore God's.

Minguillo Fasan

That devil luck favoured me again. My sister, after all her docile time, had suddenly manifested the *ninfomania* of which I had been pleased to accuse her.

Padre Portalupi admitted in a letter that it 'had been stated' that Marcella had been subject to erotic delusions about one of the lay doctors recently come to the island, a certain Flangini, about whom I made a note to seek out and make happy.

I composed the most exquisite response: '*Padre Portalupi, I see you spliced on the horns of a dilemma here. Either my dear sister's purity has been compromised by your negligence, or she is indeed subject to the* ninfomania. *Whichever is the case, dear Padre, I rely on you to inform me, so that I can take the appropriate steps for her protection. San Servolo has not served her well.*'

Was I playing with fire, enquires the Timid Reader, practically *asking* Padre Portalupi to send her off the island for her own safety? Well, yes — but that was because a zephyr of possibility had wafted to me, a brave new idea for a more permanent disposal of my sister. I was so very very tired of fending off the goodness of those doing-good Brothers.

A week later, crossing the courtyard at San Servolo, for what I hoped would be a surprising and awkward interview with Padre Portalupi – especially given my long absence from the island – I saw an energetic figure hurrying ahead of me. A young man with a head of hair like an angel. He wore surgical costume: he was not a priest. There was something about him that made me finical, that obliged me to follow him quietly, so that he knew it not. From the way he walked, confident and fast, this slender Haloed One felt at his ease on San Servolo.

I had no need to go far in my pursuit, for he turned to his right, and directly I saw his profile. Then I sagged with relief. For a paranoical moment, I had thought it was the little doctor, my sister's erstwhile sweetheart. Now I realized that I had been foolishly mistaken. No, *this* man was far more substantial, taller, and infinitely more sure of himself than the vanquished little doctor would ever be.

Gianni delle Boccole

I were that affrighted when Minguillo set off for San Servolo. There werent no time to warn Santo that he were coming. For so long Minguillo haint shone an interest in his sister or the island tall.

I watched his gondola set off from our steps. Then I realized I still had his velvet hat in my hand. I waved it at him. Minguillo were facing the Palazzo Espagnol and he were givin it a lovin look. His smiling face were turned direckly toward me. I waved the hat harder. Still he dint see me tall.

And that twere when I notist it. All these years Ide lived at his baconcall and yet Ide niver took it in. Being so powful in our lives, Ide never thought on Minguillo as a person with a weakness, what peered muzzily at the world. What should of wore spectickles. That's why he were such a poor shot, on account of his weak vizion. That were why he niver kilt Marcella with his gun. Minguillo Fasan could not hit a hole in a ladder.

249

Minguillo come home, a big grin on his face what smote my heart, and Anna's.

In the meantimes o course Ide searcht the study. But Ide found only ashes in the grate of whatever letter ud summonsed im to the island.

I dint have to wait long to find out what that letter ud sayed. That night, Santo runned into the *ostaria* panting. A dredful thing ud appened to the poor ladies at San Servolo.

'It was not me,' Santo sayed. 'I did not touch her, not even a kiss.'

He hexplained that Marcella were in a shockt state. 'She says nothing,' he wispered. 'She looks at the wall again.'

'So she can only be shockt out of it?'

'I fear so.'

I menshoned, 'I heared that Cecilia Cornaro is returned to Venice.'

Marcella Fasan

'Here you, you with the face on you.'

Cecilia Cornaro surprised me in the herb garden. Padre Portalupi, now returned from the mainland, had prevailed on his colleagues and allowed her in to see me against Minguillo's express orders. The Padre hovered in the shade of the trees nearby, his face looking punched but faintly exhilarated.

She seemed grievously altered; it was more than the years that had passed. Her fire was damped. Something had shattered her confidence, leaving a bruised wariness in its place. Even on San Servolo, the rumours had reached us: that Cecilia had been worsted in a love affair with an English poet. I wanted to put my arm around her and comfort her, yet I was afraid to pity her. No doubt she would hate me for it.

She said bluntly, 'I know what happened to you. All of it. Marcella, all those months in my studio, when I was as open as a window with you,

you never told me the truth about your brother. Then, after Piero died, you never once wrote to me to tell me what was happening to you. How could you be so cruel to a friend? Yes, *cruel*, Marcella. People who love you should be allowed to help you. They should be allowed to choose what sacrifices they make.'

I looked at her wordlessly.

'And to accept help – that does not reduce you to a Poor Thing. Yet who could not pity you here?' She gestured at the asylum walls, which must have seemed fearsome to her who so hated to be constrained in anything.

Outright compassion from Cecilia Cornaro was a thing hard to bear. I reached for her damaged hand, and held it up to the light. It was concealed inside a black mitten, but the sunlight silhouetted two fingers welded together. Anna had told me that Cecilia Cornaro bore this wound because of me, because she had once tried to help me and so incurred my brother's wrath.

And how should I reply to her? *Now you have seen exactly how my brother will act against anyone to whom I confide my trust, anyone to whom I lament my bad treatment by him. Does that not give you an understanding of my situation and my silence?*

Or should I talk toughly as she would? *Yes, you can help. And now you have a damage of your own on the outside, and some hideous pain as well you try to hide inside – perhaps you can see mine more clearly. Can I be your pet Deformity? You can be mine. Can you help, you ask? It would certainly help if you would take me to live with you. For even if I escape from here, Minguillo will leave me penniless. I can mix your colours . . . If you will let Santo-Spirito come to visit me sometime . . .*

Cecilia's voice roused me from my fantasies. It appeared she had reviewed them all herself before coming here: 'I have no need of a daughter or an assistant, or another creature under my feet in my studio. You are not of age: your brother could yet intervene in any such plan. But Piero's face keeps coming into my mind, and I know that it will not go away until I do something for you.'

'Perhaps Piero haunts you because my brother murdered him. The duelling sword was poisoned,' I explained flatly. 'You may ask the attending surgeon.'

'Would that be the same attending surgeon who came to my studio to beg me to come here?'

'Santo,' I whispered.

'The same. Do you know that he . . . ? Are you? But he has nothing. He has no power to release you from here anyway. He has chivvied me here, I believe, in the hope that the sight of me will stir you from your self-absorbed and excluding misery. Perhaps he also thought our reunion might have the same effect upon myself.'

'Will it?' I looked into her green eyes and saw actual flecks of pain in there.

But Cecilia was musing, 'There must be a solution for this. It is like finding the right colour for the shadowing of an eye socket; sometimes it is not the obvious thing. It can take something surprising, a yellow or a green. I'll be back, trust me. Now, the good Padre Portalupi is recovering his composure. I need to reduce him again. Excuse me.'

'We may not have much time,' I whispered. 'Minguillo will use . . . what happened . . . against me. As soon as he calculates his best advantage out of it.'

'Indeed. Marcella, have you ever wondered why your brother hates you so?'

'I haven't. It has been a fact of my life since before I had thoughts of my own.'

Cecilia Cornaro made a sharp snort of derision. 'Do you know Tiziano's painting of Marsyas?'

I nodded.

'When he's upside down, trussed up like a goat for the flaying, Marsyas has his mouth open. That is not simply to scream. It's because he's asking, "Why are you stripping me from myself?" That would be the intelligent thing, to *ask* why your brother insists on treating you much the same way. You might meet Minguillo's hatred halfway and parley with it, if you knew whence it sprang. Did you offend him in some way in your childhood?'

'Before or after he crippled me?'

Cecilia barked, 'Do not whine. Who told you to cooperate with his tortures? You have a tricksy bladder. It does not have you. You have a poorly leg. Ditto. A sick man pretending to be a doctor abused you. He did not even rape you. You have a mad brother. Yet who told you to go hand in glove with those who want to oppress or pity you – by being as passive and silent as you please in the midst of vivisection? You think

252

you are brave, because you do not cry to others to help you, but no one,' and here her voice broke down to a whisper, 'no one can withstand cruelty on their own. It is vain to think you can do so. There are times when it is a kind and courageous act to cry out, to tell the world what is happening, to warn other victims . . . What of your poor sister-in-law, for example?'

I looked away.

'And you have inspired adoring love, which proves . . .'

Here, she bit her lip and succumbed to dolorous memories of her own for a moment. Then Cecilia spoke to herself, as if forgetting my presence, 'Now I am commissioned to go to Vienna for some portraits of the royal family. While I paint them, I shall think what is to be done by Marcella Fasan. And by the loving friends whose help she has so far preferred to spurn.'

I wanted very much to strike her with my crutch.

'Apparently the Viennese royals are not very brilliant conversationalists, so I shall not be distracted. Now you are protected here, even from your brother, I believe. You have your Santo about you. For the moment, there is no better place in the world for you to be.'

She embraced me hard and quickly, so that I choked on mouthfuls of hair, and strode off, Padre Portalupi trotting nervously behind her. After she left, I sat on my own under the trees, thinking for a long time.

Doctor Santo Aldobrandini

Cecilia Cornaro's visit provoked a strange reaction in Marcella. At first, after Flangini's attack, Marcella had been sunk into herself. It was clear that she felt defiled, reduced. Yet now she began to show a physical resilience I had not seen in her before. More and more often she appeared without her crutch. She held her head up. She asked questions. Her radiant skin spoke the same language as her mouth. Her smile, enchantingly, reappeared, and then her irresistible laugh. The other

Tranquils were unnerved by her new, strong presence. They persisted in bringing her the crutch, as if she had forgotten it.

Meanwhile, Flangini had been flung off the island in disgrace and had disappeared from society. Padre Portalupi had believed not a word the lecher said, preferring the truth of his own witnessing – a chorus of once-Tranquil ladies all reduced to a state of piteous misery. Flangini was the worst kind of criminal, the kind who take their pleasure from inflicting mental pain. I supposed we should be grateful that he did not force an actual congress upon any of his victims. He simply confined, groped and spoke filthily, making them feel unworthy even of inspiring lust.

Of course I wondered if Minguillo had sent Flangini. Yet the man had been indiscriminate in his brutalities. There were a dozen female patients who had suffered as Marcella had. That was too clumsy for Minguillo, who cared not at all about incidental damages, but who was cunning enough to anticipate the awkward investigations that would result from such a scandal.

In fact, Flangini was his own man, just another Minguillo, just another character that you would not believe in if you met him in a novel but who nevertheless stalks this earth, hurting those in his path. In Flangini's case, it would not be for long, I consoled myself: a bluish tint of his lips and fingers indicated an advanced structural disease of the heart.

Now Padre Portalupi was saying, 'We really must let Marcella Fasan go away from this place. She has never been out of her senses, though the sweet sensibility of her nature has caused her to share the lives of the truly afflicted with an affectionate empathy. But I fear that the memories of Flangini, and of how we left her vulnerable, might indeed provoke a fissure in her equilibrium. I shall write to her brother and tell him so. I'll take this opportunity to declare her officially *risanata*. That would release her from the order from the *Sanità* that confined her here.'

Joy cudgelled the breath out of my lungs. If Marcella was officially sane, then I could marry her. But the timing would be crucial.

'She would be released into her brother's care?'

'Sadly, she is not of age,' Padre Portalupi confirmed.

How could I extract her? Images rained into my mind, of an intercepted gondola, a priest standing by, Marcella cloaked beside me at the altar of an obscure church.

Padre Portalupi's face had clouded. 'Her brother is what makes me hesitate. Sometimes I think it is the brother we should have admitted two years ago. Yet I shall write to him once more.'

Sor Loreta

At last I felt a hope stirring. I was rewarded one night with a vision in which the crucified Jesus beckoned me with His great eyes to climb up to His side on the cross. With His own hand, He gently cupped my head and drew it to the wound in His side.

'Drink, dearest Daughter,' he said in His rich, soft voice. 'Here is something to slake your thirst in ways that the human world cannot provide.'

And so, like Santa Catalina herself, I fixed my lips upon His holy wound and suckled, tasting sweet manna that refreshed all the members of my body until I felt as if I was possessed of a superhuman strength. So the Most High succours His chosen ones, feeding them with the greatness to accomplish stupendous and mysterious acts.

And therefore I was not surprised when Sor Sofia was shortly fetched away to Heaven or Hell, according to God's design. This is the Way of the Lord.

Gianni delle Boccole

Minguillo were up to summing new. Twere clear from the smile on his face n the way he hummed in the courtyard. He liked to go sit in the place where Conte Piero had died, and smell the poisonous blue flowers there. Also, from that vipery he could see all the comings n goings o the whole house, and find buckets o scuses for a trimming or a punishing. We all trod in fear. Running along corridors, walking too slow along corridors, being in corridors – all sich could bring on a slap, or worser – ten minits of his foul tong.

Come a day when I sorpresed Minguillo in his office. I creepled in silent as gilt. He were crouched by the bookshelf, looking jist like one on them orang-utang apes, and he were running his pimpled nose long a row o books on the next-to-bottom shelf. Course he needed to be that close, I knowed now. He couldn't see scut from far way. He tookt deep breaths. Twere as if each one on them books were sented with diffrint perfume.

Books was allus arriving for him, of course, wrapt in cloth and delivert in the hands of booksellers who lookt like men what boil horses' bones for glue.

Minguillo haint seed me yet, so I peered oer his shoulder at them little darlins of his. Then it struck me: pinkish brown with a fine grain to the leather – them covers was jist like that repungent book of humane skin he had got from Peru.

That's what he were collecting. Not jist poor old Tupac Amaru, but dozens of em. Books of humane leather. That's what he were spending Marcella's inhairitance on.

Brute God!

Anger n fear whipped through me. I were dizzy with feelins. Pity for the poor creechers bound round them books. Shakin with the old bull-horrors at Minguillo's happy hunting em down. Sick-bitter that Minguillo were safe here in his study spending his filthy looter on them dredful murderin goolish books while Marcella were confined on an island as a lunatick. Gilty that I, in the end, had permitted this to appen on account of my wafering oer the true will n then loosing it.

I must of huffed out loud, for Minguillo turned round n seed me.

He leaped up. But twere too late for him to hide his grin nor the things what were spred on his desk.

Twere maps of South Hamerica isnt it.

Part Four

Minguillo Fasan

Yet again the disposal of my sister preoccupied me. For the second time, I thought that God, or at least nuns, would help me. Napoleon had slammed the doors on my original intentions. But in Arequipa, in the faltering Viceroyship of Peru, I had heard there was a Dominican nunnery that would take only girls of rich Spanish blood.

Rich Spanish blood, that had a nice ring to it. And what had our family, if not blood and richness with a heaped spoonful of Spaniard stirred into it? An admixture of Venetian could only enhance the *limpieza de sangre*, the purity of bloodline that so obsessed the Spanish of the New World, threatened as they were with miscegenation of many hues at every bedpost.

The Dominicans, I thought, they would do nicely, with their Spanish and New World connections. *Domini Cani* — Dogs of God, they called themselves. Peru's own demented Santa Rosa of Lima was a creature of their order. 'The Tears of Santa Rosa' — soon to be relaunched on an eager market — would pay my sister's dowry. The Orderly Reader shall acknowledge the perfect symmetry of it all, and be pleased by it.

In any case it was well past time for me to sort my father's affairs in Arequipa. Months after he died, I received a threadbare document to say that he had been pronounced *ab intestato*, at which I had smiled wryly. My father was far from intestate. In fact, he had at least two wills. It now occurred to me that in Arequipa there was a mansion and a warehouse for me to claim, that might be turned into funds for more books of human skin and other diversions of mine.

The little matter of allowing a Venetian-born girl to enter a Spanish convent I solved easily. Among the fraternity of human-skin bibliophiles was a certain powerful cardinal in Rome, a very epicure in creature books. Within days of my sending a highly suggestive letter, I had a document with a papal seal on my desk, ready to send in advance to Santa Catalina and frighten all the humble colonial clerics into convulsions.

Meanwhile, I persuaded the *Fatebenefratelli* that it was the decent thing to do, to keep Marcella for a little longer, until I could find a way to accommodate her, without disrupting the lives of my own delicate wife and beloved little ones. I reminded Padre Portalupi that my womenfolk had been accustomed to think my sister a dangerous madwoman, and that they had not seen her for years. I could not ask them to accept her in the house without my mediating presence. The problem, as I put it, was that I myself was committed just at that moment to a business excursion. I did not mention my South American plans. I reported merely that I was going to Cadiz, which was true, as it was on the way to my real destination.

Portalupi responded that naturally Marcella was welcome until I might personally welcome her back into the bosom of our family. The fellow's tone seemed somewhat ironic, so I arranged to have him taken into the *Magistrato alla Sanità* for some more stern questioning while I was away.

I embarked on the *Star* on January 3rd 1813, to call in at Cadiz, Falmouth, Montevideo and Buenos Aires, on my way to Chile. I clutched my *Biglietto di Sanità*. That told the world that I was *fuori d'ogni sospetto di Peste* – free from any suspicion of disease. And of course, outside of Venice I was also free of any suspicion of bad character. I travelled light and happy.

At least I did so until we reached the open sea. My first sea passage to the New World had been gently uneventful. But this time – the winds they did blow, and soon blew the smile right off my face and Signor Fauno's artful tousle straight out of my hair. The Kind Reader will at this point save us both a deal of trouble: He will consult His memories of squalid sea passages done on the page by Messrs Smollett, Polo and their ilk, and put them all together with their every screeching timber, add extra vomit, stir well, and He'll have some idea of the journey now endured by myself, and shortly to be endured by my little sister.

As we approached land, the storms were fetched away to plague other less deserving voyagers. I was still churning in the belly: the thorny coasts of Argentina had no allure for me, but when we rounded the lower point of that wild continent, then I began to feel something like pleasure in the journey again. The Chilean archipelago, the lounging sea-lions and the glaciers snouting into the sea: now *that* was what I remembered. Chewing on the sinewy air, and watching the seam of our wake cleave the azure waters, I understood afresh why my father had loved this journey, and why he had spent so much time here.

The clean air made me drunk. The high skies rolled my soul over. I began to believe in the New World as I had never believed in God, if you can call Him that. The skin of Tupac Amaru seemed to thrill under my fingers, as if he too was happy to be back in his native continent, where indeed his own spirit of revolution was abroad once more. The clatter of gunfire sometimes travelled across the shores to us on the *Star*, and we saw pyres of smoke that could only be towns ablaze. The excitement was contagious. It lay on my skin all the way up the coast.

When the cranes of Valparaiso came loping over the water to meet me once again, I felt like the king of two worlds, of which the new one was the greater – and I said aloud, 'Yes, this is where I'll put her, if she survives the journey.'

Sor Loreta

After Sor Sofia passed from this miserable life, everyone gave Me hateful looks.

Sor Arabel and Sor Narcisa, when questioned by the *priora* as to Our whereabouts, swore that We had been praying together at the time Sor Sofia must have drowned in the bath. It was true. We had prayed the whole evening. Never once did We pause in Our praying.

There was no more laughter. There was a frenzy of sobbing prayers for the soul of the departed nun. I saw only sad faces, or others that appeared ugly with fright. My sisters unfairly chose to victimize *Me* for the pain they felt at the loss of their favourite, Sor Sofia. Dung was served to Me on a platter in the refectory. I entered My cell one night to find it dripping with foul-smelling liquid, and My blue spectacles trampled to tiny splinters. Instead of hunting down the offenders, Priora Mónica reproached Me for carelessness, as the convent was obliged to pay for a second pair.

Meanwhile, the heathens of Peru were once more fermenting a great wickedness. The Holy Mother Church was threatened on all sides by new rebellions. The nuns cowered within the walls of Santa Catalina, where sometimes even the women and children of the town took refuge.

God sends afflictions to the truly faithful, that they may uniquely feel the warmth of His love by finding new ways to serve His will. Just at that moment He came to Me with a fresh sign of His favour. The sign He sent was unmistakable: a heretic. The prospect of waging God's war against this new enemy renewed My ardour.

It had come out that Santa Catalina was supposed to welcome in charity a girl from Venice! That Venetian girl's father, a merchant, had already stained this white town of Arequipa with illegitimate seed. All these many years, his mistress, Beatriz Villafuerte, and her bastard boy too, had shown the impudence to attend the church of Santa Catalina every Sunday alongside devout Christians.

So now the deceased Fernando Fasan was sending us another rotten fruit of his loins. This daughter of his was supposed to be a purest virgin of clean blood, yet how far was any Venetian ever advanced in the duty of God?

These things I know, by God's design.

There are those among the Venetians who have gone nine years without confessing. Their churches are thieves' caves. Napoleon rightly laid waste to them. The Venetians are hypocritical even to build a church. Sodom and Gomorrah were more wholesome places than Venice. This is proved by the fact that Venetians have chosen to live on the murk of mud and water, forsaking the solid rock of Our most Holy Church.

When I explained these matters to the council, there was such an uproar in the room that from the outside it must have sounded as if the sisters were hacking each other to pieces with the sharp edges of their Bibles. The worst eruption occurred when I suggested a new wall to separate the areas where the Venetian might walk and where the nuns of Arequipa might roam without fear of corruption.

I was forced to raise My voice above their screams: 'Everyone knows that the private lives of the Venetian clergy would detain a hundred Confessors for a year! The churches are ballrooms and brothels! There is a sensational laxity in the convents of Venice. Do you not know the story of the *abate* Galogero who issued all the nuns in his convent with duplicate keys?'

Someone hissed at Me, 'Sor Loreta, no one wishes to hear your voice, or see you.'

'Particularly *see* you,' sneered someone else.

And so the wolves persuaded the lambs to allow the Venetian she-wolf into the House of God. It turned out that the brother of the she-wolf was already on his way to Peru: he had been so arrogant as to assume a positive outcome from the start. He was expected at Santa Catalina at any moment.

Of course Priora Mónica preened herself on gaining an Italian nun, and a Venetian one at that. Instead of the devotions due to her Bridegroom in Heaven, the *priora*'s head was full of amateur dramaticals and little exclusive salons in her chambers for the most light girls, at which Rossini's music would be played until they fell into a sensual delirium. Naturally I was never invited, though of course I would have shunned such a *bacchanalia* if I was.

I scourged Myself on behalf of all of them, as it was ever God's design that I should suffer for everyone. Only Sor Narcisa and Sor Arabel joined Me in My penances. Both were flaccid in their flagellation, for which I reproached them many times, perhaps a little unkindly.

Minguillo Fasan

In Valparaiso I revisited my former haunts with twice as much pleasure, for a mouth-watering nostalgia sharpened my old appetites. My fine new wardrobe of shot silk and satin waistcoats drew eyes stupefied with admiration. There were those in Venice who looked down on my looks, but in Chile-Peru I was always a god. I did a little business in Chilean lapis lazuli, for I had an idea to stopper special bottles of 'The Tears of Santa Rosa' with a carved spigot of blue stone when I brought it back on the market.

Then I sailed north through waters crusted with salty foam, until a rocky promontory hooked us into the grinning white bay of Islay. I hired the least noisome *arriero* on the dock. His peons put me and my traps on to donkeys, and for three days I jolted up mountains and across plains to Arequipa, with El Misti lifting his white snowy hat to us all the way. A little asymmetrical in the slanting light, the mountain reminded me somewhat of the old Doge's *berretto*.

Hats and mountains, heads and hills. The Peruvians of this zone, men and women alike, wore black hats that made them look as if they carried a tray bearing a miniature mountain on their heads. My *arriero* told me that the head-wear was indeed an homage to El Misti. And it did not stop with hats. We stopped briefly at a shrine where I saw the mummified heads of Indian ancestors – their crania had been stretched with binding and stones since babyhood, so that their very bones had grown elongated like olives, with foreheads like snowy peaks.

'There is positively no accounting for human stupidity,' I told the *arriero*. And the thought of stupidity reminded me pleasantly of Santa Catalina, the eponymous heroine of the convent I was about to visit. That blessed lady had contrived many and more jolly tortures to wreck her own body than these natives had inflicted on their babies' skulls.

Too late, I noticed that the *arriero* had misliked my words. His head jerked sharply away. I had heard that these *arrieros* could be wickedly temperamental. Losing his services at that remote spot would leave me in no small amount of trouble. He said reproachfully, 'I knew your father, Conte Fasan. I worked for him in the mines of Caylloma. He was a great man.'

'Indeed,' I remarked. 'Dear old Papà. How I miss him!'

After that, I knew the *arriero* would serve me. He began to serve immediately, dispensing useful information about my father's 'wife' in Arequipa, one Beatriz Villafuerte. The woman still inhabited my father's, that is, *my* house, as the authorities had respected her claim as his common-law wife. A grand example of local beauty, this Beatriz, apparently, and fervent churchgoer. When he died, she had paid for a mighty requiem mass in his honour at Santa Catalina. She still tended his grave with many tears.

In Venice, my father had referred to the creature as his 'housekeeper'. I made a great show of pretending that I knew all about the saintly Beatriz and that in cosmopolitan Venice such things were little thought of.

Yet it caught me off guard, indeed whipped the breath out of my throat, to hear that there was a son by her, too.

Arequipa dawned on me white as a sunstruck diamond, carved out of El Misti's foothills.

264

'*Sillar*,' explained my *arriero*, 'is white. And so are the people. More Spanish here than anywhere. White skin.'

He explained that *sillar* was a kind of volcanic tuff shrugged off by the mountains in tremors that had several times decimated the population. The city had busily renewed itself in this virgin tuff since the terrible earthquake of 1784, and was now, he claimed, more beautiful than ever. White Arequipa was burrowed in a plump elbow of the River Chili, that lay in the shadow of three snow-scabbed mountains. The *arriero* pointed: 'Chachani, the one that looks like a bride, Pichu-Pichu, that looks like a sleeping cat. Miau! And of course El Misti.' He nodded to it deferentially.

I gazed on the crumpled peak and imagined it erupting like a ripe pimple on the day of my birth.

'How many killed,' I asked fondly, though I knew the answer, 'in 1784?'

We approached the city via the Puente Real, where a soldier stopped our party and demanded our names. When I announced myself as 'Minguillo Fasan, son of Fernando Fasan', his jaw dropped. He scribbled something hastily on a piece of paper 'for the *Intendencia*, my apologies, noble sir', and waved us graciously into the city.

We passed through an area my *arriero* described as the *tambo*, a rats' nest of stinking tanneries and leather-crafters, *chicherías* selling corn beer, all establishments topped by the unmistakably inviting balconies of the town's prostitutes. Evil smells, unfamiliar accents and exciting blasphemies clamoured richly in my ears: the Travelled Reader shall of course recall that poor sanitary conditions are ever conducive to the production of the most delightful and colourful vernacular.

We climbed a shallow hill into the centre of the metropolis. Immediately I could see why my father had taken this city to his sentimental heart. Arequipa was a little albino Venice, a pearl uncontaminated by failure and fall. The main square, the Plaza de Armas, was a veritable San Marco, enclosed in three towering stone loggias and a cathedral of far nobler proportions than the sideshow that masqueraded as our basilica in Venice. A fountain gurgled richly in the middle of the square.

'Tuturutú,' my *arriero* pointed to the bronze statue of a man with a trumpet at its frothing centre. Around him crowded market traders, rowdy as Rialto. Under the galleries of the square, just as in San Marco, gaudy shops flashed glistening glass eyes on their wares.

The churches were frankly bizarre: their facades were carved with what appeared to be a conglomeration of paganistic symbols – snakes, pumas and strange creatures in feathered headdresses. I rather enjoyed them. No Venetian is more than a little Christian, after all. And myself less than most. Also like Venice, there were almost no carriages. People walked or went by sedan chair. Mules carried mountainous loads, the notoriously temperamental alpacas light ones. A few carts rattled by.

We passed a row of dead dogs laid out in lines. 'The governor has them exterminated, because of the Rabies,' my *arriero* explained. 'We have vaccine against the Small-Pox too. You should . . .'

I waved him aside, remembering my father's unfortunate brush with the newfangled vaccination methods.

I lodged myself at a noisy inn in the palmy Plaza de Armas for the first night. I sent a note to the 'housekeeper' at my father's mansion to announce my presence in Arequipa. Until this moment, I had kept the lovely Beatriz Villafuerte in ignorance of my imminent arrival. I wanted her to have just so much time but no more. I had written that I would arrive in the late afternoon of the next day, and that I expected the house to be emptied by then of any elements that might prove undesirable to the eyes of the legitimate son of the Conte Fernando Fasan. That's how I put it. I thought it had a nice ring to it. She would be up all night looting, I hoped. Much good would it do her, though.

I made short work of lodging my father's will, that is, my edition of it, with the town clerk to copy overnight. I thoughtfully provided a Spanish translation that named his first-born son Minguillo as the rightful heir to all Fernando Fasan's possessions in the Old World and the New.

When the citizens lit the resin lamps outside their houses, I took myself back to the *tambo*, and found myself a nice little bargain in flesh. I fell asleep, my fists closed up ready for my forthcoming war on my father's mistress and her bastard.

In the morning, I suffered myself to be educated by the night's whore. My *arriero* had boasted that the 'White City of Arequipa' was famous for its *limpieza de sangre*, pure, European blood. Yet down in the *tambo* Indians of all hues, and slaves, diluted the proud paleness of the citizenry. Leaning over the balcony, how many pages of the book of human skin I leafed through that first dawn, guided by my exhausted harlot.

More than half the people who passed under my window could have been rich Venetians or citizens of Madrid, if you but looked at their white hides. These were the thoroughbred Spaniards, born in Spain proper. Then there were those whose complexion was irreproachably milky but who had a tinge of the New World about their bearing – these, I was told, were the *criollos*, born of Spanish parents here. Then came the tawny *mestizos*, the offspring of Spanish fathers dallying with native women. The pure Indian people were the most appetising – delectably sculpted in rich terracotta. Then there were slaves of various hues, ranging from coffee-coloured *mulatas* and the *moriscas*, their children fathered by white men, to the half-Indian, half-African *sambas* and the deep-black *negros* and *negras*.

'What's that?' I demanded of my whore, each time a girl of a slightly different shade passed by. She cast an expert eye and her answers enchanted me.

'*Media asambada*,' she would say, 'half *samba*', of a gingerbread-coloured maid. Or '*cuarterona*', one quarter black. And '*mestiza media chola*', or '*india acholada*'.

The whites had their gradations too, of which my favourite was '*de color trigueño*' – wheat-coloured.

I rubbed my hands and slapped my whore back to bed. Yes, the book of human skin had many pages in Arequipa, and the Expectant Reader need not doubt I planned to run my finger down all of them. And if I imagined some of those sun-warmed integuments segmented, sumac'd, tooled, lightly gilded and bound around volumes, what Book-loving Reader would blame me?

Our scene is the Casa Fasan. I took care to arrive at the house not in the afternoon, as advertised, but at eleven in the morning, and just in time to see my father's weeping mistress Beatriz being helped into a sedan chair. She was a beauty indeed, even with her face swollen and discoloured by tears. There was no sign of the brat. A train of mules loaded with fine furniture

267

and carpets waited in the street. I told the muleteer: 'Let me help you to avoid a charge of assisting in a theft. Unload these stolen goods and take them back into the house where they belong.'

At this moment, a woman, the actual housekeeper apparently, erupted into the courtyard, her face, too, disfigured with weeping. 'Conte Fasan!' she whined. 'It is not what it looks like. These things were *gifts*, sir . . .'

'And are there notarized documents to prove that?'

'For gifts of love there are no documents, sir. I beg you, the lady will be destitute.'

'The *lady*, as you so generously style her, has parasited long enough on our family.'

I held out my purse to the muleteer. Wearily, he untied the burdens of the first beast, and his lackeys did likewise, and the treasure proceeded back into the house. That is, my house.

I strolled around appreciatively. The building was a fine specimen of colonial grandeur – three courtyards enclosed by low buildings, all in the white *sillar* stone, richly ornamented with architraves and friezes in a joyous miscegenating orgy of Doric, Ionian and Corinthian styles. The walls of the first courtyard were painted in an accommodating shade of buttermilk yellow. The next courtyard was a throbbing cobalt blue, the last a russet-red richer than anything in Venice. The intense colours bullied into stark highlight all the carved details of pure white *sillar* gargoyles, cornices and pilasters. Nothing could try harder to please than the decorative cobbles, the shady arbours and the riot of flowers against this crisp backwash of paint and stone. The Casa Fasan was not the Palazzo Espagnol, yet it was not shabby either. I suddenly resented all the generations of geraniums that had bloomed in those pots for the eyes of my father's mistress and her bastard, and not for my own. Why had I left it so long to claim what was mine? By rights I should have extracted some rents since the day my father died, since the day Beatriz Villafuerte ceased to serve in his bed.

'Is my chamber ready?' I asked the housekeeper. She led me to the room where my father had so extravagantly betrayed my mother and myself. It still smelled of the perfume of my father's mistress, and the bed dipped slightly where Beatriz Villafuerte had lain with him all those illicit years. I lay on that bed listening while below me in the courtyard tears were wept and teeth were gnashed and my own name was called out in rage and disgust. I felt at home already.

I did not repair immediately to the nunnery of Santa Catalina. The Travelled Reader will easily comprehend that so fine a thing as a Venetian gentleman could not be received in Arequipa without a great deal of noticing. I made sure news of my grandeur got to the convent ahead of me, with a few struts around the main square in full fig. I dressed in a cerulean piqué waistcoat and an apple-green frock-coat to attend a private duel of two bulls on a farm outside the town, an event patronized by many elegant gentlemen and ladies of Arequipa. All eyed me curiously. In that free and easy way of mine, I let it be known that I had come to set up my sister in the nun business in town.

Bishop José Sebastián de Goyeneche y Barreda received me in honour of my father, who had been his friend. The letter from my book-loving cardinal in Rome lay on his desk, the papal seal prominently exposed. I saw surprise and doubt on his face after an hour's conversation with me, but the Bishop did not refuse my request to send a *bigliettino* to the *priora* at Santa Catalina, with a recommendation to accept my sister as a novice. A certain amount of jiggery-pokery had to be contrived, he implied, but all objections to my sister's Venetian birth would be swept aside by the fact that my father had been to all intents and purposes a citizen of Arequipa for so many years.

'Where do I sign, *Ilustrísimo*?' I asked. 'How much do I pay?'

He looked at me with unmistakable distaste. 'The municipal clerk will draw up the document for you, and it will be verified by the *síndico* and the *procurador* of Santa Catalina. It shall be waiting at the convent's *oficina* when you go there.'

On my whore's advice I next betook myself to Calle Guañamarca's taverns, where the evening's hilarity was sharpened by the sombre silhouettes of the convents of Santa Rosa and Santa Teresa, of which I heard many delightful stories about nuns made to sleep in tombs with black curtains, of cruel penances and poor rations. After sampling the *chicha* in a dozen establishments, including *El Infierno* – 'Hell' – and *El Mundo al Revés* – 'The World Turned Upside Down' – I wandered east and north through the night, taking in the Indian quarters of Santa Marta and Miraflores. Then I followed the stream of shoulders tight with hope to the gambling parlours of Callejón de Loredo, where I deprived a few children of their inheritances and came away with the smell of their tears in my hair.

Finally I found a *chichería* called *El Veneno* – 'Poison' – and drank enough fermented corn to grow a field in my nethers. I finished my night back at the *tambo* with my whore, making her make good on her promissory morning kisses, stumbling home to the Casa Fasan late the next morning, to refresh myself for my appointment at the *oficina* at Santa Catalina.

I dressed in duck trousers, a taffeta cravat and a frogged jacket, with my violet velvet toque at a rakish angle. I practised regretful expressions in the mirror. Then I strode along the walls of Santa Catalina, which reared above the street in golden crescents as if carved out of Saharan sand. Over the gate, a painted stone image of Santa Catalina herself clutched a crucified Jesus like a baby doll. The door was studded with Moorish pinions. I rapped sharply on a metal nipple with my cane.

It was only when I belatedly pulled a discreet cord that a lay-porter appeared and opened the gate into a courtyard of bland aspect. I craned my neck but could detect no aspect of nunly life. I saw the wheel at the end of the courtyard, the two-tiered contraption by which goods and money were exchanged while retaining the nuns' invisibility. Where I stood was the debatable land inside the convent, where men might deliver, or parley with the *priora*. I cursed under my breath: that showy front gate was a false one. The real gate to Santa Catalina's enclosure was at the far end of this courtyard. I would not have the satisfaction of a comprehensive inspection of the grim bastion that would encase my sister. That was a thousand pities for I had counted on taking home some nourishing memories of its dark walls and glowering cloisters: something to tuck into my imagination, for later, when I thought of Marcella and the troubles she had cost me.

'Sir,' a cool, intensely feminine voice saluted me. I was ushered into the vaulted stone office of the *priora*, fragrant with the mingled scents of wax and soap. Behind a desk, I glimpsed the *locutorio* that housed the grate through which Arequipan families might make small-talk with the daughters and sisters they had buried alive inside the convent.

Beside the *priora* sat her deputy, the very ugliest specimen of a woman to have ever slimed out of a womb. I am sure I hope so myself.

She wore blue spectacles that she removed as the door closed behind me and the room settled into soft gloom. I was sorry that she had, for then I had to look at her eyes, one of which was glued shut by folds of scarified skin. She made my flesh wrinkle into tiny crevices of discomfort. When I looked at her, I swear the sweat started to pour down my brow.

The office was well appointed with excellent furniture and paintings. I smiled to notice a vase of monkshood flowers on the smaller desk. The foolish women doubtless had no idea that it was deadly poisonous. They probably thought the deep blue resembled the robe of the Virgin, or some such nonsense!

The *priora*, however, soon revealed herself as a specimen of more intelligence than I like to see in a woman. I was pleased to discover that her repulsive assistant, the *vicaria*, was a thoroughly stupid fanatic. Her habit was ridged with various penitential garments beneath. Her neck was raw. There was blood around her right ankle: she must have been wearing the cilice. Your woman obviously considered herself among Heaven's royalty, with all that suffering. I wondered if that sucked-orange face of hers was her own creation.

The *vicaria* scowled – or perhaps, with the melted features, she just looked that way at all times – while the *priora* informed me that the council and the chapter of the convent had approved my application on Marcella's behalf.

'Does your sister speak our tongue?' demanded the Melted One. The smell of her rotten, starved breath floated unwelcomely over the desk.

Marcella's Spanish, I testified, was fluent as my own. The educational requirements of a convent in Peru would present no difficulty. I mentioned a crisis that had obliged a recent sequestration in what I delicately called 'a special refuge'. I did not mention the term 'lunatic asylum' lest it raise their price or give them qualms.

'Marcella longed all her life to be a nun,' I told them. 'So imagine the shock of Bonaparte closing all the convents in Venice, just as she was about to take up her vocation! It affected her painfully. I would go as far as to say it was too much for her. As a loving brother, I found that I could not in conscience deny her heart's desire: an enclosed life in a house of God.'

'Why not a convent in Madrid or Seville?' The Deformity's cracked shrillness well fitted the ugly mouth from which it issued. 'Given your family connections in Spain?'

I let the *priora* answer. I noted that she used a tone of exaggerated patience with her colleague. 'Napoleon's conquests and convent closures have extended there too, Sor Loreta. The situation in Europe is still uncertain for those who seek a religious life. Are you not satisfied that the Pope's own cardinal in Rome sent a letter to support this application?'

That was when I saw the pure hatred between the two women, or at least on the part of the *vicaria* towards her superior. The *priora* continued, smugness enriching her voice, 'And nor is the Conte Fasan a stranger among us. Of course, the Conte Fasan's father made himself . . . a home in Arequipa as well.'

So the scandal of my father's second family had not escaped their attention. I smiled. 'I have purified my father's house. It is a respectable residence once more.'

In fact, I had that morning moved my whore from the *tambo* in there, to her gaudy delight. I had left her eating a garlic breakfast in my father's bed.

The *vicaria*'s single eye met mine and held them for an unpleasant moment. God's Breeches but that was an ugly woman! I nourish a hope that the Squeamish Reader shall never behold her like. I wiped the perspiration off my brow and passed to the meat of this conversation. 'What are your arrangements to stop the men getting in?'

The *priora* affected horror, but I was having none of it. They had a binding promise of my money now – I had the right to information.

'Come, come, the situation in Venice is well known – convent walls built of veils etcetera and so forth. And here? Pregnancies? Love affairs? Escapes?'

A triumphant smile played about the Deformity's distorted lips.

'We have nothing of that nature in this place.' Now the *priora* looked me neatly in the eye.

On the streets of Arequipa I had heard nothing to gainsay her, yet for all I knew, behind walls as thick as Santa Catalina's they could be resurrecting virginities like wintered daffodils and no one but the buyers of maidenheads would know.

'Can you prove that such things do not occur?'

'I have never been asked such a question. It has not been necessary. Yes, that is your answer.'

'So are all your nuns so ugly that no one comes after them?'

The *vicaria* showed no sign of having understood me. The *priora* stubbornly said nothing. I persisted, 'Are your doctrines so desolate that their minds are too dull for temptation?'

'Our nuns are beautiful and noble and intelligent, and they are safe. The men of this town are our brothers, fathers and cousins, for whose souls the nuns pray all day long. Our nuns inspire not lust but veneration. As for foreigners – the feet of handsome and depraved strangers only rarely make their way up our mountain.'

I looked closely at her face to see if she was flirting with me. She was not. The *vicaria* stared at me as if I was a snake in a bottle. Well, obviously, she would not be welcoming anything male into *her* cloister, that one. I let it drop. Marcella's spindly former lover was hardly likely to make it across the ocean, up the hills of Islay and to the foothills of El Misti.

The *vicaria* now held up the famous document for me to sign. It was elegantly penned on thick paper. The light streaming through the window revealed a handsome watermark of the best Almirall production.

Apparently, I had seen fit to declare: 'I therefore beseech your Excellency that my sister might be received in the convent, for this would bring much happiness to my sister and grace and blessings to myself . . .'

I skimmed its pompous verbiage until I found the part that concerned the dowry. I was stunned at their rapacity, to the extent of even being a little admiring of it. It seemed that 'I, the brother of the sister mentioned, am disposed to give, pay and after counting relinquish 2,400 pieces of assayed silver, one quarter in advance and the rest when she passes from her novitiate into the stature of a professed nun . . .'

It still rankled that I had paid Corpus Domini in full and in advance, yet never received a return of those thousand ducats when Napoleon closed the convent. A sweet thought occurred to me: if I was selling my sister's maidenhead for a second time to God, this time I was selling God a potentially defective item. While I was sure that the little doctor Santo had not got a finger in anywhere, Padre Portalupi had refused to detail exactly what the estimable Flangini had done to Marcella on San Servolo. But she was certainly not untouched.

Alongside the predictable list of scapulars, wimples and candles was a bizarre bazaar of merchandise: a cape, two burlap tunics, two doublets, two pairs of sandals, a wooden bedstead, bed-curtains, two mattresses, four sheets, two pillows, two blankets, a bedspread, a small table, a chair, a small coffer, a washbowl, a chamber pot, a candlestick, a stool, four pairs of boots and ten yards of cotton fabric.

Another paragraph announced, 'Special Supplementary Requirements for a nun issuing from Venice . . .'

Marcella was also required to supply twenty-five items of luxury, including a painting of her patron saint, a statue of same, six cushions of Venetian cut velvet, a dozen gilded Murano glass goblets, three Turkey carpets, a full set of cooking equipment, a gilded coffee service, a dinner service of decorated silver, silk curtains, a field of ten acres outside Arequipa (they knew everything of my father's fortune, clearly) and a Venetian processional lamp of at least two hundred years' antiquity. Also at least one slave girl or a maid. The items of Venetian provenance were to be sent along with my sister, so that neither one arrived without the other.

There was an equally long list of forbidden items on a separate page, down which I glanced with interest.

The human part of the dowry could be supplied locally. The *priora* explained, 'We shall train a slave or servant in our community for when your sister takes the veil. I have my eye on a *samba* called Josefa for her. The girl is strong and willing; also clever and quick with languages.'

The *vicaria* huffed audibly at that. The *priora* continued smoothly, 'How many other servants shall your sister require? On the understanding that servants stay in the convent as our, as it were, property, even if the nun herself passes on.'

'One will be more than ample,' I replied.

The *priora* raised an eyebrow. 'Many of our girls have four or more.'

I enquired, 'And I don't suppose the Venetian goods will be returned in the case of my sister herself not surviving the journey, or her stay among you?'

The *vicaria* intoned, 'Just as a wife hands over the *dominio* of her worldly goods to her husband, so does each Bride of Christ donate her marriage portion to her Bridegroom.'

With the grace to look embarrassed, the *priora* asked kindly, 'Now tell us something of your sister, Conte Fasan.'

Away from Venice, there was no limit on my invention. I nestled comfortably in my chair and began. 'I'll not deceive you,' I lied, 'she is a frail creature. I have always maintained she was defrauded of her whole health by our mother, who gave way to an indulgence for tobacco and secretly smoked a pipe in her confinement. My sister's debility, and doctors have confirmed this, was formed of the smoke she breathed in the womb.'

I was gratified to see a slightly shifty look in the *priora*'s eyes.

The *vicaria* demanded baldly, 'What kind of debility?'

'She is a congenital cripple,' I embroidered rapidly, 'with all the attendant cerebral difficulties of the species.'

A ready tenderness immediately softened the face of the *priora*. The *vicaria* appeared lost in thought.

'That aside, my sister has in fact conspired to use her weak health as a cover for . . . certain mischiefs. A true Christian would have accepted her ills, and grown even saintlier on them. However, my sister used her apparent debility as a veil for . . . a double guilt because she worked on our compassion, inspiring our pity and our leniency, just at the moment when she most deserved our most stringent observation. By a miracle, I intervened before it was too late.

'A brother must sometimes fight duels to protect his sister's good name. I have made sure at least that her name and her body are untainted, or naturally I would not have brought her here to you.'

This long and mysterious speech appeared to stupefy both the Peruvian nuns, and certainly blockaded any further questions. And thereafter I

275

distracted them with descriptions, gravid with luxury, of the gilded coffee service that would soon be on its way up El Misti mountain.

My next visit was to the humble new home of my father's mistress, to inspect my half-brother. The problem was this: if the boy was born later than myself and before Marcella, then he might well qualify as the missing will's 'next-born child'. And he was male.

The once-proud Beatriz Villafuerte was now reduced to some rented rooms in a commercial courtyard served by a common bathhouse and latrine. When I say I went to see my half-brother, I mean I went to take a secret look, bribing an ostler to let me watch him from a spyhole in the stable that gave on to the bathhouse.

On first sight, I swore under my breath for he was indeed a decade-and-a-half younger than myself, junior even to Marcella. I would have given him fifteen years at most. I saw he was my father's son, which meant another possible contender, should the accursed true will come forth after Marcella was neatly tucked away in Santa Catalina. He was damnably good-looking, deer-eyed, slender, if you like that sort of thing.

'What is he called?' I hissed to the ostler, who kept watch for me outside.

'Fernando. He's a fine boy . . .'

Fernando! My father had bestowed his own name on his Peruvian bastard, denying it to me, his legitimate heir! Or had the luscious Beatriz Villafuerte stolen the name, with intent . . . ?

But more likely, given his coldness towards me, my father himself had offered his name freely to his Arequipan spawn. He was not ashamed of *this* son. Inside the bathhouse my half-brother emerged from the water. His body was full of grace and ease. Such ugly thoughts ran through my mind that my mouth filled with a bitter flavour.

My saliva did not grow sweet again until I went to my father's grave in the little cemetery behind Santa Catalina and poured poison into the earth beneath the abundant fresh flowers I found here. I wanted that poison to go right down to his coffin, to saturate it, and to shrivel the body beneath. Then I dined copiously, as if I was trying to eat Arequipa. I had such a desire to consume the place. A dish of guinea pig splayed and battered is a thing seldom to be met with beyond Peru, and so I took the opportunity to pillage the hutches. I ate alpaca, and mountain rabbit and woodpecker, crunching on bones like a dragon on a virgin, and I would have eaten condor if they had not failed to shoot me one of the great black birds. And when I had had my fill of Arequipa, I hurried out of town, feeling queasy in every possible way. I went back to the coast, to the next ship.

I left just in time. I was barely out of the country when a new little revolution befell Peru, shaking the place even more than the earthquake of my natal year 1784. Indian rebels under a leader who called himself Pumacahua raised their standards and some Cuzco outlaws occupied Arequipa, proclaiming independence. The noblewomen of the town and the male cowards retired to the convents for safety.

But by the time I was back in Venice the little revolt was over, and its followers had gone to their grim rewards. The convents had not been troubled by so much as a broken window. There was no possible reason why Marcella should not be dispatched to Arequipa immediately.

At the Palazzo Espagnol, a letter awaited me from Padre Portalupi, as I had expected. Marcella had been issued with the papers that declared her ready to return to the world. He felt the need to remind me, '. . . *And there shall be absolutely no need for the extremity of the restraining equipment you showed me. In fact, it would be a crime to use such devices upon your sister when she has been declared* risanata.'

Ready to return to the world? Grinning, I set about assembling her dowry. I kept the mounting pile in a warehouse by the docks. The Prudent Reader will understand that I did not want anyone to get wind of my plans until the moment of their execution.

When skimming the documents I had signed, it had not escaped me that the image of San Sebastiano was forbidden at Santa Catalina, in case his nearly naked form aroused thoughts of the flesh among God's brides. It occurred to me that Marcella would find some empathetical chime in her soul for the helpless man beset by a hundred arrows. So for her saint I commissioned a sculpture of a very fine and masculine San Sebastiano, less clothed than most, but well appointed with arrows. As an afterthought, I threw in our small family Mantegna of the same saint. I had never liked that picture – the saint is too serene. A man suffering like that should show his pain much more for people to enjoy and profit from seeing it.

I booked Marcella's passage on a merchant packet. Ever thoughtful of her needs, I enquired about ablutionary matters. Marcella was always very nice as to cleanliness, especially given her little problem.

'The pot is emptied every week,' I was assured by the purser. 'Not more than three to a pot, even in the aft cabins. Unless,' he added meaningfully, his hand twitching in his pocket.

'My sister's wants consist in nothing in particular,' I told the fellow, which sent him cross-eyed with perplexity.

Whistling, I turned on my heel, and felt his hungry gaze burning my back. I had a bookseller waiting in a tavern at Sant' Antonin with a promise of a volume bound in the skin of a very young woman said to have been taken from her while yet living. I was sure that I would know, on touching it, if this tale was genuine. For the bookseller had vouched that this little erotic work was bound in the breasts of the girl, and that one opened the cover by grasping a nipple.

A few hundred of my finest francs and that dainty was mine. It cost more than sending a sister half a world away. My fingers were seldom far from that book while I awaited the documents confirming Marcella's transportation to the beyond.

When all was accomplished, notarized, paid for and receipted, my mother and wife tersely informed, I went to Marcella on San Servolo and announced what would be happening to her next. I dropped in her lap a rollicking *Life of Santa Catalina*, including all the good details of how the lady fasted, disfigured her flesh, sucked the pus out of sick women, drank from a wound in God's side and married Jesus, who gave her his circumcised foreskin as a wedding ring. A long voyage is a grateful time for good reading matter. So.

The Alert Reader will be unsurprised to hear how I commenced that interview.

Of course, I said, 'This is going to be a little uncomfortable.'

Marcella Fasan

Minguillo's long absence abroad – we neither cared nor knew where – had given us one more season to know each other, softly, safely. My diary had become an illustrated love letter. I stood straighter to be able to see Santo from further off. My eyesight sharpened because at any time Santo might come into view. My hearing grew keen enough to hear him smile on the other side of the island.

We did not have much, but we thought we had time.

And then Minguillo came back with his new masterpiece for wrecking my happiness.

'Minguillo is planning a slow murder,' I told a white-faced Padre Portalupi, 'by the hands of others, of course.'

It was our one fully honest interview, this dry-eyed conversation in which I recounted all Minguillo's abuses since my childhood, the assassinations of Riva and Piero and the ruin of my own leg.

'Why did you stay silent all this time?' asked Padre Portalupi. He was a man broken in two. In an instant, he had taken on the full burden of his unwitting collaboration. I thought of what Cecilia had said to me, and I knew that I had wronged this man, who would have loved to help me. Now at last I would show him the trust that he had earned.

'I did not stay silent. Will you take care of these for me?' I handed him the pages of the diary I had kept on the island. He opened the first page, began to read, began to weep. He turned a page, discovering a fond likeness of himself. He turned one more sheet, and came across a portrait of Santo.

He asked me gently, 'Our doctor Spirito is your doctor Santo?'

I nodded. 'But Santo has never once been alone with me on this island.'

'That does not need to be said. The young man's honour would not allow it. Unlike your brother's. I will put a stop to this,' he insisted.

I told him that he could not help me. 'Minguillo will destroy you if you try. Why should you be sacrificed too?'

I explained how Minguillo had already tampered with him, divorced him from his natural goodness by lies, and then interrupted his supervision of San Servolo with the use of repeated summonings to the *Magistrato alla Sanità*. To make trouble for Minguillo, I told Padre Portalupi, would risk losing him his place.

'You stand between the poor patients here and all the fashionable theories from Paris, and the surgeons, you know that. Marta, Fabrizia – all my friends: they need you to protect them. And you must think of your own situation. An exile and a beggar cannot help others.'

For Padre Portalupi was like a nun, bound in poverty to his vocation. If Minguillo had him dismissed, stirring up some manufactured scandal as an excuse, no one would want a disgraced monk as a doctor, laying his corrupted hands on their sick flesh.

'Is there no one else who can help you, Marcella?' he urged.

'The deed is done. I am not of age. I have no money for a lawyer. My brother has already signed me over to the nuns in Arequipa. He tells me that even my trunks are full and sealed.'

'Your artist friend, the one with the . . . strong opinions? Ce . . . ce . . . Cecilia Cornaro?' he stammered. Her name alone still inspired alarm in him.

'Cecilia Cornaro is in Vienna. I suppose this fact also entered into Minguillo's calculations. There is no time for anyone to help me. My brother tells me that my departure shall be tomorrow at dawn. And that I shall be taken directly from San Servolo to the boat that shall carry me to South America.'

Padre Portalupi stumbled up from his desk, his face compressed with pain. He rambled around the shelves of his office, murmuring to himself. He pressed herbs into my hands, 'For the journey. Dwarf thwostle – *Menta pulegium* – for seasickness, also good for ache of loin or buttock and sore of thigh. For long periods on the back of a horse.'

Then he met my eyes, 'But Marcella, this is not the kind of medicine you really need, is it? Please wait here in my office. I am sending Spirito to talk to you. A private colloquy cannot do any harm at this moment. I believe he can help you more than I can. I shall make sure you are not disturbed, for a little time.'

Doctor Santo Aldobrandini

The first kiss, the last kiss, who could tell what that was.

Gianni delle Boccole

It ud appened at last. But the timing were spektackolar bad, God-the-Murderer!

Santo ud finely at last made his dekkerashun. And Marcella had shone willing. From what I could gather, save us, there had been a kiss.

'*Baso no fa buso, ma xe scala per andar suso,*' I told him, for my own heart were dancing with happiness. 'A kiss dunt make a hole, yet it's a ladder to get where ye want, as ye mite say.'

Then I were sorry, for Santo blusht like an August sunset, and told me that jist when evrything was seeming to be goin pretty the real news were bad n worser. So much for the ladder. That partickeler kiss, as it turned out, led nowheres. Marcella ud been kissed, only to be wisked oft to some battlement up a mounting in Peru. She were alredy on the boat by the time Santo runned into the *ostaria* to give me the news, Pig ovva God.

She had not een been hallowed home one night to take leave on her Mamma, or on them what truely loved her. As usual Minguillo ud wrongfooted us like a general. There ud been nothing in his study – not a sliver o paper een – to give me a hint o his fowl plan all these weeks – jist his assence from it on misterious excursions to the docks.

Santo were convolsed with the idea that he would become a ship's surgeon on the next brig out o Venice and work his passage to Peru.

I hated for to be a damp squid but someone had to be the voice o reasoning: 'What will ye do when ye get there? She'll be shutted up in the convent and ye wunt be hallowed in by no matter o means. Ye isn't famly, and ye can't speak Span-yard.'

Marcella Fasan

All the way to South America I breathed on that kiss.

I felt Santo's lips on mine like an anchor dragging back through the oceans we ploughed.

I did not think about storms, or rowdy whales or ambushing pumas on mountain paths, or what awaited me behind the walls at Santa Catalina. I thought of Santo. When I looked into the rheumy mirror in my cabin, I saw his face. When I closed my eyes and touched my mouth, I felt his lips on mine.

The passage was tempest-strewn. Now that I had been kissed by Santo, I was afraid to die before I had got all the goodness out of that kiss. And that was my only fear every time the sea sent up jagged shards of white-tipped green and sucked them back under the boat.

I spoke to no one. I was reluctant to interrupt my contemplation of the kiss. Then, among the passengers, I was astonished to see my old friend Hamish Gilfeather, but only faintly so, as my full power of thought and feeling was still entirely fixed on the kiss.

I had not nearly finished with the kiss when Hamish Gilfeather renewed his kind interest in me. At first, enveloped in the kiss, I heard his voice as if it was echoing across a misty valley. But gradually I began to listen, for the listening was good.

Hamish Gilfeather refused to be discouraged by my abstracted silence. He chatted to me until he drew words and then gradually conversations out of my mouth. Once he had me talking, he never ceased to attend to me. In his kindness he reminded me sweetly of Piero, whose death we both flinched from mentioning in those first days. Physically, he did not, for where Piero was a delicate insect, Hamish Gilfeather was a robust warhorse of a man. Mr Gilfeather was expert at manoeuvring the wheeled chair I used for rough days on deck, and knew just when to take my arm when I faltered on my crutch.

Mr Gilfeather, who had business in Montevideo, had been told by our captain that I was on my way to a Peruvian nunnery. In his fury, he felt moved to relate to me stories of the Inca girls found frozen to death or battered on the head in mountain shrines, well fattened with meat and maize, their hair shorn off, their families far away.

'The Spanish lassies fare no better for all their pure blood,' he ranted. 'The nuns in their enclosures must wait longer for their deaths, to be sure, but 'tis certainly no life,' he declared with pity. Then he opened his rain-coloured eyes wide and enquired, 'Unless it is a true vocation you're suddenly having, Miss Marcella, that will make the whole thing a joy to you? I don't recall any such notion when ye were working on your paintings in Cecilia Cornaro's studio.'

I shook my head.

'I do not wish to be tactless, y'know,' he continued, 'yet I travel the world and I have seen my share of barbarities, and this forcing innocent little girls up mountains is the one that really sticks in my craw and wobbles the wet of my eyes. The little dearrrs! Why, I have seen displayed at Savile House in London a Peruvian lassie left to starve up in the Andes five centuries ago and so thoroughly preserved by the ice, so perfect as in life, that ye might offer her hot chocolate and hope to revive her . . . To me, any nun is just as sad a business.'

I saw a drop trembling on the end of his nose, and I handed him my handkerchief, at which he kissed my hand. That gentle kiss brought me back into the present world. Thereafter I could not be stopped from prattling to him all day and through many nights too. I told him my whole story, not leaving out any flinching detail about Minguillo, about poor Piero, whom he had loved. My explanation of the true nature of Piero's death caused Mr Gilfeather to take an abrupt solitary turn about the deck until he recovered himself. When he returned, I told him about Cecilia, and about the madhouse. For three whole nights in a row I talked about Santo's kiss.

Hamish Gilfeather listened in silence, occasionally clasping my hand, or murmuring some Gaelic imprecation against my brother. Finally I remembered to enquire, 'And how is your wife, Signor Gilfeather? She was not well when we met before.'

His wife's illness had worsened, he told me. She was now bedridden by a wasting disease. That explained his deft touch with my own disabilities, and his tact. I felt selfish then, for we had talked only of my tragedies for all these days. After that, I encouraged him to speak of his adored Sarah at every opportunity.

'Did you ever persuade Cecilia Cornaro to paint her?' I asked.

'Not yet. 'Twas the chief object of this last visit to Venice. I was sorely disappointed to find her away in Vienna. Only Cecilia Cornaro will know how to keep my darling Sarah alive . . .'

I finished his sentence silently, 'Even when she is dead.'

I had never seen a man in love with his own wife before, and it was a thing that gave me much cause for wonder.

Gianni delle Boccole

Minguillo knowed full well when he put Marcella abord the boat that them Incas had jist put up another reverlushun in Peru and marital law were imposed on the country. He told me hisself what high-jinx the Span-yards had originly did to squash the old infidel ways in the Inca breasts. They had hurted there dead loved ones, that's what they done. Een there grate hants n huncles, what they keeped preserved in there ouses for there worships, was pulled apart n jumpt on by the Span-yard conkistadoors. I were feroshus sad to hear it.

'The remains', Minguillo called em, and he laffed like ripping satin.

The remains of Tupac Amaru, for example, what had become a book on his shelf.

I wunt have bethought so hard and hurtful about it all, if I haint myself onct accidently handled that book made o the Inca's skin. I still had the dirty taste of it on my fingers, and now

I could not stop thinking about what the Span-yards were about in Peru. Swear that in them days after Marcella was tookt from us I went a little mad myself. There were no hope to fizz-sick my own soul, and I were sorry for all the poor creechers abused in this world.

If them Incas bethought a little soul clung to the dead they had loved, for why were that so bad? – for why *shunt* they be hallowed to love there deceased ones? How was them mummies diffrint from the bits o saints that the Christians like to keep in there churches? For why was they evil?

I am not so well oft for brains, but I know – sfortunately – at what point a person becomes a corpse. But at what point do a corpse become 'remains'? I mean, losing that thing which makes the living show it respeck?

Tis like to ask 'at what point does a pig become pork?'

When does skin become leather? And is it a thing ye can do in good conshens – to use humane leather to bind a book?

I were so upset that I had horrid fancies. Late at night, did Minguillo's books of humane leather talk among themselves? Did they tell the stories of there desiccrashons to each other, like old soldiers in a tavern?

There were one in English, that I could not get out of my maginings. By an English lady named 'Mary Wollstonecraft' for her pains. Twere called *A Vindication of the Rights of Woman*. I guest at the littoral meaning – were something bout the wronging and righting o ladies. I had opent that one, and lookt at its topography that were did in fine lettering. But first thing I seed was that Minguillo imself had writed a jolly note inside that sayed, '*This* particular woman's rights were perhaps slightly violated when they flayed her anonymous shoulder to bind this book.'

I dropped the poor pink-grey thing on the floor, and then sayed sorry to it a hunnerd times, each time sorryer.

Sor Loreta

The heathens were brought low as dogs after their failed revolt of 1814. I felt a little nostalgia for My childhood memories of the death of Tupac Amaru II back in Cuzco in 1781. Now it was proclaimed that the Indians would not be allowed to wear their Inca clothes – their *unco* vest or their *yacollas*, shawls of black velvet, or the *masapaycha* circlet with a tassel of red alpaca.

I had no doubt of My duty, especially with the dangerous Venetian Cripple on her way to us. The convent must be purified of all taint. There were tokens of the pagan ways in the beds and baskets of our own servants in Santa Catalina! So I had all the Indian *criadas* penned up in the grain-store by Sor Narcisa and Sor Arabel while I combed through their sacks of poor possessions. Not a few of them had garments and relics that I detected to be of an unholy nature.

I collected all these objects in a heap in the garden and then called all the *criadas* to come and watch while I set fire to everything.

Then I had Sor Narcisa and Sor Arabel hold the girls down, one after another, while I poured cold water over their heads as a kind of baptism. The young girls kicked and screamed, because they believed in their ignorant hearts that baptism was the way the Spanish spread the Small-Pox that had devastated their race and lost them their continent.

Doctor Santo Aldobrandini

I left San Servolo when Marcella did. It was unbearable there without her, especially because of Padre Portalupi's stricken looks. He had instantly forgiven me my assumed identity, saying, 'Under whatever name, you have done God's work here, Santo. I only wish I had . . .'

I went back to Venice so that I could be close to Gianni and glean what fragments of news that I might of Marcella and her journey. And to see what Napoleon's epidermis might kick up for me in the way of an opportunity to follow her to South America.

Destroyed by his Russian campaign, my old patient Napoleon was now a prisoner on Elba. Spain was lost. The Austrians were back in Venice. But some mystical quality still hung about him. No one believed that Bonaparte was really quite over. We were all waiting for him to start itching again.

I did not know if Minguillo's thugs were still keeping watch for one Santo Aldobrandini. So I kept the name of Spirito, and found lodgings as far from the Palazzo Espagnol as I could contrive. My next step was to negotiate with a Spanish madam in Cannaregio, who gave me lessons in her mother tongue in exchange for treating her whores for all the diseases to which their profession exposed them.

I had first been called there some eight years before, after one of the girls was savagely beaten. Signora Sazia was pleased with my carrot poultice and a lint saturated in warm arnica lotion that put the girl back to work in less than a week. Then I had saved actual lives when the girls were poisoned by malicious doses of 'The Tears of Santa Rosa' just before I went to the Russian front.

Signora Sazia offered me a regular position and wage. I agreed on condition that one Minguillo Fasan was barred from her establishment. She smiled bitterly, 'He already is. It is he who beat my girl and sent us the Tears. We are fallen women here, Doctor, yet we don't care to be pushed. Are you the Conte Fasan's enemy? Then you are our friend.'

She embraced me, and advanced me my first month's wages, which meant that I could for once treat Gianni to a meal in the *ostaria*.

The madam proved a happy choice as a language mistress. She had once been a working girl herself. She knew at least as much about the most hard-working items of human anatomy as I did.

And so, while Marcella's ship sailed closer and closer to Peru, I also journeyed towards my goal of being a credible doctor in Spanish. I hoped very much that my vocabulary was respectable, yet perhaps it mattered not if it was not. Marcella would understand that I preferred to treat the poor and uneducated. *Pechitos*, *chichis* and *tetitas* would do very well as words for breasts. And I rather liked *pitonguita*, little python. These honest, vivid words tasted more wholesome than some poetic euphemism uttered in a fawning voice. My brief experience of doctoring for the rich had almost disgusted me in my profession.

Sor Loreta

The *priora* was angry with Me for burning the possessions of the *criadas*. The light nuns had just re-elected her for a second term, and she was full of her own glory and eager to scourge Me with hard words.

'Graven images, *Madre Priora*,' I told her in a slow penetrating voice, as she seemed determined to stay ignorant of the most simple truths. 'The Andean peoples had not even heard of Christianity before the Spanish *conquistadores* arrived. For a thousand years the Devil ruled their minds and directed all their acts. God caused Spain to conquer the Andean peoples because their sins were so very awful that it was the best thing for them.'

She groaned, so it was My duty to continue: 'All over Peru our Holy Fathers are seeking to put an end to heathen behaviours. We must do our part. *You* are too busy with Rossini to do so. And now there is a Venetian heretic on her way to corrupt us all.'

It occurred to Me then that the worship of Rossini might well be excised in the same way. The image of a pyre of sheet music came into My mind. I must have spoken some words to that effect, for the *priora* lost her composure. She shouted in inelegant tones that the *criadas* were wild with grief for the loss of their clothes, the miniatures of their mothers, their dolls (for some of the convent servants were only children) and their sacred bits of paper they could not even read.

'The extirpation of the ancestors was a shameful affair!' she cried and I suddenly wondered if her high colour carried a taint of Indian blood. That would explain her weakness for tobacco. She ranted, 'That ugly business finished with the seventeenth century! Along with those crazed martyrs who drank pus and mutilated themselves. Decent people do not do such things any more, don't you understand? It is like a return to the horrors of the Dark Ages. You are a creature of the Dark Ages, that is what you are, and you wish to drag Santa Catalina into the darkness with you!'

I stood proudly silent. The *priora* then informed Me, viciously, that the *criadas, sambas* and even some of the nuns called Me 'the Vixen' and not 'the *vicaria*', the honour rightly due to Me.

I struggled with the temptation to weakly lament this new insult. I bore it bravely, like another scourge. It is ever thus, that God chooses his finest few to bear the ignorance and malice of the many.

I steered My thoughts towards My great task ahead.

Soon she would be among us, the sister of a brother well steeped in the Devil's arts. I had seen how he drummed his foot under the table, accompanying Satan's music inside his heart. She, of the same stock, could not but be corrupt, accustomed to wallowing in the fleshpots of earthly vice in that most depraved of cities which had spawned her.

I alone knew that soon I would be like salt and light to that ambassadress from the dark abyss of sin! How she would be amazed by Me!

Marcella Fasan

Forty-five days from Falmouth to Rio de Janeiro. There the customs and quarantine officers rampaged through the ship as we disembarked to take the air. Outside O'Brien's Hotel, I saw slaves for the first time, chained together by the dozen, bound for the flesh-shops in the market square. At the door to one of these establishments, I stopped to stare at hundreds of black-skinned children dressed indifferent as to sex in blue-and-white checked aprons. They regarded me and my crutch without curiosity, sunk in their own misery.

There would be slaves at the convent of Santa Catalina. Minguillo had complained that he was obliged to buy one for me as part of the dowry, though she would not serve me until I professed. I hated the thought of owning one of these stolen children, or any human creature. And how, I wondered, could any slave of mine not heartily hate me too?

On to Montevideo and in this passage it came on to blow. All the passengers except the well-seasoned Hamish Gilfeather, and, for some reason, myself, took greenly to their beds. We enjoyed our solitude on deck and I felt the wind blowing strength into my bones. By the time that the other passengers crawled out of their beds, we were near land again.

All my life I had seen only Venetians, or those, like myself, whose blood was a little enriched with Spanish elements. At Montevideo I was astonished by the visible blends of blood in South America, from pure Spanish down to undiluted Inca and those blue-black slaves hunted from Africa and carried here to be sold.

A group of Indian children followed Mr Gilfeather and me through the streets, chattering to us in a high, clear Spanish devoid of Old World lisping. Mr Gilfeather gave them almond comfits and bright ribbons that he unwound in great lengths from his pockets to their never-ending delight. In exchange, I was presented with a parakeet sewn up in a box of hide with a small round hole cut in, barely large enough for the bird's beak to emerge with desperate caws for food.

'How do I clean its little house?' I asked, with appropriate motions, and they laughed at me, partly for the strangeness of my own accent, but also at my miscomprehension.

'No clean. When dead, new house, new parakeet.'

When the children were out of sight, Mr Gilfeather and I ripped open the cage and liberated the bird. It flew unsteadily yet with increasing grace, singing in intense tuneless joy.

We stared after it, unwilling to make the obvious comparisons.

Mr Gilfeather and I were soon to be parted, for Minguillo had decreed that I should make a land expedition over the Andes, instead of the gentler sea journey.

'This is an outrage,' pronounced Hamish Gilfeather. 'A strong man would quail at this journey and take it only in the company of a posse of stout friends. Your brother . . .'

Although I never uttered a word on the subject, I frankly longed for Mr Gilfeather to delay his own journey and to accompany me over the mountains. But he could not prolong his absence from his beloved Sarah. A letter from her doctor had reached him in Montevideo that had tugged his heart in painful jerks. Her strength was failing and he must hurry back to see her alive.

'How I would rejoice to take you with me,' he told me. 'And don't ye think that I've not been brooding on the same thing. But your brother's signed your contract with the nuns. I would be a wanted man over two oceans if I plucked ye from their clutches. I would never trade again, and I could not support neither you nor Sarah . . . should she live.'

'It is fine enough for me that you have kindly thought so,' I lied. 'Let us talk of it no more.'

'I can offer one thing,' he told me, the day before his ship sailed. 'Whatever letters you write tonight – I shall undertake to have them delivered discreetly and safely to your friends. And should my wife's condition prove better than I hope, then I shall myself make a swift journey to Venice, to meet with them and see what can be done, my dear.'

He handed me a bundle of clean, dry writing paper.

'I am constantly in need of more glass rings and musical snuff-boxes from Venice,' he explained, lest I felt too much beholden.

In the morning, as we shared a final breakfast, I handed him my sheaves of paper, folded, sealed and addressed to Padre Portalupi, Gianni, Cecilia Cornaro and Santo. This last was wrapped in my handkerchief, which enclosed a piece of my hair that I had snipped off in the night. It was all I had to give Santo by way of a promise of myself. He already had my kiss.

Hamish Gilfeather pushed a box of cigars across the table.

·'I do not, have never . . .'

'For your peons, lassie. A cigar presented with a ceremonial degree of politeness will effect far more goodwill than any amount of tipping. Cigars are currency with men and women alike, for both genders are addicted to tobacco here. Bestow them wisely, and ye will flourish among the people whose help you need.'

He kissed my hand and pressed it hard, producing a jar of cucumber pomade as his final gift. 'Farewell, my dear. Rub this into your face when the cold burns it, keep your fingernails short and out of your mouth, never fall asleep when you are cold, and I shall like your chances of surviving, dear girl.'

Gianni delle Boccole

Nine weeks later come five letters wrapped in a big soft packet, that were sent all the way from Scotland. Twere from a man called Amish Gillyfether, bless him a thousand times, for he ud seen our Marcella alive across the ocean and into the hands o strong men what he had slippt a little summing to take her safely oer the mountings.

He last seen our girl, he writed, in brave spirits and good health. The sea-journey ud in fact fortyfied her. She ud talked of me feckshonately, and wished me to know all were good with her, at least, at last sighting.

There were a dear little note all for me alone, even, with funning tales of life at sea and even drawins to show she were in sweet humour.

The soft item that wrapped the letters were a Scottish blanket which I give to Anna, who were delighted with it. The colours was a bit rich for my blood, but she assured me twere the hide o fashion.

The letter for Santo – I delivert it myself to his digs in Cannaregio. Twere a little gift for me, to see his face when he held that packet in his hands. I saw the curl slip out of it and around his finger.

Now, thanking this Mr Gillyfether, we had summing, not hope zackly, but a candle to hold up to see if hope mite come our way.

Doctor Santo Aldobrandini

I bought a map of the South Americas. I stared at fields of ice and killing peaks.

Against my will, stubborn memories imposed themselves on that map: the deaths of our Venetian soldiers that I had been powerless to save in the implacable tracts of Russian snow.

Before they died, many snow-doomed individuals showed signs of idiocy and weakness of sight. They lost the use of their tongues for speech. They had marched on, propelled by the bodies of their comrades. But if they slipped to the outer part of the column, eventually they peeled off the core of men, and lurched into ditches of pillowy snow, where they died.

And if they were brought to a warm place, worse awaited them. For the frozen parts melted only to be seized by an instant gangrene that moved greedily over the whole body, sometimes creating a peculiar phosphorescence, very like beauty, in their skin. The individual would then suffocate with a putrid liquefication of the lungs. Other men, iced in their blood, simply fell down in front of the fire and never rose again.

Signora Sazia, frowning compassionately, taught me *los pulmones, el hielo, la gangrena, piel luminosa, la muerte:* lungs, ice, gangrene, luminous skin, death.

Marcella Fasan

For my journey over the mountains, I was accompanied by an *arriero*, three peons, and six mules carrying my dowry as well as our provisions.

Hamish Gilfeather's cigars went a long way towards ensuring my comfort. I distributed my stock with smiles on the first day. After that, the peons treated me with more kindness than they had been paid for, and even made an effort to speak a comprehensible Spanish in my hearing.

Out of town the way soon became bleak and steep. On the very first day I saw a vulture astride the back of a lame yet living horse, devouring its torn flesh while it brayed pitifully. The peon called Arce mercifully dispatched the horse with his musket. Higher up, we passed the bodies of mules mummified where they had fallen. Arce showed me how the sun and cracking wind had reduced them to paper models of themselves: he bounded off his own beast and picked up the carcass of one of the dead mules with a single hand. He urged me to dismount and try it myself. And yes, it was dry and light as a handful of corks. An hour later, Arce pointed out a human corpse on its way to the same airiness of being.

We passed our nights at wretched post houses ('*esta casa está a su disposición*') where we slept on mud floors in rooms without doors, and ate in *pulperías* surrounded by drunken local men. Changes of linen were possible only every fourth day. We ate olives in clinging oil, mutton *asados* without salt, and dried beef that tasted and reeked like strips carved off a saddle.

Green fields tidy as villa lawns alternated with dizzy passes where a false step would have dashed us to atoms on the rocks below. And with each step the way grew harder and the cold more cruel.

'Shake yourself like this!' the peons urged when we paused. They flung themselves around like dervishes, shouting '*Alalau! Alalau!*' The very words seemed warming, and I followed their example to the best of my abilities, hurtling around my crutch in a jerky dance.

The cold first retarded my circulation. The blood seemed to delay at my heart, unwilling to venture to the frontiers of my body, which became livid and bluish about the ears, nose and fingers. I felt a languor that was hard to resist. My limbs grew disobedient to my feeble will. My animal functions almost ceased. The skin contracted around the roots of my hair. The flesh of my face pocked like a plucked goose. My numb fingers lost the capacity for discrimination – a knife blade or a silk cushion would have felt the same to them. My tongue forgot how to distinguish flavours. Inside their rabbit fur, my fingers and feet shrank until my gloves and snowshoes threatened to drop off.

Drowsiness finally overtook me. I wanted to sleep at all costs, to lay myself down in the snow, just for a quarter-hour. I begged to be allowed to do so. But the peons told me that if I did, I would never get up again.

'What's she got to get up for anyway?' I heard one of them mutter. 'Poor little girl, poor little one.'

For Santo would wish it, I thought. *So that Santo may kiss me again.*

Sor Loreta

We received news that the Venetian Cripple had landed at Montevideo. As I pictured her progress over the mountains, I thought of the cold she would endure, how the wind would whip her flesh, how the altitude would poison her belly. As I did so, I scourged Myself with especial severity, to be fit for the great undertaking of bringing the Venetian devil to God.

All the light nuns were gossiping about the Venetian Cripple: what clothes she would bring with her, how beautiful she would be. Most of all they asked one another, why had her brother sent her over the Andes in the worst weather? How could she survive?

I told Myself. 'If she is a devil, then she will survive.'

Marcella Fasan

I remember a pleasant torpor stealing over me. Later I was told that the men saw me fall to the side of the horse to which I was tied, just as we approached another mountain inn.

Afterwards Arce explained it to me in stark nursery terms. They had carried me into a cold room and stripped me to my shift. Then they took turns to apply rough frictions with snow and cloths drenched in iced water. Still I lay without signs of life.

'But we refuse to let you die, girl!' Arce told me proudly. 'We say "No! No!" to Mister Death!'

When I first began to moan, they brought every kind of aromatic substance at their disposal into the room, smells both shockingly good, like roasted llama, and bad, like fermented hay. They laid me in an iron tub of cold water, careful not to break off any of my frozen digits, and when

I commenced to stir, they had me out of my bath, and onto a wooden slab where they applied volatiles and sternutatories to my nostrils. They opened my mouth and blew warm air into my lungs.

They tickled my parts with a feather. When washes of hot wine had no effect on my coma, they blew tobacco fumes up my rectum with bellows. They recommenced the manual frictions, this time with rags soaked in brandy and camphorated spirit of wine. When they could raise my head, they made me ingest a basin of tea, and then one of mulled wine, and carried me to a small room where a fire was lit. After an hour, I began to perspire and cry out at the darting pains in my fingers and legs.

'Then,' smiled Arce, 'we know you live all right, girl.'

I had not wanted to open my eyes, even when conscious. But when I felt the dignity of clothing roughly swaddled around me, I unclenched my eyelids for the first time. And saw nothing. In front of my eyes was pure white; a mist more impenetrable than the worst Venetian *caligo* – a sheet glued to my eyeballs.

'I am blind,' I wept. 'I can never see Santo again.'

When the men came to ask me what tortured me so, I added a torrent of Venetian to explain that my existing disabilities were now harnessed to this greater one, making me an entirely useless being.

'How could even Santo love me like this?' I sobbed.

'Your *santo*, your patron saint?' someone asked me. 'I think the nuns are supposed to have lady saints up at Santa Catalina.'

'Is just snow-blindness,' a kinder, invisible voice told me. 'It will pass.'

A growl from the *arriero*: 'And if it does not, it does not matter – the poor one is going to Santa Catalina. She does not need to see anything there, let alone some saint. Not even her Bible. Presumably she knows her prayers by heart already.'

'Why does she not need to see?' The mention of Santa Catalina charged the peons' voices with breathy fascination.

I recognized the *arriero*'s superior tone again, 'Do you not know what those girls do all day there? And all night?'

'Do you?'

'It is their life's work to pray for the sins of their families. They may do nothing except say *las almas del Purgatorio* to cut down the time their families spend roasting. Those girls get shut away for ever so that their brothers and fathers and uncles may commit all the seven sins all day long in complete safety of their souls. The little sister will be praying away for them, speeding their way to heaven. One nun can do a whole household, if she is the hard-praying kind. Anyway, it does a family good to know that they have their own little saint in the convent, a living one. If you can call it living.'

'You don't say! The nuns cannot do anything else? Do they not visit the poor? Or sew? Or grow flowers? Or have entertainments?'

My ears burned.

'Most certainly not. Each girl has twelve slaves, and the slaves live any life she might have, doing her cooking, her washing, her shopping – all so that she may do nothing else except sit on her knees, mumbling. She is dead to the outside world. That's why they wear black, you know. They are in mourning for their lives. The nunnery has everything – mills, water, food. It would not be good for the nun's soul to be distracted, so everything is walled in there with her, in the living tomb. I heard that in Santa Catalina they are not even allowed to look at the mountain, in case it gives them improper ideas, being so manly and rugged!'

I heard the peons sniggering and slapping each other on the shoulder.

The *arriero* continued, 'So your nun lives in the convent like a rat in a cage. Until she goes mad or dies, or both. Happens all the time. Women are not s'posed to live locked up without their natural desires being accommodated, are they? So when one goes off, another little sister is sent up to take her place.'

'We keep this poor little one alive just for that?' Arce's voice was hushed with shock.

Another peon said starkly, 'Might as well put the creature out of its misery, Pedro.'

A gruff voice interrupted, 'Let's lose the girl then, and accidentally "lose" all this dowry-treasure. We can bury it in the snow and come back to get it when the story dies down. For her, it would be a mercy. For us, our making!'

There was a cautious murmur of approval from one of the other men and a cry of protest from Arce.

A rougher new voice suggested, 'We save she life once already, and we not even nearly at Arequipa. So let us tell she this – that we drop she treasure over a cliff, unless she promise on brother's life to say prayer for each one of we. The Scotsman say brother's all she got, she father dead.

We tell she that we hunt brother down and kill he if she don't pray for us and make us path safe.'

The *arriero* asked dubiously, 'How shall we know she keeps the bargain?'

'If anything happen to any one of we, us know that she has broke she word. She has to send one up for each of we every day.'

'No! Every hour!'

'Christian prayers!' muttered one peon contemptuously.

'Well, you can't expect her to worship the spirit of Pachacamac, can you? Does not matter what comes out of the girl's mouth – the right gods hear the right prayers, say I.'

After much debate, the peons settled on a prayer for each of them every two hours on weekdays and once an hour on Sundays. There was much talk about a special prayer to Santa Gertrude, that was a sure thing to save a thousand souls each time it was said.

Arce exclaimed, 'And Santa Águeda, to stop earthquakes!'

'So she lives, but what about the treasure?'

The *arriero* shouted, 'You know nothing! If she arrives without the treasure, then those venal cows at Santa Catalina won't take her in. They'll put her in the nearest brothel. She would be worth nothing to us then. God does not hear the prayers of whores, not with all those angels singing. We may as well all rot in hell. What would you rather have, a few pieces of gold, or eternal salvation, you miserable dog? Anyway, you would never be able to sell the gold or the statues without drawing suspicion on yourselves. It's not as if Peru is overflowing with Venetian antiquities. Is it worth a hanging to be a rich man for a day?'

And so Arce's kindness and the *arriero's* prudence saved my life.

I kept my face smooth and nodded my agreement as they mentioned the possible ill-consequences for my brother if I did not say the prayers they required. It had not occurred to them that I might have little reason to believe in a merciful and listening God. Or that, however many years I would now spend on my knees, I would sooner pray for the souls of their mules than for Minguillo's.

Dinner was ready: a stringy fowl that challenged the teeth to a losing duel. They settled down to disputing the year of the chicken's birth, and I was forgotten.

'Get some on your inside, girl,' Arce told me, handing me a portion. 'We go high-high tomorrow. May be last thing you keep down.'

298

Doctor Santo Aldobrandini

Although the Bible speaks highly of the spiritual worth of such ventures, the human body is annoyed and destroyed by journeys up mountains. If she survived the cold, Marcella would have altitude sickness to endure.

I consulted John Arbuthnot, *An essay concerning the effects of air on human bodies*, 1733. He told of a journey by Joseph d'Acosta to the top of the mountains of Peru, where he and his company were seized with bilious vomitings from the thinness and coldness of the atmosphere. They gasped for air, like fish beached with the tide. Every step was made as if in lead-lined boots.

For Marcella, every step was already twice as hard as for anyone else.

Marcella Fasan

The mist lifted from my eyes overnight. When we started moving again, Arce rode beside me and told me about what they had done to save me from freezing to death the previous day. After that, I lay face-down in the cart. I could not face those men. Each one of them had looked on – even handled – my naked form. They had seen more of me than a doctor, more than Santo had.

Then, when the *puna* came upon me, it took me badly. I had lived all my life at the low level of the sea. The mountains stole all the air out of my lungs, and the world grew glassy in my eyes. I slipped back into a torpid state from which I was roused only when the altitude swooped down and evacuated my stomach. I vomited meat, water and phlegm, retching and retching till only saliva was cast up.

'*Aquí hay mucha puna*,' Arce agreed, stepping out of the way of my watery projectiles. 'Here is much altitude illness. But you should see Pariacaca,' he told me. 'There you would vomit out your own knees! Here is good *puna*. There is very bad.'

'Is Pariacaca on our way?' I asked anxiously.

'If the lady would like to see it . . .' the *arriero* joked.

When we reached the topmost point of our travels, the peons indulged in a wild neighing, just like the mules. I gathered this was the traditional way of expressing relief and joy. In the mêlée a trunk tumbled off one of the mules, and I heard the ominous tinkle of glass.

From that hill I first saw a white town glittering in front of us like a model of a city proffered in a saint's hand. As we descended, my strength grew. With mittened fingers I drew portraits of each of the peons, which they accepted with much bowing. At their request, I sketched the floating palaces of Venice and the basilica of San Marco, in neither of which they quite believed, even after handing my drawings around with solemn care.

That night, when their snores announced I was virtually alone, I drew myself a pencil portrait of Santo and fell asleep with my cheek resting on his face.

'Your brother?' Arce awoke me with coca tea.

'Not brother,' he read my face. Gently, he took the picture from me. 'I keep safe for you, girl. Not good take to convent.'

Three days later, we crossed into Arequipa over a bridge that they called 'Bolognesi'. The current rushed beneath us in dizzying spirals that slammed against the shore and snarled around pocked stones big as cottages.

I heard Arce whisper to his friends, 'What say? Show the poor one a bit of the town before bung her up for good? Let her see Venice not only city with churches.'

So they turned sharply right and around and I beheld at once two strange sights. One was a square every piece as elegant as our San Marco, and a size or two bigger. A violent wave of homesickness swept through me. Just as in Venice, there were graceful arcades on three sides and a vast cathedral on the fourth. And in one corner stood a building as foreign and pagan as anything I had ever seen in books. It was crawling with lizards and leopards and tropical insects all rendered in a pink stone that seemed alive as human flesh.

'Now *that* what we call church in Arequipa,' Arce told me.

Gianni delle Boccole

If Marcella ud survived the mountings, she would be in that Santa Catalina by now with the Peruvian priests forcing holy wavers through her lips and accusing her of evry vernal sin, pickin on her jist because she were furrin and not one on em. Poor girl, not knowing a soul in that far-oft place. If she ud survived.

Humane company I were powless to provide. Insted, I done the most hardest thing in the world for me. I writed a letter. To the *priora* at Santa Catalina. I counted on that she would have some Italian from all the Latin litergees.

I told her evrything what Minguillo had did to his sister, from the start. In my one-word way, I made a list from garden to attic. If that *priora* bethought me wanting in the head, there wernt nothing I could do bout it.

I ended, '*For all I know, what is little, your convent is a good place. How I hope so. It would be God's work indeed if ye could look after our Marcella because God knows she is nowise safe in Venice.*'

I signatcherd it, 'a friend'.

Marcella Fasan

After one mule-promenade around the square, I was handed over to the nuns.

The afternoon sun was burning holes in the sky when we arrived at the door. The convent seemed dug out of golden sand, the towering creation

301

of a dogged child at the seaside. In the road just behind me, all Arequipa whistled, trotted and gossiped past. I knew that I stood for a precious moment between two worlds, and that soon I would be lost to this living one and delivered into the infinite silence and solemnity beyond. I craned my neck, taking in the street of pale stone houses, trellised and balconied with self-confidence that belied their lowly stature. Bougainvillea blazed cardinal red, not Venetian purple, against the white stone. A peasant woman walked past, her skirt a-fidget with poppy-scarlet flowers printed on indigo cotton. I gazed on each colour greedily. All colour, all life, I thought, would now be stifled to black and white inside the convent walls.

As I climbed with difficulty out of the cart, I supposed, *this is the last cart I shall ride in, until I am dead and my corpse is taken to the communal grave.*

Goodbye cart, I thought. Then goodbyes fell on me like a net over a lion in the jungle. I farewelled all the things I might never see again: canal reflections playing under the ribs of a bridge, a ball-dress, a little boy, a shop, a party, a rabbit, a haystack, a regatta, a silvery fish swimming under water, a young doctor giving me a look that reached inside me and gently handled my soul.

And the things I could never hear now: a Venetian folksong, a lullaby, a minuet, the cry of the fishmongers, the abuse of the gondoliers, a salty argument in the street, running feet, my own voice laughing (for I knew that to speak light thoughts in a convent was considered a kind of unchastity), the voice of a young man telling me he loved me.

Then the *arriero* was pulling a bell-cord, and a door opened promptly under an arch that bore a relief of Santa Catalina herself painted in sun-struck colours. From a crack in the door, a black-clad nun peered out at us through blue spectacles. Her face was brutally disfigured, a part of her nose melted against a cheek. I lowered my eyes, sensing it would be unwise to stare. Her own eyes were unreadable behind the thick blue glass.

'The Venetian Cripple?' she asked and the lower half of her face, the part capable of expression, showed a vicious delight. It was not so much her stagnant breath, nor the hard words, but her way of saying them that sent my heart plummeting. My brow prickled with nervous perspiration.

'We have managed to save her for you,' the *arriero* declared proudly, 'though twice she nearly died of cold and the *puna* and from her own weaknesses. However, our strenuous efforts have delivered her safely.'

'God has chosen to preserve her 'til this time,' replied the nun smoothly.

'Your interventions, however strenuously you might describe them, had little or no bearing in the matter. We do not pay gratuities for deliveries, if this is what you are hinting at.'

At that word 'deliveries' I began to tremble.

I stood with my eyes downcast, desperate for the necessary room but determined that my first words in my new home would be of a higher order than '*Dónde están los . . .*'

'*Vicaria*, why do you keep the poor child fainting on the doorstep?' A new voice, low and intelligent, issued through the doorway.

A black-clad arm now reached out of the convent wall and drew me to a comfortable breast.

'You are welcome, Marcella Fasan,' said the clever voice warmly, and in Italian. In another second I was on the threshold of a vaulted receiving room, cosy with carpets and flowers and brimming with lamplight.

The *vicaria* tutted and turned her back, busying herself with barking orders to the men who carried my dowry across the threshold into Santa Catalina. Impatiently, she herself lifted a vast box from the cart and heaved it into the courtyard. The men stared: the grotesque woman was emaciated and diminutive in stature, yet she had more strength than any of them.

The *arriero* nodded at me encouragingly, and the other men smiled and waved fondly. But Arce crossed himself.

Sor Loreta

It would be harder than I thought. In His divine wisdom God had sent Me a She-Devil with a sweet face and a pitiful, limping form. She was artfully put together to glean compassion and tenderness from the weak-willed.

I alone knew the Devil in all his guises and I was not taken in.

I shuddered to imagine what transactions the Venetian Cripple had combined with the *arriero* and the men. I saw by the amorous looks they gave her that she had fanned their desires with her expert seductions. Now Priora Mónica was also seduced.

Remembering Sor Andreola's milky softness, and Sor Sofia's flower-like

303

face, I guessed that the Venetian Cripple would set out on Satan's path with an outward display of modesty and quietness in all her actions. Like them, she would dissemble devoutness with skill and guile.

How was I to wrestle with the Devil in the soul of such a subtle enemy?

Marcella Fasan

The *priora* was kind and soft as a feather bed. Her first thoughts were all for my comfort: I was quickly shown a necessary room, thereafter plied with refreshing drinks, punctuated by warm hugs. Her Italian was strongly accented but grammatically correct. She said that she loved me already because I came from the country where Rossini was born. She purred, 'I know that our dear Rossini cherishes a great affection for Venice. For the Venetians first recognized his genius.'

Then she looked at me with a quivering lip, 'Have you not seen Rossini on the stage at the theatre of San Moisè in Venice? Imagine, the maestro was but a youth of eighteen when his *Cambiale di Matrimonio* was first performed in your blessed city in 1810!'

I shook my head sadly, and she shook her head too, as if to shake away the disappointment. I decided not to tell her that girls confined to their rooms or on island lunatic asylums were not allowed out even to hear the genius of the young Rossini. Perhaps she did not know about my time on San Servolo; perhaps it would be better if she did not.

She pulled a velvet cover off a shining ebony object. It was an English piano brought from London at the cost of 4,000 francs, she told me gleefully, 'So that we may play Rossini.'

'You speak excellent Italian, *Madre Priora*,' I observed lamely.

'Of course I must speak the language of our dear Rossini! But how you must be tired! We must smuggle you into your room before the other nuns become overexcited about your arrival! Imagine! A Venetian here among us! For them, it is like a fairy tale.'

There was a tap on the door. I started to see a man of middle years enter the room, to be greeted with smiles from the *priora*.

'Do not fear, child,' she told me. 'Surgeon Sardon must examine you before we allow you to mingle with the other nuns, lest you have brought any contagious disease. And he will give you a vaccination for the Small-Pox. We are proud to have rid Arequipa of this affliction by God's miracle of modern medicine.'

The doctor's examinations were brief and discreet. Finally he made me walk a few steps without my crutch and administered the vaccine to my arm from a little bottle topped by a long needle.

'Fit to serve God,' he smiled. 'Though you shall feel unwell temporarily on account of the serum.'

With a smile, he cautioned the *priora*, 'Let her have a restful day. No dramaticals.'

The *priora* summoned a *velo blanco* – a white-veiled serving nun – to take me to my cell. 'A little something to eat will be brought to you there directly,' she told me. My possessions, she explained, had been carried there in the meanwhile, and the dowry boxes would be opened in my presence before the precious contents were stored in the *cajas de depósito* of the convent.

My arm bandaged, I followed the *velo blanco* down past the entrance offices. My farewell to colour proved premature. We made our way down through an orange courtyard with a red oleander gleaming under a bitingly blue sky. That orange fanfared like cinnabar and saffron yellow and rose madder all fighting on the palette for dominance. Such a riot of strong colour I had not seen since I was a child, looking down from the minstrel's gallery at a sumptuous spun-sugar dessert served at a ball in the Palazzo Espagnol while the French still ruled us. We passed down to another bitter-orange courtyard luminous with figs and geraniums.

I reproved myself for my surprise. Venetians do not *own* colour, though we sometimes think we do.

Cecilia Cornaro would be in ecstasies here, I thought.

Yet then again, Cecilia Cornaro, if she came here, could walk out again.

The *velo blanco* pointed ahead to the novices' quarters and my own cell. 'First, let me show you our cloisters! I should not really,' she giggled, 'but otherwise you might not see them till ... maybe till you profess. Quick quick!'

She guided me into a courtyard whose thrumming intensity of blue could only have been created by a fusion of hyacinthine and pavonated cobalt exalted by lapis. This hot blue kingdom was planted with orange trees heavy with fruit. The upper walls were frescoed with tales of divine love. The art was cheerfully bad, yet vividly full of stories: a sea angular and viscous at once, as only land-bound people paint it; a drunken fool had a black-and-white cat peering quizzically from his shoulder-bag; blindfolded angels romped clumsily; the soul lurched towards God, improbably encased in a child's wheeled walking frame.

A breath of cold air made me shiver. Like a wound in young skin, an unexpected doorway gashed one sweet, sun-rich wall. It opened into a curious dark hall with two biers like cribs, one of which held the dead body of a withered nun in full habit and holding a pastor's hook. I uttered a cry of dismay.

The *velo blanco* explained that the nun had died peacefully of old age. She would spend a day in state while her sisters celebrated her ascension to heaven. There were paintings of other dead nuns lining the walls, all with their eyes shut and their mouths a little slack. Each held the pastor's hook in a tight fist, as if it were a truncheon. Some sported a fine growth of moustache on their pale faces; others had eyebrows that rushed to join together. There were bridal flowers about their temples and a festive look to their coiffure. I leaned closer into the paintings to look at the brushwork. To be in this convent, all these women must have been of pure Spanish blood, yet the local artists had given them the exoticism of South America. How was it done? Cecilia would have diagnosed the exact shade of . . .

The *velo blanco* hurried me out of the blue courtyard and back down to the cloister of the novices. As we arrived there I saw another nun with a tray of food approaching my new cell. She paused outside the door and peered into the gloom. She saw something inside there that clearly frightened her: she placed the tray on the bench outside the cell, grimaced and ran away without another word. When I turned to ask my *velo blanco* why her sister was so afraid, she too had already disappeared.

Sor Loreta

The demon who possessed Judas and Jezebel had entered this girl from Venice, making her more powerful than the weak sisters of Santa Catalina.

And there was only Myself to keep vigilant. It was My duty to keep our foolish Virgins pure from contamination for they hovered ever on the chasm of impurity.

Perhaps I might forfend the Venetian Cripple's attack before it was launched?

These were My thoughts as I hurried through the courtyards down to the novitiate where I was to preside over the opening of the Venetian Cripple's dowry trunks. My angels flitted urgently around the walls.

'Yes, yes,' I told them. 'I shall render this daughter of Satan unto Our Lord.'

The brother of the daughter of Satan, I now discovered, had furnished Me with all the tools that I needed. So God's design unfailingly reveals Itself to the Enlightened.

Marcella Fasan

I hesitated on the threshold. My arm ached where the doctor had punctured it. My head was heavy. There was the sound of frantic activity inside my cell: as if Venetian rats scurried and gnawed in there. I peered through the window and saw the top of one of my dowry trunks open and a veiled head bent over it. I remembered the wry embarrassment with which the *priora* explained, 'We must account for your dowry, my dear. It is a sordid business but our chaplain directs us so.'

And they had a sordid nun for doing the business too. It was the *vicaria*, she who had already given me such a cruel salutation at the gate, who was presently engaged in turning my trunks inside out.

She had removed the blue spectacles and I saw that one eye was glued shut. Her face was pitted and scored. Later I would learn that when she was just a child she had plunged her face into boiling water in the hope that the scars would deter any potential husband. Yet those features of hers must have been ugly already. Her eyes were too small and too close together; her chin jowled and jutted, and her nose could not have been scourged into its hooked shape.

She thrust her mannish hands deep inside one of my dowry chests. Then she snatched them out, bleeding from fragments of the Murano glass that had shattered on the mountain. And her ankle was bleeding too, on to my stone floor – she must have been wearing the cilice around her thigh.

As soon as I walked in she rose and slapped me hard across the face. I felt a tiny shard of glass slicing my cheek and blood trickling down towards my collar.

'I suspected as much. A Venetian here! I was against you from the start. But they voted me down, out of a squalid curiosity to see one like you. You shall come straight to the bathhouse and immerse for two hours to start the cure for your *calor*. Look at that vulgar sweat on your face!'

Calor? In Venice we said '*in calore*' when a cat was in need of a husband.

I stared down the trajectory of her bloodstained jabbing finger, and discovered that it was, of course, my dowry that had got me accused of indecency. My brother had chosen San Sebastiano as my personal saint. The *vicaria* was glaring at my handsome statue of him, and the gloriously serene image painted by Mantegna.

'Obscene things!' she hissed. 'It is as I warned them, you have come to corrupt our young sisters. They would not listen.'

Minguillo must have got wind of the fact that for some reason San Sebastiano was held in extreme ill-repute here at Santa Catalina. I had been indifferent to the booty in my trunks, just as a slave feels little interest in his price. I had not suspected that even in my dowry Minguillo might find a new way to damage me.

'My brother . . .' I faltered, and then stopped. Minguillo had been here and met with them. He would have found a companionable soul in this *vicaria*. Was the apparently sympathetic *priora* also party to his machinations? I felt the full force of my isolation then. Longingly, I pictured Anna's and Gianni's faces turned towards me with loving expressions. And Santo in the garden at San Servolo, looking over the heads of the lady Tranquils to meet my eyes.

'*What* are we going to put in your *hornacina*?' the *vicaria* demanded, slapping me again, and pointing to an arched alcove apparently designed to serve as a little altar inside my room. It had been decorated around its borders with naïve paintings of flowers and leaves.

'This sacrilegious Venetian filth,' she pointed in disgust at San Sebastiano, 'will go directly into the vaults and never be seen again by decent women. If it were my choice, it would be put to the flame. Now it is God's design that *you* learn a lesson you'll not forget.'

She seized my ear and pulled me out of my cell – tumbling the tray of food to the ground in our wake. She jostled me along myriad little streets – not a soul appearing – to a low chamber where a stone tub the size of a large carriage was filled with water that did not look as if it knew the breath of a coal fire to warm it.

'Behind the screen,' she ordered curtly. 'Take off your clothes.'

The Small-Pox vaccination was coursing palpably through my body, making me slow and dull. I fumbled at my travelling clothes until they had all dropped away. I hesitated behind the blue wooden screen, unwilling to expose my naked self to her hating eye.

'What are you doing in there?' she demanded suspiciously. 'Come out this minute.'

I emerged timidly. In the goose-pimpling cool of that stone chamber, my leg scars blazed lividly, as if I had flagellated myself where it most hurt. I caught sight of a severe-looking John the Baptist in an altar above the bath. I supposed that the nuns regarded their baths as a kind of baptism. As I looked bleakly at the saint, I heard a sharp intake of breath, a rustle of indignant wool. The *vicaria* hastened around the rim of the bath and slapped my face again, so hard that I staggered to the very rim of the pool, teetering there.

'Where is your chemise, lecher?' she shrieked at me, her eyes feasting on my wounds, the fetor of her breath hot on my body.

'You said . . .' I tried to cover myself with my inadequate hands.

Reeling from yet another slap, I crouched inside the shelter of the screen and pulled my chemise back on.

'Now, get in there!' she pushed me so I toppled into the wintry water, hitting my head on the stone side as I went down. I plunged deep, hit the

309

slimy bottom with crumpled hands and rode the splashing water back up to the surface inside the clinging bubble of my shift. I struggled to right myself, grasping the side for safety. Warm blood fell down the iced rictus of my face. Through that red curtain, I searched out my enemy.

She had not finished with me.

She was pinioning one of my hands with a booted foot. I had a glimpse of her face. All humanity had departed from it. A mask of rapture stiffened her features. It was as if she was no longer conscious.

Then she leaned over and pushed my head under the water and kept it there.

Doctor Santo Aldobrandini

What I needed was money, if I was to be with my love.

Money. Such a little, sordid thing, that would not buy a clean, loving heart. A dirty thing, handed around among strangers. Yet for me, who did not have it, what a monstrous proportion money now assumed in my life.

All my days I had proudly discounted it, feeling superior to the rich noblemen whose self-indulgence I despised.

On San Servolo I had earned little, for I had offered my services cheaply in order to be sure of a place near Marcella. Though I had eaten poorly and dressed worse, I had saved nothing.

In Venice my name had been blackened by Minguillo, so I could not earn my living as a surgeon to the wealthy. (Of course, to get myself to Marcella, I would have attended even spoiled patricians.) I practised on the poor and on the prostitutes of the town, for the Spanish madam advertised my utility to her friends. I charged poor rates to poor patients. How could I do anything else? Slowly, slowly, I began to collect funds.

It was not enough, and it was not fast enough. I had a sense of my breathing impaired, because impatience made me lean forward, always looking for new ways to get money. I became mercantile, calculating.

I inscribed myself to an apothecary, concocting his electuaries. I became bold in demanding my share of the profits. I looked for other opportunities. I took in sewing, pretending that I had a seamstress for a mother: I could stitch up a shirt as well as a wound. I swung wooden crates at the docks.

Money, money. It did not seem attracted to me, but I coaxed it into my pocket, hour by hour. I heard the coins clinking against one another with a happy ear.

In dark moments, the music of the money sounded cold and tinny. Had Marcella survived the journey? If not, the money, and all the things I did to get it, would be worthless.

Then Gianni came to tell me that Marcella had arrived in Arequipa.

'Thank God,' I embraced him.

'But *how* do you know she is safely there?' I demanded, suddenly insecure.

'Minguillo pushed the cook down the stairs this morning just after a letter were delivered from the *priora* in Peru isn't it.'

I rushed to pick up my bag of ointments so I could tend to the poor cook. But Gianni held up his hand: 'Santo, twould be death for you to come to the Palazzo Espagnol, and *that* would be death for Marcella.'

Silently, I handed him some arnica lotion from my pocket.

The coins in there jingled quietly. The music of money, even when thin and tinny, is always optimistic: I had come to know that at last.

Marcella Fasan

When I awoke I was back in my cell and the *vicaria* was nowhere to be seen. Beside my bed was an opened bottle of smelling salts and a little sack of snuff. My shaking hand found a linen bandage clamped around my forehead. A woolly bladder of hot water rested on my chest, which felt raw, as if it had been rubbed briskly for a long time.

The kindly *priora* was at my side, holding my hand. She held a teaspoon of brandy-and-water to my lips and tipped it in.

311

'Welcome back,' she smiled. 'We have managed to revive you at last. And you have come through the effects of the Small-Pox vaccination to the side of safety.'

I cried out then because a brutally ugly face swam into my view, behind the *priora*. Her eyes followed mine back to the altar across the room. 'Ah, Marcella, do not be afraid. That is your new saint.'

What I had glimpsed was not the *vicaria* but a crude statue of a lady saint whose haggard face was scored with red marks. Santa Rosa of Lima, I deduced. My own San Sebastiano painting and statue were nowhere to be seen.

'What did I do, Mother?' My teeth chattered.

The *priora* explained to me that the image of San Sebastiano was specifically forbidden in the nunnery. 'Some prudish edict along the lines that his handsome face and naked torso might encourage lewd dreams and put the nuns "*in calore*".'

'We say that for cats in Venice,' I told her.

'And so cats are expressly forbidden here too,' she said mildly. 'Yet they find their own ways in and live among us Signor Rossini has even written the dear creatures a duet, so I cannot think them entirely evil. Speaking of which, I personally do not blame you for the San Sebastianos, child. Perhaps your brother did not read too closely the terms of our agreement for the dowry.'

Perhaps he did, all too closely, I thought.

'I suppose that in Venice the women may look upon San Sebastiano without restraint?'

I nodded. She looked at me searchingly, 'Is there a possibility that your brother might have wished to set you in a bad position here from the start?'

The *priora* held both my shoulders and looked into my face, 'Have you carried such a burden for long, child? I refer to the intentions of your brother.'

Her intuition astounded me. I had a mad vision of myself falling into her arms and telling her everything. But I feared to stretch her imagination to a final wall of cynicism, and have her think me guilty of exaggeration. Her tenderness would be very hard to give up even after so short an acquaintance with it. I took refuge in my accustomed vague and wondering stare, the one that had served me so well in the madhouse on San Servolo before Santo came to find me.

'This is a subject we shall explore another time, when you have seen that you have reason to trust me. I realize the *vicaria* might have damaged your confidence in the humanity of our regime at Santa Catalina. Please believe me, Sor Loreta is not characteristic of our number. She is a person more to be pitied than feared. Her faith took an hysterical turn from the start. We generally choose to be amused at her excesses. It helps us to bear her.'

She sighed, 'Perhaps we should have been less accommodating in her regard . . . But let us not talk of that now! Let me prove to you our friendly ways. Your new sisters are waiting to meet you.' The *priora* waved at a nun guarding the door.

My face was caressed by a rush of warm air, as when summer sails are unfurled. Smiling girls surrounded me, kneeling by my bed, bending over one another's shoulders, folding themselves up to get closer to me.

'So pretty and delicate!' one breathed. 'She is like glass!'

'Does she speak Spanish?'

'Yes! You know she does! We were told . . .'

'The Venetian Cripple!' giggled one, but she was sternly shushed by the *priora*. 'Her soul is perfect in the eyes of God,' she reminded them comfortably, 'and in ours too, therefore.'

A dozen gentle hands lifted my sheets and looked at my chemise, ran their fingers along the Burano lace and the satin ribbon of the collar. They exclaimed with delight at my linen, now neatly folded upon my shelves, and then fell on the little heap of my travel clothes that lay on the floor. One of them picked up my drawers – and danced them round the room, humming to an aria from Rossini. It was clear that my new companions knew that the *priora* would be indulgent to any little lightheartedness so long as it came with the appropriate musical accompaniment.

'Divided drawers!' It seemed such a thing had never been known among these girls. Another picked up my silk skirt and held it against herself, and they all gasped. '*Venetian* fashion,' they sighed.

I thought wryly: *Yes, Venetian fashion from perhaps ten years past. Minguillo did not waste money on keeping my clothes abreast of the times.*

The *priora*, instead of reproving them, allowed full reign to their joyful curiosity. I had the strangest feeling that she wished to allow them to see more of me, that she wanted me to be known for more than my twisted leg. Indeed, my crippled state was quite forgotten by them, and they were now consumed with asking me questions about *Carnevale* in Venice, and the manners of the gentlemen, and the looks of the gondoliers.

A shadow fell inside the room then, and the *vicaria*'s harsh voice cut in, 'This creature has evidently been chosen to bear the worst scourges by God. Envy her, sisters, for she has her penances already written on her flesh.'

Suddenly my lame limb was once again the biggest part of my body. The girls who were holding my underclothes let them drop to the floor. One dark-eyed novice ran a sympathetic hand briefly over my leg. Everyone else stayed motionless.

'This is not to say,' the *vicaria* continued, walking up to my bed, 'that *she* should claim more than a small share of the world's pity. She does not merit that. Does she, Sor Juana Francisca del Santísimo Sacramento? Does she, Sor Manuela de Nuestra Madre Santa Catalina? Does she, Sor Josefa del Corazón de Jesús? Does she, Sor Rafaela del Dulce? Does she, Sor María Rosa del Costado de Cristo?'

As each of the girls was named, her face drained of colour and she took a step backwards. Finally, the *vicaria*'s voice sent the young nuns scattering back to their cells: a patter of light feet like raindrops, and a sharp anxiety in the air too.

The *priora* faced the *vicaria* across the emptied room. 'Was that entirely necessary, Sor Loreta?'

'Venice's filth must not be allowed to dirty our convent. I am surprised that you allowed them to indulge their fantasies and behave indecently with the Venetian Cripple's undergarments.'

'You were spying from the outside, as usual? An unfortunate habit of yours, Sor Loreta. I wanted to create an informal welcome for our new sister. A freezing bath was not the greeting I intended. However, I need not justify my actions to you. I am yet *priora* and have been elected to that post twice by the wish of our sisters, unlike yourself.'

The *vicaria*'s single eye blazed and then fell blank.

On recovering from my near-drowning, my first duty was to attend the church. My father must have cut a great figure among them, for on my first day's attendance the church of Santa Catalina was thronged with people curious to see *la Veneciana*. This I knew from the *vicaria*'s own lips. She stared at the crowd, mumbling bitterly.

From the other side of a screen, I glimpsed an exotic congregation – women in flowered frocks and black mantillas of lace, an officer from the Peruvian army flashing golden earrings.

We nuns filed into our part of the church, constructed in a tunnel shape – 'against earthquakes' someone whispered to me – and decorated inside in buttermilk and gold. The nuns' sweet voices floated up and through the grate into the ears of kin. I saw from the faces of the congregation how the singing flowed into their hearts and made their imaginations soft and wistful.

The grate was made of wood on our side and from iron on the side of the public, as if to suggest that ours was the more fragile prison: our confinement was supposed to be of our free will.

The *priora* had told me that my father worshipped here when he was in Arequipa. My memories of him were affectionate but sparse. What would he think, to see me here? What, if any, had been his plans for me? I covertly examined all the Arequipan fathers and brothers who had put their daughters and sisters here. Once a week at least they had to come to this church and face what they had done. When they saw their womenfolk behind the turned wooden struts, I wondered, did they remember their trusting baby faces as first seen through the spindles of their cots?

I kept my own lids lowered, for the *vicaria* hovered near my side; too near, for my comfort. I heard her laboured breathing in my ear, and it reminded me of my childhood, when Minguillo used to stand outside my bedchamber, breathing through the keyhole to frighten me until I learned to lodge a pencil in there every night.

Minguillo Fasan

Conscience is like tickling. Some are susceptible; some are not.

The Scrupled Reader will find, to His distress, that much of modish literature tends to emasculate that tender organ, the conscience. Take as an example the present tale, of an incorrigible character for whom crime pays, and abundantly. If only my account were to close at this juncture, one would think the world well matured and rotted in infamies that ever go unavenged.

Just at that moment, why, everything I touched prospered! My old enemy Napoleon — a dismal failure! My sister banished! Money flowed in from my innovations in quackery. My little collection of books of human skin stretched across *three* shelves of my study. I rearranged my dainties daily, shuffling the male and female books as a skilful madam redeploys her regular girls among her regular customers for fresh pleasures.

When books of human skin were thin on the market, then I diversified, commissioning my own special additions to the library. I begot a book on hunting bound in fox-skin, a natural history of songbirds bound in a patchwork of larks, and a treatise on the Great Cats tooled in the shaved skin of one of the Palazzo Espagnol felines, whose mysterious absence was much remarked upon by the fond maids and much rejoiced in by our rats. And if anyone crossed me, the Reader will understand, it became my pleasant pastime to imagine which text would best be bound in *his* skin for the most exquisite appropriateness.

It was at this palmy time that I probably indulged most in the peccadillo of smugness. How could I not? My sister was at last beyond the reach of her aspiring lover, even if he had the least idea where she had gone. So. As for him taking Marcella to wife: *well*, I thought comfortably, *pigs shall fly in formation before that happens, and I've not heard of any wings sprouting in the sties.*

No respect to the Gracious Reader, but has He?

Marcella Fasan

Despite my offence with San Sebastiano, the *priora* informed me that I would proceed directly to the first step in my betrothal to God and become a novice. 'Your journey here has been so long,' she said kindly, 'we shall hasten the final stages for you.'

I speculated as to the battle the *priora* must have fought with the *vicaria* to win this privilege for me. I continued to wonder what lies Minguillo had told them about my life to date. He would have had a free hand. I watched and listened. From the way they treated me, it was clear everyone around me thought my chronicle and therefore my character to be as pathetically tangible and as simple as my crippled leg, and indeed that I, Marcella, had been created by this congenital defect, wearing its damage in mind, body and soul.

For the occasion of my novitiate I was re-dressed in my own clothes and conducted to the church by my black- and white-veiled sisters. At the climactic moment, a curtain was drawn across the grate for a few moments. Hands snatched at me, tearing off my clothes, swaddling me in crisp linen and wool robes. I simply did as I was told, kept my hands above my head, moving to the left or to the right as directed by whispers. When the curtain opened again, I was revealed to the audience in my white novice's habit, kneeling, and holding a lighted candle, with a dazed expression on my face that must have looked like beatitude to anyone who wished to see it that way.

The novices' quarters consisted of our cells, our own exquisite little oratory, a chapel, a common room and a small library of religious tomes. I was at least five years older than the other girls, and felt more than a century their senior. They were little princesses from noble Arequipan families, who had known nothing but a pampered and sheltered existence. And yet they took me to their hearts, sharing their childish gossip and confidences as if I were one of them.

We were under the dominion of the mistress of the novices, who was a sworn enemy of Sor Loreta and therefore inclined to be kind as spring

317

sunlight. Then again, it was her duty to entice the young girls in her charge so that they would eventually profess themselves to God without rebellion or regret. Her other role, which she fulfilled to perfection, was to keep the novices well briefed as to the horrors of the outside world.

There was no murder, no rape, no wife-beating, no death in childbirth, not just in Peru but in the whole Spanish dominion, that was not fully relayed to us in our comfortable quarters. If anything, the mistress rather exceeded her permission to make the outside world seem ghastly and obnoxious. By her account, uncloistered young girls were soon worn away to old hags by the chores and burdens of married life. Their lives were one continual shattering round of provisioning, cleaning, birthing, suckling and turning the other cheek until they died, much younger than most nuns. Our bedtime stories were of wives who found marriage an unsupportable burden and committed horrid suicides, often taking their infants with them to Hell, for the babies died before they could even make confession and receive absolution! Then there were the husbands who ran rapiers through their wives' silk dresses, not much caring if the wives were inside them or not, and who stole all their jewellery and spent it on whores. Such stories always ended in apparently spontaneous prayers to God to thank him for delivering his little nuns from such unsavoury and dangerous fates.

And yes, given my experiences, there was much to be said for a place of refuge, especially one so far away from my brother.

Minguillo's interview with the *priora* must have taken place in her *oficina* just inside the gates. The featureless outer courtyard gave no hint of the inner nature of the convent. He must have imagined Santa Catalina as a grey, silent tomb. Of this I was certain, because if Minguillo had realized how it really was inside Santa Catalina, he would never have sent me there. If it was in my fate to be a lifelong prisoner at my brother's pleasure, then it seemed a small triumph of my own that my latest and final prison should be in such a faultlessly beautiful place.

Santa Catalina was like a kingdom in an Arabian fairy tale. Breezes crisp with mountain freshness swarmed gently around flowered courtyards, winding lanes and fountains. Instead of banishing them, the convent fed the joy of all the senses. Mr Rossini's music jaunted out of the *priora*'s office. Caged birds warbled by the altar, sweetening the choir's voices.

Pleasures crowded in the perfume of the roses, the downy flesh of ripening fruit, the long fingers of dry sunlight touching our faces each morning.

Most particularly there was at Santa Catalina an unashamed and happy greed for rich food. Each of the professed nuns' apartments had its own kitchen. Hot wafts of intermingled stews and roasting guinea pigs filled the evening air. The next morning it would be the smell of pastries and hot chocolate, in the forenoon of marzipan, and, in the late afternoon, spiced bread. If you knelt down to sniff a flower in the gardens you would surely find it coated with a perfume of sugar and vanilla from the delicious *polvorones*.

To be a nun at Santa Catalina was like living in an exquisite doll's house. The colours were too simple for the real world. There were no sophisticated shades or tints, only intense pure colour.

Then there was El Misti. In Arequipo, I could not but be affected by a sensation that only a thin veil separated Earth from Heaven. The mountain's summit floated so high above the landlocked mist, so far separated from any credible land, that it seemed nothing more or less than a glittering heavenly kingdom among the clouds, a myth in itself. The *vicaria* had tried to stop nuns from looking at it, but Sor Loreta could not exterminate the mountain, however. Even if you did not stare at it, El Misti stared at you. I myself felt the mountain's presence as I would a white ermine cloak – light and delicate and luxurious and, most of all, protective. Minguillo was on the other side of that mountain, as well as across an ocean and two seas.

In this loving atmosphere, a sincere belief might actually have thrived in me. The comforts of faith might have started to sop my losses; I might even have defeated Minguillo's hopes of my utter misery by discovering a joyful vocation. Yet one thing held me back, and kept me divided from my apparently devout and submissive self.

Everyone assumed that because I was a cripple I had never known love. But the thought of Santo's kiss, and the memory of the silent promise he had whispered into my mouth on San Servolo, undermined the faith I might have cultivated at Santa Catalina. As every prayer 'from this untouched virgin of Christ' crossed my lips, it pained me that God seemed to collude blandly in the fraud. What kind of God was this to trust as my eternal Bridegroom? Who accepted hollow vows from

319

unwilling novices, who allowed brothers to stow inconvenient sisters in what Cecilia Cornaro had once called His harem?

And I had to bear in mind that this same God was also the idol of a creature as crazed as Sor Loreta, who single-handedly did more to promote profane thoughts among us, simply by her frightful example, than could the Devil himself.

Divided from myself again, I took refuge in paper, as I had done as a girl. My single-leafed diary found a safe home at the back of my candle cupboard.

Sor Loreta

By day, I sent Sor Narcisa and Sor Arabel out to gather information on the Venetian Cripple. Those girls had footsteps that weighed nothing.

I Myself walked around at night, listening, watching. I heard it whispered in the refectory that the convent had a ghost, who haunted the narrow alleyways in the early hours. The silly little girls in the novitiate had claimed that a goblin pressed his face against their windows in the early hours.

Marcella Fasan

But by night, what a difference! What a primitive place was Santa Catalina! With the bats swooping, the candles and ovens glowing inside tenebrous rooms, the Moorish domes and archways reared up in phantasmagoric silhouette.

It was at night that the darker histories of the convent soaked through to the surface of things. The very dew seemed thickened with the grim dust of the past. Suddenly I was aware that so many items that I touched, even my very bed, had once belonged to women who had been declared dead to the world when still on the edge of girlhood, and who had lived as brief phantoms in this vibrant place, only to die in obscurity.

Back, back, back in time the night took us. I was terrified by Santa Catalina after nightfall. Our ladylike community seemed to descend into primaeval times, more a tribal village than a convent, the fires burning like little red hells in the blackness.

Inside and outside became debatable. The colour was gone and fearsome shadows crept in. Suddenly the convent seemed so vulnerable, so tentative, like a mere graze in the earth, a fragile settlement in the wilderness where powerful and malevolent beasts lurked all around.

I wrote in my diary: '*All is not well in Santa Catalina. By night, I can feel it.*'

Minguillo Fasan

The Deriding Reader deceives Himself if He interprets my recent silence on the missing will as a sign of weakness or defeat. By no means.

Once Marcella was dispatched, I began investigations anew into the identity of the will-thief. Many years had passed since I found the chicken head in its place. I was tired of living with a dim worry raking up discomfort at the back of my mind. I wanted the thief found and hurt.

I set out to interview everyone who had lived in the Palazzo Espagnol, from the last occasion when I saw the real will until the time I discovered its theft. Servants, priests, pensioners, boatmen and gardeners left my study dazed and afraid: of course I was not able to ask the one real question that needed answering, so I tortured them with vague accusations, watching closely for any sign of guilt.

In my wildest hopes, the thief was already dead. But even the wildest hopes have their sagging corners. If the thief was deceased, where had he stowed his document, that is to say, mine?

Perhaps whoever had the will aspired to torment me slowly to madness? Vain hope! And what individual of such diabolical cleverness had crossed my path? I was surrounded by halfwits at every turn.

Speaking of which, I remarked to my valet Gianni, 'Do we know anyone who means me ill? I mean someone from the old days, when my father was still alive?'

If the fellow had only known what I was talking about, how he would have stood up straight and stared, instead of giving me his usual look of a fish boiling in a pan. He was the only servant I trusted to dust my study. There I strewed my private papers around with tranquil ease. For Gianni, whose head looked like the bole of a squat palm tree with a tuft of hair at the top, was illiterate and incurious as wood.

Marcella Fasan

Colour-dazed and sun-dazzled, I performed the duties of my novitiate faultlessly. I learned the stories painted on the walls. My Spanish took on an Arequipan accent and I acquired the special words that defined the place: *sillar*, the white stone that cradled us; *mestiza*, mixed blood; *criada*, servant; *esclava*, slave.

I had a new name, Sor Constanza. And a new hairstyle: a few curls clinging to my head under my white veil.

Despite that, Venetian glamour still attached to me. Novices would still take every opportunity to cross-examine me on Venetian fashions and scandals. They wished to assume that I had been at the very summit of high society, for it aggrandized them all to have a great Venetian lady among them. They could never understand why I had come to Arequipa, when I could have lived by San Marco Square and had the Grand Canal for my liquid garden. And a Venetian nobleman for my lover.

Marcella Fasan kept silent. It was Sor Constanza who smiled and asked, 'What could be more beautiful than Santa Catalina?'

322

The mistress of the novices purred in agreement and kissed my dissembling cheek.

Sor Loreta

The Venetian Cripple tried to keep herself away from Me, but I did not let her escape My vigilance. I did not consider that I had done My daily duty unless I had encountered her at least once and looked deeply into her eyes. I hoped to discover the precise nature of her sin.

The *priora* noticed that I paid special attention to the Venetian Cripple. She harangued Me like a Pharisee, 'Were you sent to destroy the peace of this convent? I rue the day the Fathers were so blind as to admit you. You should have been put in a madhouse, not allowed to drive other women out of their senses! Do not turn Sor Constanza into another Sor Sofia. You must learn to leave the younger nuns alone.'

'I do what I do in the love of God, and there will be harvest.'

The *priora* put on a wheedling voice, as if talking to an unreasonable child, 'Sor Constanza is terrified of you since you nearly drowned her the day she arrived here. She behaves perfectly, but I fear it is too perfectly. Do you consider this, that you drive the poor girl's thoughts *away* from God? That she is suffused not with piety, but with fear of what you will do to her next?'

'Her conscience is not pure – for she hides sin behind that meek face – so naturally she will be frightened of an incorruptible soul. How should it be otherwise?'

The *priora* sighed and tried to dismiss Me. I pointed My deaf right ear at her and let the insults rain down inside it uncomprehended. I stayed, for there was an angel hovering over her left shoulder urging Me to remain in her presence until she had drunk the hot chocolate I had brought her.

Gianni delle Boccole

Marcella ud been gone a year, and there were preshous little news of her. And I would know, wunt I. Because I read evry one o Minguillo's letters, allus hopin to find a sottile refrunce to my own, what I had sent anonimousely, with another merchant and a hunnerd of cash scrapt together by the servants, to the *priora* of Santa Catalina. I hopt that the *priora* might write to Minguillo with some hard questions after that. But she did not.

Minguillo aughter been happy, for he had suckseeded. No more need to go creeplin about, doing secret harm to his poor sister. But ye can't take the slither out ovva snake. He were still restless. Still puzzlin about the old will what had been took, saucespishus of evryone.

By an oirony he used *me* as his eyes, to espy on t'other members o the household. I give him hunnerds o insent details, and telled him a sack o small lies to keep him busy wonderin. And I ust the cover o his investigations to be making my own. Evry time Minguillo interfewed another suspeck, I stood stiffly ahind him, listenin, learnin n crossin off one more possible from my own list o will-thieves.

Marcella Fasan

Within a year, I was deemed ready to take my vows. I could find no argument that was convincing as to why I should not now be promoted to a professed nun, a *velo negro*, a black veil, which conferred the right to vote in the three-yearly elections. As a professed nun, I would have a larger cell, servants, and – the only thing I cared about – more privacy. I had no ambitions, but I knew it would cause a scandal if I refused the veil, and I had no wish to draw attention to myself.

If anyone looked at me too closely, I was afraid that they might see Marcella Fasan under Sor Constanza's skin. Docile Sor Constanza did not show any desire for the life beyond the walls of Santa Catalina. But Marcella Fasan's vivid existence continued on paper. Behind the candles in my cupboard were the pages on which I truly lived. In those pages, Santo was like the lining of my heart, indivisible from me. I did not wonder if he still loved me. I knew that he did.

So when I professed myself betrothed to God, I did so in a provisional way, committing myself to Him only until I might be married to Santo, even though there presently seemed no practical possibility of ever seeing him again.

At the height of the special mass I laid my body on the floor in the shape of a cross and recited the words that bound me to the order. Then I knelt before the smiling *priora* and pronounced my flimsy promises. Through the window of the choir, the priest handed me the black veil. Other nuns helped me draw it on, patting it down to perfection. A bride must be beautiful for her husband.

Only when my wedding ring was drawn over my finger did I flinch away from the priest, drawing a gasp from the watching public.

I held out my hand, telling myself, *It is a rehearsal, for my real wedding.*

Then I was crowned with roses, and led in triumph back into the cloisters for a fiesta that was scarcely spiritual, given the number of cakes consumed by us all; except for the *vicaria*, of course, who was in the tenth day of one of her lengthy fasts.

I turned the ring around on my finger. On the way back to my cell I plucked a blade of grass, which I curled up and inserted between the gold band and my finger. The ring did not quite touch my skin.

Doctor Santo Aldobrandini

Gianni had found a letter from the *priora* at Santa Catalina on Minguillo's desk. The occasion for her writing was to inform him that another part of the dowry had fallen due because Marcella had become a professed nun.

I stumbled out of the *ostaria*, sick at heart. I leaned against a wall, the coins in my back pocket sharp as knives against my thigh. Married to God? That meant she had married someone else but me.

Why had she not contrived to stay a novice, or to become a tertiary, a lay sister?

Gianni followed me out, otherwise preoccupied. 'Now,' he mouthed gloomily, 'Minguillo says that she gets a slave of her own. He has to pay. How can them Peruvian servants understand her like Anna and me?'

'Why did she do it?' I agonized. 'How could she take the veil when she knows I . . . ?'

Gianni thumped my back, 'Maybe she crossed her fingers behind her when she vowed? Maybe 'tis all a big imposture! Maybe' – and his voice darkened – 'they drugged her.'

Maybe they beat her, we both thought. *Maybe they locked her up and tried to drive her mad*. We had no reason then to think that Santa Catalina was any kinder than the cruellest convent in Venice. After all, Minguillo had chosen it.

I had never seen Marcella dressed in black. How pale must her skin look against its harshness. Doctors attending nuns will notice that the black colour of their habits gives nuns special cutaneous problems, their murky costumes swallowing up the rays of the sun while impeding the healthy transmission of heat away from the body. Particles of disease and unhealthy accumulations are more readily absorbed by dark clothes. The metaphor applies to the stifling of the whole bodily economy: for to be a nun is surely a kind of dying? Dead to the world, the nun's body quietly decomposes unseen by loving eyes.

Meanwhile I had been right about Napoleon: it had not proved so easy to stifle his itch. My old patient had risen from his own ashes and stormed off Elba. Soon he was back in Paris, planning to take back everything he had lost, except his youth and health, already irretrievably spent.

At that moment I wished that Napoleon might leave off scratching his itches with Old World corpses, commandeer a ship and take up his rampages in Peru. For then there would be call for doctors by the hundred to amputate and sew up his victims. And all the convents in South America would be forced to release their poor hostages from their grim cells, and divorce them from their heavenly Bridegroom.

Marcella Fasan

A week after I married God, I was led from my old cell to the new one. A sturdy *velo blanco* carried my possessions, except for the little sheaf of diary pages I had hidden in a shawl and insisted on carrying myself. The *velo blanco* walked ahead to show me the way, for I was now to live in a part of the convent that I, as a novice, had never before been permitted to visit.

We crossed the blue courtyard diagonally and entered a cluster of buildings with the air of an ancient village. We passed Calle Cordoba, with its white walls decked with red geraniums. At the end it thinned down into Calle Toledo, a canyon of terracotta buildings, flat and simple. On our right were shattered and mutilated walls slanting out of the ground like a mouthful of rotten teeth.

'The earthquake in 1784,' said the *velo blanco* briefly. 'Sor Loreta arrived on the same day. We have never been able to fully recover from that catastrophe.'

She guided me to a sudden right turn into the Calle Sevilla, lined with walls red as meat, and rising up in white steps towards the entrance of an old church surmounted by a bell.

'Here,' the nun pushed me gently through the first doorway on the left. 'This is where you shall live now, Sor Constanza.'

327

I entered my courtyard through a pair of low wooden doors, each hewn out of a single mellow plank with the sheen of roasted butter. Above the door was inscribed the name of a previous occupant, M. Dominga Somocursio.

'What happened to Sor Dominga?' I enquired.

'She is with Our Father and Husband,' I was told. 'The Small-Pox. She was afraid of the needle and refused the vaccination. Her parents ordered the cell sold and the proceeds used for masses for her soul. Now your brother has bought it for you.'

My brick-paved courtyard was painted a vivid cobalt blue. Three long stone seats lined the walls, and there was a small flowerbed in the centre. The kitchen opened off to the left and my bedchamber straight ahead, with a pot of geraniums foaming white at either side of the door. How fortunate I was, I thought, to have a beautiful courtyard of my own. Later I would discover that all the professed nuns' quarters boasted private gardens, some far grander than mine.

The courtyard seemed steeped not in Christian elementals but the flavour of the East: the graceful arch over the door, the low golden stone pocketing the sky.

'Earthquakes,' commented the nun, following my eyes.

I smiled to myself. I'd already drawn cartoons of the proud white Arequipans who did not like to admit to the Arabic influence from the Moorish conquest of Spain. Earthquakes were invariably blamed for the oriental shapes of their buildings. Here in this far-flung colony, outnumbered by native people and seared by foreign light, the white Spanish treasured their pure blood and their Catholic religion more than the citizens of the places where such things went unquestioned – except by the risen-again Napoleon Bonaparte.

I followed the *velo blanco* inside a large airy room. Its terracotta floor had been cleaned in readiness for the silk carpet that was part of my dowry. It had a vaulted ceiling with little windows and alcoves, and a creamy, detailed architrave. And a compact black girl, who curtseyed to me.

'What is your name?' I asked.

'Josefa,' she replied and curtseyed again. 'I am your servant cook maid slave.'

'You have just one,' observed the *velo blanco* condescendingly. 'Most of the professed nuns have three at least. Margarita the pharmacist has twelve!'

Josefa observed sturdily, 'I can do a leetle somefing-somefing for my mistress, though.'

328

'Then show her the new quarters,' ordered the *velo blanco*. My belongings were deposited on the divan and the serving nun departed.

Josefa stared at me unblinking. 'So,' she announced, 'here tis your new house. Here tis this, and this, and this' – she pointed at the fireplace, the chimney, the bed, with studied formality.

Then, when the footsteps of the *velo blanco* had faded, Josefa's face opened up into a delicious grin. Hands on her hips, she said, 'The other servants talk. They say you be good mistress. In that case I be good servant, and perhaps slowly by slowly I shall love you. I think is passable.'

'I very much hope so,' I smiled, 'I already feel quite fond of *you*.'

'Sgood then,' said Josefa. 'You look-look some. I put your fings in order.'

My new *hornacina* was already inhabited by the unpleasant statue of Santa Rosa. Her ragged red face looked down on her luxurious new accommodation dismissively, as if to say, 'All things on earth are the same for me. I live for the world beyond this one.'

'Ugly cow, she,' observed Josefa.

'And dismal with it,' I concurred. Josefa yelped with mirth.

Below Santa Rosa was a cupboard for candles, already well stocked. My diary would be safe behind the wall of wax. Encloistered opposite was a large cupboard with four doors and two deep shelves. I was amazed at this capacity – what personal possessions might a nun accumulate to fill such a space? Hidden behind some curtains on the opposite wall I found my bed. As in the novitiate quarters, it was in an arched alcove, to protect me from earth tremors. A stark cross hung above the bedhead. There was a space where I supposed my desk and chair would go. The divan was plumped up with cushions. The large kitchen could be approached both from my room and the courtyard. It was furnished with a capacious oven on which Josefa was already stirring something fragrant.

'Smell good, yes?' she asked.

I nodded. 'Where do you sleep?'

She pointed to a pallet bed beside the oven. 'Hot-hot like Africa.'

I could positively *ramble* through my new world. It was more like a miniature country house than a cell. Noticing a door near the *hornacina*, I poked my head through it, discovering yet another room that was nearly as large again as my new parlour-sleeping-chamber.

I called Josefa, 'What is this other room for?'

'For what you likes, madam,' came the answer.

There came into my mind's eye the image of Santo writing at a table in that room, looking up to smile at me, reaching out his hand.

Sunshine washed in from the courtyard and a barred tall window that looked down into the innumerable little streets. There was no glass, just wooden shutters.

So this would be my kingdom and my cage. As yet, it seemed a cage as wide as the world and full of pleasant possibilities.

With even a whole room for 'what you likes'.

Doctor Santo Aldobrandini

I imagined Marcella looking up at the walls of the convent of Santa Catalina, gazing towards the snow-topped mountains. I felt her shivering in the thin Andean air. She had promised to be married to those walls: she had promised that she would never more leave that place. The promise went beyond her death, for I knew that nuns were destined to be buried within their cloisters when they died.

I could not evict that image from my mind's eye: Marcella, with God's ring on her slender finger, gazing up from her stone cage high in the sky of the New World.

Did she think of me? Of the ring I did not give her before she was sent away?

With whom did she talk? Did the nuns force cruel penances on her? Would they hate her for a foreigner, despise her for a cripple?

And the servants? Perhaps Gianni was right to worry. Why should the servants in Arequipa love Marcella? More masters and mistresses are poisoned by their servants than is realized by people outside the medical profession. I have seen plump noblewomen reduced to skeletal children by slow and gradual administration of arsenic, or swiftly dispatched by aconite.

My Spanish madam pronounced herself delighted with my progress in her language. There was no part of my body I could not name, no rash

330

or spot for which I lacked the Spanish word. But would I ever use my knowledge now?

Marcella – or Sor Constanza, as Gianni told me – was married to God. Would she consider bigamy?

Marcella Fasan

At first the daily life of a professed nun proved little different from my existence in the novitiate. We were woken by a wooden rattle just before five in the morning and we made our way promptly to the central fountain in Plaza Zocodober, all the while reciting our rosaries. We would observe the morning's canonical hours and attend one chief mass. After that we would go to our cells to take rest, and to recite psalms, counting off the anniversaries of important saints and using psalters to remember any of our number who had recently died. At eleven-thirty, we dined, usually in the refectory, after which we returned to our cells.

In the afternoon we were back in the choir for *vísperas* and *completas* and the silent recitation of the rosary. The rest of the day passed in alternating periods of prayer, reading of the Bible and *Lives* of the saints. The peons had been partly right. We were expected to pray specifically to save the souls of our loved ones from the endless tortures of Purgatory. I murmured my prayers audibly, for the *vicaria* was known to prowl the streets, listening under our windows.

Minguillo's name did not cross my chanting lips. Piero's, yes: I devoted my prayer hours to him. Gianni, Anna, and even my mother and nieces figured in my devotions. Nor did I forget my promise to send up the required prayers for the peons and especially Arce.

As for Santo, the thought of him was a prayer of its own kind.

While my lips were busy with prayer, I sketched: Josefa busy in the kitchen; the other nuns bent over their hymnals in the church; my vivid little garden. I longed for colour pastels and paint. But I dared not ask for them.

Food, in profusion or deprivation, marked out our hours and days. Unlike women married to mortal husbands, we did not concern ourselves at all with provisioning, cooking, serving or clearing away. We were served just like men. Our relationship with food was therefore more spiritual, or so the sermons said.

We 'fasted' every Friday, which meant eating only potatoes and cereals or fish. This was too greedy for Sor Loreta, who would berate us for our luxuries, and who frequently reminded us that 'the infant Catherine of Sweden consented to suckle at the breast of her mother only on days when there had been no conjugal relations between her parents'. Another of her favourites was San Nicola. Even when he was a baby, San Nicola was so holy that he took just one breast on Fridays.

'While you gorge your gullets,' sniffed the *vicaria*, 'I myself will feast only on Christ's Body and Blood at communion.'

'Cannibal Princess!' someone observed, and I craned my head to see who so dared, but all the nuns' faces appeared smooth and guiltless.

Our staple was *locro*, a stew of lamb, beef, peppers and potatoes. On Thursdays we would be given our rations of *manjar blanco*, a milky dessert, and a chicken stew, wine and fruit. Between Ash Wednesday and Forgiveness Week, we were given a dish of chickpeas cooked in honey. On Sundays we had two pastries, rice pudding, two different fish dishes and potatoes. During Holy Week we fed on two honeyed desserts with peaches and quinces.

We were expected to make a daily attendance at one of the confessionals off the main cloister. We climbed up four steps to a tiny cupboard with a door we closed behind us, so we sat in airless darkness to confess ourselves. The grates were cut directly into the wall of the public part of the church: our voices floated through the holes into the place where our bodies were not allowed to go. After each confession – at which Marcella Fasan invented for Sor Constanza a repertoire of mild sins – I emerged blinking into the cloister with its red ochre arches and carmine geraniums.

We were permitted to look after our own gardens, growing flowers for our *hornacinas*. Our servants might go out of the convent to buy seeds and kitchen supplies for us. And of course they came back with ears full of town gossip, items of which were traded like cards in a highly staked game.

Friendships between the nuns could be managed, it seemed. I heard giggles and conversations from behind wooden shutters as I made my way down the Calle Toledo. Yet no one in those first few months of my professed life invited me into their cell, or sat beside me confidentially in the choir. I divined that the *vicaria* had made the other nuns afraid to talk to me.

Like many of the nuns, I made a pet of a living flea in a green glass flask. Indeed, his antics were companionable during the long hours of prayer. The convent fleas seemed much delighted by the *limpieza de sangre*, the purity of the blood that they sucked from the nuns at Santa Catalina.

Josefa would pick them out of my bedlinen with iron forceps and line up the corpses on my *hornacina* as an offering to my ugly Santa Rosa, observing, 'Shame they can't bite her. She like that, eh?'

Doctor Santo Aldobrandini

When the Waterloo'd Napoleon was transported down to the island of St Helena in the South Pacific, I had the strangest revelation. Marcella was now physically closer to Bonaparte than she was to me.

While I marked out all my days of loss, I began to feel a bizarre kinship with my old patient in his last decline. Did he, like me, quite fail to kill the hope that his life might be given back to him? Did he dream of release, just as I dreamed of rescuing Marcella? Did his mind trace the waves pleating under his ship's prow, all the way back to his finest hour on the battlefield, just as I remembered my finest second, that in which my lips had been joined to Marcella's?

Unbeknownst to the generals who had fought and feared him, Napoleon was all along nursing inside his own belly the enemy that would be his nemesis. A prepyloric ulcer was carving out a long niche that would eventually be occupied by a cancerous tumour.

By the time Napoleon was confined on St Helena, the tumour was already on its invisible march north, south, east and west inside him. To mitigate his intestinal cramps, his doctors set about killing him slowly with colonic irrigations and vomits induced by antimony potassium tartrate. Repeated doses left him with the flow of blood to his brain interrupted by scattered bursts of heartbeats, like gunfire in battle.

Napoleon had no friends on St Helena. In his circumstances, a doctor, however constant his attendance at your side, is not a friend. That doctor is the person who will document your death, ache by ache, gasp by gasp.

Did Marcella gasp on the mountain air? Or was she nourished by its purity? Did they allow her paper to keep her diary? To draw on? Did she have a doctor? I found myself searingly jealous of the unknown Arequipan surgeon who would have the privilege of touching Marcella's leg, and standing in such proximity to her luminous skin that his own astonished face would be bathed in light.

Marcella Fasan

Josefa gave me to understand that she would scrutinize my behaviour for a provisional period before allowing herself too many familiarities.

'Noble girls strange,' she said. 'Seem nice, then sudden mean and stuck up.'

'I would never . . .' I protested.

'I spose not,' she acknowledged. 'But I just wait a leetle-leetle.'

Josefa was still the only person, apart from my confessor, with whom I spoke. Chatter in the convent byways was quickly silenced by the *vicaria*, who seemed omnipresent, gliding from corners or breaking away unexpectedly from a still silhouette on a stone escarpment. On catching a nun alone, she would destroy her with personal criticisms. I suffered many such humiliations, and overheard many more outside my window. So assiduous was Sor Loreta in discerning imperfections, it was as if we were all hollowed gourds held up to the light. Yet how wrong she was too, accusing quiet girls of garrulity and thin girls of vanity. The *vicaria* loved my limp as a living parable of my undoubted sins, urging other nuns to imitate my penance by putting sharp stones into their shoes. Here again, Sor Loreta was deluded, for of course it was not God but my brother who was the author of my mutilation.

Returning from my confession on the first day of Lent, I was horrified to see the *vicaria* walking towards me in close colloquy with her two fawning retainers, Sor Narcisa and Sor Arabel, in front of whom she rejoiced in humiliating the other nuns. She had not yet seen me, so I had time to steal into the nearest doorway. Still I heard her voice grating closer, and so I withdrew deeper into the unknown room, backing over the narrow stone threshold until I could find a place out of sight.

My eyes were squeezed closed with terror. My back pushed through curtains and into a room that smelled deliciously of cigar smoke, wine, flowers and linseed oil. I felt for a moment that I was back in Cecilia Cornaro's studio in Venice.

When I opened my eyes, they fell on a girl lying negligently on an elegant divan. I knew that face. I had glimpsed it in the refectory. Otherwise I would never have thought her a nun. She was smoking a cigar with an expression of highly focussed bliss. Instead of her habit, a morning gown was carelessly tied around her waist, half open and showing a petticoat that was none of the cleanest. A silk shawl was dripping off her shoulders. Her hair hung down her back in two supple brown tails and her feet were encased in splendidly dirty silk stockings, one of which was loitering down towards the ankle. Utterly unruffled by my unexpected appearance, she grinned, 'Ah, *la Veneciana*! Do shut the doors, be a lovely.'

I pushed a hand through the curtain and grasped the handle, pulling it shut. Then I turned back to her just as she enquired, in a casual drawl, 'So would you like to see a dirty picture?'

And she pulled from her bosom some dozen little cards, on each of which was painted a nearly naked San Sebastiano.

Minguillo Fasan

My perfectly methodical investigations had failed to reveal a will-thief. With this conclusion of my probing, I felt a kind of relief. I had subjected my entire household to an empire of fear, and nothing had emerged. I was able to reassure myself that the thief was no more, and that his opportunity to hurt me was buried with him.

Yet still I was afflicted with discontent. My wife Amalia was the new object of my opprobrium. She had failed to produce a son.

This was getting to be a little uncomfortable. I wanted a baby boy to sit on my knee, to dress in miniature imitation of me, to teach how to shoot as well as me, to show every corner of the Palazzo Espagnol. My boy-baby hunger struck me every time I saw a squalling infant in the street. It put me in a fever, made me feel a temporary inmate in my own home, made me walk into low taverns and hold cool bottles against my hot forehead.

Like Adam, I blamed my wife.

The Excitable Reader asks why I mention this posture of affairs?

The Reader should calm Himself, and put away any suspicions.

If there's anything a writer should not be doing and ought to be snubbed for, it is laying a red herring. It tends to get a writer disliked.

Doctor Santo Aldobrandini

The one thing I would not do for Signora Sazia was to kill babies in the wombs of her girls. I saw the mothers to term, and I brought those infants into the world as kindly as I could. I tried to find homes for them among other patients, those who longed in vain for a child. I would not permit a single baby I had midwived to go to the orphanages run by former nuns. Rather, I would walk the streets with an infant under my arm until I found someone who would take a baby for love alone.

Great and opulent families are more inclined to sterility and are more often disappointed in the gender of the offspring if it proves female. So there is hardly a prosperous quack-midwife who does not boast herself able to foretell a boy or a girl child. Hippocrates states that a woman who is to bear a boy will have a good colour to her skin, and be merry all through her pregnancy. The male foetus, he adds, prefers to lie on the right side of the womb, while the female cleaves to the left. So the son-bearing mother shows a heavier, firmer right breast and favours her right foot. Others claim to tell the gender of the foetus by the preternatural cravings for particular foods on the part of the mother. An English midwife, Mistress Jane Sharp, has happily recorded that 'Some Women with Child have longed to bite on a piece of their Husband's Buttocks', a sure indication of a boy child fattening inside.

I do all I can to discourage such talk among my patients. There is danger in this foolishness, for both mother and child. There are those fathers who insist on a boy child, who will go so far as to procure the death of the unborn baby, through violence or poison, if these falsely painted signs point to an unwanted girl child forthcoming.

A steady flow of coins now conjured up a smile in my back pocket. I went to the docks to make enquiries about a passage to Peru. A few months more of drudgery and starving economy, and that passage would be within my grasp.

Marcella Fasan

This girl with the pictures of San Sebastiano was none other than the famous Rafaela, universally admired and adored as the wickedest nun in the convent.

'Where did you . . . ? Were you allowed . . . ?'

'No, lovely! No one is *allowed*. I happen to know that you have been punished enough to understand that already.'

'Where did you . . . ?'

'I did not get them. I made them.'

'You painted these?'

'And I would value the opinion of a former citizen-ess of the City of Art on my brush skills, if you please.'

I glanced over my shoulder, trembling. Just to be there, talking to this scandalous girl, was all kinds of wrong. To look at her San Sebastianos was surely a capital offence. The *vicaria* would nose me out any moment. This cell was perilously close to the bathhouse, where she might even now be punishing some poor novice.

The girl seemed to know exactly whom I feared. 'The Vixen won't be showing that thing she calls a face in here. We've got an understanding.'

As she uttered those words, her face filled with an indescribable bitterness. Then she shook herself like a cat, grinned, and demanded, 'Now seriously, do tell what you think of my little daubs.'

She laid them out on a table in front of the *hornacina*, which was beautifully painted but held only a simple iron cross. Her cell was luxuriously appointed, with the finest Turkey carpet underfoot and a pyramid of cakes from the best bakery in town, still in their waxy wrappers, fragrant on the window sill.

Her folded arms and set mouth gave me no freedom to refuse her request. Nor did I wish to limp out of that cell straight into the arms of the *vicaria*. So I fanned out the little cards on her table.

The paintings were fine, truly fine work. I told her so.

'But . . . they *let* you paint?' I asked.

She pointed to an easel. Displayed was a saint so pallid and deeply etched with suffering that it would gladden even the heart of the *vicaria*. The detail was realistic, the *chiaroscuro* perfectly balanced. The *sfumatura* of the complexion was as good as anything Cecilia Cornaro might have done.

'Now turn it over,' she ordered, 'and lift the first layer of canvas. All my paintings are doubles.'

On the back was a perfect San Sebastiano, handsome as the sun. The most abbreviated shade of a meagre fig-leaf drew attention to his thighs rather than concealing them.

338

'Dear God!' I whispered.

'I work to commission,' she said proudly. 'The other nuns want San Sebastiáns mostly. Or babies. You've no idea how much pale pink paint we run to here!'

She pointed to a particularly hideous Santa Rosa of Lima, drying in the sun on her window sill. I lifted it up and carefully prised off the second skin of canvas at the back. There was a perfect pink cherub of a baby, holding out his hands and almost audibly gurgling with his rosebud mouth.

Given my physical difficulties, I had never raised my ambitions to motherhood, not even when I fed on Santo's kiss; or perhaps just momentarily. Mere normal function had always seemed a thing above rubies. But, looking at Rafaela's baby, I could suddenly understand what the nuns in here, and the nuns everywhere, had been deprived of. What a cruel irony was imposed on the poor girls! They were made to worship the image of a baby, as the desire and joy and salvation of the whole race: a little pink, perfect baby with fat hands and wise eyes. And yet a real baby was the one thing that they would never be allowed to have or even hold.

Rafaela seemed to read my thoughts. 'Cruel, aint it? And nuns aint supposed to be *jealous* of the Madonna, but to venerate her. It's a bloody wonder that Marys the world over are not regularly defaced in convents, aint it? Most of the time she looks such a prig. So smug. "Look what I've got! My own little fat pink saviour. *And* I get to stay my own woman with no man to treat me like a serf and get me pregnant every year!" '

Rafaela cradled an imaginary baby Jesus with her cheeks puffed out satirically. Then she growled, 'I've been itching to add a moustache or a beard to a couple of pompous virgins around here myself!'

I wanted to ask her if she spoke of living or painted virgins, but then a quiet step outside Rafaela's door drew the blood from my face. I rushed to cover the painting.

The footstep passed on and we smiled at one another.

'I . . . I paint a little too,' I offered.

'Really?' Rafaela drawled. I had offended her. Perhaps she believed I wanted to compete?

'Have you heard of the artist Cecilia Cornaro from Venice?'

'Who has not? Did she not have doings with Lord Byron and Casanova too? Did the English milord not break her on the wheel . . . and what a painter!'

339

'Well, she is my friend. And she taught me a little . . .'

By now the nun had leaped to her feet. 'Cecilia Cornaro! You gem! You diamond! You softest part of a cat!'

She shuttered her window quickly and in a practised motion set a wooden pail of mossy slime from the fountain in front of the door, so that anyone opening it would stumble. She took me by the shoulders – I smelled vetiver perfume on her skin – and sat me down in front of the easel. She put a paintbrush in my hand, and a small square of clean canvas in front of me. 'Show me what you can do.'

The stem of the paintbrush remembered my fingers like a living thing. How good it felt to dance the quiff of fur in the soft pigment! I rapidly sketched Rafaela's face, adding some colour and shade to it.

She whipped the canvas from my hands and pulled out a sliver of prohibited mirror from under her mattress. She compared the painted and the reflected images, then danced around the cell with my picture so that the wet paint sprayed coloured tears down the white walls.

'It's true! We shall paint together! Sor Constanza . . . are you not really named Marcella?'

'Yes.'

'Marcella and Rafaela. We're sisters now.'

At the word 'sisters', Rafaela's welcoming smile suddenly closed down in grief. She said more quietly, 'Welcome to the family business.'

She thrust the paintbrush back in my hand. With its tip dipped quickly in black, I sketched another image of Rafaela. I still have it: she's shown as a mischievous little mountain hare stretched out in a shaft of sunshine, and winking at me.

Sor Loreta

There was fresh sin in Santa Catalina. I could smell it as clearly as if someone had thrown a dead mouse behind My bed, a thing that had happened to Me more than once, as it was God's design to rain testing misfortunes down upon his Most Devout Daughter.

340

Of all things I feared, the worst had happened. The Venetian Cripple had allied herself with the depraved Rafaela, the one nun I might not touch with My discipline, for reasons that God does not choose to reveal.

This Rafaela might say with impunity outside My window, 'Pray do not disturb Sor Loreta. She is having a nap. Sorry, I slander her. Sor Loreta has of course taken to bed with the weight of her own insupportable holiness.'

'May your tongue cleave in your mouth for saying that!' lisped someone else, in a perfect imitation of the voice of Sor Arabel.

And Rafaela's retainers giggled like sparrows chirruping over stolen bread rolls.

With Rafaela and the Venetian Cripple at Satan's work together, I knew that it would not be long before I was obliged to carry out God's work again.

In the meantime, I took comfort In My little garden, where I planted My special seeds in faith, flowed anointing blood upon them, and awaited My harvest. Monkshood must surely be a holy plant, given its name and its powers and its beautiful blue colour.

There was a saying at Santa Catalina: *cada flor es una monja*, every flower is a nun. Like San Francesco, I spoke to My speechless little sisters, the flowers, and I told them of My great plans. My blue flowers came up like the Virgin's Robe, like the colour of Heaven, like San Francisco's own cowl, drenched in a deep pious blue.

Marcella Fasan

Rafaela's sprawling cell was designed for two. She said that she had originally shared it with her younger sister, who had died. About her death, Rafaela was at first tight-lipped.

'That is a whole other subject,' she said. 'I cannot come to it cold. I let my slaves sleep in my sister's room. I enjoy their company.'

She smiled, and suddenly looked more like Cecilia Cornaro than it was easy for me to bear.

Her *samba* Hermenegilda and *criada* Javiera were devoted to her. I saw

341

that in their shining, smiling faces when Rafaela presented them. I was sure it was not common practice at Santa Catalina for a high-born nun to introduce her slaves, especially by name and with a fond arm around their shoulders.

Rafaela's cell became even more complicated at the back. Her blue courtyard led to, of all luxuries, a private necessary room, laid out with her washing things. And then there was the kitchen, amply equipped with pots for boiling water. Rafaela told me that her slaves always had a hot basin ready for the moment when she had to do her penitential bath.

'My sister . . .' Rafaela choked on some inaudible words.

'How did she die?' I ventured, for it seemed Rafaela had opened the door to that question, and there was no staying on the outside.

Rafaela eyed me starkly, 'Well, I suppose it is for the best that I tell you sooner rather than later. If you are to be my collaborator and friend, you must share my fortunes. My sister Juana – Sor Sofia – died from a forced bath. I heard you were welcomed to Santa Catalina the same way.'

'The cold bath? Did your sister misbehave?'

'No, she was an angel. The opposite of me. She actually had a vocation. The day our parents brought us to Santa Catalina was the best of her life, the worst of mine. She asked even *me* to call her Sor Sofia – she was happy to give up her real name. I had to get used to it. She always told me we were lucky to be here, safe from the horrors of the world. That's the bitterest irony of all. The worst horror of the world lives in Santa Catalina.'

'You mean the *vicaria*?'

Looking at Rafaela's *déshabillée*, the cigar dangling from her finger, it was not hard to see why the *vicaria* might have singled her out for punishment; but why her angelic sister?

Rafaela kicked the wall savagely. 'The *vicaria* had a passion for Sofia. My poor sister always told me that we must show understanding to the woman, and that when she was at her most vile – that was when *we* should be most kind and gentle with her. But the *vicaria*'s passion for Sofia was not kind or gentle. It was hideous, devouring, dangerous! And when it was thwarted – she was forbidden to see or speak to my sister – then it turned to hate.'

342

Her voice cracked, 'In the end my sister died of it. The *vicaria* – and I claim the honour of coining the title "Vixen" by the way – waited until my sister was laid low with a stomach upset. Sofia had a weakness in that part. As far as I can trace the events, my sister was walking back from the infirmary that night. She never arrived here.' Rafaela's words were swallowed by a tearing sob, 'What a beast I am!'

I wanted to put an arm around her, yet I did not know if she would welcome it. I murmured, 'It is surely not you who is the beast.'

Rafaela flung the tears off her cheeks with a violent shaking of her head. 'Wait! You do not know. I can never forgive myself that I let it happen. Hermenegilda came running to tell me that Sofia was in the bathhouse with the Vixen. The evil thing is that I thought for a moment *good!* for this meant that the Vixen had broken the rule of keeping away from my sister. So at last there would be an excuse for the *priora* to forcibly sequester her and remove her from office.

'I thought, *this will end it, once and for all.* For all these years Sor Loreta had been following my sister, lurking in wait for her around corners, contriving to have "accidental" meetings. When she could not see Sofia, Sor Loreta spent all her time praying for my sister's soul, which she claimed had been taken by the Devil. My sister was a gentle creature, not vengeful, and she did not even hate Sor Loreta for this oppression. She always said simply, "The poor woman is mad. We must be compassionate."

'I was thinking about the madness of Sor Loreta, as Sofia described it – which I saw simply as badness – and I was pacing the cell, counting the minutes Sofia had been in there with her. Suddenly I knew it was too long. We've all had the Vixen's baptisms. She makes us sing hymns until she pushes us under the water. I opened my door and leaned out. I could hear Sofia singing across the pathway, her voice growing weaker and weaker. Then I think – oh, I have played this over so many times in my head! – that I heard the splash.

'I began to count again, but then I could bear it no more and I ran out of my cell and over to the bathhouse. Why did I wait? I as good as colluded . . .'

Rafaela turned to the wall, as if she could not bear to be witnessed in recounting the last part of the story. I knew the comforts of a wall to stare at, so I sat patiently. Over her shoulder, she told me, 'It was already

343

too late. Sofia was floating face-down in the water. I leaped into the bath. When I turned her over, I saw her lips were cut and bleeding. There was no breath. Her eyes were half-closed and her tongue appeared between her teeth. I held her in my arms and tried to breathe life into her with my own lips. I turned her around and began to squeeze water out of her chest. The Vixen just looked down on me and smiled. She was in a state of rapture, gone from this world. She did not even look human. She did not know who I was. That demented, brutal smile must have been the last thing my sister ever saw.'

Rafaela faced me again. 'There was a bottle floating on the surface of the water, broken at its mouth. There was a story that the Vixen used a lachrymatory bottle to store the tears she wept for Sofia's soul. She must have forced Sofia to drink those tears before she drowned her. That's why my sister's lips were bleeding.'

Rafaela fell silent, overtaken by memories. When I judged that she could speak again, I asked, 'Why has the Vixen still a place among us? Should she not be in prison?'

'That is what I thought at first, of course,' Rafaela continued, 'but when I shook off the stupor of grief, I did some thinking, for once: thinking that I should have done much beforehand. *Thinking* would have saved Sofia. I bear guilt, for I did more than anyone to drive the Vixen mad. I laughed at her, I made others laugh at her. I thought she was a joke for my personal entertainment. I hate to be confined, so I made her the butt of my frustration. And I underestimated her madness, jabbed at her feelings constantly . . .'

'Even if that is true, why should you not tell the *priora* what happened? No one would blame you as you blame yourself.'

'If you had seen the Vixen's face that night, you would know why. Her soul had left her body. I am perfectly sure she remembers nothing of the deed: she has buried it in an unvisited part of that mind of hers that is so distorted by starvation and flagellation. She would be able to put her hand on the Bible and swear she knew nothing.

'Also, there were no witnesses. Sofia is not the first girl to die of cold baths here. There have been cases of genuine pneumonia and heart failure in the winter. Sofia was always delicate in her health. Even if the *priora* believed *me* – a known troublemaker with a history of mocking Sor Loreta – I doubted if the *vicaria* would be punished properly. The only

344

punishment suitable for what she did is a hanging. The *priora* would not wish to deliver a nun – even this one – to the world outside for a murder trial and a public execution.

'Santa Catalina would never survive the shame if the whole story came out. Monseñor José Sebastián de Goyeneche y Barreda would close us down and send us all to Santa Rosa, where we would have to sleep in tombs. We would each of us be as dead as my sister, who would never be avenged. And the only person who would be happy would be Sor Loreta, who would be ecstatic at the martyrdom of a violent death. She would be in *calores* on the scaffold! At last the whole world would see how starved and mutilated she is! Why should I make her that gift she desires above all others?

'I decided to keep quiet and use the information I had to my own advantage. The first thing it did was to confound the Vixen. Perhaps it has confounded you too?'

'No, I perfectly understand!' I whispered. 'You *had* to be silent.'

Just as I, as a little girl, had known that my parents would never deliver the punishment that Minguillo deserved, and had therefore resolved on a dignified, mystifying silence that also protected those who loved me. Yet had that only provoked Minguillo to worse outrages? And Cecilia Cornaro had told me that I was cruel to withhold the truth from those who loved me, and that it was vanity to suppose I could manage without their help.

I asked how the *vicaria* had responded to Rafaela's own silence.

'All through Sofia's lying-in at the *sala de profundis*, I felt her eye on me, confused. She is mad – she does not understand anything or remember anything. But she instinctively feels that I know something to her detriment. Ever since Sofia died, she ignores all my transgressions, never enters my cell to search it, never addresses a word to me, let alone a hard word. She leaves me alone and persecutes other girls, though she dares not go too far now. I have made sure that my friends Rosita and Margarita know what happened to my sister too – so if the *vicaria* tried the same with me, they would go straight to the *priora*. Now, *Veneciana*, I have you, too, to help me.'

'Yes,' I replied eagerly, 'you have.'

I did not yet feel ready to confide it in her, but I had already decided that Rafaela's story would be recorded in Marcella Fasan's illustrated diary, alongside my chronicles of Minguillo.

As I slipped out, I noted that Rafaela's cell was well positioned for what she happily described as her 'life of crime'. It looked on to the Zocodober fountain, all carved with Moorish patterns, around which the servants conducted their 'souk', exchanging goods brought in from the outside world. With the babble of voices and the rushing of the water, it could have been the Rialto. Rafaela's servants, she had told me, had special double-bottomed baskets, in which they secreted perfumes, cigars and other contraband items, the more secret exchanges taking place by the slaves' latrine.

In the following days, when I discreetly and shyly asked other nuns about Rafaela, I heard it said that every company of women needs a naughty girl, to be brave for all the faint-hearted ones and enact the wildness in their hearts. The worst that was said was that such a spirited creature would likely meet a bad end. Yet even in those words there was certainly more regretful affection than malice. All expressed tearful sorrow for the loss of Rafaela's sister, Sor Sofia.

From the time of our first acquaintance, I visited Rafaela almost every day during the afternoon hours that were free for contemplation and 'spiritual activities'. I sat sketching and painting, all the while drinking in the sound of the stone fountain playing outside the window, with my Venetian ears that craved the music of water.

My new studio was Sofia's room, where the slaves slept. Two doors and a right angle from the entrance, it was ideally placed for secrecy, should anyone take it upon themselves to spy. One of Rafaela's loving servants was always posted in between, well rehearsed in delaying explanations.

Painting, as Rafaela had said, was not prohibited at Santa Catalina. It was only our secret subject matter that put us at risk. Our pictures were supposed to be of saints, and indeed we painted a great many of them, as a cover. We even painted in *mestizo* style, adding green parrots, flamingos and Peruvian *kantu* flowers to our backgrounds. We twisted feathers of birds-of-paradise and Inca ornaments into the hair of our lady saints and decked them with necklaces of Chilean malachite. The Peruvian Jesus was broad in the nose, dark-skinned and dark-eyed, had brown bowed legs and wore a lacy skirt – the traditional *mestizo* undergarment – instead of a loincloth.

Yet under cover of these legitimate arts, we also made secular

346

portraits for sale. Later I would discover that some of these pictures were smuggled out to the world, and sold with 'artist unknown' in the masculine form as the only signature. For the serving nuns of the convent, we made *mestizo* portraits of the baby Christ. For the pure Spanish nuns, we painted stern Santa Rosas and Santa Teresas, behind which we secreted San Sebastianos, sensual as pagan gods. We painted seductive girl-saints for those inclined that way, using the likeness of their reigning favourite.

'And this is the wickedest thing of all,' gloated Rafaela, 'not only because of the Sapphism but . . .'

Cecilia Cornaro had told me why not. I finished the sentence, 'Because a nun must never have her portrait painted unless she is dead.'

Minguillo Fasan

The Indulgent Reader will forgive me for returning to a subject that vexed me in that period.

Without noise, nosegays or notoriety, the Alert Reader will already have guessed what I, in my innocence, only now began to suspect. Amalia did not *want* to give me a son. It was her petty revenge for certain slights done to her. My lack of a son was, I told my quack, all the fault of my wife's recalcitrant womb. Your woman might not have much by way of a mind, but her uterus was set on flouting me.

'Dose her,' the fat quack suggested, pointing down to my pretty garden.

If that womb were set on its girlish ways, then it was not a matter of heartbreaking consequence if it would bear no more.

Any stick will do to beat a dog, I thought.

'My dove,' I said that evening, 'drink this.'

Sor Loreta

The convent gossiped about petty thefts, which were surely just a case of careless light nuns displacing things by accident. Meanwhile, from outside the walls I heard continual news of Satan's work in Arequipa. There was a very shocking incident in the town. Two women brawled, and one of them held the other down and lifted her rival's skirts and threatened to introduce hot peppers into her private parts. I thought on this often, and it in turn made Me think of the sinner Rafaela and the Venetian Cripple, and whatever they were contriving by way of obscenity and devilment. My own purity caused Me to be extraordinarily sensitive to the vibrations of sin, and now I felt them coming most powerfully from the cell of Rafaela.

I felt perfectly alert for the first time in a very long period. I realized now that for many months I had stumbled around the convent half-blinded with grief for Sor Sofia. Since Sor Sofia's death, all My ill thoughts of her had dissolved into regret and loneliness. My hatred was now fixed on its proper objects: her sister, and the Venetian Cripple.

Sor Narcisa and Sor Arabel could not console Me for My loss. I spoke harsh words to them and in this way, slowly, I unconsciously turned them against Me, though I would not see the effect until very much later.

Marcella Fasan

I was not Rafaela's only disciple.

Most days there assembled in her cell a community of friends, the flower of intelligence and liveliness in the convent.

I was surprised to find among them some nuns who were, though

348

relatively young, figures of authority at Santa Catalina. There was Margarita, the pharmacist, trained since childhood in all the healing arts. Margarita was a *criolla* born in Bolivia. She had been at Santa Catalina since the age of two. Like Rafaela, she enjoyed an amicable rapport with her slaves.

Rosita, the *portera*, was a *gachupina*, a Spanish-born Catalan nun. She held the keys to the tradesmen's entrance and the front gate. She also operated the *torneras*, the revolving wooden shelves by which items were brought into the convent without physical or ocular contact between the nuns and the outside world.

The four of us sat in Rafaela's cell, unmolested by the *vicaria*, dangling our legs over the edges of the beds, recounting our past lives and the delightful gossip from Arequipa and as far away as Lima. The convent's own scandal in those days was all about some grisly relics that had gone missing – the heart of Brother Mariano Moscoso, Bishop of Tucuman, and the tongue of Luis Gonzaga de la Encina, eighteenth Bishop of Arequipa. It was said that the Bishop's tongue had been indefatigable in preaching, and tireless in praising God.

'Who would want such horrors?' asked Rosita.

'The gardener might have sold them to Pío Tristán,' mused Margarita, explaining that this rich Arequipan nobleman was mad for religious relics and statues.

'What about the manual of poisons, gone missing from the pharmacy?' wondered Margarita.

Once I asked Rafaela, 'Why do you not pursue an office? It would give you privileges and independence, like Rosita and Margarita. All the clever girls rise here. Do you not want one day to be *priora* or at least serve on the council?'

Rafaela scowled, 'I don't want to believe I'll stay here. I do not want to get used to it.'

The other girls laughed and embraced her, yet there was sadness weighing down the paint-scented air that day too. I put it down to compassion for Rafaela's restlessness. No one could imagine how she might leave the convent. Her father had negotiated a dowry that would revert if she were to fail as a nun.

It was in this affectionate company that I told the story of my own life so far, of Minguillo's assaults on my happiness and health, and of my various imprisonments. I even confided in them my time at the madhouse.

I should have noticed that they did not appear too much surprised at the earlier part of my tale, but I was intent upon the clamorous relief of full disclosure.

Finally, with much squealing encouragement, and some admiring whistling, I told them about Santo.

Outside the fountain played and played, and yet nothing interrupted the violent lime green of its surface. Rafaela whispered to me once, 'It's distilling poison, to help me kill the *vicaria*.'

There was killing to come, but not the killing that Rafaela envisaged.

Minguillo Fasan

I threw myself into business, all the better to fatten the inheritance of my boy baby whenever (and from whichever, as it were, channel) he should make his way into the world.

It seemed to me the *ne plus ultra* of human grandeur that I should begin to sell our Peruvian medicines in England and Scotland, the jewel of Albion, whose doughty soldiers had trounced Napoleon and whose markets thrived, unlike those that had felt the pain of succumbing to Boney's desires. The revived 'Tears of Santa Rosa' would look well with a brave tartan ribbon to sash the bottle, I thought.

Reports had come to me of an excellent Scottish merchant with the gift of languages and the stomach for travel, with connections already established in the New World and the Old. He was known to voyage between Montevideo and Manchester without the least qualm. This Hamish Gilfeather I now summoned by letter – to propose bestowing upon him the honour of becoming my international agent.

What? What's that? The Reader asks, why a Scot?

I had always liked Scots. They aren't pretty, but they do not lie. If the Musical Reader ever desires a moment of pleasure, he should ask a Scotsman to say '*prego*'.

Anyway, this Mr Gilfeather was by coincidence a regular visitor to Venice, it turned out. Dealing in hairy rugs in wide-awake colours, I had heard; and doing the act of darkness with our famous Venetian whores, or so I divined.

Marcella Fasan

'Why,' Rafaela mused, 'does your brother not come to see you, lovely? Even male relatives may come once a month to the *locutorio*.'

I turned on her in painful confusion, 'After all I have told you, how can you wish *that* on me?'

'Not the vile Minguillo. I mean your Arequipan brother.'

'My *what*?'

Rafaela looked at me in perplexity and wonder. 'You don't know, you truly don't know, do you?'

Then she muttered, 'Of course, how could it serve the odious Minguillo to let her know she has another family to love her?'

As kindly as possible, Rafaela explained about my father's mistress – 'a nice woman, not excessively clever but devoted to your papà', and about the son who was, it seemed, very close in age to myself. Mother and son were now living in near destitution over a *chichería* in a bad part of town. Minguillo had evicted them with all possible humiliation from the house they had once shared with my father.

'Do you know, they came to witness your novitiate and your profession? That must have been hard for them. The whole town was watching them, when it was not watching you! They were very dignified, Marcella. They looked at you so kindly – almost longingly. They must guess you are as much your brother's victim as they are.'

My heart leaped at the thought of someone bound to me by blood who was not Minguillo. 'What does he look like, my half-brother?'

'Not like you – he is dark like his mother. Really quite delectable in a young, bruised way.'

'How do you know all this, Rafaela?'

'Well of course I've seen 'em myself in church. As for the rest, Hermenegilda goes about the city, and brings back all the news. But there is not much to be said of your half-brother and his mother. They have no money now to display themselves or get themselves talked about.'

'What is my half-brother's name? Do you know that?'

'Fernando, like your father.'

'So my father saw him as a real son.'

'And Beatriz Villafuerte as a real wife. He adored her. Your father's tenderness for his family was famous. The town is still rather proud, to tell the truth: that a great Venetian nobleman should choose a second wife from our women, and have a son whom he brought up as a gentleman. Did your family in Venice have no idea?'

'We always wondered why my father spent so much time here, except that Venice was so . . . sad in the last years of his life, after Napoleon. When I saw the Plaza de Armas, I thought it looked so much like our San Marco, but better. Venice was disgraced, ruined – this was my father's new country, where nothing was spoilt.'

'They say your father was happy here. Perhaps he was not happy with your own mother? You never mention her, lovely, which tells me rather a great deal about her, in fact. As does the rest of your story. Anyway – before the public eviction by your brother Minguillo – young Fernando and his mother were figures in society. They were liked and respected. Beatriz spread her good fortune around the town. So when Minguillo came and ruined them . . . well, he was not well thought of for it. Now the lovely Casa Fasan is all shut up, the servants dismissed. There were many went hungry as a result.'

'I am sorry,' I murmured.

'It would not have hurt your brother to allow his father's mistress and his son to live decently. They had to rent rooms in the house of Benito del Rosario Condorpusa . . . one of the worst *chicherías*.'

'It *would* have hurt him. But my brother and his mother – what do they live on?'

'Fernando apprenticed himself to a shoemaker. Can you imagine? Once he was a little lord in this town. Now he mends the shoes of peasants.

352

Yet I will say this for him too, he has never been heard to complain, and applied himself, and quickly exceeded all the other shoemakers in skill. In fact, his shoes are in demand.'

'The *priora* knows all this? Josefa knows?'

'Of course. Like I did, they must both think you know, and that it is a sore subject, or they would have talked to you about it!' Rafaela exclaimed. 'What a caper! We must contrive for Fernando to come to the *locutorio*. I'll discuss it with Hermenegilda. Beatriz Villafuerte's *samba* is her cousin. But you can see Fernando himself, any Sunday worship. He's always there, and he's always looking at you, lovely. Have you not felt it?'

'I keep my eyes down. The *vicaria* . . .'

'Next Sunday, I'll show you.'

Santo, I thought, *Santo, we have a half-brother now.*

Minguillo Fasan

It crossed my mind that Marcella now lived within a loud moan of our bastard half-brother Fernando. There were times when that seemed too cosy-cosy for my liking. Then I thought again, and was more pleased.

The Reader fails to comprehend my pleasure? Would the Reader like to keep up, please!

The impoverished bastard Fernando must have known of his half-sister walled up with all the noble virgins of Arequipa. Your boy would naturally resent her for being born on the right side of the sheets. All the money and Arequipan land that had bought her place at Santa Catalina – it might have been his. Perhaps, resentful as all bastards are by nature, he would even pretend a superior knowledge of her, try to damage her with made-up stories, more fatal than bullets in a small town like Arequipa. In the end I found that it comforted me to know Marcella was close to a half-brother who must hate her, as I could not do the job myself adequately from this distance.

Mr Gilfeather responded to my letter. He enquired if I was the same Minguillo Fasan who traded in chinchona from Peru. How far my fame had spread! He showed some of his native reserve in that he agreed to meet with me when his business would bring him to Venice. And not before. The fellow did not commit himself to becoming my creature, writing of '*an interview to establish mutual interests, if any*'.

I told myself that Gilfeather was cautious because of all the revolutions fermenting in Bolivia and Mexico and Chile and Paraguay: no place for a merchant, where the natives are fighting their Spanish superiors. The wily merchant no doubt wished to see if I would offer him protection, letters of introduction to eminent *mestizos* (should things fall out their way), and promises of safe houses should it not.

Yet

The cold gall of him! But I decided to be amused by it, and hoped to be still more amused when I met him in person. A date was finally set, one month from my wedding anniversary.

Marcella Fasan

Josefa fussed with my veil. 'We make you pretty-pretty for you brother today.'

In the church I surrounded myself with friends in the hope that the sight of me would be blotted out from the *vicaria*. Through this shield of female amity, I would peer safely at my half-brother and his Mamma.

For I could not trust myself not to manifest legible emotion when I met his gaze. All week, while I had waited for this Sunday's mass, my heart beat its wings like an insect in a little box, and tears jerked into my eyes at unexpected moments.

Rosita, Margarita, Rafaela and I arrived early, so that we might take the seats nearest the grate, with the best view of the lay worshippers.

The *vicaria* bustled in next. I was horrified to see that she chose the chair immediately opposite mine. We had counted upon her taking her usual position in the centre, and upon Rosita and Margarita subtly leaning forward to screen me.

All was not lost: Rafaela, ever resourceful, had invented a sign language for us in advance. 'If I ball up my right hand, look right into the nave. If I ball up my left hand, look left. Fernando always sits close to the front, so as to have a good view of you. If I show you eight fingers, he is in the eighth row. From there, it's up to you, lovely.'

I tried to keep my eyes downcast and fixed on Rafaela's fingers. As the church filled up for the mass, her hands stayed unnaturally still in her lap. My stomach churned as the people of Arequipa trickled into the church from the side door that opened up to the street. A shaft of glittering sunshine fell through the entrance, lighting each person theatrically as he or she arrived. I snatched the briefest glance each time I heard a new footstep on the stone threshold.

The church was nearly full, and yet Rafaela's hands remained unmoving in her lap. Given that she was a notable fidget, I worried that her motionless posture would draw Sor Loreta's attention. Rosita and Margarita had the same concern, I realized, from their tense faces and their eyes fixed on the dreadful stillness in Rafaela's lap.

'Look somewhere else!' I longed to urge them, for I was terrified that their eyes would draw the *vicaria*'s straight to the one place we did not want them.

Then Rafaela balled up her right hand. When she was sure I had seen that, she showed me four fingers unfurled.

Gianni delle Boccole

There had been roomers, save us, of course there was roomers. When a Venetian lord spends the bigger part o his life and breathes his last in a strange country, there must of been summing to tug n tie him there. Now I knowed what. Twere a woman, and twere a

355

son. Not a son like Minguillo, but a proper boy, a child to be proud of, to love, a boy to leave to the world with pride.

I had finely workt my way into a strongbox I found up the chimney in Minguillo's study. Twere full of scribblings, like he were writin a book bout his life, as if anyone would want to read *that*! About what he had purpletrated in Venice, I knowed all too well, so I spent my preshous short espyin time on his writins bout his time in Peru. That's where I found out bout the half-brother in Arequipa.

My first thought were naturally o the lossed will. Could it be that the next-borned child menshoned in it were alredy alive when my old Master Fernando Fasan wrote the will? Could this Arequipa son be the legal hair?

The son were called 'Fernando', which sayed a great deal. As done the fact that Minguillo throne the boy and his Mamma out on the streets, poor insents that they surely was. Minguillo exsalted in the fact that the boy had took to making shoes for his bread. The son of my old Master Fernando Fasan a cobbler! God-on-a-stick!

I bethought straitway if young Fernando hated on Minguillo, which he surely did, then that lad could be a friend to Marcella. Why, he mite go and visit her and keep her company through the bars o the talking parlour.

Yet perhap he dint know that she existed? Minguillo had kickt the dirt oer his sister's livin grave too many times afore. Now she were shut up in a convent like she were alredy in her coffin. Were there any trace o her in Arequipa for this boy to know bout?

Minguillo had give out that private letters was forbid at the convent of Santa Catalina. So he told his Mamma, anyway, and she were in fact reliefed.

There haint niver been no answer to my letter to the *priora*. Perhaps that merchant niver delivert it? But now I could write to the young Fernando! I wondered had he took the Fasan name? His Mamma, I read, were one Beatriz Villafuerte. How many women o sich name lived in Arequipa? All the Span-yard names sounded ixotic to me. There mite be a hunnerd o them Beatriz Villafuertes out there, Dog ovva God!

Meanwhile the Contessa Amalia were giving us all cause for worrit. Her face was bluish and her fingernails turned black and she tookt to her bed, poor girl, languid as a lilly. The usband were nowhere to be seed most of the time. Twere as she had turned odorous in his sight.

Swear Minguillo made his peerances only to supervise the Contessa's dinners.

Marcella Fasan

Rafaela, as arranged, had at this moment distracted the *vicaria* by dropping her hymnbook loudly on the floor. Rosita and Margarita recollected themselves and our plan. While the citizens of Arequipa filed forward for communion, the two girls simultaneously addressed the *vicaria* with whispered liturgical questions we had prepared in advance. The *vicaria* looked flattered to be consulted on such an elevated matter and failed to silence them. Instead, she leaned forward towards Rosita and sketched a crucifix with her hands, whispering in an animated fashion.

I dared only a few seconds of silent ocular contact. The boy was slender, tall and he had my – our – father's brow and lips. Our eyes met. I saw that my half-brother Fernando understood that at last I knew who he was. His face paled, then flushed. His eyes filled with tears, but remained steadily fixed on my face. My own gaze travelled quickly to the pretty, plump woman beside him. My father had loved her, perhaps more than he loved my mother. He had neglected our family in Venice to be with them, leaving me to Minguillo's care, without a protector. Yet they had suffered too, at Minguillo's hand, been humiliated and made homeless and penniless. I found I wished these two nothing but good. I nodded as slightly as possible, and they both nodded back, wonderingly. The mother clutched the son's hand, and he put his other arm around her. Her shoulders shook.

Rafaela nudged me with her foot. It was no longer safe to look.

I returned my eyes to the floor, yet my heart was dancing.

Doctor Santo Aldobrandini

In Spanish and Italian, it goes by the bland name of *aconito*, which gives no warning of its powers.

They say that *Aconitum nepallus* was named 'monkshood' by the English pharmacists, because the flower folds upon itself like the cowl of a friar. Among its other names are 'helmet flower' and 'soldier's cap'. Then there are those who call it wolfsbane, because it is used to bait and murder those creatures.

The effects of monkshood poisoning are well known to those whose duty it is to investigate suspicious deaths. When someone vomits, sweats copiously, froths lightly at the mouth and suffers a blurring of the sight, then an adult portion of monkshood may be suspected. Tiny doses, regularly administered, will weaken the heart, nerves and stomach, any one of which will fail comprehensively after a certain time or with one conclusive dose.

Gianni told me things about the Contessa Amalia that worried me – but given the scandal that Minguillo had invented, that I had lusted after his wife – I was the last person to be able to make tender enquiries on her behalf. What if Marcella found out that I had intervened? Amalia, I feared, would ever be a sore spot between us.

Yet the more I heard from Gianni, the more I became convinced that my reticence would connive at a murder. And what kind of doctor would I be, suspecting as I did, yet never intervening as Minguillo and his quack droppered a distillate of monkshood into his wife's increasingly tiny meals?

I assembled remedies for all the poisons that Minguillo might employ. One by one, I gave them to Gianni, who had Anna administer the herbs infused in water and milk.

Gianni did not conceive, and I did not force on him, the ironical realization that, in funding these remedies from my own pocket, franc by franc and day by day, I unwillingly delayed my passage to Peru.

Marcella Fasan

The next day Fernando presented himself at the *locutorio* and asked to see me. Via the swift-running *criadas*, the rumour ran from the *locutorio* through the first terracotta courtyard to the novices' cloister, bounced out of there and into the courtyard of the oranges, down Calle Toledo and up Calle Sevilla and straight into my cell on Josefa's full, pretty lips.

I dared not follow the rumour back to its source, and nor could I sit still, so I went to Rafaela, who was already smug and replete with the glad tidings.

'I told you.'

'But can this be good? Will the *priora* allow me to talk to him? Does she know what happened in the church?'

'This is Arequipa. Everyone knows everything about everyone.'

There was a shuffle outside the door.

The *priora*'s *criada* knew where to find me. My painting business with Rafaela was thriving, and we were now openly accepting commissions even from outside the convent. A tithe of our visible earnings was taken for charitable causes; the rest we spent on paint and canvas, and cigars for Rafaela. I had blushed to hear the *priora* singing our praises at the refectory more than once. She liked to say of us that 'our two artist-nuns are to be much admired and perhaps a little indulged for the piety of their paintings'.

The Vixen had snarled when she heard that, visibly snarled.

That ruined face was in my mind as I hurried up through the courtyards to the *priora*'s office. Her expression was kind as I entered. 'Sor Constanza, you have had a visitor.'

I wondered how best to dissemble astonishment, but she quickly and kindly spared me the trouble of trying to lie to her. 'I am sure that the fact of your father's second family and your half-brother is generally known in Santa Catalina already, my dear. The more interesting question is how we are to proceed.'

I nodded.

'Of course, it was an immoral situation that is not to be condoned. Naturally it would be better if such things did not happen in the world.'

To mitigate the severity of this speech, she winked at me. 'However, Signor Rossini has seen fit to write divine music to accompany even acts of marital infidelity, so we must allow that they happen from time to time, and that a few extra years in Purgatory are reckoned worthwhile as payment by those who participate in such sins. Who are we to punish them further here on this earth? Now, the real question is, should we let you meet your half-brother Fernando?'

'If the decision were mine, I would say yes,' I said boldly, 'for he is innocent. The condition of his birth was not chosen by him.'

'As would I say yes, with all my heart. Yet I must think about how the world will judge us. So far my deliberations go in this direction: the boy Fernando is known to be a good and devoted person. He is pious, hardworking and supports his mother in every way. Moreover, the accident of his birth has borne no bitter fruit in his character as it sometimes does.'

We were both thinking, *The character of the other brother is bitterer than any fruit.*

'In cases like these,' the *priora* continued, 'for hot Spanish blood has frequently generated such scandals, I rehearse the world's opinion on my *vicaria*, as there could be no severer censure than hers.'

'She is sure to say no!' I protested.

'Of course she is,' responded the *priora* tranquilly. 'The question is how to make her "no" seem wrong-minded. You must leave this with me a while to ponder. I shall in the meantime act as a friendly embassy to young Master Fernando so as not to dash his hopes of meeting with you. I have a feeling that this means a great deal to him.'

'I have heard they are desperately poor and subsist only on his earnings as a shoemaker,' I said. 'I wish there was something that I might do for them, some act of charity.'

'You refer to your dowry?'

'All that silver! How is it fair . . .'

'But that is the convent's property now. It was given to Santa Catalina in your name, and is not mine to distribute as I wish. Such alms as we give

360

are carefully regulated. Go now, child. Please send in Sor Rosita to play the piano for me. I think much better to the accompaniment of Signor Rossini.'

Minguillo Fasan

The Uxorious Reader will know the problem.

My second wife was proving more difficult to run to ground than the first. There were noble families in Venice who would not even entertain my overtures, seeming somehow alarmed at the fact that I began them before Amalia had actually died. And then an officer of the *Sanità*, alerted by some tittle-tattle, actually came to my door, demanding to see my wife.

I had him taken up to Amalia's chamber, where he took copious notes of her rather listless condition. The Reader shall be amazed by my composure, which was historic. Indeed, I felt a sweet calm at my core. I knew that nothing could be proved by her visible state.

Yet after the man shuffled off, I found myself briefly disintegrating into raving shards of impotent anger. Someone had made a bid against me from the infinite shadow of anonymity, from that same menacing place where the will-thief dwelled. And the visit of the officer would cause talk. The Sensitive Reader knows how vile it is to feel the hot breath of a town whispering behind its hands about Him.

It made *me* feel defiant, to think 'to Hell in a tub' with all of them.

One day is a mother, the next a stepmother. The Reader and His hard-working informant must trudge through both. So.

More than ever, I craved a new, son-bearing wife. In my accounts, I had already made provision for my second wedding: a table of opulence to strike my fine guests dumb, and a shower of small coins and dry bread rolls for the poor outside the church. A wedding would cost nearly as much as a book of human skin!

The intriguing Mr Hamish Gilfeather was due in Venice very shortly. I found myself wondering if your man had a fecund daughter or two fathered on some drag-tailed wife in his craggy Scottish castle. If not a Venetian mother for my son, then a foreign one would do as well. She would have the advantages (to me) of ignorance and isolation.

Doctor Santo Aldobrandini

The *Sanità* had acted on my anonymous *denuncia*, but only with an official inspection of Amalia in her sickbed. They did not even send a doctor to see to her. Then I realized with a sickening pang that it was only if Amalia died that my *denuncia* would have any power.

With those medicines that cost me so dear, we continued to keep Amalia alive day by day. Sometimes I feared that we but prolonged her agony: death might have been a merciful release for a girl trapped in marriage with Minguillo Fasan.

Gianni meanwhile had become obsessed with the half-brother he had discovered in Arequipa. He was convinced that we should write to the boy, and tell him what evil had been done to his sister. The good man seemed agitated, kept muttering something about 'the hair' from which words could be prised neither meaning nor possibility.

The impetuous Gianni also had wild hopes of the Scottish merchant who was coming to Venice for an interview with Minguillo. This merchant had known Marcella in the days when she had painted with Cecilia Cornaro. Then he had arrived back in Venice providentially, in time to see her safely across the ocean to South America. It was true that he had ensured delivery to me and Gianni of the only letters we had ever received from Marcella. Certainly, this Hamish Gilfeather *seemed* to be more than an obliging courier.

But I could not wax so enthusiastic as the trusting Gianni. The problem, for me, was that this Hamish Gilfeather countenanced dealings with Minguillo Fasan: for that alone I deemed him a potentially obnoxious and untrustworthy person.

Marcella Fasan

'As good as a "yes"!' Rafaela was jubilant.

'As good as a "not yet" anyway.'

The next Sunday in church I was able to exchange a definite nod with Fernando and a shy smile with his mother. I saw from the radiance of their faces that the *priora* had indeed encouraged them to hope for a good outcome.

The next time the *priora* summoned me, it was to say, 'Your brother is in the *locutorio*. Go to him now. I personally will supervise the exchange, but my ears and soul shall be full of Rossini, so you may consider this a private meeting.'

'How did you . . . ?'

'Settle with the *vicaria*? It would be better for you not to know, child. I do not wish to compound her humiliation or her dislike of you.'

Relief made me tremble. I knelt and kissed her ring. I did not want to make the mistake with her that I had made with Gianni, with Cecilia, with Padre Portalupi. I wanted her to know that I needed her help and that she had earned my grateful trust.

Did my new brother know that I was a cripple? That was my first thought as I limped into the narrow room with the grates, to the accompaniment of loud piano music from the *oficina*. Instinctively, I tried to hide the dragging of my right leg.

Fernando was standing at the grate, his fingers laced through the metal.

'Sister? Marcella?' His tears were falling quietly upon the iron.

I looked at the boy, reading my father's dimly remembered loving expression on his gentle face. I could not speak.

'Marcella,' he whispered with a reverence in his voice, 'or must I call you Sor Constanza?'

His Spanish was of the New World, but I had learned to understand the inflections. I felt the eyes of the *priora* upon me, through her grate at the end of the room. Fernando's knuckles were white on the bars. It was up to me to observe the proper courses. If I did not, then I might not see this precious boy again. 'I am Sor Constanza, Fernando. I am so very happy to know you.'

At this he broke into noisy sobs. I stood one foot from the grate, watching his shoulders shake. I longed to reach out and touch one of his slender fingers. But I knew how much depended on my restraint.

'Our father must have loved you very much,' I said soothingly. 'He would be so proud of how you have grown up and how you look after your mother. Here in the convent I hear nothing but good of you.'

He gasped, 'And out in the streets . . . there are terrible stories of what that *cerdo* Minguillo did to you . . .'

'Hush.' I inclined my head towards the grate where the *priora*'s intelligent eye glittered in the lamplight.

'I wanted to say . . . I mean to say, sister, that you have been so alone in the world, and I want, my mother and I want . . . for you not to be alone any more. We want you to know that we already love you.'

At this all my resolve crumpled and with it my weak knee. I fell back against the bench, sobbing as loudly as the boy had done.

Fernando misunderstood the nature of my emotion. 'For you,' he moaned, 'it must be such a cruel exile, to be driven out of *hermosísima* Venice and sent to the end of the world. Venice! Yet Santa Catalina is safer than Venice for you . . . and *we* are here. If you will accept our protection, we shall be your guardian angels outside the walls of the convent. Nothing bad shall happen to you again while I am alive to protect you.'

The irony of this situation forced me to exclaim, 'It is not your fault! Our father chose to spend more time in Arequipa than Venice. Yet you were deprived of what he would have wanted to provide for you. I feel guilty,' I blurted, 'that you live in penury while I have such comforts here.'

'I am grateful every day to be the son of Fernando Fasan. I do not need payment for it.'

'You are so thin . . .'

'Oh Marcella, even with that veil . . .'

I heard the *priora*'s gown rustle warningly. I must not acknowledge any physicality in the room.

'Brother Fernando, if we can behave decorously I believe that the kind *priora* will allow us to meet again.'

'Yes, that is what I want more than anything.'

I heard the door opening behind him, and the *priora*'s voice calling through the grate, 'Go back to your cell, Sor Constanza. We shall talk later.'

Fernando whispered, 'Next time, bring me outlines of your feet, sister. On paper.'

Sor Loreta

Priora Mónica went against every decency and allowed the bastard half-brother Fernando Fasan to visit the Venetian Cripple in the convent.

'No good can come of this,' I warned, intercepting her in the main cloister where she stood enjoying the sun in a very sensual way. My angels were very active that day, spurring Me to brave defiance, even though I knew that the *priora* detested this kind of intervention.

'And what bad?' she asked Me, humming a vulgar little snort of Rossini. I thought she might have stopped that since the Corsican had been defeated and sent to an island in the South Pacific to rot.

'The boy wants to make his sister some shoes to support her crippled leg. Even your God would allow that blameless act, I trust, Sor Loreta.'

Sor Narcisa and Sor Arabel were of the opinion that these shoes would be the agent of mischief. I told them not to distract themselves with crazed conspiracies, but to secretly watch over the Venetian Cripple herself with redoubled attention.

Priora Mónica came to Me, furiously angry. 'Why do you have poor Sor Constanza followed by your jackals wherever she goes?'

'Because she is sure to reveal herself in sin, sooner or later,' I answered tranquilly.

At this the *priora* appeared to be taken with some kind of convulsion. She lost control of her temper, and shouted at Me: 'Sor Loreta, I sicken at the sight of you! You do everything you can to put other nuns in a bad light. Is that charitable? Is that loving? Your nature is contentious and rivalrous like a man's. An evil man's! Quite apart from your hideous appearance, you must ask yourself, "Am I the kind of bride that God would choose for Himself?" '

With that blasphemy, Priora Mónica compounded her other notorious insult: her wish that I should crucify my tongue. In fact, all these months past, the other light sisters had never let Me forget it, for they counted the days lost in which they did not remind Me of it in subtle, wicked ways. Now it burned afresh in My mind, that felt lit from within with a new, clear fire.

Marcella Fasan

Back in Rafaela's cell, a clamorous company of my friends cross-examined me about the meeting.

'Fernando must be gasping to find out about Venice, about how your father lived there, about what Minguillo did to you.'

'Of that, he seems to know something. Which has made me curious, Rafaela. What did you know of me before we met? My brother has always written my biography in advance. I thought that he told the nuns only that I must be sent away to a New World convent because Napoleon was closing those of the Old World.'

Rosita answered pertly, 'We already knew that he shot you and crippled you. That he had locked you up in a madhouse. And that the madhouse would not have you, as you were patently not mad, so he sent you here, hoping you would die on the way. But we did not know about your Santo until you told us.'

'How . . . ?'

'There was a letter. An anonymous, illiterate letter that was sent to the *priora*. In Italian, but a rough kind.'

Rafaela reminded me, 'Rosita has Italian, because of the Rossini.'

Rosita herself took up the story, 'I was waiting in the *oficina* to play the pianoforte. The *priora* was delayed. The letter was right in front of me. Where was I to put my eyes? Can you guess who wrote it?'

I could.

'The writer – he did not think to give an address or a name so the *priora* could write back to him. He seemed a dear creature, and most certainly he loved you like his own child. But he was upset and disorganized. Or perhaps he was frightened of discovery?'

'With reason.'

'But now Fernando can write to him!'

It was as if someone had led me to a well, and that well went right through the earth to the other side, where Venice lay shimmering.

I brought the outlines of my feet to Fernando as he asked. The *priora* allowed me to pass the sheets of paper through the grate. Waiving the normal rules, she also permitted my brother to return just two days later. Through the grate, he showed me a pair of boots. The one that would house my club foot, he explained, had been built up in the heel, a fact subtly disguised by the leatherwork. The other would support my wasted leg.

'I believe that these will help you to walk,' Fernando said as he demonstrated his work. 'Please try them for a few days and then bring them back to me for any adjustment that might be needed. It usually takes several fittings to perfect such boots.'

The *priora* nodded, and Fernando fed the boots through the *torneras* one by one. Back in my room I discovered that the boots were lined with paper. When I pulled it out, I saw words addressed to myself. Fernando had written, 'I hope very much that the boots fit you, dear sister, but it would be more useful if they did not. For then you can bring them back to me. I, in turn, shall hope to find something inside of interest . . .'

I pulled the boots on and took an experimental step. Fernando was a genius! My limp was perforce eliminated. I ran across the room and flung my crutch through the door to the courtyard. Josefa emerged from the kitchen with a questioning face, and then, when I read the letter out to her, she snapped her fingers with joy. She ran out to retrieve the crutch, and handed it to me: 'Now you must pretend limp.'

Three days later I was back at the *locutorio*, crutch under my arm, shaking my head and handing one boot over to Fernando in the dim light of the alabaster window.

'I need you to look inside, brother,' I tried to sound plaintive. 'There is a portion that jars the tender arch of my foot in there. Could I trouble you to scrape away a little at what is inside?'

My letters and my loving sketch of him and his mother crackled audibly as Fernando took the boot in his hand with a smile.

'My love to your Mamma,' I said softly.

Gianni delle Boccole

Then I *did* hear summing. A letter for me come from, believe this! – the half-brother in Arequipa!

He hisself finely writed me, the boy, Fernando. Save us, but een his handwritin were zackly like his father's. His letter were full o sweet feckshon. And his Italian were that good, with many little words n turns of frase that was jist like my old Master Fernando Fasan.

'I have not yet met you, dear Gianni, but I feel that you are one of us,' this new Fernando Fasan writed.

My old Master must of taught his Peruvian son our tong. In doing that, he had give him more time than he ever give Minguillo. I blessed my old Master's good judgingment. He *knowed* his Venetian son to be a bad lot. He *knowed* to content hisself with the good one in Peru.

But I have runned way with myself. The reason I heard from Young Fernando were that he had seed Marcella, and talkt to her! She had talkt sweet n loving on me! My letter to the *priora* had been safe delivert, and read, and evryone knowed bout it, een Marcella. The *priora* ud saved it and give it to Fernando to read, een!

Marcella had askt Fernando to write me, to tell me n Anna that she were doing well. That Santa Catalina was not tall a beastly place, that she had friends, and she had the protection ovva good *priora*.

Fernando writed, '*She says you must believe Santa Catalina is nothing like the Venetian convents. There is no cruelty to the sisters, no cruel penances. The nuns are kindness itself, except for one mad one, and my sister is well treated, and even permitted to use her talent for painting. She has made a dear friend called Rafaela, with whom she paints. This Rafaela takes care of her like a sister. What else can I tell you of Marcella? I know you will be hungry for news. Her physical condition is good. She asks after her friends, Gianni and Anna, and a Doctor Santo, and the artist Cecilia Cornaro, in Venice.*'

That made me start up in my chair. Twere time to go and tell Cecilia Cornaro what were appening. After some time – in Scotland, they sayed – she were jist arrived in Venice and working on a poortret of her lover, Lord Byron. That were the gossip. Better still, I decided, Santo should go to her. I were a little nervous. Ide heard she were increasing on the wildcat side o nature. And there was no hairs on that one's tong, as ye mite say, to stop the rudeness fallin out o her mouth.

Fernando ended his letter with the name of a street in Arequipa. '*You may write to me here, and the contents of the letters shall be faithfully transmitted to Marcella. We have found a way . . . She in turn longs for news of you and all whom she loves in Venice.*'

All whom she loves. Swear that I were in charity with the whole world that day. Anna n I hogged and danced in circles like creeking old toys, Sweet God!

I ran to Cannaregio and pulled Santo out o his room.

'She is not lone,' I raved, hoggin him close. 'She is safe!'

In that, as in all things, I were wrong.

Marcella Fasan

Rafaela was beside herself with joy for me, and perhaps her irrepressible high spirits at my adventure made her now take a risk that was outrageous even for her.

All the nuns at Santa Catalina nursed a tender place in their hearts for the *priora*'s shocking reproach to Sor Loreta, 'Why don't you crucify your own tongue?'

News of the insult had spread on breathless wings, had roosted comfortably in Sor Loreta's legend, and it was often muttered in her wake. It was on the first day of the shoes that Rafaela sketched a picture that made me lose two heartbeats with shock. It was an unmistakable portrait of Sor Loreta, her mouth grotesquely stretched by a crucifix holding it open. In this picture, the *vicaria*'s cheeks were fat as those of a hog, and her neck bulged with three plump chins. Into the aperture of her lips, she was throwing roast chickens, spicy sausages, *polvorones* and wild potatoes.

'Destroy it!' I urged Rafaela. 'It would be very dangerous if anyone else ever saw it. Or someone told Sor Loreta about it.'

'Not much point now, lovely. I would have to destroy the copy I pinned in the refectory. And the one I nailed inside Sor Loreta's favourite confessional. And the one I stuck between the shutters of her cell.'

Doctor Santo Aldobrandini

An irascible woman is a shoreless ocean, as we say in Venice, and Cecilia Cornaro's reputation for raillery went far beyond the horizon.

But Gianni urged me, 'Go and see her before she takes off again to another place.'

A ball of oil-soaked rag hit my shoulder as I entered the room. I noticed full trunks labelled 'Cadiz'. I had caught her just in time, it seemed.

'I am . . . the friend of . . . Marcella Fasan,' I stammered, at the end of Cecilia Cornaro's long tirade on my birth (entirely true), my clumsiness, my irrelevance and my timing. Then she looked at my face.

'Indeed,' the artist observed, wiping her brush on a filthy rag and walking around me as if I were the prey and she were the hunter.

'Ah yes,' she pronounced, 'I remember you.'

As I explained our news of Marcella, I caught a glimpse of Cecilia

Cornaro's naked left hand. Last time I had seen her, when I fetched her to Marcella on San Servolo, the damage had been concealed inside a black mitten. Now I saw the truth: a fine webbing had fused the two burned digits.

'Then you will remember that I am a doctor,' I said.

'And this concerns me how?' she asked tartly.

'I think I could do something for your hand.'

She flushed and snatched it behind her back. 'What makes you think I need your services?'

'The way you hide the deformity. Your face as you speak of it.'

'What could you do anyway?' She attempted to preserve a casual tone.

'It will hurt a great deal, but I believe I can separate your fingers, if you'll let me. Marcella would want me to at least try.'

She fell silent. I feared she would turn me away. It would be natural. She had grown used to her injury; no one, or few, are used to surgical pain.

Then she spoke: 'I have a sitting now. Come back this hour tomorrow with your instruments of torture. I'll supply the brandy and the swearing.'

I returned with my little case the next day. Cecilia Cornaro had already medicated herself with spirits, and swayed towards me with a vague expression. I sat her at the cleanest table, washed the paint off her hand and bathed the fingers in carbolic acid and olive oil. To put her at her ease, I tried to talk to her. 'I heard there was a fire in your studio. But why did you get burned? Did it happen while you were asleep?'

I pointed to the *divano*. Its yellow silk coverlet was torn and slightly blackened. It was partly covered by a blanket of Scottish plaid, well sprinkled with cat fur. The beast himself stretched out asleep on top of it.

'I do sleep here sometimes, when I work late at night and there seems little point in walking back to my house at Miracoli. I was asleep when the men broke in.'

'It is true then, that the fire was started deliberately?'

'Only in that they deliberately broke my door, they deliberately tied me up, they deliberately poured oil over my paintings and deliberately set a taper to them.'

'And you knew who they were, and who sent them?'

'Persons unknown in pantaloons wearing masks,' she slurred on her sarcasm. 'Nothing to pin anything on anyone. They imagined, or their *capo* did, that I would die.'

'But you managed to untie yourself?'

'I work with my hands. I am dextrous. After the men left, I got the ropes off.'

'So how is it that you got burned?'

'I did not leave immediately.'

'Why not?'

'I had people to save.' She gestured at the paintings and sketches that were pinned all around the walls, some still singed.

'Paintings to save, instead of your own life?'

'I managed a few. But I stayed a moment too long. I was trying to save Lord Ponsonby for his wife. The man had cancer, which she knew not. The portrait was to keep her company after his death.'

My surprise at this compassion must have shown in my face. She growled, 'I know what you're thinking. And you're right. I'm not kind. I dream of revenge.'

I made my first cut then, and she sighed rather than cried out. I drew my knife along the webbing, gently cleaving it in two, right down to the fork of her fingers. The blood emptied thinly into the basin I had placed on the table. Cecilia Cornaro looked down, muttering, 'I must have cochineal beetles inside me – look at that colour, that is what I call a *proper* red . . .'

Then she fainted.

I brought her round with salts, but only after I had bandaged and splinted her fingers, and cleaned the floor of her blood. The webbing had been so fine that it would soon dry out and fall off. I wrapped the Scottish blanket around her shoulders and propped her up against her *divano*.

Cecilia Cornaro started talking as if we had not been interrupted. 'I dream of revenge, I told you,' she said, with no mention of the surgery she had just endured. With her good hand she reached for a sketchbook on the floor and flicked it open.

'This is what I've drawn at night, since it happened.'

Minguillo's face appeared again and again on the page: in profile, in three-quarter view, a glimpse of his cheek from over a shoulder. Each likeness was perfect, the madness bristling out of him, and the badness inscribed in his features like the pits of the pimples in his skin.

'If I could forget how much I hate him, then these pictures would remind me,' I exclaimed. 'You have caught his nastiness exactly.'

'Then you too dream of revenge?' Cecilia Cornaro examined her bandaged fingers, running a thumb down the newly created vacancy between them. The pain must have been hideous, yet her mind remained focussed upon her enemy.

I confessed, 'I have a particular voluntary dream that soothes me. It is quite complicated.'

'I enjoy complications.'

Her green eyes met mine, drawing the words out. 'When I was training to be a doctor, my Master was a surgeon who had an obsessive interest in warfare by disease. And secret ways of spreading it.'

'You mean, like the Plague?'

'The Plague is all but gone from us. Yet we still have the Small-Pox. Diseases of the skin are my special field, you see. And I take an interest in the history of them. The Small-Pox helped the Spanish conquistadores suppress the Incas.'

'You have taken a particular interest in South American matters recently, I imagine.' She smiled the way a cat yawns, but there was warmth in it too.

'An intense interest,' I acknowledged, 'so I can tell you that there have been two great Small-Pox epidemics in the Americas, in 1775 and 1782. In Arequipa, free vaccinations are given now. Marcella is safe from that, at least.'

Cecilia Cornaro possessed formidable powers of intuition. She asked, 'But you, I mean your *imagination*, remains interested in the Small-Pox as an agent of revenge? How does that function?'

'The Small-Pox diffuses itself from person to person in tiny fragments of dead skin – that is, in flakes of the scabs from the sores that are the most visible symptom of the disease. My former Master, Surgeon Ruggiero, was obsessed with an idea carried out by Sir Jeffery Amherst, a British general. Fifty years ago, Amherst wished to kill off the Ottawa Indians of Pennsylvania. He set off a Small-Pox epidemic among them, by causing their supplies to be dusted with a few powdered scabs from Small-Pox victims.'

'So only a small amount of the Small-Pox is required?'

'Almost invisibly small, if we speak of the *Variola confluens* strain, which is the most fatal. The unusual thing about the Small-Pox is that it may be transmitted by paper – between pages of a letter, for example. Lovers have been known to end their romances involuntarily, by sealing up a fragment of the Small-Pox in their love letters.'

'How intensely fascinating,' breathed Cecilia Cornaro. 'But how in the civilized world does one get one's hands' – and here she held her repaired one out – 'on an invisibly small amount of the Small-Pox?'

'Ruggiero made a habit of shearing the scabs off his Small-Pox patients, drying them in peat smoke. He stored the pieces in camphor underground. Against a difficult day. He was an ill-tempered man with enemies of his own . . .'

'I see the direction of your so-called voluntary dream. It involves a pestilential brute – Minguillo Fasan, for example – receiving a particularly dusty letter . . . Ah, one does not have to be a poet to love poetic justice!'

I thought she pronounced the word 'poet' with bitterness.

'But I am a doctor. I have sworn an oath. Anyway, to carry this idea out, well, then I would be like *him*.'

'We are all like him to a certain extent.'

'The difference is that we do not act upon that tendency in ourselves.'

Cecilia Cornaro let me know that I was dismissed.

But as I left, she enquired casually, 'Your old Master, Surgeon Ruggiero – did he have his portrait painted ever?'

Marcella Fasan

The *priora* must have guessed what was going on, for a shoemaker of Fernando's reputation could never have contrived so many mistakes. However, she tolerated without comment the exchange of boots –

though I was soon on my eighth, then twelfth pair. Even though I no longer needed it, I kept using my crutch as supporting evidence for my continued need for refinements in the construction of my boots.

Or perhaps it was not deliberate blindness: it could have been her ill health that caused the *priora* to overlook our transactions. On two occasions she had fainted in the refectory. She barely ate, and her skin had lost its healthy lustre. I was sorry to see dear Priora Mónica unwell, but I was busy with my own rejoicing.

Via the boots, I learned that Santo was nearly fluent in Spanish now, and working every way he could to find a passage to South America. What he would do here was not yet clear, but I grew delirious with happiness merely to think of us breathing the same air.

Hope had fledged in me: hope, with which I had barely been acquainted in my life. I developed a friendship with that cheerful stranger. I began to nourish vague but vivid dreams.

Until the morning Josefa arrived in my cell, her smooth black cheeks polished with tears.

'Rafaela is no more,' she told me.

Part Five

Doctor Santo Aldobrandini

I should never have breathed my reprehensible fantasies aloud. After my conversation with Cecilia Cornaro, I was drowning in guilt.

Death by drowning occurs when fluid enters the air cells of the lung, thus preventing the due oxygenation of the blood.

The post-mortem appearance of a person deliberately drowned usually shows the signs that indicate death by asphyxia – lividity of the cadaver with the nose, lips, ears, fingertips almost black in colour and a protruded tongue – together with the following symptoms, peculiar to murder by drowning: excoriation of the fingers, with the skin of the assailant under the nails; fine froth at the mouth and nostrils.

If the victim is examined by a surgeon, the frontal cut will reveal lungs ballooned with water, and froth, sometimes bloodstained, abounding in the air tubes. Such signs must not be mistaken for pneumonia, but identified as the true evidence of foul play, if justice is to be done.

Sor Loreta

One day it became clearly apparent that Priora Mónica could no longer govern, due to an indisposition that had stolen up on her over the past weeks, no doubt due to her sensual excesses. She no longer had any appetite for the rich foods and tobacco that she once craved. Naturally, I assiduously avoided power and glory in temporal life, but at this time the Lord asked Me, in My humbleness, to take sole charge of Santa Catalina.

Our Holy Fathers outside the gate did not intervene. When I personally explained by letter just how things stood in the convent, they praised Me for My vigilance, and accepted that their unaccustomed presence in our community would cause upset at this difficult time of the *priora*'s illness.

'*Please continue your good work, Sor Loreta*,' they wrote to Me. '*Make sure to keep us informed of events*.'

I did not feel it was necessary to trouble the Holy Fathers with some items that would have seemed of little importance to them. Nuns die, like anyone else. I simply asked the priests to send one of their number to officiate at the funeral of a nun who had expired that same day of a sudden fever following a cold bath for her *calores*.

Marcella Fasan

Limping as fast as I could towards the Zocodober fountain, I passed nuns knotted in intense conversations.

Hermenegilda and Javiera were already laying Rafaela out with hands trembling with immeasurable tenderness. I embraced them both. Then I kissed my friend's cold cheek, her closed eyes, her wet hair, her bruised nose and her blackened ears and fingertips.

Margarita and Rosita quietly let themselves into the room. They stroked Rafaela's hair and then each took one of Rafaela's still hands.

'Have you heard? The *priora* is dangerously ill,' murmured Margarita.

Too late, we stared at each other with a simultaneous realization. The *priora*'s health had gone into decline without any of us remarking on it, nor becoming suspicious as to why she had grown so pale, lacked an appetite and so frequently fainted.

Margarita, Rosita, Rafaela and myself: our friendship had sealed us in a bubble of hilarity. We had thought ourselves so witty, mocking the *vicaria*'s fanaticism. We had been too busy ridiculing Sor Loreta to see the danger of her heightened madness.

'Was the drawing of the crucifixed tongue,' pronounced Josefa, walking into the cell with a mass of roses and herbs. 'That what done it. You laugh, Rafaela laugh, we all laugh. We sorry now.'

Minguillo Fasan

I know who you are! You are that Derisive Reader who's kept sneeringly aloof from me.

What? What's that? You told yourself that you continue to put up with this wickedness only in the sure hope of witnessing my come-uppance? But there's no sign of that coming, is there? You say, and you may even *think* you've kept your distance, but I note that you're still here with me at the thin end of the book, when everything has gone my way – except perhaps one. Or two. Think on that.

Well, the Derisive Reader may be happy now. There is trouble come to beset me.

Amalia did not quite die. I saw this as a delay, not a foreclosure on my plans, but a nagging grievance to me, just the same.

And then the Scottish merchant Hamish Gilfeather proved a disappointment. What a mealy pillar of rectitude! Call him fifty years old, call him a prude and a Puritan. He had a dead wife, as I had hoped to, and precisely no daughters. Being of a narrow and grudging nature, I doubt he would have put them at my disposal anyway.

The wife's death was recent, and the man was still in a lather of sentimentality over it. The Pillar loomed up straight and cast a long thin shadow over my desk when I suggested some highly qualified Venetian whores for his cheering up.

He was precise and stiff-lipped at our one meeting, giving me searching looks that felt to rove my mind, in a highly uncomfortable fashion. He glanced at Amalia's portrait over the mantelpiece and then at me, and audibly muttered something insulting about an old Chinese proverb he had picked up on his travels.

To my disappointment, he cared only for pursuing his own interests in Peru, on which he did not elaborate, though I tried in every way to extract some idea of them. He was not to be drawn, tempted or threatened into a partnership with me.

'Now that my beloved Sarah is gone,' he murmured — as if I might care — 'I have few ties to my native shores.'

My dreams of a Britannic empire were fading away to nothing in the course of one conversation. The fellow had a hurry on him too, that made him peremptory, that made him unwilling even to take a drink with me, even though I had prepared a special cup of liquid amity for him.

'I'll be wishing you good morning, Conte Fasan,' he said, rising abruptly at the sight of the rosy glass.

'You shall take some "Tears of Santa Rosa" back to Scotland with you,' I explained. 'The first consignment will be at my expense. You shall see how the Scottish ladies will love it, and be back for more directly.'

'I cannot stop you sending it, I suppose?' he enquired.

'No,' I gloated.

'And I suppose very few people decline your offers?' your man asked me, with an unreadable look on his face. 'I had heard it said of you, Conte Fasan, and I wanted to see for myself.'

Marcella Fasan

While Rafaela's body was laid out in the *sala de profundis*, the *priora* hovered between life and death. Her coma was profound. She responded only to painful stimuli, fluttering her eyelids open for a second. Then she started anxiously, as if she feared attack, but soon lapsed back into unconsciousness.

Priora Mónica's servants kept Margarita by their mistress's side, succumbing to violent hysterics if she showed signs of wishing to attend to her duties in the pharmacy. As long as Margarita was there, the Vixen stayed away and had no possibility of finishing her task. Sor Loreta was to be seen haunting the lane outside the *priora*'s quarters, her face skeletal with tension, her dry hands rubbing against one another.

She was waiting like a hyena for the death, counting on the likelihood that the Holy Fathers would then appoint her *priora*, whereupon she would cover up her crimes with all the devilish skills of her madness.

When not in the public safety of the church or refectory, the nuns stayed in their cells, afraid to be caught out on the streets. In hurried colloquies by the fountain, Rafaela's *criada* and *samba* kept Josefa informed of what was going on. And she informed me, relaying information also to the *sambas* of Margarita and Rosita.

A secret meeting was arranged, with Javiera despatched to detain the *vicaria* with an invented tale of an Indian man seen in a far corner of the convent grounds.

First Margarita, then Rosita slipped into my cell. The servants followed, one by one. Time was too short for us to lament our losses, or to indulge in recriminations about our failure to recognize the danger of the *vicaria*. Nuns, servants and slaves talked starkly, as equals. Whispered bursts of information were exchanged like musket fire.

Sending a *criada* or a *samba* to the Bishop was quickly dismissed as an unworkable plan, as was the idea of whispering the truth to a priest at the confessional. Sor Loreta had won the clergy's confidence. No one would believe the lurid tales of a coloured servant, or an anonymous denunciation at the confessional, especially of such an unwelcome tale, for it was one that would cast the Bishop and his priests in a ridiculous light for their long-standing ignorance and grave misjudgment in their choice of *vicaria*.

'It will be for you to denounce the Vixen, Marcella. You know the whole story. The *vicaria* tried to do the same thing to you. You are high-born. You'll be believed,' Rosita explained. 'But not till the *priora* is safe and can corroborate your evidence. The Vixen's position is too strong. We must make our own unassailable before denouncing her.'

Margarita reported, 'In the meantime, I am trying to discover which herbs were used to poison Madre Mónica.'

'But if Madre Mónica does not . . .'

Josefa interrupted Hermenegilda, 'And what you all do for to protect *my* mistress?'

My *samba* looked at me, her eyeballs veined with fear, 'You is surely next victim, madam, you know that, does not you?'

Doctor Santo Aldobrandini

Hamish Gilfeather was an angel in a dour guise. This man, on the pretext of a meeting with Minguillo, had brought hope and joy to all of us – to Gianni, to Anna, to me.

'After my dear wife died in my arms, I came straight here to see what can be done for Marcella,' he explained. 'My Sarah urged me on. Why, she never tired of hearing about the girl. She said, "Hamish, when I am gone, you must be a hero for someone else." That's what she said.' Mr Gilfeather's face grew dim.

I did not have to warn him about Minguillo. Marcella had explained everything, even the death of Piero Zen, who had been his friend. Hamish Gilfeather had parleyed with Minguillo only for the purposes of seeing the enemy at first hand, and gleaning useful information. As for the latest news, of Amalia's journey to the fringes of death, Hamish Gilfeather had already drawn his own conclusions.

'I saw the lady's portrait in that grim great house,' he murmured, wiping away a tear. 'Poor wee pretty pretty girlie. I can see why *he* wanted her ... the Chinese have a proverb for it. "Ugly Frog longs to eat flesh of Heavenly Goose," they say. But what made *her* entertain him as a husband? Did her mother knowingly send her to a fiend's bed? D'ye ever see the monstrous tic of his leg, beating like a timpano on the floor? And the flocculent skin and the mad eyes on him! 'Twere it my daughter had been sacrificed like that, I would have slit the man from heid to pluck.'

For me, Amalia was still a painful subject, so I changed it. I enquired, 'And what are your plans, Signor Gilfeather?'

The merchant was now going west to Spain. There he would meet with a trusted courier who made regular journeys to Peru, and who would make sure 'any letters ye care to furnish' reached Fernando, for their final journey inside those miraculous boots to Marcella.

Every day for a week I took new letters to Hamish Gilfeather at his

384

inn by Rialto, for how could I put into one letter all I had to say to Marcella? Once I had tried to put it into a single kiss.

Hamish Gilfeather was often out. When I asked the innkeeper where he was, I was treated to a wink and a smile. 'Very interested in Venetian *art*, our Scottish merchant,' he hinted.

The next time I saw Hamish Gilfeather, I enquired after Cecilia Cornaro's hand. I had not seen her since I carved her fingers apart.

'It does famously! She would not tell ye, but she is grateful.' He turned slightly pink about the jowls. 'She has a good heart. D'ye know she actually came all the way to Edinburgh when my wife lay dying? It was too late for a portrait, which I so badly wanted. But when my darling Sarah passed, Cecilia let me talk and talk to her of my miseries. She said that she liked the Scottish accent.'

Hamish Gilfeather's trunks were dispatched back to Scotland heavy with Murano glass tucked up in Burano lace. He told me with a long face that Minguillo would be sending a great box of 'The Tears of Santa Rosa' to follow, despite his protests. And I forthwith set him extremely straight as to the nature of that liquid.

'I would have suspected as much if ye had not told me,' he growled. 'Have no fear: the pernicious stuff shall be destroyed.'

Venice seemed empty without Hamish Gilfeather. He had left me a note in his strictly grammatical Italian: 'I have no small doubts that I'll be seeing you in Arequipa one of these fine days, and every hope that it shall be with our dear Marcella on your arm.'

I doubled my working hours so that I barely dozed between jobs. If Marcella was to be on my arm, I wanted to be able to buy her a dress with sleeves of silk.

Marcella Fasan

I made my usual abridged and fanciful confession. The priest dismissed me with a light penance: clearly he had no idea of the drama being played out on our side of the grate. Then I slipped across the courtyard to the *sala de profundis*, knowing myself under the observation of the Jackals.

I joined a group of frightened nuns singing *Salve Regina misericordiae* in quivering voices around Rafaela's corpse.

My friend lay in the wooden catafalque with a large candle at each of its four corners. Rafaela looked unfamiliar in her full habit: in real life she had been so assiduously negligent in the wearing of it. Seeing her encased in black and white was almost the only way to persuade myself that she was truly dead. White roses had been placed at her temples by her loving servants, and their perfume mixed with the smoke of the candles.

Around her were the old portraits of dead nuns.

You may not paint a nun until she is dead. A hundred years ago, back in Venice, Cecilia Cornaro had told me that. Rafaela and I had laughed about it. Suddenly it seemed the bitterest fact in the world.

I had brought with me paper and pastels. I did not think the Jackals would stop me – even they must have had their fill of our pain that day. Rafaela's face I had sketched many times, but never like this, still, sad, almost ugly with surprise, as if the *vicaria*'s unforeseen lurch back to violence had truly astonished her. The hollow of one eye was blackened, with red and purple shadows. The side of her head that the *vicaria* had smashed against the bath was swollen: you could see the distortion even beneath her veil. Hermenegilda had scorned to cover the damage with flowers. I propped my crutch by the door and prepared my materials with a shaking hand. After I had recorded every detail of Rafaela's injuries, Rosita and Margarita quietly signed and dated my picture as a true likeness. Then I began a picture of Rafaela as I had known her.

In knots of two and three, the nuns came cautiously to pray and weep by Rafaela's corpse, and to watch me draw. Hermenegilda and Javiera made sure my vigil was never solitary. Everyone seemed to understand that there was a safety in numbers: I was often in a large company of mourners. Apart from her Jackals, the *vicaria* had no supporters inside Santa Catalina, but there were plenty who feared her enough to turn a blind eye to their doings.

In the middle of the night, when all the other nuns were locked out of the *de profundis* hall, the *vicaria* brought in a barber from the *tambo* and ordered him to cut out Rafaela's heart, to be buried separately in a lead casket. Before dawn, every nun in Santa Catalina knew about this butchery.

386

The next morning, the church filled with citizens come to mourn the untimely passing of Rafaela. Separated by the grate, we nuns stared in silent agony at the sombre father and friends who thought Rafaela snatched from life by an illness, not a murderess. An elderly priest intoned the well-worn words with resignation.

All through Rafaela's funeral rites, I felt the *vicaria*'s eye upon me through the blank blue of her spectacles. At her feet was a small wooden box. I guessed it contained my friend's heart. I stared with compulsion at the mound on Rafaela's breast, a wadding of bloodied cotton which left a sticky residue on the black fabric of her unaccustomed habit. On their side of the grate, the Arequipans had only a distant glimpse of their lost daughter. They had no reason to suspect the desecration in that coffin.

Why, having mutilated our friend, had the *vicaria* not ordered the coffin closed? It was a mad risk to take. Behind any conscious motive, I understood, because I understood Minguillo, a darker, unconscious reason. A part of Sor Loreta wanted the nuns to behold what had happened: the image of Rafaela's plundered breast was her sharpest instrument of terror. She wished us to be aware of what could befall an enemy of hers, even beyond death. It was little wonder that none of us stumbled forward to cry out the truth to the congregation. The nuns were still too shocked and too cowed even to weep aloud for Rafaela. The *criadas* and *sambas*, however, bawled and ululated their distress, and the well-bred citizens of Arequipa sobbed on their side of the grate.

After the service, Sor Loreta tucked the box under her arm and led the way to the convent's cemetery. The great wooden doors opened and all the nuns followed her through. Rafaela's coffin was carried to the graveside by two gardeners, careful to keep their eyes firmly on the ground before them.

The priest took his position at the head of the grave. The *vicaria* bustled to his side, interposing herself between all of us and the man. She laid the box by her feet, to free her hands for prayer. At the last minute, as the coffin lid was shut, and just before Rafaela was to be lowered into the moist earth, a *samba* came for the *vicaria*, who looked ferociously angry. I clutched Josefa's hand, reading my own hopes in her wide eyes: had the Bishop somehow received news of the true nature of this death? Would the Holy Fathers all come now, and examine Rafaela's body?

The priest, his duties over, was already turning towards the gates.

Leaning too far forward, I stumbled then, and I saw him glance at me curiously: mine was not an Arequipan face. He must have guessed that I was the celebrated Venetian cripple. He had probably taken my confession many times, hidden behind the grate.

'Get on with it!' Sor Loreta barked at the two gardeners, who held the coffin suspended on their ropes. Then she hurried away towards the *oficina*.

The coffin departed slowly into the darkness. The lead box with Rafaela's heart still lay on the verge above the grave. I supposed that the *vicaria* had planned to fling it in on top of Rafaela; or worse, to keep it for herself, to gloat over. Everyone's eyes were threaded on Rafaela's coffin descending. With my crutch, I drew the little box towards me, and tucked it under my skirt. The gardeners began to spade earth over the coffin, and the nuns, freed from the *vicaria*'s presence, fell into one another's arms to weep.

Hermenegilda caught my eye and winked. She and Josefa stole close to me, and on the pretext of retying a shoe, Hermenegilda reached beneath me and scooped the box into her apron just as the *vicaria* bustled back among us, asking petulantly, 'Is it done then? Where is the box?'

'Buried, madam,' chorused the *criadas* and *sambas*.

Sor Loreta's eyes burned angrily. So she had indeed meant to keep Rafaela's heart for herself. She shouted, 'Why are you all still here? About your duties, smartly!'

Josefa muttered audibly, '*Me cago en la putísima madre que te parió*, Sor Loreta!' which caused a distracting eruption among the nuns, for it meant 'I shit on the whore of a mother who gave birth to you'.

Under cover of Sor Loreta's shouting, '*Who* said that?' Hermenegilda stole away with Rafaela's heart.

That afternoon I had Josefa take the lead box outside the convent, along with a handful of coins from me. I had Rafaela's heart preserved in embalming fluid and set in a silver casket. When Josefa smuggled it back from the undertakers, I kept it at the rear of my candle cupboard with my diaries.

One day, I vowed, *I will take you away from this place, Rafaela.*

In the meantime, with the help of Josefa, Javiera and Hermenegilda, I had to try to keep myself alive.

Gianni delle Boccole

Jist when we was drunk with joy bout Amish Gillyfether's visit, we heared from Fernando that Marcella's friend Rafaela were dead, and in a vilent way. Rafaela were one she painted with, and loved. Piece to her dust.

And the good *priora* were tookt bad, probly at the hand of this holey mad nun called Sor Loreta, ugly as a gargle, what had seized powr.

Santo jumpt to the same concludings that I done. His soul were fishered with worrying. But the next letter were the one that finely decided him. The posts being what they were, it arrived one week after the first, tho twere dispatcht many days later. Fernando writed with a shaky hand, '*I hate to frighten you. And I never thought that I should write such a godless thing, to conspire to take a bride of Christ out of the House of God. But I have reason to believe that to leave Marcella at Santa Catalina would be tantamount to abetting her murder.*

'*I can turn to no one here. In Arequipa, those in power will have a vested interest in turning a blind eye, even if it all comes out. Honourable Gianni, I know you are indentured to Minguillo and may not travel. Is there someone else you can send?*'

Was there, Fool-God!

Fernando finisht: '*We have the beginnings of a plan, an outrageous plan, but a plan, to save Marcella. My sister invented it herself, or I should never have dreamed of imposing its horrors on her. It is necessary that the man you send is a doctor or a priest, or if possible both.*'

I lookt at Santo, reading oer my shoulder, 'Time to make yerself sparse!'

Santo were out o the room like a bird out ovva cage, with hope flopping his wings. I lookt at his back provingly, notin it were broader than afore. And he ud also growed some bones around his heart out o the strength of his loving Marcella. Now he were ready to go to war for her.

Marcella Fasan

Rafaela's servants watched over me day and night, sharing shifts with Josefa. They made sure I was never alone, even when I went to Rafaela's grave to chant the psalm *Libera me* at the foot of her tomb, which must be done for eight days after the burial, according to convent custom.

Though Sor Loreta and her Jackals were just three, and we nuns were nearly eighty, the murder of Rafaela had kept us in a numb and passive state. We clung together, waiting for our spirits to return. Meanwhile, I worked hard on Josefa's Italian, until we could communicate fluently in what might become a necessary secret language. Josefa rewarded me one day with a perfect sentence in immaculate Italian. She had just returned from a visit to Fernando, and her very apron seemed puffed up with hope.

'Embrace me, madam,' she ordered.

'*Volentieri!*' I answered. In my arms Josefa crackled like a roaring fire. Her clothes were lined with letters, from Gianni, including three dictated to him by Anna, from Hamish Gilfeather, and no less than seven from Santo, each more superb than the last. Josefa spent the next day quietly excavating a new hole behind the coal bucket. Into that hole, reluctantly, I placed my letters, but only when I knew every word of Santo's by heart.

'Just one,' I pleaded, 'just one to hold at night?'

Josefa was stern, 'Just one letter all the scuses the Vixen need, if she find.'

Outside my cell, my friends were also busy. If the *vicaria* approached the Calle Sevilla, Rosita and Margarita devised crises for her to attend to. Sor Loreta's thirst for power became my only shield of safety: we could make it seem that there were more important things for her to do than to kill me. Yet in the end Sor Loreta would come for me. We all knew it, and we all knew what would happen when she did. All our hurried conversations were as to the how and when.

Two weeks after Rafaela's death, I was distractedly reading Santa Teresa. A story caught my attention, a horrifying tale of a nun in Salamanca who escaped her prison by feigning death, buying the body of a woman already dead to substitute for her own. It drew my memory back to a passage from *La Religieuse*, Mr Diderot's terrifying novel of convent cruelties, a gift from Minguillo when he first told me he had sold me to the Dominicans: 'Why, amidst all the wild ideas that pass through the mind of a nun driven to desperation, does that of setting fire to the convent not occur to her?'

Now it occurred to me. With a body, with a fire, I could feign my death, just like the nun in Salamanca.

When I explained my idea to Rosita and Margarita, they squealed and covered their mouths with horror. 'I could *never, never* do that.'

I could do that, I thought. *I could do that.*

But I was not so ignorant of the world that I did not realize desperation was not enough – I needed money.

Rosita suggested, 'Say that you wish to pay for a month of masses for Rafaela. That means you'll be entitled to unlock your dowry chest.'

Margarita exclaimed, 'Rosita! Remember *who* must attend the unlocking of the trunks!'

Josefa interrupted, 'Is a little somefing-somefing in the storeroom what was yours, madam. What could be turned to cash money on the outside?'

I kissed her cheek. Josefa was right. There was another source of wealth available to me: the precious Mantegna painting of San Sebastiano and the sculpted saint that languished in the depository at the displeasure of the *vicaria*. Rosita the *portera* was in charge of the keys to every secret and forbidden part of the convent. This would not be the first time she had quietly removed contraband items for sale outside the convent walls on behalf of nuns inside.

'Not the slightest problem!' she assured us. 'Here's how we shall bring it off. Josefa must be seen, for the next days, to be carrying large heaps of old linen for the *criados'* church which is raising money for orphans of their class. She must be noticed by the Vixen, and she must not lose her nerve if the Vixen hauls her in for questioning as she passes through the gate, and goes through the linen.'

'We shall all collect linen,' Margarita added, 'things that are torn or stained. We shall stain and tear them as necessary, until the Vixen takes the bait. Oh, she will rip through Josefa's bundle, looking for mischief, and she will find nothing but ruined goods fit only for a poorhouse. The day *after* that is when we shall hide the Mantegna painting and the sculpture among the linens, for the Vixen will not bother a second time.'

Josefa duly transmitted to Fernando, who waited half-mad with anxiety, the news that two valuable objects were to be delivered to him to be turned into funds for my flight. The means of my escape I sketched in words on a piece of paper that I sewed with jagged stitches into Josefa's skirt. Merely to put the plan in writing had embedded the horror of it under my skin. I dared not put this message in a boot.

Fernando's reply came to me in the same resewn slit in her dress.

'Dear sister, you know I would not accept a "soldo" from you, but on your behalf I have already negotiated a ludicrously high price for the Venetian sculpture of San Sebastián from an agent of the Tristán family. I know that the most horrible part of the plan in execution rests with you now, my poor Marcella. I apologize in advance for the grimness of your task.'

A few days later Josefa brought a new note from Fernando, sewn into the lining of her hat. He wrote, *'Joyful news, sister. We have a new accomplice for our plan: he shall be arriving with us shortly. I believe you are already somewhat acquainted.'*

Gianni delle Boccole

The letters come thick n fast from Cadith, from Prayer in the Cape Verde Islands, from Montyvidayo. There was no surgeon jobs, so Santo ud gone for a sailor, working his passage like a seadog. Good winds without stint ud blown him to South Hamerica in quick order. On arriving safe in Arequipa, he writed to me. *'So beautiful here, you could not imagine it, Gianni, this town is like a pearl.'*

Santo had took imself strait to the home of young Fernando and his mother. He were welcomed like a son. And the next morn Fernando brought him direckly to the church so he could see Marcella ahind the grate. And she could see him.

'We renewed our unspoken vows,' he wrote me. I could picture it, like they was lone, insted of in the big theatre o the church.

Santo straitway begun doctoring in Arequipa. Fernando ud set up evrything while Santo were yet on the seas. There were patients lined up from the first day.

But in his black robes (he were too poor for any fine soot) and o course with his extreme devoutness in attending evry church service at Santa Catalina, he were assumed to be a Holy Man. Santo judged it best not to naysay this. Seein how it went, Fernando and his Mamma fattened up a roomer that Doctor Santo were come direck from the Vatican. Venice were niver menshoned in his regard, so as not to draw saucespishons.

There was no medickle schools in Arequipa, meaning all doctors n blood-letters allus come from outside. So Santo were not mistrusted on sight as a furriner. Santo writed to me that his Spanyard were serving well, and that I must go to thank the Spanish madam in Cannaregio on his behalf.

He were in high humour: '*Occasionally in Arequipa I am caught out by an anatomical vulgarity that Signora Sazia fervently assured me to be the correct and respectable term for some particular organ. To maintain my dignity, I have to explain with a straight face that in the Old World this word is used exclusively by the aristocracy*.'

The Vixen were still in charge of Santa Catalina but she ud arrogated her rule sufficient to allow visits again. Santo deducted she were too prudint to exude the famlies from a sight of there daughters, in case they snifft a rat. Fernando saw Marcella from time to time at the talking-parlour. Not too often, so's not to draw tension.

Better yet, there were an akshual plan afoot for her escape, but twere too diffuse to tell me as yet, Santo sayed. I burned up not to know it. It hinged, he hinted, pon his personal gaining the confidence o the twitchin Vixen. In the meantime, the grate thing were to keep Marcella alive long nuff for this misterious plan to git carrid through.

Santo had speedy made hisself evryone's favrit doctor in Arequipa, nowise sorpresing given his gentle ways, clean fingers, safe fizz-sicks and low prices. This meaned he were also getting to be the doctor what pronounct the deaths among the poor. And this, for the plan, were more important than anything, he writed me.

What kind o plan could that be? It sounded dredful grim. I clinched my teeth. So much appening in Arequipa while I anguished way in Venice, servin a Master what seemed to be loosing the grip of hisself. Minguillo ud took to sittin up in the tower at the back of our *palazzo* where no one ud been for sentries. What he doed up there, no one knowed, but he come down agin with hair like a haystack and his eyes starin in diffrint direkshons.

Sor Loreta

It had come to My attention that a holy man had arrived in Arequipa, a man of great sanctity adorned with the highest virtues. He naturally chose Santa Catalina as his place of worship.

He practised as a doctor, but was also a priest. The populace took him to their hearts. The Ignorant even brought him the mummy corpses that were sometimes found in the higher reaches of the mountains, as if he might bring those ancient pagans back to life.

He was come from Italy, the home of the Pope, and so it naturally entered My head that I should meet him and be allowed to partake of the beneficence of holy rays that would surely issue from his glance. He in turn would be illuminated by intercourse with Myself. My secret hope was that a holy man would be able to see My stigmata that had remained invisible to the unenlightened nuns who surrounded Me, and that he would affirm the existence of My angels, denouncing the other doctor who had called them 'ocular spectres'.

If this Doctor Santo pronounced My stigmata and angels to be real, then the malicious tongues of the Ignorant would be silenced and people would start to take note of My life, and write it down for the instruction and inspiration of posterity.

And perhaps the stupidly protracted illness of our careless *priora* would make it an obvious thing for Me to summon this Doctor Santo to our convent to minister to the sick woman.

Who else should receive him but the *priora*'s trusted deputy, now acting in her stead, who had never been accused of a moment's lightness?

Marcella Fasan

Santo was in Arequipa. A mere wall of stone separated us, and one murderous, mad nun. That was all. Minguillo was not here to grasp and crush my happiness. I had one appalling act to perform, and I would be free, and with Santo. Beyond that act, in my imagination, the rest of the future glowed a radiant white like the sun at noon.

And each morning at mass I married Santo with my eyes across the grate. 'I love you,' I sang instead of the words to the hymns.

'I love you,' Santo sang back to me.

Still the *priora* remained unconscious. A quiet spirit of resistance was beginning to suffuse the community of nuns, *criadas* and *sambas* who adored her. The love we bore her meant that we could not conceive of a future without her: we pinned our hopes on her recovery.

'Give the *priora* a bell,' I had suggested, 'tied under the covers. Then it will ring if someone lifts the blanket.'

'How did you learn to be so vigilant?' Rosita asked.

By now the whole convent conspired to keep Sor Loreta running around. The nuns invented small disputes upon which she must arbitrate. They sacrificed themselves by deliberately misbehaving so that she would be distracted by the joys of punishing them. The *vicaria* had taken on the *priora*'s *samba* as her own. But the girl was loyal to us, and kept us fed with information about the Vixen's movements. The treasurer nun was also recruited to our side. She now made a daily incursion to review senseless figures with the Vixen, who had to pretend to comprehend them so as not to lose face. Rosita invented a lost key and a vast inquiry was launched as to its whereabouts, with every sister in Santa Catalina to be personally questioned by the *vicaria*.

In this way, for several more weeks, we avoided her coming for me. Fernando visited as often as he dared and turned himself into a piece of glass – by which I mean that he generously effaced his sweet self so that I might commune directly with Santo.

'There is talk of an Italian holy man in the town,' Fernando told me. The Vixen sat listening to our conversation, eager for an excuse to terminate it, her one good ear pressed visibly against the grate.

'Have you met him?' I enquired casually, in the shadow of the ear.

'Indeed. He seems to be a searching kind of soul,' Fernando smiled. 'His quest is his whole passion . . .'

Then I saw Sor Loreta's blue spectacles flash behind the grate.

Good, good, I thought, for whatever interested her in Santo was only grist to our plan. I shuddered too: it was as if I was offering him to a spider.

Josefa meanwhile brought me yet more letters in her skirts and in the false flap of her basket, and took missives from me in return. Santo begged for more information about the *vicaria*. I wrote down everything I could remember – her obsession with Christ-the-infant, her invented stigmata and her so-called angels.

The one thing I forgot to mention was her astonishing physical strength.

Minguillo Fasan

I began to look with more interest at my daughters, and to urge food upon them. They could be breeding by the age of fifteen. If not a son, then a grandson for my beloved Palazzo Espagnol! I had to be patient, however – everyone who knows anything at all knows that little girls are far too inclined to frustrate the plans of their owners by miscarrying or producing stillborns.

I suspected someone of going through my belongings again. There were signs of disturbance in my study, of someone slipping in like a weasel to spy on me. I feared for my precious books of human skin.

It struck me that children are known book-murderers. To avoid any unpleasantness among my daughters, and by means of *adapting* a fairy story for their consumption, I made the pale little ghosts severely afraid of entering my study evermore. Their trembling gifted me another idea: I plucked hairs from their heads and inserted them between certain pages of the books, so I would know if anyone other than myself had visited my little colony.

No respect to the Gracious Reader, but even *His* esteemed fingers would not be allowed to partake of that part of my library. I could not bear for anyone but myself to lay a hand on those books. The very thought of it made my flesh creep as if a thousand ants were burrowing underneath it.

I became so fearful for my books that in the end I carried them up to the Palazzo Espagnol's tall tower where I might be among them privately without fear of interruption or discovery. I laid special pieces of dust on every seventh stair, so I would know if anyone tried to spy on my haven.

Marcella Fasan

My reprieve could not last for ever, I knew that. Yet I was not at all ready when Sor Loreta's *samba* came running to tell us that the *vicaria* was on her way to my cell, and that she was wearing that face that was not hers, but a mask of rapture.

Josefa put our feeble little plan into play immediately.

'I so sorry to do this to you, madam, so sorry,' she lamented, as she hit me on the temple with the Bible, hard enough to bring up an authentic bruise and swelling.

'Lay you down, is good like that,' she whispered tenderly as I crumpled to the floor, my head on the cushion she had prepared for me.

The *vicaria*'s footsteps rang through my silent courtyard. Those steps proceeded up to my side, until I felt her shadow cooling my body. I kept my eyes shut, breathing slowly and deeply, as if unconscious. Her sandaled foot nudged me. I smelled her dank breath. But when she turned her back on me to question Josefa, I looked up. There was a pouch of herbs hanging from the Vixen's belt. I glimpsed her profile, and it took away my breath. Her ecstasy had wiped away all the fretfulness and anger

397

her features normally wore, rendering her face strangely blank, like those of a painted wooden puppet.

'Sor Constanza did fall off her crutch, see,' Josefa was explaining. Was her tone too defiant? 'Hit the head. Out cold.'

The *vicaria* did not go away. I watched from under my lashes as she untied the strings and handed the pouch to Josefa. 'Boil this as an infusion,' she told the girl. 'Spoon it into her lips even if she does not wake up.'

Sor Loreta rocked slightly, with her arms wrapped around her. She crooned joyfully, 'It is what the Venetian Cripple needs.'

Josefa nodded soundlessly and took the poison carefully into her hand.

'Go . . . go and *boil the kettle*,' insisted the Vixen. Josefa's face drew tight like a bud.

Sor Loreta is going to wait and watch the deed done, I thought. *She is going to force my poor Josefa to murder me.*

'Fire is out,' Josefa protested.

'Then make it,' the *vicaria* sang.

Doctor Santo Aldobrandini

It is said that in the old times only the Andean nobility were permitted the narcotic pleasures of *Erythroxylum peruvianum*, which the natives call coca. The leaves, once dried in the sun, are stored in pouches. The method of ingestion is by chewing, which releases a pungent but not bitter flavour. These days, when altitude sickness strikes, or hunger, or sadness, Peruvians of all classes take refuge in the coca leaf's pleasant power to deaden all troublesome sensations without killing the person who suffers them.

Later, when it all came out, I could scarcely breathe when I pictured what happened next. Only Josefa's quick thinking saved Marcella's precious life. While she stoked the fire, the *samba* contrived for the *vicaria* to turn her back for a moment. 'Is someone at the door!' she cried, kicking the coal bucket behind her.

While the *vicaria* ran to investigate the imagined knock, Josefa emptied the pouch of poison into the fire, substituting coca leaves from her own apron. She was stirring the mixture in a pot when Sor Loreta bustled back. The Vixen slapped Marcella's face to rouse her from her faint.

'It's ready, give it to her now!' she commanded Josefa.

Then she watched the boiling infusion being tipped down Marcella's throat, savouring every last drop.

I pictured that moment – the weeping Josefa holding the cup to her beloved Marcella's lips – and Marcella drinking, not knowing if she would survive to the end of the draught.

The coca infusion sent Marcella into a swift delirium. Her symptoms – clammy skin, blurring eyes and gastric convulsions – convinced the *vicaria* that her work was done, or at least in unstoppable progress. She left.

Josefa stayed with her mistress until she was halfway to being herself again. Then Hermenegilda kept vigil, while Josefa ran to tell us what had happened.

We sat around the scarred old table: myself, Fernando, a tearful Beatriz and the still-trembling Josefa. She urged, 'You need act quick-quicker now.'

Two days later, one of my patients died. She was the right kind of patient: a destitute young Indian of no family; a slight creature, slighter even than Marcella. She had been found unconscious in a field on the edge of town. Even though just such a body – deceased – was the object of all my desire now, I had tended the woman with all my skill. I would not have killed by negligence, not even to free Marcella. How could I ask her to marry a murderer?

My patient succumbed to a sudden haemorrhage that could not have been anticipated. She had been carrying the beginnings of a dead child inside her, which I was about to remove in the hope of saving the mother at least. My knife revealed that the little corpse had turned putrid in the womb. I sat by the girl as the life ebbed out of her, holding her hand, and thanking her silently for what she was about to do for Marcella and myself. I did not even know her name.

I sent a messenger to a peon whom Marcella had advised me to take into our confidence. In twenty minutes this Arce had driven up with a cart. He pulled a creased drawing out of his pocket and compared it with my face. Then he smiled, 'Up on mountain, Marcella draw you,' he explained.

He received the woman's body with respect, crossing himself as he laid her in the cart. He waved away the coin I offered him.

'To get one alive girl out, I happy take one dead girl in that place.' he smiled. 'And that one, your one, she is very alive, I think!'

I watched the cart lurch down the street towards Santa Catalina.

Sor Loreta

The holy man had sent a messenger to say that he would be honoured to attend Me. He hoped I would find an evening appointment convenient as '*our days are mutually though separately beset with precious cares God obliges us to discharge. As to the precise evening, I am afraid it must be dictated by the exigencies of my patients*'.

I wrote back, '*You need not advertise your arrival in advance, Doctor. At any hour of the night you shall find Me doing God's work.*'

When the bell rang outside the gate just after supper the next evening, I knew it could only be the holy man from Rome. I quickly rubbed a little pepper into the points of My stigmata, only to make them easier to see in the candlelight. Then I rushed into the courtyard in time to forfend the *portera*. There was disappointment in her face when I told her that I would answer the gate Myself.

'Stifle your vulgar curiosity,' I ordered, 'or your work will be given to a sister more deserving of the honour.'

She shrank away, trembling visibly. Her reaction was so exaggerated that it gave Me pause for thought. I wondered: what did Sor Rosita have to hide? As I hurried towards the gate I resolved to look into the matter.

He fell on his knees when he saw Me, and clasped his hands together – right there out in the dirty street. Then he exclaimed in a Spanish with a strong Vatican accent to it, 'The stigmata! I had heard there was a holy one between these walls. It was worth a journey over oceans just to see such a thing with my own eyes!'

I lowered My own eyelids modestly and begged him to rise and enter Santa Catalina as My guest. He followed Me into the *oficina*.

When I finally looked up at him, I noted straightaway that the holy one was of a troubling boyish demeanour. His face was slick with sweat as he looked at Me. His impatience and his nervousness spoke to Me of some unresolved longing in his spirit. Of course, I could read his afflictions with a clarity and acuity that is denied to those who live their lives in a dulling cloud of sensual satisfaction.

I locked the door from the inside so that We might talk undisturbed by light nuns who were anyway that evening rioting at their latest feast. That night I had chosen not to reprove those foolish girls running around wild with the smell of meat and the constant tinny tinkle of Rossini, which they all hoped, in their shallow way, would penetrate the sleeping ears of their *priora* and bring comfort to her bed of pain.

'Let Us kneel,' I told the young man, gathering My skirts. 'Before you go to attend to the *priora*, We two should pray together. And let Us take communion. I have here the holy wine prepared for you.'

I was so exalted by the moment that I neglected to drink My own wine, but Doctor Santo swallowed obediently from the chalice when I held it to his lips.

Doctor Santo Aldobrandini

Her painted stigmata glowed hotly with a recent application of some corrosive. Yet worse were the melted nose and the striated skin of the unexpectedly powerful hand with which she gripped mine, and the voice, deep like a man's. The tight grin of mania stretched her face to odd angles.

I tried to calm myself by consulting my medical memory of the annals of self-harm. Self-mutilation is the joy of the self-obsessed. That encyclopaedia of maladies, Napoleon, tumbled into my mind immediately. Once, I recalled, he nearly infected himself with Bubonic Plague, just to prove a point. His troops stumbled into it at Jaffa in March 1799. Napoleon decreed that buboed groins were nothing more

401

than a sign of moral feebleness. Therefore his own brave soldiers could not possibly catch the Plague by mere contact with the sick. Napoleon inspected a mosque that had been turned into a hospital. He even handled a corpse and touched a bubo.

And what if a fragment of contaminated dust exhaled by the dead man's cooling body had made the leap and bedded itself in one of the many small fingernailed rips in Napoleon's own itching integument? Just imagine – Marcella would still be in Venice, or, more likely, dead at Minguillo's hand. And the Old World would have been at peace these last fifteen years.

Sor Loreta sighed a little impatiently, drawing my mind back to the present with her foul breath, characteristic of fasters. Then a ripple of incomprehension rumpled her ecstatic expression for a moment. I hoped I had not overheated my little pantomime of 'recognizing' her stigmata. It seemed to have gone down well. She told me in a confidential tone that there was much that we could do together.

Indeed, I thought. For I must engage her in fascinating conversation long enough to allow the secret delivery of the Indian girl's body, and then I had to persuade her to take me to the *priora*, so that I might save the woman's life.

I allowed myself to indulge in a brief vision of Marcella, Marcella herself in person, just yards from me, somewhere beyond the wall of the *oficina*. I sipped the *vicaria*'s proffered communion wine without thinking. It was only the bitter aftertaste that reminded me that I was sharing the goblet with a poisoner. The effect was instantaneous – numbness and tingling of my lips and limbs, retching convulsions in my stomach, and froth forming in my mouth. She had used monkshood.

I knew that I should put a finger down my throat to induce a vomit, but I was already experiencing difficulty in breathing. I had emetics in my bag, but no longer the power even to focus my eyes on the clasp. As I began to feel drowsy, she hurried me out of her office, her forceful arm clenched on my elbow to keep me upright. I had a sensation of swimming through seaweeds at the bottom of the ocean. My rippling skin burned hot and cold.

We arrived at a cell of great beauty and complexity, at least, it seemed so to my blurred eyes. Sor Loreta's intention was apparently the same as my own: to have me at the *priora*'s bed.

'The Doctor Santo, make way,' she hissed at the cluster of nuns who guarded the entrance.

The nuns looked at me hopefully – I dimly understood, through the miasma that was enveloping my senses, that these were Marcella's trusted friends, trying to help me play my part that night. I was powerless to speak – the monkshood had frozen my tongue. The nuns must have thought that I was still an active part of the plan. And I was unable to tell them that this plan had been kidnapped and run away with.

Marcella Fasan

As Santo was approaching the main gate, Josefa was to be slipping out the back. She was going to meet Arce, the peon who had saved my life on the mountain, who would bring the poor dead Indian woman.

I could not help with the delivery. It was essential to the plan that I should be highly visible elsewhere at that moment. So I had been making an unaccustomed fiesta towards the end of supper in the refectory, talking loudly and laughing immoderately. And so I had succeeded in getting my face slapped by the *vicaria* as she hurried back to her office. She had shown no surprise at my presence, and had given no appearance whatsoever of remembering that she had so recently tried to poison me.

'Good, good,' I had muttered, clutching my burning cheek. I thought, *She will enjoy remembering that. She will remember that the clock was striking the halfway point of the ninth hour when she punished me. She will remember that was the last time she saw me alive.*

A few minutes later Rosita, via Javiera, reported the Vixen approaching the *priora*'s office. It was one quarter before nine. Santo, I knew, was due there very soon, and she would want to scourge herself savagely before receiving him. I walked with dragging steps to my cell to start the most strenuous and grim part of the evening. Josefa was waiting, her eyes glittering, her breast heaving and sweat shining on her brow.

The corpse must be heavy, I thought, fearfully. *Of course, she had been with child.*

'Is it done?' I asked Josefa.

'Yes, is there, in the pumpkin vines,' she whispered.

'Thank you,' I breathed. 'And Santo?'

'Rosita has told Javiera, has told Hermengilda, has told me, is gone to the *vicaria*, is all as planned. Now, madam, we remember us through this part one time more?'

'Just the part for . . . after what happens here,' I whispered. What I was about to do I could not bear to hear in words.

The *samba* said, 'When you is finished your . . . business, madam, you go up to back gate. The *portera* Rosita leave it open for fifteen after ten of the night. She dare not leave it longer. *Vicaria* come to see doors and keys four times each evening. Close you the door behind you, for the sake of *portera*, she beg you, and slip the key under where she can find and return to its place quick-easy.

'When you leave the gate . . . turn you to your right, madam, walk swift but not run. You don't run good, draw attention. Steady-steady walking, in two minutes you reach Plaza de Armas. Fernando he be there, he be wait in sedan chair by cathedral. And the doctor Santo, he be wait by statue of Tuturutú. The peon Arce, he hide-hide under tree in case of trouble. When you see Santo and Fernando, run, madam, run. To the doctor Santo, will help you to the chair. If you is followed, then the peon Arce make distracting. You still run to sedan chair.'

I listened respectfully, all the while thinking, 'Santo is in the convent.'

If the plan went awry at this stage, the presence of an unidentified corpse in my cell would be impossible to explain in any decent way. We might both be accused of murder. The *priora* lay dying in her cell, while a dead woman lay in the pumpkin vines. If my courage failed now, I would imperil Priora Mónica, Josefa, Rosita, Margarita, Fernando, Beatriz and Santo too.

Santo was in the convent.

'Come, madam,' urged Josefa. 'Now we have a little somefing-somefing we must do together. It is now.'

I looped a heavy blanket over one of her arms and took the other, picked up my crutch and crept out of my courtyard to begin our task.

Sor Loreta

As I led him towards the *priora*'s bed, I watched him. His pale face was innocent like an angel surrounded by a golden halo of hair. So had Sor Andreola's been. So had Sor Sofia's been once.

Into the young man's eyes came a faraway look – a look of the Flesh and the Devil, just as I had suspected when I first laid eyes on him.

His mouth was forming words that did not emerge.

But the young Fiend refused to quail. He refused to give up. Though he looked so fragile, Satan's power in him was stronger than anything I had ever seen. So the Devil's power becomes most shockingly manifest in the last living moments of those possessed by Him.

Marcella Fasan

I did not even know her name.

One arm on my crutch, I tried to drag her upper body out of the bushes, with Josefa tugging at her feet. We made no impression on the woman's dead weight. I hid my crutch in the vines and dropped to my knees. Using both arms, I succeeded in sliding the shoulders and head over the heavy blanket we had laid out on the cobbles. Josefa swung the lower body into place.

Out of the shadows, the moon lit up the corpse with a pale, searching light. I closed the folds of the blanket over it, covering the blank face in the patterned wool. She was my own age, pretty, with a broad nose and delicate brows. She was slighter even than myself, otherwise we should never have managed to move her an inch.

Josefa took one corner of the blanket, grunting, 'Now – now, madam!'

Using every atom of my strength, I pulled on my corner. Finally, the body, like a vast seed-pod, began to slide through the courtyard, and to the right, into the main part of the convent. Pain swept through my damaged leg, making me sway.

I am sorry, I thought, as I jerked the girl's head over the threshold, *I do not even know your name. You were so pretty. What were you going to call your baby?*

The streets of the convent were empty. In cells all around us, the festivities raged. We saw no one and no one saw us. I wept silently, for the dreadful thing I was doing, for the pain in my legs, for the danger of discovery, for the poor dead girl and her lost child.

The riskiest part of all was in front of the *priora*'s own cell, which lay yards from me at the conjunction of Calles Granada, Burgos and Sevilla. For, if the plan was working, both the *vicaria* and Santo were in there now. Santo would be trying to save the *priora*'s life with all the skills in him. The *vicaria* would be trying to stop him, with all the evil in her.

It was then that I realized what I had forgotten to tell Santo. I had neglected to warn him about the bizarre physical strength Sor Loreta harboured in her skeletal form. I stopped dead, overcome with fear, but Josefa urged me on.

There was a hum of voices and darting candlelight at the window of the *priora*'s apartments. I yearned for it, but I did not hear Santo's voice. *He must be at his work*, I thought. *Let him save Madre Mónica. He shall do it, if anyone can.*

We dragged our seed-pod past the *priora*'s room and to the first pair of steps, where it thumped fruitily, then ten paces to the next pair of steps followed by three more pairs before we could propel it into my courtyard, where we allowed ourselves the luxury of stopping and catching our breath.

We pulled the woman into my room and up over the dais to my bed, where I laid her down with her head on my pillow.

Josefa threw herself into my arms, and we held each other for a few moments, each absorbing the long shudders and gasps of the other. I rested my chin on the top of her head, and forced myself to look at the Indian woman on the bed. The blanket had fallen open.

Santo has tended to this woman, I thought. *His hands have touched her.* Gently disengaging myself from Josefa's embrace, I walked over to the woman, raised one of her hands and kissed it. I twisted off the ring of my betrothal to God and slid it on to her limp finger. My own finger was still stained green with the blade of grass I always wore between myself and that ring.

'Madam . . .' Josefa was holding out a hymnbook for me. She had a Bible in her other hand. We busied ourselves tearing them up. We ruckled each page and tucked them between the Indian woman's legs, her arms and her body, around her neck. Flowers of paper bloomed around her as if she was on her bier. I would need to set fire to many parts of her at once so that she would burn quickly.

'Now Josefa,' I said firmly, 'your work is over for a little while.'

'Madam, I could still . . .'

'It has been agreed, Josefa. If we are discovered now, it is best that you are not seen to be part of it.'

'But, madam . . .'

I shook my head. Josefa lifted to her lips a little green bottle that Margarita had provided. It was a sleeping draught that I would later be accused of administering so that Josefa would not interrupt me at my task. Margarita had promised me that it would cause no lasting damage.

Josefa's bright eyes clouded over. I kissed her and led her to her bed in the kitchen of the cell, and settled her on her pallet. She was already asleep. Stroking her hair from her forehead, I almost envied her. She would not even have to see what I was about to do.

I went out to the drain outside my courtyard, and pulled the string to lift up the flat bottle of brandy that Margarita had procured for me from the pharmacy. Returning to my room, I poured the brown liquid over the woman.

Had she enjoyed spirits in her short life?

Her face did not change as the fumes of alcohol reached her face. Over her head I now placed a rag soaked in brandy.

I told her, 'I am sorry.'

When I set fire to her torso, I turned my back immediately, but not fast enough to miss her body contracting with the flames, as if she danced, grotesquely, on her back. Her bones creaked as they snapped into a simulation of life. Her chemise burned away, revealing a neat trail of black stitches where Santo must have sewn up the incision he made in trying to save her from the infection of the dead baby inside her. Then the stitches themselves caught fire.

I ran to the door, desperate to flee this scene. Yet I forced myself to stand with my hand on the frame. I had to wait until she had burned properly and was truly unrecognizable. And I had work to do in the meantime. I reached to the back of my candle cupboard and pulled out a rolled-up portrait of myself, painted with the help of Rafaela's sliver of mirror. I stretched it on four prepared pieces of wood, and set it in the stone *hornacina* in the furthest corner of my bare second room, where the flames would not reach as there was no fuel for them. I looked at my painted face, spectral in the candlelight. Josefa had gasped when she saw the portrait, saying, 'Madam, 'tis you to last hair.'

The portrait and the smell of burning reminded me of Cecilia Cornaro. She would damn my work, out of habit, but it was infected with her skill. I had painted myself lively, and loving. My expression was the one I would have worn if I had been looking into Santo's face.

I had not dared to prepare a bag before I committed the deed. Who knew when the *vicaria* might take it into her head to enter my cell abruptly in the hope of finding punishable mischief? But I had visualized my list and the order of gathering my belongings. In minutes I had brought the sketch in my mind to life: my diaries, my drawn evidence of Rafaela's murdered face, a change of clothes, some coins and a pair of Fernando's wonderful shoes all crammed inside a sack. The very last item I added was Rafaela's heart in its silver casket.

'Your heart is to get your heart's desire,' I told her tenderly, 'to leave this place.'

I forced myself to return to the burning bed, which crackled and fumed merrily, releasing a smell horribly like roasting guinea pig. I had counted on that. For guinea pig was the dish of the evening, and in cells all over our convent the nuns' *criadas* and *sambas*, having fed their mistresses, were still turning the little beasts in rich gravy and licking their lips at the thought of their own suppers.

I little wanted to take a closer look at the burning girl, but I needed to see if the fire had done its work properly. I edged near, holding my head as far back on my neck as I could and looking gingerly down my cheekbones. My Indian sister was but half-eaten by flames. The cloth across her face was just ashes now. I raked them aside – the features had melted away like wax, like the *vicaria*'s. For the first time, I thought of the pain the madwoman had inflicted on herself when she was just a child. She had been mad, even then.

The Indian woman felt nothing, of course. Hot blood suddenly trickled down through the void where her eyes had been. I retched. I forced myself to check the legs and arms. I did not want any traces of her vivid skin visible. Tatters of flesh still clung to her limbs.

The bottle of brandy was empty. Despairingly, I stared around the room, and then seized the lamp. I emptied its oil over the woman's torso and dropped a piece of paper over each leg. The fire took hold with renewed vigour. I could trust it now. I did not want to raise a huge conflagration, for Josefa lay sleeping in the next room, and I could not bear the risk of her being harmed.

Santo was in the convent, keeping the *vicaria* occupied and saving the *priora*. In minutes, perhaps, I would see him.

I tore off my habit and spread it over the flaming bones. From under Josefa's mattress I pulled out a thin street-dress with a flowered skirt. Fernando's boots were not hidden by it, I worried. Nor did my skirt quite cover the thinness of my deformed leg. We had not thought of everything. My self-portrait gazed at me trustingly. I stared back for a moment. Then I whispered, 'Goodbye, Sor Constanza.' I kissed the sleeping Josefa one last time.

Santo was in the convent. Soon, soon, both of us would be outside it.

Climbing the steps back up to the conjunction of Granada, Sevilla and Burgos, I pattered through the courtyard and up to the gate.

Doctor Santo Aldobrandini

To my inexpressible horror, the *vicaria* dismissed all the other nuns. Unfortunately, they had been reassured by my presence and agreed to leave their beloved Mother in my care. How could they know that I was numbed and dying of monkshood?

A deathbed is a place for the quietest words. Perhaps they thought I swayed with feigned religious fervour as I stood over the *priora*'s still form, mumbling with scant breath. Only one nun gave me long looks, and edged closer to observe me better. Her intelligent face swam in front of my eyes.

'Bless you, Father,' she whispered.

Of course, Fernando had thought it prudent to have the whole town think that I was truly a man of God. Those poor women saw what they wanted to see, a saviour, not a drugged man struggling to breathe.

Then I thought of Marcella, with her wasted leg, dragging the remains of the Indian girl down to her cell with only Josefa to help her. Did they have the strength? I had lifted the woman in my own arms to my bench – her dead weight was considerable. Josefa had told us that the body must pass the *priora*'s cell to reach Marcella's. Was she passing even now? Had she passed? Or was she too failing?

I sniffed the air for burning. Yes, the smell of roasting flesh – guinea pig – flooded through every door and window of the convent, sending a vivid wave of nausea undulating through my stomach.

The *vicaria*'s face loomed close to mine. Her eyes were empty of recognition. Her expression was devoid of humanity. The woman had slipped into a rapture and no longer knew what she did.

Yet I understood what Sor Loreta was about to do: perhaps her poison caused my thoughts to run dementedly parallel with her own. In the privacy my presence had sanctified, the *vicaria* was now going to kill the *priora*. Afterwards, when she came to her senses, she would denounce me as the incompetent agent of her victim's death. She would tell the world I had attended the convent in an intoxicated state. And that in my drunkenness I administered erroneous, fatal drugs to the suffering *priora*.

Doctors are required to cure, not kill. There's little mercy to be expected for one who lets a helpless woman of God die under his criminally careless fingers. Sor Loreta had the confidence of the priests. I was a foreigner, with a secret that would soon be exposed. How would I defend myself?

Then I realized that I would not have to. There would be two corpses found in this cell tonight: the *priora*'s and my own.

Sor Loreta would not need to find an explanation for that fact. By the time our bodies were found, she would be back in the *oficina*. She would be able to truthfully manifest complete surprise at the two terrible deaths at Santa Catalina, for she was not really in this room at all. Whatever had taken over her mind was stronger than sense and it was certainly stronger than a dying man.

Marcella might escape to the outside, but she would find herself there without me.

Marcella Fasan

It was nearly three years since I had seen outside the walls of Santa Catalina. Yet Arequipa had burned an impression into my brain that day I first arrived, when the *arriero* and his peons had allowed me one last turn around the main square before they delivered me.

I pushed the door open and slid outside, flattening myself in the shadow of the wall. The street was empty. I closed the door behind me and locked it, sliding the key back underneath.

'Be safe, Rosita,' I whispered.

'Turn you right,' Josefa had said. But to my right a pair of soldiers were now approaching, and they were already peering in my direction. Left was empty, and so I edged along the wall in that direction. I could hear the soldiers whistling and swearing.

One slurred, 'Sthat a woman? By the convent wall?'

'If it is, she is too skinny for *me*. Go on, help yourself.'

Their pace quickened. But the beer made their legs as incompetent as my own and one stumbled into the gutter. They fell into incoherent argument.

I fled up an alley, keeping in mind that I was parallel to the square, that I must turn right to find my way back. I limped and lurched. I could not find a passageway to my right.

My thoughts pounded in my head.

What if the *vicaria* worked out what had really happened? I feared that Josefa, slow with drugs, might be maltreated in the process of Sor Loreta's investigations. She might not be able to escape.

'Tuturutú,' Josefa had told me. 'Santo will meet you under the statue of Tuturutú.'

411

Doctor Santo Aldobrandini

I sank to my knees. The nausea had invaded all my senses; even my hearing sickened so that my head was invaded by a sound like bees swarming. I think now that this must have been Sor Loreta singing to herself. Sharp pains racked my stomach, as if my intestines were wrapping around my liver. Strange fluid forms swam across my vision. Death craved my complicity, welcoming me with a promise of relief.

I turned my back on death. I crawled away from it. I took hold of the hem of Sor Loreta's habit and dragged her down to the floor. I threw my body over hers, grinding my torso over the part of her skin that was most fragile, her thighs, wrecked by the cilice. I punched the section of her thorax that housed her gall-bladder, which her fasting would have filled with bile. She grunted.

An intense, sensual joy filled her face. Her pain seemed somehow to feed her sinews and her lungs. She shrugged me off, stabbed my belly with her knife of an elbow, and shuffled on her knees back to the bed. The *vicaria* bent over the *priora*, her hands outstretched above her neck. I raised my head and saw all the signs of imminent death on the sick woman's face. The *vicaria* had but to apply a simple pressure to that wasted throat and the thing would be done.

My arms had knotted in a solid contraction, but my right leg retained some sensation. I kicked the knees from under the *vicaria*. I heard her head smack against the bedpost. She lay still on the floor.

Then she surged up like a dark wave, reaching her emaciated, trembling hand towards the bed again.

The *priora* opened her eyes.

In a clear voice she asked Sor Loreta, 'So you intend to murder me, then? Let all our sisters witness the act.'

From under the covers she dragged a bell and rang it. Suddenly the room was full of nuns, who cried out in one voice at the sight of the *vicaria*'s hands being snatched away from the *priora*'s neck.

412

The nuns surrounded the Vixen. One of them, who seemed to be in authority, called out, 'Remember our plan!'

In the midst of the shouting and screaming, another nun ran to me and tipped a bottle of castor oil to my lips. I felt it rush down my throat. Next she dosed me from a bottle of black suspension. Then she pulled me outside, me crawling like an animal. In the garden, she hoisted me to my knees, gently holding my head as I alternately swigged on the powdered charcoal in water and vomited copiously into the grass.

'Keep on, Doctor Santo,' she said encouragingly. 'I'm the pharmacist Margarita,' she explained, 'Marcella's friend. One of the other pharmacy nuns told me about the froth on your mouth and how you seemed to be retching and shivering. I guessed the symptoms of monkshood poisoning. It's one of the Vixen's favourites. Her garden is full of *Aconitum nepallus*. And other poisons too – cardinal flower or *Lobelia cardinalis*, and crown of thorns, *Euphorbia milli*.

'The ... *vic* ...' The words jerked out of me mixed with vomit and bile. 'Thank ...'

'The *priora* is still alive. And if you had not come, and occupied the Vixen,' said Margarita, 'there would have been no cover for what Marcella is doing now.'

'Has ... she?'

'I cannot tell you. I do not know. She refused help with the actual deed because she did not want to implicate us if everything went wrong. If it has been done, it is over now. She will be outside – you must go to her.'

From inside the *priora*'s cell came the sound of Sor Loreta screaming like an animal and younger voices speaking to her angrily.

I rose unsteadily, 'I mus ...'

'No,' insisted Margarita. 'If Sor Loreta becomes violent – well, she is not the only one with access to stupefying herbs. Her two assistants sleep peacefully now, thanks to something from the pharmacy garden. We can take care of everything now: we Santa Catalina nuns have a most particular way we wish to proceed.'

A nun who called herself Rosita took my shoulder. 'I'm the *portera*,' she explained, producing a bunch of keys from her belt. She led me through meandering ways to the front gate.

'Marcella will have used the back gate; you must leave this way,' she whispered. 'Now go!'

The fresh night air hit my face, waking all my senses up, most of all the one of love.

Marcella Fasan

I limped down a long stone lane, turning right at the first opportunity. But this street was crowded with taverns and their rowdy patrons. I could not be looked at and remarked upon by people whose curiosity and tongues were loosened by corn beer. I doubled back, found a nightsoil alley, stole along it, into another road that led away from Santa Catalina, and at last a turning to the right.

Two priests were strolling towards me, deep in conversation.

One of them was the man who had officiated at Rafaela's funeral. He had stared at me then, the Venetian cripple – he might remember my face! And if not that, my limp. I stilled my body, forced myself to crouch down, pretending to tie a loose lace of my boot.

Footsteps approached me. The priest spoke, 'This is no place for a girl to be out alone. Does your mother know where you are?'

My head lowered, I shook my head. I dared not speak: he would recognize my Venetian accent from the confessional.

The two priests passed on, grumbling. I doubled back and turned right. Or should it have been left?

How long had I been galloping around Arequipa, lost? Had they given up hope on me, Santo and Fernando?

Then, unexpectedly, the magnificent square opened up in front of me, and there, in the middle, was the fountain and the little man with his trumpet pointing up to the sky. And under him was a figure that I recognized. His back was to me. He was splashing his face and mouth with water from the fountain – why? Between splashes, he stared intently in the direction of the cathedral. He had expected me to come directly from Santa Catalina – he could not have anticipated the diversions that the soldiers and priests had forced on me. How must he have felt, those dragging minutes, thinking I had failed?

The ground was not beneath my feet as I ran across the square to him. When I reached him, I did not dare to salute or touch him. I breathed quietly behind him, until he turned around and took me into his arms, as if it was the most natural thing in the world to kiss and caress the weeping eyes and smoke-filled hair of an escaped nun and madwoman with a stain of green around her finger.

Doctor Santo Aldobrandini

For a moment I could not hear Fernando's voice for the colour of Marcella's eyes.

He was calling, 'Come! Quickly! Bring her to the sedan chair!'

He was asking me to gather Marcella in my arms and carry her?

I thought then, *Once I pick her up, she will have to plead with me to ever let her feet touch the ground again. And even then I may deny her.*

Marcella Fasan

In the confusion that followed the discovery of my supposed charred corpse, Josefa too slipped out of the convent, having first rescued my crutch from the pumpkin vines. She brought with her a handful of the ashes of the poor girl we had burned. We gave them a loving and respectful burial beside the dead foetus that Santo had taken from her body.

Josefa was instantly installed as the dearest member of our household, excepting Santo and my new mother Beatriz and my brother Fernando. Oh, that was everyone! Well, we loved her and would never forget what we owed her.

Hermenegilda came to us full of the latest news from behind the walls of Santa Catalina. Within hours, every nun in the convent knew exactly what had really taken place in my cell and in the *priora*'s. Rosita and Margarita had not been able to keep their secrets, though they were steadfast to our plan of allowing the *vicaria* to stay in her position, in name only and carefully guarded, until the *priora* was well enough to resume her post.

'People *know*?' I trembled, for what if Minguillo heard of my flight?

"Carse they do. A good story is good story, make talk. Is no problem,' said Josefa imperturbably.

Even Sor Loreta must have known, in some part of her distorted brain, though she chose not to. Hermenegilda had told us that, rather than admit the scandal, the *vicaria* had written to my brother that I was no more, just as I had hoped.

'Did she send the portrait to prove it?' I asked.

"Carse she did. Quick-quick. She did not want it around place to haunt, hoo hoooo.'

'But if people know, won't someone tell the Holy Fathers, and won't they come to take me back to the convent? Did I burn that poor woman for nothing?' I wailed.

Josefa laughed. 'O no, not nothing. Needed burned dead lady to get buried for you. So Sor Constanza proper dead. But the priests they cannot let out know truth too-too late. Make them look so crazy-fool-stupid. So many times the nuns of Santa Catalina make them look stupid already! Is men, like any other. Proud. Must stand on dignify, pretend don't know nothing.'

So that would be an end to it. Sor Constanza had gone to her wedding night with God. She would be seen no more on this earth. The Bishop had been informed. A death certificate for Sor Constanza had been lodged with the notaries. For such an irreligious death, and remains already self-cremated, a scanty service in a poor church had been considered more than sufficient. We discovered that Sor Constanza's ashes, apart from the handful rescued by Josefa, had been quietly buried in an unmarked grave in unconsecrated ground.

Marcella Fasan could marry whom she wished.

Santo saw trouble from a different quarter: 'Your brother will come after the truth. The lure of getting back your dowry will bring him here, but more than that, curiosity and frustration. That you died apparently at your own hand and not his: that will drive him into a frenzy. We are not free of him yet.'

416

We were also stricken with worry for Gianni and Anna – we had not judged it safe to warn them in advance of the plan and its accomplishment. But how agonizing for them, if they heard of my apparent death, now that it was successfully accomplished! We could only hope that our letter reached them before Sor Loreta's to my brother, informing him of my supposed end, with the portrait as evidence.

We had already decided to live as a public couple in Arequipa. Marcella Fasan had no papers of her own for the notaries, and the last person I wished to see was a man of God, even to marry me, even if we could have afforded the outrageous sums the local priests charged for weddings.

So we married each other.

Mother Beatriz made me a veil sewn with rosebuds, and gave me her best dress to wear, the seams much taken in. As she stitched me into it, I breathed perfume that my father had brought her from Venice and the Old World. Arce arrived with his cart decked in vines and ribbons. In a field on the city outskirts, we gathered a bouquet of wild flowers. Under the high sky, Fernando gave me away, producing two silver rings he had fashioned himself from Beatriz's last bracelet. Santo took me to his wife. Josefa pronounced us married. There never was a happier wedding. For our wedding feast there were beans and day-old bread. We could afford nothing else. We took my flowers to the grave of the unknown mother and her baby.

For our wedding night, there was peace and privacy, and an endless, light-soaked dawn.

Minguillo Fasan

So suddenly without a scrap of notice I received this portrait of Marcella from the nuns. If a letter had ever accompanied it, that letter had been lost in one of the numerous passages the painting had taken. And, as the Retentive Reader will recall, I at that time knew absolutely nothing of any arcane layings-down as to when and how nuns might have their faces painted.

I had not commissioned any portrait of my sister. It was confoundedly odd that Marcella should wish to send me an image of herself, when she had spent her life trying to hide away from my attention.

I placed the ailing, flaking thing in my study and used it to frighten my daughters for a few days. Then I took it up to the tower and surrounded it with my books of human skin in a tight circle. I thought their clamorous presence would soon sink the life that somehow shimmered in that portrait.

But it did not. The light still sparkled in her eyes.

Then I got to wondering. One hundred and seventy-five steps to visit Marcella and the books – each step a new speculation. And then I got to be tortured, with my brain raking for whys and hows, each doubt like a knife stuck in the small ribs. *Why* would my sister send me a portrait of herself? *How* could she contrive to have it painted and dispatched? Such a fine piece of work: it must have cost a fine piece of money. Where did she get her hands on *that*? I had trimmed her *peculios* to the bone.

I wrote to the nuns in Arequipa, but subtly. The way I phrased it was, '*Is all well with my dear sister?*'

Three months later I had my reply, smelling of gunpowder from its passage down the coast. For a general called Bernardo O'Higgins and one José de San Martín, who had 'liberated' Argentina, were currently blasting their way to Chilean independence. It was rumoured that Peru would soon be heading in the same direction.

There had also been a change of regime at Santa Catalina. A new *priora* replied tersely, in handwriting that was wild and odd, '*Sor Constanza does as well as she deserves.*'

I could not read her signature. I noticed that she used the capital 'M' for 'Me' when she explained how the top position had fallen to her. It was clear that Marcella had gravely displeased her and that she rejoiced sternly in some misfortune of my sister's.

But what misfortune? That intrigued me. My sister had misbehaved then, and they were punishing her. That, I had to see. I had missed Marcella's misery, I realized. It would do me a power of good to be near it again.

Anyway, I had pharmaceutical business in Peru to tickle up, and pleasures to renew in Valparaiso now the Chilean revolution was safely over, by all accounts. I had not been to the South Americas for three years. At the thought of the mountains, the cranes, the white walls and red bougainvillea of Arequipa, I felt a tug of desire in every inch of my body, especially the inches.

I had a yen not to be on my lonesome for this long journey. Now that I had seen the ways and valleys and peaks, they would not detain my entire interest a second time. And it would be useful to have someone to test any food that my nose judged guilty of adulteration. I called in my half-wit valet Gianni and told him, 'We're going to Arequipa.'

And watched his jaw drop five inches in one second.

Gianni delle Boccole

The poortret of Marcella got me worrit more than anything. There were a message in them sweet eyes for me, yet I were too stupid to read it. For why a picture of her now? Did nuns get thereselfs painted? It went round n round my head like a rat in a trap, that there were summing not right bout this poortret. Ide heared nothing from Santo nor Fernando to make sense of it.

Minguillo spent most of his time up in the tower now, hardly niver come down een to eat. We was told to leave trays on the second landing. Sumtimes they were untoucht the next morning. He dint scarcely talk to us, just baconed with his hand. When we seed him, he were a thing to behold. His eyes on storks. His skin lookt like a dirty tablecloth. Them three shelves was empty in his study now, and the poortret was vanisht, so I guest he had got them all up there with him, them bein his real famly, that's what he ud made of it.

When Minguillo told me that we was oft to Peru I were torn atwixt laffing n crying. Laffing that Minguillo ud given me the one thing I wanted more than anything else in the world. Crying because Minguillo were going to Arequipa, and that were surely for to do more bad to Marcella.

For himself, he wunt lay his cats upon the table, what he were up to. Wunt say nothin bout the why. It were all bout the when. 'WHEN can you get my trunk packed? WHEN are you going to get that stupid look off your face?'

Yes, I were daydreamin all the time them days. For I ud painted myself a dream: that the misterious plan was all eksecuted, that Santo n Marcella was alredy safe and happy in Arequipa. That they was marrid and they expected a little one.

I *had to* paint a dream. There was still no letters, Beast ovva God. Silents like death. I brewed on that silents. It fomented in my mind.

I was that firstrated that I went to see Cecilia Cornaro, to tell her bout the poortret. But she weren't there – one of her signs sayed, 'Gone to Cadiz to do minor Bourbons. Feed the cat.' Her studio door were open so I walkt in. Puss were in residence, looking feroshus mean. I went to the butchery next door and bought him some livers for his trouble, and he condesended to eat them in my presents. I strokt his big old head and lookt round the studio.

There was two poortrets still wet on seprit eezles. One were a picture of the famous English milord, the wicked poet Byron, what were knowed to be Cecilia Cornaro's lover. Lookt like a one. T'other were unknowed to me, but she ud painted a little floatin banner under his breast in the old style. It sayed 'Doctor Ruggiero of Stra'. A miserable, septical cove he lookt, holding a little glass

420

flask o brown dirt up to the light by the scuff of its neck. Stuck to the eezle I were sorpresed to see a reseet for a large sum from one o them horse-boiling booksellers what Minguillo favoured.

When I got home I found Anna in my room, kneelin on the floor with a pile of my clean small-clothes aside her. She were linin the bottom o my small travail-trunk.

'Men never know how to pack,' she sayed.

I catched sight o summing at the bottom jist before she put my small-clothes in.

'What's that?' I spluttert.

Marcella Fasan

Now Josefa washed my married sheets, as she had once washed my nun's sheets. She cooked for us; she took what coins Santo earned and turned them into food. There was nothing left over for clothes or wine.

Fernando had rented us a pair of clean rooms next to their own, using the proceeds of the sale of the statue from my dowry that he had saved for this purpose. Those funds were now spent and gone. We agreed to save the Mantegna as our last resort against destitution. To live in poverty was a new thing for me. In my worst days at the Palazzo Espagnol or on San Servolo I had wanted for nothing, materially. And nuns do not wonder where the next meal will come from, or whether there will be candles enough to light their tables.

To the curious eyes of the Arequipans we turned oblivious cheeks flushed with happiness. But our joy infected their spirits. Santo's patients pushed him extra coins, saying, 'Buy something pretty for that little wife of yours. We all like to see her smile.'

What we bought was canvas, and paint. I began to revive my old business, the one I had started with Rafaela back in the convent. However, instead of saints, I painted the cheerful sinners of Arequipa – the *criados*, the *sambos*, the *mestizos*, *mulatos*, *criollos*, for whatever they could afford, be it our slops emptied for a month or a basket of potatoes cool from the

421

earth. Arce drove Santo out to countryside patients in a cart, and ferried my subjects to our rooms to be painted. He brought paper for Santo's writings, and the stumps of candles to for him to write by. The peon would take no other payment from us than to eat at our meagre table occasionally.

'I did good, girl,' he remarked often, patting my hand.

'Very good,' I embraced him.

As I worked, my memories naturally flew back to those cheerful days in Rafaela's cell, painting our secret commissions together.

Rafaela's heart in its silver box I kept by me.

'One day,' I promised, 'I will take you to Venice.'

Margarita and Rosita wrote to us via the hem of Hermenegilda's skirt. The chapter of offences had met secretly with the council. All had voted to let Priora Mónica recover her strength before having her quietly reinstated – recovery from monkshood poisoning should leave no permanent effects. Santo and Margarita had agreed on the safest course of treatment.

Rosita explained, '*Then we shall hand the* vicaria *over to the Holy Fathers and the Intendant. We shall present the problem and the solution at one time, as a* fait accompli, *perfectly done. We shall let them think that they have managed the thing from beginning to end. Meanwhile all the sisters are set to inventing particularly colourful confessions to keep the chaplains distracted.*'

Margarita observed, '*And if those priests even think of interfering, we shall remind them that we still have some uncles!*'

She continued, '*I am still tending the poisonous plants in Sor Loreta's garden, for evidence when the time comes. The Jackals have agreed to be her guards, and this will be taken into consideration when the case is finally brought against her. No one else wants the task, anyway. In fact, she does not require much guarding. For she sits quite still all day, talking to herself harmlessly. She is always mumbling about "fire and flame", "burning pain" and "mutilated beyond any recognizable humanity*, Deo gratias".'

Rosita opined, '*She is jealous that you died so horribly – as she thinks. She wears your ring, you know – she had it taken off the corpse. We have started taking her up to the* oficina, *where we lock her up for a few hours of the day, guarded by the Jackals. The priests and the delivery men see the nun with the blue spectacles through the window, and think all is as before.*

'*We are taking our time here, dear Marcella, hoping to resume life as it was, but better. And you too must resume the life that your brother tried to break. But*

422

better. Just think, you, the weakest among us, had the strength to do the most hideous and hard deed.

'In years to come, this will be the one astonishing story that everyone will remember about Santa Catalina.'

Gianni delle Boccole

Anna wernt tall contrite bout what ud appened with the will.

'How was I to know what it was?' she sayed. 'You did not tell me you had mislayed a will.'

Twas true, o course, that Ide kept numb on the subjeck. And twas true poor Anna haint got her letters. One peace o paper were the same as the next for her. She ud found the will where Ide hid it in a pile of old clothes rolled up under my bed. She had tidid the clothes and put the will with all t'other loose papers she keeped for linin the travail-trunks o my Mistress Donata Fasan and my old Master Fernando Fasan. Turned out that the will had been sevral times to the Fasan villa in the country oer the years, and een onct to the Foscarini *palazzo* on the Brenta when Donata Fasan past a summer there. Each time it ud been brought back safe to Venice, unpacked with the clothes, smoothed out and keeped for the next journey.

I read it agin. I had been right. I had not dreamed it. Minguillo were not the legal hair o my old Master Fernando Fasan. Not tall.

With a grateful shutter, I slid the bonyfied will into my nightshirt sleeve. All those years ago, I ud messed my chance when twere offered me, humming and whoring and then loosing the preshous document like a squirrel looses a nut. Now I were takin it to Peru, and I would find the young Fernando Fasan, and I would put it direckly in his hand, so he could help Marcella get what were riotously hers. For onct, I wunt esitate.

The last thing I did were to write to Amish Gillyfether for to tell him all our news.

The journey were pieceful. The sea were in its best humour. I were niver sick – a Venetian is allus borned with his sea-legs attatched. The land-going were harder. The mounting nights affrighted me, dark as a stack o black cats. Our paeans was kindnuff fellows but I felt loanedsome among em.

Evrywheres I saw the countryside ravished by earthquakes and grate mountings moan down by irruptions. In that way Peru were like my mood, what grew more dissolute by the hour. For Minguillo were too happy, like someone ud presented him with a cart o gold bouillon. I haint heard him laff like that since his Papà died. Of course I were the buttock of all his jokes, what come in through the back passage at evrything.

Minguillo's happy inhevitable meaned Marcella's sad.

If Santo ud suckseeded then Minguillo would of been foul of temper. Instead, he wistled, he chortled, he saw laffs in evry corner. All oer the briny for weeks on end, and then updown the valleys, jolting on horses that had my back dislocratered from collarbone to breakfast – all that way he keeped sniggering to hisself een when we gasped in cold to cut a man's nose clean oft, so that I were happy to bury my hands in the shag of my mule what had a stink you could hang yer hat on.

It seemed like an age, for it were tortshure to be constantly in his hellarious company and I were back-to-belly tired of distimulating to be a fool in front o him. Yet our journey past more quickly than anyone could of hoped. Twere less than sixty days from leaving the Palazzo Espagnol to when I saw El Misti Mounting lift his white hat at me, *how de do, sir*.

Doctor Santo Aldobrandini

There were times when I luxuriated in a lyrical kind of sadness for the life I had lived before Marcella became mine. Sometimes I thought that it was truly I who had lived the nunly life. I had existed – for it cannot truly be called living when it is without human affection – until I met her. I had known neither fraternal nor parental love, nor truly a friend, except Gianni and Padre Portalupi, who were my conduits to her. Then I had been married to my hopeless love of Marcella for so many years, rather like a nun married to the Christ she believes she will join only at her death.

Now I was married to happiness. I warmed my skin on it, shin to shin, nose to cheek. I breathed that cure-all medicine, laughter, day and night. I was now a hopeless addict of it. In Marcella's presence, I knew every flavour of love, from fond to frantic, from hair-raising to hilarious, sometimes all in the course of ten minutes.

I knew not what the future might bring to us. But Marcella spoke too often and too fondly of Venice for me not to be aware that she wished to return there. As did I. The pages of my manuscript multiplied nightly, and the book would soon need a Venetian printer to set it to type.

But how to get home? With what? And the brother? Venice was contaminated with his presence. How could we return to live in the same town where he breathed?

Minguillo Fasan

The servants at the dusty Casa Fasan did not break their hearts with joy to see me. The whore at the *tambo* remembered the colour of my money.

There being no invitations forthcoming for better entertainment, I went straight to Santa Catalina the first morning. Casting dubious looks in my direction, a little serving nun admitted me. I stormed past her into the vaulted office of the *priora*.

At the desk, I recognized the old *vicaria* of the melted face, she whose cruelty I had known as one knows a new family member on sight. So your woman was now the *priora*, the author of the odd signature and the capitalized pronouns. Revolutionary times indeed! A repulsive nun stood either side of her, like gargoyles on a roof.

The *oficina* being dimly lit, her blue spectacles were on the desk, and the woman's face was naked for the reading. Now I saw that she had advanced in ugliness since I last beheld her. Her eyelids were thick, as if carved out of yellow *prosciutto* rinds, the sparse eyelashes protruding at rare intervals like bristles. At the sight of *me* she flinched and paled, her skin pocked like beaten pewter. Then she stood up. The two tall nuns moved closer to her. One put a restraining hand on her shoulder.

The Deformity jeered, 'Why did you come here, Conte Fasan? What possible good can it serve at this stage?'

'I demand to see my sister.'

'Well, that is hardly possible.'

'Now I'm fond of a joke, but I ask you, madam! Bring her to me.'

'Your sister has left this miserable life. How is it that you do not know this?'

I took a step backwards. A hole opened up inside my viscera and let the bile flow out through my veins. I shouted, 'Why did you not tell me?'

'I did. In my letter, I told you that she was as well as she deserved. Which was, of course, dead and in Hell. And I sent you the portrait to prove it.'

'To prove it?'

'A nun may not be painted when she is alive, sir. If you did not know that simplest of God's truths, then I cannot be held accountable for your ignorance. I always thought Venice was a pagan town: you yourself, sir, are living proof of that.'

Her two retainers exchanged glances and one of them positively forced her back down into her chair. Her one open eye glittered madly. The woman had lost her senses, I realized. Why had the priests allowed her to remain in power?

'Yes, you can be held accountable,' I made my voice low with menace. 'You forget that Monseñor José Sebastián de Goyeneche y Barreda was my father's friend. So my sister is . . . dead? When did this happen and how?'

The *vicaria* showed not one trace of fear. In fact, she had a look of glassy hilarity about her as she announced, 'Your sister died besmirched. She took her own life. Having first committed the sin of vanity by painting that portrait of herself.'

The portrait had been startlingly accurate. Cecilia Cornaro's lessons had served my sister well, I thought.

The ugly nun was now telling me of the fire and my sister's corpse reduced to gristly ashes in her own bed. She dwelled on details of the state of Marcella's blackened face, the arms and legs flayed to the bone by the flames, the hair frizzled off her scalp — until even I was disgusted, though it clearly took more than a roasted corpse to reduce the composure of the *vicaria*'s sturdy attendants.

The *vicaria* held out her hand. 'Look, I wear the ring we took off her burned body. *She* never deserved to wear it.'

I demanded, 'I should be given that ring.'

'You deserve it no more than your sister did.'

'Then take me to her tomb.'

'She defiled the body God gave her and our convent too with a sacrilegious act of self-murder. The Church forbids cremation: she chose to cremate herself! In killing herself, she stole a soul and a bride from Christ. It was not for us to sanctify such desecrations with an honourable burial among our holy sisters.'

I pointed out, 'Do not fanatics like yourself spend their whole lives seeking death? How is that different from my sister?'

Her lips quivered but no sound issued forth. I said impatiently, 'Now, where is the grave?'

The nun waved a dismissive hand in the direction of the walls.

'I was told that a peon took the remains away on a cart,' she said spitefully, and it was then, the Understanding Reader will forgive me, that I struck her across the mouth so that the blood came. Her retainers made no move to defend her, I noticed, but appeared rather gratified.

She mumbled on the blood and fixed her eyes on me in a crazed, flickering way.

'If I cannot take my sister, then I shall at least make this journey worthwhile by reclaiming the dowry,' I declared. 'I would like two thousand four hundred of your best pieces of silver brought round to the Casa Fasan, for a start.'

'I think not,' said the woman, wiping her mouth. 'Sor Constanza married God here, and she did not leave the convent, except in spirit. So her dowry

427

stays where it was bestowed,' she concluded firmly. 'Indeed the manner of her death caused such expensive damage to her cell that we sold her slave to pay for it – or we would have done. But the creature somehow escaped.'

Then she was ringing a bell and before I knew what was happening, her two retainers had bodily pushed me out into the street with such force that I found myself prone in the gutter.

I lay there some minutes, my apricot satin frock-coat irreparably stained with alpaca dung. I was not quite ready in myself to rise to a man's stature. A sweltering brew of feelings tumbled through me. Marcella's was as bad a death as I could have dreamed up for her. But this was all too sudden, and the worst of it was that it had happened outside my hegemony. How wretched had her life been that she had been forced to end it? It irked me that someone else had hated Marcella, and had done badly by her, had brought her down, and had done so more comprehensively than I ever did.

No respect to the Empathetical Reader, but I cannot really expect Him to understand. A part of me was missing, the part that had owned Marcella's fate. That had been taken from me violently and without my knowing. I had been deceived and led on. Marcella's death was the one thing I had always desired, yet in the way of its achieving – I was left hollowed, empty.

Gianni met me at the door, his face full of questions and alight with the thought of glimpsing his little darling Marcella behind the grate in the church the next day. Just a few hours before, I had told him that he might accompany me to the morning mass where the nuns sang 'like them serifs in heaven', as he had put it.

I brought the fellow down to earth, and then considerably below it, in a few terse words.

Gianni delle Boccole

Dead? Dead by burning herself? No, twere not a possible thing, God-the-Murderer!

Could the holey mad nun of driven my darling Marcella to *that*?

From the timing I could work out, it ud appened when they sent that curst poortret. Fernando and Santo must o writed to me, but reverlushons n quarantys was holding up all the post in the ports. By the time there letters must of arrived in Venice, Minguillo and me was alredy on the boat for Peru. I keeped thinking on how Santo must of suffert, to be come all this way just for to marry a burned remain!

The servants in that house knowed summing. They closed there lips wheniver they seed me or the bastert brother approach. They was busy shakin the mould out o this smart edifis what had been shutted up like a tomb for three year. I were sartin it must be knowed in Arequipa zackly persay what ud appened to Marcella. Ide have it out of em. My bit o Span-yard were getting better by the day, tho in front of Minguillo it were o course non existing, like my scill for readin n writin.

Inside the ouse twas loathsome to be. For now that he knowed that Marcella ud past on, Minguillo were full of sorry for *himself* as if he was the antagonist in some trudgical story. He were not morning for Marcella, nowise was he. Swear he were morning that he did not kill her himself. Conserquintly he ud got a temper on him to take lumps out of ye and I were always the scrapegoat for all his umbrage.

He forbid me to leave the house.

Not that I cared what he bethought now. A grate change ud come oer my feelins, seein him like this. Twere as if I ud been frit of a bad god with powr over the hole world. But now, with Marcella dead, there were nothing left to be affrighted of in Minguillo. What were he? A little spotty person in terrible clothes. A person what couldn't hardly see beyont his ugly nose. A monster, what dint know scut bout what were good in this world, who were not invinsible no more, and knewed it.

I desprit wanted to find Fernando, and Santo. But een with Minguillo reduct to a ornery mortal in my eyes, I were cowardly fraid to go out on my lone in that white city o Span-yards, with them foreboding mountings all round. And that volcano above us seemed to be a-watchin me like a vulture in his airy when I lookt out o my window.

How many bits o girls is lying up there sacrificed to make there kin feel better? That's what I askt myself.

Minguillo stalkt round the house, rubbing his hands, makin strange little moans like a drubbed dog.

Marcella leastwise were free of his tortshures at last, and I tried to feel happy on it. But I could not. I could not. Save us, half the time I could nowise een believe it.

Marcella Fasan

It had happened. Minguillo had come to Arequipa. Josefa brought home the story that the *vicaria* threw him out of Santa Catalina. He was among us, and he would shortly hear about us. Then he would come for us.

These were the thoughts that ran around my head in tight circles. The afternoon was already thinking sombrely of evening when Josefa came with the news. I put down my paintbrush and sat at our planked table with my head in my hands until the sun's light grew wan and then died.

Yet there was one piece of news that was not evil. Gianni, my beloved Gianni, was in Arequipa too. I roused myself to dispatch Josefa with a message, that he should meet us in the square. We could not have Gianni inadvertently drawing Minguillo to our home.

In the meantime Santo came from his rounds, looking like one condemned. He too had heard about Minguillo's arrival. We sank down to the floor together, holding each other, trembling.

Gianni delle Boccole

A girl black as a burnt ouse come to see me. She told me in a soup o languages that she were the servant of Marcella. Marcella ud taught her Italian. Marcella were lovely, lovely, she sayed. Marcella were still alive, and living in Arequipa with her husband Doctor Santo. I were mazed n knee-trembling with so much good news, tumbling on me like kisses n kittens. I wanted to pick up that little black girl and plant one on her volumptuous pommygranite lips.

'Take me to her,' I sayed. The strength of my wish made me lordly.

'No, it is impassable, is not safe,' the girl told me and then she went mute as a statue.

I shone her with evry bit o my body that I were desprit.

'They will come to meet you in the Plaza de Armas tomorrow at three of the afternoon. Is safer that you does not know where they lodge . . . in case of prablems. So far all Arequipa make sure-sure your Mister don't know he sister still alive. Must keep like that some time more.'

'Ye can trust me,' I told her, feroshus proud.

'Passably,' she sayed. 'But not your Mister. *Cabrón!*'

I felt a sharp pain in my hand. I lookt oer my shoulder where she were looking, n a shutter runned down my spine. Twere Minguillo a-zigzagging down the street wiv his most begrumplt spreshon on his face.

'I told you to stay indoors,' he said, cuffing me hard on the ear.

Then he lookt at Josefa and askt, 'How much? Supposing I'm even interested.'

That much Span-yard I could unnerstand.

She giggled, tussled up her hairs, swung her hip and answered perter n a canary, a big price. She added to me, in Italian, 'Can't your Mister keep his foot still?'

'But she haint . . .' I protested.

431

'Save your breath to cool your cutlets. All women are for sale. You can't afford her, oaf,' Minguillo told me. 'Get on inside and stay there. Now you, missy, how does a little black *bastardina* like you come to speak Italian?'

I heared the girl's mocking laffter n footsteps patterin way. I longed to follow her.

Marcella Fasan

Josefa patrolled the edge of the square, always keeping my eye.

We had all come together, Fernando, Beatriz, Santo, Josefa, Arce and me, to give Gianni the warmest welcome of his life. Such embraces, so much kissing, so many exclamations!

Santo was explaining to Gianni, 'So Marcella is legally dead. That's the perfection of it. Even though the whole town already knows the truth.'

Josefa joined us, saying, 'Everyone know, is safe anyhows.'

Then she looked Gianni up and down, and up again.

Poor, sweet, dazed Gianni looked from one happy face to another, until his eyes came to rest on Josefa, where they stayed a long time. He asked, 'But what do you live on?'

'Love!' we all cried at once.

'And doctoring,' said Santo seriously.

'And painting,' I murmured proudly.

'And beans!' added Josefa.

'And shoes,' shouted Fernando.

Gianni said, 'There is something else, Miss Marcella. There is a piece of paper that you need to see. That you needed to see, many years gone.'

He unfolded a yellowed packet of parchment. He moaned, 'This is your father's true handwriting, Miss Marcella,' and his face crumpled up in a howl.

'Tis the relief!' he wept.

432

I took the paper in my hand.

Last Will and Testament, it said, in Venetian.

Gianni delle Boccole

The frale old will were past from hand to careful hand as I walkt home rejoysing with Marcella's new famly. Marcella dint use the crutch tall no more, but walkt hippety-hoppety on Santo's lovin arm.

I tookt glad eyefuls of all o them. Marcella . . . what can I say? Ye niver saw anyone what lookt less like a nun! She had her smile back, the one from when she were a child. Santo was growed two feet taller, and the two o them niver hallowed more than an inch atween em. As for lookin at each other, they was still catchin up on that too.

Young Fernando were the spit of his father, so very much more so than Minguillo. I seen it in the brow n mouth partikeler. I tookt to that boy like lightning. He were hevidently bout a year younger than Marcella, so she were still the next-borned child of the bonified will.

As for Beatriz Villafuerte – I could nowise unnerstand a word she warbled, but Sweet God that were one handsum woman. ('Well did!' I silently congraterlated my old Master.) And more to the point, she were alredy a loving mother to Marcella, much more than her real Mamma had ever been. I got a teary feelin evry time I saw that Beatriz Villafuerte put an arm round Marcella and draw her in for a hog, which were plentiful often, though she had to share her with Santo. Then there were Josefa, the girl with the volumptuous lips and smart tong inside em.

Twere not long, the will. Marcella translated it into Span-yard for them while they made a festa ovva small plate o brown bread n sour oil like it were surgeon-in-cream with oisters n brandy. We talkt late into the night.

Twere Josefa, what knowed evrything about evrything, what told us that in Span-yard law women has the same inhairitance rights as men.

So Minguillo mite not fight that will, not in Arequipa. All the silver, the ouse, the warehouse o the famly, they riotously belonged to Marcella now.

Marcella sayed quickly, 'But whatever comes to me, comes to us all. We are family.'

Yet we needed a lawyer to prove it and lay it out afore the important ones in charge.

A lawyer cost money. We – I were a part of it now – haint got none.

They could barely feed thereselves. They was fat on love, but love dunt heat any susspans, do it?

Josefa – that's how ye say it *Hrhrhrhr-seff-ha* – she told us, 'Sell me, you get two three four five hundred pesos. With you can buy you best lawyer in Arequipa, even Juan Pío de Tristán y Moscoso. He get satisfaction from the brother.'

'I could never sell you!' cried Marcella, and took the little *samba* to her breast. It lookt a very nice thing to do.

'Passably,' sayed Josefa comfortably, 'but you is able sell me to some folks from Cuzco for a little somefing-somefing. Then I run away back here to you. It do happen all the time.'

There eyes growed wide at the thought.

When I made a move to leave, young Fernando sayed, 'Where are you going, Gianni? This is your home now.'

I lookt round at its tinyness and humbleness. Marcella were alredy on her feet, making me a nest o blankets by the fire.

Yes. Let Minguillo wonder, I bethought, *where I am and for why*.

And it did appen, that Josefa razed four hunnerd pesos oft a merchant from Cuzco who were travailing back with ten donkeyloads o best Arequipan brandy. I were sorry to see her go, and I dint like the looks that merchant were giving her.

But with that money we did indeed have hopes of buying the services of one o the clevrest and richest men in Arequipa, Juan Pío de Tristán y Moscoso, jist as Josefa ud suggestered. By the time his eminents ud agreed to give us one quarter-hour o his time, Josefa were back again, with her soft black eyes n clouds o tussled black hair n her way o filling up the room with comfort. There was beauty for ye, that Josefa. There wernt a maid in Venice what could hold a tapir to her.

I bethought that at leastwise one on them soft black eyes rested on me kindly.

Marcella Fasan

They said that he was worth a million pesos. In Arequipa, only the Tristán and the Goyeneche families had fortunes of that kind. They did not need our little business, I feared. Yet Santo argued that only people of that kind knew all about haggling for wills, and understood what could be got out of them.

It was Josefa who suggested that we offer Juan Pío de Tristán y Moscoso not just our pesos but also the little Mantegna painting of San Sebastiano from my dowry. My forbidden sculpture of San Sebastiano had already, of course, made its way to the lawyer's collection. Fernando took the picture round to the Tristán residence the next morning, wrapped in a Venetian shawl. He did not stay to haggle a price, leaving the luminous little canvas to plead its own case more eloquently than he could.

We sent the will itself to Juan Pío de Tristán in the hands of Gianni, dressed in his Venetian valet's outfit. Gianni was instructed to say that he came from 'the heir of the great Fernando Fasan', which would surely get him in the door.

If Juan Pío de Tristán y Moscoso's butler thought Gianni, with his best Spanish, referred to Minguillo, that was not our fault.

Gianni delle Boccole

'*Tragado como media de cartero*,' Josefa told me. 'S'all right. S'good.'

That means 'swallowed like a postman's sock', I know that now. It's Span-yard for to have fallen hopeless in love.

She knowed afore I did. She come to me in my nest by the fire on the night o the day I perswaded Juan Pío de Tristán y Moscoso to take our case, and lifted her dress oer me, and swallowed me like a postman's sock.

Doctor Santo Aldobrandini

In less than a week, Juan Pío de Tristán y Moscoso strode into our rooms brandishing a sealed document. Doubt shrivelled his smile when he saw our humbleness, but his pride quickly reasserted itself. For he had won our case: using the Venetian will, he had proved Marcella the rightful heir of her father.

Pío Tristán's friend, the Intendant, sent soldiers to evict Minguillo from the family house. No sooner had the soldiers set foot on the road to the Casa Fasan than Josefa – to whom every rumour flew on greased wings – dropped the laundry and rushed off to attend the spectacle, along with a crowd of ill-wishers. Josefa came back panting to tell us how my brother-in-law had been dragged out of the house by two officers, dropped in a cart and the horse slapped in the direction of the *tambo*.

Josefa said, 'He keep a-hollering, "My sister is a dead woman!" The officers say, "Any more threats of murder and it will be the prison not the brothel for you!" And they had to got a second cart for all his costumes throwed out of house with.'

Beatriz and Fernando took possession of their old home the very next day. We scorned sedan chairs and walked proudly through the streets with people clapping us along the way. It was a joy to watch Beatriz embracing her sobbing servants, running her plump hands along her beloved curtains, opening wardrobes to sniff inside. In a trunk in the cellar we found all her dresses, carefully folded in paper. The housekeeper had hidden them, hoping for her safe return.

Although we happily joined the homecoming procession, Marcella and I did not stay at the Casa Fasan. We returned to our poor rooms. We needed nothing more, and truth to tell, we were almost afraid to leave them. The place was hallowed to us. When we moved, we agreed, it would be back to where we belonged, to the Old World, to Venice.

Exhilarated by his victory, Juan Pío de Tristán y Moscoso talked now of taking on the Venetian side of our business, for a taste of the value, of course. But we were confident that we would be able to establish the rights and wrongs of the situation without a voluble Peruvian lawyer to entangle the case.

In the meantime, letters were flowing fast between Cadiz and Arequipa. Cecilia Cornaro offered us her house at Miracoli, so as not to embarrass my new mother-in-law and sister-in-law with the shock of our arrival. Marcella was too kind to say so, but we both entertained few hopes Donata and Amalia Fasan would welcome me into their family. They had been fed the lie that I aspired to be Amalia's lover. Amalia herself, meanwhile, would have no idea that I had saved her from Minguillo's poison. And she was a Foscarini, after all, with eight hundred years of arrogance to uphold. She would not rejoice to see a humble doctor at the head of her table.

Marcella insisted that she had nothing but sisterly feelings for Amalia now. But the Contessa had been implicated in the plot that had so nearly sundered our love. How could Marcella feel quite easy under the same roof? And there were Minguillo's little daughters to think of: they had been trained to think their aunt a madwoman. I was hollow with homesickness for Venice, but no, I was as yet in no hurry to be an inhabitant of the Palazzo Espagnol, where I had been so starkly humiliated and could expect more of the same.

Cecilia had written, '*The beds shall be aired at Miracoli. It's yours. I shan't be able to witness your billing and cooing without vomiting. So I shall withdraw to my studio until the Palazzo Espagnol is revolutionized and ready to receive you.'*

She had also sent some money orders to be drawn on a Spanish bank: *'How better to use the fees from Bourbon faces? An advance for your passage home to us.'*

Marcella packed her few things, including the silver box with the heart of her friend Rafaela. We began to reminisce together about the play of water reflections under bridges and the cries of seagulls at dawn. We spoke of visiting our friends at San Servolo; of gondola rides on summer evenings.

Gianni was torn. Venice was his mother and father, but he had fallen in love with the young *samba* Josefa. She loved him back, her every inch. Marcella and I discreetly watched them at their mutual discoveries with almost parental delight. Gianni asked me, 'How did I get to forty year without never the once falling into love?'

'Perhaps because you never met Josefa before?' I mused.

He put his head in his hands, 'What to do bout it, though?' he moaned joyfully.

I solved the problem for him easily.

'Marry her,' I suggested, for marrying of course seemed to me the solution to every hurt or ill, 'and you shall both come back to Venice with us.'

He stared at me as if I was a vision of the Virgin Mary.

'Would she have me?' he asked in an awed voice.

'Does she not have you quite thoroughly already?' I smiled.

Then Josefa trotted in, placing a proprietorial hand on Gianni's flank. Giving it a thorough feel, she remarked, 'Is ructions at Santa Catalina. The *priora* is good healthy again. Is all up with Sor Loreta at last.'

Sor Loreta

The forces of lightness and profanity triumphed again. It came to pass that I was driven out of My position at Santa Catalina.

One day the Holy Fathers filed into My office with some ruffians and told them to tie Me up and carry Me to a storeroom behind the novitiate. I was chained to a sack of flour. They told Me that I was to be given up for prosecution by the magistrates in Arequipa for the murders of Sor Sofia and Rafaela and the attempted murder of the *priora* and the Venetian doctor. I was even accused of dropping a tile on the head of one of the infirmary nuns who had denied Me access to the sick, back in the old century, and of drowning another infirmary nun in the bath that same year. They showed Me a drawing of the godless nun Rafaela, without her veil, her head all bruised and beaten on one side.

'How could you?' someone spat.

'I am deaf,' I told them. 'I do not hear lies or blasphemies.'

I was paraded through the street, tied to an ugly horse, on My way to the trial. The people shouted: 'Take her and burn her at the stake, and make sure to roast her crisp!'

It was no less than the contumely heaped on the saintly heads of Santa Rosa and Santa Catalina. I rejoiced for I was at last going to follow in their paths. *Deo gratias*.

In the court I spoke clearly, and told them all about My invisible stigmata and My halo and the angels who came to visit Me in sunlight, and the many miracles I had wrought, and how I alone had carried out God's designs at Santa Catalina all these years. Silence descended on the courtroom then, and the jeering faded away to wonderment. Everyone started mopping their faces with their handkerchiefs.

I shouted, 'Teresa of Avila longed to go to the country of the infidel Moors that they might behead her and so allow her to fully exhibit her blessed faith. I ask no more than Santa Teresa. Behead Me! I shall but the sooner lie with Him, My Amorous Bridegroom in Paradise!'

I added, 'Let My head be buried with My face downward outside the cathedral, in front of the main entrance, that men may trample upon Me and I may serve them as a stepping-stone to the House of God.'

Then I grew rather vague, and said some other things that I can no longer remember.

The magistrates seemed to realize that they had no power over Me. They refused to behead Me. They sent Me to the Virrey José Fernando de Abascal y Sousa. Yet he denied Me an audience and had Me taken in chains to the Bishop. However, Monseñor José Sebastián de Goyeneche y Barreda was no friend of Mine, for I had shown him as a fool who knew nothing of the goings-on inside Santa Catalina all this time.

They took Me back to the grain store at Santa Catalina.

And there I found a corded stack of old dowry documents, extravagantly written on one side only. Feathers there were aplenty from the dead geese and chickens that were hung up in that room before cooking. When I asked for ink, the nuns laughed and brought Me colourless white spirit-of-vinegar.

'You have said quite enough,' jeered the pharmacy nun Margarita. 'Have some of your favourite drink instead!'

The Bishop dictated a letter to Me. He said that nothing had been proved against Me because I was held to be insane. There was no lunatic asylum in Arequipa. The hospital of San Juan de Dios would not look after Me, he stated, because I was considered too dangerous, and My parents would not bring Me back to Cuzco, so I must remain at Santa Catalina but live therein as an anchoress in a prison cell with no persons to visit Me or look on My face.

I was suffused with joy as I read, for this meant that there would be no one to supervise what I ate or drank, or did not, nor what penances I performed upon Myself, nor what I wrote with goose feathers dipped in white spirit-of-vinegar on the backs of those old dowries.

At last the Lord God has found a sufficiently glorious death for Me, far from the sneering eyes and taunting mouths of the light nuns. All My consolation lies with the future world which shall welcome Me as its Noble Queen. *Deo gratias*.

Gianni delle Boccole

Josefa n me sat in the court to listen n stare at the wicked nun. I dint unnerstand one word in ten, but Josefa wispered in my ear. Some were plain to see anyways. At sartin moments, the nun's hideous face changed and she become summing not tall humane, but full of dredful joy.

Insted of hanging her head, that nun objerkated evry soul in the room. She invade agin all her enemies, what seemed to be evryone in this earthy life. She stuck out her withy-cragged neck and the breath on her were so ghastly it made everyone lean backward in there seats. We was alredy swetting like pigs at the sight o her.

Josefa n me was torned atwixt laffing and being frit to death when Sor Loreta begin to rave n caper bout in the accused box. That nun sang like a sworm of bees and she curst all the present company as she was drug oft, screamin that they should be her vessels not her judges and shouting that the Fissure of Souls would come and collect his Dews from the lot on them n that Arequipa would be swallowed up into the earth and that Santa Rosa of Lima would come and kick all there corpses to Hell.

Minguillo Fasan

Our scene is the humble room in the *tambo*.

All the way back there, I had kept my head down for there were slivers of quartz locked into every piece of *sillar* stone that spat hurting white light straight into my disbelieving eyes.

I was still whispering, 'My sister is a dead woman,' when I opened the door and lurched into my whore's room. People in the crowd had shouted things at me. Scraps of their words were, against my will, assembling themselves into a long, coherent, repellent sentence in my mind. It made my skin feel hot and rigid like an iron pot full of boiling tar.

Marcella had not died: she had escaped from the convent and married the little doctor, and someone had found my father's real will and given it to the authorities to make use of against me. I was comprehensively ruined.

My little bed-maggot eyed me dubiously. She knew already. Even while I had lain with her the previous night, she had known my sister was living, and she had said nothing at all. And yet she was too stupid to fear me in this moment. Her face showed only curiosity and her eye hovered at the level of the purse in my pocket. She did not know if I could afford her any more, and she was not about to do me courtesies out of the love of her commercial little heart.

This is going to be a little uncomfortable for her, I thought.

It could be made more exquisitely so if she was naked. And a temporary holiday from my troubles would be achieved by putting my Devil into her Hell a while. So I threw some coins on the bed. She began automatically to disrobe at the sight of them, murmuring tenderly '*Desafortunado* . . .'

And that's when the door thundered, cracked open and a familiar face appeared.

Now of course the Reader loves it when the long arm of coincidence reaches round His shoulders and draws Him in to witness a scene like this – but for my part, I was unpleasantly astonished to see one Hamish Gilfeather standing in my doorway with a parcel in his hand. The man did not like me, and I did not like him to see me in these ignominious surroundings.

'For Minguillo Fasan,' he said quietly, pointing to the packet. 'Passage paid.'

'What,' I demanded, 'are you doing here?'

Our business together had not flourished. Your man had for some reason taken against me. So what had brought him all this way up a mountain to find me?

'Anyone may come to Arequipa,' he remarked, glancing around the sordid room with the air of someone who expected just what he saw. 'In fact, I have dear friends of my own here and I wished to pay them a visit.'

442

'Friends? In Arequipa? You never mentioned that before.' I was naturally excluded from the circle of 'friends'. I felt bile tight-lacing its bubbles in my stomach.

Silently, Hamish Gilfeather handed me the parcel.

'Who's this from then?'

'From Venice,' he replied insolently, as if that was a proper answer. 'I was coming to inform you that our business relations – that never started as far as I was concerned – are absolutely at an end. I thought I would make this delivery at the same time.'

'You – you – *dismiss* me?'

'I was disgusted to learn from a real physician what filth you put into your so-called "Tears of Santa Rosa" that you wished me to sell to respectable ladies in Scotland! Fortunately, I discovered the truth before poisoning any of my countrywomen wi' lead. I destroyed every bottle.'

'It is no problem of mine that you did not turn a fortune on "The Tears of Santa Rosa". Everyone profits from it, who chooses to. You'll still pay me for what I supplied,' I parried in a quiet, threatening voice.

He handed me a purse. 'Pray do not agitate yourself. I had not planned to negotiate wi' the likes of you. It would soil my hands. This settles our accounts. I'll be on my way now. Good evening to you, sir, madam,' he said with the barest civility to me and a sincere smile to the whore.

The ripostes fizzled acidly in my throat, instead of making a clean exit through my lips. Hamish Gilfeather turned on his heel unanswered and uninsulted, and left.

Throwing the purse on the sagging bed, I sent the whore away. It appeared that I had mislaid the usual urge. Anyway, there was surely more entertainment in the mysterious parcel than in her well-ransacked treasury. Its shape and size gave me reason to hope for something that would lift my spirits. I picked up my gift, which was addressed in a lively hand I knew not, and divested it of the string, paper and linen that bound it. A cloud of brown dust rose as I lifted the dense little book out of its swaddling. I buried my nose in the fragrance of its cover, breathing deeply, searching out the familiar scent: yes – and surely the truth shall have already crept upon the Reader – my eager eye, my nose and fingers told me that this was a volume bound in human skin.

443

It was a book of gynaecological matters, beginning with a treatise on virginity by Severus Pinæus and concluding with a tract on conception and childbirth. Illustrations showed the female parts stretched and dissected. It had been printed in Amsterdam in 1663, but the binding was newer.

Which of my faithful booksellers, my slave-traders, my rind-pimps, I wondered, had dug up this little dainty of anthropodermic bibliopegy?

The cover was golden brown, tessellated like a snake's back and much beset with delicate gilding. Inside, my anonymous correspondent had inserted a slip of paper on which was written: '*The doctor who owned this book had it rebound in the skin of a female patient. He thought it "congruent". She was a white woman, yet the doctor had it tanned to a darker colour using sumac, presumably to extend his joke. This seems to us to be your kind of a joke.*'

I was already smiling when I read that, and then a shiver took hold of my body. How could this person – no, these *persons*, for they had written 'seems to *us*' – know exactly what would amuse me?

Yet how incompetent were my correspondents! Did they not know the rules of the chase? Before handing over such an item, all my usual booksellers would have tempted me by an account in writing, teasing up my fantasies to entice my purse wide open. I swelled with my sixth sense – that of getting a bargain. I would beat them to the ground for this item.

Then an involuntary tremor fluted up and down my spine. I looked around me. Was I observed? Was someone enjoying the spectacle of me at work with my hands on a book of human skin? Were there other messages for me?

I leafed through that dusty old book so fast that it promptly and unkindly cut me right across the palps of my fingers on both hands. A paper cut is notoriously more painful than a sword injury! I sucked my wounded fingers and looked at the diagrams of female reproductive organs, speculating. I tasted the dust of the street suspended in my own sweet blood, and it brought back a memory.

All those years ago, in our country house in Venice, I had damaged my fingers when I shot Marcella's knee. Dirt had invaded a trifling wound. That was how I lost my favourite finger. Here in filthy South America, might I not be tempting fate to suck on bleeding digits after touching a book that had travelled the world unwashed? I pulled those affectioned pieces of myself out of my mouth with a plop and stared at them as if they were friends who had just revealed themselves as enemies.

Too late I sniffed at the linen and the paper in which my taking-away gift had been enclosed. I only throw it out to the Investigative Reader, this strange and simple fact: those wrappings smelled of oil paint.

Doctor Santo Aldobrandini

When Hamish Gilfeather walked through our door, I was speechless with surprise.

Not so Marcella, who threw herself upon him with a delighted shriek that made him drop his parcels. For one moment I was pierced by a salty little stab of jealousy. To know Marcella was to love her. Hamish had known her long years. They had voyaged together – I had not yet had that privilege with my wife. Drawing back a little, I watched to detect clinical symptoms of sentimental guilt or complicity. I can plead only this to excuse my unreasonable and unbecoming jealousy: I had not yet grown accustomed to the safety of love.

The Scotsman held her back from him a moment, and ordered, 'Do that thing again, lassie.'

She ran back to where she had been sitting, then leaped out of her chair and into his arms again.

'Where's yon limp of yours, child?'

'Shoes. Magic shoes. My brother Fernando . . .'

'Shoes and a wee something else, I would say,' Hamish Gilfeather smiled hugely. 'You have resolved to allow others to help you, I see.'

And I must allow Marcella to love, I reminded myself. *It is what she is made of.* Now I too embraced Hamish Gilfeather with heartfelt warmth, exclaiming, 'How? Why?'

'I received a letter from the good Gianni. So I knew Minguillo Fasan was on his way here, and I feared that could mean no good for Marcella. He said that you, Santo, were here already, and well,

445

I thought it was time for all those wi' a soft spot in their hearts for young Marcella to bide a while together and see what could be contrived for her good.'

He looked at our thin silver rings, and our transparent happiness, and said, 'I see that the very best thing has already been contrived. It was worth ten stormy voyages to see this done.'

He kissed the top of Marcella's head and gathered up his scattered parcels. 'I bear gifts,' he murmured, 'from Cecilia and myself.'

'Cecilia and yourself,' I repeated meaningfully – and here he flushed a little.

'Aye, I met wi' her in Cadiz on my way here. She is making portraits of the local Bourbons, ye know. She entrusted me with a few errands in Arequipa – deliveries and shopping, ye know women. She has a yen to grind some Andean lapis lazuli into her blue paint . . .'

'Deliveries?' I asked sharply. 'Do you have a letter for me?'

I dreaded a confession, that she had been to my old Master, Doctor Ruggiero in Stra, that she had embarrassed me with a foolish attempt to make use of my Small-Poxed dream of revenge.

'No letter for you, Doctor Santo, just her best regards,' and he winked. I did not like the mischievous look of that wink. Was it Cecilia Cornaro's wink, duly transmitted, or his own? Was he intimate enough with the artist to have been treated to an account of the shaming thoughts I had revealed?

But what could I say to shake all the secrets out of that wink? In retrospect, I could have said many things, and acted decisively, and prevented . . . but I did not. I was too ashamed to expose my filthy fantasy to Marcella and Hamish Gilfeather when such a thing seemed in that joy-filled moment quite unnecessary.

The merchant was opening a large packet. 'This is for Marcella, from Cecilia,' and he unfurled a roll of linen with two dozen pockets, each plump with a bladder of oil paint or a pair of squirrel-fur paintbrushes. I breathed a sigh of undeserved relief. Cecilia Cornaro might spit fire like a dragon, but she had simple kindness in her heart.

Hamish Gilfeather embraced us one last time and turned to the door, shaking another of his packets so it gurgled like an empty stomach. 'Now where is that young villain Gianni? I have a grand desire to tip a dram of some scurrilous Scotch whisky down his throat, and put the wobbling boots on the chap. I have brought the necessary particularly for that purpose.'

Minguillo Fasan

One day after Hamish Gilfeather made his delivery, I had more than a memory of gangrene. Morning punched me in the face with unbearable illumination: those paper cuts festered and that ominous tingling began again just as it had when I was a young man fresh from shooting his sister. From my skin arose that luminescence that announces the disease: just such a luminescence, I recollected, as was promised by my 'Tears of Santa Rosa'. Before nightfall the Spanish surgeon Sardon was climbing the stairs with his imperfectly serrated saw and a belated bottle of carbolic acid to stop the putrefaction.

After the first surgery, I burned with a fever and my throat and face grew fat with putrid liquors. The very soles of my feet crisped as if on hot coals. I quacked myself with brandy, letting it suck on my pain. And, as I closed up the hatches of my skin and curled in a ball, I noticed a new patch of red spots rising out of the black hairs on my abdomen.

I drank my dinner alone that night, for my buffle-headed valet had deserted. Gianni sent me an illiterate kind of note – turned out he could write after all! – to say that he 'risined' from my service. Then I realized that he had never really been in it, had he? He was Marcella's creature, right from the start. They all were.

I had travelled to Arequipa with him at my side, I had paid his passage, fed him and watered him: and all the while he must have been carrying my father's real will in his shirt. I tortured myself with wondering how he had found it: perhaps even in one of the searches I commissioned myself?

Outside in the street I heard some Indians muttering '*chapetones pezuñentos!*' Stink-hoofed Spaniards. It seemed that another little revolution was brewing in Arequipa, one of those slow-boiling ones that end up with the cauldron turned over in the fire and all destroyed. The old city seemed destined to mirror the great events of my own life with its upheavals.

I began to scratch the hillocks on my torso, which felt like pieces of shot under my skin. Then, unwillingly, I looked at my face in the mirror. I leave the Reader to supply suggestions for the curses I employed upon myself now for refusing the Small-Pox inoculation on my first visit to Arequipa, only insisting that the epithets are vicious and profane. My whole belly suddenly heaved and I was left looking at sour stars of ill-assimilated food on the floor.

I felt the grave's maggots tickling under my skin.

This was going to be a little uncomfortable.

Gianni delle Boccole

Josefa come rolling in to the tavern where I were taking my luncheon of beans and bread. 'The Minguillo is took ill.'

'Ill how?' I askt happily.

'With the spotty swelly smelly sickness. Plus, his fingers is rotted and bein cutted off.'

'The Small-Pox? Do that make your fingers rot I dunt think? But there haint no Small-Pox in Arequipa. I bethought ye was all innokulerated agin it here.'

'He got it by a present from Venice, Santo says. From a dirty dirty book with pus crusts on its inside. I don't know passably why, but Santo is verrrrrry upsetted about it. And here is a letter for you from Cadiz too. Has took its time to come. Three months.'

I ripped oft the seal and scanned the contens. It were a fairy's writin, a fairy with a hysterkal habit of the drink, Ide say. It tookt me a minute to unnerstand that this were the hand o the artist Cecilia Cornaro.

She writed, '*For safety, I send this letter separately from the item of our mutual revenge, and in anticipation of it, so that if anyone thinks I am wrong to do this thing, there is yet time to intercept Hamish Gilfeather and have the item destroyed.'*

I jumpt near out o my skin. By an oirony, *this* letter ud been held up in a quaranty, allowing its plaguey friend to arrive before it, Grate Rascal ovva God!

We sat round the table that night, workin the story back to the bone. Santo ud give Cecilia Cornaro the idea, he admitted it, the day he split her fingers what Minguillo's thugs had soldered together with the fire.

'And if I were to go to her studio now, I know I would see the portrait of the doctor from Stra, the one who collects Small-Pox scabs, and I would know how he paid for it, and that this transaction was brokered by me.'

Marcella clutched his hand. He bowed his head.

'Would that be one Doctor Ruggiero?' I askt, partly to cover the bowel howls that come from all them beans what we ate.

Santo nodded and lookt down.

Next to him, Amish Gillyfether put his head in his hands. 'Cecilia!' he moaned. 'She told me that her cat liked me. The trouble was I like *her* a great deal more than the little beast could know. With Sarah gone, I was . . . I could not keep away from Cecilia.'

Amish Gillyfether admitted that he haint askt Cecilia what were in the packet he were to take to Minguillo – 'I did not want to know, I suppose now, lest it stop me from making the delivery. I showed a pathetic amount of courage, for I rather hoped it would be something that would upset the fellow a great deal,' he sayed quietly. 'I see my guilt now clearly, in that I did not tell you, when I first arrived, that I had already delivered a parcel for Minguillo, did I?'

Then we all lookt down. Fernando offert, 'We did not ask either . . .'

But twere no good. The more they deducted of the way things ud run, the more each o them hated on thereselves, completely missin the point that anythin that hurted Minguillo were all to the good for *them*.

Amish Gillyfether moaned, 'And most of all I blame myself for letting my sweet Cecilia take the burden of all our ill wishes, and acting on them.'

Marcella sayed nothin, but lookt like a sorry ghost, one hand in Santo's. Josefa sat by me, givin me the snuggle-up. I sayed nothin too.

My betters was looking like morners. Yet I burned to shout this – that Cecilia Cornaro had did what all t'others wanted in there secret hearts to see did, but would of scroopilled to do, out of goodness. Which niver got anyone anywheres with Minguillo Fasan.

Cecilia Cornaro, with her unfearing hate, had sent Minguillo a pestilents, that were in its doings very like them callus acts that he ud visited upon evryone he knowed in this world.

Een now, my quill refuses to shed one tear of ink oer Minguillo Fasan!

Brava Cecilia Cornaro, says I. She is a grate lady, for she knows how to hate proper on who should be hated on proper. She should be famoused for all prosperity.

Doctor Santo Aldobrandini

Josefa brought us more detailed news of how my brother-in-law had lost his fingers. It was nothing to do with the Small-Pox, of course. He had fallen to a medical misfortune that was new to me in all my years of doctoring: in leafing through the guilty book he had cut his fingers. The paper cuts had admitted dirt that ushered in a gangrene that devoured those rifling digits one by one.

While his hands now showed him for the monster that he was, Minguillo would not die of lack of fingers. But the Small-Pox, now that was a different matter.

I had ministered to Small-Pox patients often enough.

In the usual course of the disease, in its more rabid *Variola confluens* strain, the incubative period lasts up to twelve days from the reception of the poison. The primary stage has all the symptoms of an inflammatory fever. These include chills, burning skin, a frequent pulse, a thickly furred white tongue. Blood drawn from the veins has an effervescent quality.

The patient complains of thirst, headache and a feeling of bruised pain all over the body, especially in the back and loins. His appetite declines. Just before the first eruption, there is generally nausea and vomiting. The breath smells peculiarly disagreeable at this point, the looks are heavy and sometimes one or both cheeks of the face will glow with a sudden colour.

Some patients are attacked by a harassing cough and defluxion. Fever increases at night. On the third or the fourth day, the unmistakable lesions begin to appear upon the face, and subsequently upon the extremities. Initially, they are red and hard, as if there are fragments of shot under the skin. So Minguillo might not notice them at first, given that all his adult life he had continued to suffer from an unfortunate adolescent complexion well supplied with pimples that resembled the macules, papules and vesicles of Small-Pox.

The next evening there is generally a paroxysm, followed by more pimples, which become painful and inflamed. The face begins to swell, and there commences a suppuration of the sores into pustules that spread universally, even joining up in masses. The contents begin as watery and clear but gradually change to a yellow matter. It is at this point that a vile odour sometimes begins to emanate from the patient's entire body. A secondary fever attacks as the pustules ripen.

If the patient is to survive, then the pustules dry and fall off in the same order in which they made their appearance. By the twelfth or fourteenth day, the patient is well again, though disfigured, initially by purple stains and later by indelible depressed scars, called vulgarly 'pits'.

Naturally I did not attend Minguillo Fasan. Yet as the days passed, I *thought* him through the primary, eruptive, suppurative and *confluens* stage.

On the thirteenth day we heard that Surgeon Sardon was presently pricking all the pustules on his patient's face with a needle dipped in carbolic acid to reduce pitting. Then news came that Minguillo had been smeared in olive oil and glycerine, and painted with a thick paste of cream and flour to prevent light acting on the pustules to deepen their colour.

Marcella Fasan

Santo and Gianni and I stayed indoors. Josefa, whose cousin was a *samba* at the *chichería*, brought us daily news of Minguillo's travails. At first it seemed that he could not survive the gangrene, the amputations and then the Small-Pox. On two occasions a priest was called to his room.

The fingers had been cut off one at a time. Minguillo would not allow the surgeon to do a clean job. He clung to each one until it was black. Finally my brother was left with just one digit on each hand, the little finger of the left and the thumb of his right. By that time he was too deep in the Small-Pox fever to know what had happened to him.

I wished that I could sink into the same state of delirium. Josefa could not understand my misery: 'Why you sad, mistress? Is bad all through, your brother, is better he die horrible death. So?' Josefa flicked her fingers, 'Simple easy, he get boil in big black pot in Hell.'

Santo understood; we said nothing, yet I read my own thoughts in his agonized face.

We are not killers, our eyes appealed to one another, *we did not kill Minguillo.*

But, our eyes answered, *we feed on carrion, if Minguillo dies.*

I remembered how, on my journey to Arequipa, I had promised the peons that I would pray for them, lest they should hunt Minguillo down and hurt him.

I prayed now. For Minguillo.

I prayed not because I loved him, or because I wished him better, but because I was terrified that his death would cast a dirty shadow over our joy.

Gianni delle Boccole

Finely Josefa's cuzzin let it be knowed that in Minguillo's room there were sich a stink that the Fiend in Hell would cower in a corner if he got hisself a whiff of it. And that Minguillo coughed up his innards hour by hour.

'*La tosse xe 'l tamburo de la morte*,' I exsalted. 'The cough is the drum of death.'

Then I were sorry, not for Minguillo but because I could see that Santo n Marcella were torned up in peaces. I were not so pure of heart as they. I osculated back n forth: some days I hoped his death would be quick, and other days hoped it would be long. Main thing was, he had one hoof in the coffin alredy. I were only on tender hooks for the end. Then I hoped they would leave his corps out in the hot sun for the aunts to dine on.

Amish Gillyfether were sad too, because he bethought hisself an assassin. He also bethought hisself a fool. He were dissolute at the idea that Cecilia Cornaro dint love him, that she had courted him for his uses, made a murderin porter out o him.

'Women!' I told him at the tavern. 'They turn ye oer.'

Tis true, there is times when women is the devil, een when ye love em to affinity. Josefa ud took agin me the night afore when I wunt swallow a ginny pig did up in its own gore what she had cooked speshal for me. Eyes, nose, little whiskers still there, dripping on the plate, breaking yer heart. Would ye put sich a thing in your mouth, I ask ye?

I threated her with Anna's squid in black ink back in Venice, and all ovva suddenly poor Anna's painted as my fancywoman – long with evry thing else that daggled a pettycote in Venice. I kickt myself for it, but I een ust Anna's scar to hexplain why there wernt niver nothing romantical atwixt us. But Josefa were in an umbrage and wunt listen. Then she set to wondering what got into her eyes and blinded her the night she agreed to be with me.

'*Imbécil!*' she shouted. I wernt sure if she were reefering to herself or me. I dint know if she had any love hid inside her beautiful chest for me still. All my sartinties slipt way, like I were falling through the branches of a big tree. Till that hour I haint een bethought on the so many years atwixt our ages, for they ud melted away in the throws o pashon as ye mite say. But now I felt two seprit pains – one, that I ud waited too long for love, like a *cacca* fruit what drops n splodes on the forist floor the very moment tis perfeck ripe. And second, that for all my forty year, and my heducation and my travails round the world, I were still not wise nuff to catch the preshous fruit safe in my hands.

Amish Gillyfether's big craggy face were full o pain too. 'If you let them, Gianni, women will turn your life right way up or upside down.'

'To the laydies!' I razed my glass, full of oirony and pisco, the local drink to which I had took quite a pleasant fancy. 'And to Minguillo Fasan bein tuckt up by a spade!'

Amish were fond of a Chinese proverbial, and he give me one then. He sighed, 'Do not beat a drowning dog, not for the sake of the dog, but for the sake of the soul of the beater.'

Marcella Fasan

At last, when it seemed too late, I was doing as Cecilia Cornaro had bid me. I was trying to understand why Minguillo hated me, why he had tried to strip me from myself. The will – which he must have known about all along – did not explain it all.

Now I forced myself to think back. What I found was this: no one had ever liked or loved Minguillo, not his parents, not his wife, not his daughters, not his servants. He was therefore not constrained to avoid hurting or disappointing or shocking anyone.

It is deforming to the soul to be the object of odium. Perhaps it disinfects the sense of good or bad? I remembered the hollow, hateful misery in my ribs when I used to sit at the most obscure part of the table, shunned by my family. Santo remembered the nuns who had raised him with whips, and sharper still, slighting looks and cutting words.

Gianni was in a raw mood, for he and Josefa had just proved their love by a first quarrel. Blackly, he insisted that Minguillo was always 'rotting', even as an infant.

'Was he treated badly?' I asked Gianni. 'Were my parents cruel?'

'They jist wanted to keep out of his way, like any sensible folk isn't it,' replied Gianni. 'Where is your thoughts going, Marcella? Ye cannot be repining for him. He never wanted *you* safe, nor happy, nor well, nor even alive. He's been a-murderin ye for years.'

Gianni hoped to kindly bluster me out of what he called my 'Stew of Despond'. He could not. Minguillo had fixed himself at the core of all my thoughts. This was perhaps his last evil act against me: he had succeeded in one cruelty he never managed before: to make me hate myself.

For I could not forget my childish desire to have him dead.

All those years, I'd repeated stoutly to myself, 'There is only one just penalty for Minguillo's crimes: his putting-to-death.'

I had fervently wished it. I had been coolly 'a-murderin' Minguillo in my mind for years. I had infected Santo with the same desire. And Cecilia. And Hamish. And now, while I did not wish to be the actual authoress of my brother's death, nor did I in truth wish him to continue blighting this world with his existence. I would have to learn to live with this knowledge about myself.

Hamish came to see me, his eyes full of leaving. I waved to Arce waiting below with the buggy to take him to Islay and the coast.

I hugged Hamish hard and long, telling him, 'And Cecilia loves you too. I am sure of it.'

'I am going to her now, to find out,' he said.

Doctor Santo Aldobrandini

Typically, Minguillo thought himself recovering, when really he was still failing. He had advanced to the cosmetic treatments well before his pustules ceased seeping, thereby infecting them anew. He drank copious quantities of brandy and smoked cigars to hide his own stink from himself. His lungs collapsed under such a barrage of cruelty.

The *samba* told Josefa that his arms wore flour-cream paste like gloves up to his elbows, except where the finger-parts were cut off.

'Looks like *monstruo*,' Josefa reported, 'like somefing borned wrong.'

On his chest he insisted on keeping the book of human skin that Cecilia Cornaro had sent him.

Josefa said, 'The surgeon after him to burn he book, he hats, he clothes, for he must of bringed the Small-Pox to Arequipa with. He refuse, however. *Imbécil!*'

At the word '*imbécil*', she threw an imploring look at Gianni, and received a melting one in return.

Ah, I thought, *soon healed*. Already Gianni and Josefa can no more live without one another than can Marcella and myself. I made a note to include in my book a paragraph about the perdurability of love even when its skin is scribbled over with angry scars.

There came a knocking at the door. It was Minguillo's surgeon, Sardon. He desired to consult the great Italian doctor about his unruly patient. I had expected and dreaded this summons.

I helped Sardon save himself. I suggested that sea air would be beneficial for his patient. In fact, what I implied was that, as death was probably imminent, it would be better for the surgeon himself if Minguillo were out of Arequipa and upon the ocean when it happened. Then the death could not be blamed on his doctor. In fact, the very absence of his doctor might be seen to have caused the death, which would give the surgeon's reputation a fillip among the credulous Arequipans. Sardon gave me an anxious, knowing frown, and rushed away.

So Minguillo was carried on a stretcher to the coast. The cool, fresh air of the mountains seems to have been his salvation. By the time he was at Islay, he was sitting upright. A brig was leaving for Valparaiso the same afternoon. Minguillo walked aboard on his own two feet, hooking his remaining fingers over the ropes above the plank.

Sardon had accompanied Minguillo to Islay, and indeed escorted his patient all the way to the ship, not from affectionate concern, but because he feared losing his fee that showed no sign of being paid. Finally he had to bargain for his wages, using as his currency some information I had provided. For I had asked Surgeon Sardon to convey the probable provenance of his disease to his patient. I was afraid that Cecilia Cornaro's book of human skin would infect others in the close confines of shipboard life. My dream of revenge had already created too much reality.

Surgeon Sardon told me afterwards that Minguillo had listened, pulled the book from his pocket, and cried out, 'Cecilia Cornaro!'

And he muttered, 'So they're all like me, after all.'

Then he threw the book into the sea, shouting, 'I too am cured. Like leather!'

Marcella Fasan

Minguillo was right. Like the men and women who gave their skins to cover his beloved, hateful books, we are all cured but in a different way. I am cured of being a Poor Thing with a Defiant Thing secretly festering beneath her skin. And I am cured of hiding pain inside me, when others, who love me, take it as a gift to help me.

Santo is cured of being an orphan, and of despising people just because they are noble or rich. Gianni is cured of being a secret thief. The torments of prevarication and self-hatred have all been flushed out of him too, with the triumphant revelation of the will. Fernando and Beatriz are cured of being a second and a secret family. Josefa is cured of being a slave.

457

Minguillo, however, was wrong about one thing. He is not cured of being Minguillo. He is just less capable of being Minguillo than before. And his unwitting accomplice, Sor Loreta – she is not cured either. She has the fanatic's impermeability: she will never change, not in this life, anyway.

We have sent letters to Hamish and Cecilia, assuming they are together, to tell them that like us they are cured of blood-guilt: Minguillo has survived.

And now we speak to Josefa only the Italian tongue and we are teaching her Venetian as fast as she can absorb it, which is very fast indeed. For the quarrel between her and Gianni has been cured with kisses, and soon she will be on the boat with us to Venice, where she will reign like Nature's royalty that she is. Anna and the other servants will make her welcome. And I smile to think of my mother's hairdresser confronted with those magnificent black curls. That smile weakens a little at the thought of my mother, and with what little enthusiasm she will greet her returned daughter. But I have ambitions in her regard. I wish to take her into our affection, and to let her be my mother, as she used to be in those days when I was a child, when Minguillo stayed away in Valparaiso and we shared an idyllic summer with Piero Zen.

We shall not need to live as exiles in Cecilia's house, after all. The Palazzo Espagnol awaits us. Amalia's mother, the Contessa Foscarini, has relented. Amalia has fled the place where Minguillo tormented her and gone to live in an apartment of her parents' vast home. She has taken an assistant husband, by coincidence a member of the Zen family. I wish her well. Her mother, the Contessa Foscarini, did not permit her to take Minguillo's daughters with her. I hope that she will allow us to raise them as our own, and that it is not too late to give them a childhood. My greatest fear is that Minguillo will summon the poor little creatures to him in Valparaiso, and maim their lives for ever.

Fernando and Santo have become brothers in every sense. They feed each other information, like two little boys trying to piece the world together. Fernando's knowledge of the human foot is more detailed than any doctor's. He has decided to establish a small hospital, giving free treatment to the poor Indians of Arequipa. He will make shoes that correct limps caused by rickets, mine accidents and birth deformities. Meanwhile, Santo has imparted to him every bit of knowledge about skin conditions that affect the human foot and legs, from the little growths that creep up between the toes, to rashes that signify a more serious malady.

And Beatriz too has her part to contribute: she now visits the poor of the city, among whom she dwelled for so many months. In her fine yet simple clothes, she goes not as Lady Bountiful, but as a friend. Perhaps she happens to leave a basket of food by the door in the poorest houses, or a good dress of the exact right size where a young woman despairs of finding a husband. Women and men of every hue, from *limpieza completa de sangre* to the darkest *negro*, are welcome in the Casa Fasan. I wonder what my father would have made of it? I like to believe he would have thought well of his house full of Arequipan laughter and smiles. After all, he came to Arequipa and made a son here.

And I? Well, I hardly dare say it yet.

But one thing is certain: when we are back in Venice I shall gather all my secret, scattered selves – the pages kept by my dear Anna, by Padre Portalupi and those dusty heaps behind the armoire in Minguillo's room. And I shall put them all together so that Santo can one day read the undivided truth. Even the thought of that cleans my feelings, like a confession.

Why are we all doing our best to become angels? It is perhaps because we shall always have something shadowy in our consciences, even though Minguillo has lived, well, partially lived.

Sor Loreta

I overheard the light nuns gossiping outside the grain store. And so I learned how the wicked brother of Sor Constanza has been afflicted with both the gangrene and the Small-Pox. He has been sent out to sea to die. It is God's design that Minguillo Fasan does poorly, for he sent his sister the Venetian Cripple to destroy all My great works at Santa Catalina.

It is known that many devout people live wretched and lonely lives in this world while, in contrast, evil villains enjoy much honour and great comforts.

Yet sometimes the situation is reversed and the true Daughter of God trumps Her enemies.

Therefore, any good Christian who reads this document should know that I, Doña Isabel Rosa López de Tapia, known as Sor Loreta, swear by the holy cross that all that is written here is true, for I saw it and it happened to Me, and I write it, albeit in colourless white spirit-of-vinegar, to the honour and glory of My Lord Jesus Christ.

Outside My cell, which abuts the street, I hear the Indians talking. They speak of bad things, of revolution and bloodshed and of throwing off the Holy Mother Church for ever. I am glad that I shall be martyred before this happens. The pain of My death will exceed even the torment planned for herself by Margherita of Cortona. That saint's Confessor prevented her from cutting off her nose and lips at the last minute, but I shall not quail in My purpose.

In preparation, I broke My blue spectacles and used the shards to sharpen two twigs that God left for Me on the window ledge of My prison, by the agency of an innocent sparrow. I have used pieces of blue glass to line the hardwood plank that serves as My sleeping place, for thus did Santa Rosa lie in a bed of excruciation in the last weeks of her life. I have unpicked some threads from the flour sack to which I am tied. I have all the tools I need. The *priora* will suffer the most exquisite torments when she discovers that I have followed to the letter the cruel instructions she once gave Me, and shall die of them.

Meanwhile, I have purified this dirty room by breathing in it. I am now more Spirit than Flesh. It is so long since I have eaten that I have ceased to have bodily functions at all. As I approach the longed-for flowery bed of My Sweet Spouse, My Virgin body, weightless and incorruptible like that of Teresa of Avila, gives off a scent of lilies. This is God's seal of approval on My spiritual and moral perfection – He allows even Me to smell the beautiful blooms of My glorious Eternity in anticipation. I have a sense that I am hovering above the ground, ready for My flight into His Arms. There shall be no agony of death for Me, nor the flames of Purgatory. I shall fly direct to His Embrace. And those poor sinners left behind Me on earth will one day travel leagues to venerate My cradle and My grave.

These quiet days, when no one comes to see Me, My head is full of memories of the death of Tupac Amaru II, all those years ago in Cuzco when I was a child.

Gianni delle Boccole

Josefa loves me agin, Sweet God! I finely talkt my way back into the middle o her heart, after dying days on the outside edge of it.

Twere Venice that done it, all my tales o the lacy stone palaces n the emerald-green canals bestrid by bridges, and the slender gondolas flying greaseful oer the waves. Perhap I were carried too high on the wings o poitry, for she wanted to know when was the breeding season for the gondolas and how many eggs they layed.

Arequipa is a fine place, swear tis a vegetable paradise in many ways. I wunt say it haint growed on me. Jist to breathe here gives a hunnerd pleasures – the air in Peru pisses on the air in Venice for purity!

But tis also true I can hardly wait to get back home. Jist telling Josefa bout Venice made a homesick hole in my heart. I think of sittin with Josefa n Anna in the window seat o the kitchen, watching the days shortening and the old Canalazzo growing vilet n green in the evening shadow. I want to sleep in my own bed with Josefa in my arms. I help her pack the trunks, and re-joys each time we seal one shut. Santo has gathered many good Peruvian erbs, specially the chinchona bark, to help people in Venice. No more 'Tears of Santa Rosa' to rut there guts!

Anyway, Marcella n Santo is expectin, and there child must be borned in Venice, must it not? The Palazzo Espagnol needs a son. The old one wunt be coming back. It haint nuff to be dispossest o the Devil. Ye need to put summing good in the hole what Beelzebub left for to make good the damidge. And far as I can see tis jam on both sides, for my Josefa will be the key to the turning out o all the tapeworm hants n huncles n nevvies n kneeses what has been a-parasitin on the rooms o the poor old ouse for sentries past. They couldn't stomach to share a roof with a black girl – they dunt give nothing to the world, but they still thinks they is above it. Josefa will be the powful emetic to flush out the festering – and then, slowly by slowly, we can bring the Palazzo Espagnol to rights agin.

First thing we'll do is pull apart Minguillo's study and bedchamber too, and raise their insides to the ground. Their paper n traps have breathed his bad air all these years. Marcella has told us that ahind the wardrobe in his bedchamber are *her* diries n drawings that allus so mistificatingly dispeared. How clever she were! All them years I hunted the will of Fernando Fasan, and I niver bethought of anything so smart as that!

Meanwhiles I have told Marcella n Santo evrything bout Minguillo's own direy and bout the dozens on dozens of orrid n orrible books of humane leather that Minguillo collected with her himbezzled inhairitance and finely put up in the tower. I hoped twould help there poor sore consciences to know of that high corner o Hell in our home, for in what wise did Minguillo deserve to live, in the light of *that*? They was both quite feint with shock when they heared the numbers o books and the kinds o titles and there skins.

When he could talk agin, Santo spoke ovva Greek satire called Marsy-ass who set himself up as better n a god. That satire were punisht by havin the skin flayed oft his body. 'I was writing of it only today,' Santo whispered, 'in my own book.'

'Well, Minguillo set himself up as better than God,' I sayed stornshly, 'and so he has got himself riotously skinned for it.'

'But what of the books?' Marcella asked quietly.

Santo had a solushon, o course. He tookt my shoulder and sayed, 'Gianni, we shall take them to church, each member of the household carrying a book in his or her arms, gently and kindly. And we shall have a mass said for their mutilated bodies, and set their souls free. And then we shall take the books to the new cemetery island that Napoleon made at San Michele, and we shall bury each book decently in the earth.'

Marcella lookt at him with pride n love, and he give her then the most oxorious kissing that can be had in the Old World or the New.

Minguillo Fasan

So they have finished me off. The phlegm's ruttling in my pipes like waves shivering over stones and I'll ever after be cursed with vegetarian whores who'll not eat my meat at any price because of my Small-Pox pits and missing digits. I am the flayed man of whom nothing remains but a wound all over.

And I'll never more see my Palazzo Espagnol – *that* I can also put on their account. How could I expose my fingerless, fortuneless self to the ridicule of the Venetians?

Valparaiso is my home now.

The loss of my fingers was actually perpetrated by the artist Cecilia Cornaro. I can almost respect your woman for the symmetry of her revenge. The portrait painter has painted my face irretrievably pitted, and more. I had burned her art and disfigured her own hand, as the Retentive Reader will remember. An eye for an eye, or rather eight fingers for two fingers, though perhaps, the surgeon tells me, it may not stop there. For today there's a blackening at the base of my one remaining thumb. Without it, how shall I address my perpetual itches? My new itches and the old itches of a man who has lived his skin to its limit. The brute batterings of the stubs of my arms shall not suffice for relief. And as for turning pages of beloved books, I shall be resorting to tongue and teeth.

I'm told, as the Reader has no doubt heard, that Cecilia Cornaro acted alone.

Does the Reader think me simple?

Who taught the artist the art of epistolary murder by Small-Pox scab?

Who taught *him* the Spanish that got him to Arequipa?

Who made sure that the book reached my very hands?

And who had hoarded and finally dragged into the light the will that has now wrenched my adored Palazzo Espagnol out of my bedraggled grasp?

And in whose name did all the foregoing company conduct their outrages upon me?

Once, many chapters back, I totted up the list of my enemies and lamented the weak showing. I do so again, with the same dismal result augmented only in numbers – a female artist, a Scottish trader in little frilly nothings, a Spanish madam who, I now discover, had supplementary skills in language instruction. A valet who stole wills. Not very impressive, is it? Yet they somehow contrived to pitch their petty little hatreds and their small talents together, in order to bring down the Colossus.

It eats inches out of my heart by the hour – that if my enemies are shamefully pathetic, my downfall's also freighted with the dead weight of allies distinguished only by their incompetence. The ugly *vicaria* planned to do me the unconscious favour of killing my sister, and yet her fanatical stupidity left her exposed. Now she is shut up for murder. They say that in her cell they found hidden the heart and tongue of two different bishops, stolen from the convent's treasury, among piles of damp empty paper that she claimed was 'The Life of a Great Saint penned by a Forthcoming Angel'. And that when she was confronted with her theft, she crucified her own tongue with two twigs tied by pieces of cotton unpicked from a flour sack.

The Spanish madam in Cannaregio has been to the magistrates with tales repeated by whores with whom I passed delirious minutes many years ago. I totally repudiate all charges against me in the matter of Riva Fasan, Conte Piero Zen of facetious memory and even my wife Amalia, who remains stubbornly alive. (Yesterday evening I received a missive from Venice requesting my attendance to answer charges on those matters, as well as the kidnap and false incarceration of my sister. Never has Valparaiso looked so beautiful as this morning.)

My own fat quack, who should have been making me rich in Venice – doubly important now that the old will has been dragged into the light – has spilled the secret of the formula for 'The Tears of Santa Rosa', staking it in a card game, his fatal weakness. Now he too languishes in prison in Venice – and worse, he's gone down with *my* reputation firmly nailed to his concoction. That 'The Tears of Santa Rosa' contains not the weeping of nuns but instead deadly acetate of white lead is a fact known universally now and likely to stay

464

fresh in the public's memory for some time. My quack's alembic and our bottles have been pitched into the Grand Canal by servants preparing the Palazzo Espagnol for its returning mistress and her circus retinue. My wife's already deserted. My mother and my daughters shall probably die of shock, which would be convenient, as they would be a sorry drain on my depleted purse just now. More likely, they shall be put out on the street.

For now I am actually, literally, miserably poor, exsanguinated by greedy booksellers, all blood-feeders on what's left of my fortune. My post consists only of letters from creditors wishing to draw attention to enclosed accounts which have no doubt escaped my attention, and who shall be glad if I can favour them with settlement at my earliest convenience and oblige etcetera and so forth.

Yet how my desires effloresce even as my prospects congeal!

My heart is ripped when I think on all the items I can no longer afford, particularly the latest English novelty, *Frankenstein*, written by the woman of the English poet Shelley. She is called Mary. One of her mother's books, some nonsense about the rights of ladies, is already in my collection bound in a bit of a lady. How apposite that the strident bluestocking's own flesh should join her there on my bookshelf! From what I hear, this *Frankenstein*, about an evil creature brought to life from a corpse, cries out to be covered in human skin and added to my collection – and what will happen to *that* when Marcella returns, and the little doctor Santo takes possession of my library? At least Tupac Amaru, my first and best beloved, lives with me in this exile, which is for him, of course, a kind of homecoming.

I won't embarrass myself by thanking the Reader now for His continued attendance. We both know that I am better than that. Yet I have one last morsel for Him to chew on before I close.

I invite the Reader to place His face within the glimpse of a mirror. I challenge Him now: *Tell me that you did not love what I wrote*.

'Gentle Reader . . .' coaxes the lady novelist, flatteringly. *My* Reader's interest was not fattened and flavoured on milky pap like that! Do you see any Gentle Readers around here? Your actual Gentle Reader would have thrown down my words in disgust in the early minutes of perusal.

When you started to read this tale, you took into your home a cur dog from the street, enjoying his fangs bared, riding on his power when he made little girls cry just to look at him. You pretended you were shocked by me. You loved to be shocked and you craved more. Do not tell me you did not flick through the pages, eager to be revolted. And do not tell me that I failed to provide a vividness to console you for the pale commonplace of your own real life.

Did I not take you, as promised, on a long walk in the dark, and did you not choose me as your guide, by reading on? Is not the act of reading a congress as intimate as any carried on between lovers: with only these two parties, the Reader and the Writer, behind the closed doors of the binding, alone and raptly conjoined? You must own how deeply I burrowed my way into your affections with my picturesque atrocities, because you were first entertained by them, and then embraced them.

And so, Dear Reader, my crimes became yours.

The Reprobate Reader would like some conclusive remarks, I am sure, and I make haste to satisfy Him.

I would quote from the wise, that is, from the Venetians who once had wit enough to manufacture such sayings: *Dio ha mandà l'om per castigar l'om.*

God created man to shame man.

This is all I designed to say in this tale. Shall we now declare a truce in this war of compliments?

What? What's that? The Reader has more questions? That's fighting talk!

The Reader has but to wait. The previous issue of this book having been so rapidly exhausted, the author wishes to inform the Nobility, Gentry and Public generally that he is now at work on a new edition, all revisions calculated to enhance its value and utility. Early each morning, before the scorpions are stirring, I scratch out a little more of the tale.

I know this information is going to be uncomfortable for you.

Historical Notes

The Fasan family and other characters

The noble Fasan family of Venice is this author's invention, as much as Minguillo's use of the title '*Conte*', not infrequently assumed on spurious grounds by Italian patricians.

A purely Venetian family would not have been allowed to own silver mines in Peru, as Spanish colonial trade policies were notably restrictive. But I have taken the liberty of presuming that the Spanish blood of my Fasan family would have facilitated trade in Peru, even if through local *factores*, or agents. Peru was a rich source of silver, particularly from the mines of Potosí, where the precious metal was first discovered as far back as 1547. However, by the eighteenth century Mexico was proving even more productive.

The invented characters: Gianni, Cristina, Anna, Amalia, Santo, Piero Zen, Marcella, Minguillo, Donata and Fernando Fasan, Hamish Gilfeather, Beatriz Villafuerte and her son, Sor Loreta, Rafaela, Josefa and the other servants and slaves of Santa Catalina. However, the names of the sisters recited by Sor Loreta (when she dismisses them from Marcella's cell) are those of nuns who really were at the convent of Santa Catalina in this period. For these beautiful names, I am indebted to the Arequipan historian Dante Zegarra.

Cecilia Cornaro has appeared in two previous novels of mine, *Carnevale* and *The Remedy*. In this one, she is true to her invented life: a feisty painter of portraits who endured a painful love affair with Lord Byron after a joyous one with Casanova.

Padre Portalupi and the Rossini-loving *priora* were real people, though their actual words are invented. A Pío Tristán really was one of the richest and most influential citizens of Arequipa during the time when this novel is set. The unfortunate Bishop Chávez de la Rosa was also a real historical character, as was his successor. M. Dominga Somocursio's name appears above the cell I chose for Marcella but her biography is invented.

467

One Matteo Casal did indeed attempt to crucify himself in Venice in the early 1800s.

Venetian curiosities

The Palazzo Espagnol does not exist, under that name at least. There is an exquisite little Palazzo Contarini-Fasan on the Grand Canal opposite the church of Santa Maria della Salute. The Palazzo Contarini Corfù has a tower rather like the one described in this book and rambles in rather the same way as the Palazzo Espagnol.

The Venetian artist Giambattista Tiepolo was commissioned in 1740 to paint Santa Catalina of Siena and Santa Rosa of Lima, together with Sant' Agnese of Montepulciano, at the church of Santa Maria del Rosario (known as 'Gesuati') on the Zattere, finishing the work in 1748. In the painting, the three saints are shown worshipping the baby Jesus as the Virgin Mary appears to them.

Nuns and convents

It is true that many of Venice's nuns were forced into convents against their will, installed there for the sake of financial expediency (a nun's dowry was a fraction of what was required for a noble match). Not surprisingly, these unwilling nuns were sometimes inclined to licentious behaviour. The walls of some Venetian convents were notoriously permeable for nuns who wished to conduct romances. Sor Loreta correctly cites the case of the *abate* Galogero, who was dismissed from the convent of Santa Chiara in 1758 for issuing the nuns with duplicate keys to the gate.

Not all nuns were unwilling. Marriage to a mortal man at the time of this story could turn even a noblewoman into a kind of serf. Some women genuinely preferred to take the veil than subject themselves to the domination of a husband. Parents, particularly in the more dangerous outposts of the Catholic world, might sincerely believe the convent to be a safe repository for daughters spinstered by a scarcity of suitable men. And some women, of course, entered convents with a true vocation; some even with a religious fervour.

The Nun, a remarkable novella by Denis Diderot (1713–84), tells the story of Suzanne Simonin, a strong-minded girl forcibly incarcerated in a series of convents and subjected to sadistic treatment and sexual abuse.

Suzanne is trampled by the other nuns as they come out of church – just as Sor Loreta craves to be at the end of this book.

The Nun was typical of a body of literature that captured the public's imagination in the late eighteenth and early nineteenth centuries, sensationalizing the cruelty of powerful clerics and the essential unhealthiness of one-sex confinement. Diderot's book, published in 1796, is a searing indictment not of the Catholic religion – for Suzanne remains devout throughout – but of the system of confining women in segregated communities where power was easily corrupted and the weak and innocent were especially vulnerable. Suzanne asserts: 'It is a certain fact, Sir, that out of every hundred nuns who die before fifty there are exactly a hundred damned, and that taking no account of the ones who in the meantime lose their reason, get feeble-minded or go raving mad.'

What happened to the nuns when Napoleon disbanded the convents of Europe

In the early stages of the French Revolution, it became fashionable to think of nuns as the victims of oppression. Later, the nuns and monks were regarded with suspicion as forces of conservatism and potential royalists.

For information about the demonization and executions of nuns in France I am indebted to Mita Choudhury's excellent book *Convents and Nuns in Eighteenth-Century French Politics and Culture* (2004).

There were at least several thousand nuns in Venice by the time Napoleon began to disband the city's convents in 1806. Records show that dowries totalling three million ducats had been paid into the Venetian convents during the second half of the eighteenth century alone.

That bounty was probably not far from Napoleon's mind when he went to war against Venice's religious institutions. By 1810 he had closed thirty-two of the forty parish churches, closely followed by the convents and monasteries, confiscating their buildings and turning them into barracks, hospitals, warehouses and museums. Some churches and convents were pulled down. Many more had their fates sealed by Napoleon, for the abandoned ecclesiastical edifices soon degraded into an irreparable state, and were later demolished. The Austrians continued with the process of militarizing the lagoon's religious architecture or letting it rot away. It was only in 1965, when the Italian army finally gave up its hold on the lagoon islands, that it was possible to see what a tragic and far-reaching disaster Napoleon had visited on the built environment of Venice.

Venice's written and painted history suffered too. Both the archives and the great art treasures of the churches and convents had been emptied into state galleries like the Accademia, into damp warehouses and wrecked churches, or carried off to Paris. Many items never returned, or were damaged beyond repair by careless storage.

As this story records, the convent of the Penitential Sisters of Saint Dominic in Venice (known as Corpus Domini) was closed in 1810 on the orders of Napoleon and demolished not long afterwards.

What happened to the thousands of nuns evicted when Napoleon closed the convents is a mystery that has never been properly investigated. The scholar Silvia Evangelisti, author of *Nuns, A History of Convent Life, 1450–1700* (2007), suggests that they were returned to their families, some with and some without pensions. In other places nuns were allowed to live in the convents until they died – if those convent buildings escaped the pickaxes of Napoleon's demolition teams. The convents were then renamed '*conservatori*'. There are accounts of parents hiring a building so the nuns could live in secular communities almost identical to their former religious ones.

When researching this book I wondered if many of the unwanted noble nuns might have ended up as '*dozzinanti*', noble paid-for guests on San Servolo. But when I examined the admission records of the asylum during Napoleonic times, it appeared that very few of the nuns were sent there.

Napoleon's health

Santo's observations are based on the dictator's actual medical records. I found immensely useful for my research the following books: Napoleon Bonaparte's own (or at least attributed) *Manuscript of St Helena* (written in 1817), translated from the French by Willard Parker (1924); Arno Karlen's *Napoleon's Glands and Other Ventures in Biohistory* (1984); David J. Markham's *Napoleon and Doctor Verling on St Helena* (2005); and George B. McClellan's *Venice and Bonaparte* (1931).

Napoleon died on May 5th 1821 on the South Atlantic island of St Helena, where he had been sent into perpetual exile by the British. Many colourful theories about the cause of his death have been promoted by different historians – notably one about wallpaper poisoned with arsenic – but it is now generally agreed that he died of stomach cancer, as his father had done before him.

San Servolo and the Archipelago of Maladies

The Archipelago of Maladies was as described by Minguillo and Santo.

San Servolo was in 1714 a military hospital for '*reduci*' (amputees). It was run by the *Fatebenefratelli*, originally from Portugal. In 1804 the island became the city's insane asylum for both male and female patients. The female lunatics were moved to the Ospedale Civile in 1834 and to the nearby island of San Clemente in 1873.

L'archivio della follia, edited by M. Galzigna and H. Terzian (1980), examines the rich archive of documents including '*cartelle cliniche*' of patients at San Servolo, and provides excellent background to the practices and people on San Servolo. The museum of asylum artefacts, which opened in 2006, was also very helpful in my research.

The *cartelle cliniche* were introduced in the 1820s (so I have anticipated them in this book) and gradually became more and more prescriptive, so that by filling them out the doctors ended up with a diagnosis. It was probably better for the patients in earlier days when the doctor-priests started with a blank sheet of paper and an open mind.

The admission book was as I describe, kindly shown to me by Professor Luigi Armiato when I first visited the archives of San Servolo for research in 2007. Also the documents of admission, with their logo of the *Regno d'Italia*, are as seen by Marcella.

The idea of isolating lunatics for their own good is a longstanding one. At the time this book is set, Venice herself might have been described as mentally unstable. She had in a dozen years been a Republic, a *Municipalità Provisoria*, French, Austrian, French again, and now she was a feather in the hat of the inglorious *Regno d'Italia*. So, I suspect, it was all the more important to keep any individuals with visible mental fissures from presenting themselves as metaphors for the city's cracked and limping existence. The police were ordered, by each successive authority, to be vigilant for such elements and to hustle them speedily across the lagoon and out of sight.

Many of the people confined at San Servolo suffered from physical illnesses that threw up symptoms of mental disorientation – pellagra, scurvy and rickets, all of which were endemic among the poor underfed classes. A wholesome diet at the island soon cured them.

The practice of isolation remained prevalent through the nineteenth and twentieth centuries. It was only in the last quarter of the twentieth century that it became fashionable, or perhaps expedient, to release the patients of mental asylums 'into the community'. This occurred in Italy in 1978 and in the United Kingdom in the 1980s.

William P. Letchworth, in *The Insane in Foreign Countries* (1889), wrote: 'In Ireland, there was Glen-na-galt, or the "Valley of the Lunatics", beautifully situated in County Kerry, not far from Tralee. To this vale it was believed that every lunatic would eventually gravitate if left to himself. The process of cure consisted in drinking the cooling waters and eating the cresses that grew beside the spring.'

Cold-water cures were also identified in the same source: 'It is recorded, that, not many years since, lunatics were denuded and thrice dipped at midnight in Lochmanur, in the far north of Scotland.'

Philippe Pinel (1745–1826) is regarded as the father of modern treatment for the insane. He was the first to institute a relatively humane regime at the infamous Bicêtre and La Salpêtrière hospitals in Paris. Under his care, patients suffering from what was then diagnosed as nymphomania were not shackled, purged or bled as a matter of course. Pinel also made a practice of talking to them about their problems.

George Man Burrows, in his 1828 work *Commentaries on the Causes, Forms, Symptoms, and Treatment, Moral and Medical, of Insanity*, observed that all lunatics had a 'peculiar odour'. He said, 'It has been compared to the scent of henbane in a state of fermentation; but I know nothing which it resembles . . . I consider it a pathognomonic symptom so unerring, that if I detected it in any person, I should not hesitate to pronounce him insane, even though I had no other proof of it.'

Burrows was among those that claimed that hysteria (aggravations of the womb) could manifest in excessive saliva, tears and urine. 'Affusion of cold water' was one of his recommended cures.

Jean-Étienne Esquirol (1772–1840), Pinel's student and successor, noted bad breath among his patients at La Salpêtrière, but this might have had something to do with rampant scurvy there due to the poor diet: the disease causes rotting of the gums.

In *Practical Remarks on Insanity* (1811), Bryan Crowther urged close supervision of the excretory functions of all lunatics, who were inclined to withhold bowel movements and urine. Applying leeches to the pubis was suggested by John Millar, in his essay on amenorrhoea, 'Hints on Insanity' (1861).

The custom of putting inconvenient women in mental asylums has been observed in fact and fiction before. William P. Letchworth, in his aforementioned work, noted, 'A grave abuse connected with these receptacles for the insane lay in the fact that they were resorted to by the powerful and unscrupulous as conveniences for getting rid of any relative who might happen to stand in the way of their selfish aims.'

The notion that certain physiological traits predisposed women to immorality was championed by the nineteenth-century Italian psychiatrist Cesare Lombroso. His ideas were similar to those cited by Minguillo, although he is of a later epoch.

The chain device that Minguillo designs for Marcella is based on the equipment used to confine an unfortunate prisoner known as James Norris at Bethlem Royal Hospital, London, for fourteen years.

My descriptions of the postures of the mad were partly inspired by Raymond Depardon's moving black-and-white photographs of the inmates of San Clemente towards the end of the last century.

Santa Catalina (St Catherine of Siena)

Catalina Benincasa was born in 1347, the twenty-third child of a family that lived near the Dominican church in Siena. She became a nun in 1363. She never learned to read or write but dictated a visionary work known as *The Dialogue* to her followers. She crusaded to bring Pope Gregory XI back from Avignon to Rome.

Sor Loreta's account of Santa Catalina conforms to the hagiographies written in or close to the saint's time. Catalina threw herself into a boiling spa in order to disfigure her face and body and thereby discourage future suitors. She deprived herself of sleep and ate almost nothing, sometimes sucking the juice from vegetables before spitting out the pulp. One witness described her pushing twigs down her throat to help her vomit up food.

Fasting appeared to lessen her need for sleep. She poured her energy into great feats of housework, rather like Sor Loreta's cleaning of the convent. Despite her own eating 'infirmity', as she herself described it, she performed feeding miracles for the destitute and also fed them with charity. She drank the pus of a diseased tertiary, describing it as exquisite. Yet the odour of her own body and of her clothes was always described as remarkably sweet. Santa Catalina claimed to have received the stigmata, though no one saw the marks until after her death. At times she would drink only the blood of Christ, in other words, the Eucharist wine. She also had visions in which she was encouraged by Christ to suckle on the wound in his side.

In 1366 she had a vision of a mystical marriage to Christ, in which he offered her a wedding ring made of his circumcised foreskin. Santa Catalina's marriage is depicted in paintings by Michelino da Besozzo (at the Pinacoteca in Siena), Barna da Siena (Museum of Fine Arts, Boston), Giovanni di Paolo (Metropolitan Museum, New York), several by Lorenzo Lotto (Galleria Nazionale d'Arte Antica, Rome, and the Alte Pinakothek, Munich) and Filippino Lippi (San Domenico, Bologna), among others. Some show Catalina marrying a baby Jesus; in others her bridegroom is adult. Saint Catherine of Alexandria also had a mystical wedding with Christ, often shown in art.

Santa Catalina died at the age of thirty-three, after a fast in which she gave up even water.

Santa Rosa of Lima

Isabel De Flores y Del Oliva was born in Lima, Peru on April 20th 1586, and died there on August 30th 1617. It is thought that Rosa modelled herself on Santa Catalina of Siena. She was beatified by Clement IX in 1668, and canonized in 1671 by Clement X, the first saint of the New World. She is the patron saint of Lima and Peru, and also of the Philippines, India, florists, gardeners and people ridiculed for their piety. She is often depicted with a wreath of roses around her head and keeping company with the Christ Child. One account of Santa Rosa records how when she gazed adoringly at a portrait of Christ, the painting began to sweat.

Fasting and fast-tracking to sainthood

If Sor Loreta had lived in the sixteenth century or earlier she might have actually succeeded in getting herself beatified.

Some mediaeval Catholics believed that it was Adam and Eve's sensual gluttony, in eating the forbidden apple, that had humankind exiled from Paradise. Therefore to refrain from food was to 'feed' Christ, who had fed mankind by literally sacrificing his body for its redemption. Some female saints, including Catalina of Siena, believed that by suffering bodily torment like Christ's they would be able to save souls, just as he had.

Central to Christian ritual is the concept that Christ literally fed his followers directly from his body. Partaking of Christ's sacrifice is symbolized in the consumption of the wine and wafer, his body and blood, at the Eucharist.

In Venice, Quirizio da Murano (fl. late fifteenth century) painted Christ offering a Eucharistic wafer and also opening his robe to show the wound at his breast to an eager praying woman, as if inviting her to suckle. Other paintings show Christ projecting the blood from his wound directly into a communion chalice.

In mediaeval times, a woman was not permitted even to touch the Host, yet the visions of many female saints portrayed them grasping it. Several saints, 'purified' to a state of heightened perception through starvation, claimed to be able to distinguish a false Host from a real one, as Sor Loreta does. Benvenuta Bojani claimed that she received her only food from an angel who dispensed it with his own fingers from a luminous vase.

Through such audacious visions, women created an opportunity to dictate or write religious tracts, positioning themselves somewhere between God and humanity, acting as his primary messenger. This was a role denied to most women by the patriarchal church up until very modern times. It is still denied in some places.

Fasting women also took themselves beyond the authority of their families, their sister-superiors in the convent and male doctors by establishing that their relationship was directly with God. Claiming special honour in his sight, they felt empowered to overrule any human intermediary.

The female saints mentioned by Sor Loreta, and their painful food-oriented penances, are all as recorded in various hagiographies. In the early modern period, one of the main ways women could 'prove' an advanced spirituality was by demonstrating a supernatural amount of control over their own bodies, manifested in starvation, hyperactivity and flagellation. The cruelties these women practised on themselves from childhood or puberty more or less guaranteed that they would have short lives of constant pain: headaches, stomach aches, boils and difficulty in breathing. Mental disorientation and hallucinations were also likely symptoms.

Some female saints adulterated the food that they did consume with ashes or gall to ensure no sensual enjoyment. Some, like Angela of Foligno and Catalina of Siena, ate filth and pus, which they claimed tasted sweet to them. Angela tried even to eat the putrefied flesh of a leper that came away in the water when she was washing him (but choked it out). Caterina of Genoa boasted of eating lice as big as pearls. Several, including Teresa of Avila, deliberately induced vomiting. Perhaps the most extreme was Veronica Giuliani, who fasted assiduously. But if a plate of food arrived at her place in the refectory mysteriously spattered with cat vomit or adulterated with rodent parts or containing a whole leech – then Veronica would fall on it voraciously. On the orders of an abusive confessor, she also licked the spider webs and spiders off the walls of her cell.

In her magisterial work *Holy Feast and Holy Fast: The Religious Significance of Food to Medieval Women* (1987), Catherine Bynum explains food's central role in both life and religious observance. Yet it was exclusively the women who devoted a great deal of their time to preparing or dealing with food. Even rich women at least supervised the production of food in the home. If they fell pregnant, they literally became food for the babies growing inside them. After giving birth, they fed babies from their breasts.

If food was women's kingdom, sometimes it was also the only part of their lives over which they exercised authority. As Bynum points out, 'human beings can renounce, or deny themselves, only that which they control . . . It was far more difficult to flee one's family, to deny a father's plans for one's betrothal, or to refuse sexual relations to a husband than it was to stop eating.'

The onset of fasting was generally at puberty (though some, like Veronica Giuliani apparently, refused their mothers' breasts on fast days even, in infancy). In mediaeval times, twelve or thirteen was the age when families began arranging husbands for their daughters. Some of the young would-be saints used fasting and other disfiguring methods to make themselves physically unmarriageable prospects. (For those who starve themselves do not merely become thin: they, like Sor Loreta, also develop foul breath, unpleasant symptoms of bloatedness, limp hair, dry and cracked skin. They also stop menstruating and are unable to conceive.) Others insisted on removing themselves from any possible contact with men, sometimes walling themselves up in small rooms.

Yet a rejection of burgeoning sexuality was surely not the fasters' only motive. Nor does it seem likely that adolescent self-starving can be retro-explained satisfactorily by Freudian and post-Freudian theories about anorexia: those neatly summarized by Rudolph M. Bell in his excellent *Holy Anorexia* (1985) as 'refusing an oral impregnation fantasy involving the father's incorporated phallus'.

For many of these girls also rejected family life altogether, striking out for independence. Or they took refuge in a convent, where they would no longer be subject to domestic chores imposed by parents or husbands. Stories of some female saints show them in violent conflict with their parents, particularly their mothers. In extreme cases, mother–daughter rivalries would be conclusively settled by the death and sainthood of the younger woman.

Nuns, married to God, had different relationships with food from those of their sisters who were married to men. Firstly, fasting or eating special foods were part of a nun's ritual and faith. The central, symbolically charged role of food would no doubt attract young girls to whom food – or the avoidance of it – had become something of an obsession. Some religious women devoted themselves to the poor, taking on motherly feeding responsibilities for them. And several female saints were credited with replicating or imitating Christ's food-stretching miracles for the starving. Scarcely credible feats of energy were also attributed to these women in such pastoral activities. (Sor Loreta, born at Cuzco's high altitude, would have been naturally endowed with a powerful heart and extremely large lungs.) Yet many saints who concerned themselves with feeding others paradoxically chose to starve themselves and deprived themselves of sleep, often in cruel and unusual ways. Benvenuta Bojani, for example, would bathe her eyes in vinegar to keep herself awake.

Given that dramatic food-orientated self-mutilations were really over by the mid-sixteenth century, I would argue that in the time when this novel is set, a propensity of young girls towards ecstatic visions and obsessive worship might also have been a sign of a lack of emotional maturity, fatally combined with a fierce pheromonal surge of competitiveness. And a convent could be a hothouse of all such feelings.

The end result of dramatic fasting, whether inside or outside the convent, was that the girls became dangerously thin. Some additionally flagellated themselves or invented other scarifying penances for their flesh, such as sleeping on bundles of thorns. The reason and desired outcome for all these tortures, according to the fasters, was to unite themselves with Christ, by sharing his torments. But there was another, more tangible result. Such dramatic self-torture drew attention to the sufferer. A saintly woman reduced to an asexual child's proportions, perhaps mutilated at her own hand, might receive veneration for her piety.

There's no doubt fasting captures the public's imagination, now as then. Disempowered men have also used hunger-striking to make a point: the IRA and Gandhi, for example. Although fasting is no longer theologized in the Christian faith, it remains a way to draw attention – sometimes reproving, sometimes covertly admiring – to those who practise it. Today's size-zero models and actresses are rewarded with massive publicity for their ability to abstain from food. The gossip columns also like to record which stick-like starlet partied 'til dawn: another echo of the saints who deprived themselves of sleep and yet showed frenetic energy.

There has been much discussion as to whether the chaste, self-harming, starving female saints were early sufferers from anorexia. However, mediaeval women were not under cultural pressure to look thin: emaciation was not thought beautiful. Dieting to reduce weight was unknown. In those days, breasts symbolized food and feeding: today the prevalent iconography is erotic.

True parallels cannot be drawn between the present and an age without anaesthesia of any kind, antisepsis or birth control. Today's woman is offered products to make her thinner, to suppress any pain, to avoid conception. She is urged to eat a variety of aspirational food, such as (ironically) 'extra-virgin' olive oil and organic products – whereas would-be saints like Santa Catalina desired to feed only from Christ, treating his wound as a breast, becoming joyfully inebriated with the blood that they drank.

Certainly, some of the female saints showed symptoms that we would today quickly label anorexia or bulimia. And it's interesting to note that many of the fasters saw their not-eating as an illness – it was described so by the biographers of Colette of Corbie, Walburga, Joan the Meatless, Alpaïs of Cudot and Santa Catalina herself. There's a superficial correspondence between saintly fasting and modern anorexia in the physical symptoms of starving: sleeplessness, dangerously low pulse, bad breath, light-headedness, tactile insensitivity, euphoria and depression. However, as Caroline Bynum explains, it is not possible to know if spiritually led fasts *caused* the symptoms

478

we now know as anorectic, or whether fasting was a result of physical illness or any of the psychological manifestations that are currently ascribed to both the symptoms and the causes of anorexia: self-hatred, anger and masochism.

Sor Loreta's feeling on marriage – that it would be like martyrdom by being tied to a rotting corpse – was actually proposed by the Spanish writer Pedro Galindo, in his *Excelencias de la castidad y virginidad* (1681).

Starving and chastity were not sure fast-tracks to sainthood. Failure to truly imitate Christ's sufferings could result in a mystic being exposed as a fake. Fasters who retained the bloom of health were regarded with suspicion: perhaps the Devil was feeding them? Could it be that a familiar or incubus was providing devilish sustenance? Some non-eaters were accused of the sin of trying to commit suicide. Also taken into account against a supposed mystic were any bouts of mental illness, or a tendency to alienate people.

Some would-be saints countered accusations by insisting that they themselves were persecuted by demons. Veronica Giuliani was beset by head-slapping, flatulent demons who trashed her room and hissed like snakes. These demons were even said to impersonate Veronica, so that she was able to appear in two places at once.

Stephen Haliczer, in his fascinating book *Between Exaltation and Infamy* (2002), discusses the rise and fall of female Spanish mystics. During the Inquisition, a woman like Sor Loreta might have suffered one of two fates: to be allowed to martyr herself by penances, or to be denounced as a false saint. Interestingly, over seventy per cent of the women recognized for sanctity in Spain were of rich or noble families. Lower-class or poor women were more likely to be accused of being impostors.

Peru in the early nineteenth century

The death of Tupac Amaru II was as described. His revolt against colonial rule, however, was not nearly as simple as its depiction by Sor Loreta. Although the rebel claimed to speak for everyone who was not Spanish, the Inca nobility of Cuzco, for example, who were treated with relative respect by the Spaniards, did not support his pan-Andean ambitions. Meanwhile, Tupac Amaru II himself claimed the Spanish king's support for his revolt.

Tupac Amaru II had renamed himself after an Incan ancestor beheaded in 1572. He was in reality a relatively prosperous member of the middle classes – not a peasant, as snobbish Sor Loreta sniffs. His letters and declarations speak of undoing unfair tax regimes and ridding Peru of bad government, but he never explicitly expressed a nationalist or independence agenda. The revolt did not end tidily with his death, but continued for several years.

While establishing Catholicism in Peru, the Spanish deliberately suppressed the Inca faith and the idolatry of mummies. The Spanish did what they could to break the old traditions, often humiliating the mummies in public, to make them unfit objects for worship.

By the late sixteenth century there would have been few mummies left to hunt out. The Indians had certainly learned to hide the ones that remained. So an eighteenth-century exposure of a mummy, as Sor Loreta describes, would have been a rarity.

Cuzco, the former Inca capital, is still rich in Inca relics and architecture. The foundations of many colonial buildings – secular and ecclesiastic – are indeed set atop monumental Inca stone blocks.

At that time, up to eighty ships a year sailed from Peru to Spain and the Old World, usually carrying at least some Jesuit's bark. Silver from the famous Potosí mines would have been channelled out via Buenos Aires. Travel from the Old World to the New was often arduous. I used near-contemporary accounts for my itineraries. The French feminist Flora Tristan (1803–44) travelled to Arequipa from Bordeaux via Praia, Valparaiso and Islay. The inimitable Flora wouldn't have been Flora without catastrophic contretemps to dramatize her account. So a journey that should have taken eighty days took her 133, due to storms and other setbacks. She found Islay closed because of typhoid. The modern port for boats is at nearby Matarani. From there the visitor travels the same land route that Flora (and Minguillo) took to Arequipa.

The New World offered many novelties to travellers from Europe. Charles Brand, in his *Journal of a Voyage to Peru* (1828), was shocked to see ladies in Callao wearing silver spurs, riding astride and smoking cigars. He was revolted by the one-eyed veils and tight skirts, observing that the women encased in the latter seemed like walking mummies. Minguillo, I was sure, would have had a different reaction.

The population of slaves or at least negros was very large in Peru. The viceroyalty recorded 89,000 slaves in 1812. These people would have been mostly third or fourth generation descendants of tribes kidnapped from Africa's coasts and transported to America. The word '*sambo*' (or *zambo*) was used in eighteenth-century Peru for anyone of pure or mixed African descent. There were various shades of *sambo*, from *negro* (the darkest) to *pardo* or *moreno*. Lima had the biggest population of *sambos*, but Arequipa too had its share of slaves.

Of course, all the convent slaves were female.

Mountains

In the late eighteenth century, mountains became fashionable in Europe. The romantic spirit was very appreciative of the agreeable frisson of terror inspired by the wild, frightful aspects of glacial, craggy peaks.

Until then, there had been a tendency to think mountains somewhat pagan and rather unseemly. There are records of travellers deliberately closing the blinds of their carriages so as not to be contaminated with the sight of the alpine savagery. This extract from Canto III of Byron's *Childe Harold's Pilgrimage* is typical of the outpourings of his time:

> *All that expands the spirit, yet appals,*
> *Gather around these summits, as to show*
> *How Earth may pierce to Heaven, yet leave vain man below.*

In Peru, mountains were sacred to the Incas: as such, they were not places of tourism. They were inescapable, and life-shaping, in more than just an environmental sense. The mountain-shaped black hats so despised by Minguillo are still worn by the Peruvians and are known as *collahuas*. The flatter broad-brimmed hats are known as *cabanas*. The suggestive shape of the mountain was in earlier times mimicked by the Peruvians in a very unusual form of body-sculpting. Using stones bound tightly with fabric to the sides of the head, they stretched the skulls of certain people from infancy in order to create an elongated cranium that resembled a mountain.

Of course, mountains have always been a popular site for convents and monasteries too. As Hamish Gilfeather observed, there has been a long tradition of taking young girls up mountains to sacrifice them, in one way or another. The Museo Santuarios Andinos in Arequipa hosts the body of a young girl christened Juanita, who was found frozen on the slopes of Mount Ampato. The girl was between twelve and fourteen when she died, around 1440. Scientists have established that she fasted one day before her death, which was due to a violent blow to the head. It is believed that she was taken up the mountain and sacrificed to the mountain god Apus, rather than left to starve to death as Sor Loreta's servant relates.

There was a preserved Peruvian woman on show at Savile House in London in 1828, as described by Hamish Gilfeather.

The white city of Arequipa

Beautiful, elegant Arequipa is a delectable surprise to the modern traveller, who might not expect to find a baroque square finer than San Marco in Venice, 7,500 feet above sea level and eighty miles from the ocean, surrounded by snow-topped volcanoes and yet verdant with flowers and palm trees.

At the time this novel is set, Arequipa was a two- or three-day journey from the port of Islay. Overland it was six days from Puno on Lake Titicaca, and ten days from Cuzco. In this period, the population of the city would have numbered something less than 30,000 people. Venice's population was many multiples of that.

The name does mean 'Yes, stay!' in the local Quechua dialect. The colonial city was founded by García Manuel de Carvajal, a lieutenant of the Spanish *conquistador* Francisco Pizarro, on August 15th 1540.

When Cuzco revolted against the Spanish in 1814, there was some support from the Arequipans of the lower classes. The leader, Mateo Pumacahua, briefly occupied Arequipa. The intendant, José Gabriel Moscoso, was executed for failing to support the rebel cause. By this time it was not just the Indians who were no longer prepared to put up with a system, whereby the best of everything was claimed by the 'white' Spanish settlers and those of mixed blood were deprived of power and status: all the different castes and creeds were ready for a change, including many of the *criollos*, prosperous Spanish-blood citizens born in Peru, whose ambitions had been persistently thwarted over the centuries. Others were terrified of losing the stability that Spain's protection brought: the Tupac Amaru revolt had shown what bloodshed might occur in the event of Spain losing control. In the end it was non-Peruvians who secured independence for the nation: Simón Bolívar and his general San Martín. By 1821, three years after the close of this novel, Peru was declared an independent nation.

One of the best accounts of the town in this period comes from Flora Tristan, whose father was from Arequipa. By the time she arrived in

Peru, the country had been independent for over a decade. Flora Tristan's account of Arequipa is flavoured with her personal issues. She had gone there to claim her father's inheritance from her uncle, and was disappointed in that. Her father's brother was too canny for her. He was in fact the wealthy Juan Pío de Tristán y Moscoso mentioned in this novel. He served as intendant between 1814 and 1817 in Arequipa, after the murder of José Gabriel Moscoso. Given his wily ways with Flora, I felt it reasonable to assume that he would be expert in matters of wills.

Flora took a somewhat chary, superior attitude towards Arequipa, always comparing it rather unfavourably to Paris. She admitted to the beauty of the town, and recorded many details like the gutters that ran down the centre of the streets. She also commented that the women of the town barely walked because they had a superstition that it would make their feet larger. The only place that truly charmed Flora was the convent of Santa Catalina, where she stayed for some time, and where she was greeted with delight by the nuns, just as Marcella is in this book.

The Arequipan writer and politician Mario Vargas Llosa novelized Flora's life, and that of her grandson, the painter Paul Gauguin, in *El paraíso en la otra esquina* (2003). Vargas Llosa has described the city of his birth as being well known for its 'clerical and religious spirit, its lawyers and volcanoes, its clear sky . . .' Indeed, in Arequipa there is sunshine at least 360 days a year. But Vargas Llosa also admits to a certain kind of personality 'disorder' among the locals, who suffer from *la nevada*, or 'snowfall' – a bad mood brought on during the few days when the snow in the mountains sends black clouds over the town. The cloudiness, allied to an increase in static electricity, can make Arequipans behave wildly, broodily or violently. It usually happens in February, March or April. The writer also claims that his townspeople have always been the butt of jokes by other Peruvians: they are seen as arrogant and even mad. Vargas Llosa diagnoses these criticisms as 'the result of jealousy', citing the marvels of the town's architecture, rich history and naturally beautiful setting.

Earthquakes have changed the landscape of Arequipa several times. The damage of the 1784 quake is still visible in the convent of Santa Catalina. There were serious quakes in 1958, 1960 and 2001. The last caused the loss of one of the magnificent cathedral's twin towers. It has now been restored.

A note regarding Arequipa's cemeteries: in the early 1800s a Bourbon decree prescribed that tombs should no longer be inside church buildings and that citizens should be buried in land on the outskirts of the city – for example in the Miraflores cemetery, situated on a pampa, which is now a housing estate with shops. Some rich citizens continued to bury their dead stone tombs inside the churches, and in small cemeteries behind them: I have claimed this right for Fernando Fasan senior.

Arequipa was granted World Heritage status in 2000. Visitors can see a number of houses belonging to rich families – including the Tristán and Goyeneche dynasties. The Casa Fasan is of course invented.

The convent of Santa Catalina in Arequipa

When the Spanish *conquistadores* colonized the New World, they were quick to re-create the institutions of the Old World there. Among the earliest institutions were churches, and with those came monasteries and convents.

The Dominicans were the first to bring the Catholic religion to Arequipa. The Jesuits followed. Santa Catalina was founded in 1579 by a rich widow, María de Guzmán. The convent thrived, and soon occupied two city blocks. Inside its golden walls wind streets and cloisters in vivid colours, as described in the novel: yet another surprise for the modern traveller.

Like all the convents in Peru, Santa Catalina housed the daughters of the conquering Spanish, and performed the same social function as convents in Europe – solving the problem of permanent protection for daughters for whom acceptable husbands could not be found, or for whom secular dowries would be too expensive. The convents also accommodated laywomen, often wealthy widows, who wished to live the monastic existence without taking vows, and who paid for the protection of the convent walls, agreeing to respect its rules of behaviour. Girl boarders were sent to convents to be taught by the nuns. Given that most of the nuns came from rich families, the young women were accustomed to servants: these were supplied inside the convent too. Slaves were often part of the dowry paid to the Church for the admittance of a novice. The noble novices usually progressed to being 'choir nuns' or 'professed nuns'. At this point they adopted black veils to symbolize the fact that they were dead to the world, and that the world was dead to them. There was a second echelon of '*velo blanco*' or white-veiled nuns, who were often from a lower social class, or of mixed blood. They undertook the humbler duties of the convent, and could not rise to high office.

I am indebted for the descriptions of monastic life at Arequipa to the excellent book *Santa Catalina, el monasterio de Arequipa* (2005), edited by Cecilia Raffo, Isabel Olivares and Alonso Ruiz Rosas, and to Isabel and Carmen Olivares personally for sparing the time to talk to me about the convent's history and answer my many questions.

Marcella's description of the daily routine of the nuns is based on a letter written by the *priora* Sor Paula Francisca del Tránsito to Bishop Chávez de la Rosa on April 1st 1791, which is published in the above book. The regime at Santa Catalina was kind, and nuns had a certain amount of freedom in their choice of mystic path to heaven. A series of paintings of Santa Catalina might inspire them to mortify their bodies with prolonged fasts and scourging, and to deprive themselves of sleep. Equally, they might choose to live comfortably in their luxurious surroundings.

Arequipa's Santa Catalina, like most convents, offered able and active women professional prospects that were not available to their sisters outside in the world, where marriage remained the only acceptable career for the high-born. At Santa Catalina the following positions could be achieved by ambitious nuns: *priora*, her assistant the *vicaria*, mistress of the laywomen, mistress of the novices, choir mistress, sacristan, gatekeeper, grate-keeper, treasurer, procuress (of goods), chief nurse, pharmacist, wardrobe mistress and secretary. A woman with a competitive streak might possibly turn into a bully or a fanatic like Sor Loreta: closed convent society might shelter cruelty with privacy, as in Diderot's novel.

There is no record of a nun like Sor Loreta at Santa Catalina, but Luis Martín, in his *Daughters of the Conquistadores* (1983), recounts an episode of a homicidal Peruvian nun in the seventeenth century. At the convent of La Encarnación in Lima, a fiery and unstable nun called Doña Ana de Frías stabbed a fellow nun to death, and wounded another. The Pope himself intervened and she was judged mentally unfit. Condemned to six years in the prison cell of the nunnery, she died before her sentence was completed.

Marcella's escape is based on that of the nun Dominga Gutiérrez Cossío in 1831, not from Santa Catalina, but from the nearby convent of Santa Teresa, inhabited by the Discalced Carmelites. This is vividly described by Flora Tristan in *Peregrinations of a Pariah* (1838), although Flora alters the story – for example, saying that Dominga (a cousin of hers) was incarcerated at the very severe convent of Santa Rosa. This is possibly because Flora visited Santa Rosa herself and was able to conjure a moving description of its austerities. Compared to Santa Catalina's free-form beauty and sense of personal freedom, Santa Rosa indeed seemed a cold prison, with the nuns sleeping in black-curtained tombs in dormitories, and social snobbery rampant.

With the kind and enthusiastic help of Santa Catalina's excellent guide, Laura Salazar García, I identified a route by which Marcella might have conducted her escape from the cell we chose as hers. Today there are several entrances to the convent, each with an inner courtyard of 'debatable land', where men might enter to make deliveries without actually penetrating convent grounds. Both these areas feature the '*torneras*' – two-tiered wheels on which money and goods were brought into the convent without ocular contact.

The annals of Santa Catalina do include one anecdote of an escaped nun. She left the convent through a dry irrigation channel – out of curiosity, to have a look around the town. When she tried to return she found that the channel was full of water. She went to the bishop. He came to Santa Catalina and said that he had heard that a nun had escaped. He ordered all the nuns into their cells, where they had to stay with the doors shut. The escapee was brought back and told to do the same. The bishop then told the *priora* that everyone was accounted for and that the story of the escaped nun was a false rumour.

Flora spoke of the nuns of Santa Catalina wearing a pleated veil, which seems not to have been true. She spoke of the cells as miniature country houses and the nuns living in a great deal of openness and relaxation, keeping chickens in their own courtyards, growing flowers, and enjoying an intimate, gossipy social life more like a girls' boarding school than a convent. The *priora* at Flora's time was a cousin of the Tristán family – as was her severe counterpart at Santa Rosa. Santa Catalina's portrait of Manuela de San Francisco Xavier y Rivero shows a woman with a high forehead and a mouth that seems to express a subtle irony. Mismatched brows suggest an inner complexity. It was she who loved Rossini and imported the expensive piano.

The *priora* of Santa Catalina changed every three years, but she could be re-elected many times, serving on the council in the 'fallow' period. The nuns were tended by two chaplains. Around four aspirants or novices were accepted every year.

Marcella enters Santa Catalina in 1816. The *priora* at Santa Catalina at that time was Sor Fátima de Nuestra Señora del Carmen y Araníbar, who was succeeded in 1817 by Manuela de Santa Cruz y León. However, I have used instead the name Mónica. The personality of my *priora* is confected from the portrait painted by Flora of her relative, and, of course, from the imperatives of the story.

The process of admission would involve an interview with the *priora* and then an agreement on the dowry, as explained in the novel. The contract would be signed by the father who consigned the nun – she would only sign it herself if she was over twenty-five years old. Girls were admitted at the age of fourteen or fifteen usually, and remained novices until they were allowed to profess at the age of eighteen. The act of profession was deliberately theatrical, like a wedding, as described in the novel.

In theory, the nuns were supposed to enter the convent of their own accord, but there would have been a certain amount of family pressure. In the revolution-torn unstable times of the early nineteenth century, Spanish fathers would consider that they had delivered their daughters into safety if they consigned them to a convent. And there is, of course, a certain amount of self-interest in a family entrusting a daughter to a convent: given that the nuns were supposed to pray continuously for the souls of their family members, in order to lessen their time in Purgatory.

At this time there were around fifty-three of the *velo negro* (black-veiled professed nuns), twenty-eight of the *velo blanco* (white-veiled serving nuns), twelve laywomen who had invested their fortune in a retired life and sixty-two lay people working in and around the convent for its maintenance. There were seventy servants and slaves of every variation of blood: *mestizas, negras, mulatas, sambas* and others.

As previously mentioned, some real names are used in the book. The nuns came mostly from Arequipa and the surrounding areas. But Dante Zegarra's list of nuns who entered Santa Catalina between 1810 and 1820 includes a Sor Juana Francisca from Lampa, a Sor María from Cuzco and a Sor Manuela from Lima. One *velo blanco* nun is listed as *hija natural* (illegitimate daughter). The *velo negro* nuns were generally of pure Spanish blood, though born in Peru. There is a record of a nun born in Spain being admitted to Santa Catalina in 1964.

The dowries were tailored to the fortunes of the families of the nuns.

Many girls brought as dowry pieces of land that were rented out to lay farmers. The convent sometimes traded dowry objects and even slave girls to keep the convent fed, warm and supplied. The dowry letter Minguillo signs in the *oficina* is based on a document that is still preserved in the museum at Santa Catalina.

I have taken the names of some of my nuns from the friends that Flora made, even though my story takes place almost fifteen years earlier. For example, a Margarita from Bolivia was thirty-three in 1834 when Flora was there. She had been at Santa Catalina since she was two.

As described in the novel, visitors were allowed by permission of the *priora*. They would be escorted to the *locutorio* (*parlatorio* in Venice) which was inside the first courtyard. The nuns would arrive at the narrow chamber via the second courtyard. Facing them were five grates. All conversations were supervised by the *priora*, whose office had a grate into the *locutorio*, or by another nun.

It is true that a real cult of the baby Jesus arose among enclosed nuns in the New World and the Old. In some convents, the nuns were even allowed 'baby Jesus' dolls to cradle and dress up. This does not appear to have been the case at Santa Catalina, but the cult of *El Niño Jesús* was certainly strong there. I have invented the excess to which Sor Loreta takes this matter, though Veronica Giuliani recorded a similar phenomenon, in her case with a painted icon of the Madonna and Child.

It appears that certain pets were allowed, and it is true that at Santa Catalina some nuns kept fleas in bottles, partly to show their devotion to all living things. A beautiful green flea bottle (*pulguero*) is displayed in the convent's museum.

There was no lunatic asylum in Arequipa at the time this novel is set, and nor was there a medical school. Sick nuns were attended by doctors and blood-letters in the *oficina* of the *priora*, or cared for in the convent's own infirmary.

Sor Loreta's accounts of the trials of Bishop Chávez de la Rosa reflect the historical facts. The noble nuns were very active in claiming and maintaining their rights. For example, they later also demanded and upheld the right to have their sisters buried within the convent walls, even when this was challenged on health grounds. Now they are buried in a crypt in the grounds. The relatively luxurious existence so deplored by Sor Loreta at Santa Catalina continued until strict reforms were imposed in 1859, bringing the lifestyles of the nuns more into line with those in European convents.

Santa Catalina was declared a National Historic Monument in 1944, which saved it from some radical and destructive rebuilding plans proposed in the 1930s.

In the 1970s, a far-ranging programme of careful restoration and building work took the convent back to its original structure, with a new area provided for the modern nuns, which meant that tourists could be permitted to visit the older parts of the convent during certain hours. The colours of the convent were carefully restored to the lowest stratum of paint found during the repair works. It was at this point that the internal streets of the convent were given their names: these were not in use at the time this book is set.

The convent opened its doors to the public on August 15th 1970, the 430th anniversary of the founding of Arequipa. The visitor may now wander through two hectares of winding alleys, cells and cloisters. Some cells are fitted out with furniture from the sixteenth and seventeenth centuries. At a café near the back gate (through which Marcella escapes) visitors can eat biscuits and cakes cooked by the nuns. A wonderful recent innovation is to allow candlelit visits by night, a truly chilling and moving experience, when the convent seems to plunge back through four centuries of history.

The *sala de profundis*, used for wakes, still contains thirteen portraits of dead nuns, painted between the seventeenth and nineteenth centuries. Most are painted with their eyes shut, though one shows Sor Juana Arias with her eyes open, as they were when she was found dead in her cell. Many nuns are crowned with flowers, particularly roses, like Santa Rosa of Lima. The historians Dante Zegarra and Alejandro Málaga Núñez-Zeballos concur that nuns were not painted in their lifetimes during this period.

In other parts of the New World, for example in colonial Mexico, portraits of nuns, both alive and dead, were actually very popular. The paintings of *monjas coronadas* reached quite extravagant heights, with the nuns shown in exuberant jewelled crowns and towering headdresses of multi-coloured roses.

Marcella's faked self-immolation would have been regarded with horror. The Catholic Church relaxed its dictate against cremation only in the 1960s.

The treasure of the convent, in the form of valuables from the nuns' dowries, is now displayed in the old infirmary, in the arches that used to protect the beds of the sick from earthquakes. It includes beautiful china, paintings, lamps, statues and silver. A wonderful collection of art hangs in the former dormitories of the serving nuns, with many examples of the so-called Cuzco School of the seventeenth and eighteenth centuries: Christian imagery subtly adapted to local tastes by indigenous artists. Compared with contemporary ecclesiastical art in the Old World, these New World Christs were darker-skinned and wore Peruvian clothes. The Madonnas wore pyramidal robes that very much recall mountains. These paintings were often bordered with patterns of South American flowers and birds.

Today, a part of Santa Catalina still functions as an enclosed convent. But since 1985 nuns have been permitted to go out into the city, if accompanied, for specific tasks. They still occupy themselves with needlework, and examples can be purchased in the convent's shop. Pope John Paul II visited Arequipa in 1985, and beatified one of the convent's most beloved nuns, Sor Ana de los Ángeles Monteagudo (1602–86).

Gioachino Rossini

Rossini's first operatic success took place in Venice and he harboured a lifelong affection for the city. The famous *Duetto buffo di due gatti* – funny duet for two cats – is attributed to Rossini, but it appears to have been compiled from fragments of his opera *Otello* (1816) by another musician about ten years later.

Remedies

The fox pasting given to Marcella in the country and the recipe used by Minguillo to conceive a male child come from Sextus Placitus' *Medicina de Quadrupedibus*, which suggests all kinds of cures using animal parts.

The folk medicines stocked at Minguillo's *Novo Mondo* apothecary were among the items given much popular credibility as cures and prophylactics in the early nineteenth century.

All the books quoted by Santo are real, and can be found in the British Library or the Wellcome Library at London's Wellcome Collection. Santo would have loved the great works on dermatology published by Robert Willan, *On Cutaneous Diseases* (1808), and Jean-Louis-Marc Alibert, *Description des maladies de la peau* (1806), but he would not have been able to afford them.

Monkshood or aconite is indeed a deadly poison, and the flowers, and the effects of ingesting them, are as described. There is no known cure for a serious poisoning.

'The Tears of Santa Rosa' is an invention of the author's.

Disinfection of mail, and transmission of smallpox by paper

Smoking, perfuming and dousing in vinegar were supposed to purge letters of yellow fever, leprosy and plague ... which, as it turned out, could *not* be transferred by paper. The only killer disease that can be transferred by paper is smallpox. To destroy it requires an intense heat treatment, such as the determined application of a very hot iron.

V. Denis Vandervelde, founder of the Disinfected Mail Study Circle, writes:

> While disinfection was practised against half a dozen infectious diseases in the early nineteenth century it was quite ineffective against almost all of them. Smallpox was so widespread that it was not normally a cause for disinfecting mail, but it *could* have been conveyed on dry paper at this time in Arequipa. We have reliable records of smallpox in Chile from 1554 and in Peru from 1802. The Spanish authorities in Latin America were keenly promoting Jennerian vaccine against it from the first years of the nineteenth century.
>
> In the year 1804–5 there was a worldwide alarm about yellow fever and it is likely that travellers from the New World would have been detained in a Venetian lazzaretto, and any mail would probably have been 'perfumed' (in a box with sweet-smelling herbs). More serious treatment, including scorching, was reserved for plague mail.
>
> There was much less concern then until 1814–16, when there were outbreaks of plague in the Kingdom of Naples, the Ionian Isles and Malta. Yellow fever was much less of a threat until 1819, when the Spanish and Portuguese resumed splashing suspect mail with vinegar.

Smallpox is remarkably resilient. Spores kept at room temperature can survive for years. Frozen samples of the virus can be revived decades later. A British doctor records scabs dried in peat smoke and stored in camphor being viable for inoculation procedures eight years later.

There are also historical cases of people spreading smallpox deliberately, by using powdered scabs. Santo correctly cites the case of the British general Sir Jeffery Amherst, who in 1763 sent 'sundries' to the Ottawa Indians of Pennsylvania, having first sprinkled them with powdered scabs. There is another story, from the 1860s, of a grave-robber who serviced a medical college in Cincinnati. Fed up with pranks played on him by the anatomy students, he infected a number of them deliberately, by delivering to them the corpse of a smallpox victim for dissection. A case of a love letter transmitting the disease was recorded in 1901, when a woman in Saginaw, Michigan, was infected by a *billet-doux* posted from her sweetheart in Alaska.

For my medical research, I used as many contemporary sources as possible. Santo's wisdom is imperfect, and of its time, being based on what he might have read himself in Charles Roe's *A treatise on the natural smallpox, with some remarks and observations on inoculation* (1780) or Robert Dickinson's *An essay on cutaneous diseases, impurities o[f] the skin. And eruptions of the face* (1800) or Lorenz Heister's *Medical, chirurgical, and anatomical cases and observations* (1755).

The reader will of course realize that the gangrene infection in Minguillo's fingers has nothing to do with smallpox, though both are brought to him courtesy of the book of human skin, the first via paper cuts and the second via breathing in the powdered scabs. Santo's account of the progress of the disease does not conform to modern observations. The lesions of smallpox evolve through various stages – from maculae to papulae to vesicles to pustules to scabs – but remain discrete and do not coalesce.

One other thing to note is that the concept that a bacillus could cause human disease did not really originate until later in the nineteenth century. It was only in 1898 that a French scientist, Paul-Louis Simond, made public his research that showed that the plague bacillus was transmitted to humans via the fleas of rats. At the time this story is set, it was believed that the plague was spread by contaminated dust inhaled, ingested or absorbed via skin lesions. The plague has never completely disappeared: the last major outbreak was in India in 1994. I am grateful to William Helfand for referring me to the vital text on this matter: M. Simond, M. L. Godley and P. D. Mouriquand, *Paul-Louis Simond and His Discovery of Plague Transmission by Rat Fleas: a Centenary* (1998).

Nor was the blame for spreading malaria squarely laid upon mosquitoes until the latter part of the nineteenth century: at the time of this novel medical theory concerning the disease was dominated by the fashionable theory of 'miasmas' of malignant fragments.

Books of human skin

Human skin has more uses than one. Stories of its extracurricular roles are as numerous as they are hard to verify. It was claimed that girdles made of human skin were worn to facilitate childbirth in mediaeval Bavaria. It is said that the Hussite general John Zisca ordered his skin to be made into a drum for frightening his enemies after his death. A Paris surgeon is rumoured to have presented a pair of human-skin slippers to the *Cabinet du Roi*. Hermann Boerhaave, the Dutch physican, was said to have in his collection of medical curiosities three full human skins and a shirt made of internal organs, as well as a pair of high-heeled ladies' shoes in human leather. An executed convict had furnished the skin; his nipples were used to decorate the instep.

Since a fashion emerged in the seventeenth century for domestic display, tattooed skin fragments of sailors and slaves have found their way into 'cabinets of curiosity' in the private homes of 'ordinary' people. And in recent times Dr Gunther von Hagens has made a fortune from his show of 'plastinated' corpses – treated, flayed and displayed.

Human skin has been displayed for martial reasons for far longer. Herodotus records that the ancient Scythians flayed and tanned the skin of their enemies. There are accounts of marauding Danes who pillaged Christian churches in Britain being skinned and their hides nailed to the doors of the churches they had violated. (Even if this was not true, it was no doubt a discouraging story for other Danes who might have contemplated attacks.) There is one hideous incidence of flaying in early modern Venetian history: Marcantonio Bragadin was skinned alive by the Turks after the Battle of Famagosta in 1571. His body was stuffed with straw and paraded through the city. Eventually the loyal Venetians mounted a raid on the Turks' arsenal in Constantinople and stole Bragadin's skin. It now reposes in a black marble urn on his tomb at Santi Giovanni e Paolo, with the actual flaying depicted in pastel paint above a bust of the hero.

A slave called John Brown was used for experiments by a doctor, Thomas Hamilton of Clinton, Georgia, who subsequently made a fortune with a quack cure for heatstroke. Among other things, over a nine-month period

Hamilton flayed skin from the slave's body, in order to see how deep the black pigmentation went. Brown's sufferings were recorded in his memoir *Slave Life in Georgia*, first published in 1855.

A set of playing cards made of human skin was among the exhibits at the Centennial Exposition in Philadelphia in 1876. It was said that the cards had been captured from an Indian tribe.

Books bound in human leather – by a practice known as 'anthropodermic bibliopegy' – have always been a rather specialized item. But then book collectors have ever been known for their unusual ways. Leon H. Vincent, in *The Bibliotaph and Other People* (1899), wrote: 'Yet the most hostile critic is bound to admit that the fraternity of bibliophiles is eminently picturesque. If their doings are inscrutable, they are also romantic; if their vices are numerous, the heinousness of those vices is mitigated by the fact that it is possible to sin humorously.'

Harry Lyman Koopman, in his 1916 work *The Booklover and His Books*, observed: 'The binding is, therefore, a part of a book's environment, though the most intimate part, like our own clothing, to which, indeed, it bears a curious resemblance in its purpose and its perversions.'

The Bibliothèque Nationale is said to hold several volumes that incorporate human skin: a thirteenth-century Bible (fonds Sorbonne no. 1297) which was supposedly made of *peau de femme* but is more likely to be actually wrapped in the parchment from a stillborn Irish lamb; another thirteenth-century Bible (fonds Sorbonne no. 1625) and a text of the Decretals (fonds Sorbonne no. 1625) seem more likely to be bound in human skin.

The first well-known examples of the human-binding craft are from the late sixteenth century. Often there was a thematic link between the binding and the contents of such books: for example, Brown University's John Hay Library owns a 1568 anatomical work, *De Humani Corporis Fabrica*, 'On the Fabric of the Human Body', by Andreas Vesalius, as well as two anthropodermic editions of the *Dance of Death*.

Anthony Askew, an eighteenth-century physician, was reputed to have had his *Traité d'anatomie* bound in human skin. American doctors began to show an interest in anthropodermic bibliopegy in the nineteenth century. Joseph Leidy had an 1861 edition of his *Elementary Treatise on Human Anatomy* with the following inscription: 'The leather with which this book is bound is human skin, from a soldier who died during the great Southern rebellion.' Dr John Stockton-Hough, who first diagnosed trichinosis in Philadelphia, used the skin of patients he lost at the Philadelphia Hospital to bind various volumes of medical texts, including two on fertility issues for the human female. Dr Stockton-Hough observed that the skin of a woman's thigh was difficult to distinguish from pigskin. Two of his books may be seen in the Philadelphia College of Physicians' Library, along with Joseph Leidy's.

It is not known if the original owners of the bindings gave their permission for such use. Some of the human leather used for these medical and religious books is likely to have come from poor patients whose bodies were unclaimed after their deaths in hospital.

Harvard's Langdell Law Library has a Spanish law manual from 1605 bound in human skin. An inscription explains that the binding is the skin of the owner's dear friend, one Jonas Wright, who was skinned alive by an African tribe in 1632. The book, 'being one of poore Jonas chiefe possessions', was returned to his friend along with a piece of his skin for the binding.

The French Revolution, which provided a wealth of corpses, appears to have inspired a number of human book bindings. Several copies of the French constitution of 1793 were said to be bound in the skin of some of the revolution's countless victims. Royalists spread the rumour that the revolutionaries kept a vast tannery of human skin at Meudon. It was alleged in 1794 that in Angers human skins were also tanned to make riding breeches for army officers.

The early nineteenth century saw new sources of human leather emerge from the law courts. In Great Britain, wealthy book collectors were able to buy the skins of criminals who had been executed and anatomized. It was considered a part of the punishment that the offender would know in advance that his body was to be dissected by the surgeons. This was the fate of the notorious grave-robber William Burke, executed in 1829. After a public dissection, a piece of his body was tanned, and made into a wallet.

Sometimes the skins of criminals were used to bind accounts of their deeds and their trials, execution and eventual dissection. This was the case with John Horword, hanged for the murder of Eliza Balsum in 1821. A copy of his book – in every sense – is at Bristol's City Record Office, inscribed '*Cutis Vera Johannis Horwood*' and decorated with skulls and crossbones. At Moyse's Hall Museum in Bury St Edmunds, there's a similar volume on – and in – William Corder, the infamous killer of Maria Martin in the 'Murder in the Red Barn' scandal of 1828. The museum also displays Corder's scalp and ear. Two copies of the memoirs of the irrepressible highwayman James Allen, alias George Walton, were bound with his own skin in 1837 with a stamped inscription '*Hic Liber Waltonis cute compactus est*'. Walton had requested that a copy be given to one John Fenno, one of his victims, who had impressed the criminal with a brave resistance when attacked. The other was given to his doctor. Fenno's family eventually gifted the book to Boston Athenaeum's library.

There is one story of a woman requesting that her skin be used to bind a book. A young noblewoman was dying of tuberculosis, a disease which, in its latter phases, sometimes shows erotic symptoms. Although they had never met, she became obsessed with the French writer and astronomist Camille Flammarion, who had captured the public's imagination with his works on the stars and his theories of life on other planets. One version of the tale claims that the woman summoned him to her, announcing that she planned to bestow a gift he could not refuse. Another account insists that she had her hero's portrait tattooed on her back, leaving orders for her doctor to cut it out of her when she died so that it might be tanned and sent to Flammarion to bind his next book. Whatever the truth of the story, it appears that a copy of Flammarion's *Les terres du ciel* was indeed bound with female skin in 1882. In a gilt inscription, the binding is described as 'a pious execution of an anonymous vow'. In a letter, Flammarion claimed that the woman was unknown to him, but acknowledged that he had received the skin. He observed 'this fragment of a beautiful body is all that survives of it today, and it can endure lastingly in a perfect state of respectful preservation'.

The Grolier Club of New York owns a volume entitled *Le Traicte de Peyne: Poeme allegorique*, published in Paris in 1867. The flyleaf is inscribed in pencil, 'Bound in human skin', though this claim has not been verified.

A young German named Ernst Kauffmann sought a similar immortality. Despairing of success as a writer himself, he put together a book of *Two Hundred Famous Men* illustrated with woodcuts, requesting that it should be bound in his own skin after his death.

Human skin scandals abounded at the end of the nineteenth century and the beginning of the twentieth, feeding a new taste for the macabre in a reading public desensitized by Jack the Ripper and other cases described in lurid details in the popular press. In 1883 the infamous Tewksbury Almshouse in Massachusetts was accused of selling the skin of its wretched inhabitants – principally the pauper insane – to local tanners. A whole industry in human hide was suspected. There was a tale of some French medical students being dismissed after being caught selling the breasts of dead female patients to the binders of obscene books in the Faubourg Saint-Germain. This led to an alleged sighting of the Marquis de Sade's *Justine et Juliette* bound with a pair of human breasts.

The Wellcome Collection in London has a gynaecological treatise that was originally printed in Holland in 1663. The title page reads: *De Virginitatis notis, Graviditate & partu*. It consists of a number of illustrated essays on the female reproductive tract, the first of which is a piece by Séverin Pineau on virginity, pregnancy and birth. At some point the volume was acquired by a doctor, Ludovic Bouland, who had an interest in bookplates and artistic bindings. Bouland was born in Metz and had graduated in medicine at Strasbourg in 1865, thereafter practising in Paris. Dr Bouland had the book rebound in the skin of a woman which he had obtained when he was a medical student.

Bouland wrote inside: *'This curious little book about virginity and the generative functions of women seeming to me to merit a re-rendering congruent with the subject, has been re-dressed in a piece of the skin of a woman tanned for myself with some sumac.'*

The identity of the woman is unknown. My descriptions of Gianni's reactions to the book are based on my own, when I went to examine this volume at the Wellcome Library.

It is not known what happened to the skin of Tupac Amaru II after his parts were displayed in different towns in Peru: the book bound in it is an invention.

There are no records of *Frankenstein* or *Pride and Prejudice* being bound in human skin. However, both novels were first published in the period when this novel is set and Minguillo would have heard of the sensations they caused. Some novels have suffered human bindings, including a tattooed copy of *The Three Musketeers*, which belonged to a French doctor at the turn of the last century. (This same doctor is said to have had a copy of Mercier de Compiègne's *L'éloge du seins des femmes* – *In praise of women's breasts* – bound in the skin of a human breast, with the nipple clearly visible in the centre of the front cover.) There is also the case of an 1852 edition of Milton being rebound in the skin of the Exeter rat-catcher George Cudmore, who had killed his stepdaughter.

And so it is very possible for an innocent book to have its original binding torn off and replaced by something more alarming. There may be many books of human skin as yet unidentified in public and private libraries around the world. The tanning process tends to darken human leather so it is indistinguishable from normal book bindings. A microscope and some expert knowledge are required to tell it apart from pigskin.

Michelle Lovric,
London and Venice, March 2010

Acknowledgements

This book's research in Venice, Cuzco and Arequipa was completed with the help of a grant from the Arts Council, England. I would particularly like to thank Charles Beckett for his encouragement through the long process of writing this novel.

I am indebted to William Helfand, Vladimir Lovric and Jane Topple for checking my medical history, to Dr Christopher Rowland Payne for casting his kind professional eye over dermatological detail, and to Kristina Blagojevitch for Spanish translations and editorial assistance.

On the island of San Servolo, I was given generous access to the *manicomio* archives by Professor Luigi Armiato of la Fondazione I.R.S.E.C. Simon Chaplin at the Hunterian Museum in London was generous with time and advice.

Dennis Vandervelde, President of the Disinfected Mail Study Circle, advised me on the quarantine procedures, and organised an unforgettable trip to the deserted island of the Lazzaretto Vecchio in Venice's lagoon during the summer of 2008. Alessandro Fuga and Roberto Roselli from the Consorzio Venezia Nuova were kind enough to show us around the island, along with Dottore Umberto Bocus.

For access to materials and people in Arequipa, I thank Francesco Bandarin and Luis Sardón and also Giovanna Salini at the Peruvian Embassy in London.

I am grateful to Silvia Evangelisti and Mary Laven for their expertise on Venetian nuns.

In Santa Catalina, I was given every variety of help a writer and researcher could desire by Bradley W. Silva, then director, by Isabel and Carmen Olivares, restorers at the convent, and most particularly by both Dante Zegarra and Alejandro Málaga Núñez-Zeballos, historians of the city of Arequipa. The Santa Catalina guide Laura Salazar García helped me find physical contexts for all the turns of my plot inside the convent. I am also grateful to Mauricio Romañes for background on Arequipa and its history.

The historians Kathryn Burns and Sarah Chambers were both generous with advice and help, though any factual errors that cannot be conveniently attributed to deliberate artistic licence remain my own.

As ever, I am endlessly grateful to Victoria Hobbs at A.M. Heath, who does so much more than I ever thought an agent would. It's been a very happy experience to work with Alexandra Pringle, Helen Garnons-Williams and Erica Jarnes at Bloomsbury, and with Audrey Cotterell, the copy-editor.

The manuscript was given a thorough cleansing, battering and revivifying by my writing friends, Pamela Johnson, Cheryl Moskowitz, Mary Hamer, Mavis Gregson, Carol DeVaughn, Geraldine Paine, Annabel Chown, Paola de Carolis, Ann Vaughan-Williams, Sarah Salway, Jane Kirwan, Sue Ehrhardt, Jill Foulston, Patricia Guy, Carole Satyamurti and Louise Berridge.

As ever, I am grateful to the staff at the British Library, London Library and most particularly the Library at the Wellcome Collection.

A NOTE ON THE TYPES

The text for this book is set in the following types:

Perpetua is an adaptation of a style of letter that had been popularized for monumental work in stone by Eric Gill. Large scale drawings by Gill were given to Charles Malin, a Parisian punch-cutter, and his hand cut punches were the basis for the font issued by Monotype. First used in a private translation called *The Passion of Perpetua and Felicity*, the italic was originally called Felicity.

Guardi was designed by Reinhard Haus of Linotype in 1987. It was named after the Guardi brothers, Gianantonio and Francesco, the last famous artists from the Renaissance Venetian school of painting. It is based on the Venetian text styles of the fifteenth century. The influence of characters originally written with a feather can be seen in many aspects of this modern alphabet.

Caxton was designed by Leslie Usherwood in 1981. Caxton is an Old Style design with small serifs, and short ascenders and descenders.

Berling roman is a modern face designed by K. E. Forsberg between 1951 and 1958. In spite of its youth it does carry the characteristics of an old face. The serifs are inclined and blunt, and the g has a straight ear.

Bell was designed in 1788 by Richard Austin while working in John Bell's British Type Foundry. Bell, impressed by the clarity and contrast found in contemporary French typefaces cut by Firmin Didot, wanted his foundry to offer a British version. Austin, a skilful punchcutter who first trained as an engraver, produced a sharply serifed face, like Didot in its contrast of thick and thin strokes, but more like Baskerville in its use of bracketed, less rectilinear, serifs. Stanley Morison later described the face as the first English modern typeface.

Bembo was first used in 1495 by the Venetian printer Aldus Manutius for Cardinal Bembo's *De Aetna*, and was cut for Manutius by Francesco Griffo. It was one of the types used by Claude Garamond (1480–1561) as a model for his Romain de L'Universitë, and so it was the forerunner of what became standard European type for the following two centuries. Its modern form follows the original types and was designed for Monotype in 1929.

Not
The End

Go to channel4.com/tvbookclub for more great reads,
brought to you by Specsavers.

Enjoy a good read with